COSMIC FUSION

COSMIC FUSION

GORDON EKLUND

WILDSIDE PRESS

Published by Wildside Press LLC.
www.wildsidepress.com

A NOTE REGARDING
COSMIC FUSION

I wrote *Cosmic Fusion* what now seems like a great long while ago. (Likely because it was.) According to the final (1226th) ragged page of the original typescript, the writing occupied the period between January 1973 and September 1982. I think that may be a bit of an exaggeration. While the first lightning flash of inspiration might well have struck as early as 1973—there's a strong hint of the central gimmick in my story "The Ambiguities of Yesterday," written around that time—the actual writing—beyond the initial few-chapters-and-synopsis that earned me a nice contract, the biggest of my career up till then, with a major New York publishing firm—didn't really get going in earnest until late 1978 or early '79. Three-plus years (and three drafts later), I turned in the completed manuscript, all 1226 pages worth, received a check for the remaining portion of the advance payment owed me, and settled back to await the eventual publication of the finished book.

It turned out to be a long wait. The book was never published until now.

The years I spent writing *Cosmic Fusion* were chaotic ones for me. My marriage, which hadn't been in good shape for many years, finally disintegrated for good. I moved from the San Francisco Bay Area, where I'd been living since the middle sixties, back to my old home in the Pacific Northwest. In fact, I made the move not once but twice. (The second time it stuck.)

But whatever the chaos in my private life, the day-by-day writing of *Cosmic Fusion* acted as a kind of a psychological salve for me, a refuge from the strife swirling around me. The book was largely born out of a sense of frustration at how my writing career was going. By 1978, after several early novels of promise, I'd settled into churning out a succession of commissioned commercial projects that I found increasingly difficult to put my full heart into. These included two *Star Trek* TV novelizations, four posthumous "collaborations" with Edward E. Smith, the inventor of the space opera subgenre, a genuine primitive genius of sorts, but not one I felt much kinship with, three quickie SF adventure novels (one of them taking all of nineteen days to write) for the publisher of the ever popular Harlequin romance series. I wrote all these for the quick money, to support myself and my family and enable me to continue writing full time. The trouble there being that writing full time meant writing things I didn't really want to write and writing them quickly because that was the only way I could make enough money to allow me to write full time. A conundrum in other words.

Cosmic Fusion was intended to be the book that broke me out of all that. It was the Big Ambitious Novel I was going to write because I wanted to write it. Consequently, I threw myself into it. More than that, I threw everything else into it too. (Except maybe for the old secondhand living room sofa, though if you look close enough it may be in there too right next to the kitchen sink.) Some days, in fact, it's rather painfully obvious—at least to me—who and what I was reading the night before. Because all that's in there too. I kept on writing though, banging furiously away day after day on a succession of used manual typewriters—I went through them fast—until the novel was done.

So why then was the book never published?

The funny part is, I really don't know. Nobody ever told me.

I suppose I could venture a guess or two.

For one thing, as often happens in the publishing business, the editor who'd originally commissioned the book had by the time it was finished long since moved on. Her replacement had no particular stake in me or my writing. That sort of stuff happens everywhere all the time in all walks of life. Ask anybody who's had his or her beloved boss quit or, worse, been canned with the arrival of the new regime. (I've been through that one too a couple of times. No fun.)

In addition—and perhaps more significantly—by 1982 the business of science fiction publishing had changed dramatically from when I first started writing and selling SF as a twenty-four-year-old boy wonder back in 1970. By the early eighties, the *Star Wars* movies had happened. (And changed everything, according to some; I won't argue.) Science fiction was no longer a marginal publishing genre appealing to a handful of oddballs, cranks, and devotees. It was big business. There was money to be made in those imaginary star-lanes out there in the galaxies of long ago and far away, and where there's money to be made there's also money to be lost—and less tolerance for the oddball, the crank, the weird.

"A 300,000-word comic novel about sex and death and science fiction" is how I described *Cosmic Fusion* in the introduction to my story "Chambers of Memory" in Michael Bishop's definitive anthology of pre-*Star Wars* 1970s SF, *Light Years and Dark*. (A story that turned out to be the last one I'd write for a decade.)

It still strikes me as a fairly apt description of the novel, even if it does exaggerate its eventual length by about a third. (It's still pretty long though.) And as summary it may well help explain why the book was never published. It was too long, too different, too quirky, and way too goddamn weird. And *comic*? What's science fiction got to do with comedy? Nothing funny here.

After *Cosmic Fusion*, for all intents, my science fiction writing career was done. When people asked, as they sometimes did, what goes on, I told them I had a writers' block. In a sense I did. But it wasn't so much that I *couldn't* write as that there was nothing I particularly *wanted* to write. Especially science fiction. Which was all I was known for writing. Yet another conundrum, in other words.

In the end it took me fifteen years of fitful effort to finally finish the one remaining novel I was under contract to write. (No great shock when the publisher—yep, that same one again—promptly bounced it.) I did eventually write and publish a juvenile/YA SF novel, and an occasional short story of mine also appeared over the years, but that was pretty much it. I found a job (one of those real ones I'd only heard tell of before—the kind that paid regularly and eventually quite well), I raised my son, I enjoyed my life, I fell in and out of love a few times, read a little SF now and then to keep my sense of wonder intact, kept in sporadic touch with my many friends in and around the field, even attended the occasional SF convention.

As for *Cosmic Fusion*, eventually I must have gotten the manuscript back from someplace, because it ended up in a cardboard box (a big one) in the back closet where I keep things paper I don't know what to do with otherwise, and there it stayed until John Betancourt of Wildside Press, who'd somehow seen the manuscript as it was making the rounds of a few other New York publishers, called about something else and happened to ask in passing whatever happened to that old big novel of yours.

And here it is now. Somewhat revised and mildly updated around the edges; still pretty much what it was to start with. Still weird after all these years.

One final question then: ah, but is it any good?

On that I'm going to take a pass. In all due candor, I'm the last one you ought to ask. I can say, reading through it for the first time in thirty plus years, I was often taken by surprise. Sometimes pleasantly, sometimes less so. I will say that I wish it was a bit funnier.

But I wish that about pretty much everything else in the world these late days too.

—Gordon Eklund, October, 2016

CAST OF PRINCIPAL CHARACTERS

Desmond Blue—*detective*
Gordon Schwerner (Dr.)—*scientist*
Alfie Jarrett—*healer*
Peter Mark—*future Bishop of Rome*
Nadia van Hauten—*aka Arnold Hope Grimthorpe*
Crystal LaFleur—*sanest person around*
Lacy Bach—*redhead*

IN EAST AFRICA

Darby Spock—*white hunter*
Mohammed Bello—*devout believer*
Maria Vincente—*woman loved by Darby Spock*
Charles Vincente—*proponent of Intensive Love*
Nylun Bobutu—*wise man*
Waldo—*brain*
Carmen—*heart*
Phillip—*eyes and ears*
Talia O'Brien—*soul*

IN SAN FRANCISCO

John Hartford Hennesey—*cockeyed optimist*
Tess Hennesey—*inventor of faster-than-light space drive*
Susannah Hennesey—*virgin & robot*
Reynal—*smartest "robot" who isn't*
Henry—*his motto: to serve man*
Mary-Margaret Munro—*retired striptease artiste*
(Cobbler) Tom Griffith—*former British Prime Minister* (C)

IN WINESAP

Roy Goldman—*pulp fiction writer*
Theda Goldman—*not who she seems to be*
Ginger Cunningham—*constant reader*
Lucius B. Washington—*last of the old time catfighters*
Oscar Stovall—*literary critic*

Jayne Stovall—*refuses to work in Pearson's back rooms*
Hiram Evers—*town bandmaster*
Samuel Brady—*owner of Winesap's second largest secret library*
Bob Jones—*pimp*

IN TIBET

Bludoni—*wise ass guru*
Georgi Gustanov—*pilot who brought down the slug*
Louie Roth—*dental patient*
Ling Chi Ho (Dr.)—*tooth extractor*
Mario Donatello—*opera's most perfect tenor voice*
Isaac—*computer nerd*
Brother Xavier—*colorblind monk*
Irwin Jacob Levitsky—*crank sociologist*
Nora Malloy—*psychic*

ALSO

Vasily Andreev—*vishee*
Sally Marx Berryman—*gold-digger*
William James Berryman—*grievously wounded at Belleau Wood*
Bimbo—*dancing bear*
Scarlet Tewkesbury Cipriano Blue (aka Emerald Blaze)—*ex-wife*
Pierre Chabrol—*traveling salesman of intimate apparel*
Marcel de Sarnot—*author of* Mysterion, *a memoir*
Eric/Petra Fassbinder—*accountant*
Richard Benjamin Ford—*God's diligent pilgrim on Earth*
Carlotta McCoy Hennesey—*astronaut*
Koko—*clown*
Rosie Kovacs—*dog-faced lady*
Victor/Herman Lindstrom—*former Nazi*
Queenie O'Rourke—*Aussie gun moll*
Anna Provosky—*prima ballerina assoluta*
Jorge Renaldo—*evolutionary theorist*
Meredith Savard—*modern artist*
Simon & Beatrix Schwerner—*Los Angeles science fiction fans*
Sergio I (Roncallo)—*leper*
Felipe Taglia—*equipped with marvelous appendage*
Hugo von Schneider (Baron)—*sadist*

About suffering they were never wrong,
The Old Masters: how well they understood
Its Human position; how it takes place
While someone else is eating or opening a window or just walking
    dully along;
How, when the aged are reverently, passionately waiting
For the miraculous birth, there always must be
Children who did not specially want it to happen, skating
On a pond at the edge of the wood:
                    —W. H. Auden, "Musee des Beaux Arts"

"As I understand it, it is a theory of theirs," answered Flambeau, "that a man can endure anything if his mind is quite steady. Their two great symbols are the sun and the open eye; for they say that if a man were really healthy he could stare at the sun."

"If a man were really healthy," said Father Brown, "he would not bother to stare at it."

                    —G. K. Chesterton, "The Eye of Apollo"

"Ever been bit by a bee?"

                    —Walter Brennan in
                    the Howard Hawks film
                    To Have and Have Not

BOOK ONE

ALL THAT IS THE CASE

"You're a mess honey. You've been eating too much candy."

—Marlene Dietrich to Orson Welles
in Welles's film *Touch of Evil*

1

The door dilated and Dr. Gordon Schwerner stepped through the gap. A thin rigid intense man of twenty-four years dressed in a dapper white linen suit, Schwerner carried a manila envelope under one arm.

Inside the dank sweltering room Desmond Blue, the world's greatest detective, sat cross-legged on the hard earthen floor. A dog, an Afghan hound, slept at his feet. As the door folded shut behind Schwerner, Blue raised his shaven head and glared through hooded eyes. "Damn you, Doctor," he growled. "I left strict word not to be disturbed."

Schwerner sniffed the air meaningfully.

The sweetly pervasive stench of opium filled the tiny basement room. It had been months since the last of Blue's private dope-buying excursions away from Arabia Deserta—the geographically inaccurate name by which he called his Saharan home—but his stash never seemed to diminish. Blue, a giant of a man, six-four, close to three hundred pounds, bulbous-nosed, red-eyed, gripped the bowl of a long-stemmed pipe.

"If you're busy," said Schwerner, "I suppose the matter could be postponed." Sweat beaded his brow and chin. Outside beneath the savage Saharan sun the heat could hardly have been worse.

"I thought you intended to go fishing in the moat," said Blue.

"When this came up I altered my plans."

Blue shut his eyes and recited in a nasal tone: "'You will find angling to be like the virtue of humility, which has a calmness of spirit and a world of other blessings attending upon it. We may say of angling as Dr. Boteler said of strawberries: "Doubtless God could have made a better berry, but doubtless God never did"; and so, if I might be judged, God never did make a more calm, quiet, innocent recreation than angling.'"

Blue opened his eyes and heaved a heavy sigh. "I quote here from Izaak Walton. Go fishing, Doctor, and to hell with the rest of it."

"This is important, Desmond."

"If you insist." Blue extended a hand. "Let me see what you have there." On occasion in the past—between cases—Blue had been known to lapse into torpid inactivity. After a year's retirement, he was worse than ever.

Schwerner slipped the envelope behind his back. "I want your full undivided attention, Desmond. I need you to be alert."

Blue smiled and when he did the pallid flesh of his cheeks and throat smoothed out, giving him a peculiarly child-like appearance. "I am alert, Doctor. Sunnyside-up. Like a fried goose egg. Now let me see that envelope of yours."

"The opium…"

"So? What of Coleridge and his stately pleasure dome decreed? Surely you are not daring to insinuate that the most profound of English romantic poets was not alert."

"I wouldn't know," said Schwerner drily. "I've never been especially fond of verse."

Blue chuckled grimly, focusing on the pipe in his hand. "Nor have I now that I think of it. I'm a practicing detective, you remember, and a retired one at that. Now give." Blue reached out to take the envelope.

Schwerner scurried back a few steps. "I really ought to brief you first."

Blue shrugged ponderously. "As you wish." He patted the hound. "Good Baskerville, good dog."

Schwerner spoke hastily, fearing he might have pressed his advantage too far. "As you may recall I have recently been monitoring the efforts of a certain scientific cabal in Switzerland to probe the mysteries of time. Only today has definite proof come into my hands indicating that these efforts have met with success."

Blue's eyebrows rose questioningly. "A time machine?"

Schwerner shook his head. "A time camera. One capable of taking photographs of the past."

Blue nodded with more interest than he had shown before. "And you've obtained evidence?"

"I have. The initial successful experiment occurred some six weeks ago. The device was placed inside a sealed laboratory, the shutter activated from without. The resulting photograph depicted the room not as it was but rather as it had been exactly one year before. The fortuitous presence of a wall calendar provided confirmation."

"Six weeks ago?" said Blue. "And I wasn't informed until now?"

"The degree of secrecy surrounding the project has been quite extensive. Even today fewer than a dozen people outside the inner cabal are knowledgeable of its success."

"A dozen plus us," said Blue.

Schwerner beamed with pride. "Our espionage network remains second to none."

"In spite of my retirement?"

"I have assumed you'd wish to remain in touch with global developments."

Blue again reached for the envelope and this time Schwerner handed it over. Blue flipped open the flap, then paused. "Consider the possibilities," he said. "Helen of Troy in her bath. Caesar and Cleopatra in the act of physical love. The private lives of public figures."

"I think you ought to look at the evidence, Desmond."

Blue shrugged and removed a dozen still photographs from the envelope. He examined the first closely. It showed a frail bearded young man nailed to a wooden cross.

"These couldn't be faked?"

"Do you think so?"

"From the poor devil's expression it's either real or else they've uncovered the finest dramatic actor in history."

Blue studied the second photograph. Another bearded man—Lincoln—an instant before the bullet.

The third photograph also depicted a violent encounter: John Kennedy at the moment of fatal impact. The fourth, in an abrupt alteration of mood, showed Christopher Columbus (who else could it be?) wading ashore on San Salvador.

Blue turned the photograph toward Schwerner. "Was it necessary to move the device each time a new scene was recorded?"

"The camera had to be present at the event's actual location, yes."

"What if it was observed?"

"Apparently it couldn't be."

"They seem to have gotten around quite a bit in only six weeks."

"The project is well funded. A consortium of twenty or so surviving wealthy men and women including the San Francisco multimillionaire John Hartford Hennesey."

"So the very rich are back with us again," said Blue. Moving rapidly on, he skimmed the remaining photographs: an Egyptian pharaoh, presumably Cheops, gazing proudly at a half-built pyramid; the Battle of—Blue guessed—Gettysburg; the beheading of Louis XVI; Mohammed entering Mecca at the head of his desert army; the signing of the Declaration of American Independence; the execution by fire of the deranged martyr Joan of Arc; Moses descending from Sinai with his tablets of stone. The twelfth and final photograph was yet another snapshot of murder: a bloody spook in a stained toga surrounded by a mob of knife-wielding assassins.

Blue clucked his tongue sympathetically. "Poor Caesar, yes, but not in the act of love."

Schwerner reached into his coat pocket and removed another photograph, "I held this one out because I didn't understand it. Do you know who or when it's supposed to be?"

Blue examined this last photograph. It showed a wild-eyed little man with a stubby brush of a moustache. A crowd of uniformed retainers hovered nearby.

"Adolf Hitler in the bunker. May 1945, I would suspect."

Schwerner shook his head. "Who?"

"Hitler, the German leader during World War II."

"I'm afraid I'm not familiar with the man."

Blue nodded. "I'm surprised you recognized the others, Doctor. Your education was rather single-minded and you did not—"

Blue stopped suddenly. His jaw slackened and his hands shook. He emitted a gasp of shock.

"Desmond, what is it?" said Schwerner.

Blue shook his head. In the thirteenth photograph—the one of Hitler and his henchmen—the figure of a blond-haired pinch-faced man could be seen lurking in the background. "Notice this fellow here?" said Blue.

Schwerner nodded, "Yes. But who—?"

"And this one?"

In the photograph of the Lincoln assassination among the theater-goers the same blond-haired pinch-faced man.

"My God," said Schwerner, stunned.

"Then you see it too?"

"I…yes. Those two men—they're—"

"One and the same," said Blue. "They're identical."

A PROFILE: THE SLUG OCCUPATION

They arrived in the sky over Earth one fine April day in their ships the color of gold. Seventy-seven ships ranging around the circumference of the globe, ships that seemed to chase the rising sun.

In their wake, the golden ships left a wave of devastation, destruction, and (at least for a time) death.

Among the cities, towns, and villages annihilated: San Francisco; Rome; Joplin Missouri; Dar-es-Salaam; Minsk and Kiev; Padua; Paterson NJ; Quebec and Geneva; St. Louis and St. Petersburg (Florida); Venice in California and Venice in Italy; Salt Lake City and Mecca; Springfield Mass and Springfield VA; Benares, Mecca, Kyoto, and Austin Texas; Mukilteo, Washington; Pittsburgh PA and Pittsburgh CA; seventeen obscure villages along the upper Yangtze; and three of the five metropolitan boroughs of greater New York City.

Among the towns and cities spared: London and Athens; Bangkok and Baghdad; Tangier, Paris, Berlin, Moscow, Tijuana; and Winesap, Illinois.

Pocatello, Idaho was razed.

Shanghai China was undisturbed.

Portland, Maine was obliterated.

Portland, Oregon was unscathed.

Although much of incorporated Los Angeles County was leveled, Hollywood and Malibu were not touched.

Seventy-seven ships the color of gold—all in a single April day.

Not only were certain towns, cities, and villages destroyed but anyone and everyone within their borders either died or else disappeared without a trace.

In 17% of the affected areas the entire human population was struck instantly dead.

Three days later all of the dead returned to "life" again. In most respects the resurrected corpses remained oblivious to the ordeal they'd gone through. They walked, they talked, they laughed, they cried—the same as always.

One thing they didn't do—since technically they remained dead—was breathe. Nor did they sleep.

Rather than allowing themselves to be referred to by such viciously derogatory canards as zombies, golems, vampires or worse, the resurrected dead insisted on being called simply "spooks."

"Spooks we are and damned proud of it too," a spook spokesperson in the ruins of Brooklyn declared.

Spook pride! became a popular teeshirt slogan among the dead and many of the living alike.

In time people began to notice that the spooks never seemed to age. Or become ill. Or die. (Except by their own hand.)

In general spooks preferred keeping to their own kind. Privately operated "spook reservations" sprang up around the world to cater to their wants and needs.

Oh, and they smelled. They stank. They reeked of death. Drugstore sales of cheap perfume reached record levels near the spook reservations.

In the remaining 83% of the towns, cities, and villages left in ruins by passing of the golden ships, no human remains were ever found. Blue ribbon teams of United Nations pathologists scoured the ruins without success. The people who had lived there had simply disappeared, vanished, gone kaput.

Where had they gone? Who had taken them? Why and what for?

None of these questions could be answered.

The "taken" became for a brief time the popular way of referring to the missing millions, spurring a short lived religious revival among Christians and Moslems alike.

But then these "taken" began to reappear. To come back. To return.

Strange, previously unknown people dressed in tattered rags began to appear in growing numbers in the devastated areas. "Savages" they were at first deemed based on their ragged attire and steadfast refusal to respond to inquiries, official and unofficial alike. DNA samples surreptitiously obtained from a number of savages soon led to identification. The savages, it turned out, were the former residents of the destroyed areas thought to have vanished. When confronted by evidence of who they used to be, the savages were dismissive. They continued living their brute hand-to-mouth lives in the ruins of the destroyed towns, cities, and villages regardless of who or what they may have been before. No clear pattern could be detected in where or when a particular savage might return. A man who'd vanished in the destruction of San Francisco might show up years later as a savage living in the ruins of St. Louis while his beloved wife of twenty years reappeared in devastated Brussels, while his ten-year-old son was in Salt Lake City and his six-year-old daughter the Upper Yangtze.

Largely because of the presence of so many savages, few others ("lifers" as they were called) evidenced much interest in resettling the devastated areas. In addition, popular superstition held that the destroyed towns, cities, and villages were somehow cursed and should be shunned.

In addition to those living in the ruined areas, several distinct categories of people also vanished that day.

Among these were:

All major political leaders wielding actual rather than virtual power whether visible or invisible including various kings, princes, sheiks, presidents, premiers, emperors, judges, justices, speakers of houses of parliament, county assessors, and party chairpersons.

All recognized leaders of organized religious faiths or factions from popes to preachers, from shamans to swamis, from rabbis to television evangelists.

All military officers above the rank of army colonel and several hundred below including in Paraguay two corporals then plotting a coup.

All scientists and engineers whose normal daily work involved (if only peripherally) the creation or maintenance of weapons capable of inflicting mass death upon other human beings.

(The weapons of mass destruction themselves simply ceased to exist as well. *Poof.* Gone in an instant as the golden ships flew over were all stores and stocks of H-bombs, A-bombs, death rays, chemical and bacteriological agents. Rifles, handguns, knives, and swords remained untouched. For any nation wishing to start a war against a neighbor, these crude devices were the only remaining means with which to wage it. Unsurprisingly, world peace soon reigned throughout the globe.)

Of the scientists and engineers who survived the passing of the golden ships, none admitted having even the vaguest notion of how to go about building replacement weapons of mass destruction. "I think I did used to know something about that," said one physicist, a veteran of the Second World War Manhattan Project, "but it seems to have somehow slipped my mind in the interim."

Seventy-seven ships the color of gold, all in a single April day, wreaking destruction wherever they passed.

And then they were gone.

With one exception.

Near Moscow a MiG-21 fighter piloted by the highly decorated Captain Georgi Gustanov of the Soviet Air Force managed to penetrate in series of deft tactical maneuvers the invisible defensive shield surrounding the golden ships and with a single well-placed missile sent one of them hurtling down toward the earth below.

According to witnesses on the ground, a living entity was pulled from the flaming wreckage and immediately whisked away covered in woolen blankets to an undisclosed secret location by senior Soviet security officials.

Three days later a brief bulletin from the Soviet News Agency TASS confirmed the capture of "the biggest, ugliest, nastiest, slimiest, green-skinned, yellow-bellied banana slug you ever saw in your life." (In rough translation from the original Russian.)

Interrogations of the captive were said to be continuing apace with further announcements promised as soon as difficulties in language were resolved.

This was the last official word ever heard concerning the captured entity.

In the wake of the Soviet announcement, the unknown beings operating the golden ships previously referred to as everything from "fallen angels" to "devils in disguise" and "scary monsters from the void" were now universally known as "the slugs."

To confuse matters further, a team of Dutch-German astronomers soon issued a report based on a meticulous study of stellar positioning which stated that the Earth was now some sixty-seven days ahead of where it should have been in its current revolutionary route around the Sun.

In other words, the scientists declared, sixty-seven days in the history of the world were now unaccounted for.

To add to the growing confusion, vast numbers of people now came forward reporting that they had all experienced the exact same dream the night after the golden ships passed by. In the course of this dream, time itself was observed to run in a reverse direction. The present became the past, the future stretched endlessly farther into the distance, the sun set in the east and rose in the west, people grew younger by the hour, the dead rose up out of their graves while newborn infants returned to the womb, and a milk glass if you dropped and broke it immediately reconstituted itself.

In a survey of voting age adults conducted by the Gallup Organization 93% of all respondents reported having experienced this same dream. (The remaining 4% either didn't know, couldn't remember, or had no opinion.)

A book entitled *The Slugs Own Us!* by the self-described Fortean philosopher Phineas K. Bump theorizing that the missing sixty-seven days were in actuality a period of occupation during which the creatures in the golden ships—called "slugs"[1] for convenience sake—after first sending the human population back through time to get them out of the way, made a number of significant alterations to the world they occupied. "The slugs did this," wrote Bump, "because they own us and wished to improve the value of their property."

The book became an immediate (if somewhat controversial) international best seller.

Proponents of the Bump Hypothesis pointed to widely shared public feelings of anxiety and discomfort in the wake of the slug attack. Great numbers of people described feeling as if they had just entered a familiar room in their own home after a brief moment's absence and sensing that somehow things had been changed, moved around, altered without their knowledge or consent.

Pharmacists reported an increase of up to 900% in the number of prescriptions for anti-anxiety drugs being filled.

2

The elevator rose with the effortless ease of a shark through water. Within lurked a pint-sized rat-faced man of twenty-two years with a wiry clump of black hair and long sensitive lashes. When the elevator stopped and the doors slid open the young man sprang forward into the hall with the delicate caution of a cat on the prowl.

Directly opposite him another young man in a linen suit stood stiffly in front of a thick oaken door. When he saw the first man pounce from the elevator this second man scowled and shook his head curtly. "Desmond can't see you, Alfie. He can't t see anyone now."

"Bullshit, Schwerner," said Alfie Jarrett, continuing forward. "Desmond's always willing to see me."

Dr. Schwerner looked smug. "As a matter of fact he specifically instructed me to tell both you and Peter to keep out."

"Do you really expect me to believe that?" Alfie placed a hand on the brass doorknob and gave a quick jerk. The knob caught and held.

Schwerner beamed triumphantly.

Alfie wheeled. "You bastard. Why didn't you tell me it was locked?"

"Because it wasn't me, Alfie. Desmond must have done it himself. From the inside. I told you he doesn't wish to be disturbed."

"Okay," said Alfie, some of the anger leaving his face. "I'll bite. What goes on?"

"I'm afraid," said Schwerner, "that I am not at liberty to disclose the details at this time."

"Oh, yeah?" With a quick grin Alfie reached inside his leather jacket and removed a stiletto. He flicked open the six-inch blade. "You sure you want to make an issue out of this?"

"Don't be an ass, Alfie. You're hardly going to use that thing on me."

"Says who? It's happened before. The hand can always slip. Just an accident but the poor sap's still dead."

"If you ever harmed me," Schwerner said stiffly, "Desmond would send you off to prison where you rightly belong and you know it."

With a knowing wink Alfie let his jacket fall shut and looped an arm around Schwerner's shoulders. "So how about a little hint then? Peter says he caught Desmond throwing away a basket full of good dope. That's not normal behavior, you know."

Schwerner squirmed until he succeeded in breaking free of Alfie's grasp. "Please don't do that. You know I don't like to be touched."

"Then how about spilling some beans?"

"All right." Schwerner adjusted his garments. "I suppose it can't hurt to reveal this much: I definitely believe it's going to be a case."

"No kidding," said Alfie, pleased. "So what's it going to be this time? Murder, kidnap, extortion, gang rape, what?"

Schwerner looked vague. "It's nothing like that. This is something totally different from anything we've ever handled before. It's big, Alfie—bigger than you can imagine. Even if I had the liberty—and I don't—I couldn't begin to explain. Desmond will have to tell you in his own good time."

"Which had better be soon." Alfie shook his head. "I don't know about you, Schwerner, but one year of doing nothing is plenty for me. If I wanted to go stir crazy I'd have stayed in prison."

Schwerner nodded his head in the direction of the door. "He's not alone in there either."

"Nadia?" said Alfie.

"Crystal and Lacy too. The three of them. For more than an hour now."

Alfie's smile grew wider. Nadia, Crystal, and Lacy were Desmond Blue's confidential secretaries. "I'll tell you what, Schwerner, I'm going down and tell Peter the good news. If anything happens you come and get me right away."

Schwerner looked glum. "I wouldn't anticipate anything so soon. This is a particularly complex case. It might be days, weeks even…"

"Just let me know. Okay?"

"All right."

Alfie took the stairs two at a time going down. As he approached Peter Mark's room in the east wing of Arabia Deserta, the flutter of guitar music reached his ears from an open door. He rapped twice on the wall, then entered.

The room was small and cluttered, stacks of books piled everywhere. Peter Mark sat on the edge of a narrow cot, guitar balanced on a crossed knee. As Alfie entered, Peter laid the guitar aside and beamed a greeting with liquid blue eyes in the expressionless steel mask of his face.

"You don't have to stop on my account," said Alfie. He made a bare spot for himself on the floor and sat cross-legged. "I enjoy listening to you play."

"That's all right," said Peter. "I want to know about Desmond. What did you find out? Anything?"

When he spoke Peter's voice emanated from a speaker embedded in his throat. He wore corduroy jeans, a plaid checkered shirt, and brown suede shoes. Underneath the clothes his body was composed of skin and blood, flesh and bone. Only his face, head, throat, and hands had been damaged in the accident and consequently recreated out of hard steel. "Did you manage to talk to him?"

"He's holed up in the study with the three ladies. I couldn't get in. The door's locked."

"Isn't that rather odd?"

"Schwerner was standing guard. He says it's going to be a case."

"Is he positive?"

"He acts like he is."

Peter smiled with his eyes. "That's tremendous." He leaned back on the bed and placed his steel hands behind his steel skull. "Did Gordon tell you what the case involved?"

"'I am not at liberty to disclose the details at this time,'" said Alfie in a voice mocking Schwerner's own. Both men laughed. "You can believe that if you want but I say he's just being tight-assed."

Peter shook his head disapprovingly. "Gordon has had a difficult life, Alfie. We all ought to try and show compassion."

"No tougher life than yours or mine."

"That's not for us to judge. The deaths of both parents, the horrible isolation of that dreadful island. Did you know that all he had to read during the years he was growing up were scientific texts and fantastic novels?"

"And no little girls to diddle around with either."

"You're not being fair, Alfie."

"Maybe. But sometimes the guy grates on my nerves."

"I wonder when Desmond will be able to tell us more."

"According to Schwerner maybe not for weeks. So who knows? Remember the case with the crazy coot going around chopping up kids with an axe and mailing the bloody body parts to the parents? Desmond accepts a huge fee and then sits on his ass upstairs alone in the study for three weeks. Then one day he rings for you and me and we fly off to Nova Scotia. Desmond walks up to some fatso eating an ice cream cone on a street corner and puts the grab on him. The fatso confesses. 'Yes, I did it. I'm sorry I did but I couldn't help myself. Can't you understand? It wasn't my fault.' How did Desmond know? 'My methods are not subject to review.' Christ, Peter. This might turn out to be another one like that."

"But you don't think so," said Peter with his usual quickness of mind.

"No, and neither does Schwerner. If this really is a case, then it's got to be something as big as the Pacific Ocean. Remember, Desmond retired because he said there weren't any more challenges. Well, I'm giving him twenty-four hours and if he's not out of the study by then I'll kick down the door and drag it out of him."

"So what are you doing tonight?"

The abrupt change in subject took Alfie by surprise. "Tonight? I don't know. Playing poker with Crystal and Lacy, I suppose. If they're out of the study by then."

"Then why not come downstairs with me instead? I'm going to preach a special sermon to the beastmen tonight. I'm sure it's going to do them a world of good."

Alfie felt embarrassed. Peter was his best friend—maybe his only real friend—and he hated having to say no, but those things down in the basement—the so-called beastmen Schwerner had taken under his wing—they turned his gut. The beastmen were failed experiments, demented creations of a genuinely mad scientist Desmond Blue had put out of business some years ago on a remote island far beyond Hawaii. The scientist had been attempting to transform wild animals into civilized human beings by various arcane vivisection methods but it hadn't worked out—not completely—and the beastmen had emerged neither fully human nor fully animal. An organization devoted to the cause of protecting supposedly defenseless animals had hired Blue to investigate certain rumors. He had gone to the island and arrested the scientist but instead of destroying the beastmen—which any sane person would have done—because of a plea for mercy from Schwerner, who wasn't normally so softhearted, he had agreed to bring them back to Arabia Deserta and install them in the basement. The only animal Alfie had ever had any use for was Blue's Afghan hound Baskerville and that was only because Baskerville was so stupid you couldn't help liking him. Animals that walked on two legs and spoke broken English made him queasy. "You wouldn't want me in there. The beastmen hate my guts anyhow."

"If they do, Alfie, it's only because they don't really know you. And you don't know them. The beastmen are truly innocent—pure unfallen spirits. For them all experience is intense. There are no gradations, no shadings. They either love or hate with nothing between."

"You're a lot more lovable than I am, Peter."

"You shouldn't sell yourself short, Alfie. The divine spark resides equally in all of us."

"Don't give me that old crap, Peter. You know I'm an atheist. I've committed far too many sins in my life to start believing in God and his good buddy Jesus. I've got enough real problems without worrying about going to hell forever."

"That's a self-limiting proposition, Alfie. God would surely forgive your sins as He's forgiven so many others. That's the meaning of Jesus, you know."

"If he was any sort of decent god He wouldn't forgive me anything. I don't forgive myself. Why should He?"

"Because your soul emerged from His special essence. The same as all of us.

"Including the beastmen?"

"I—yes. Including them."

"Look, Peter, I—" Alfie broke off. From the hall he heard the click of boot heels approaching. "Listen—it's one of the ladies." Bounding to his feet Alfie hurried to the door in time to see a petite raven-haired woman whose skin seemed to glow with a peculiar sheen sweep past.

She wore thigh-length black leather boots, a purple satin blouse, and denim shorts that clung to her slender hips like glue.

"Hey, Nadia," he said as she went past.

Nadia van Hauten was the senior of Blue's three secretaries, all gorgeous and, more importantly, equally whip smart.

Blue liked to say that surrounding himself with smart beautiful women made his own longtime celibate state more meaningful.

"What's up, Alfie?" she said, striding past.

"Where you going, Nadia?" he called after her.

"Crazy," she said.

Peter hovered behind Alfie. "It must be the library," he said softly.

"Doing researching on the case. Come on. Let's follow her."

"Nadia won't tell us anything without Desmond's permission. You know that."

"Who said anything about telling? We're detectives, aren't we? Let's detect."

The two of them followed the woman at a circumspect distance until she disappeared through a door at the end of the hall. It was the library, all right. Alfie darted forward and positioned himself to one side of the door. He gestured at Peter to stand on the other side.

Five minutes passed before the woman reappeared balancing a pile of books in her arms. As she came through the door her eyes lit on Peter and she turned quickly away only to discover Alfie inches from her elbow.

He grinned. "So we meet again, gorgeous."

"Just my rotten luck."

Nadia hurried quickly on down the hall.

"Well?" said Peter as the sound of her boot heels faded way. What did you see?"

Alfie shook his head. "You're not going to believe this."

"Why not?"

"Because those books she was carrying—you want to know what they were? History books—illustrated histories—all about Hitler and Russia and that sort of stuff."

Peter rubbed the curve of his steel chin thoughtfully. "But it's got to be about the case. Desmond wouldn't take time out for anything else right now."

"If it is," said Alfie with a shrug, "then it sure must be a damned old one."

3

In the privacy of his study observed only by the coolly efficient eyes of his three confidential secretaries Desmond Blue, a mountain of a man and a brilliant detective as well, balanced his round chin in his meaty palms and wondered whether he ought to be laughing or weeping aloud. Dressed in a shabby yellow dressing gown, sunk deep in the folds of his favorite easy chair, Blue did neither. On a tray near his elbow rested the newest batch of time photographs obtained by Dr. Schwerner—an additional twenty-one to augment the original thirteen.

On this same tray lay a sheet of paper, the master list Blue had just finished compiling. He gave a heavy sigh. The facts were now clear; only a single interpretation remained possible: this was a case, all right, maybe the biggest case in the history of the human race. For that reason alone—the enormous significance of the matter—Blue didn't know whether he ought to be stricken with despair or overwhelmed by joy.

"Nadia," he said, lifting his head and gazing at the secretaries who sat neatly hip to hip on the loveseat across from him. Nadia was the brunette, Crystal the blonde, and Lacy the redhead. The three enjoyed his total trust and confidence.

"Yes, boss," said Nadia, already on her feet.

"Go down to the library and fetch me some books. I want histories. Photographic histories. Bring as many as you can carry at one time."

"Will do." She headed for the door.

Blue observed her pert rear end clearly outlined under the thin denim fabric. He felt nothing—no lustful stirrings. The urge is gone for good, he thought. After all these years of torture and suffering I ought to feel pleased.

As Nadia slipped through the door, Blue caught a glimpse of Dr. Schwerner lurking in the hall. Damn the man, Blue thought, with a sudden rush of emotion. Damn Schwerner and his bloody espionage network. Do I really need this case?

Blue had been retired—reasonably content—stoned out of his gourd most of the time—for a year. And now this—this challenge.

For the past twelve months Blue had steadfastly refused all offers of employment. His last case, fumigating the human vermin in a Rocky Mountain town gone rotten to the core, had brought in a cool million dollar fee. With no financial worries he had elected to say the hell with it for good. The Rocky Mountain town: it hadn't been a case—an intellectual puzzle—it had been a small scale war where one either killed or else died. Blue had not died but his spirit was grievously wounded, his last cherished dreams annihilated. In his mind's eye through the many years he had practiced the art of detection he had always envisioned confronting opponents as worthy as the Doctors Moriarty, Mabuse, and No; Red Scharlach; or Flambeau the master thief before the priest Brown convinced him to pursue the straighter path.

What he had long sought was simply a nemesis equal to himself but the Rocky Mountain town had seemed to put an end to that quest. Forty-seven dead, three times that number in jail, and not one man worthy either of a bullet or a cage. As a consequence, Blue had lapsed into retirement, sickened by the corruption of his labors.

It was true that on a few occasions in the last year he had surreptitiously slipped away from Arabia Deserta to investigate certain interesting situations brought to his attention through private sources. None of these leads had developed into a firm case, however. If a woman had been found stuffed inside a chimney, if a viper had struck through a solid wall, if a purloined letter or Maltese falcon had needed finding Blue would have returned eagerly to the game afoot. But he knew by now that these visions were mere fantasy while the other—the bloody slaughterhouse of a Rocky Mountain mining community—represented brute reality. He demanded the former but only the latter existed in reality.

Until now. Until fantasy had become reality and the world's greatest practicing detective—himself—at last discovered an opponent as cunning and diabolical as any that might have crept from the pages of the most fantastical literature.

Blue removed the master list from the tray and read it over once more. There were three handwritten columns on the page. The first—definite appearances of the pinch-faced blond man he had spotted with Hitler and Lincoln—now totaled four.

The second column dealt with a swarthy, darkly beautiful woman: so far she had turned up in five of the photographs. The third column listed the appearances—also five—of a hatchet-faced narrow-eyed man who seemed to favor political disturbances: Blue had positively identified him in first century Jerusalem, in Petrograd 1917, and in Charleston South Carolina April 1861.

Still, as damning as the evidence was, the master list told only part of the tale. Blue's initial hypothesis based upon an earlier, less complete version of the list had failed to build a sufficient case. Science has invented a time camera (he had reasoned) so why not at some future date a legitimate time traveling machine as well? These three recurring figures might therefore represent nothing more sinister than visitors from some future age come to observe the more remarkable events of the past.

An admirable theory. Neat and acceptable.

And then—an hour ago—Schwerner had arrived with the second batch of photographs.

At the top of the pile lay another snapshot of the crucifixion, a somewhat earlier glimpse in time.

Two Roman soldiers pounding spikes into the palms of the condemned Messiah. Two soldiers, one turned facing the camera.

In horror Blue had recognized the now familiar countenance of the hatchet-faced, narrow-eyed man.

It was then that Blue had first experienced those conflicting emotions: joy and despair.

It was a case—God was it ever!—a genuine case.

Could he crack it?

Blue laid the master list aside and whispered a single word: "Evil." Melodramatic? Perhaps. But these people were not mere observers of history; they were participants. One of them had helped kill Jesus Christ.

If not evil then what else could they be?

When Nadia returned from the library Blue told her to leave the books near his chair where he could easily reach them.

He took the topmost volume off the stack and wrenched it open.

A Pictorial History of Twentieth Century Warfare. Suppressing his monumental pity and disgust Blue turned the pages. Finishing the book he reached for another—*Great Criminals of Yesteryear*—and again examined each blurry photograph. He went through the lot. Every book. Only at the end did he reach a definite conclusion. They simply were not there—none of the three—pinch-faced man, narrow-eyed man, darkly beautiful woman. Clearly they had managed to avoid the pages of official history.

Which could mean only one thing: these people were not merely evil; they were also intelligent and cunning.

The case was definitely firming up.

Blue rose from his chair.

From the loveseat the secretaries eyed him expectantly. "Something else, Desmond?" said Crystal, the least patient of the three.

"Yes. One thing. I want you to place a person-to-person call for me. To the Vatican. Do you think you can do that?"

She looked confused. "To the what?"

Blue shook his head. "No, of course not. You wouldn't be likely to know. Have Nadia explain. She's old enough to remember. In fact forget the call. I'm sure the number wouldn't be listed. You three can go to bed."

Blue headed toward the door. Lacy, the youngest and newest of the three, hastened over and held it open for him. As he passed Blue patted her cheek and smiled.

In the corridor Dr. Schwerner waited expectantly.

Blue brushed past him and hurried toward the stairs.

Schwerner, after a moment's hesitation. hastened in pursuit. "Any instructions, Desmond? Anything I can do?"

"Yes," Blue called back over a shoulder. "Fetch Peter. If he's asleep rouse him. Warm up the aeroplane. I want to go as soon as possible."

"Go? Go where?"

"Rome."

"In Italy?"

"There's a man I must see."

"Who?"

"The Pope."

"You mean there is one?"

"The last I heard there was, yes."

They headed down the stairs, Blue in the lead, Schwerner following close behind. "But what do you want with the Pope?"

"A client, Doctor. As you ought to be aware it's a serious violation of professional ethics to investigate a case without specific authority. The Pope strikes me as a good first bet not only as an employer but also to provide a few early clues as well."

"Then it is a case?" said Schwerner.

Blue burst through the door leading to the ground floor hallway. "It is indeed," he confirmed. "We have a case."

A PROFILE: DR. GORDON SCHWERNER

Even as a child Gordon Nathan Schwerner was a shy, nervous lad who seldom smiled and never laughed. He was nearly four years old before he felt the need to utter his initial words and these were numbers—seven, eleven, thirteen, nineteen—for reasons never fully understood.

Gordon was the first and only child born to the union of Simon and Beatrix Schwerner, Caltech educated engineers who had married fairly late in life—he in his forties, she in her middle thirties—even though they had been business partners for a number of years before. Perhaps because of the tardiness of their son's arrival in terms of their own lives Simon and Beatrix tended from the beginning to watch over him with an obsessive protectiveness. Gordon was never allowed outside the precincts of the Schwerner home in Phoenix Arizona—where both parents also worked—and no one was ever permitted inside except for a pediatrician named Alvah Silberman who came by once each week on Thursday afternoons without ever finding anything significantly wrong with the basically healthy young boy.

By the time Simon and Beatrix had married both were independently wealthy from the many various inventions they had together built during their professional collaboration. Several years earlier they had developed a device which when fitted to the carburetor of an internal-combustion engine allowed an automobile to travel up to five thousand miles on a single tank of gasoline. The patent on this invention had been sold to a major multinational oil firm for a sum in excess of two hundred million dollars. The device was never heard of again, a fact which did not noticeably disturb the Schwerners who were by then much involved in an entirely new project and who rode bicycles or walked everywhere they went.

This new project of theirs was the invention of a practical household robot, a computer in human form but many times more intelligent and efficient than any flesh-and-blood man or woman. Once the invention had been perfected the Schwerners sold all legal right and title to the speculator John Hartford Hennesey who intended to market the device on a worldwide basis and bring about a second industrial revolution. Hennesey paid the Schwerners in excess of three hundred million dollars for the patent but the seventy-seven golden ships of the slugs soon appeared in the sky overhead and spoiled his marketing plans.

By the time of the robot patent sale young Gordon Nathan Schwerner was approaching five years of age and in the considered opinion of his parents was at last old enough to travel beyond the boundaries of the family home. Perhaps as a consequence of this Simon and Beatrix also reached a decision that the time was ripe to follow through on a vow they had exchanged at the time of their marriage to eventually quit the world of science and business and seek private sanctuary elsewhere. After secretly purchasing an uninhabited island in an isolated corner of the South Pacific, they quietly moved all their belongings and soon followed with their son and five robot prototypes, their possession of which they had managed to conceal from Hennesey. One of the robots had not only been taught to read and write and perform basic housekeeping chores but was also skillfully programmed in the medical sciences.

Among the possessions the Schwerners moved to their island retreat was a library numbering some thirty thousand volumes, mostly scientific texts but also including an exhaustive accumulation of nearly all the science fiction and fantasy literature ever written. Both Simon and Beatrix were confirmed devotees of the genre, an interest which had first brought them together as members of a science fiction fan society in Los Angeles California.

A month after the Schwerners set up permanent housekeeping on their private island, the golden ships of what became known as the Occupancy appeared in the sky and in the course of a single day one hundred twenty million people around the world vanished. Among these—likely due to the estimated half-billion dollars deposited in their bank accounts around the world—were Nathan and Beatrix Schwerner.

Gordon Nathan Schwerner was not harmed. Noting the disappearance of his parents, Gordon asked each of the five robots in turn to offer a possible explanation as to what might have become of them but since the Occupancy was in no way explicable they were unable to come up with anything suitable.

As a result, Gordon Schwerner spent his formative years alone on his parents' private island accompanied only by the five robots and the library of thirty thousand books.

In the course of his voluminous reading—likely owing to his utter lack of experience in the outer world—Gordon displayed a confusion in separating fact from fiction. Among his more bizarre beliefs was the conviction that the planet Mars—which he soon learned to pick out in the nighttime sky—was peopled by a savage race of six-armed green-skinned monsters who waged continual warfare upon one another with swords and spears and antigravity devices.

In order to survive when his supplies of canned food ran out Gordon taught himself to fish and with the help of the five robots designed, built, and launched a small wooden boat. Along with reading, angling thus became a major passion in his life.

Gordon Nathan Schwerner remained alone on the nameless private island with the five robots until he was seventeen years of age. It was then that a helio-plane landed on the beach one afternoon and an enormous fat man resplendent in a traditional African dashiki leaped out and began calling out to him by name.

This fat man turned out to ne the private detective Desmond Blue who had been hired by a law firm in Arizona to unravel the complexities of the Nathan and Beatrix Schwerner estate. No one had ever suspected that the legitimate heir might still be on Earth but Blue had managed ferret out the existence of the private island and journeyed to the South Pacific in search of the truth. Gordon accompanied Blue back to Arizona to claim his rightful inheritance but within a month he had been arrested on a morals charge involving an underage girl in a city park in Phoenix. (Likely a prostitute but as the judge himself remarked that's no excuse, son.)

A somber Blue visited the young man in his jail cell. It came as no surprise to him to discover from the psychiatric reports that Gordon Schwerner's sexual development had been hopelessly stunted through a combination of early sensual deprivation and an overdose of romantic literature. Gordon had attained the age of seventeen before being first exposed to the intimate details of the physical sex act (while viewing a pornographic film in his hotel room shortly after his return to so-called civilization) and the shock had apparently been too great for him to cope with.

"When the innocent savage is removed from the primordial environment," Blue told the sympathetic judge hearing the case, "then the remover not the savage is to blame for the consequences."

Gordon Schwerner was released in the care of Desmond Blue who put him in charge of the sophisticated crime laboratory that occupied an entire top floor of Arabia Deserta. It was Blue's devout belief based upon his own personal experience of many years of celibacy that only a good strong dose of hard work could relieve the brute tensions of an overactive sex drive.

Blue took to calling his new employee "Doctor." When Schwerner protested that he had never been awarded a university degree Blue tapped his forehead and stated that the only degree that mattered to him was the one implanted in the little gray cells of the brain.

There could be no argument that Gordon Nathan Schwerner was a scientific genius of the first order. He began to indulge in private research in the fields of biology, chemistry, and genetics as well as assist Blue in his casework.

Dr. Gordon Schwerner was not a happy man by any stretch of the imagination but it seemed possible to those who knew him well that he might have found a stable niche in life.

4

Dressed casually in torn jeans and black leather jacket Alfie Jarrett stood with his shoulders resting against a concrete pillar and observed as Jesus Christ, the self-proclaimed savior of humankind, preached to the two dozen or so hissing purring beastmen who made their home in the basement of Desmond Blue's Saharan mansion Arabia Deserta. It was a grotesque tableau, one made even more bizarre by the harsh torchlight that illuminated the high-ceilinged stone-walled chamber, casting giant distorted shadows everywhere. The raw animal scents of sweat, urine, and excrement clung to the air while Jesus himself, a lean young man with a thick black beard, steel-gray complexion, and round blue eyes like water, leaned forward on his makeshift podium and waved both gloved hands excitedly overhead. Jesus wore tattered white robes, frayed leather sandals, and a garland of holly around the fringe of his skull. In spite of the fervor with which he spoke the vast majority of the beastmen managed to ignore him entirely. Even Alfie—his devoted friend—found it difficult to listen for more than a few moments without his attention flagging. Instead to keep his mind occupied he concentrated instead on a private mental exercise: identifying the original bestial antecedents of the various creatures gathered in the big room.

The pair of white-haired moon-faced balloon-breasted females squatting a few feet in front of him were relatively simple: sheep for sure. Dogs, pigs, cows, and cats were also readily identifiable but certain others—the yellow-whiskered beady-eyed old male curled up in a corner for instance—were more difficult. If Alfie had been forced to venture a guess he would have tagged the old one as either a panther or a cheetah but he was probably not even close. Another male with skinny arms and a stub of a tail could have been almost anything. The arms were definitely monkey-like but the ears were long and pointy and made Alfie think of a horse or mule instead. He could have walked over and asked of course but he didn't want to do that; he hated the damned beastmen. If it hadn't been for Jesus—or Peter Mark—he would never have ventured down here of his own free will. Not in a thousand years. Or a million.

Only one of the beastmen—a hunchbacked male with big wet eyes, probably a former dog—seemed to be paying much attention to Jesus. Now and then he would interrupt the flow of the sermon to ask questions in a shrill insistent voice more like a small dog's yip than any human sound. "But, sir," the beast yipped at Jesus, "isn't saying that a slave should adore his master the same as asking a sheep to love a wolf or a mouse to love a cat?"

"And what is wrong with that, my poor child?" Jesus asked patiently. "Isn't it written in the holy book that a day will surely dawn when the lamb and the lion lie down with one another?"

"How strange that you should mention that, sir," said the dogman, looking suitably impressed. "Why, only last night here among us I saw a lion and a sheep touching and fondling—"

"Exactly, my friend," said Jesus hastily. "And isn't it also written that all creatures regardless of birth are brothers of the spirit in the sight of God? Do not be misled by mistaken delusions fostered by the devil. There are no slaves or masters in the eye of the Lord."

The dogman looked confused. Alfie could well sympathize. Slave or master, god or devil, it was all pretty much the same brand of gobbledygook to him. "I'm afraid I wouldn't know very much about that part, sir," the dogman said apologetically. "We beasts have never learned to read, you know." He tapped his forehead. "Our brains aren't big enough, they say."

"I think you're missing my point," Jesus said, exasperation showing through. "And please stop calling me sir. How many times do I have to tell you people? I'm not a man. I'm the son of—" Jesus broke off. A bell was trilling nearby. Alfie turned his head and looked at the far wall. The elevator light was flashing. Now who? he wondered. So far as he knew except for Lacy whose job it was as the newest employee to feed the beasts nobody ever came down here anymore.

Jesus tried to go on with what he had been saying but even the loyal dogman wasn't listening now. With the sound of the bell the beasts had turned in unison to watch the flashing light. Alfie wondered why. Perhaps they were so stupid they expected to be fed again or maybe they just welcomed any sort of relief from the awful tedium of their drab pointless lives.

When the elevator doors opened it was Dr. Gordon Schwerner who emerged. As soon as he did the beasts let out a frightened howl and scampered to the most distant corners of the room. Alfie laughed out loud. When the beastmen had first been brought to the mansion Schwerner had conducted a number of rather painful experiments involving them and ever since the survivors had been frightened senseless at the sight of him.

Pointedly ignoring the beastmen Schwerner came over to Alfie. "I certainly didn't expect to find you down here."

Alfie nodded at Jesus. "Peter asked me."

"Well, it's him I really need to see. Desmond wants him right away."

Jesus climbed down from his wooden crate and approached Alfie and Schwerner. It was Peter Mark of course—cleverly disguised.

The Jesus costume, Peter had told Alfie earlier in the evening, was the one way he had so far found of grabbing the attention of the beastmen for any length of time. From what Alfie had seen tonight it appeared that poor Peter was going to have to find another gimmick.

"Did you want me, Gordon?" said Peter. "It's not the case, is it?"

Schwerner spoke softly as if the beasts might eavesdrop. "It is the case, yes. Desmond wants you to fly him to Rome right away."

"Me? What's wrong with Crystal?"

"Nothing that I know of. But Desmond said to fetch you."

"Is he in the study?"

"No, he's out on the airstrip. He doesn't want any delay."

Peter glanced over at the cowering beasts and let out a sigh. "I suppose it doesn't matter. They weren't listening to me anyhow."

The three of them turned to the elevator.

Alfie punched the button for the ground floor. Peter disembarked first and headed for his room. The others followed. "You do intend to change clothes, I hope," Schwerner said, tagging along behind.

"Does it matter?" said Peter. "Even in Rome nobody knows Jesus anymore."

"The man you're going to see there does."

Peter glanced back at him sharply. "Who's that?"

"I don't know whether I ought—"

"Oh, cut the crap, Schwerner," Alfie said. "Peter's going to find out soon enough. If you know something, spill it."

"Well…" said Schwerner, apparently still not convinced. "Have you ever heard of the so-called Bishop of Rome?"

"The Pope? The Holy Father?" Peter stopped in the doorway to his room and turned. "You can't mean…?"

Schwerner nodded. "The Pope is our prospective client."

"Good Lord," Peter said reverently. He looked down at himself. "Then I had really better… He might regard this as blasphemy—or even worse."

"See?" said Alfie when the door had shut. "Peter's got something going for him that you and me can never hope to have, Schwerner. Peter actually gives a shit what somebody else thinks."

"The Pope is merely another man," Schwerner said.

"Actually," said Alfie, "I was thinking less of the man more of his God."

"God doesn't exist. The Occupancy proved that much. No omnipotent God would have allowed that."

Alfie laughed. "Well, be careful not to mention that to Him when you two meet up in heaven. He might get pissed and send you down to hell instead. Then you'd end up having to spend all of eternity cooped up with me."

"That would be a true damnation," Schwerner said.

"Don't be nasty, Doc," said Alfie.

5

Hands thrust deep in his trouser pockets Dr. Gordon Schwerner stood shivering in the crisp Saharan dawn and watched the shiny red- and blue lights of Desmond Blue's private tri-motor aeroplane fade from view. So now they were gone, he thought, taking a deep breath. So now the case was truly on at last.

Turning, Schwerner crossed the roof and slipped through an open trap door. He went down a ladder and through a door that led to the third floor corridor. Often when awake this early in the morning he liked to go down to the moat that circled the mansion for a bit of quiet angling—he had personally stocked the stream with rainbow trout and big mouthed bass—but today he was too exhausted even for that. His laboratory, offices, and personal rooms occupied the bulk of this floor. Schwerner opened a door, passed through one empty room, and drew up in front of another door. Removing two keys from a pocket he unbolted the heavy padlock and stepped inside. Fluorescent lights winked on at his entrance. The room was spacious with two wooden benches, a Formica-topped table, and a pair of steel cabinets serving as the only furniture. Identical handwritten notices had been attached to both cabinets. The signs read:

DANGER!

High Explosives!
Keep Clear!

Pleased by his own ingenuity in devising the warnings, Schwerner crossed to the nearer of the two cabinets and stood motionless in front of it. Reaching out with sudden decision he grasped the combination lock and twirled the dial. Tumblers clicked. Back and forth three times. The door popped open with a squeak.

Inside she stood. The female. Absolutely naked. Complexion as cool as ice. Smooth unblemished skin. Blonde hair. Blue eyes. Well-rounded breasts. The neat curlicue of the navel through which she had once fed. Schwerner felt the air rush from his lungs as he stared at her marvelous beauty. He had created her. By himself. Grown her starting from a single cell in a laboratory test tube. No one else knew. Not even Desmond Blue. Schwerner had fathered this woman. She was his child in every sense of the term. His daughter.

He extended a hand and gently caressed the pale skin of her throat. Suddenly with a soft cry she moved her eyes and looked straight at him.

"Doctor Schwerner," she said.

"Lai," he said, the sound of her name sticking in his throat.

"No," she said with a slight smile. "I am not Lai. Lai is asleep. I am Jai."

He smiled back at her. Names were something both of them seemed to have trouble comprehending. They frequently confused one with the other.

"Come here," he said, stepping back. "I want to look at you."

With a nod she stepped gracefully forward, muscles rippling beneath the white sheen of her skin. She stood in front of him. "What is our purpose today?"

"Do we need to have a purpose?"

"We always have before." Her voice, free of accent or inflection, was still somewhat machine-like in tone. He thought it was her only significant flaw. "Do you wish to instruct me further in the multiplication of numbers?" she asked.

"Not right now, no. I want…I think I ought to examine you."

Even to his own ears the words sounded transparent. Lai seemed to be smiling again. Had she seen through his subterfuge? No, he decided, that was not possible. Mentally and emotionally Lai was no more sophisticated than a five-year-old child.

"My God, you're lovely," he said all at once. "You're gorgeous."

This time her smile was more definite. "Why, thank you, Doctor." She accepted the compliment as her natural due.

Lai—and her twin in the opposite cabinet, her male counterpart, Jai—were the climactic consequences of a series of genetic experiments Schwerner had been pursuing in secret the past few years. His original inspiration had come from the example of the beastmen in the basement but unlike the renegade scientist who had created them Schwerner had elected to commence work from the beginning, with the true essence of life, a culture, a spore, a unicellular form. His interest had not been in changing animals into men; that, he believed, was nonsensical and absurd. He had wanted to build life—to create—and with Lai and Jai had succeeded beyond his wildest imaginings. Lai and Jai were not simply human duplicates; Schwerner was no latter-day Dr. Frankenstein. Lai and Jai represented a truly new species—their own separate and distinct form. It had taken almost a year after their bodies grew to full size before they took their first halting steps across the laboratory floor. A few days later they spoke their first words. Now they could not only converse in excellent English they could read at a fairly proficient level and perform basic mathematical exercises. The teaching had not proven difficult. Their mimetic capabilities verged on the awesome. Perhaps they were just that, Schwerner sometimes thought. Awesome. As superior to ordinary human beings as humans were to the beasts of the jungle.

Suddenly unable to control himself Schwerner lunged forward and before he knew what he was doing had placed his hands on Lai's bare shoulders and lowered his face to her chest. She smelled so clean—so purified—her scent made him delirious. His mouth opened. His tongue brushed the bud of her right nipple.

She made no effort to resist. Deep in her throat she moaned gently.

With a tremendous effort of will Schwerner forced himself back. "I'm sorry," he said, panting like a beast. "I didn't mean to do that. I shouldn't have…"

"Why?" She held her hands out in apparent sympathy. "I was not harmed."

He took a step back from her, shaking his head. "You don't understand. What I did was wrong—terribly wrong. I took advantage of you. It was a crime." He wished Desmond were here. Desmond was a man of the world. He would be able to understand and explain. But Schwerner knew he could never tell Desmond about any of this. With his desperate belief in God's reality, Desmond would surely regard what Schwerner had accomplished in his laboratory as an arrogant usurpation of the Creator's domain. Blue would want to have Lai and Jai destroyed and Schwerner could never permit that to happen.

He shut his eyes and turned his back on the woman. I am no less a child than she, he thought, with sudden clarity.

His own parents—Simon and Beatrix Schwerner—how deeply he despised them. Thirteen years alone on that dreadful island with only the metal hulks of robots for company—how thoroughly that stunted life had twisted and distorted his own in turn.

He remembered when Desmond Blue had first brought him back to the civilized world and the lawyer in Phoenix had been explaining how wealthy a man he was and wasn't there anything special he wanted to do with all that money and the only thing he could think of was the two of them—Simon and Beatrix and their robot servants; even that early on he had come to loathe them. "I would like to hire someone to go back to the island and destroy the five robots that are there."

The lawyer looked surprised. "But, Mr. Schwerner, those robots are valuable property."

"I thought you said I was rich."

"Well, yes…"

"Then it's my money to spend. I should be able to do whatever I want with it."

"Of course."

"Then that's what I want. I want those robots destroyed."

"But you could sell each—"

"Have you got a dollar?" said Blue. He was looking at the lawyer.

"Well, certainly but I don't see—"

"Give it to Mr. Schwerner—I'm sure he'll pay you back—and then he can give it to me. The dollar will serve as my retainer. I'll leave for the island tonight and see that the robots are destroyed."

Shaking his head in dismay the lawyer handed Schwerner the dollar.

He hadn't seen Desmond again for several weeks. Not until after the incident with the poor girl in the park.

Desmond came to visit him in his cell.

The first thing Schwerner asked him about was the robots on the island.

"They're gone," said Blue.

"Dead?"

"I took them apart personally bolt by bolt, screw by screw, and threw the pieces in the ocean."

Schwerner experienced a tremendous sensation of release—and pleasure.

Opening his eyes now, he turned back and discovered Lai watching him intently. The fixity of her gaze made him shift on his feet. "I think you'd better get back in the cabinet," he said. "I'm tired. I need sleep."

She didn't move. "Are you sure that's what you really want, Doctor?"

"I—yes." What was happening? She had never contradicted him before. He tried to edge past her to the cabinet. "Just let—"

Then she assaulted him. There was no other word to describe it. Her arms locked around his shoulders, her body pressed against him, her lips sought his, her tongue entered his mouth, her breasts—

"No! Please!" Somehow with the last ounce of strength he possessed Schwerner managed to push her away. His knees were as weak as water. "Lai," he gasped. "Lai, why did you do that?"

Her eyes never wavered. "You asked me to."

He shook his head. "No. I didn't. I never did anything of the kind."

"Are you sure?" Her mouth was an oval.

"Don't say anything else. Don't deceive me." He pointed at the cabinet. "Get in there. Please, Lai. We can talk about this later."

"I'm not Lai—I'm Jai. See?" She touched her left breast.

Schwerner had not noticed before. Slightly below the nipple could be glimpsed a faint blemish, an indentation, like a birthmark in the shape of a five-pointed star. He remembered seeing such a mark on the man's chest but never on hers. What could its appearance mean?

"Please." Again he pointed. "Get back in your cabinet."

"All right—if you're sure." With a shrug she obeyed. Once she was safely inside the cabinet Schwerner slammed the door and spun the combination lock.

Alone at last he crossed the room, went out, locked the door carefully behind, and staggered to his bedroom on the opposite side of the corridor.

After undressing he dropped down on the hard mattress and shoved his face deep into the soft folds of his pillow. Bright sunlight streamed through the windows; true daylight had arrived with a vengeance. Schwerner tried to concentrate on the case, on anything except Lai and what she had done and said, but before he could shape any clear thoughts he was sound asleep.

He began to dream.

6

Watch your step, Peter," cautioned Desmond Blue, pointing to a dark brown splotch on the pavement. "I don't believe these streets have been cleaned recently."

Peter Mark edged around the wet brown pile. "I'm surprised anybody here can afford to keep a dog."

"They can't. Humans also excrete."

"The sewers—"

"Clogged years ago, I'm afraid. Useless."

"That's disgusting."

"Of course it is—but do come ahead."

They turned a corner and proceeded down a dark alley. Peter had to close his nostrils against the stench. None of this was what he had expected to find here in Rome, the former capital both sacred and profane of the entire Western world.

In his dreams Peter had always conceived of Rome as resembling a glittering jewel—a diamond.

Instead on this his initial visit Rome had been exposed as no different from any other of the empty devastated cities left behind by the slugs after their occupation.

"You'd think at least some of these houses would have lights," Peter said as he stumbled in the dark. "It can't be much later than nine o'clock. Don't savages need to see too?"

"No electricity," said Blue.

"Well, a candle or two anyhow."

"Unsafe. In an area such as this it's never wise to draw attention to the fact that one is alive. Someone else might feel envious." Blue stopped so abruptly that Peter bumped into him. "A match," he said, snapping his fingers.

Peter struck the match against the curve of his chin and handed it to Blue.

A post stood in the middle of the alley, spots of worn paint showing traces of faint numerals. Blue leaned forward, trying to read. He grunted. "I think this may be it."

"Are you sure?"

"Unless our informant lied. This way, I believe." Blue edged away. Peter followed his dim shape. In situations such as this with the quarry close at hand Blue often seemed to develop a sixth sense that immunized him against even darkness. Peter still found it difficult to believe that His Holiness, the Bishop of Rome, Vicar of Jesus Christ, Successor of St. Peter, Prince of Apostles, Pope Sergio I could be living here in this foul fetid slum but Blue appeared convinced that his information was accurate.

"I think we may have arrived." Blue stopped. Past his bulk the outline of a doorway could be glimpsed. "I'll knock but if there's no immediate response you'll have to kick it in."

"Are you sure we ought to do that?" Peter couldn't help feeling that the Pope—even in these reduced circumstances—deserved a certain measure of respect.

"I sympathize with your feelings," Blue said soothingly, "but I'm afraid that His Holiness may attempt to flee and it's imperative that I speak with him at once. You are surely aware of the magnitude of this present case."

As a matter of fact Peter was not aware of anything of the kind. Blue hadn't said a word to him about the case since their departure from Arabia Deserta more than two days ago.

Blue raised a fist and knocked three times in rapid succession. Peter listened intently but heard nothing from the other side of the door. Blue waited only a brief moment more, then stepped back.

"Kick it down."

Peter took a deep breath, backed off several steps, and launched himself at the door. His shoulder struck solidly. It was only flesh and blood—unlike his hands or had—but the door was brittle. Swinging inward, the door carried Peter forward into a dazzling splash of light. Momentarily blinded he tripped and fell to his knees.

A shadowy shape—Blue—darted past him. A voice—again Blue—shouted, "Woman, quickly. I seek the Holy Father. I demand...oh."

This last was uttered in a stunned whisper. Hands grasped Peter's shoulders and hauled him to his feet. "I believe we have found our man," said Blue.

Peter blinked furiously until his vision cleared. The room was small and cheaply furnished. The light emanated from a single lantern hanging from a beam in the ceiling. The windows were covered with heavy curtains.

The woman Blue had addressed wore a loose peasant's blouse and a gray flannel skirt. A black hat and veil covered the top of her head and concealed the upper portion of her face from view. Peter's glance passed swiftly over her and came to rest on a knot of soiled blankets in a far corner of the room. The blankets suddenly twitched and an arm protruded from the pile. The fingers were stubs of raw flesh. Then a face like a savage mask appeared beside the arm. The black lips moved. "Who...?" said a voice. "Who are you?"

"My God," Peter said softly.

Blue nodded. "Yes, it's him—Sergio I."

"But what...what can...?"

"Leprosy. You need not fear contagion. Schwerner can provide us antidotes when we return."

"You knew?"

"Rumors had reached me." Blue approached the ragged shape on the floor. "Your Holiness, I am Blue—Desmond Blue." The Pope's dark eyes, strangely alive, followed his progress. Blue knelt down, took the Pope's bleeding hand in his, and raised the fingers to his lips.

There was a tawdry brass ring on one finger. Blue kissed it. "I am deeply honored, Your Holiness."

"As am I, Mr. Blue," said the Pope. "Your accomplishments in the secular sphere are not unknown even in this humble abode."

"I am flattered."

"But what has occasioned this invasion of my privacy? Surely I am no longer pursued by goblins from my criminal youth. Tell whoever sent you that time will soon wreak its inexorable vengeance upon Sergio. I am an old man, Mr. Blue, with only a few bare days in which to live. Let God punish me as he sees fit for the multitude of my sins."

Blue remained on his knees. "I have come for reasons of my own, Your Holiness, to seek your assistance in a matter of grave importance to believer and unbeliever alike." Blue kept his voice hushed. Peter drew closer in order to hear better. Behind him the veiled woman unfurled a broom and began to sweep the floor vigorously.

"I am willing to aid the cause of justice in any manner possible," said the Pope. "What is it specifically that you require from me, Mr. Blue?"

"Information only. You are cognizant, I have reason to believe, of the existence of a secret conspiracy designed to spread evil throughout the world."

The Pope's rotting teeth showed as he struggled to smile. "There are many such conspiracies, Mr. Blue."

"I refer in particular to one which is known to have had a hand in the crucifixion of your master, Jesus Christ."

"The Jews?"

Blue shook his head. "We both know better than that."

"Then you…" The Pope stiffened. "Then you know of the Sect?"

"By that name, no."

"But how…?"

"I am a detective. It is my business to know such things."

"And you intend…?"

"To destroy them." Blue's chin trembled with the force of his indignation.

"It is not possible."

Blue shook his head. "I admit that I will require some assistance—yours to begin with. What can you tell me of this conspiracy—this Sect?"

The Pope considered. "I can tell you this much, Mr. Blue. It is the opinion of my church over the centuries that such a conspiracy exists and that its agents are the conscious associates of Satan on Earth."

"But they are men also? They can be confronted, battled, wounded, slain?"

"They can."

"Then their origins are of little interest to me. Forgive my bluntness, Your Holiness, but I am less concerned with gods and devils than with human evil."

"In that event, Mr. Blue, it would appear that you and I have little in common."

"Perhaps," muttered Blue. His hands shook and for a moment Peter feared that anything—even violence—might occur but Blue's voice when it came again was as gentle as hymn. Need I remind Your Holiness that in twenty-odd centuries of active conflict your church has failed to eradicate this menace? Questions of philosophy aside, do you honestly wish to prevent me from playing my own hand?"

"Satan cannot be conquered by one who is less than his equal. Even you, Mr. Blue, do not claim to be a god."

"I am a man, Your Holiness."

"And a man is nothing."

"I have a right to try!"

The Pope shrank back from the fervor of Blue's passion. He regarded him intently for a long moment. "I suppose you do. Experience is the one great humbler."

"You will assist me?"

"As far as I am able, yes."

"Then tell me what you know, everything you know regarding this conspiracy."

"That is very little, I am afraid. My memory is no longer what it once was. I find, in recent times that I am able to recall minute details from my boyhood with more clarity than the contents of last night's dinner."

"Then allow me to examine the documents."

The Pope looked surprised. "What makes you believe there are any?"

"Logic and deduction. This conspiracy has been in existence since before the time of Christ. The Catholic Church has long been noted for its methodical and systematic ways. At some point in history something must surely have been set down on paper."

"There is nothing here," said the Pope, indicating his modest surroundings.

"Then where?"

The Pope hesitated. "In recent years as our monetary resources dwindled it often proved necessary to sell many of the church's valued possessions to wealthy collectors and scholars."

Blue shook his head grimly. "You are toying with me, Your Holiness. Such documents as these would not have been casually disposed of, even in the early corrupt years of your reign."

"These are secrets, Mr. Blue. Sacred secrets."

"Then share them with me." Blue leaned closer to the pile of blankets. "Trust me. I implore you. For the sake of humanity—if not that of God."

"There is a group…" the Pope began.

"An organ of the church?"

"A secular organization. A group of men and women." He paused. "I assume, Mr. Blue, that you recognize the dark nature of our present age."

"Not necessarily a dark age—an exhausted one. We human beings reached our limits at too youthful a stage in our history."

"Then you hold out some hope for the future?"

"I do. As the prophet said, 'This too must pass.'"

"In that case the group to which I refer is one that shares your general optimism. They call themselves the Preservation Society. An organization of scholars and social scientists dedicated to the task of preserving the wisdom of the past for the use of future generations. The documents you seek were handed over to them a number of years ago."

"By whom, may I ask?"

"By me personally."

"And where can I find this Preservation Society?"

The Pope's voice grew hushed. "I'm sorry but I cannot tell you that. For reasons of security the exact location of the society's head-quarters has long been kept secret—even from me. A former brother in the church, the monk Xavier, handled the transfer of documents. Xavier is, I believe, a leader among the Preservationists. During his years with the church he took a strong personal interest in the history and methods of the Sect."

"And you have no idea where I can find this Brother Xavier either?"

"Alas, our final meeting occurred the day I turned the documents over to him. He told me then that he could be reached through certain friends in Kabul. The impression I received was that the society's headquarters also lay somewhere in that general region."

"And who were these friends through whom he could be reached?"

The Pope shook his head wearily. "I do not recall, Mr. Blue. I am sorry."

"Then I must begin my search in Afghanistan."

"I would think so, yes. Other than that there is little I can tell you. I have not read any of the documents you seek. So far as I am aware, except presumably for Brother Xavier, no one alive has either."

"That is why you need me," said Blue.

"Perhaps. You are unquestionably a wise man, Mr. Blue, and there are few such nowadays who are also honest men. I wish you... luck." His head dropped back on the blankets. He seemed drained of energy, spent.

Blue gripped his arm. "One more moment, Your Holiness. There is another minor matter which must be settled. In order to commence my investigation of this case I require a sum of money."

The Pope opened his mouth and made a noise. He may have been trying to laugh but the sound that emerged was more like a strangled cry. "Please forgive my bad manners, Mr. Blue. But money? Money from me? From the church? You must be joking."

Blue held up a finger. "I ask for only a lone dollar. In order for me to undertake the case professional ethics demand that I first have a client. One dollar will suffice as a retainer."

"You wish the Catholic Church to hire you as an investigator?"

"Not the church, Your Holiness—yourself only. This will remain a private matter between us."

The Pope's diseased hand disappeared under the blankets and reappeared clutching a single crumpled bill. "Here—take it."

"One final matter then," said Blue. "Although it deeply pains me to mention it I have received the unfortunate impression that you do not expect to live much longer."

The Pope did not flinch. "A few weeks at the most. However, I am not unready to face my Maker."

"What measures have been taken toward determining your successor?"

"That is hardly my prerogative. The College of Cardinals must convene in sacred conclave following my death and decide who—"

"No," said Blue, shaking his head grimly. "That would prove a grievous mistake. My investigations indicate that all but a few of your cardinals are hopelessly corrupted with many openly engaged in criminal pursuits—prostitution, narcotics, gang warfare. Even those whose piety cannot be questioned seem lacking in the strength of character necessary to undertake such arduous decision-making as the election of a new pope."

"I am not unaware of the truth of what you say, Mr. Blue, but unfortunately the procedures must be followed."

"Not necessarily. Are you aware that the present conclave system of papal election was not established until Pope Gregory X issued his Apostolic Constitution in 1174? As a matter of fact prior to the reign of Nicholas II in the eleventh century popes were not even chosen by the cardinals but rather by the clergy and citizens of Rome. And St. Peter, as you know, was designated by Christ personally to head His church. I see no reason why you should not also name your own successor. The cardinals will no doubt dispute your authority but I am convinced that future generations will affirm the wisdom of your decision."

The Pope looked sad. "But there is no one, Mr. Blue. The cardinals are as you said either corrupt, weak, or both."

"Then do not limit your selection to them alone. Pope Gregory X was neither a cardinal nor a consecrated priest but merely papal legate in Syria."

"But still…who?"

Blue pointed over his shoulder. "Peter here would make an excellent pope."

"That—that robot?" The Pope scowled. "That is blasphemy, Mr. Blue, sheer blasphemy."

"Peter is no less a man than you or I," Blue said stiffly. "Some years ago he was involved in a serious aeroplane accident. The mask he wears, the steel hands, are superficial coverings only. Underneath, believe me, Peter Mark possesses a heart, blood, bone, sinew—a soul. Furthermore he happens to place more faith in the existence of God than any man I have ever known."

"Is he Catholic?"

"Holy Father," said Peter, interrupting, "my faith has led me in certain—"

"He is a Christian," Blue finished. "Which in this day and age ought to be more than sufficient. I do not offer this suggestion for selfish or whimsical motives, Your Holiness. I am totally serious. Once you are gone to your holy reward I am convinced that certain criminal elements will move at once to subvert the papacy and subjugate the church. Peter can be trusted to withstand such forces. He is young, honest, intelligent, and absolutely devoted to the teachings of Jesus Christ."

The Pope looked past Blue to where Peter stood. "Tell me, young man," he said. "Are you willing to perform the sacred duties of this high office as required?"

Peter felt totally bewildered by this unexpected turn of events but heard himself answering the Pope without hesitation: "I am, Your Holiness."

"And are you further willing to accept the grave responsibilities of functioning as God's chosen representative in this world?"

"I am, yes."

"With all the burdens, spiritual and material, that that must necessarily entail?"

"He refers to chastity," said Blue.

"Among other things," said the Pope.

"I have no...no compunctions or doubts about that," said Peter.

"Then come here, my son. Mr. Blue, you are either a most convincing man or I am an enormous fool or both."

Peter crossed the room and took the Pope's outstretched hand. At first touch a feeling of electrical intensity passed through his frame.

"I name you," said Pope Sergio, "my chosen and legal successor on this Earth. Upon my death you shall reign in my stead as Vicar of Christ."

"I…I…" Peter searched his soul for some way of expressing his emotions but before the proper words came the Pope's hand slipped from his and the old man's weary eyes closed. "Sir?" said Peter, suddenly overwhelmed by the weight of the burden he now carried. "Sir, are you all right?"

The Pope's eyes opened slowly. "Merely tired, my son, very tired. An official proclamation will be issued forthwith. There may be trouble—the cardinals, as Mr. Blue stated, are weak men entrapped by the temptations of the carnal world. My housekeeper will see that—"

"The housekeeper!" shouted Blue as if stricken. Spinning quickly he cried, "Peter, grab her."

But the woman was already out the door.

Peter raced in pursuit but his eyes had grown unaccustomed to the dark and once he passed beyond the open door he was as good as blind. Stopping to orient himself he tried to use his ears to locate the woman but at that moment Blue came bustling out after him and the two men collided. Peter felt his feet slip out from under him and he landed heavily on his rump.

Fleeing footsteps echoed from the end of the alley.

"That's her!" cried Blue. "There she goes!"

Peter scrambled to his feet and sprinted after Blue but the woman had gotten too much of a head start. By the time they reached the mouth of the alley the street beyond was silent and empty.

"Damn," said Blue. "Damn, damn, damn."

"Who was she?" asked Peter. "What made her run away?"

"I should have known. I sat there a dozen feet from her and never bothered to look close enough to know her. Peter, how could I be so stupid?"

"But who is she, Desmond?"

Blue shook his head. "I'm sorry. I forget that you haven't yet seen the photographs. The swarthy woman with a dark beauty—that was her, I know it now." He placed a hand on Peter's shoulder. "She is deeply involved in this case. I'll explain later. Come. We'd better get back to His Holiness."

By the time they reached the Pope's rooms the old man had fallen asleep. Blue dropped to the floor and sat in a cross-legged posture of stoic indifference.

"You'd better fix the door," he told Peter dully. "Look for a hammer and nails. We shouldn't leave him like this."

Peter went into a back room and after a brief search found what he needed. "I'll take care of the door, Desmond. You go ahead and rest."

Blue gazed up at him. "Rest, I'm afraid, is the part of the problem not the solution. It was that retirement of mine. The little gray cells in my brain have atrophied. Next to me a moronic toad is a genius."

"Isn't there anything we can do? The woman could not have gone far. The police…"

"Not them, no. Not in a case of this magnitude. The woman has learned everything of importance and has no doubt gone to inform her colleagues. It's too late to alter that now. The one real advantage we possessed was the element of surprise and that's been allowed to slip through my clumsy fingers." He shook his head mournfully. "We're in trouble, Peter—trouble as deep as an ocean trench."

Knowing there was nothing he could say to console Blue when he was in this mood Peter went to the door and began to hammer it back into place. The sound of the hammer was like rapid gunfire but oddly the Pope never stirred. His breathing was smooth, regular, comforting. Blue remained seated on the floor, never twitching a muscle.

A PROFILE: POPE SERGIO I

Sergio Roncallo was born in that state of grace commonly referred to as obscurity.

In the case of young Sergio this obscurity consisted of a village of farmers and fishermen in the northern part of the island of Sicily. His father (or so Sergio believed as a boy growing up) was a cobbler and his mother a kind, generous, pious woman but both were shot dead by a band of assassins when Sergio was fifteen, an act that made it seem possible that his father might have been involved in activities more nefarious than simple shoemaking. (His father's brother

Sandro was acknowledged even by Sergio to be engaged in several forms of criminal enterprise.)

Thus tragically orphaned Sergio was taken in hand by this uncle who removed him from school, taught him a trade, and put him gainfully to work in his own employ. Sergio soon became quite proficient as an assassin and when he was seventeen shot and killed his first man and by the time he reached twenty had killed at least four others, all at his uncle's instigation. The following year Uncle Sandro himself perished in a bloody gun battle and Sergio found it expedient to remove himself from the island of his birth and for a time adopt a different name.

His first new home was Naples where he fell instantly under the spell of the cool azure beauty of the crystalline bay. Deprived of the patronage of his uncle Sergio drifted into the less violent byways of criminality. For several months he labored diligently as a pickpocket and later helped manage a chain of brothels owned by a man named Angeloni.

When he was twenty-five Sergio married a pregnant prostitute whom he had come to know in the course of his work. She was a far from beautiful or loving woman but his devotion to her became legendary. Two years after the birth of a child, a daughter, the woman left Sergio and went to live with the leader of a rival gang. In one of the few acts of personal pique in his life Sergio shot and killed this man and shortly afterward left Naples, taking his wife's young daughter with him. (The wife herself was never heard of again; her descent into obscurity proved as complete as it was rapid.)

Sergio subsequently settled in a village not far from Rome where he found somewhat fewer opportunities for criminal employment than in Sicily or even Naples. Nevertheless through hard work, perseverance, and a willingness to assume the most unrewarding tasks he was able to maintain himself and the child in comfortable surroundings.

When the slugs appeared in the sky over Earth the criminal classes were spared any form of retribution except for those few who had amassed immense quantities of personal wealth. What the disappearance of these men brought about was a vacuum at the pinnacle of the profession and this in turn led to an outbreak of internecine warfare which continued until the vacuum was filled. Sergio was one of those who quickly moved up several rungs on the ladder of power although in his case the ascent was neither violently effected nor especially lofty.

Another vacuum had also been created within the hierarchy of the Roman Catholic Church since even the humblest parish priests had been taken by the Occupants. Helping to fill this vacuum Sergio along with many of his criminal compatriots became a member of the priesthood. Although a personally devout Catholic who always attended mass and made certain that his step-daughter did the same he apparently felt no shame at assuming this undeserved role. The leading criminal bosses of Italy, France, and Bavaria had meanwhile transformed themselves into cardinals and bishops so that as usual Sergio appeared to be doing nothing more drastic than following the direction of his superiors.

It was this characteristic in fact—his loyal and devoted nature—that led to Sergio's eventual ascension to the papacy. Had one or the other of the criminal cardinals been chosen to fill the supreme position, a new outbreak of violence would almost assuredly have followed. The cardinals thus decided to elect a figurehead to stand at the helm of their church. That figurehead turned out to be Sergio Roncallo.

During the initial months of his reign Pope Sergio I served his cardinals faithfully by doing absolutely nothing to interfere with their activities.

It was during this period that the treasures of the Vatican standing unprotected in the devastated ruins of Rome were systematically looted, many precious works of art being sold for a pittance of their true value. Only an occasional soft voice of protest was raised against this rape of the church. Like all organized religions the Roman Catholic church had now become largely a faith without followers for it had proven difficult for people to interpret the slugs and their Occupation s anything other than a message that churches were no longer an acceptable means of worship. Unfortunately God had neglected to indicate any alternative path that might be followed in safety and as a consequence most people simply chose to ignore religion entirely.

It wasn't until the third year of his reign that Pope Sergio I underwent a dramatic spiritual awakening. The chain of events began with the serious injury of his beloved step-daughter in a bicycle accident near St. Peter's Square. Sergio accompanied the girl to the nearest hospital and for many hours prayed on his knees, pleading with God to intervene mercifully, but in the end the child nevertheless died. Leaving the hospital with hatred burning in his heart Sergio was accosted by a blind mendicant, a savage returned to the streets of Rome, who begged for morsels of food. Unable to contain his anger and bitterness Sergio lashed out savagely at the sightless man and struck him a brutal blow in the face. As soon as his knuckles came into contact with the man's flesh a fiery ball of brilliant white light engulfed them both. When it cleared the blind beggar began to shout, rub his eyes, rant, and weep. It took Sergio a moment to comprehend. The blind beggar could see again. A genuine miracle had taken place before Sergio's own eyes.

Convinced that God had thus spoken to him Sergio summoned the cardinals to the Vatican the following morning. "God visited me last night," he told them, "and indicated that the time has come for us to change our ways. He struck down my beloved daughter to show that I had sinned and then restored the sight of a blind beggar to prove that he was also merciful. Come, let us join together to dispose of our ill-gotten gains and spread the gospel of God and Christ from shore to shore in a spirit of charity, humility, and sincere faith."

The cardinals were silent for a long moment. Then all together they erupted into laughter. "You've lost your fucking mind," one of them told Sergio in confidence.

Despite this failure Sergio remained convinced of the rightness of his plea. In the ensuing weeks he became a familiar figure in the savage districts of Rome with his flowing papal robes, Vulgate Bible, and voice that never ceased crying out the word of God. It was during this period that the Italian government—a newly established one at last—moved against the gangsters who had seized control of the church. Several powerful cardinals were arrested and the Vatican ruins were assaulted and held by a battalion of soldiers. Thus forcefully evicted from his home Pope Sergio took up residence in a modest boarding house. He existed on what alms he could earn by begging.

Soon enough he disappeared from public view.

One rumor had it that he'd contracted leprosy and was dying.

Another stated that he had fallen back into his old ways and joined a band of spook traders operating in East Africa.

A third rumor said that Jesus Christ had come down from heaven to personally escort Pope Sergio, still breathing, through the gates of paradise.

Only one of these rumors proved accurate.

7

Among Desmond Blue's retainers only Alfie Jarrett was truly a dreamer but the nightly visitations that came welling up from his subconscious constituted some peculiarly purposeful phenomena as if deliberately instigated and molded by unknown means. Alfie himself understood only this much: that whenever he dreamed he was never taken by surprise; he always seemed to know in advance exactly what to expect and greeted each successive vision as it appeared like an old and trusted friend.

Tonight for example there was the gray woman in the rocking chair. Alfie had experienced this dream many times before. "*Mother*," he moaned as he slept, although the truth was that Alfie had never known a real mother, though this old gray woman would doubtlessly serve. And not just a mother either: Alfie had never known a father or brother or uncle or cousin or aunt or sister. As far as he knew he had been born without family at the age of seven in the company of Zeke and Bess and the old gas-guzzling Pontiac they used to crisscross the southern and western American states.

Zeke was a wizened monkey of a man aged perhaps forty, country bred, slow talking, sly, a dozen times in and out of various jails and prisons. Bess, an enormous giantess of a woman with legs and arms like the trunks of trees and a knot of brown hair wrapped around her head like a swami's turban. Bess was a city lady all the way, had once danced in the burlesque theater, dreamed often of a career in the movies or on television.

The when and why of how the two had come together—and acquired young Alfie—remained a mystery.

For Alfie was a healer.

How real had that talent been? It was hard to remember now that the power had long since vanished but Alfie was inclined to think that, yes, he actually had been a healer. That might even explain his missing mother, for becoming gradually aware of the power her son possessed she might have come to fear him as a devil or demon and eventually cast him from her life. The laying on of the hands. The healing embrace. The kiss of life. As a young boy, for as long as he could recollect, Alfie had plied the healing trade. He saved lives.

Then took them.

It was a simple procedure.

Repeated endlessly. (So it seemed.) The old Pontiac chugging down yet another country lane. The big old house looming ahead. The dying man inside. (Sometimes a woman.) Wrinkled piss-stained sheets. Musty stench of death. Rich farmers. Retired storekeepers. More than a few wealthy bankers.

Zeke would stand at the foot of the bed, Bess off to one side, Alfie down low on the other.

"We come here as soon as we heard tell of your plight, Mr. Kincaid," said Zeke. "This here boy, he can do what the doctors can't, cure you, save your life, I'm guaranteeing you that. Run that goddamn cancer clean out of your belly. The boy's got power, that he has, and if you don't believe it, if you think this is just a way of stealing your money, then don't give us one red cent till you're up and about and the doctor's begging your pardon and saying how it's a miracle."

And Mr. Kincaid would say (if he could—sometimes they just nodded): "James Ericson wrote me and said you'd saved his life."

"A fine man, Ericson." (Zeke never failed to speak well of the dead.) "Alive and kicking his heels even as we speak. Tending his corn patch. Hitting hardballs with the grandkids. We got one condition only. You don't tell anybody we're here. A housekeeper, any farmhands—get rid of them. Bess here can clean and I'm not half bad at burning a beefsteak. If word ever got around what Alfie here can do we'd be hounded halfway to Albuquerque and back again. We like to save folks' lives when we can but it's got to be done in a private and dignified manner."

Mr. Kincaid would nod, saying he thought that was only right and proper. And why not? The poor sap was dying. And then the pain would overcome him, the aged body stiffening, eyes filled with tears. "Jesus Christ, man, you've got to help me. You've got to save me. I'm dying. I can't—you must understand—I'm not ready to die yet."

How come? Alfie wondered even then, aged no more than ten or twelve. Why did they all want so much to live? The whole world round people kicked off hundreds by the hour and every one of them went clawing and wailing and saying how he or she wasn't ready—not yet—please give me ten more minutes of life.

What was the big deal? Shut up and die, Mr. Kincaid. Slip gently into the deep dark night. It's not as if anybody really gives a hot holy damn how long you live once you're old and worn out and useless. It's not as if anybody's going to mourn your passing ten minutes from now any more than they do already. Thirteen billion years since the Big Bang of creation. Alfie had read that somewhere. Thirteen billion years and old Mr. Kincaid really believed that a few extra minutes of one man's life was something worth shedding tears over.

Zeke would look properly sympathetic. "What about it, son? Think you can save this man?"

"Sure can, Zeke."

And so he would. Invariably—without fail. Mr. Kincaid and Mr. Ericson; Farmer Lipscomb and Banker Hughes. He'd lay on his healing hands. Kiss the kiss of life. The dying men would live. Get up out of bed. Walk around. Kick their heels high in the air. Go to see the doctor in town and be told it must be a miracle.

And maybe it was.

Until the day would come when Zeke would pick his nose and say, "Well, Mr. Kincaid, I've been thinking. We've helped you out and glad to be of service but you're a man of high position and must have many acquaintances around the state. Maybe a fellow you met up in Omaha or Lincoln, somebody who's ill himself. Maybe an old army buddy you'd like to see saved."

And Mr. Kincaid (now cured) would write Mr. Spencer (dying) and tell him of the miracle that had destroyed the cancer and saved his own life.

Then Zeke and Bess would kill him. Old Mr. Kincaid that is. Alfie had nothing to do with this part. The chosen method was usually poison—Bess knew plenty about that—but sometimes when they were in a hurry Zeke might use his hands. They were powerful strong hands, small as he was, and could wring the life out of anyone in a couple minutes flat. The specific technique didn't matter. The deed was done. Mr. Kincaid, who had lived, died. It was as simple as that.

Why kill them? Greed of course. For Zeke and Bess the fat bushel of green cash they'd received from Mr. Kincaid in his initial burst of gratitude was never enough.

There was always more hidden around the house.

Valuables to be hocked. Furnishings to be stripped.

Many, many people died this way. (Alfie never kept track.)

It wasn't as if any of them weren't going to die anyway.

The end came at the house of a certain Mr. Newman, a baldheaded liver-lipped druggist in rural Minnesota. The healing had already been accomplished—the laying on of hands, the kiss of life—the town doctor consulted, miracle pronounced, letter of introduction written and mailed, and now the big old house was being systematically looted. Upstairs Mr. Newman lay bound and gagged on the bed. The poison had been administered and might take another fifteen minutes to work. Zeke and Bess were outside loading the Pontiac with valuables. Alfie sat in the downstairs parlor hurling a stiletto— he called it his shiv—against the wall. When the blade caught in the soft plaster he'd stand, retrieve the shiv, sit, and throw it again.

He was about to come to his feet when a voice spoke from behind his ear. "Freeze as you are, young man."

Alfie turned his head an inch—but only his head.

An enormous fat man loomed in the doorway, black gun clutched in one big hand. Alfie's shiv, stuck in the wall, was too far away to reach. "Who the hell are you, fatso?"

"Blue's the name. Desmond Blue."

It rang no bells. Alfie didn't follow the news. He started to call Zeke and Bess then realized that would be stupid. This man had entered through the front door and if Zeke and Bess were just outside they would have stopped him and since they hadn't that meant they weren't just outside.

Desmond Blue seemed to read Alfie's thoughts. "Your friends have been taken care of."

"You killed them?"

"No. If I had you would have heard the shots and fled and it's you not they who interests me." The gun jerked in his fist. "Now shall we proceed upstairs?"

"How come?" Alfie put on his most innocent expression. "There's nothing up there."

"Mr. Newman is."

"But he's dead."

"Move, Alfie."

Alfie moved—though reluctantly. The sight of the dead or dying disturbed him.

Upstairs in the big dark bedroom Mr. Newman lay bound and gagged, his frail body twitching in agony, racked by spasms as the poison worked its will. Alfie had never before realized the amount of sheer torment involved in the simple act of dying.

"Save the man," said Blue with a brisk nod.

Alfie gaped. "Are you nuts? I can't just—"

"You've done it before."

"That was different—cancer, disease, shit like that. Everybody knows cancer's ninety percent mental. This guy's shot full of poison. It'd take a miracle to save him."

"Then perform one."

"I'm telling you it can't be done."

"And I'm telling you it will be."

There was something in Blue's matter-of-fact tone that convinced Alfie further resistance would prove futile. So he mounted the bed, straddled Mr. Newman's chest, and loosened his gag. The old man's pale lips were covered with pink spittle and his big wrinkled nose dripped green mucus. It was a foul disgusting thing to see and Alfie was damned if he was going to touch him but Blue waved the gun and looked adamant and said, "A miracle, Alfie—a miracle right now."

"You're nuts, Fatso."

The gun rose jerked another quarter inch, "Please."

Alfie leaned over, shut his eyes, held his breath, and administered the kiss of life. When it was over, gagging, retching, he sprang to his feet and wiped his mouth with the back of a hand. "There, you big fat bastard, I did it. Now are you satisfied? Now do you believe what I told you?"

"What did you tell me?"

"I can't work miracles."

"Then how would you describe that?"

Alfie looked back at the bed. Mr. Newman wasn't writhing anymore. The spasms had passed. His body lay still, eyes clear, breathing short and shallow. Mr. Newman looked at Desmond Blue and wet his lips as if to speak.

Fortunately, Blue cut him off before he could say anything. "Conserve your strength, Mr. Newman. The situation here is well in hand. I apologize both for myself and my young friend for any inconvenience you may have endured. Alfie, shall we slip silently away? I believe Mr. Newman needs to rest."

They went out. Mr. Newman wasn't dead. Alfie found it hard to believe. Poison was poison. You couldn't just make it go away.

In the downstairs parlor Blue tucked his gun away in a holster, reached out, and placed both big hands on Alfie's shoulders. He looked him straight in the eye. "You face a choice, young man. Either go to prison for life with your accomplices or else come and live with me. I need an answer right away. Which shall it be?"

"What are you talking about?" This had to be some kind of idiot joke, he thought.

Blue did not appear amused. "I'm talking about a job offer, Alfie. An honest job. A real home for you."

Alfie could have pulled a knife. What Blue didn't know was that he always carried a little one stuck way down in the left front pocket of his jeans. He could have drawn the blade, rammed it into Blue's big plump gut, and been out of the house and gone in thirty seconds flat.

"What kind of job?"

"I'm a private detective. You'll assist me in my casework."

"Why me?"

"Because you're quick and bright and capable. I've been considering for some time taking on a retainer but you're the first person I've run into who could handle the job."

"Now I know you're bullshitting me."

"No, I'm not."

"Then…" Alfie felt his head nod before he knew what he was doing. "Then I'll take the job."

Blue dropped his hands. "In that case you may also keep the knife."

"The one in the wall?"

"And the one in your left front pocket as well."

All this was some years ago. As for his healing powers, apparently the exertion of exorcising the poison from Mr. Newman's system had put too great a strain on them. Afterward, Alfie was never able to cure a thing—not even a hangnail.

Alfie was dreaming once again. "Mother," he whispered as he slept. "Mother, I can see you."

But he was mistaken. It wasn't Mother. Not at all. The woman who stood naked in front of him was blonde-haired, blue-eyed, lean-waisted, and young. There was a tiny birthmark in the shape of a five-pointed star on her left breast slightly below the pink bud of her nipple. Alfie rubbed his eyes. He had never dreamed of a woman like this before.

Seeing Alfie's eyes on her the woman advanced toward him. Her feet didn't seem to make a sound as they glided across the carpet. When she reached the bed she bent down, drew the blankets aside, and climbed in beside him.

Alfie always slept in the nude.

Her eyes were bright and watchful. She did not make a sound.

Hesitantly Alfie put a hand on her shoulder. She certainly felt real enough. Her long hair brushed his face and throat as her head moved downward. She caressed his chest with her lips. It's just a crazy wild dream, Alfie assured himself. Her tongue licked his navel. Christ, I haven't dreamed like this since I was twelve years old.

Her head dipped lower. Her lips went around the head of his penis. She began to suckle him smoothly, gently, silently.

Alfie swallowed hard. His throat and mouth felt dry as the desert sands outside. Only a crazy wet dream for sure.

He watched her head rising and falling in the pale moonlight that seemed to tiptoe into the room like an unexpected visitor from a distant land.

He was feeling things that had nothing to do with lust or passion. It wasn't only a simple blow job, he thought. Not with a woman like this. She was too pale and pure for that.

What the hell kind of dream was this anyway?

Suddenly past the woman he noticed a second figure in the room. A naked man. Tall, blond-haired, well-built. He could have been the woman's twin.

"Jai," the man said. "Jai, you must come with me."

She lifted her head and looked at him. "Why?"

He pointed at the open window. "We need to go."

"But I want him." She meant Alfie.

"Not now. You can do it later with me."

"But that's different."

"Jai, we must run."

Still without a word to Alfie the woman slipped from his bed. He watched in wonder as the two of them, the woman first, then the man, left through the open window.

None of this is real, Alfie thought. It's all a goofy dream. He pinched himself and said *ouch*.

The dream was over.

Alfie got up out of bed, crossed to the window, put his hands on the sill, and thrust his head out into the cool night air. The green lawn maintained by Blue at vast expense was as vacant as the empty land beyond. Palm trees stood here and there like vigilant sentries and the artificial moat that circled the mansion bubbled gently in its course. Alfie turned his head and looked at the glass enclosure of the greenhouse where he kept his personal collection of flora—his roses and Dutch tulips and fuchsias. There wasn't a trace of a cooling wind.

He took a step back and laughed out loud. I'm looking for my own wet dream, he thought.

Then he froze. On the ill lay a clue so minute and insignificant that only a trained detective such as himself would have noticed; a few snarled strands of blonde hair. Alfie held them up to the moonlight. The hairs glittered like threads of gold.

A noise from beyond the window attracted his attention. He looked out again and saw in the sky, still distant but drawing closer, the shiny red and blue lights of an approaching aeroplane.

Blue, he thought.

Blue and Peter back from Rome already.

He turned from the window, found his clothes in a clump on the carpet, and began to dress.

If Blue was back that meant there would be work to be done.

He could hardly wait.

The case was on.

8

It had been far too long a time since Desmond Blue had last experienced the pleasure of seeing his study jammed full of people. To celebrate the occasion—and the commencement of his latest, most challenging case—he lifted a clay mug to his lips and swallowed an enormous gulp of sudsy brown beer. Blue wasn't normally a drinking man—medicinal herbs being more to his liking—but it was indeed an excellent sensation the way the beer coolly stroked the insides of his throat going down. He settled back in his easy chair, placed the empty mug on the floor at his feet, and sat with his hands on the knees of his dressing gown like a majestic bear. With quick darting eyes he surveyed the room. Across from him snuggled together on the loveseat sat his three confidential secretaries, Nadia, Crystal, then Lacy, each with a hand poised above a notepad ready to scribble at an instant's notice. Beyond them Alfie Jarrett leaned against the wall, an unlighted cigarette dangling from his lip, while Dr. Gordon Schwerner paced restlessly nearby and Peter Mark sat cross-legged on the floor, the hound Baskerville curled up beside him. The golden rays of the morning sun pierced the curtained windows. It was shortly past dawn. Blue and Peter had returned from Rome mere moments ago. This meeting had been convened without delay.

"Ladies and gentlemen," said Blue, "I do not wish to prolong this indefinitely. The reason I have gathered you here at this admittedly barbaric hour is a simple one: we have a new case on our hands and the time to begin its pursuit is now."

None of them looked especially surprised.

Nadia jotted a quick note on her pad. Crystal and Lacy remained still.

"Well, what?" said Alfie, coming away from the wall. "Damn it, Desmond, are you going to spill the beans or not? Schwerner knows what's up and since Peter's been hanging around with you so he probably does too. You always tell the women everything. That makes me the only ignorant one in the room and I don't much like it."

"We are all ignorant, Alfie," Blue said solemnly. "Some more than others to be sure—some in different ways—but all ignorant. That's what makes us human."

"Bullshit," Alfie grumbled.

Blue pretended he hadn't heard. He focused his mind on the situation at hand. "I believe that the best way for me to introduce our present case is to relate certain details of a much earlier matter. The one to which I refer dates back to a time when I wasn't much older than any of you and only just commencing my career as a practicing detective. During those youthful years of struggle the bulk of my work came to me through various criminal lawyers who would engage me to investigate certain ambiguous aspects of their clients' defenses. The one I wish to relate—the Robert Feeney case—was one of these."

Alfie moved to interrupt but Blue caught his eye until Alfie subsided into sullen silence. Once he had gained center stage Blue seldom cared to relinquish it until he finished. In this instance—for dramatic reasons—he preferred to relate his story in as much of a single burst as possible.

"Robert Feeney," said Blue, "was an ordinary man living in an ordinary small city in an ordinary corner of the United States who one day for no apparent reason shot and killed a total stranger who was no less an ordinary man than Feeney himself. Charged with the crime of first-degree murder Feeney was examined by the usual gaggle of psychiatrists and pronounced sufficiently sane to stand trial. As the date approached Feeney informed his attorney that he wished to enter a plea of not guilty by reason of self-defense. The attorney was understandably skeptical and retained my services to establish the veracity of whatever claim Feeney wished to raise. I accepted the case, went to the county jail, and met with Robert Feeney in his cell.

"I started out by asking bluntly what he thought he could prove by claiming self-defense in the slaying of an unarmed man he had never set eyes on before the killing. Feeney argued that the victim's identity had nothing to do with it. I asked him to explain what did then. He gave me a strange look and offered to tell me the whole story. There was no other way I could fully understand, he insisted.

"It had all begun, Feeney told me, some six months before at a time when his own life was in such a serene state that he seriously regarded himself as perhaps the happiest man on the face of the globe. He was an artisan, he told me, a successful silversmith specializing in medallions, bracelets, and belt buckles who owned his own shop in an exclusive development and whose annual income exceeded mine several times over. At home—a comfortable ranch-style dwelling in an expensive suburb—he had a wife he dearly loved, three fine children of varying ages, two electric beetle buggies, an all-terrain recreation vehicle, and a sailboat, this last in spite of the fact that the city where he resided was located several hundred miles from the nearest substantial body of water.

"The first calamity—this was Feeney's preferred term—to alter this seemingly Utopian mode of existence was a tornado. Such meteorological phenomena are not uncommon in that part of the world but this one seemed unique in that it struck only a single locale: Feeney's house. No one was home at the time so that Feeney's only loss was financial and that largely covered by insurance. When he finished telling me about the tornado Feeney smiled crookedly and said, 'What I didn't know was that the bastards were saving their best shit for later.'

"That 'best shit' included the second calamity which occurred a few days after the first. Feeney and his older daughter, a lovely girl of nineteen, had gone downtown to view a touring art exhibit. As they were leaving the gallery located in the ground floor of a high-rise building, a window washer several stories above happened to drop a metal bucket which went spiraling downward toward the street below. Just as the daughter reached the curb the bucket struck her solidly on top of her head. Her skull split open and portions of her brain oozed out. She was pronounced dead on the spot. Feeney who was walking several paces behind was not injured.

"Due to the loss of his house Feeney and his family had been staying with an older brother. This brother, a shy sensitive man, took Feeney's ill fortune as his own and began drinking heavily. The night before the daughter's funeral the brother passed out in a stupor and the cigarette he had been smoking fell into his lap. When Feeney woke in the morning he found his brother's charred remains. The fire had stopped there oddly enough. The firemen told Feeney it was a stroke of luck that the entire house had not caught fire and burned.

"The daughter's funeral went ahead as scheduled. During the course of the ceremony a gentle rain began to fall. By the time the funeral party reached the cemetery a storm was raging. There were only two recorded instances of lightning striking that day. One bolt struck at the gravesite—killing Feeney's wife—and the other struck in the city, burning Feeney's silversmith shop to the ground. In addition, Feeney's best friend—a man he had known since boyhood—caught pneumonia while attending the funeral and died a week later from complications.

"I won't try your patience with a complete recitation of the remaining events. Feeney's youngest child, a girl of eleven, accidentally cut her hand on a broken cup while washing dishes. The wound became infected and her arm had to be amputated at the elbow. While leaving the hospital she slipped on a banana peel—this has been definitely verified, by the way—and fell under a passing automated lawn mower. The blades slashed her body to shreds. Three days later the surviving child, a son, was bitten by a rattlesnake. He might have survived except that the taxi taking Feeney and the boy to the hospital attempted to take a shortcut through an old part of the city and crossed an abandoned sewer line which collapsed under the weight of the vehicle. By the time the boy could be extracted from the wreckage he was dead. Feeney himself again suffered no injury.

"Nor did he ever. When I visited except for the obvious effects of incarceration Robert Feeney was a man in the prime of health. He described to me a total of fourteen other deaths—family members, friends, close acquaintances—as well as a considerable number of injuries, illnesses, and accidents. By the time he finished my notebook was a mass of scribbles. I then asked him, assuming everything he'd told me was true, why had he decided to kill a man he had never seen before?

"'Because I just couldn't take it any longer,' His eyes gleamed with passion. 'If there had been any kind of pattern, a design, something I could get my hands on, hell, I might have been able to accept it. But there just wasn't anything of the kind. It was all…coincidence. What else could I do? You tell me. I figured I had to do something just as crazy, just as irrational, just as coincidental as all the stuff that was happening to me. If my life was insane—if the whole universe didn't make sense—then I had to adjust to it. I had to become mad too. So I went out, bought a gun, and shot and killed that poor man.'

"'Did it help any?' I asked.

"He leaned back in his chair. 'Actually, yes, it did. From that point on the calamities stopped.'

"'Then you must be satisfied now?'

"'I'm not, no."

"'Why? If it worked, if the murder of that man ended all your troubles you should at least be pleased.'

"'Ah, but did it?'

"'You just told me it did.'

"'Yes. But for how long? How do I know this isn't another coincidence? If it can happen one way, why not another?'

"I couldn't answer that. Robert Feeney was tried, convicted, and in due time executed for the crime of murder. I didn't attend the trial. I don't know whether he ever offered his plea of self-defense or not. His attorney thought it was mad but attorneys are generally of a dull logical mind."

"I guess don't get it, Desmond." Dr. Schwerner was the first to speak when it became clear Blue was done. "What does any of that have to do with this new case of ours?'

Blue gazed at him with sympathy. "The connection, Doctor, is the fact that Robert Feeney was right. That's what I need for all of you to understand. Robert Feeney enjoyed the rare privilege of seeing the true character of the universe we inhabit, a domain ruled by coincidence and chance where anything can happen and sometimes—though not often—it does. Poor complacent Feeney learned his lesson well but in trying to adjust to the irrationality around him he managed only to bring about his own demise. What Feeney failed to realize is that while the universe may indeed be mad it's imperative for human survival to act as though it isn't."

"Aren't you forgetting God?" Peter broke in to ask.

Blue smiled. "Perhaps I am. But the point I wish to reiterate is the relevance of Robert Feeney's life to the case at hand. If the universe is not rational while the human race is, then how do we explain the madness of history?"

"I think you ought to be more specific, Desmond," said Schwerner. He glanced back at Alfie. "You can't expect everybody to follow a complex philosophical argument."

"All right then," said Blue. "Information has come into my hands proving beyond any measure of doubt that the apparent madness of human history is an illusion. In this instance—unlike the Robert Feeney case—the calamities we have always regarded as coincidental are not. A conscious conspiracy does and always has existed."

"What sort of conspiracy, Desmond?" This was Alfie who looked as he always did when a new case was at hand—bright-eyed and eager to begin.

"A conspiracy of evil," said Blue. "For the past several thousand years this conspiracy—known simply apparently as the Sect—has inspired, directed, fomented, and encouraged everything that has gone wrong with human history. They helped kill Jesus Christ, inspired Adolf Hitler, instigated the Children's Crusade, introduced the first plague germs to the European continent. Our case will devoted to uncovering this conspiracy and if possible crushing it."

Alfie whistled softly. "That sounds like a big order to me, Desmond."

"Indeed it is, Alfie." Blue looked at his secretaries. "Nadia, I gave you some papers earlier. The time has come to distribute them."

"Sure, boss." The raven-haired woman rose to her feet and removed three fat manila envelopes from inside her blouse. She handed one each to Alfie, Peter, and Dr. Schwerner.

"What's this?" said Alfie.

"During my return flight home from Rome," said Blue, "I jotted down the facts pertinent to the case. Besides these notes each of your envelopes contains your specific assignment. This case is so vast and complex that I believe it will demand the total involvement of all four of us for some time to come."

"Then we will be leaving Arabia Deserta?" said Schwerner who looked worried.

"I'm afraid so, Doctor. Is there any reason you would prefer not to?"

"I…" Schwerner shook his head quickly. "Not at all, Desmond. It is merely my own work, a few modest experiments. Sometimes it is difficult to leave matters partly finished."

"I fully sympathize, Doctor, but in this instance I believe it will prove necessary. I have arranged transport for each of you leaving Tangier later today. If any of us should fail to return within a reasonable length of time—and this includes myself—I have left instructions with Nadia on how to proceed."

Alfie held up his envelope to the light.

"When do we get to peek?"

"As soon as you wish. In private of course. You'll have several hours at your disposal prior to departure. Everything I gave you should be burned as soon as you've memorized the specifics. Before letting you go I only wish to emphasize one further point. Do not under any circumstances trust a single solitary soul outside the seven of us. As deeply as it chagrins me to admit it our mission has already been compromised. The Sect is almost certainly aware of who we are and what we intend while we as yet know little of them. I have tentatively identified three of their number—you'll find snapshots enclosed in your envelopes—burn these also—but there may be dozens, even hundreds of others involved. Please—as deeply as I love the three of you—take care."

"What about reporting procedures?" asked Schwerner, a practical man as always. "I gather we shall be traveling to widely divergent locations. How do we keep in touch with you if we uncover anything of importance or value?"

"Nadia, Crystal, and Lacy will remain here at Arabia Deserta. If absolutely necessary, you may contact them by coded cablegram. I in turn will endeavor to communicate with them as regularly as possible. Are there any further questions?"

There were none. The three men looked down at the envelopes they held as if impatient to begin.

"Then let me say only this, my dear retainers: we must not fail. This case differs dramatically from any we have previously pursued in that should we fail the result will not merely be that a criminal evades justice but may well lead to the eventual extinction of the human race. Each of you has good reason not to love that species. You have suffered at its hands and a degree of bitterness naturally lingers. All I can say is this: if humanity perishes, what other species will rise to take its place and do better? And please keep in mind that the conspiracy we now move to confront has been like a disease infecting every cell of the human organism. Envision please the Earth as we know it today: a planet ravaged by past excess, bathed in human waste, filth, and suffering. Who is to blame? Some will say God. A few evoke Satan. Most will tell you it's the fault the slugs and their apparent Occupation of the planet. The wisest will point a finger at humanity itself. But I say to you that it is entirely conceivable that none of these solutions is correct. The conspiracy we face—the

Sect—is old and powerful. I have in my possession evidence indicating that certain of its members have enjoyed tremendously long spans of life—they may in fact be immortal. Now try please to envision a world in which this conspiracy has been eradicated. It could be a paradise. I am therefore beseeching each of you to ignore your private grievances and join me in helping bring about the vision I have described. What can be glimpsed in the mind can be transformed into reality. The thought must always precede the deed. Let us strive together then to accomplish our common goal, for beside it all else pales to utter insignificance."

Blue leaned back, all emotion spent, and for a moment simply exulted in the stunned silence he had brought about. They never knew the old boy still had it in him, he thought with delight.

He came to his feet and headed for the door. With a hand on the knob he paused and looked back. "While you study your assignments, should any questions arise, I will be in the basement."

"Not the dope room again?" said Peter, aghast.

Blue chuckled thinly. "As a farewell gesture only. I shall not imbibe." He clicked his tongue and slapped his thigh. "Come along, Baskerville. Heel, boy, heel."

A PROFILE: DESMOND BLUE:

To be utterly candid from the outset: at the time he commenced his investigation into the case of the Conspiracy of the Sect Desmond Blue was without question the greatest detective in the world. In point of fact this was a position Blue had occupied for a good many years.

The only detectives who might profitably be compared with Blue in terms of intelligence, sensitivity, intuition, insight, and deductive reasoning were those like Hercule Poirot, Philo Vance, Father Brown, Ellery Queen, Nero Wolfe, and of course that genius of geniuses, Mr. Sherlock Holmes.

The crucial difference: Holmes, Poirot, Brown etc. were fictional creations; Desmond Blue was a flesh and blood human being.

Standing six feet four inches in his stocking feet, tipping the scales at a cool two-ninety-five, bulbous-nosed, keen-eyed, the greatest practicing detective on the planet Earth.

Desmond Blue emerged from rather peculiar beginnings.

Born in the state of New Mexico, U. S of A., his mother a brilliant physicist who would have collected a Nobel Prize years earlier except for the defect of her gender, Father never specifically identified. (Blue himself chose to forgo investigation; if pressed he would imply that his father was a disinherited prince from one of Europe's more notorious royal families.)

Shortly after the birth of her only child Desmond Blue's mother had disappeared along with her infant son from the government project where she had been working, eluding an FBI dragnet in the process. A month later she was found one morning in the bedroom of a plush Beverly Hills hotel suite, her throat and wrists slashed with a razor, the baby Desmond fast asleep in an adjoining room. Before taking her own life the mother had established a trust fund from savings to guarantee her son's future education.

Young Desmond thus grew up encircled by various relations— maiden aunts and grandparents predominated. He was a reclusive child who began to read on his own at age three. His favorite reading as a child were Arthur Conan Doyle's stories of the great Sherlock Holmes.

By the time the boy turned five everyone acknowledged that he was a genuine prodigy.

At ten he announced that henceforth his last name would be *Blue*.

At fifteen he was graduated from one of the nation's most prestigious preparatory academies. At eighteen he obtained a master's degree in modern literature from the University of Michigan. (Another in psychology followed one year later.)

His favorite recreational pursuit remained the reading of mystery and detective fiction. He put together a private collection of such work of enviable proportions including a complete run of the hard-boiled pulp magazine *Black Mask* although he himself was more partial to the classical school of detection.

Deciding to become a psychiatrist he entered medical school and finished at the top of his class.

He was subsequently accepted into a renowned psychoanalytic institute in New York City. During this period Blue also went through his first physical love affair with a slightly older woman named Nora Malloy, a renowned experimental researcher among certain psychotropic chemical compounds. It was thought by many that during the course of their affair Nora and the young Blue may have ingested some of these chemicals together and perhaps made love while under the influence.

After five years Blue left the institute. His private psychiatric practice in Manhattan soon flourished. His patients included such celebrities as the female astronaut Carlotta McCoy as well as more ordinary people including the divorced middle class housewife Scarlet Tewkesbury Cipriano whom Blue later married.

Desmond Blue was a kind, honest, and generous man. Those who knew him well (never a great number) liked and respected him.

When the slugs occupied Earth Blue was at the time in Copenhagen attending a seminar. His beloved wife Scarlet was among those struck dead (if only temporarily) when the golden ships passed over Salt Lake City where she'd gone to attend the wedding of a favorite niece. Like the others who died Scarlet Tewkesbury Cipriano Blue was reborn three days later as a spook, though she and her husband never reestablished marital relations. (Few of the reborn, as it turned out, felt any lingering interest in those who'd failed to undergo the experience of death.)

Whether because of this or something else Desmond Blue began to change.

Not that he wasn't still a kind, honest, and generous man: he was indeed all of that.

He closed his psychiatric practice.

He began smoking marijuana and hashish.

Soon he was also using opium.

He sniffed cocaine, chewed peyote, and twice injected heroin into his veins.

After several months self-indulgence he applied for a license as a private investigator. The license was granted. (In the immediate aftermath of Occupation most surviving governmental agencies were easily susceptible to bribery; almost anything could be had at the right price.)

Things did not always go smoothly for Desmond Blue private eye in those early years. He hired a confidential secretary, Nadia van Hauten who, it was said, more often supported Blue than vice versa.

(Nadia was a prolific and successful freelance writer of escapist fiction under the pseudonym Arnold Hope Grimthorpe.)

Blue's first well-publicized case was a murder investigation in Old Detroit where a cooperative workers group was attempting to reopen the old Ford Motor Plant to produce a new model of electric beetle buggy. When the first new machine rolled off the assembly line in full view of hundreds of witnesses and the doors were hurled open a dead body toppled out.

Blue deduced the one and only way in which such a crime could have been perpetrated and fingered the guilty party.

As time passed Blue's reputation as a detective steadily grew. Such remarkable successes as the cases of the Burmese snapping turtle, the Argentine labyrinth, and the disappearing wombats of Bangladesh brought new clients to his doorstep by the eager dozens.

Desmond Blue became a man of considerable wealth and fame. He was able to hire an additional pair of confidential secretaries to work side by side with Nadia van Hauten. He moved his base of operations to the Saharan Desert after purchasing the vacant mansion of an eccentric oil heiress who had vanished like most others of her kind in the Occupation.

Later Blue decided to take on a few retainers to help with his caseload. associates. Alfie Jarrett was the first of these—a young man with vast energy and a quick mind.

Dr. Gordon Schwerner was the second; his genius though of a radically different kind rivaled Blue's own.

Peter Mark was the third associate. Blue had rescued Peter after a horrible accident and felt it only proper to find a beneficial use for the remainder of his life.

He also acquired a dog, an Afghan hound he named Baskerville.

After a number of years Blue came to feel increasingly alienated from the tone and tenor of his detective work. His decision to retire from active practice was motivated largely by a scarcity of worthy opponents. Catching crooks had become so simple it wasn't much a challenge anymore. Except for a few sojourns under the cover of private dope-buying excursions Blue had not left the grounds of his Saharan estate in more than twelve months.

Thus the case of the Conspiracy of the Sect arrived like a beacon of light in an ocean of darkness. n excuse had been found not only for Blue to begin work again but also to go on living. (Suicide had hovered close to his consciousness in recent days.)

So that afternoon following the departure of Alfie, Peter, and Dr. Schwerner for Tangier Blue packed a suitcase of his own.

When Crystal returned to the mansion after ferrying the others to Tangier aboard her helio-plane, he informed her that she would now be flying him to Kabul, Afghanistan after one brief stop along the way.

BOOK TWO

SECTARIANS

Historians undertake to arrange sequences,—called stories or histories—assuming in silence a relation of cause and effect. These assumptions, hidden in the depths of dusty libraries, have been astounding but commonly unconscious and childlike; so much so, that if any captious critic were to drag them to light, historians would probably reply, with one voice, that they had never supposed themselves required to know what they were talking about.

—Henry Adams,
The Education of Henry Adams

1

By turning in his seat and gazing out the window Dr. Gordon Schwerner could observe the wide blue slash of the Congo River as it snaked through the dense forest below. This part of Africa had even now been only lightly touched by the iron and concrete ravages of modern civilization so that at least as seen unblemished from twenty thousand feet up aboard the East African aeroliner *Shaka Zulu,* it must have resembled the wild country first visited by the explorer Henry Morton Stanley more than a century before.

As unique as the view undoubtedly was it failed to hold Schwerner's attention for long. Natural wonders had never possessed much attraction for him; give Schwerner a good abstract mathematical equation any day of the week—now that was real beauty. His flight had originated in Tangier with stopovers along the way in Timbuktu and Nairobi before reaching its final destination in Zanzibar. Most of Schwerner's fellow passengers were well-dressed white men and women presumably here in Africa for reasons of business or commerce. There would not likely be many tourists among them. The slugs had largely brought an end to that onetime popular activity.

When a person left his or her own home voluntarily they did so under the assumption that it would remain intact until their subsequent return and the slugs had demonstrated that this was no longer always the case.

Directly across the aisle from Schwerner sat one of the few Negroes on board, a lean black-bearded man with heavy hips, a square jaw, and gold-rimmed spectacles perched on the nub of a flat nose. The man kept glancing furtively in Schwerner's direction as if he thought he might know him. It annoyed Schwerner who was not much fond of Negroes to begin with.

Who could the man possibly be? One of the Sect conspirators hot on his trail already? Schwerner struggled to dismiss the thought as patently absurd. There was no conceivable way anyone could have learned he would be aboard this particular flight. Besides, the Negro had already been on the plane when it landed in Tangier.

Schwerner lowered his gaze back to the book in his lap and made another effort to concentrate on reading. The book was a novel, *Heart of Darkness* by the Polish-English writer Joseph Conrad. He had read a portion of it a number of years before at Blue's instigation—there had been a period when Desmond had tried to broaden his knowledge of the so-called liberal arts—but remembered little except that the story took place in Africa. The few pages he had so far managed to trudge through had served only to remind him that the region of Africa involved in the story was the old Belgian Congo not the eastern savannah where he was presently bound. As such reading the book seemed to him largely a waste of time.

After a few more minutes of struggle he gave up, closed the book, and turned back to the window. The Congo River had vanished now, leaving in its wake only a broad expanse of yellow-brown grass punctuated by an occasional brief flash of blue, presumably a stream or small lake. They would be arriving soon. His orders from Blue had instructed him to fly to Zanzibar and check into a particular hotel but said nothing else. What was supposed to happen next? he wondered. Would somebody contact him? He assumed so but had no way of knowing for certain. As usual Blue's mysterious secretive ways were a distinct annoyance.

The aeroliner landed with a bump and a jerk that snapped Schwerner from his reverie. He looked out the window and saw a handful of dilapidated hangars, a rather seedy-looking main terminal, and large numbers of apparently idle native workmen. If this was a typical view of Zanzibar then he wasn't much impressed.

As Schwerner emerged from the plane and crossed the runway through the clinging heat a putrid odor like rancid meat assaulted his nostrils. He stopped briefly and glanced around in an attempt to locate the source of the stench. Huddled near the main terminal, restrained by a rope barrier, stood ten or so black men. They were spooks plainly—those who had perished in the slug attack on nearby Dar-es-Salaam and then come back to life three days later. Schwerner had never seen this many spooks in one place at any one time before. Usually they kept to their own reservations out of sight of the living. Feeling vaguely repelled Schwerner lowered his head to hurry quickly past but had covered only a few paces when the Negro from the plane rushed past him and began shouting at the spooks in an unfamiliar tongue. With a brisk wave of the hand he indicated to them to follow him and led them off toward a distant building across the way. The foul stench of death hung in the air in their wake.

By the time Schwerner entered the terminal the other passengers were already passing through customs. The agent who beckoned at Schwerner more closely resembled an Arab than an African. He had tan skin, a narrow moustache, tiny dark eyes, and a bright red fez for a cap. The agent stamped Schwerner's passport, flipped quickly through the pages of the Conrad book and handed him a dozen malaria pills. "You are welcome to remain in Zanzibar for as long as you wish."

Schwerner was about to move on when something—perhaps his detective's sixth sense—caused him to linger. He looked back and saw there was no one in line behind him. "Back on the runway," he said in a hushed tone, "I happened to notice a number of spooks. They seemed to be waiting for a black gentleman who was aboard the aeroliner with me. Do you know anything about him?"

The agent shrugged. "The spooks are a foul stinky bunch, that is for certain. I order them to wait outside so they cannot stink up my upholstery." He nodded in apparent pride at the adjoining waiting room, a few battered couches covered in ragged plastic. "I hope you were not made ill."

"No, I'm fine. But what about the man they were waiting for? Do you know who he is?" Schwerner extracted a crumpled bank note from his wallet and passed it surreptitiously to the agent. The two of them were alone now; the other passengers had gone ahead.

"Mohammed Bello," the agent said with a wink that seemed to indicate that everyone knew who Mohammed Bello was.

"What's his connection with these spooks? Does he…ah…does he own them?"

The agent scowled. "There is no slavery in Zanzibar. It is barbaric practice—for barbarians only."

"But the spooks work for him?"

"That is true. Many of the dead, they work for Mohammed Bello at no pay. That is an entirely different matter—not slavery at all. Bello owns a large plantation near Kilimanjaro. He grows coffee. Some say it is coffee. Others say…" He winked.

Schwerner produced another bank note. "What do the others say?"

"Poppies."

"Opium?"

"A new strain, they say. Only spooks can work in the fields. Others who try go quickly mad. It is some very powerful shit, this new opium strain."

Schwerner thanked the agent for his time and moved off. The air conditioning did not appear to be working and his shirt and jacket clung to his skin like paste. He retrieved his luggage, a single suitcase, and stepped outside. Mopping his brow with one hand he raised the other and gestured at a line of beetle buggy taxis parked across from the terminal. A one-seat electric that was barely more than a chassis, windshield, and three wheels broke from the pack and squealed to a halt beside him. Dropping into the passenger seat Schwerner instructed the driver, a light-skinned Negro with carrot-orange hair, to carry him into town.

"You got no hotel, *bwana*?" the driver asked in clipped English. "I can maybe fix you up for cheap. Everything's full this time of year. It is a dreadful mess. Can get you a hot girl too if you want. Black, white, mixed race, you call it, *bwana*."

"I have a confirmed reservation at the Hilton Inn," Schwerner said stiffly. "You may take me directly there if you wish." He seriously doubted the hotels could possibly be anywhere close to full.

The driver smirked as if the two of them shared a secret. "Begging the pardon, *bwana,* but you look much like a military man. Army officer? Colonel maybe? That correct?"

Schwerner was aware that he did not in the least resemble an army officer. "I'm a scientist," he said with what he hoped was an air of dignity.

The driver beamed. "One Dr. Schwerner maybe?"

He turned in surprise. "Why, yes. How did—?"

The driver stepped on the accelerator and the little beetle buggy sprang forward. A vehicle this size would be fortunate to reach thirty miles per hour at top speed. The driver seemed intent on reaching level in the least amount of time possible.

"If you the doctor, then I got a message for you, *bwana,*" the driver said as he whipped around a corner onto a narrow blacktop road. Clasping the wheel lightly in two fingers he dropped a crumpled wad of paper into Schwerner's lap.

Schwerner unfolded the message. The paper contained only a typewritten name: *Darby Spock.*

The driver was weaving through light traffic, mostly motorbikes or beetle buggies not much larger than his own. The landscape on both sides of the road consisted of a wearying collection of ramshackle huts and hovels.

"Did you type this?" Schwerner asked. He had to raise his voice to be heard about the whining electric motor and the rush of hot wind.

"No, sir. Given to me by another, *bwana.*"

"By whom, may I ask?"

"Great fat dude."

"This Darby Spock perhaps?"

The driver giggled. "Darby Spock don't pass no messages to me, that's for sure, *bwana.*"

Schwerner concealed his annoyance. He was certain the driver was poking fun at him—he had said *bwana* far too many times otherwise. "Then who is this Darby Spock person who doesn't pass messages?"

"Spock is your big fix-up man in Zanzibar. You go to him and he fix you up with thrills. Safari to the mainland, shoot and kill the biggest of game. Lion. Hippo. Tiger."

"There are no tigers in Africa," Schwerner said curtly.

They had entered the confused winding streets of the town proper. Bleached white buildings nestled snugly together, walls touching walls. There were numerous shabby little shops, their windows filled with assorted glittery junk. "Besides, I have no interest in hunting. Angling is my sport of choice."

"Then stay away from Darby Spock. He's one great white hunter, that's all." The taxi bounced to an unexpected halt. "You want to purchase ivory trinkets, *bwana*? Fine lace? Intricate native carvings? Picture postcards for a lady friend back home? Dirty ones perhaps? Got some hot stuff in here for sale cheap."

Schwerner frowned at the rapidly clicking fare box. "I wish to be borne to my hotel immediately."

"Darby Spock waits on you there." The driver accelerated with the same vigor as before. "Down in the bar. Better hurry quick though. Spock gets stinking drunk and you no see him for ten, twenty days."

Schwerner had been thinking about something the driver had said earlier. "This fellow who gave you the message for me. You said he was a large man?"

"Fat *bwana*, sure."

"Was he—?"

"Desmond Blue, right again. Big daddy of the private eyes."

Schwerner was taken aback. Blue—here already. But why? If he had somehow flown straight from Arabia Deserta he might well have reached Zanzibar first. But that still didn't explain his motive. "Do you happen to know if he's still in the city?"

"Nah. He rings me at home. I'm in bed humping white college girl no longer a virgin when I'm done but answer and say hello. Meet me at the aeroport, Blue says. Old friend of mine from way back, Blue once save my tail from a real pickle. I go and he give me message to pass to you the doctor and then leave."

It hardly seemed to make sense for Blue to have come all this way only to pass a message he might have whispered in Schwerner's ear back at the mansion but Blue's methods were often tangled. Schwerner tried to figure out what if anything this might mean.

The shrill blast of the bug's horn shook him loose from his reverie. He looked up just in time to see a man's contorted face only inches from the windshield. There was a thud as the bumper struck the man and his body vaulted up and over top of the beetle.

Schwerner swung his head and saw the man lying in the street behind them.

"Good God, you've killed that man!" he cried.

The driver seemed oblivious. "Can't kill what's already dead, *bwana*."

Schwerner swung his head again to be sure. The man was already back on his feet again, weaving unsteadily from side to side. As Schwerner watched another car clipped him a glancing blow. He slumped to his knees, regained his feet, and staggered off.

The car turned a corner. "So that was a spook we struck," said Schwerner.

"Dead man, sure."

"But what was he doing down here?"

The driver shrugged. "Working in a shop maybe. They do heavy work, loading and unloading. Sweaty work but the dead don't sweat." He tapped his forehead. "Stupid ones mostly. Brain scrambled by being dead too long. Walk into traffic all the time, get hit by beetles."

Schwerner repressed a shudder.

"Here we go, *bwana*," the driver said a short time later.

* * * *

The Zanzibar Hilton Inn appeared little different from the rest of its ilk, a product of the decadent years of an earlier century. Schwerner paid the driver and lugged his suitcase into the lobby, a big colorful room, the walls decorated with garish paintings of native African wildlife. The registration desk huddled beneath a six-by-six foot representation of a trumpeting bull elephant.

Schwerner rang the bell and waited for a clerk to appear. The bar, a shadowy room, lay off to the left. A stooped aged Arab at last emerged from behind a beaded curtain and after a tedious search through his desk sullenly confirmed Schwerner's reservation. A bellboy was summoned and led Schwerner to the third floor. He inspected his room carefully for snakes and other vermin then dismissed the boy with a modest tip. Alone he stripped to the buff and took a shower. The water was refreshingly cool and invigorating. He put on clean underwear, a fresh shirt, and his wrinkled linen suit. Then he went back downstairs and into the bar.

The room was sparsely populated, the few occupied tables containing only a single customer each. Schwerner let his eyes adjust to the dimness then crossed to the bar. There was a lone figure seated here on a tall stool. Schwerner decided this must be the man he was looking for. He wore knee-length khaki shorts, soiled white socks, and a bush jacket with a torn sleeve. He was smoking tobacco in a curved pipe and wore a .45 revolver in a holster at his hip. The walrus moustache on his upper lip was brown and bushy.

Schwerner waited for the bartender to arrive and take his order then shifted his weight and peered more closely at the man beside him. When he did he nearly cried out. The man was clearly a spook.

"You must be Dr. Schwerner, I presume," the man said in unexpectedly soft and gentle voice. In life he might well have been a typically a florid-faced man with a red nose and ruddy cheeks. In death he retained only his large girth, big knotty hands, and tanned muscular forearms.

"I am Gordon Schwerner, yes."

"Spock's the name. Darby Spock. I'm a doctor too if you want to make something of it but I bloody well don't." He reeked of the powerful scent of cheap perfume. "Blue phoned me last night and said I should wait for you here. I suppose you'll want to be leaving as soon as possible. It'll have to be the day after tomorrow at the earliest though. I'm having trouble obtaining sufficient petrol for the long trip. Damn slugs took it all away with them, you know."

Schwerner found that if he didn't actually look directly at Spock it was not terribly different from talking to a normal living person. He let his eyes hover a few inches above Spock's left shoulder. The bartender arrived now with his drink—a glass of supposedly French Beaujolais.

"Fill mine too," said Spock who was drinking straight whisky. "You'll have to get the tab," he added in an aside to Schwerner. "I seem to have forgotten my bloody wallet again."

"I ought to warn you," said Schwerner after the bartender had come and gone again, "that I don't know quite as much about this case as I might like. I don't know how well you know Desmond but he prefers to divulge information only when he deems it vitally necessary. Perhaps you could tell me exactly what it was he told you."

"Not a whole hell of a bloody lot." Spock's words were somewhat slurred and Schwerner realized with a start that the man was more than a little tipsy. "Said you were an associate of his coming to Zanzibar on a big case. Said I should meet you here at the Hilton. Said you'd want to visit the mainland and I should act as your guide. Said if anybody asked what was going on I should say we were touring the freshwater lakes. Do you care much for fishing? I find it a dreadful bore. Much prefer hunting big game for sport."

"I fail to see the sport in killing innocent animals."

Spock shrugged. "Once you've been dead yourself you find there's many worse things than getting killed."

"Such as?" said Schwerner.

"Such as being alive," said Spock with a laugh. He reached for his drink. "Blue said you'd be wanting to visit the Renaldo Castle. Did I get that part right?"

"I guess so. If that's what Desmond said. Did he...uh...did he happen to mention why I was going there?"

"Not a word. I figured you'd know."

"Who is this Renaldo?"

"Blue didn't tell you that either?"

Schwerner looked away, embarrassed. "He didn't, no."

"Well, he's not anyone now. Renaldo's long dead. And buried. At least his bones are. That's about all that was left of him when they got through." The bartender passed by. Spock beckoned and held up two fingers. "Want to hear more?"

Schwerner shrugged. "I suppose."

"Well, he came from South America originally. I forget which country if I ever knew. Jorge Renaldo, his wife, and two children. They arrived in the old Tanganyika Territory damn near a century ago now. Rich as Rockefeller, so the story goes. Carried a bag of uncut diamonds big as your nose hooked to his belt. Claimed he was a psychiatrist. Said he'd studied under the late great Dr. Freud personally. Likely bullshit but who knows? For some reason—a bribe would be my guess—the colonial authorities granted him a big plot of land in the interior. Renaldo took the family and went out there to live. He was gone maybe a dozen years. It was wild desolate country without another white person a hundred klicks around. In time though the rumors started drifting back—damned nasty rumors. The governor got curious and sent a detachment of soldiers to find out what the hell was going on. The soldiers never returned. Which made the governor even more curious. So he sent out five companies this time. They managed to get to the bottom of things."

"What things?" said Schwerner.

Spock shook his head, suddenly reticent. "I wasn't there so I can't really say. All I know is what I heard. One version had it that Renaldo wasn't a native South American but a Romanian or Italian or some other kind of dago. I suppose you're familiar with the hoary old myth of the vampire, a dead man who drinks the blood of the living in order to survive." He grinned. "Sort of like me except that I prefer Scotch whisky."

"But that's simply a legend based upon a genuine psychological disorder."

"Right. I don't happen to put much credence in it myself. The whole thing reeks of superstition and unlike you lifers we spooks are largely free of such idiocy. Another version though says that Renaldo was a German, knew Hitler personally, gave him a lot of his ideas."

"I don't know very much about Hitler," Schwerner admitted. He recalled the little Blue had told him. "He started one of the world wars, didn't he?"

"Among other horrors, yes. But I'm speaking more of his treatment of the Jews."

"What about the Jews?"

"Hitler tried his damnedest to exterminate the lot of them. There were six million dead in Europe before he was done. Well, Renaldo set up his own miniature version of the Third Reich out there in the bush and since there weren't any Jews around he substituted tribesmen instead."

"Are you saying he slaughtered them for no reason?"

"I'm not saying anything. That's how one version of the story goes and like I told you I wasn't there and can't rightly say. The third version is the one I personally prefer. Renaldo was interested in psychic phenomena—you recall he claimed to be a psychiatrist—brain waves and all that sort of rot. He used the natives in the course of a series of experiments that went awry with the result that the natives were driven slowly but hopelessly bonkers. Renaldo then killed them all. Maybe out of pity or remorse or maybe just trying to cover up what he was doing out there. When the soldiers arrived they found mass graves all over the landscape, bleached bones sticking up out of the turf."

"So Renaldo was arrested?"

"At first, yes, but then—this is something I've never heard of otherwise—the colonel in charge turned Renaldo over to a tribe of Goniani, a fierce warlike bunch from the southwest. All I can say is that what Renaldo did must have been pretty damn horrible for any white man to do that to another white man. The Goniani took care of poor Renaldo."

"How?" Schwerner heard himself ask though he was far from sure he really wanted to know.

"Well, first they whipped him with strips of giraffe hide until his flesh was a bloody pulp. Then they buggered him, one after the other, maybe three dozen in all. It's an old Goniani expression of contempt. Then they took what was left of his body and covered it with a coating of soft clay and allowed that to harden. They poked air holes for the mouth and nostrils and then hung it suspended over a low fire. They baked him alive in other words. Then they made his wife and children—who'd been forced to watch the whole thing happening—made them eat his baked remains for lunch. I've been told it's a common religious rite among the Goniani. Who can really say? Afterward they killed the three of them, cut off their heads, fed the bodies to the crocodiles, and that was the end of it."

"My God," said Schwerner who was feeling slightly sick to his stomach. "That's appalling."

"Is it? I wonder. The Goniani weren't necessarily being cruel. They may have simply wanted to be sure that the dead remained dead. As one who's learned that that's not always the case I can't help sympathizing."

"All of this was apparently a long time ago," said Schwerner. "What possible relevance does it have with anything now—with me?"

"I'm afraid you've got me there, old man. The big house Renaldo built out there in the bush is still standing. It's made completely of stone, a marvelous architectural structure really. They call it the

Renaldo Castle now. Has to be seen to be believed. How Renaldo managed to build it out there in the middle of nowhere, God alone knows—whether he imported the stones from somewhere else or forced the natives to dig them up. For years after his death no one would go near the place. I tended to steer clear of it myself. Then a year or two back—time tends to get jumbled when you're dead— a man named Charles Vincente and his wife Maria showed up in Zanzibar with the woman claiming descent from Renaldo through a sister he had left behind in South America. The government checked on the claim and it appeared valid. The couple demanded their house and land back and the government said if they wanted it they could go out and get it. They did just that, setting up housekeeping. More than that they started up a special school— a home for disturbed children, they called it—and began receiving clients from as far away as North America. They were both educators. The government checked on that too."

"It sounds harmless enough to me."

"I'm not attempting to draw a parallel with Renaldo. As a matter of fact I've visited the Vincentes on several occasions and they struck me as bright, friendly, idealistic people, Maria especially. The children seemed healthy, cheerful, and damnably well-behaved."

"Then I still have to wonder why Desmond wants me to go out there."

"As I said your guess is s bloody good as mine. But I can tell you this much: something funny is going on out there. The last time I was in the vicinity I decided to pay them a visit. I couldn't get in. Barbed wire had been strung all around the place and signs erected in four different languages warning everyone to keep away. The natives were whispering again and seemed restless if not outright frightened. I couldn't get a damned thing out of them. As I said I'm not a superstitious man. Once you've seen what lies beyond the grave, life holds few remaining terrors. But frankly that place bothers me. It's got too much ugly history in it. I was thinking of taking another trip out that way on my own when your boss called."

"But you know nothing specific? Not since the death of this Renaldo and his family?"

"No, nothing. Maybe the Vincentes simply want some privacy. I could understand that if they weren't the only white people within miles. And Charles is a queer sort of duck to begin with."

"In what way? Nothing like Renaldo, I hope?"

Spock shook his head. "You'd better wait till you meet him and make up your own mind." Spock looked down at his empty whisky glass. "As I said we can leave day after tomorrow at the earliest. We'll take the ferry across and from there I have a petrol-driven jeep and an old van waiting. I'll engage a few of my regular boys to accompany us."

"That will be fine," said Schwerner. "How do I contact you? Are you registered here at the hotel?"

Spock laughed heartily. "The Hilton prefers not to accommodate the dead, I'm afraid. They claim we stink up the joint, you know, even when we bathe in perfume to please you lifers. I had to slip the bartender a twenty just to sit here till you showed up. I don't need a room anyway. We dead can go for years without sleep. I have to fill myself with dope to pop off for more than ten minutes at a crack. I'll come by and fetch you when I'm ready to leave."

"As you wish," said Schwerner.

Spock slid off his stool. His balance seemed precarious as he stood flexing his knees. "Don't forget to settle the tab. I'll reimburse you later of course."

Without a farewell he sauntered toward the exit.

Schwerner watched him go then turned back and finished the rest of his wine. He paid for the drinks—Spock had apparently had several before his arrival—then headed off back to the sanctuary of his room. He opened his suitcase and sat down on the bed. From a hidden pocket he extracted a dog-eared magazine and flipped through the pages, glancing at the familiar lurid photographs. His mind however refused to concentrate on the glories of undraped youth and kept drifting instead to other matters. He thought about the case. There was still so little he knew even after the meeting with Spock. A local atrocity tale, decades old. A stone castle located in the middle of nothingness. The sudden presence of barbed wire where none had stood before. What did any of this have to do with the conspiracy he had supposedly been sent here to confront? Were the Vincentes members of the Sect? But if so how did Blue know? Schwerner tried to recall the various intelligence reports that had passed through his hands the previous few months. Anything concerned with East Africa? Nothing he could recall offhand. Blue of course had his own private sources of information—a network of loyal informants who refused to deal with anyone but him. Perhaps one of them had told him something about the Renaldo Castle or the Vincentes that had aroused his suspicions. Yes—but what?

Schwerner realized he was simply too tired to think clearly. He came back to his feet and yawned. It was definitely time for bed. As he undressed he could hear through the window the piercing cry of some strange native fauna. He threw open the window and inhaled the cloying scent of cloves. It had begun to rain again. The sound reminded him of the patter of a child's first hesitant footsteps.

He shut the window, climbed into bed, and was soon asleep.

2

The big lumbering aeroplane that carried Alfie Jarrett across the broad Atlantic and the elongated sward of the North American continent refused to set down at his intended destination San Francisco because that once fabled city no longer existed—the slugs and their golden ships had seen to that—and instead landed in the bustling environs of Nuevo Sacramento where a hardy band of urban pioneers had for the last few years labored to establish an independent city-state after the pure Athenian model. At least that's what the brochure Alfie had been handed as he left the plane informed him. He scanned the first paragraph, came to the part about the pure Athenian model, wrinkled his nose, shrugged, and tossed the brochure aside. He had nothing against pure Athenian models but it was hard to see one from where he presently stood.

The Nuevo Sacramento aeroport consisted of two parallel strips of dingy gray concrete, a couple of aluminum hangars, and a tin shack for customs and baggage. In spite of the primitive appearance of the place customs turned out to come equipped with its own intricate filing system which promptly turned up evidence of Alfie's criminal past which meant it took him an additional hour of explanations and phone calls before he was allowed to make his official entry. By the time he escaped the tin shack and reached the outside world there wasn't a beetle buggy taxi in sight. His suitcase was heavy in his hand, his stomach cried out for nourishment, he was dog-tired, it was cold and dark and miserable, and he still had another hundred miles to go before he reached San Francisco. Alfie swore softly to himself, wondering whether he ought to go back inside, curl up on the floor, and wait for morning.

He was about to do exactly when the limousine rumbled into view. He stared in wide-eyed wonder as it drew close and gradually slowed down. The limousine was black except for a couple acres worth of glittering chrome and about the size of an average ocean aeroliner. It was a Lincoln Continental, he was pretty sure, a breed as supposedly extinct as the woolly mammoth.

The limousine bumped to a halt directly beside him. The front door swung open silently and a woman in the passenger seat stared out at him. Alfie transferred his own gaze from the car to her instead. She wasn't simply gorgeous; she was ravishing. Coal black hair, blood red lips, tiny heart-shaped tattoo on her left cheekbone, and a body whose marvels could only be imagined in the dark interior of the limousine.

"Mr. Jarrett?" said the woman in a voice like butter.

"I've been called that." He grinned. "Among other things of course." The joke sounded dumb even to his own ears.

But she laughed—a tinkling noise like a xylophone. "I'm Tess Hennesey. My father asked me to come and meet you."

"Your father?"

"John Hartford Hennesey. Won't you please get in?"

Hennesey was the person Desmond Blue had sent him here to see but nobody had said anything about a daughter. He started to climb in beside the woman—he assumed the seat was roomy enough—but she pointed him toward the back—with a radiant smile. Reluctantly, he opened the back door and slid in. "I imagine you'll want to stretch out and relax after your long trip," she said by way of explanation.

Alfie pretended not to mind. The seat was as soft as a bed of feathers and as wide as the continent of Asia. He stretched his legs as far out as they'd go and still fell inches short of touching the seat in front.

"This is one swell car," he said.

"It's an original replica mid-twentieth century model," she said, turning and peering at him over the top of the seat. Her eyes were green and she was wearing some sort of thin satin garment. She smelled nice too—perfume, he guessed. "I find it rather ostentatious but Father adores it and the highway between here and San Francisco is in such dreadful shape it's safer and more comfortable to drive a big car."

He ran his hands across the soft leather seat.

"It feels as good as new. Must have cost a fortune."

"I'm sure it did," she said drily. She turned to the driver who so far hadn't uttered a word. "Henry, I think we can be on our way now."

"As you wish, Miss Tess."

The limousine accelerated so smoothly and silently that it took Alfie a moment to realize they were moving. At the same time he noticed something peculiar about the driver: he wasn't human. From the back it wasn't easy to tell for sure but the hands clutching the steering wheel were steel pincers and that seemed a pretty good indication. Alfie had never seen such a human-like robot before. He knew they existed, knew Schwerner's parents had developed a functioning model years ago, but hadn't been aware there were any still around in operating condition.

Tess Hennesey was smiling back at him again. "I wanted to say how delighted I was to discover you'd accepted Father's offer to come and work with him on the project. He's basically a gregarious man and I know it's difficult for him to live as much by himself as he must because of the work. Whenever I'm able to spend time with him he talks my ear off and he's even harder on the robots like poor Henry here." She reached out and patted the machine on its brainless skull. "I should explain that Father would have come himself to pick you up but the project is in a delicate phase at the moment and he didn't want to leave unless there wasn't any choice."

"I'm looking forward to meeting him." Alfie was being deliberately vague. As usual he knew only the barest framework of his assignment and had to play things by ear till further enlightenment came. Blue's written instructions had been terse: go to ruins of San Francisco, meet a man named John Hartford Hennesey who will be expecting you, and watch him like a hawk till you're instructed otherwise.

Alfie hadn't known that anyone except a few savages still lived in the ruins of San Francisco and with the kind of money Hennesey appeared to possess he clearly was not one of those.

"The telegram you sent Father excited him tremendously by the way," said Tess. "He made me read it as soon as I arrived from Hollywood where I live. I hadn't spoken to him in several days and wasn't aware he'd fired his previous assistant. He told me there was no question in his mind you were the perfect person for the job, the one he'd been looking for all the time."

Alfie put on what he hoped was a modest grin. "I always try to make a good first impression."

"I think it was your idealism more than anything else that convinced him." She shut her eyes and appeared to quote from memory: "'The stars in the sky are beacons placed by the hand of God to beckon to the spirit of man.'"

"That's what I wrote?" said Alfie, appalled.

"Don't you remember? It's the exact sort of thing Father is always saying himself."

Alfie looked at her intently. Was she making fun of him? It wasn't easy to tell. Her eyes were as cool as a couple of emeralds. "I hope I can live up to what he's expecting from me."

"And you're young too. The others—your predecessors—were always older men. Father used to say that only those with long memories still knew how to dream. Apparently your telegram changed his mind. I understand one of your ancestors was a ranking official in the Apollo moon project."

"That's what I've heard too." Alfie assumed this was another of Desmond's lies.

"Father was surprised that he'd never heard of him. He was an Air Force officer himself, you know, and tried to volunteer for astronaut training. NASA rejected him for medical reasons—there were questions about his stamina even then—but he always kept up on space developments."

Alfie felt it might be a good idea to change the subject before he got in too deep to get out. Damn Desmond Blue and his obsession with secrecy. This could turn out to be sticky. "What about yourself? I bet you've led an interesting life too."

"Me?" She seemed amused. "What makes you think that?"

"Well, not everybody gets to ride around in a limousine like this one."

"But that's not me—that's Father."

"Then what about him? I'm sure he's got to be an interesting character too."

So Tess told Alfie about her father. As he'd already pretty much deduced on his own John Hartford Hennesey was an immensely wealthy man. After his forced retirement from the Air Force because of a heart murmur he had gone into financial speculation and by an uncanny anticipation of future trends and developments had made a bundle before the slugs came. Hennesey always dealt strictly in paper, Tess said. He had no interest in acquiring property. What he'd do was buy a chunk of stock in one company, sell it at a profit, then buy a bigger chunk of stock in another company. By the time the golden ships appeared in the sky Hennesey was among the five or six richest men on the planet.

Alfie was confused. "In that case I guess I don't understand. I mean, the slugs took all the rich people on Earth away with them. How come your father's still here?"

"You said it yourself. All the rich people on Earth."

"I guess I still don't get you."

She smiled. "Father wasn't on the Earth when the slugs came. He was in space—in orbit."

"Oh."

"It was a secret, you see. A privately financed space mission. No government was involved. Father hates governments. He thinks they only foster mediocrity. As soon as he returned to Earth the first thing he did was buy San Francisco and start work on the project."

"He bought it?" said Alfie. "He bought a city?"

"There wasn't that much left of course. But he did pay the United States government—what little of that remained intact—a fair sum in gold bullion. Father never liked San Francisco when it was full of people, he told me. Disreputable lot, full of moochers and looters."

"And you've lived there ever since?"

"Father has, yes. I come and see him whenever I have the opportunity. And he has his robots of course. Father purchased the original patent a short time before the slugs came. He intended to manufacture and sell them on a worldwide basis but there wasn't much of a market left with so much of the world in ruins so he just made enough for his own use."

"How many was that?"

"Around five hundred, I believe."

Alfie shook his head. "Five hundred robots? What do they all do?"

"Oh, Father's found uses for them. Wait till you see the city, or at least the part that Father's fixed up, then you'll understand. One of his passions is American history and he's tried to make everything totally authentic. It's really an impressive creation."

"What about the savages? Don't they give you any trouble?"

"Very rarely. Father tries to take care of them in his own way and there's also a wall built around the compound where we live. It's primarily a security precaution—because of the project—but it also keeps the savages on the other side."

Alfie wondered exactly how much he was supposed to know about this mysterious project. From what he gathered Hennesey had hired him to work on it. He decided not to reveal his ignorance by questioning Tess any further. Presumably Hennesey would explain things more fully when they arrived.

Lights began to appear off to the left of the highway. Tess turned and pointed. "That's Berkeley over there. The funny thing is Father has more trouble with those people than he does with the savages. They're always sending emissaries wanting to look over the grounds. They're afraid of Father, I think. And envious. Don't you agree it's human nature to fear anything that's radically different?"

"I hadn't thought of it before."

"You should. It's what Father always says too."

"Sounds like he's a smart guy."

"Oh he is. No doubt there."

* * * *

A short time later the limousine veered hard to the right and a long steel and concrete bridge came into view. The frame was bent and crooked, the roadway warped and rutted, but the bridge was apparently sturdy enough to support the weight of the limousine. Nevertheless, Alfie sweated the whole long way across. The water below visible through occasional gaps in the roadway looked dark and deep and awfully cold. He'd never learned to swim and even avoided baths when he could.

At the far end of the bridge lay the ruins of San Francisco. More remained of the old city than Alfie had anticipated. Many of the buildings, including a number of the taller ones, stood intact.

The streets, though torn, gouged, and strewn with rubble, seemed passable.

"How far is it to your place?" he asked as the limousine climbed a tall hill, swerving frequently to avoid jagged chunks of broken concrete.

"The compound's located out near the ocean beach where the big park used to be—Golden Gate Park. Father says he likes the fog—especially when he wakes in the morning. It helps clear his mind."

Alfie peered through the dark and noticed a flash of furtive motion just outside the window and then another darting shadow slightly farther ahead. Savages, he assumed. He'd once spent several days in the ruins of Pocatello, Idaho, tracking down a psychopathic killer who'd gone into hiding there among the savages. He'd gotten his man eventually but there had been a several unpleasantly close calls along the way.

The wall Tess had mentioned rose up in front of them all at once. It stood perhaps fifteen feet high, sloping gradually outward from bottom to top, and capped with interwoven strands of barbed razor wire. The flat stone surface had been polished smooth and looked impossible to scale. Probing searchlights beamed down from perches along the wall. As the limousine approached, a big steel gate in the middle of the wall swung inward and the limousine drove through the gap.

What lay a short distance ahead on the other side of the wall was enough to make Alfie's jaw drop open in amazement. He had to blink to be sure he was seeing what his eyes insisted he was seeing. The limousine might well have passed through a portal in time.

It was a city street—a broad paved boulevard—but not any city street of today, not Bombay or Shanghai or Paris or Chicago. This street was something out of another era. Neatly painted wood buildings lined both sides of the avenue. Alfie saw mostly small shops, some food markets, a single large department store, and even a few individual residences. Electric streetlamps illuminated the sidewalks and there were deep parallel ruts in the pavement that puzzled him until a trolley went swaying past, bell jangling, and then he understood.

Tess Hennesey regarded him with delight. "Well, what do you think?"

"It's...weird." He swung his head from side to side. A shop window on the left advertised genuine horsehide boots. Another opposite had a display of derby hats. Alfie spotted what appeared to be a motion picture theater. The marquee boasted that a customer could expect to view five separate films plus a juggling act for the single admission price of five cents. "What is this?" he asked. "Some kind of museum?"

She laughed. "I suppose it is in a way. What you're looking at is San Francisco as it was in 1912. We call it Market Street though it's not intended to be a specific replica of any particular street. 1912 was Father's favorite year in American history and he's done his best to evoke the shape and feel of that time totally."

"Why 1912?"

"Because of what happened immediately afterward."

"What was that?"

"The federal income tax amendment. Father dates the decline of American civilization from that point."

The numerous pedestrians strolling back and forth along the avenue were, Alfie now saw, robots. Most were decked-out in the fashions of an earlier time—billowy skirts, buttoned shoes, straw hats, bow ties.

"It's only three blocks long so far," Tess explained. "I know Father would like to do more but the project takes up so much of his time he hasn't had the chance lately to work on it."

The limousine rolled sedately down the avenue and finally glided to a stop in front of a pink two-story gingerbread Victorian house near the end of the third and final block. A tall man with a thick head of steel gray hair stood on the sidewalk waiting for them. He was dressed in a long frock coat, striped pants that bulged at the knees, red satin vest, and string tie. His moustache was an ornate handlebar and he clutched the head of a wooden cane in his left hand. John Hartford Hennesey in the flesh, Alfie presumed.

Tess sprang out of the limousine and hurried up to the man. Draping an arm around his shoulders she pecked him fondly on the cheek. Alfie let himself out the back and walked up to them. Hennesey peered past his daughter and fixed Alfie with a penetrating stare. After a moment's hesitation he nodded his head in apparent satisfaction and stepped forward. His left foot dragged as he walked. "Mr. Jarrett," he said, extending a hand, "it is indeed a pleasure."

"Thank you, Mr. Hennesey." Alfie looked up the street in search of something pertinent to say. "This is quite a place you've got here, sir. I wouldn't have believed it if I hadn't seen it for myself."

"Just a hobby, son," said Hennesey. He nodded toward the darkness beyond the last street lamp. "My real work goes on out there."

Alfie assumed this was a reference to the mysterious project, "Tess said you'd been busy lately."

"Busy isn't the word, lad. Consumed would serve better." Hennesey reached inside his vest and extracted a gold pocket watch. "As a matter of fact I was about to head out that way when they called from the wall and said you were here. If you want you can tag along and get your first look at how things are progressing. Now that the car's here we'll take that."

"Sounds great to me," said Alfie.

Turning to Tess, Hennesey said, "Dear, why don't you go inside and whip us up a quick snack while we're gone? Susannah's still not fully recovered from her last illness though Reynal's doing his best to get her back on her feet. I'm sure Mr. Jarrett must be famished after his long trip."

"I'd really like to come with you, Father. I haven't had a chance to take a good look at things lately."

He touched her cheek paternally. "This is apt to turn out to be a lot of dry technical business, darling, and I don't want to see you bored for no good reason. I'm sure there's plenty enough right here in the kitchen to keep you busy till we get back."

Alfie caught an angry glint in her eyes which she tried to conceal from her father. "I'll see what I can do in the kitchen," she said smoothly.

"Shall we go?" said Hennesey, beckoning to Alfie. He leaned on his cane for support as he walked to the car. It took a moment for Alfie to realize Hennesey's left leg—at least the portion below the knee—was an artificial limb. Holding his cane, Hennesey slid into the back seat without assistance and Alfie dropped down beside him.

The robot driver—Henry—accelerated at once. The paved avenue went on for only a short distance and then there was nothing but hard bare dirt. The limousine bounced and swayed, tires kicking up a fine spray of dust and sand.

Hennesey reached into his coat pocket and removed a long black cigar. He lit the end with a kitchen match and puffed contentedly. "Care for one?" he asked.

Alfie was trying hard not to cough. "No, thank you, sir."

"Not afraid, are you?"

Alfie shook his head, "Not really. But tobacco isn't supposed to be healthy, is it?"

"So certain people would like to make us think." Hennesey snorted. "Or maybe what I ought to say they'd like us *not* to think. One fact you should always keep in mind, Alfie—you don't mind if I call you Alfie?—is that governments are devoted to the principle that no individual is capable of using his own brain."

"Then you're not worried about cancer—or heart attacks?"

"I didn't say that. What I said is that I've got an opinion of my own. If you've got a contrary one you're welcome to it. The important thing, son, is the right of every man to make up his own mind. I smoke cigars because I damn well like to smoke them. You don't. Neither of us needs a pack of braying halfwits telling us what we ought to do for our own good."

Alfie wasn't entirely won over by Hennesey's argument. What he seemed to be saying sounded a lot like playing baseball without an umpire. Not that Alfie had much use for governments himself: too many of them wanted to put him in jail. But they had their uses—he could see that.

The roar of the pounding surf reached his ears as the limousine slowed, the headlights picking up the shape of a wooden shack looming ahead. "There it is," said Hennesey, pointing. "That's the place."

"What place is that, sir?"

"The project site." Puffing smoke Hennesey grinned. "Don't let appearances deceive you, son. There's more to that old shack than meets the eye."

The limousine slid to a halt a few yards in front of the shack. Hennesey held the door open for Alfie. Apparently the shack wasn't kept locked.

Inside Hennesey switched on a light. The interior consisted of a single empty room. The floor was a sheet of solid hard concrete.

"Well, what do you think?" said Hennesey.

Alfie assumed he was supposed to feel bewildered. "I don't get it, sir. There's nothing here but an empty room."

Hennesey chuckled. "An excellent observation, lad. I can see you've got a sharp head on your shoulders. If this place is good enough to fool somebody as keen as you then it's probably good enough to fool just about anyone. Not very impressed, are you? An empty shack at the edge of the ocean. Looking around, you wouldn't think this is the single most important chunk of real estate in the whole blessed Solar System, would you?"

Alfie shook his head. "No, I guess I wouldn't."

"Then take a gander." Hooking his cane over one wrist Hennesey reached inside his coat and withdrew what appeared to be an electronic remote control. He pressed down hard with his thumb and the remote emitted a shrill whistle. As it did a pair of intersecting cracks appeared in the concrete floor. Alfie skipped back as the cracks widened and a portion of the floor slid aside, exposing a gap six feet square.

Alfie looked at Hennesey. "There's another room down there."

Hennesey beamed. "More than that." He pressed the remote again. The whistling was of a slightly lower pitch than before. A metal platform emerged through the gap in the floor and dangling underneath came a series of pulleys and then a thick strand of steel cable. The platform continued to rise until it banged against the ceiling of the shack. The cab of an elevator slid into view through the floor.

"Shall we proceed?" said Hennesey.

They entered the elevator. Hennesey jerked a lever on the control panel and Alfie's stomach turned a flip flop as the elevator dropped with a lurch.

"Once we're out of the way the floor seals automatically behind us," Hennesey explained. "Some people might say I'm being overly cautious but I think after you see what I've got down here you won't be so sure."

There was no telling how far they descended. A half-minute at least passed before the elevator halted its plunge.

When the door opened Alfie followed Hennesey out.

They stood at the bottom of an enormous, brilliantly illuminated underground cavern. Flashing electronic panels occupied the entire length of the wall nearest him. Tilting his head, he looked straight up but the ceiling was obscured by distance and shadow. Two robots wheeled past. There were several more of them standing by the electronic panels.

Then Alfie looked at the rocket. The sight took his breath away. The rocket balanced on a trio of tail fins stood in the center of the cavern. It was a good one hundred feet in length.

Many more robots clustered around the base of the rocket and others could be seen partway up its length perched precariously on wooden scaffolding. "Is this the project?" said Alfie.

"This is it, yes," said Hennesey.

"A rocket?"

"A spaceship."

"A real one?"

"The *Lazarus*. I built it myself, son—me and five hundred robots. Nearly five years of exhausting labor it took, not to mention the months spent hollowing out this cavern."

"It must have cost you a fortune."

"More than one."

"And you think it'll actually fly?"

"I'm sure of it."

"Where to?"

"Anywhere you might want to go."

"To the Moon?"

Hennesey snorted. "The Moon, hell's hinges. That's a dead world, son. Why would anybody want to go to the Moon?"

"Then what's the rocket for?"

"Not the Moon. Not the planets either. The *Lazarus* is bound for the stars—for Alpha Centauri and beyond."

Alfie wasn't exactly a rocket scientist but he'd hung around Schwerner enough so that an occasional bit of knowledge had rubbed off. "Wouldn't that take years, sir—centuries. The stars are a long way off."

"Not anymore they're not."

"But the speed of light—"

"—is 186,282.3976 miles per second. And that's all it is. Never mind what that poor deluded Jew Einstein tried to tell people. Do you see that crew of robots way up there? Not the first bunch, the other crew, the ones way up near the nose cone."

Alfie peered as high as he could. The platform with the robots on it was hardly more than a dark speck. "I guess I see them, yes."

"That's where the Hennesey Drive is being installed even as we stand here and speak. I told you it took five years to build the *Lazarus*. But it took twice that long to build and perfect a faster-than-light drive. It's the dream of a lifetime, son—my dream, my lifetime."

"I thought it was supposed to be impossible to go faster than speed of light. I thought that was Einstein's theory."

Hennesey looked at him fixedly. "Einstein was mistaken, son. Not his fault. A great mind, yes, but limited. Nothing is impossible. If you can imagine it you can accomplish it."

Alfie wasn't so sure about that. There were a lot of things he had imagined in his life he didn't think could ever be accomplished—or ought to be.

"Are you saying you've invented a way to go faster than light?"

"That's what the Hennesey Drive does, son. It doesn't so much go faster than light—I won't argue with your Einstein there—but it goes around it."

"Around light?"

"That's correct."

"And you did this yourself?"

Hennesey looked modest. "I could scarcely claim that. I'm a businessman, not a scientist, but I'm also a rich businessman and if nothing else wealth grants a person certain freedom of choice. I served as a catalyst only. For twenty years I picked a little from one man's brain and a little from another. I employed the best minds of our pathetic day and paid them good money for their work. I made sure none of them knew a thing about what the others were doing. Everything was done piecemeal. In the end when the parts were fused to form a whole what I had on my hands was a workable functioning star drive."

"But you haven't actually tried it yet?" The rocket looked new and shiny.

"My chief project engineer, the robot Reynal, has done some preliminary tests. As far as it's possible to do them here on Earth. The results have been positive. The real test will come when the *Lazarus* leaves the Solar System."

"What I don't understand," said Alfie, "is how come nobody ever came up with this space drive idea before. They used to pour tons of money into the space program, didn't they?"

"Governments did." Hennesey spoke as if he were delivering a curse. "It's individuals who have imagination, Alfie, not governments. Collaboration is the father of mediocrity. If you take two smart men and stick them in a room with a problem to be solved, what will emerge at the end will be at the very least a compromise. That's why in developing the Hennesey Drive I deliberately kept people apart. A government is nothing more than compromise multiplied by the millions. I'm an anachronism, Alfie—I admit that freely. I'm the last liberal capitalist left on this globe. But I love the Earth—I love the human race—and before I die I want to give it something to remember me by. I want to give humanity a future, Alfie. I want to give them the stars."

Alfie was gazing at the rocket—at the starship. "Whoever goes up in that thing is going to have to have plenty of guts."

"A few more days, son, not many more, and I intend to be on my way."

Alfie turned his head. "Your way?"

"Who else? It's my project—my dream. I wouldn't trust it to any other man."

Alfie struggled to be tactful. "But aren't you kind of old for that, Mr. Hennesey?"

"I'm eighty years old, Alfie, and I don't deny a year of it. I've got one good leg and a heart that's about ready to conk out at any minute. But I'm tough. And smart. In my youth I was a fighter jockey for the USAF. Graduated from the academy in Colorado, fought in more little wars than I can count, always did my part until the crackpot doctors decided to toss me ashore on my ear. I know about hard times, son. Maybe I am old, maybe it will kill me, but like I said it's my dream and nobody can take that away from me."

"But what good will it do if you die?"

"I've thought of that, son." Hennesey reached out and laid a hand on Alfie's shoulder. "It's why I don't dare go it alone. If I die there has to be somebody to carry on the mission without me. That's where you come in, Alfie. Any man who can write what you wrote in your job application is a man who shares my dream. I want you as my co-pilot, Alfie. I would regard it as an honor."

Alfie stared at Hennesey in shock while inwardly cursing Desmond Blue in every fashion imaginable. Nevertheless, he knew he didn't have any choice. It was the case—if it hadn't been, Blue wouldn't have sent him here—and the case was his job.

"Sure, I'll go with you, Mr. Hennesey," Alfie said brightly. "It's always been my dream too. To the stars and back."

3

The heels of his shoes making a crunching noise in the gravel like a towheaded boy chewing peanuts, Peter Mark strolled along Elm Street in downtown Winesap Illinois. Around him twilight slowly fell like a first act curtain while fireflies twinkled, crickets played, and a gentle breeze stirred the air like the hushed breath of a slumbering giant. Peter had left the town's block-long central business district behind only a short time before but despite pausing beneath the flashing neon sign of Pearson's Family Drugstore to solicit directions he was already hopelessly lost. He moved through an area of stately two-story wood frame houses set behind white picket fences and neatly shorn lawns. The gates in many of the fences stood as if in welcome and he could see indistinct figures sitting and rocking on the broad front porches, their murmuring voices floating out to reach his ears like the bells of ice cream wagons on blistering summer days. Children played freely in the spacious yards—tag, crack-the-whip, and kangaroo—and dogs glanced up curiously at his approach, at last wagging their tails in farewell as he passed on.

At the corner of Elm and Poplar Peter came upon a vacant lot where a game of baseball was in progress. He paused to observe as tee-shirted boys raced gracefully through the darkening twilight in pursuit of the dim white sphere which rose lazily at the crack of the bat before plummeting sedately into the waiting outfielder's patient glove. Peter hadn't watched or played the game in more years than he could recollect and barely remembered its complex set of rules but there was still something so innately serene in the orderly procession of pitch, hit, and run that he found it difficult to tear his eyes away from the makeshift field. A billboard he had observed from the bus as he first entered town had proclaimed Winesap as the "Heartland City of the Real America" and thus far Peter had seen nothing to contradict that claim. The town seemed to him like a place where the very existence of evil was unthinkable and it was not easy to keep in mind that it was evil that had surely caused Desmond Blue to send him here in the first place.

The sound of approaching footsteps forced Peter to turn away from the ball game at last. A man and woman were coming toward him hand in hand from the opposite direction. As they drew closer Peter steeled himself for the anticipated reaction of shock and dismay when they saw his steel hands and face but like the man in front of the drugstore downtown—like everyone he had so far set eyes in Winesap—their expressions never wavered. The man seemed older than the woman although that might have been partly an impression created by her girlish attire—open-necked middie blouse, short pleated skirt, cotton knee socks, and low-heeled brown-and-white saddle shoes. She was an attractive woman too, Peter thought, with short sandy hair, a round freckled face, and a button of a nose. Observing her approach he felt a sudden gentle stirring in his loins and almost cried out in surprise. It was not often in the years since the accident and his subsequent decision to seek God and Christ that he reacted this way toward a woman.

He was so flustered in fact that the man and woman had reached him and the man spoken before he knew what was happening. "I— I'm terribly sorry," he stammered as the bat cracked and the ball flew behind him. "What did you say?"

The man was smiling at him in a good-natured way. "I merely wished you a good evening, friend." He spoke in the twangy nasal tone common to the region.

"Oh, of course," said Peter. He kept his eyes focused on the man's open non-descript features. "Yes, it is a magnificent evening."

"Need some help?" asked the man.

"Help?"

He chuckled amiably. "Afraid I couldn't help noticing you were a stranger in town—we get few visitors in these parts—and wondered if you were perhaps looking for someone or something in particular."

"Well, yes," said Peter. "I asked at the drugstore for directions but I seem to have lost my way nevertheless."

"Oh, that's just old Mr. Pearson. He loses his own way half the time even though he's lived in Winesap sixty years now." The man extended a hand. "I'm Bob Jones by the way and this is Miss Laurel Brady. I assist Mr. Pearson at the pharmacy so I know him well."

Peter shook hands solemnly, noting that Bob Jones unlike most did not flinch at the contact of hard steel. "I'm Peter Mark," he said. "I was looking for the Fire House."

"Oh, I know who you are," Laurel Brady broke in. She stopped suddenly as if startled by her own voice. A sweet aroma clung to her, the scent of freshly washed clothes. "Fire Captain Brady is my father. He mentioned at breakfast he was expecting a new man today."

"Well, I'm him," said Peter, looking down at his feet. "I got off the bus just a few minutes ago."

"Then at least you're headed in the right direction," Bob Jones said. "Knowing Mr. Pearson, it's fortunate he didn't send you off toward Hawaii." He pointed up the street. "Just go three more blocks this way then turn left on Abraham Lincoln Way. The red brick building on the corner. It's the one with the fire truck parked inside."

Peter nodded his thanks. For some reason he seemed reluctant to move on. "You certainly have some beautiful weather around here."

"In my opinion," said Jones, "it's always beautiful in Winesap."

"Oh, Bob," said Laurel.

"No, it's true. Not perfect, mind you. I didn't say that. Sometimes it rains too much and there's always a little snow in the winter. I'm not talking about the weather anyway—I'm talking about beauty—and to me the most beautiful place in the world bar none is right here in Winesap."

"So far I like it very much too," said Peter.

"You were wise to move here," said Bob Jones.

"It was largely because of my health that I came." Peter was repeating the lie Desmond Blue had instructed him to establish.

"Oh, are you ill?" asked Laurel as if surprised that such a condition existed.

"I was in an accident. During a fire. My hands and face were badly burned."

"I did notice your, uh, your scars," Bob Jones conceded, "It must have been a dreadful thing to have happen."

Peter shrugged. "I suppose I'm used to it by now."

"All I can do," said Bob Jones, "is guarantee you'll be treated like anyone else here in Winesap. I was born and raised in this town and so was Miss Laurel here though she's never been away and can't appreciate home the way I do. I spent a week in Chicago once. Terrible place. The people mean as whipped dogs."

"Whipped dogs have a reason to be mean," Laurel said.

"Those people in Chicago didn't. No danged reason whatsoever."

"It's certainly different here," Peter cut in quickly.

"You can say that again," Bob Jones said. "In Chicago people won't even look a man in the eye. Can you believe that? I never felt more alone in my life. When I went to work for Mr. Pearson I straight out told him I'd do anything he wanted except go to Chicago or any other big city like that. Not now, not then, not ever. I told him that straight out."

"Well," said Peter, taken aback by the force of Jones's passion, "thanks for your help."

"Glad to give it." They shook hands again. "I suspect we'll be seeing a lot of each other." He glanced over at Laurel. "I seem to be spending most of my evenings at Fire Captain Brady's house these days."

"Oh, Bob," said Laurel.

Peter nodded a farewell and moved on. Partway down the block he looked back and saw the two of them—Bob and Laurel—still standing, holding hands now, watching the ball game.

* * * *

Peter reached the town Fire House without further incident. It was a square one-story red brick building located on a tree-lined street. The big front doors stood open and Peter could see the shiny bulk of a red fire engine inside.

He walked up and went through the doors and noticed a man kneeling and polishing the left front fender of the truck. Peter cleared his throat. The man glanced up at him and rose to his feet. Again there was no indication of shock or horror in his expression. His smile was warm and authentic. "What can I do for you, young fellow?" He was in his late forties or early fifties with a tanned leathery face, wrinkled eyes, and thin graying hair.

"I'm Peter Mark. I believe I'm supposed to go to work here. I got into town a short time ago and thought I ought to report right in."

"We've been looking out for you." He gripped Peter's hand firmly. "I'm Fire Captain Sam Brady. How was your trip? Any problems finding us?"

"No, sir, everything went fine. I met your daughter on the way here and she told me where to go."

"Laurel is a lovely girl. Was she alone when you saw her?"

"No, sir. There was a gentleman with her."

"Bob Jones, I'll bet. Well, a person could do worse for a son-in-law. I was married twenty-seven years before my wife passed on. Life hasn't been the same since, let me tell you."

"I'm a single person myself."

"Not for long you won't be." Brady chuckled. "Not in Winesap anyhow. We must have the world's largest collection of eligible spinsters. Young ones, old ones, pretty ones, homely ones—any sort of single woman you care to mention. A nice young fellow like you, I'll bet the phones have been ringing off the hooks since you stepped off that bus."

Peter nodded politely to conceal his puzzlement. Surely these people weren't blind to the fact that his face was a steel mask. "I try putting all my energies into my work."

"Do that around here and you're going to have to go out of your way. There's only the one fire truck in the whole department and ninety percent of what we do is coaxing housecats down out of trees. I hope it's not going to prove too dull for you."

"I'm not worried about that, sir," Peter said, touching the side of his face meaningfully. "I could do with some dullness for a change."

"Had an accident, did you?"

"Yes, sir. I was burned pretty badly."

"Why don't you come in and let me introduce you to the boys?" He moved around the truck and opened a door in the back. "There's six regulars in the department plus myself. The rest are volunteers.

Two are on duty now and four off. You'll be the odd man out but we can figure out something later."

Peter followed Fire Captain Brady into a cramped room lined with metal lockers full of firefighting gear. Four men sat playing cards at a table. Brady introduced Oscar Stovall and Hiram Evers first. These were the two regular firemen presently on duty. Stovall was a youngish man with a blank open face while Evers was as old as Brady with keen observant eyes. The other two men—Albert Jenkins and Stanley Short—were volunteers. Jenkins, a lanky man in denim coveralls, announced that he was so far ahead on points it would take the others a month of Sundays to catch him. He asked Peter if he wanted to sit in. Peter said he wasn't sure he knew the game. Jenkins said, "In that case we'll have to start teaching you right away. It's a violation of city ordinance for any man to belong to the Winesap Fire Department and not know how to play gin rummy. Ain't that right, Captain Brady?"

For several minutes Peter stood beside Brady observing the rapid fluctuations of the cards. Conversation drifted languidly around the table. There was talk of a town parade later in the month and mention of the possibility of a traveling carnival reaching Winesap in a few weeks. Albert Jenkins said he thought it was the same carnival a local girl named Cindy Dee had run off to join the year before. Apparently Cindy had fallen in love with a handsome barker but had returned home only a few weeks later. "I'll bet you one thing for sure," said Jenkins. "That barker won't dare show his slimy face around here again. If he does we'll organize us a little tar-and-feather party for him."

Captain Brady winked to show Peter the men were only the kidding, then wandered off. Peter lingered another few moments and followed.

Brady was now polishing the right front fender of the truck.

"What did I tell you?" he said without looking up from his work. "Didn't I warn you it was dull as molasses around here? Those boys run on worse than a ladies' bridge club sometimes, I tell you."

"Oh, I don't mind," Peter said. "A friend of mine once told me that only the best people gossip because only the best people care enough about their friends and neighbors to want to talk about them."

"I suppose that's one way of looking at it," Brady said grudgingly.

"But I was wondering if you could help me out, sir. I'm going to need a place to stay here in town. Is there a good hotel you can recommend, one where I can get meals too?"

"Hotel?" said Brady as though the concept was foreign. He laid down his rag and stood upright, shaking his head. "I'm afraid the last hotel in Winesap shut down ages ago. We don't get many visitors here. We're kind of off the beaten track."

"Then where can I find a place to stay?"

"Let me see what I can do. Hold on just one second, will you?" He went into the back and returned a short time later with Oscar Stovall, the younger of the two regular firemen.

"Oscar here says he can fix you up with a place to stay."

"Sure can," said Stovall, his voice less than emphatic. "Jayne and me have got another spare bedroom upstairs. There's a little girl that's been staying with us too but she don't take up much room either. I'm hardly ever home anyhow."

"Oscar's a dedicated fireman," said Brady. "Sometimes I've got to kick him in the butt to get home to go home at all."

"I don't wish to intrude," said Peter.

"It's no intrusion," said Brady. "Tell him so, Oscar."

"It's no intrusion at all," said Stovall.

"All right," said Peter. "If you honestly don't mind."

"I don't mind," said Stovall, speaking for himself this time.

"Then go ahead and run him over and get him settled," Brady told Stovall. "Peter, I'll want to see you again tomorrow afternoon around five. You can pull your first shift then."

Peter and Stovall went outside. The twilight had deepened to full evening and a huge complement of stars like silver pinpricks graced the cloudless sky. Stovall crossed the street to his beetle buggy, a two-seat electric sedan parked beneath a massive maple. Peter slid into the front seat beside Stovall. "I'll need to get my suitcase. I had to leave it at the bus depot."

Stovall grunted and turned the ignition.

There seemed to be an underlying sullenness to his silence that made Peter wonder whether he had made the right decision in accepting the offer of a place to stay. Of course Stovall might only be tired or distracted or even just shy, the latter an affliction with which Peter was intimately familiar; shyness often came across to others as covert hostility, he knew.

The drive through town was sedate and unhurried. With the advent of darkness the people Peter had observed earlier on their porches or in their yards had vanished from view. The front windows of the houses they passed now flickered with brightly colored reflections emanating from within. Curious, Peter pointed to one of the windows and asked, "Do you have a local television station here?"

Stovall shook his head. "Better than that. It's the tridee."

"I don't think I've ever actually seen that." Three-dimensional hologramic television had barely been launched as a practical concept when the Occupation occurred and interrupted its commercial development. Although flat television had largely reestablished itself as a prime entertainment vehicle, the tridee concept had for the most part become the exclusive property of the remaining few wealthy. Desmond Blue refused to allow it to be installed at Arabia Deserta; he said the medium itself was depraved. For art to exist, he insisted, there must be artifice. Tridee was as real as life—more real in many ways—and bigger. "I thought it was supposed to be quite expensive."

"I guess it is most places," said Stovall. "In Winesap every house has its own receiving box. It's absolutely free. Doesn't cost a dime. The mayor sees to it—Mayor Washington."

"Who provides the service? Is it a company?"

"Nope. That's the mayor too. It's all part of the city charter."

"But who pays for it?"

"Taxes do, I guess."

"Your taxes must be awfully high."

"So?" Stovall swung his head and looked at Peter blankly. "It's worth it, ain't it?"

"What about people who may not want it?"

"Everybody wants the tridee," Stovall said in a flat tone.

Peter wasn't entirely convinced of that. "Are the programs really that good?"

"They're great," said Stovall, his expression dreamy. "They're the greatest thing there is or ever will be."

While Stovall waited outside Peter went into the bus depot and retrieved his suitcase from the station agent. He carried it out to the car and started to toss it in the back when the worn strap snapped and the lid popped open. He caught it in his hands before anything could spill and placed the suitcase on the edge of the front seat so that he could close it again.

"Hey," said Stovall, his voice sharp as a knife. He leaned over and pointed inside the suitcase. "What's the hell's that thing there?"

Peter looked down. "This?" He pushed a few seldom worn neckties aside to reveal what lay underneath. "It's only a book." He showed the spine to Stovall. It was *Don Quixote*, a personal favorite he brought with him everywhere.

Stovall flinched back as if the book might burn him. "You can't have that here," he said in a shaky voice. "Not in Winesap you can't."

"But it's just a book. What's wrong with it?" Peter turned the book in his hands, pretending to examine it closely. "It's a famous classic. You must have heard of it."

"I don't give a hoot what it is." His voice rose crazily. "It's in the city charter—article seventeen—it's the law. Nobody in Winesap can have a book."

"Which book?"

"Any book. It don't make no difference. They're all about the same anyway aren't they? A book is a book, ain't it?" He was almost shouting in his excitement. Peter looked back and saw that two men had emerged from the bus depot and were watching them curiously.

Feeling ill-at-ease he dropped the book back in the suitcase, closed the lid, and slid into the seat. "Maybe we ought to go," he said in a tense voice.

Stovall who had also noticed the men watching nodded tightly, He started the motor and pulled quickly away from the curb. He drove with haste for several blocks, then slowed. "You mean you really didn't know about how books are treated here?" he asked as if he had been thinking about the matter the whole time.

Peter shook his head, "I'm afraid it doesn't make any sense to me. How can you have a law like that? How can you force people not to read?"

"People can read all they want. It's even taught in school—sixth grade and up—just like adding and subtracting numbers. You just can't read books is all."

"I didn't know that. I'm sorry."

"I guess everybody just figured since you were a fireman you had to know better."

"What does being a fireman have to do with it?"

"Well, it's your job, ain't it?"

"My job?"

Stovall turned his head and stared at Peter. His eyes were cold and hard. "What is it you think a fireman does?"

"Well, he puts out fires of course," said Peter, totally bewildered now. "What else could—?"

"Uh-uh," said Stovall, shaking his head firmly as if Peter had just failed an exam. "Not here. Not in Winesap. Here firemen start fires."

"But how—?"

"Books," he said softly, his gaze dropping to the suitcase. "We burn books."

Peter felt an ugly chill. He wasn't entirely sure why but the concept of burning books disturbed him at a deep level. "But why? What's wrong with books?"

"Books are bad for people, that's what's wrong with them. Books make people feel like they're dog poop. There's enough trouble in the world without books making it worse."

"But books can help people too. They can—" Peter broke off all at once, intimidated by the wild glint in Stovall's eyes as he glared at the suitcase beside him. What was going on in this town?

Peter decided his prudent course would be to keep quiet and see what he could find out. Desmond Blue had sent him here with instructions to observe and listen, not to argue matters of principle with a man who did not seem entirely in his right mind. "Nobody said anything to me about the law," Peter finished. "It's not that way where I come from. We just put out fires."

"I've heard that," Stovall said curtly. He was driving slowly now, his eyes fixed on the suitcase rather than the road ahead. Fortunately, there did not seem to be any other traffic on the road tonight in Winesap. "Most places don't seem to care about people's happiness. That's what makes Winesap a special town. Did you know that a man named George Washington was the father of the whole country? Well, Mayor Lucius Washington is another just like him. He wants nothing except to make people happy."

"Then what do you think I should I do?" said Peter. "About my book. Should I turn it over to you?"

Stovall considered, then shook his head. "If you did I'd have to tell where I got it from and I don't want to get you into trouble. You just got here after all. You didn't know no better."

"Should I throw it away then?"

"That'd be best. Throw it away. Then tomorrow somebody will find it and turn in the alarm and we can go out and burn it."

"Here?" asked Peter, glancing out the window.

"I don't think so. If you throw it out here a little boy or even a girl might come across it in the morning on the way to school and not know the right thing to do. You wouldn't want something like that on your conscience, would you?"

"I guess not," Peter said meekly.

"I know a better place. It's a big old house way up in the hills where nobody's lived for years. The Berryman place. They say it's haunted." He chuckled. "You can toss it out there and then in the morning I'll pretend I saw it driving by. That way Fire Captain Brady will have to let me take the truck up there myself and do the burning." His voice took on a different, almost feverish edge. "I love the burning. The way the pages blacken and crinkle. It's like an old person's skin. Then they turn to ash and float away on the wind. It's beautiful. It makes me feel happy seeing it."

Stovall gripped the wheel firmly, accelerated, and swerved around the next corner. In no time at all the lights of the town lay below them. The car climbed a winding road and at the crest Stovall gestured toward the door and said, "Here—throw it out here."

Peter already held the book in his hands.

When Stovall gave the signal he hurled the book out. It landed at the edge of the road, bounced once, and came to rest on top of a pile of brush.

"Nobody ever comes up here," Stovall explained as he made a neat U-turn and started back down the hill. His chin, cheeks, and forehead were beaded with sweat. "I won't have any trouble finding it in the morning."

Peter had already decided to keep quiet about the fact that *Don Quixote* was not the only book he had brought along with him. There were several others tucked out of sight in the suitcase beneath various articles of clothing. Like *Quixote* all were personal favorites he enjoyed reading again and again: *The Brothers Karamazov, Heart of Darkness, Voyage to Arcturus, The Idiot, Last and First Men.* He also had a copy of the New English Bible and a translation of the Gnostic Nag Hammadi manuscripts that Nadia had lent him. He wondered whether the firemen of Winesap were expected to burn these too.

"What about Bibles?" he asked as they glided through the empty streets of town. "Do you burn those also?"

"Why? Have you got one?" The feverish tone had entered Stovall's voice again.

"Oh, no," Peter said hastily, "but I suppose some people must."

"How come? The slugs got rid of all the preachers, I thought."

"Well, yes, but there are still some people who follow the old religions."

Stovall seemed puzzled. "Not around here they don't. That stuff always sounded weird to me. Why would anybody care whether there was a God or not? I suppose if we ever found a Bible we'd have to burn it but so far we never have that I know of."

Peter struggled to conceal his outrage. Quite plainly his initial impression of Winesap had fallen short of the truth. If this town was as he had originally surmised a veritable Garden of Eden then it was an Eden long since contaminated by a taint more corrupt than original sin.

The house in front of which Stovall parked resembled almost any other in Winesap. It was a two-story wood frame building encircled by a white picket fence. As Stovall strode up the concrete walk his pace gradually quickened as if in anticipation. Peter followed, carrying his suitcase. The by now familiar pattern of flickering lights could be glimpsed through the wide front window.

The door was not locked. They entered a hallway. "I want to grab a couple minutes tridee before I go back to work," Stovall said. "Want to join me?"

"I think I ought to get settled in first if you don't mind."

"Then I'll send Jayne out." Stovall frowned. "She can show you where to sleep, I guess."

Stovall disappeared through the first open doorway to his left. After a few moments Peter overheard his voice talking excitedly and another somewhat gentler voice replying in kind. Curious, he peered around the corner.

The room was large and unfurnished and filled at the moment with naked bodies—men and women both—cavorting in various suggestive poses. It took Peter a moment to understand that none of this was real. The bodies were mere figures, translucent images.

In the center of the room a flesh-and-blood woman knelt on the floor. Stovall stood over her, waving his arms and talking in a loud voice. The woman kept shaking her head. She was plump, blonde, with wide clear eyes. She did not have any clothes on.

Averting his eyes Peter stepped quickly back before he could be seen.

A short time later Stovall reappeared. His face was flushed and he seemed angry. "Jayne says she can't come help you. She's watching one of her shows and says she wants to see how it comes out. I'll show you up to your room myself."

"The program she's watching must be pretty interesting," said Peter as they mounted the stairs.

Stovall shook his head. "Just the same old junk she's always watching."

Peter's room was at the head of the staircase. It was good-sized with a made-up double bed, a chest of drawers, writing desk, and chair. Stovall asked Peter if there was anything else he needed. Peter said he was tired from his trip and would probably go directly off to bed.

"I guess I'm not going to get to watch my tridee after all," Stovall said in a sullen voice. "If I stay here any longer Captain Brady is going to start wondering what happened to me."

"Do you think there'll be much work to do tonight?"

"Nah. Not tonight." Stovall looked glum, then suddenly brightened. "But tomorrow there'll be a book that needs proper burning."

"My book you mean?"

"That's right. And I've got you to thank for it, don't I?"

When he was alone Peter opened his suitcase on the bed and put his clothes away in the chest of drawers. He carefully separated the books he'd brought and slipped them temporarily under the bed.

When the suitcase was empty he went around the room looking for a more permanent hiding place. He finally came across a badly warped floorboard in the rear of the clothes closet, pried the board loose, and looked underneath. There was a gap a foot deep under the floor. He retrieved the books and managed to stuff them one after another into the hiding place. When he was done he replaced the board and pounded it shut with the heel of his hand. Satisfied with his work he went over and sat on the edge of the bed. Desmond Blue, had he known, would most certainly have been displeased. Peter was aware that the smart thing would be to get rid of the books right away but if what Stovall had been telling him was true, there had already been too much burning of books in Winesap and Peter couldn't bring himself to add to it.

He yawned. His eyes were growing heavy. He suddenly realized he was a lot more tired than he had imagined. Turning on his back he let his eyes slide shut. In a few short moments he was fast asleep.

* * * *

He woke to the blinding light of the electric bulb burning overhead. For a moment he could not recall where he was, then the word "Winesap" popped into his head and he remembered that was the name of the town—the town where firemen burned books.

He looked at the watch on his wrist, saw that it was past four, and managed to stagger to his feet. He went to the door, opened it a crack, and listened cautiously. He could hear nothing from below.

Peter decided to venture forth in search of a bathroom. He opened the door wider and took a step out. Then he saw the woman. She lay curled on her side on the hardwood floor. It was the same woman he had seen earlier below—Jayne Stovall presumably. Her nude body appeared tense with none of the usual slackness of sleep. Peter was concerned she might be ill. Crouching at her side he reached for her arm.

Then he noticed that her eyes were open.

His hand hung suspended in mid-air.

"Who are you, pretty boy?" Her voice was flat and empty of emotion. She made no effort to move.

"I'm Peter Mark. Didn't your husband…?"

"The new fireman? Then one from out of town?"

"I—yes. I guess I'm going to be staying here awhile. Is there— can I help you in any way?"

She thought for a moment then nodded, raising her head slightly. She wet her lips. "You could fuck me."

Peter stared, unable to believe she had actually said what he seemed to have heard.

She sighed. "You don't want to, do you?"

"I'm sorry but I…"

"Figures. No luck, that's me. Oscar doesn't want to fuck anymore either. All he wants is to watch tridee and burn books. He likes the shows with the killing and torture in them. I like the shows where people fuck all the time. That's how we're different, I guess. Now go away and let me sleep. I'm tired."

Peter went back into his room. It took him a long while before he fell asleep again.

A PROFILE: THREE SECRETARIES

The three confidential secretaries employed by Desmond Blue all possessed certain characteristics in common: all were female; all were intelligent; all were efficient; and all were beautiful.

Nevertheless, the three were not in any sense identical; they were not even similar.

Nadia van Hauten was the senior member of the trio. Age un-specified. Hair raven black. Not tall but slender. Narrow hips and narrow waist. Skin that glowed with a translucent sheen.

Several ago earlier while working the night shift as a waitress in a diner across from the shuttered General Motors assembly plant in Youngstown Ohio recently turned into a reservation for refugee spooks from the ruins of New York, Nadia first made the acquaintance of Desmond Blue.

What was Blue doing in the Youngstown? (He had come there in search of his dead and reborn wife.)

Had he succeeded in this search? (To a certain extent, he had.)

Was he pleased as a consequence? (No, he most definitely was not.)

What was his basic spiritual attitude as he entered the diner, found a vacant booth, and ordered a cup of black coffee? (He was deeply, perhaps suicidally depressed.)

What did he do when the coffee arrived in front of him? (He took a tentative sip, gagged, spit it out. "Worse coffee I ever tasted," he later said.)

A short time afterward Blue and his waitress (Nadia) became involved in a spirited discussion.

It was Blue's contention that human civilization had reached its apex during the Age of Pericles in ancient Athens while Nadia, hotly disputing his premise, declared that the Greeks had stolen every idea they'd ever had from the Egyptians of the Middle and New Kingdoms.

Blue was suitably impressed. He'd rarely met anyone regardless of position or gender capable of matching him at an equal intellectual level.

Nadia informed him that if he wished to remain in the diner any longer he would have to order and pay in advance for a second cup of coffee.

Blue pondered. He had no desire to see such an interesting conversation concluded abortively yet neither did he wish to wound his sensibilities (not to mention his stomach) with more of that loathsome brew.

"You could always order food," Nadia suggested.

Blue shook his head. It was one of his strongest beliefs that if the coffee repelled, the food would do worse.

So in order to continue the discussion Blue offered Nadia a job. "I've never had a secretary," he said. "People tell me I could use one. How would you like the job?"

"What does it pay?"

Later that day as the two of them hitched rides through the hills of western Pennsylvania Nadia asked Blue what it was he did for a living.

"I used to be a psychoanalyst," he replied, "but now I'm thinking of becoming a consulting detective. I like searching for things—especially the truth. What do you think? Is that a worthy idea?"

Nadia said she thought that was a smashing idea.

They'd been together ever since. Through the thick and the thin, the deep and the shallow, the worse and better. Good times. Bad times. Mediocre times.

During the early struggling years Nadia churned out a series of lurid romance novels for a French Canadian publisher at two thousand dollars a clip to help meet their mutual needs. Years before, she explained to Blue, she had been a modestly successful author of science fantasy escapist fiction under the pen name Arnold Hope Grimthorpe. After the Occupation nobody wanted to read stories of that kind anymore. They were deemed too close to reality for comfort. "So I became a waitress," she said. "It helped pay the bills."

The second of Blue's secretaries, Crystal LaFleur, had entered his employ a few years later. Blue and Crystal first met in a dingy bar in a rowdy district of Ulan Bator where she worked as an exotic dancer. At the time Blue preferred to do his serious drinking in the shabbiest surroundings possible—and few were shabbier than this Mongolian dump—since he'd long ago noticed that one would seldom be bothered by the other patrons in such places because they too were invariably serious drinkers who wanted nothing except to be left alone to enjoy their poison of choice. Blue had come to the Mongolian capital incognito in order to investigate the activities of one Hapgood Wyatt, a former Irish soccer star who'd recently recruited a large mercenary army, proclaimed himself Khan of All the Mongols, and announced his intention to conquer the world. Progress on the case had so far proved minimal—Wyatt's position in Ulan Bator seemed unassailable—and Blue was deeply despondent as a result. Attracted by Crystal's surprisingly innovative and sensitive dance routines and feeling a rare need for human company Blue invited her to join him at his table. Quite unexpectedly she recognized him underneath his intricate coolie disguise. She was quite the admirer, she said. She'd followed all of his cases in the local English language papers—including especially his brilliant solution of the Puzzle of the Patagonian Preterite. Later she confided in response to his gentle probing that she had indeed until recently been employed by Hapgood Wyatt as his personal pilot but the relationship had soured when she broke his nose one night when he insisted on pressing certain unwanted advances. "I thought being as how he was the supposed Khan of All the Mongols he'd have got beyond all that carnal crap. But I guess not."

Blue quickly assured that he had remained personally celibate for some years now.

Then he offered her a job. "Confidential secretary," he said. "I already have one excellent woman in my employ but could always use another. You'll have to move to the Sahara Desert where I now make my home and, oh, while we're at it, can you type?"

She could. And also pilot aerocraft of all varieties.

That night Blue and Crystal, both blind drunk, ended up sharing the same narrow cot behind the bar and Blue never made a move to lay a finger on her. In the morning as she dressed Crystal shared certain confidential information that led to the arrest and imprisonment of the reigning Khan of All the Mongols who turned out to be a renegade Baptist minister and embezzler wanted by the law in thirty-nine of the current forty-three Semi-United States of North America.

Oh, and Crystal took the job. (She had been with him ever since.)

The third of Blue's secretaries, Lacy Bach, had not come to work for him until just recently.

Lacy was the redhead: long-legged, small-busted, with wide round innocent eyes that seemed to radiate compassion and concern.

As the junior secretary Lacy was stuck with such menial chores around Arabia Deserta as cooking the meals, scrubbing the floors, washing the clothes, emptying the wastebaskets, answering the phones, and feeding the beastmen that lived in the basement.

She never complained.

Lacy first came to Blue's attention on the mean streets of downtown Hollywood here he'd ventured in the guise of a blind mendicant to probe the Strange Matter of the Indigent Horde.

For the past several months each Sunday someplace in Beverly Hills a number of seemingly homeless men and women would suddenly appear as if from nowhere in their ragged street garb, unwashed faces, and foul filthy fingernails—perhaps as many as fifty of them in total. Invading a plush house apparently selected at random, these vagrants would take the residents captive, lock them in their own usually spacious clothes closets, and then spend the remainder of the day and night making themselves at home. They would eat, drink, snooze, revel, watch tridee and television, swim laps in the pool, lounge on the lawn, tell vulgar jokes on the patio. The following Monday morning come dawn they would depart as unceremoniously as they had arrived, always taking careful pains to clean up whatever mess they might have made.

On a few occasions suspicious neighbors alerted the police of a possible disturbance; wholesale arrests resulted.

Nevertheless, come the following Sunday the horde undiminished in number would again descend on another location.

The residents of Beverly Hills eventually banded together and hired Desmond Blue to solve the mystery and put an end to the menace.

His investigation soon led him to the enigmatic personage of Lacy Bach. He first took notice of her during one of his initial forays into the skid row area off Hollywood Boulevard, for Lacy was a difficult person to miss when accompanied by a ragtag collection of down-and-outers she prowled the pre-dawn alleyways, peering inside the overflowing garbage bins and extracting an unused head of lettuce here, a packet of unconsumed pancake batter there.

What particularly intrigued Blue was the manner in which she was dressed: white satin evening gown, fur stole, string of pearls glittering at her throat.

In due course Blue traced Lacy to a ramshackle hovel constructed of corrugated cardboard and perched at the edge of a secluded pond in Griffith Park. The first impression he received when he went inside was how clean and homey it was: there were thick shag carpets on the floor, subdued contemporary furnishings in the one room.

Lacy sometimes fed as many as a hundred individuals daily from the scraps she collected each morning, he learned.

She was also the ringleader of the Indigent Horde. It was Lacy who planned each invasion. It was Lacy who provided the men with bus fare and trench coats in order to infiltrate Beverly Hills.

Blue arrested Lacy one Saturday following a meeting at her home during which she announced the end of the invasions. We have attained our goal, she assured her followers. From now on the citizens of Beverly Hills can never again ignore us. Each Sunday like clockwork they will be reminded of our existence automatically as they were once reminded at church of the example of Christ.

Blue lingered after the others left. He then took Lacy into custody, charging her with the crimes of kidnap and unlawful entry.

She accompanied him without resistance or protest.

Blue had not gone two blocks toward police headquarters in his rented beetle buggy when he pulled it over to the curb, cut the engine, and looked at the young woman beside him dressed in her typical finery.

He offered her a job. In return for her freedom.

She accepted with alacrity, stating that she'd always wanted to do something interesting with her life and working for a famous consulting detective while living in a mansion in the Sahara Desert did indeed sound intriguing to her.

"By the way," he said, "can you type?"

She could not.

"Well," he said, "we'll find other things for you to do."

They had and she did and had been with him ever since.

Three secretaries: Nadia, the loyal; Crystal, the rational; Lacy, the compassionate.

Together they made a team: a whole greater than the sum of its parts.

They served Desmond Blue well.

4

In the upstairs study of Desmond Blue's desert mansion a trio of women lay sprawled in various postures of languid relaxation. Although these were the same women who served as Blue's confidential secretaries it's doubtful anyone—perhaps including Blue himself—who had known them only in their official capacities would have recognized them now. Discarded were the satin and silk, leather and lace. Gone were the false eyelashes, sweet perfumes, and fragrant powders. With Blue and his three retainers absent from Arabia Deserta for the first time in over a year the three women were at last set free to assume their own natural identities. Nadia van Hauten wore a red flannel nightgown that dropped past her ankles like tent; Crystal LaFleur, unkempt blonde hair cascading down her back, was dressed in a shapeless gray bathrobe; and Lacy Bach's chosen mode of apparel for the day consisted of a pair of men's blue jeans cut off below the knee and a ragged green-and-gold sweatshirt emblazoned with the emblem of a defunct American League baseball team. In truth seen this way none of the three women was precisely beautiful. They weren't ugly by any means. But they were only themselves.

Music was playing in the background, the quartet from *Rigoletto*, the role of the Duke sung by the great Italian tenor Mario Donatello. The recording was Nadia's choice. She was the opera buff among them while Crystal preferred free jazz and Lacy was fond of late Bob Dylan and early Rolling Stones.

Nadia, the senior member of the trio, occupied Desmond Blue's favorite chair with the hound Baskerville curled at her feet. Her eyes moved back and forth between the other two women as they conversed.

At the moment it was young Lacy who was speaking: "I honestly wonder if we shouldn't have told Desmond about those two poor things Schwerner had locked up his laboratory. I know Desmond has his limitations but he's no ordinary male. He might have understood why we did what we did."

"Uh-uh," said Crystal. "Sure Desmond's smart as a whip. No one would argue that. But he's still a male. If we'd told him about Schwerner's little experiment he'd have wanted to give him the Nobel Prize. We three are the only ones here who could possibly understand what it's like to be treated as some man's slave."

"I don't believe they give out the Nobel Prize anymore," Nadia said.

"Well, you know what I mean," Crystal said. "It's just that Desmond is a male and to a male achievement is of supreme importance. Since Schwerner succeeded in created human life in the laboratory and nobody had done that before—except Dr. Frankenstein in a million movies—then it must be something worthy of a prize. We did the only right thing possible. Besides—" she smirked "—did you get a look at Schwerner's face after he saw they were gone? I thought he was going to have a panic attack till Lacy shot him with the anti-memory drug."

"Speaking of which," said Nadia, turning to Lacy, "there won't be a relapse, will there? The memories won't come back."

"No. It's permanent. Every memory of Schwerner's concerning the two in his closet has been wiped clean. Desmond's used the drug on himself too, you know. It's worked for him."

"What memories did Desmond have that he wanted to erase?" Crystal asked.

"He didn't share that part with me," Lacy said.

"I'm not surprised," said Nadia, the one who'd been with Blue the longest and knew him best. "He's a deeply private man."

"A private man who's also a private eye," said Crystal with a laugh.

"Don't ever call him that to his face. Desmond hates the term private eye."

"What about shamus, sleuth, gumshoe, elbow?"

"Avoid those too. Being a simple detective is good enough for Desmond."

"For the rest of us too," said Crystal.

She was the one who'd discovered the man and the woman imprisoned in Schwerner's laboratory. The discovery had come about through happenstance, although Crystal at Nadia's direction—and presumably Blue's—had long made it a practice to now and then take quick snoop through the private rooms of Alfie, Peter, and Schwerner—treachery though highly improbable from such devoted retainers was never a total impossibility—but until this most recent occasion had never come across anything more remotely interesting than Schwerner's extensive collection of crude pornography and Peter's many Bibles.

The discovery had taken place the night before last while Blue and Peter were still in Rome seeking the Pope. As soon as Crystal entered.

Schwerner's back laboratory with a set of duplicate keys, her attention had been drawn to the cabinets by the absurd warning signs Schwerner had affixed to them. Using the blade of a knife she pried open one of the doors and discovered a naked woman inside like a slumbering goddess. Moving on to the second cabinet she found a similarly god-like man. When Crystal reached out and touched the man on his cheek he came awake and spoke to her. She did the same to the woman who also woke. The man said his name was Lai; the woman that hers was Jai. Both explained how they'd been brought to life by Schwerner ("our dear father") in the course of a biological experiment.

Instinctively repulsed Crystal ordered the two of them out of the cabinets. Leaving them there in the laboratory she hurried off to tell Nadia and Lacy what she'd discovered.

Both of them concurred with her point of view: Lai and Jai were being treated as slaves. They should be set free.

But how and when? That was the dilemma.

Crystal said: "I think if we're going to set them free, the sooner the better. I can fly them to Tangier first thing in the morning and leave them there."

"That's a horrible idea," Lacy said. "From what you say they're still like children. A place like Tangier they wouldn't last a week."

"Then what do you suggest? We can't hide them here. Once Schwerner finds them missing he'll tear the place apart."

"No, he won't," Lacy said. "Not if he doesn't remember anything about them."

That was when she told the others about the memory erasing drug Blue had obtained and used on himself.

"But that still doesn't solve the problem of how and when to set them free."

"It doesn't, no," Lacy admitted.

In the end it was Nadia to whom they turned for direction. Leaning forward in the easy chair she scratched Baskerville behind his ears and said, "Crystal's right but so are you, Lacy, and that's the dilemma. It's like when the European imperial powers were finally forced to give up their ridiculous colonies in the middle of the twentieth century. What we need to do is come up with something like commonwealth status. I say fly them to Tangier and set them free. But one of us—Crystal, it'll have to be you—is going to have to stay with them until they're able to survive on their own. They're smart, I'm sure. They pick up things extraordinarily fast. Maybe a month—two—and they'll be fine. We'll have to come up with some excuse to satisfy Desmond as to why you're not here but that shouldn't be difficult."

"You could tell him I'm pregnant," said Crystal.

"With Alfie's child," said Lacy.

Crystal let out a string of loud retching noises.

"Knock it off, the both of you," Nadia snapped. "This is serious business. Crystal, go get them. The time to act is now."

But when Crystal went back to Schwerner's room as soon unlocked the door she sensed something was wrong.

"Jai?" she said, stepping inside. "Lai? Where are you?"

Then she saw the open window. The curtain flapped in the hot wind.

She crossed over and looked out. In the soft dirt under the window she could make out two parallel sets of footprints. They moved away from the wall, past the greenhouse where Alfie kept his flower collection, and toward the moat that circled the mansion and the barren inferno of the Sahara beyond.

She sucked in her breath and held it for a long time.

Then fighting off a chill she hurried off to inform Nadia and Lacy of what she had discovered, that Lai and Jai were already free.

5

In a drafty public meeting hall in one of the foulest slums of Kabul Afghanistan a fat man dressed in a dingy gray smock and torn leggings sat cross-legged on the warped apron of a bare stage.

This fat man was a self-proclaimed guru and prophet whose white-brown hair fell in matted clumps clear to the small of his back. His eyes were a blazing blue, his skin burned as brown as the earth, the flesh of his face creased and wrinkled like a lunar landscape. Those gathered closest to the stage to hear the guru speak—perhaps four dozen in all—were almost uniformly youthful, clear-skinned, and well-dressed.

Each had willingly coughed up the flat sum of three thousand dollars for the hour-long lecture. (A combined discount rate of five thousand dollars had been made available to those couples able to prove they were legally married.) The fat guru, whose name was Bludoni, had only recently arrived in Kabul at the conclusion of a seven years' trek on foot through the holy places of east Asia. It was said by some that he had not only scaled the north face of Mount Everest but had lain submerged beneath the sacred waters of the Ganges for three full years. All agreed that during the course of his journey Bludoni had achieved an insight concerning the specific nature of cosmic existence.

It was in order to share the details of this insight that the present meeting had been convened.

Bludoni spoke: "I have come before you this evening, my fellow seekers, to make a confession. In all true humility I must concede that my long journey of which you have no doubt heard proved in the end utterly without value or purpose. For seven years I wandered, a pilgrim in search of enlightenment, and for seven years I failed miserably in that quest."

There was a confused stirring in the audience. Clearly this was not what any of those present had paid several thousand dollars to hear. The guru allowed the stirring to become a noisy rustling and then silenced it with a benign smile.

He held up one plump finger.

He went on: "It was not until I had attained the outskirts of this very city we presently inhabit, a sad and disillusioned man, that true enlightenment was at last bestowed upon me. It was then and there that I chanced upon a wizened beggar who lay supine upon the roadway apparently struck by an errant vehicle. I paused and administered aid and later in gratitude for my kindness the beggar man offered to tell me a particular story. I had heard a great profusion of stories during the years of my quest and in the beginning anticipated nothing remarkable. Yet when the beggar finished, my eyes were filled with tears, my heart beat in my chest like an enormous drum, and my soul soared outward till it seemed to fill the void of the cosmos. It is this story I wish to relate to you tonight."

The audience was hushed and expectant now. This was more like what they had come to hear.

"The story," said Bludoni, "concerns one Felipe Taglia, a man of mixed Italian and Spanish ancestry born in Paris of noble though impoverished parentage in the early years of the eighteenth Christian century. Felipe's mother and father came to London when he was yet a child and it was there that he grew toward adolescence. When he was still some months shy of his sixteenth birthday both parents were carried away in an outbreak of cholera. The orphaned Felipe was described to me by the beggar who had heard the tale from one who had heard it from one who had heard it from one who had heard it from one who had heard it from one who had heard it from one who had heard it from one who had actually known Felipe in the flesh as tall, willowy, dark of hair, and somewhat oily of complexion. He was not, it appears, a notably handsome man nor was he particularly intelligent. The one extraordinary characteristic Felipe Taglia possessed— and one of which he was as yet entirely unaware—was his sex organ, his penis. When erect that member measured a full thirteen inches in length with a girth slightly in excess of four inches. It is this organ and only this organ which makes the life, career, and philosophy of Felipe Taglia such an illuminating study."

Bludoni paused at this juncture and surveyed his audience as if in anticipation of some form of protest but the crowd remained attentive and silent, plainly eager for him to continue.

Bludoni smiled thinly.

"For a lad of his youth few avenues of employment existed in the London of the time. It was by no means surprising therefore that Felipe soon drifted into service, obtaining through friends of his late father a position as coachman—Felipe was always fond of horses—in the home of one Sir Melville Smythe, a respected merchant with interests on three continents. It was some seven weeks after Felipe's arrival in the Smythe household during a period in which Sir Melville was away at his country estate that the Lady Smythe, a portly blonde woman of forty summers, first commanded Felipe to appear in her private bedchamber. The other servants smirked knowingly when this summons was relayed to the boy but Felipe was even more of an innocent, an ingénue, than his meager years might indicate and was merely puzzled and confused.

"When he entered the room and discovered the Lady Smythe still abed his bafflement increased. In a rather abrupt voice she bade him to loosen and remove his trousers and undergarments. Felipe who had been taught never to question the eccentricities of his betters moved with fumbling fingers to obey. As soon as he had removed the final barrier concealing his organ from view the Lady Smythe sat up in bed with a start and emitted a yelp of astonishment so loud and forceful that it must have echoed throughout the house. 'My God!' she cried. 'My God, what is it you have brought for me?'

"Felipe could only peer down anxiously at himself. 'My lady, why do you stare at me so?'

"'My God, it's huge!' she went on, eyes bulging. 'I have never gazed upon its equal!'

"'To what does your ladyship refer?' asked Felipe meekly, his puzzlement in no way diminished.

"'To your cock, my boy! Good Lord, I refer to your great huge horse cock!'

"'But I have seen many much larger ones in the stables, my lady,' said Felipe who was in truth far more knowledgeable concerning the organs of horses than of men.

"'Well, it's certainly large enough for me,' said the Lady Smythe with a broad grin.

"She promptly instructed Felipe to scrub and cleanse his organ in a tub of soapy water. When this was accomplished to her satisfaction she ordered him to approach the bed. Lying on one side with her neck craned slightly she took the boy's organ between her hands and began caressing it gingerly. In no time at all her ministering fingers had brought the organ to a state of ripeness. Edging forward the Lady Smythe then attempted to insert the bloated head between her lips. It was a difficult maneuver owing to the immense size of the erect organ and after a few moments valiant effort the Lady Smythe contented herself for the time being with merely licking, kissing, and suckling the swollen tip. Within a relatively brief period to his great consternation Felipe felt a peculiar burning sensation spread through his loins and soon thereafter he ejaculated into the Lady Smythe's waiting mouth. When he was at last drained she fell back on the bed but continued to observe his organ with rising interest. As time passed to her enormous delight the member failed to wilt in any noticeable manner. After several additional minutes had passed and the organ remained as upright and stiff as a dutiful soldier the Lady Smythe leaned forward once more, opened her lips as far as they would go, and this time thrust a portion of the organ directly within the cavity of her mouth. When some minutes later after Felipe had ejaculated a second time and there was again no diminishment in the size of his organ the Lady Smythe could restrain her wonderment no longer.

"She pointed. 'Does it stay hard that way all of the time?' she asked.

"Felipe glanced down at his stiff member. 'Hard, my lady?'

"'Does it not ever go soft and remain that way?'

"'I—I don't know. I've never made it hard like this before—not on purpose.'

"'Then we'll have to see what we can do,' said she.

"Removing her nightdress underneath which she wore nothing the Lady Smythe positioned herself on the bed, raised her legs, and instructed the boy to place himself strategically between them. At her urging he thrust forward and entered her all at once. The pain of this initial invasion was not insignificant but the Lady Smythe soon adjusted herself to the presence of the thick shaft and in a short time had experienced a number of trembling orgasms of her own.

"The boy Felipe stayed with her all of that day and night. In total they experienced complete congress fourteen separate times and never once did the rigidity of the boy's organ fail.

"Felipe was later to insist that the majority of what he knew of the art of physical love had been taught to him that same day and night. 'All that came later,' he wrote in a letter to an intimate, 'was mere dressing on the salad of my first knowledge.'

"Felipe Taglia remained in the Smythe household another three years during which time it was whispered that his services were most frequently required in the hours between dusk and dawn. This was a period of relative enlightenment in sexual mores and thus one can be certain that Sir Melville Smythe was never less than fully cognizant of his wife's dalliances which he no doubt tolerated in return for equal freedoms of his own. In due time however Sir Melville became aware of certain rumors circulating among the servants concerning the specific nature of young Felipe's allure and acting from a well-tempered skepticism he determined to strike at the root of these fantastic tales. He chose one evening therefore to summon both Felipe and a young servant girl to his private quarters where he bluntly instructed them to perform an act of fornication upon the floor. While Sir Melville observed in growing wonderment Felipe stripped off his clothes and took the not unwilling girl without further prelude.

"When they were finished Sir Melville dismissed the servant girl with a distracted wave and sidled closer in order to see clearly what next transpired. After a lengthy period of time had passed Sir Melville was forced to shake his head slowly in candid awe. 'My God,' he said in a somewhat stricken voice, 'then the bloody stories are true. Does it not ever...ever grow limp?'

"Felipe who had shed much of his timidity in the past months smiled reassuringly. 'It shrinks, sir, only when I will it to be small.'

"'And only then?'

"'That is correct, sir.'

"'And this talent...it can be taught?'

"'No, sir, it is, I believe, a special gift although I know not from whom or where it comes nor why I was chosen to be so benefited.'

"Sir Melville, a man of considerable cunning, concealed his subsequent thoughts. In recent weeks he had suffered a series of financial reversals which threatened untimely ruin. Since he had long ago learned that what was extraordinary was also often times profitable and since there could be no dispute that Felipe's organ represented a most extraordinary phenomenon, then there most likely had to be a shilling to be turned here somehow.

"After several moments due consideration Sir Melville ordered Felipe to dress and together they journeyed by coach into a fashionable district of the city where they gained entrance into a particularly splendid house.

"Now in the London of that time there existed a number of exclusive social clubs catering to select tastes and this dwelling happened to house the most notorious of these clubs. While Felipe waited in an anteroom Sir Melville bargained long and hard with the proprietor, a Persian eunuch, and after Felipe had been summoned and made to verify the nature of his gift Sir Melville departed in possession of sufficient funds to recoup his past losses and right himself financially. The Lady Smythe was naturally heartbroken over the sudden and unexplained disappearance of her favorite coachman but through the soothing ministrations of time and a West Indian lad procured by Sir Melville as a replacement she soon recovered and was her old blithe untroubled self once more.

"As for Felipe Taglia his own words may here serve best, for I happen to have on my person a manuscript given to me by the wizened beggar which purports to be in Felipe's own hand and describes his years in the eunuch's employ."

Reaching inside his smock Bludoni extracted several sheets of yellow parchment and holding them close to his face read in a monotone:

"'At the social club of the Persian eunuch I was provided a large and well-furnished apartment in the upper story of the house, a vast improvement upon the modest quarters to which I had become accustomed while serving Sir Melville and her ladyship. Although the windows were securely barred and an enormous Nubian armed with sword and dagger prowled outside my door I never regarded myself as a prisoner, for prisoners are those restrained contrary to their wishes while I was never less than willing to remain where and as I was. The eunuch demanded only that I remain in a state of constant readiness to serve the needs of his clientele but often as long as a fortnight would pass with no call for my services which had been priced at a rate most flattering to me. It was during these otherwise unoccupied hours that my true education commenced as I read extensively from the eunuch's personal library concentrating upon works of a philosophic or theological bent and attempted to channel my thoughts in similar directions. It was during this period also that I came to view my physical attributes in an entirely different light and to understand that the size and vigor of my organ had been bestowed upon me not merely for my own purely selfish ends but rather as a means by which to help those less fortunate. Certain revered saints of antiquity had been gifted by God with the ability to heal physical deformities while I had been similarly endowed through my organ with the power to cure spiritual ills. I came to envision myself as a sort of physician of the soul, my clients appearing before me filled with inner anguish and departing revived and renewed.

"'Who were these clients? you might well inquire. In what manner and sense did I revive and renew them? Many of those who visited me were, I recall, gentlemen of inverse persuasions to whose defense I must now rise, for even though the Bible speaks of such as abominations in the eyes of the Lord my own experience has shown them to be no more or less human than anyone else. A goodly portion of those I served were in fact quite content simply to observe as I stroked my own organ to completion while others were equally willing to perform that act upon themselves with no expectation or demand of recompense. It is true that many did prefer to minister orally to my organ and yet only a few ever bade that I perform such a deed in reverse despite my stated lack of hesitancy in that regard. In other words the majority of my services were of a purely benign nature as I was seldom called upon actively to perform: my patients would thus heal themselves in my presence.

"'Another large group of clients consisted of those who wished to be beaten, restrained, flagellated, or otherwise abused by me. At first I was frankly not charmed by these gentlemen but soon attained a revelation that it was not the sensation of pain that pleasured them but rather their inward response to it—their suffering. Even Christ is widely revered because of the terrible agonies He suffered upon the cross and my clients in attempting to follow his divine example could only be regarded as committing acts of genuine piety. The minimal role played by my organ at these times impressed me further as additional proof of the spiritual nature of these encounters.

"'Most of my remaining clients were men whose faces I never directly glimpsed. A chamber in the lower story of the house had been fitted with a mirror designed to permit those in an adjoining room to view what went on within while no one inside could see without. At least once each month—and usually more frequently—the Persian eunuch would order me to this room to copulate with others in his employ—sometimes a woman, sometimes a lad, sometimes various combinations of both. In the beginning I found little to involve me in these sessions but then one evening while performing with a pair of slender-waisted Chinese maids one of the most peculiar experiences of my life occurred. I suddenly found myself floating free of my own body and was able to will my spirit to pass through the wall so that for the first time I actually observed those who had previously been hidden from me. As I did I seemed for an instant to merge with their general essences and thus comprehended the sincere pleasure each derived from watching me perform and came consequently to the realization that these men—like all my clients—were those who received pleasure from the pleasure of others, an attitude I could not but regard as holy. In fact when upon occasion various ladies would appear at the club and seek my—'"

Bludoni broke off, raising his eyes. A freckle-faced redheaded boy of ten or twelve years had entered the hall through a side door. Bludoni hastily folded up the Taglia manuscript and thrust it inside his smock.

"Ladies and gentlemen," he said, coming to his feet, "I deeply regret to inform you that our time has come to an end. So if you would please be so kind as to..." He waved both hands briskly in the direction of the exits.

The audience responded with a low angry murmur. "Now wait just a cotton picking minute," said a stern-faced middle-aged woman at the front of the hall. "I paid a considerable amount of money to come hear you speak and all I've heard thus far is a filthy anecdote."

"Filthy?" said Bludoni, freezing in apparent shock. "To what filthy anecdote do you refer, madam?"

"To that dreadful thing you were just telling us—about that Italian person and his—his phallus."

Bludoni bowed his head somberly. "My good woman, if that to you was a filthy anecdote then you have very far to go in your spiritual quest—very far indeed."

"Well, personally I'd like to hear the end of it," said a young man seated directly behind the woman. The majority of those present nodded their assent.

"And so you shall," said Bludoni, his expression growing strained. "Tomorrow night. Same time, same place, I shall endeavor to procure the hall for a supplemental lecture. Now if you would please be so—"

"Impossible!" cried the middle-aged woman, rising to her feet. "I have reservations for a different talk then. I imagine that most of us do. The third Swami Mitra is arriving in Kabul on the morning train. Surely you knew that."

"It must somehow have slipped my mind," said Bludoni impatiently. "In that event I will attempt to meet with each of you personally. I am presently occupying rooms at the New Bengali Hotel. You may visit me there at your convenience and I will see that you are provided with copies of the Taglia manuscript."

"It's still not the same as hearing it read out loud," a young woman put in from the rear. "Couldn't you make it for the night after tomorrow? There's nothing else happening then that I know of."

"Please, I—" All of a sudden Bludoni's eyes rolled back in his head. He threw up his hands and grabbed hold of his temples. "Ladies and gentlemen," he cried in an excited voice. "I believe I am receiving a significant message from the astral plane beyond. Please, I must—you must—I need privacy in order to concentrate."

The urgency of his plea seemed to reach the audience. After only a brief hesitation they rose to their feet in mass and—despite frequent anxious backward glances—filed from the hall.

Bludoni remained upon the stage in a posture of rigid expectancy until the room had almost emptied. Then he dropped his hands, sprang from the stage, and pointing a finger advanced upon the one person who had lingered behind.

It was the redheaded boy of ten or twelve.

"Damn you, Louie Roth," said the fat guru. "This had better be important. I don't want Brother Xavier connecting you with me."

"Why? What's up?" The boy's voice was deep and powerful, that of a grown man. "Xavier didn't show up here tonight, did he?"

"As a matter of fact he did not." Bludoni halted a short distance in front of the boy and released his breath in a sigh. "Except for that one idiotic woman I don't think there was a person in the hall much past thirty years of age."

"Only kids still got that old time religion, huh?"

"It is not a religion, Louie," Bludoni said stiffly. "A religion is long and slow and tortuous and complex. What these people desire is something quick, simple, and utterly without pain."

"From what I heard at least you were giving them a good time. I was starting to get a little hot myself there for a while."

"That, Louie, is your problem, not mine." Bludoni frowned. "Now come. What is it you've brought me?"

"It's him, all right—Xavier." The boy—actually, it was by now clear, a dwarf in disguise—paused deliberately. "I think I've found him for you."

"Excellent," said Bludoni who was in truth none other than Desmond Blue the detective, also in disguise. "Tell me where."

"Not so fast." Louie Roth took a backward step. "I don't do this for the good of my soul, you know."

With a scowl Blue reached inside his smock, extracted a thick roll of bills, and peeled off several which he passed to Louie. "Now spill it."

Louie was counting the money. He nodded his head at Blue's bulging midriff. "Did you pull all that in just tonight?"

"If I failed to charge a substantial fee no one would take my message seriously."

Louie shook his head admiringly. "Maybe I ought to take up this guru racket myself."

"You appear to do quite well picking people's pockets—including mine. Now—enough idle chatter. Where is Brother Xavier?"

Louie pointed at the floor. "Right here—in Kabul."

"Then you've seen him?"

"Not me—a friend did. I ran into the guy about an hour ago down at Madam Castillo's opium den and when I showed him that photo you gave me he said he remembered him right away. Seems he bumped into Xavier just this afternoon. He was a lot older than the picture but he said he was sure it was him."

"On the street?"

"Better than that. In his dentist's office."

"Xavier would hardly be there now."

"Not necessarily." Louie was grinning. "According to my pal, Xavier wasn't there getting his teeth fixed. He was living there. In a back room. My pal wandered in while the doctor was talking on the phone."

"Does your friend make a habit of wandering through other people's homes?"

"Sure. You know the type. He likes to check out the lay of the land."

"You mean he likes to steal anything that not nailed to the floor."

"Not from this guy he wouldn't steal."

"The dentist?"

Louie nodded. "This guy ain't no regular dentist. This is Dr. Ling Chi Ho."

Blue whistled softly. Dr. Ling Chi Ho, an old acquaintance who had at one time been regarded as the criminal mastermind of the entire Orient. Blue's confrontations with Dr. Ling had been of legendary proportions. "It was my understanding that the good doctor retired from illegal enterprises a number of years ago."

"Thanks to you, yeah, but he still keeps a hand in the dental racket. There isn't a crook in Kabul who'd go to anybody else."

Blue nodded thoughtfully. Dr. Ling, he recalled, was a man of considerable intelligence, cultivation, and breeding. It was not impossible—now that he had adopted a law-abiding stance—that he might be attracted to an organization such as the Preservationists. "I believe the next obvious step is for you and I to pay a call on Dr. Ling."

"Me?" Louie did not look pleased. "Uh-uh. You're not dragging me into this any deeper."

"I'm afraid I have no choice, Louie." Blue took a quick dancing step forward and wrapped one hand around Louie's wrist. He headed toward the door, hauling the struggling dwarf behind him. "My teeth, you see, happen to be quite false while yours, I note, are not only real but rather obviously in need of some repair. We will make a late night visit to the doctor for an emergency extraction."

"Nobody's pulling my teeth. Not for nothing."

Blue thrust open the door with his free hand and hurried out. "Would you rather then that I turned my dossier on you over to the local authorities? It's quite disgustingly thick, Louie. Thick enough to guarantee you a good twenty or thirty years at hard labor, I would estimate."

Louie uttered a strangled moan. "Goddamn you, Blue. Goddamn your eyes."

And the two of them—the fat detective in the guise of a guru, the protesting dwarf in the garb of a child—hastened onward through the teeming nocturnal streets of old Kabul.

6

Since time immemorial, thought Old Man Mose (born Richard Benjamin Ford—but that was a dead name), since time immemorial he had wandered the burning blanket of the Sahara as God's diligent pilgrim on this earth. Giggling merrily as he loped along perched high on the dromedary hump. Time immemorial? Well, not that long maybe. Maybe only four centuries. Or two. Or twenty years. Twenty years was a far piece for one man to live without company, some might say. But Mose knew better.

Mose knew he was never truly alone. For God Himself dwelled out here. God driven in divine revulsion from the heathen temples of mankind to make a last stand here in the wilderness. God dwelled in the Sahara. Mose did too. Thus neither was alone.

Water was the one necessary thing for survival. Mose was careful never to lose sight of that. Even drinking no more than as he did scarcely a mouthful a day he could never carry enough for more than two months, maybe three at the most. Not that he counted the days. Time meant nothing to the diligent pilgrim. The sun rose and set. God bless the sun, he thought. In the Sahara the sun reigned almighty. Unwinking eye of God. God made fast in in the sun's burnt orb. Seeing all. Seeing Mose. Seeing him as a diligent pilgrim.

He drew up long enough to survey the lay of the land. Rolling dunes. White sheets of blistering sand. The oasis of Zbatzu looming fifty-two kilometers north by northeast. Mose knew the numbers, didn't have to think. Forty-six kilometers as the crows flew but since certain places between (cursed places) had to be avoided fifty-two was the number. He shook the canteen. More than enough water until then. No fool Mose. Mad, oh yes indeed, but never foolish. Fifty-two kilometers to go.

He prodded the camel, rode on.

Oh the things he had seen out here. Seen sinners burnt alive, seen demons eaten raw. Seen mountains that talked. Seen the burning bush. Seen the pillar of fire. Seen his own namesake, seen Moses of the Israelites, seen him striding down from heaven with tablets of stone. Seen a golden chariot ablaze with the eye of God aboard. Seen Jesus. Seen most everything.

When old Mose first came out here to the desert he dug a hole deep in the sand and planted a pole forty feet long and nailed a platform on top and dwelt there forty days and forty nights with only a canvas sheet to ward off the killing sun. Heathens came from afar to point and stare. "I am the holy pilgrim!" he cried to them. "The slugs were sent by Satan! I defy them to come for me! I wait unafraid!" Forty days and forty nights he waited and they never came. On the forty-first God appeared in the form of a dove and said *Go forth, Old Man Mose, and serve me well.* Then he came down from the platform. Bought a swaybacked camel from a heathen with a boy in his bed. Rode forth into the desert, "You will die, madman!" they shouted after him. Not Old Mose. Mose didn't die; Mose flourished. God showed him the path that was blest. He'd wandered there ever since. Served God throughout the breadth and length of this blistering land. None ever knew the Sahara like Old Man Mose. He needed no map, no compass. The stars were his beacons. Knew them well. Fifty-two kilometers. He drank more water.

His skin was as black as a crow's feathers. His eyes were narrow slits in a raw burnt face. His beard, snow white, drooped to his chest, A grizzled man. Crazy-looking. Wore the *galibiva*—the loose-fitting robes of the desert dweller. Mose came first from San Bernardino in California in the United States of North America on the planet Earth in the Solar System in the Milky Way in the Local Group in the Universe in the Cosmos of God. Came from there to the great white desert where God now lived. Came to speak with the Lord and spread His word.

Twenty years earlier when Mose was still Richard Benjamin Ford he had a wife and two young daughters. So long ago now he scarcely remembered their faces. Dead now. Went to San Francisco to visit only to be struck down by Satan's hand. Dead and then brought back to wander. He found them once in the ruins of another city. Hollow eyes filled with sin. He ran from them to the desert, to the Sahara, to spread the word of God. Lived forty days and forty nights on a pillar of salt. Visited by God in the guise of a dove. Went forth. Crazy man. Dead that weren't dead. Well, Mose lived.

He pulled back on the reins, slowed the dromedary to a trot, scanned the terrain. Fifty-two kilometers to go. But he knew this place. Big house where the fat man lived. The fat man and three women and three men. Mose had stopped here often. Spoke with the fat man and the women. Shared food. Drank wine. Nearly died first. The women nursed him back to life. Beautiful women like his dead wife and two young daughters. Mose wept at the memory. There were things he could not forget. That was one.

"So you're Old Man Mose the desert fool," the fat man said after the women had nursed him back to health. "I've heard of you. You're a legend among the desert dwellers."

"You think I'm mad, do you?"

"I think somebody is but I'm not sure who."

Mose stayed clear of the big house now. He feared the fat man. Too many tears. The burning bush. Pillar of fire. Mose had seen all this and more besides twenty years wandering the desert.

Then cresting a dune, the camel balked. There they were. Two of them. A boy and girl. Sitting in the sand. Holding each other. As naked as the first day of creation.

Mose hopped off the camel, hurried over, tossed a blanket over them. "What in God's name are you doing out here?"

They looked at each other. "Who is this God you call to?" said the boy.

"Never mind that. You're in the middle of the desert. The middle of nowhere. You'll die out here without help."

"Then help us," said the girl.

"Help you how?"

"Take us to the place where the people live."

"The house of the fat man you mean?" He could see the roof rising over the next hill.

"No. To the city. To Tangier."

Mose tugged on his beard. "Tangier is a far piece. Farther than a crow can fly. Who are you anyhow? How did you get here?"

"I am Jai." the girl said.

"I am Lai," said the boy.

He let them ride on the camel's hump, clutching the reins, walking. Gave them clothes to ward off the sun. Shared his water. Not enough for three. Someone would die. He knew it would be him.

Thirty-nine more kilometers to the oasis at Zbatzu. God would guide. God would prevail.

He shut his eyes, prayed silently, walked on.

Come nightfall they stopped to rest. His tongue in his mouth like a clenched fist. Dying he knew. He slept and did not wake.

In the morning, the two of them rode on.

BOOK THREE

THE DESMOND BLUE BLUES

"Science is progressive. What was useful two centuries ago is now become useless."
—Thomas Jefferson

1

For Dr. Gordon Schwerner the motorized trek by jeep and van across the uncivilized wastes of mainland Africa proved even more tedious and less easily endurable than he had feared. During the sweltering daylight hours progress was fitful at best with mechanical breakdowns frequent while in the evenings camped around a blazing fire Darby Spock, reeking of cheap perfume, would sit puffing on his pipe and relating endless tales of his past exploits as a white hunter, hand-to-jaw combat with leopards and lions, savage tribal rites, a boy raised among anthropoid apes, a visit to the legendary haunt of the elephants graveyard. Schwerner received the definite impression that Spock had been telling these same pointless idiotic stories over and over for years and the way the native boys invariably broke into spasms of giddy laughter the moment he launched into one only served to confirm his suspicions. As soon as it was possible Schwerner made an effort to slip off into one of the tents and go to bed. Spock on the other hand never slept. At least by the time Schwerner woke in the morning he was always there squatting wide awake beside the dead campfire, whisky bottle clutched in his hand. Despite his drinking Spock never seemed any the worse for wear. It was no more than a five-day jaunt to the Renaldo Castle, he had informed Schwerner when they left Zanzibar, but when the fifth day arrived conceded that they still weren't close. The landscape day-by-day seemed changeless. Sometimes a leafless tree or a gnarled bush would materialize to break the monotony of the grassy plain but usually not even that. One morning Spock excitedly pointed to what he claimed were two distant elephants and on another occasion the jeep drove right past a gathering of six grazing zebra. The bigger herds, Spock insisted, preferred to remain farther north in the lakes region of Uganda or else close to the cooling slopes of Kilimanjaro. This was where you'd find your lions and leopards, he assured Schwerner, hundreds of them. On the afternoon of the fifth day they rounded a curve in the dirt path they were following—only Spock would have had the nerve to refer to it as a road—with their view blocked by a grassy knoll—when Spock slammed down on the brakes of the jeep. The suddenness of the stop hurled Schwerner forward and he cracked a leg on the dashboard. "*Ouch*—damn it!" he yelled, holding his kneecap.

"For God's sake shut up," hissed Spock.

Schwerner turned his head in surprise. Spock pointed mutely ahead. At first Schwerner assumed it was simply a small gray mountain rising in the middle of the road but then he noticed that the mountain possessed two long curving tusks, a pair of tent-like ears, and a serpentine trunk. As Schwerner stared the trunk rose stiffly in the air and a small pink mouth gaped underneath.

"An elephant," said Schwerner. "An adult African elephant."

"Sit still," said Spock. "Try not to move."

Absolute and total silence had fallen around them. Until now the noise of insects and birds had been a constant chorus. Beside them the van had also stopped. Through the tinted windshield Schwerner could see the wary frightened faces of the native boys.

"Elephants aren't dangerous, are they?" Schwerner asked tentatively.

"This one may be—I think he's a rogue."

"A what?"

"A rogue bull. It's a disease—a must. Drives them mad with the itch. They'll trample anything that comes near."

The two elephants Schwerner had previously seen had been mere specks of gray in the distance, totally unthreatening. For the first time he was made aware of the sheer enormity of the beast, the massive power contained within its frame. The ears were like sails in the wind, the tusks glinting scimitars, the legs the trunks of primeval trees.

"Can't we back away?" he suggested. "Or go around it?"

"Not if we want to keep on breathing. Elephants have rotten eyesight. I doubt the bloody thing can even see us now. If we try to move though it'll spot us for sure."

"Can't we outrun it?"

"No more than you could outrun a horse on foot. I saw a rogue go after a bulldozer once. The bulldozer was wrecked, two men dead, and the bloody elephant waltzed away like it was on parade."

"Are you going to shoot it?"

"With a .45? I might as well stick a hatpin in its toe."

"My God, man, we can't just sit here all day."

"Well, we're going to—unless that bull decides otherwise."

But the elephant seemed quite content to remain exactly where it was. Gazing into those tiny fluid eyes Schwerner found it difficult to believe that he wasn't being observed in return. Strangely it was less madness he saw reflected there than calm cool reason. The elephant was patient, serene.

It could wait till the world passed by, wait till the end of eternity.

One minute passed. Then two. Five. Ten.

Schwerner's forehead, arms, and chest itched horribly from the sweat he was shedding. He reached to scratch himself but Spock cleared his throat and glared pointedly and Schwerner let his hand hang in mid-air. A fly landed on the tip of his nose. He had to endure it. Fifteen minutes went by. The elephant had not moved.

The silence was broken all at once by a loud noise from beside them. It was an engine revving up. Gears clashed. The engine revved louder.

"Bloody fools," muttered Spock, still motionless. "They'll get us killed for sure."

Schwerner managed to glance over without fully turning his head. Through the van's windshield he could see the driver's tense features as he struggled to put the machine into gear. Without warning he succeeded. With a noisy squeal and a spray of dust the van shot off in reverse. Wavering like a drunken man it left the narrow path and smacked into the side of the grassy knoll. Doors flew open in an instant, disgorging a half-dozen khaki-clad Negroes. Without a backward glance they raced across the open plain.

Schwerner looked at the elephant. To his relief it seemed unmoved by the sudden tumult of action nearby. Schwerner released his pent-up breath in a sigh of relief and started to remark that they were apparently still safe. Just then the raised its trunk and emitted a low trumpeting cry.

Then it lumbered forward like a freight train.

"That's it," said Spock. "Run for your bloody life, man."

It was the only warning he gave. A moment later Spock leaped over the side and took off running at a surprisingly rapid rate of speed.

Schwerner sprang down and dashed off in the opposite direction. Even as he ran he swore he could hear the elephant's thundering footsteps only yards behind but knew better than to look back. He spotted a rare stand of scrub trees directly ahead, zigzagged through them, then headed across the broad featureless veldt. Finally turning his head he caught sight of the elephant just as it reached the jeep.

The beast paused only long enough to give the jeep a quick bump with its head. The jeep flew through the air like a feather in a hurricane and landed upside down in a tangle of steel and broken parts. Schwerner ran even harder now, his head thrown back, his heart slapping furiously at his chest.

The elephant came after him. When it reached the trees it barreled headfirst through them in a splintering of wood.

Schwerner knew he could not expect to out-distance the elephant. It didn't appear to be running especially hard but because of its size even at a slow steady trot it was more than able to gain ground on him. His only chance was to circle around and try to take shelter in the wreckage of the van.

Just as he was about to make a quick turn to the left his right foot caught fire. Shrieking with pain he looked down and saw that his boot and lower leg were covered in red. For a moment he couldn't connect the redness with the pain, then realized what must have occurred. In his frantic rush to escape the pursuing elephant he had unknowingly stepped in the middle of an anthill and the damn things were eating him alive. With the realization of what the red splotch signified came another bolt of agony. Schwerner howled, swung his foot in the air, and lost his balance completely. As he fell he glimpsed the elephant closing in. The moment he hit the ground half-blinded with pain something enormous blotted out the sun. An instant later the sky also vanished. It was the elephant. It was going to step—

The boom was like the shattering of the world. For an instant Schwerner was certain it must be the echo of his own death. The problem was he didn't feel particularly dead. He could see and smell and hear and more importantly the pain in his leg was as intense as ever. A second booming noise followed closely after the first—just as loud but duller, more like a thud. For a moment the ground shook, then subsided.

Dead or alive Schwerner couldn't endure the pain in his foot a second more. He struggled to sit up and tore frantically at his trousers and boot. When he got them off he staggered to his feet and used both hands to swat the ants still clinging to the bare flesh of his rapidly swelling limb.

The elephant lay on the ground only a few yards distant.

Two round holes gaped in the middle of its broad forehead.

Blood spurted from the wounds and formed a crimson pool underneath. Someone had shot and killed the elephant. But who?

A whirring noise drew his attention to the sky. Looking up he discovered hovering overhead the outline of a helio-plane. From the glass bubble of the cockpit an object caught the light of the sun and glinted. It was the barrel of a large rifle.

"My God, man, I thought you were done for sure." It was Darby Spock, pipe clenched in his teeth. Watching the helio-plane Schwerner had not noticed his approach. "Here, better let me give you a hand up."

With Spock's assistance Schwerner managed to limp across to the van where he sat on the edge of the running board with his bare leg extended in front of him. His whole right foot and lower calf stung dreadfully but the sight of the dead elephant reminded him of how grateful he ought to be that at least he was alive.

"Who are they?" he said, jerking his head at the sky where the helio-plane continued to hover.

"Got me," said Spock. "Game wardens, I suppose. There aren't many left these days. We'll find out soon enough though. I think they're coming down."

The helio-plane descended slowly, finally settling to earth on a patch of ground halfway between the dead elephant and the van. Two men emerged from the cockpit, both black. One—the shorter of the two—waved his hands excitedly over his head and came hurrying toward them. To his amazement Schwerner recognized him. He was the same man who had sat across the aisle from him on the plane and been met at the aeroport in Zanzibar by the spooks.

Spock also seemed to know the man. "Bastard," he muttered darkly. "Bloody pissing lifer bastard."

When the man reached them he clasped his hands under his chin and bowed with stiff formality. He wore khaki shorts and a matching bush jacket, both of which appeared as if they had been cleaned and pressed only moments before. "Darby, old friend," the man said in excellent clipped English, "it does appear that I chanced upon you and your companion in the proverbial nick of time."

"Nobody asked for your damn help, Bello," Spock said.

"Ah, but it is those gifts which we do not solicit that we often most cherish." The man turned to Schwerner and executed another formal bow. "Mohammed Bello, sir. I do not believe that I have had the pleasure of your introduction."

"Schwerner. Dr. Gordon Schwerner. I wanted to say how much I—*ouch*." The pain in his leg had flared again.

Mohammed Bello clucked his tongue sympathetically. "I was not aware that you had been injured."

Schwerner looked down at his bare legs, not wholly unaware of the indignity of his present posture. "It was when I was trying to get away from the elephant. I must have stepped in the middle of an anthill."

Bello laughed sharply then caught himself.

"I must apologize for seeming to find amusement in your pain, Doctor, but isn't that a perfect example of the irony of human condition? To be attacked within minutes by both the largest and tiniest of nature's beasts. We are haughty creatures, we men, and yet they—our mindless subjects—bring us nothing but torment and pain."

Schwerner saw nothing amusing in any of this but Mohammed Bello had saved his life and he knew he ought to feel grateful. "I want you to know I do appreciate what you did for me, Mr. Bello."

"Oh, it was not I," Bello said modestly.

He waved a hand at the helio-plane and the tall black man who stood beside it. "It was my faithful retainer who fired the fatal shot.

I am a follower of the traditional religion, Doctor, and cannot bring myself to do harm to any of Allah's living things."

"Faithful retainer," Spock muttered. "Bloody slave, you mean."

"I'm sorry, Darby." Bello cocked his head at an angle. "I'm afraid I failed to catch that last remark."

"Forget it," Spock said gruffly. "Anyway, Bello, do you usually go around carrying an elephant gun with you in your helio-plane?"

"That bit of good fortune must be ascribed to the sheer fate," Bello said glibly. "In fact I wasn't even aware that the weapon was aboard—I abhor guns—until my pilot pointed it out."

"Then I guess we don't owe you a damn thing," Spock said, placing himself between Bello and Schwerner like a protective parent. "So if you don't mind I've got some natives to round up and an expedition to get on with."

"Expedition?" said Bello, eyebrows rising quizzically. "What sort of expedition, may I inquire?"

"No, you may damn well not," said Spock. "But since you're so bloody curious it happens to be a fishing expedition. Dr. Schwerner here is a devout disciple follower of the art of angling. We're touring the freshwater lakes hereabouts."

"But I know of no freshwater lakes in this region."

"It's the ones nobody knows about that we're out to visit. Now why don't you get the hell out of my sight before I lose my bloody breakfast looking at you?"

"But, friend Darby," Bello protested, "I was about to extend the services of my helio-plane. Neither of your vehicles appears in a particularly operable state and your native bearers if I know the breed are by now scattered from here to Pretoria. Dr. Schwerner, to be brutally frank, does not seem to be in the peak of health. There is danger from ant bites, I assure you, a distinct tendency toward infection. I seriously recommend that both you gentlemen accompany me to my home where a medical expert may inspect Dr. Schwerner's wounds and render a professional judgment. I can then send out a party to retrieve your belongings and hopefully repair your van and jeep."

"Your home?" said Spock. "What are you talking about, Bello? Your home's hundreds of kilometers from here."

"Ah, then you have not been apprised of my most recent change of address. My current residence lies less than one dozen kilometers from this very spot."

Spook's eyes narrowed. "What happened, Bello? Your neighbors finally get up the good sense to run you out?"

"Nothing so dramatic as that, dear Darby. The decision to move was purely my own. A matter of finance. The present price of land near Kilimanjaro is relatively high; in this region it is quite low. I sold the former, purchased the latter, and turned a handsome profit."

"You can't raise poppies here, I hope you know. There isn't sufficient water."

"Alas, how true. My days as a gentlemen farmer seem for the moment to be at an end."

Schwerner's leg was beginning to ache even worse than before. An agonized moan escaped his lips involuntarily. Spock, glancing over and seeing the pain written on his face, relented at last. "All right, Bello, for once you seem to be making sense. We'll go with you. But just for tonight and only because of poor Schwerner here. I don't want you thinking I've altered my opinion of you because I damn well haven't."

"Of course not, Darby," said Bello with a quick bow. "I know you as a man of absolute unshakable integrity."

Schwerner was struggling not to moan again. He looked down at his naked legs. "Darby, I was wondering. Would you mind very much fetching my pants for me?"

Spock grunted and stalked away, marching past the helio-plane and its pilot without a sideways look. After retrieving Schwerner's pants and giving them a few healthy shakes he went over to where the dead elephant lay and bent down to examine it. He moved one of the big ears aside and ran a hand over the wrinkled skin underneath. When he returned he said, "That was damned peculiar. There's no sign of must on the carcass. Usually if it's bad enough to turn the buggers rogue the stuff's all over their skulls."

"Nature can be a very peculiar creature indeed," said Bello.

When Schwerner was dressed Bello offered the support of his arm and together the two men crossed to the waiting helio-plane. "Dear Darby does not fully approve of me," Bello whispered as they walked. "I employ the dead and it is his opinion that I thus exploit them. But I ask you candidly, Doctor: if I did not employ them, who would? Unlike Darby most spooks did not have lucrative occupations to which they could return after the disaster of the aliens."

Schwerner was in too much agony to feel much interest in discussing economics. With Bello's assistance he reached the helio-plane and dropped into the front seat. The pilot who had saved his life turned out to be a spook with a terrible body odor. In spite of the repugnance he felt Schwerner made a sincere effort to express his gratitude. He had not proceeded far when Bello broke in and assured him it was hopeless.

"I doubt the poor thing can understand a word you're saying." He tapped his forehead meaningfully. "His brain was sorely damaged by the three-day absence from our material plane. Not an uncommon experience among the dead, I believe."

"But a damn profitable one for bastards like you," said Spock, reaching the helio-plane and swinging into the rear seat. He had stopped at the van and Schwerner noticed the neck of a whisky bottle protruding from his jacket. "Bello likes to employ spooks with scrambled eggs for brains," he told Schwerner. "That way he doesn't have to concern himself with paying wages."

"Friend Darby as a typically indomitable member of the English race managed to pass through the veil of death without so much as batting an eyelash," said Bello.

"Nothing happened worth batting an eyelash at," Spock said distantly. He pulled out the whisky bottle and took a long swallow. "Let's get on with this." He glanced at the pilot. "It stinks in here as if you didn't damn well know."

At a tap on the shoulder from Bello the pilot turned the ignition, the big propeller began to churn, and in a few moments the helio-plane rose from the ground. Spock tilted forward in his seat and gazed at the landscape below searching for something, presumably his missing natives.

"There's one thing about this that still bothers me," he said after a while. "I know this area better than the back of my hand and there's nothing around here but grass and dirt. How did you manage to locate a place to live, Bello?"

"Surely you must be familiar with the Grand Safari Hotel."

"The Grand Safari Hotel went out of business years ago. The place is a bloody ruin."

"It was when I purchased it, yes, but now…well, my employees and I have made a number of repairs and improvements. I'm sure when you see it you'll be deeply impressed."

When Mohammed Bello's home came into view even Schwerner through his pain could not help being impressed. The central building—the hotel itself—was a sprawling three-story structure laid out in the shape of the letter "T" with gardens in front and back, a swimming pool off to one side, and several concrete rectangles that appeared to be tennis courts on the other.

"You have done a quite job here," Spock conceded with obvious reluctance. "I admit I hardly recognize the old place."

"I deserve little personal credit," Bello said. "My employees did the majority of the work with only basic direction from me. As a matter of fact I've only recently returned from a sojourn abroad."

Schwerner had not mentioned seeing Bello on the plane and since Bello did not appear to remember him saw no reason to say anything now. The helio-plane, descending in a dwindling spiral, set down on a patch of green lawn fronting the central building. A number of wood huts lay scattered at various locations around the grounds—housing for Bello's spook employees, Schwerner guessed—as well as a large square concrete building, a warehouse of some kind.

Another native spook, this one in formal attire and copiously perfumed, opened the helio-plane doors. Bello assisted Schwerner to the ground and with Spock following headed into the hotel lobby. He left Schwerner and Spock by the door and hurried across to what once must have been the front desk, returning in a short while with two keys, "My finest rooms," he told them. "A large suite for each of you."

An elevator deposited them on the third floor. Schwerner's suite consisted of two adjoining rooms with a bath overlooking the swimming pool. The rooms were good sized, lushly furnished, and although undoubtedly unused for many years, clean and fresh smelling.

Schwerner lay down on one of the two beds in the first room and propped his aching foot on a pillow.

Bello promised to send the doctor up right away. He pointed to the wall and said, "If you need assistance in the meantime, please press that button. My employees will be instructed to serve you promptly."

"You ought to throw the old place open for business," said Spock in a sudden burst of good humor. He was sitting on the other bed. "You could make yourself a bloody fortune."

"But I've already done that once in my life, Darby. Several fortunes as a matter of fact. Besides as we both know times have changed. The era of the safari, the white hunter, the endless slaughter of defenseless wildlife, all this now belongs to a dim and distant past. Would you care to have me show you to your room now, Darby?"

"I imagine I can manage to find it on my own," Spock said, plainly annoyed by Bello's unflattering reference to his profession. "I'll stay with Schwerner till your own doctor shows up."

"As you wish." Bello bowed. "I'll send a party of men out right away after your belongings. When they return I'll see that your suitcases are brought to your rooms."

"And you can tell your men for me," said Spock, surly as ever, "that if I find one thing missing I'll take it out of their bloody hides with a whip."

Bello frowned. "The dead have no reason to steal. You of all people should know that, Darby."

* * * *

After Bello had gone Spock came to his feet with a muttered stream of curses and began pacing the room, stalking angrily back and forth. Overcome by the incessant pain in his leg Schwerner lay back, closed his eyes, and attempted to concentrate on the warm place at the core of his inner being. This was the technique used by Oriental mystics to obliterate the pain of physical suffering but in Schwerner's case the primary difficulty was that he couldn't seem to locate any such warm place at the core of his inner being. Perhaps that was an Oriental characteristic only. Like their slanted eyes and yellow skin.

"I don't like this," said Spock, in a loud voice. "I don't like this one damn bit."

Schwerner opened his eyes to find Spock looming over him. "But why, Darby? It seems to me that Bello has treated us royally so far."

"That's exactly what I don't like. What's his game is what I want to know. I've seen that bugger in action more years than I care to remember and he never lifts a finger without a bloody good motive. He's setting us up, I tell you. I wouldn't trust Mr. Mohammed bloody Bello any further than I could throw a bull hippopotamus one-handed."

"I think you're being irrational. I understand that Bello may have offended you by implying you were little more than a barbaric anachronism but are you sure you're not letting your emotions carry you away?"

"Yes, I'm quite bloody sure. If you ask me this whole thing has smelled from the outset. That elephant for instance. I told you I didn't think it was any rogue. And Bello himself. How damnably convenient. He just happens to come flying by in a bloody helio-plane precisely at the right instant to rescue us. Why was that is what I want to know. A man like Bello doesn't go soaring around in the sky for no good reason. He never did tell us what he was doing out there."

"We never really asked."

"Then you should have. I can't think of everything. You're supposed to be the bloody detective."

"Look here, Spock, what is it you're trying to get at? Do you think Bello and the elephant are in this thing together, that they planned the entire course of events in advance, that it's all part of one complex scheme?" Sarcasm was a tone Schwerner rarely indulged in but the pain in his leg was making him impatient. "Besides," he added, "why would Bello wish us any harm? Even if what you say about him is true that doesn't make him anything more than a typical cunning businessman."

"What makes you sure Bello isn't mixed up in this case of yours?"

The fact of the matter, Schwerner admitted to himself, was that he couldn't be certain. Bello was not one of the three conspirators whose photographs Blue had made him memorize but that hardly proved his innocence either. "My case concerns the Renaldo Castle and as far as I know there's no connection between it and Mohammed Bello."

"I can tell you one possible bloody connection. Bello's now living way off down here in the middle of nothing and the castle isn't a damn sight far off either. That story he gave explaining why he packed up and moved didn't make a whit of sense. The man was making thousands in the north with his poppies and cheap labor. Why would he suddenly give it up and come here unless he had a bloody ulterior motive?"

There was a furtive knocking at the door. Spock went over and hurled it open. An ancient shriveled swaybacked black man barely more than three feet tall stood in the doorway. He wore a shiny shark-skin suit, a wide-brimmed hat, and carried a black vinyl bag. There was a stethoscope hanging from his neck. The doctor? A pygmy? The little man scurried past Spock into the room, crossed to the bed, and pointed at Schwerner's wounded leg.

Reluctantly Schwerner rolled up his pants. The doctor leaned forward and examined the foot and leg without actually touching the swollen flesh. He clicked his tongue in apparent sympathy, stepped back, reached down into his little black bag, and extracted a hypodermic syringe.

"Now wait a minute," said Spock, hurrying over. "What have you got there? What's the bloody idea?"

The doctor glanced up at Spock impassively, winked an eye, and went back to preparing the syringe. Apparently he did not speak or understand English. Spock let loose a torrent of syllables in another language—Swahili most likely—but the doctor failed to respond to that either. He filled the glass syringe with a pale fluid.

"I'm sure it's probably just a simple painkiller," said Schwerner hopefully. "It must be safe."

Spock grunted. "Well, it's your bloody leg," he said, turning on a heel and storming from the room.

Schwerner was not terribly sorry to see him go. The pain in his leg was simply intolerable. He didn't care if this pygmy doctor was a crackpot lunatic who ended up killing him. At least that would put an end to his suffering.

Still silent the doctor bent over and jabbed the needle into the meaty part of Schwerner's calf. There little or no pain as it went in. Schwerner found himself losing consciousness almost at once. The doctor's tiny wrinkled face bobbed in front of his eyes. Then there was darkness.

Later, when he woke, it was to a steady pounding on the door.

2

It was late by the time Alfie Jarrett and John Hartford Hennesey returned to the replica of old San Francisco after visiting the underground project site and Tess Hennesey was nowhere in sight. Calling his daughter's name in an oddly singsong voice Hennesey limped up the front walk leaning on his cane for support and entered the two-story pink gingerbread Victorian house. Alfie followed a short distance behind. The furnishings of the house put him even more in mind of a museum with their softly cushioned chairs, garishly shaded lamps, and thick patterned carpets. A huge, rectangular, apparently genuine oak table took up the entire center of the living room floor. Hennesey wandered past all this and into the back kitchen where another, much smaller table partially surrounded by three chairs occupied a corner of the room beside the far wall. In another corner sat a potbellied black stove held upright by four ornately shaped iron legs. Alfie crossed over and looked at the stove while Hennesey went to the table and picked up a sheet of paper. He held the paper close to his face, frowned, and tugged at his big moustache.

"The stove only burns wood," he said, glancing at Alfie. "I prefer to avoid using electricity whenever possible. It's a question of authenticity."

"Where do you get the wood?" Alfie asked politely. "Not from around here, I guess."

"I usually buy it from the good citizens of Berkeley but the last time I sent Henry over there the superstitious fools refused to sell any. They're afraid of me, you know—afraid of science and progress—afraid of the future. All the people with brains moved out of this area after the slugs destroyed the old city and the ones left aren't much better than savages themselves. Worse in many ways. I had to drive down the peninsula and find my own wood to chop."

"That sounds like a lot of trouble to go through."

"Not if you like your food cooked properly—and an electric stove isn't doing it properly." He glanced at the sheet of paper again. "Speaking of which I'm sorry to say this appear to be a note from Tess. It seems she—ah—she decided to go to bed and apparently— ah—neglected to prepare us anything to eat." He balanced precariously on his good right leg. "I guess we should try and whip together something ourselves." He looked at the stove but did not seem especially eager to begin.

Alfie shook his head quickly. "No, don't worry about it, sir. I wasn't all that hungry to start with." He was finding himself strangely in sympathy with the old man. Apparently Hennesey was rich and powerful enough to control most facets of his existence except for the stubbornness of superstitious fools and the whims of his own daughter.

"As you wish, young fellow," Hennesey said making no attempt to disguise his relief. It was clear he wasn't much in the habit of whipping together his own meals. He wadded up the note and put it away in a pocket of his frock coat. "If you'll follow me I'll show you to your room."

They proceeded upstairs. Hennesey went first, clutching his cane tightly in his left hand and holding a flickering candle in a brass holder with his right. Alfie wondered how it was possible for somebody who was so full of enthusiasm for the future to be at the same time so totally wrapped up in the past. He guessed it was just the present—the time he happened to be living in right now—that Hennesey didn't much care for.

Alfie's room was clean, spacious, and comfortable looking. A canopied bed occupied the side of the room nearest the double windows. Hennesey drew back the fringed purple curtains that surrounded the bed and pointed with pride. "These pillows are made from genuine goose down and the lovely quilt was stitched together by my daughter Susannah strictly by hand."

On the wall above the head of the bed hung an oil portrait of a sharp-nosed sallow-faced smooth-cheeked man dressed in a funny-looking jacket.

Hennesey noticed Alfie looking at the painting.

"That's the great John Randolph of Roanoke," he said, "Statesman, horseman, philosopher, and duelist. One of the great men of American history in my opinion. 'I love liberty and hate equality,' Randolph said. Words worth repeating today."

"I thought I recognized him," Alfie lied. He'd actually thought it was Washington or Franklin, one of those other old presidents they used to put on paper money. "He was a wonderful guy all right."

Hennesey nodded. "It is our misfortune that the lessons Randolph taught were far too long ignored. He held that the government ought to serve the ends of its citizens and not the other way around."

"That's exactly what I believe too," Alfie said. It was late and he was tired and another dumb argument with Hennesey was the last thing he needed. Besides he wasn't entirely sure he knew what the old man was talking about.

Hennesey smiled. "I could tell just looking at you, son, that's how you'd feel. I don't believe I've told you yet how pleased I am to have a man of your quality here assisting me."

"It's kind of you to say that, sir," Alfie said, touched in spite of himself.

Hennesey slapped him suddenly on the shoulders. "By God, boy, you and I are going to have us a hell of a trip to Centauri, aren't we?"

The smile left Alfie's face. He swallowed hard. "I'm definitely looking forward to it, sir."

Hennesey seemed reluctant to leave. The candle splashed light on his face, revealing a myriad of tiny wrinkles and creases that showed his real age. "I was wondering about another thing, Alfie, wondering if you might mind answering a quick question for me. It's kind of a personal matter and I hate to intrude."

"No, sir, go right ahead." Alfie sat down on the bed. The mattress was soft and inviting. He stifled a yawn. "Is it about me, sir?"

"Well, no. It's more about me—about Tess actually. You're obviously a man of the contemporary world and I sometimes worry that I can't say the same for myself. I've spent too many years cooped up in the compound here, too many years wrapped up in my project to the exclusion of anything else. Why do you think Tess acted so…so impetuously tonight?"

Alfie pretended to consider the question.

"I don't know, sir. I guess she just got her feelings hurt. When you wouldn't let her go with us to the project site. I think she wanted to tag along."

Hennesey seemed puzzled. "But why would she want to do that? She's been out there often enough before. She's seen the *Lazarus* grow from dream to reality. She's even helped me now and then in her own little fashion. She went to pick you up in Nuevo Sacramento for instance. She knows how much I hate leaving the compound. It saved me a lot of time and bother to boot."

Alfie spread his arms. "Well, women are different than us, sir. That's one thing I have learned. They like to feel they belong, that they're part of our world too even when they're not."

"You seem to believe that men and women are inherently different."

"I suppose I do. I mean they better be, right?"

"But if men and women are different—and we definitely agree there—then it follows that one has to be superior to the other. Correct?"

Alfie sighed. In spite of himself here he was in the middle of another of Hennesey's philosophical arguments. "I suppose that's the way it has to work, yes, sir."

"Then which is the superior? Men or women?"

He knew the answer Hennesey wanted. "I guess it'd have to be us, sir."

"Tess wouldn't agree."

"Well...everybody has a right to their own opinion, I suppose."

Hennesey stared at him. His eyes narrowed. Then suddenly he reached out and slapped Alfie on the back again. "Damn it, son, I don't think I could have put it better myself. You have the makings of a born diplomat."

"I do?"

"Damn straight you do."

With that Hennessey shuffled across to the door, threw it open, and went out, balancing on his cane.

To his surprise Alfie noted it was now Hennesey's right leg that he was favoring.

* * * *

Alone at last, Alfie sprang to his feet, undressed quickly, tucked his shiv out of sight under one of the big fluffy pillows, then blew out the candle, hopped into bed, pulled the curtains shut, and slipped between the covers. As he lay on his back waiting for dreams to come and whisk him away Alfie pondered the subject of Hennesey and his starship project and what connection it might have with the case at hand. Clearly Hennesey was not himself one of the Sect conspirators. He was eccentric and perhaps a little touched in the head but there wasn't an evil bone in his body. As for Tess she didn't seem a likely suspect either. She was about as devious as a Mexican fighting bull even if the comparison didn't quite make sense. And there was nobody else here except the two of them and a lot of robots. So why was here? Alfie pondered the question, then gave a mental shrug and turned on his side. He wasn't going to let it throw him. He'd gone through cases like this before and invariably enlightenment arrived. Like one of Peter's omnipotent gods Desmond Blue sometimes chose to weave his miracles from mysterious threads but somehow they always seemed to make a perfect fit in the end.

* * * *

The patter of bare feet jerked Alfie into sudden wakefulness. At first he had trouble remembering where he was. The whole thing— the darkness, the bed, the sound of gentle footsteps—reminded him too much of that nutty dream he'd had his last night at home. And there was a pervasive odor in the air now too—heavy and musk-like.

But this was San Francisco. It all came back to him now. And it wasn't a dream. There was somebody else in the room with him— somebody very real.

Careful not to make a sound Alfie slipped a hand under the pillow next to him and grabbed hold of his shiv. He gave the knife a quick flick of the wrist and felt the blade slide into place. The curtains were drawn around the bed on three sides. He turned himself slowly so that he was facing the open end, knife in hand. Then he waited for the intruder—whoever and whatever he was—to make the next move.

He could hear soft footsteps drawing closer now. He tensed, waiting. Suddenly the shape of a pale hand appeared overhead. It moved toward him—closer.

That was when he pounced.

The momentum of his leap carried him past the curtains and into the room beyond. His arms closed around something—someone—soft and pliant. Something in the touch, the feel—something unexpected yet familiar—made him blunt the thrust of his knife. The blade passed harmlessly through empty air. At the last moment he'd recognized the heavy musky odor. It was Tess. Tess Hennesey. Tess sneaking into his room.

"*Oof!*" she cried from underneath him. "What are you trying to do? Kill me?"

Alfie rolled aside and quickly tossed the knife under the bed as he did. "Gosh, I'm sorry, Tess. I didn't—what are you doing in my room anyhow?"

She picked herself up off the floor, looked at him standing in front of her in all his nakedness, and laughed. "Damn, I guess I must have startled you."

"I guess you did," he said.

"Do you always sleep like that? Without a stitch on?"

"Yes, I do. What of it?"

"Nothing except that it tends to get rather chilly at night in San Francisco."

"I hadn't noticed. I was asleep." He was rummaging around now, trying to remember where he'd put the candle. When he found it, there were also matches in the bowl underneath.

In the candlelight he suddenly noticed something he ought to have been aware of before. From touch alone.

Tess was as naked as he was.

"My God," he said.

"Why, thank you." She bowed her head, stepped past him, and jumped into bed. She pulled the bedcovers up to her chin. "Care to join me? I told you it could get rather chilly around here at night."

He didn't need any further invitation.

Once they were both tucked snugly in bed together she rolled over on her side facing him. "I really am sorry. Father always says I'm much too impetuous for my own good. When I saw you drive up—saw you from the window—I decided I couldn't wait any longer."

"Wait for what?' he said.

"What do you think? There's nothing wrong with me, is there? If you want another look I can always oblige."

She started to pull the bedcovers down but he caught hold of her hand before she could. There was certainly nothing wrong with her. That much was plain. If anything she was even more beautiful than he might have expected.

But he was here on a case. Undercover. Desmond would be sorely distressed if he allowed himself to be distracted and messed everything up so soon.

"What if your father walked in on us right now? He might get the wrong idea, you know."

"I doubt that."

"So do I. And that's the problem. I came here to work, to do a job for your father, not to—"

"Not to dally in the valley?"

"Something like that, yes," he said.

She sighed. "Somebody told you about Mr. Flanagan, didn't they? Who was it? Reynal? That darn robot. He's so protective of father it turns my stomach."

Hennessey had mentioned Reynal earlier. His chief project engineer. And a robot.

"Who's this Flanagan? I don't think I've heard of him before."

She had a distant look on her face. "Mr. Flanagan was Father's previous assistant. The one before you. Father fired him."

"Why?"

"Why do you think?" She laughed. "He slept in this room too."

"Okay, that does it," he said, sliding out of bed now. He grabbed the candle and held it up. "You're going to have to get out of here. I'm sorry, Tess, but I can't jeopardize my job even if you are the most gorgeous woman I've ever seen in my life."

She was glaring at him. Angrily. "I really wish you wouldn't call me that."

"Call you what?"

"Tess. It's not my name, you know."

Then it hit him. In the dim candlelight he'd missed it before. She wasn't the same woman. She was close—as close as sisters could be—almost as close as identical twins—but she wasn't the same.

"Then who the hell are you?" he said.

"I'm Susannah of course. Susannah Hennesey. I live here. Tess doesn't. Tess lives down in that horrible Hollywood with all her stupid snooty friends."

"But it was Tess who came and picked me up in Nuevo Sacramento, right?"

She seemed to be pouting again. "I suppose. Who can keep up with her? She gone now though. She left hours ago."

While he was out at the project site with Hennesey apparently. As for Susannah now that he thought about it there had been a mention of someone with that name earlier. "Your father said you'd been ill."

"I was. I am. Reynal says I suffer from obsessive-compulsive narcissistic personality disorder. He says it's quite incurable."

"Sounds to me like this Reynal's on the right track."

"He has to be. He's a robot. He's supposed to be smart."

"And you're Tess's sister? Her twin?"

"Bingo," she said. "Now that hat's settled will you please get back into bed and copulate with me. Don't worry about Father barging in. I slipped a little pill into his bedtime hot chocolate. You're safe. After Mr. Flanagan I learned to be careful."

Alfie put down the candle and looked at the girl in the bed. Christ, he thought, but this was tempting. He wished he was Desmond Blue or Peter Mark or some other saintly celibate who could say to hell with his natural biological urges and pretend the whole thing didn't exist. "I still don't think it would be a good idea."

Her face fell. "You don't like me? I'm not Tess and you think I'm ugly?"

"No." He shook his head quickly. "That's not it at all. It's just..." That was the problem. He couldn't think of any way of explaining that would make sense to her without revealing too much.

"Are you gay? Homosexual? Reynal said that was always a possibility. If you are I could try to help change you." She giggled. "At least for tonight anyway."

Alfie considered the possibility of telling her he was. But that was too easy—and also risky. Too many things could happen to indicate otherwise.

"I'm like you," he said. "I'm ill—sick. I have an affliction. Something that might harm you if we—if we copulated."

"What?" she said, nearly sliding all the way out from the covers in her eagerness. "Tell me. Is it something horrible?"

"Dropsy," he said. "I have dropsy. It's not only catching but it can kill you. It's in my—my testicles."

"They look fine to me,' she said, staring at him. "A little saggy maybe but if I remember right from Mr. Flanagan that soon goes away."

He resisted the impulse to cover himself up. That would be ridiculous. But what else could he do? He didn't dare hop back into bed with her. That would be dangerous, dropsy or no dropsy.

He went over, sat down in a chair, and crossed his legs. "It's on the inside," he said, "where you can't see it. But it comes spurting out with—well, you get the picture, right? I just wouldn't want to cause you any harm. And you just got over whatever it was you had before so it would be doubly dangerous for you right now."

"Mumps," she said.

"What?"

"That's why I was sick. Mumps. Father says it's going around again. It's pretty awful. You can barely even swallow."

"Dropsy's even worse though. It's so bad I can't even explain half of what it does to you. It's that horrible."

"Reynal could cure it, I bet." She sat up then, revealing her breasts. "He cured my mumps and he can cure your dropsy. That's what we'll do. First thing in the morning he can examine you and I bet by the time it's dark again tomorrow night you'll be totally cured and ready to copulate."

Alfie was stunned. That was the last thing he needed. To be examined by a robot quack. "I've already been to a doctor and he said the best treatment is to do nothing and it'll pass on its own."

"When?"

"When what?"

"When will it pass?"

"Ten days. It's a ten day disease. Like a kind of flu."

"How long has it been already?"

He did some quick calculating, trying to determine what he could get away with. "Only one day," he said.

"You mean you just caught it?"

"Since the symptoms began to show. Right before I left to come here. That's why I've got nine days to go yet."

There was more. Susannah Hennessey like her father was never at a loss for words.

But finally he managed to get her out the door—standing cautiously aside with his eyes averted as she swept past.

He blew out the candle, got back into bed, and hoped he could get calmed down enough to manage to fall back asleep.

* * * *

Apparently, he did fall asleep. There was the barest fragment of a faint dream-like image but it so nearly resembled recent reality that he couldn't be sure exactly what was producing it, his conscious or subconscious, fantasy, reality or dream.

Then someone was rapping softly at the door.

Alfie opened his eyes, rolled over and groaned.

The knocking came again, more insistent this time. He had no choice. He got up, crossed over, and hurled open the door.

Susannah Hennesey stood in the hall wearing a flimsy thigh-length nightgown that looked as if it had been stitched together out of bits and pieces of wind. "Do you always receive visitors dressed so formally?" she asked, looking down at his nakedness.

Alfie jumped back automatically, then stopped himself. "Look, what is it this time?"

She wrinkled her nose. "Nothing in particular. I felt jumpy and couldn't sleep. I wondered if you might be having the same problem.

And what do you mean this time?"

He looked at her more carefully. Christ, there it was again—that minute, almost indiscernible difference. "You're Tess," he said, moving back out of the way and letting her enter.

"Who else could I be?" She swept past him, went straight for the bed, stopped long enough to light the candle, and then sat down on the edge of the mattress, throwing one long bare leg on top of the other. Too tired to feel especially self-conscious anymore Alfie came over and sat beside her.

"I thought you were your sister again," he said.

She stared at him. "My what?"

"Your sister. Susannah."

"Oh, her." She smiled. "Susannah isn't really my sister."

"Well, she certainly looks a lot like you."

"Of course she does. She's supposed to. Father had her built that way on purpose—with malice aforethought, so to speak. Susannah's the good obedient faithful daughter I've never quite managed to be."

"Did you just say 'built'?"

She nodded. "Last summer. Reynal did a hell of a job, didn't he?"

"Then Susannah's a...she's a robot?"

"Why? Couldn't you tell?"

"Well, I...I..."

She patted his knee sympathetically. "Don't feel silly about it. I'm sure I'd make the same mistake if I wasn't already living inside my own skin. Imagine the shock I felt the first time I set eyes on her. Happily, personality-wise, the two of us are as different as pigs and possums."

"Your father said you'd gone back to Hollywood. Susannah said it too."

"Father was just trying to save face. I told him in my note what he could do with the pathetic snack he wanted me to whip up. As for Susannah she's an inveterate liar. Reynal programmed her that way deliberately. I think he wanted to make her more realistic."

"She knows she's a robot then?"

Tess put on a thoughtful look. "You know, that's a good question. I suppose somewhere deep inside she has to but since she's been programmed not to let on, well...who can say? Just, for God's sake, don't say anything like that to her. She might have another of her breakdowns. The imbecile Father had here before you did something like that and it's taken weeks to get her functioning again." She looked at him quizzically. "What did Susannah want with you anyhow? I hope you weren't dressed like you are now when she showed up. That was another problem she had with that moron Flanagan."

Alfie decided it was best to keep the details of Susannah's visit private—at least for the time being. "She just wanted to say hello was all."

She smiled to let him know she knew there was more to it than that. "Now aren't you going to ask me why I'm here?"

"You said you couldn't sleep."

"True. And you're awake now too."

"I am, yes."

"Perfect."

She reached behind her back, pulled on something, and a moment later the nightgown fell into her lap. She stood up, wriggled her hips, and let the gown drop to her feet. She stepped away then and stood naked in front of him. "So which do you prefer? Me or Susannah? Woman or robot?"

There was no need to think that one over.

"That's what I thought," she said, looking down at his lap.

After that Alfie let Tess Hennesey use him as she willed.

A PROFILE: ALFIE JARRETT

So what still remains to be narrated from the life and times of Alfie Jarrett that has not previously been related at length whether in the form of verse, tale, song, story, ballad or play?

The mystery of his name perhaps: how exactly did he come to acquire it?

Well, Zeke Jones and Bess Smyth gave him the name. Either the first or last came from an old movie Zeke remembered seeing on television when he was a boy and the other—first or last—because Bess thought it had a lovely bell-like tinkling sound to it. In later years in prison neither could specifically recollect which part derived from which source and Alfie himself professed not much to care. According to him a name was a name was a name. If Zeke and Bess had chosen to call him Rose, well, in that case, yes, then he might have been curious to find out more but as it was, since he was only an Alfie and not a Rose, other problems took precedence. For example, how to make the rare Patagonian Blue Cactus flourish in the blistering heat of the Sahara Desert.

So then what about this famous healing power he once possessed? Was it genuine or just a myth?

Answer: Absolutely, totally genuine. Alfie encountered men and women perched upon death's precipice and bestowed upon them renewed life.

Question: Then why wasn't that talent exploited to its fullest extent in terms of money, fame, power?

Answer: Because both Zeke and Bess were already wanted by the law on previous murder charges and didn't dare show their faces publicly.

Question: So what happened that day when Alfie first encountered Desmond Blue and his psychic powers up and disappeared?

Answer: Nothing happened, for his psychic powers did not vanish. They're still there inside him—strong as ever.

Question: Then could he use them whenever he wanted?

Answer: Damn right he could. If confronted with a real need, yes, he could heal the sick and dying same as always.

Q: And what was his need before?

A: The need to survive: had Alfie ever ceased healing, Zeke and Bass would no doubt have killed him too.

Q: Then will Alfie ever use his powers again?

A: More than likely, yes, though not for a long time and not in this story.

Q: What about his love life?

A: At the time he entered the employ of Desmond Blue Alfie Jarrett was a virgin in all matters sexual. Shortly after their first encounter during the course of an exhaustive interview conducted while winging across the broad Atlantic, Blue first learned of this and upon arriving in Tangier immediately conducted Alfie to the city's most notorious brothel. "I want you to get all that out of your system right now, Alfie," Blue told him. "Because once we reach Arabia Deserta and set to work there won't be time for such ephemeral activities."

While Blue sipped beer in the downstairs parlor listening to the boogie-woogie piano player pound out a robust beat, Alfie proceeded to have sex with six different women at least twice each during a four-hour span.

His stamina, an informant later confided to Blue, was awesome but his technique lacked imagination. This was satisfactory to Blue who maintained that imagination belonged more properly to the spiritual rather than the carnal sphere. It should be kept in mind, however, that Blue himself was by then a devout celibate.

Afterward between cases Alfie would often visit at his own expense brothels as far removed from Arabia Deserta as Bangkok, Boston, Buenos Aires, and Brisbane. Whenever he returned after one of these forays he would invariably describe to his chosen confident Crystal LaFleur exactly what had transpired in explicit detail. (Crystal who'd heard it all before many times concentrated on the cards in her hand and scooped up another pot.)

Q: But that's his sex life not his love life.

A: The one woman Alfie Jarrett ever loved was the aforementioned Crystal who of course barely cared enough for him to offer him the time of day. Platonically speaking, Alfie loved Blue and Peter and even in odd ways Schwerner. But none of that counts.

Q: It's not very romantic either.

A: No, it's not. But what about this then?

Q: What about what?

A: Once upon a time in a year not far removed from today Desmond Blue sent Alfie Jarrett to the town of Gonzaga, a lawless frontier settlement in Western Australia, where a gang of brutal thugs held sway terrorizing the honest citizenry. This was only a short time before Blue's (temporary) retirement from active detective practice and since he was already sick to death of gangs of brutal thugs he allowed Alfie to pursue the case completely on his own. (Blue later conceded this to be among the more serious errors of his career.)

Alfie strolled into Gonzaga one sweltering afternoon and stopped the first thuggish looking person he saw—a seven-foot aborigine with a bone through his pierced septum—and asked who was running things hereabouts.

"That'd be Queenie," said the aborigine. "You want her try the Holy Bitch Saloon. But watch out. Queenie's in a foul mood today."

"Why? What happened?"

"Nothing happened, brother. Queenie's always in a foul mood."

The Holy Bitch Saloon when Alife stepped inside was packed to the rafters with heaving, sweating, stinking human flesh.

Alfie sprang deftly to a tabletop, kicked four glasses of beer on the floor, and announced in a voice that quaked like thunder (or so he hoped): "I'm looking for the woman who calls herself Queenie."

"Well, you've found her," said a mild voice to the left of his right boot heel.

Alfie looked down, blinked, looked again, and fell madly in love on the spot. The Holy Bitch Saloon was a true hellhole. The lighting was lousy. Alfie was dead beat exhausted after an overland mule ride from the coast. Nevertheless, it happened that way, all in a sharp infinitesimal micromoment. Love at first sight—the purest of forms.

Queenie O'Rourke was maybe nineteen years old, tiny as a will-o'-the-wisp, with ratty brown hair trimmed close to her scalp, and cruel black eyes like bottomless lagoons.

Queenie took one quick look at Alfie Jarrett and fell instantly in love with him too.

Immediately, they retired to her room in the back and for two weeks never emerged.

During that time—in between bouts of physical lovemaking sufficiently repetitious to be passed over quickly—Alfie spoke more words than he'd ever uttered at one time in his life. He told Queenie everything. About Zeke and Bess and the old Pontiac they drove. About healing people who were dying. About Desmond Blue and Crystal LaFleur, Peter and Schwerner and all the rest. He even told her about the time he'd killed two men with the stub of a wooden toothpick.

He told Queenie he'd come to Gonzaga to put her and her saloon out of business for good.

When it was over, when the two weeks were up and he'd told her everything there was to tell, she crawled out of bed, slipped back into the ratty gown she always wore, and said, "So what are you planning to do now?"

"You won't come away with me?"

"Nope. I like it here."

"But I thought you loved me."

"Oh, I do. But what's that got to do with anything?"

"I guess I'm going to have to take you then," he said.

"You can try."

They both reached for their weapons at the same time. Queenie carried a two-shot derringer tucked in her gown. Plus she was fast—blazing fast.

Her first shot nicked his cheek, drew blood.

She never got off the second.

The blade of his shiv pierced her throat as cleanly as cutting cheese.

Alfie stepped over the body, unlocked the door, and went out. He told the people waiting in the saloon below that they all had one hour to get out of town and never be seen in these parts ever again.

"What does Queenie have to say about that?" said one of those at the front of the crowd.

"Why don't you go in and ask her?" Alfie said, stepping aside.

When Alfie got back to Arabia Deserta Desmond Blue could see in his face right away that something momentous had happened while he was away.

They went upstairs to the study.

"Well," said Blue, "is she dead or isn't she?"

Alfie nodded. "I had to kill her."

"I was afraid that would happen."

And Alfie (who also must have known it would happen, perhaps had known instinctively since that first moment he saw her, felt death in the air alongside love, felt them mingled and fused, and then went right ahead and did it anyway, loved her anyway, knowing that nothing would come of it but death, Alfie broke down and wept like a baby.)

Blue let him finish then came over and embraced him. "Now you know not only what it's like to love but more importantly what it's like to be loved in return."

"It hurts like son of a bitch," said Alfie.

"That it does," said Blue, hugging him. "That it does."

3

April, observed the poet, is the cruelest of months but, thought Peter Mark, the poet must not ever have set foot in Winesap Illinois, for how could April possibly be regarded as cruel when the sky beamed as bright and cheery as the smile on the face of a pigtailed girl at her fifth birthday party, when a breeze as sweet and fluffy as cotton candy blew night and day, when the sun radiated benevolence like hot toast on a Saturday morning? In Winesap April was as kind and loving as the widow next door who served milk and home-baked cookies when you were nine years old and went tapping shyly at her door on lazy summer afternoons.

Today, Sunday, was Peter's fourth day in Winesap and he stood outside the Fire House catching a breath of air and luxuriating in the feel of the sun on his face and the wind in his eyes.

It was another marvelous day—another absolutely perfect day—and in spite of the continued revulsion he felt at the thought of burning books he had so far discovered nothing else even remotely unpleasant about the town of Winesap or its denizens. And he had kept fairly busy too, engaging in gin rummy games with the men at the Fire House, strumming his new Gibson guitar—a gift from Fire Captain Brady when Peter mentioned in passing that he liked to play—reading from his hidden store of books (though cautiously) and even going so far one evening to join Oscar and Jayne Stovall in the living room for an hour's worth of tridee viewing. (The experience had proven too intense for sensitive Peter with cowboys and Indians rampaging bare inches from the tip of his steel nose but he saw no obvious harm in it; for others it might well be great fun.)

He had also met and tried to get to know Ginger Cunningham, the skinny freckle-faced twelve-year-old who was also staying with the Stovalls. Ginger seemed rather odd. She didn't attend school or have any friends among the other children in town nor did she appear to be related to either Oscar or Jayne. Peter had been unable in fact to determine who she was or where she was from or even why she was here. When he tried to question her she either ignored him completely or else answered in uncommunicative grunts and nods. The afternoon before when he caught her on the front porch smoking a cigarette out in the open where anyone could see and took the deadly weed away from her she called him a stupid tinhead who ought to go back to the land of Oz where he belonged. Peter thought that was a strange thing to say—especially when he remembered that Ginger never seemed to watch tridee—but when he asked if she'd ever read the original book *The Wonderful Wizard of Oz* by L. Frank Baum she just looked at him blankly and said "What's a book?" But whether Ginger Cunningham was a secret reader or not hardly seemed likely to explain why Desmond Blue had sent Peter here to Winesap in search of the Conspiracy of the Sect. He was still totally in the dark there.

Just as he was about to turn and go back into the Fire House to rejoin the gin rummy game a hissing noise sounded from close by. Peter stopped and listened and the sound came again.

"*Psst.* Hey, you. Over here."

Peter looked around. A tall hedge stood off to his left. Peering over it he discovered a round-faced man with a crew cut and thick glasses crouched on the ground on the other side. "Is it safe?" the man hissed, glancing up at Peter. "Are you alone?"

Peter looked over his shoulder. "I am but—"

"Then you'd better get down here with me. Quick. Somebody might see us from the street."

"Who are you? What do you want?"

"I'm a friend. Please. We have to talk." Feeling more than slightly ridiculous Peter climbed over the hedge and crouched down beside the man.

"I'm Roy Goldman. You're Peter Mark, right?"

He nodded.

"I would have come sooner," said Goldman, "but I had to be sure I wasn't being watched."

"Watched? Who by?"

Goldman chuckled grimly. "In this town it could be darn near anybody. Fire Captain Brady, Evers, Bob Jones, Oscar in particular. He's crazy, you know—too much tridee destroyed his mind years ago. He hates me anyhow because of Jayne. She and I were childhood sweethearts. And Lucius B. Washington of course. Our dearly beloved mayor would love to hang me."

Peter was perplexed. "Have you done something wrong?"

"You bet I have—I'm a writer."

"And you live here? In Winesap?"

Goldman smiled weakly. "I know it must be difficult to understand but I grew up here and I'm old enough to remember what it was like before the Mayor showed up and all this insanity started. I moved away to Chicago for a while but last year after I got married I decided I wanted to come back and wrote and told the Mayor straight out that I was on my way and he and his henchmen weren't driving me away this time. So far as you can see I'm still here."

"But what do you want with me?"

"I want to help." Goldman squeezed Peter's arm excitedly. "I want to help you break your case."

Peter felt a chill. He glanced back over the top of the hedge to be sure no one was listening. "Case? What case?"

"You work for Desmond Blue, don't you?"

Peter considered telling a lie but it was always painful for him and he was not very good at it. "I do, yes."

"I knew it." He laughed. "Heck, there can't be that many people with a steel faces and steel hands. As soon as Jayne told me about you I figured it had to be the same fellow."

"How do you know about me?"

"From Mr. Blue—Desmond Blue. He told me about you in a letter a long time back when you first went to work for him. He and I have been engaged in correspondence for many years."

"You know Desmond?"

"I'll say I do. He was the one more than anyone else who first encouraged me to start writing. Now he's one of my biggest fans. The last time he was here in Winesap he showed up dressed in a funny disguise like a Chinese peasant. But I recognized him immediately. He and I sat around and talked until dawn one night. About books and literary things mostly—we always argue about Edgar Allan Poe—but I also told him about a little scheme I came up with to blow this town wide open. He knows all about what's going on in Winesap. He first came here another case years before."

Peter shook his head. "That must have been before I went to work for him."

"The Case of the Berryman Ghosts, he called it. A big old abandoned house up in the hills. A haunted house, some say. People kept disappearing mysteriously. Blue got hired to get rid of the ghosts and I guess he must have. Right after that I left town and started pounding a typewriter. Who is it this time? Who's your chief suspect? Fire Captain Brady, I bet. Is that why you're working undercover as a fireman? Jeez, I hate that old hypocrite."

"Do you have reason to suspect him?"

"Sure. He's the type, isn't he? Power mad. A born killer."

"Killer?" said Peter, confused again.

"This isn't a murder case? I didn't think Blue would bother with anything less. What is it then? A jewel robbery or something? A heist?"

"Well, not exactly, no." Peter saw no reason to reveal too much to this man he hardly knew.

"But look," Goldman said, "we really shouldn't talk here. Not out here in the open like this. I'll tell you what. My address is 451

Spruce Street. That's three blocks east and two north from the Stovall place. You can't miss it. A blue stucco house. It used to be white but so is every other house on the block so I painted mine blue out of spite. The houses on both sides of me are vacant. Nobody wants to live next door to a writer." He laughed. "They're all scared to death there's going to be a big fire someday. But I'm careful. I've got hiding places so secret you wouldn't believe me if I told you."

"Well, I don't know," Peter said. "I have to be careful too."

"Oh, sure, I understand. But you know you can trust me." He put a pudgy finger to his lips. "I won't breathe a word. Heck, I haven't even told Jayne and you know how close we are."

"Uh, no," said Peter. "How close?"

Goldman winked. "Real close. As close as two—"

"Well, howdy there, Roy. Fancy meeting a fellow like you in a place like this."

Peter looked up at the man leaning over the hedge watching them. It was Hiram Evers, one of the regular firemen. "Hunting for fishing worms, are you?"

"Not exactly," said Roy Goldman. He came to his feet and brushed the dirt off his pants. "I was taking a shortcut through here and some coins dropped out of my pocket. This man was helping me look for them."

"Coins?" said Evers. "Money? Hell, I never knew they gave money to people like you who don't work for a living."

Goldman flared angrily. "I make more money in a month than you'll make in a lifetime, Evers."

"At least I earn mine honestly, not by making up a bunch of shit-faced lies and fobbing them off on people too stupid to know better."

"There's no law against writing books, is there?"

"Nope, but in the opinion of a lot of decent folks in this town—including me—there damn well ought to be."

"You don't make the laws, Evers."

"But I keep them."

Goldman was beginning to look less sure of himself. "Well, so do I and I haven't—"

"All I know is the last time we answered an alarm at your place we found seven hardcover books hidden inside your underwear drawer. You ask me, there's plenty more hidden where those came from. We'll be back for them someday too. You can count on that."

Roy Goldman stepped back, his mouth open as if he intended to say something in response, but instead he turned and raced off, breaking into a dead run.

Hiram Evers bent over and slapped his knees. "Can you beat that, pal? Old Roy's as yellow as the rose of Texas."

Peter hands were shaking. "I don't think you had to be that rough on him. He didn't mean any harm."

"Maybe not but Roy's still the biggest yo-yo in town. He didn't give you that baloney about him being a writer, did he?"

"He may have mentioned something like that."

"Well, it's a line of bull. He's got an old typewriter he bangs away at all day instead of holding down a real job the way he should. But the stories he writes—crazy stuff." Evers made a sour face. "Crap about elves and witches and goblins and demons. Fairy tales. It's enough to make a grown man puke."

"But some of it's been published, right? That what he said anyhow. You haven't read any of them have you?"

"Hell, no," said Evers with disgust. "I'm a law-abiding man. Got article seventeen stitched on the seat of my long johns."

"He seemed harmless enough to me."

"Maybe so." Evers held up a fist. "If he is though it's because the rest of us keep him that way. Come on, let's go back inside. There's still a card game to play."

* * * *

That night on their way home Oscar Stovall seemed unusually animated. His eyes burned with a peculiar ardor and he kept humming broken snatches of the same hypnotic tune over and over. Peter was reminded of the way Stovall had looked and acted that first night when he found the book in Peter's suitcase. But he could see no reason for him to be acting that way now.

As they passed by the living room Peter looked in and saw Jayne Stovall dressed in a terry cloth robe lying on the floor on her back as the huge translucent tridee images flowed over and around her. Involuntarily he stopped and stared at the four-foot high face of an incredibly beautiful woman with platinum blonde hair, bright red lips, and a tiny star-shaped tattoo on her left breast. he response he felt looking at her was intellectual not physical; there was no stirring in his loins as he'd experienced with Laurel Brady. The woman's huge face broke into a sudden smile and Peter heard merry tinkling laughter. The gesture only made her seem even more beautiful. Peter watched for a long moment and then somewhat reluctantly moved on.

Dinner waited in the kitchen on aluminum trays. Stovall sat down across the table from Peter and began shoveling food into his mouth at a rapid clip. It was the first time either of the Stovalls had joined Peter for a meal and he was surprised. "Aren't you going to watch tridee tonight?" he asked.

Stovall shook his head in short nervous jerks. "Nope—and you better not either." His voice was hushed, barely more than a whisper. "We've got to stay rested up—for later tonight."

"What about later tonight?"

"Just make sure you sleep with one eye open is all I'm saying." He chuckled softly. "Cap Brady gave me a hint on the sly. There's something brewing—something big. If it's a multiple alarm job he said he'd be calling you and me before anybody else."

"But how could he know about a fire in advance? Is it arson?"

He laughed. "You bet that's what it is. Arson, all right. A little job of book burning." He started humming that hypnotic ditty again.

Peter excused himself and went upstairs.

Passing the living room, he heard a man's voice scream in agony. Two shots rang out and Peter smelled gunpowder. Another cowboy and Indian show, he guessed, or possibly a crime program. He didn't dare look in to see, knowing how addictive tridee images could be.

Up in his room Peter shut the door and picked up his guitar. After a strumming a few tentative chords, he put it down again and lay back in bed, fingering the wooden cross he wore around his neck. As he did his thoughts turned naturally to Pope Sergio in Rome. How much longer did that poor saintly man have to live? he wondered. And after he died, then what? Thanks to Desmond it would be Peter's turn to serve. Yet how could he? Peter knew he wasn't worthy. There were certain facts—unknown to the Pontiff—events from his early life—that made him unfit for any such holy office. I shall refuse the honor, Peter thought. Yet even as he did he knew he couldn't. What if it was fate—destiny—the will of God? How could he dare refuse?

His thoughts drifted back to the moment when he had first come to know God intimately. He sat at the controls of his aeroplane high over the pale blue Mediterranean and then with a twist of the wrist turned and went swerving far out over the tawny desert. At twenty thousand feet the engines died. The plane dropped, spiraling nose first toward the earth below.

When his body was pulled from the flaming wreckage there was barely enough unburned flesh to sustain the illusion of a human being.

Two men hovered over him: one tall, fat, and grim; the other younger, slim, stiff with tension.

"The poor deluded boy," said the fat man. "A suicide, it appears. We can only hope the end came quickly for him."

"Hold on, Desmond." The second man held a knot of charred flesh—what was left of Peter's right arm. "I can feel a pulse."

"Impossible, doctor!"

"No, I'm telling you I feel it. It's weak—damnably weak—but he's alive. We'll need blankets. To keep him warm. He's in shock. It may kill him yet."

"But surely there's no chance—"

"If we move swiftly there is."

"But his body...the burns..."

"There are certain advanced techniques. Surgical grafts. Remember those experiments I conducted last year involving mice. If only he can—"

"This is a man, damn it, Doctor, not a rat!"

"I do think I can save him, Desmond. Don't we have to try?"

And he had. Tried and succeeded. God and Dr. Schwerner working together or perhaps more accurately God working his will through Schwerner.

A month after the crash Peter opened his eyes and saw a thin-lipped man in a white medical jacket peering down at him.

"Welcome back to life, young man," he said gently.

Peter began to cry.

"Don't," said the man. "You'll rust.

* * * *

Now, lying on his back in bed here in Winesap, Peter realized he must have fallen asleep.

He had been having a dream.

Now someone was knocking on the door.

He got up, went over, opened the door a crack. It was the odd little girl who had the room next to his, Ginger Cunningham. She was in her pajamas.

"They want you downstairs," she said.

"Why? What is it?"

"A fire, I think. Oscar said to come and get you."

"There's a fire?"

"I think it's that friend of yours Roy Goldman."

"What makes you think we're friends?"

"I saw the two of you whispering together over at the Fire House today. You looked pretty friendly to me."

"But I didn't—"

"You better go," she said, breaking in. "Oscar goes wild when there's fire. He might run off leave you behind unless you hurry."

4

Petite and slender in sweater and jeans, Meredith Savard leaned forward and examined the painting that dominated the wall in front of her. It was oil on canvas, twelve feet by ten, and from a distance appeared to be nothing more than a sheet of unremitting whiteness. Seen from closer up though, the painting revealed a single wire-thin line of aqua blue running from the upper right corner to the lower left. Spotting the line, Meredith nodded appreciatively and without removing her eyes from the painting said, "I like it, Alice. I definitely do. It's a fun painting, full of joy."

"I'm flattered you'd say that," said the other woman in the room. Older than Meredith—perhaps by twenty years—she had the dignified bearing of someone comfortable in her own shoes. "I've titled it 'Mr. Blue' of course. I've already been offered forty thousand for it but I'm not selling—not yet anyhow."

"Good for you, Alice." Meredith smiled, looking away from the painting at last. "I say that, you realize, as someone who's never sold anything in her life."

"From choice, not talent."

"And because I can afford it." She walked back to where the other woman was standing. "But that's not why you wanted to see me, is it?"

When Meredith Savard had first come to Paris almost twenty years earlier the other woman—Alice Reardon—had been the world's most famous painter. She was still the best known, though only because so few cared about art of any kind anymore. At the time they first met Meredith had regarded Alice as the epitome of intelligence, sensitivity, and natural beauty. They'd slept together several times. Meredith was nineteen, Alice close to forty. But it had never developed into a real affair. Only a fling. Now they saw each other maybe once or twice a year—almost always in public.

"You're not in need money, are you?"

"Actually, I am. But not from you."

"I wouldn't mind." Money was the one thing Meredith had way more of than she'd ever need. Most people thought she was fortunate in that. She was never quite sure herself.

"But I would. I'd mind, that is. And of course I could always sell this painting. Or another. I'm not without resources."

"I know. I remember." She reached down and squeezed her hand.

"You enjoyed yourself then, I hope? When we knew each other before?"

"Oh, yes. I did. Immensely."

"I've often wondered about that." Alice stepped forward now and looked more closely at her own painting. She sighed. "I have a feeling I may not have it in me to do another one like this." She held up her hands, those extraordinarily delicate fingers. "These are still eager but the rest of me isn't. The ideas don't come easily anymore. I have to bang my head to get them going. That's why I wanted to see you."

"I'm afraid I don't understand, Alice."

"This painting—I want you to have it."

"Me?" Meredith failed to conceal her surprise. In their years together—even the early intimate ones—Alice had never given her anything. The nature of their relationship had ruled against it.

"Why not? You're one of my dearest friends, aren't you? Please. Give it to your new protégé if you'd rather."

Meredith smiled thinly. So that was it. Clearly Alice had only just heard. "Ah, then you know?"

"And naturally I'm curious. I understand no one has ever seen the girl before."

"No. This is her first time in Paris."

"And she's attractive, I hear."

"Oh, very."

"And young?"

"Well, yes."

"But can she paint?"

"I think so—yes. She shows considerable promise."

"Lanier tried to tell me you'd found her in a brothel in Africa."

"In Tangier actually." Meredith met the older woman's gaze unflinchingly, "Do you find that…sordid?"

Alice threw back her head and laughed. "Good Lord, no. I'd do it myself but it would mean leaving this house and I prefer not to do that unless I have to."

"I've heard you've become somewhat reclusive."

"That's one way of putting it, yes. I prefer to think I've become more selective in how I use my remaining time."

"You're not really that old."

"Old enough to know better." She laughed. "This girl though—your new love. What name does she use?"

"Lai."

"And the rest of it? Her last name?"

"I don't know if she has one. I've never asked."

"Ah, a woman of mystery. Excellent. I want to meet her. I'm having a small gathering tonight. My first in months. You're welcome as always. But do bring her with you …bring your Lai. That way everyone can meet her and have their curiosity sated."

Meredith looked at the floor, her courage ebbing. "No, I don't think so, Alice."

"Why not? I'll delegate someone to drag you here if I have to."

"I need to go, Alice." Meredith edged toward the door. "It's getting late."

"Until tonight then?" Alice chased after her. "You can collect your painting then too."

Meredith hesitated in the doorway. "We may not be able to stay long."

"I quite understand, dear." She was smiling. "Please stay only as long as you wish."

Outside it was raining—pouring. The rain formed dark puddles in the cobblestone streets. Meredith had not gone far when a figure emerged from under a cafe awning and came sprinting after her.

"You didn't have to follow me," she said when the girl caught up with her.

"I was lonely without you." Lai was blonde and blue-eyed with a round smooth face and soft pale skin. The rain ran down her forehead and into her eyes.

Meredith pulled her close so that the umbrella shielded both of them. "I'm glad you came," she said. "I missed you too."

"Was it as awful as you thought?"

"Actually, no. Alice was quite...polite."

"Then we're going to her party?"

Meredith looked at her sharply. "How do you know about that?"

"Lanier told me."

"What was he doing there? Snooping around when he knew I'd be gone. The bastard."

"I like Lanier. He's funny. He said we should all go. He said we'd show them a thing or two."

"I'm sure we could."

"Then we are going?"

"I suppose. If you really want to."

"I do. Very much."

"But why?"

"I want to meet more of your friends."

"They're not really my friends. Some of them—like Alice—are excellent artists. But the world they inhabit, it's so incredibly competitive."

"Is that why you never try and sell your own paintings."

"It's one reason. The other is that they're not very good. Not as good as I'd want them to be."

"That isn't true. I think they're very beautiful—all of them. When I go into your studio I feel like I could stay there forever and just look."

Meredith appreciated the girl's loyalty and her praise, whether deserved or not, but no one was more keenly aware of her deficiencies as an artist than she was herself. Any genuine talent she might once have possessed had long ago eroded under the influence of too many others. Alice Reardon was one of course—though not the only one.

"I finished my painting right after you left," Lai said.

"You'll have to show it to me as soon as we get home."

"I do hope you'll like it. If you don't you'll say so, won't you? If it's bad don't try to tell me it's good."

"I'm sure it's very good." And if it isn't, she thought, you'll be the last to know. Art was too precious these days to permit the luxury of candid criticism. And besides, this was the girl's first.

In the few days since their arrival in Paris Lai had worked twelve to fifteen hours daily, carrying her paints and easel into the tiny courtyard behind the flat even though the view from there—the brick wall of an adjoining building—did not strike Meredith as particularly inspirational. In the studio yesterday Meredith had done a little work of her own for the first time in months: two quick paste-ups and a pencil sketch of the girl's profile.

When they reached the flat the girl led Meredith into the big room in back. Three walls were covered with a portion of Meredith's private collection: there was a Manet, a van Gogh, two Picassos, a rare Vermeer, others. She'd obtained them over the years as one art museum after another closed its doors.

Meredith looked at the girl. "I give up. I thought you were going to show me your painting. Where have you hidden it?"

She pointed at the back wall. "I put it there. That one. The one with the pink and blue."

Meredith looked again. The painting the girl meant—the one that occupied the center portion of the wall was a Picasso. Perhaps his most famous of all—except for the *Guernica,* which the Reina Sofa still clung to—*Les Demoiselles d'Avignon.* How had she failed to notice it hanging there before?

The painting was a marvelous work. But it wasn't hers. She didn't own it. No one did.

Les Demoiselles has been lost since the slugs destroyed Manhattan. "But where…?"

The girl took Meredith's hand and led her across the room, laughing lightly as she did. "There—now you can see it better."

Meredith reached up hesitantly and let her fingertips brush the canvas. They came away wet.

"You painted this?"

"Don't you like it?"

"I—where did you get the idea?"

"I don't know. It just came to me. I like people and skin and the color blue. I think they're swimming—or taking baths."

"You didn't see it in a book?"

"Oh, no. I just shut my eyes and painted what I saw."

Meredith examined the painting again. Even as a copy the work was remarkable. Perhaps with the original in front of her she could have detected the discrepancies but not from here, not from memory.

The girl pointed at the two distorted masklike faces in the right of the painting. "Do you understand these? I don't. I wish I did. I think they're ugly...horrid."

"Then why did you paint them?"

"Because that's how I saw them. In my mind." She bit her lip, looking at Meredith. "You don't like it. You think it's monstrous."

"I think it's exquisite," she said truthfully.

The girl grabbed Meredith then and kissed her full on the lips. The abrupt unreasoning passion of the gesture took Meredith's breath away. "I'm so happy you said that," the girl said, pulling back. "I'm so glad I could make you happy."

"You have, Lai. You have."

The girl looked at her solemnly. "Is something wrong? Do you feel all right? You look...pale."

Meredith forced a smile, shaking her head. "I'm fine. It's...something to do with your painting. Not that I don't like it—please don't misunderstand me—but...well, I'll show you what I mean later."

"I'll start dinner then."

"No." Meredith caught her arm as she tried to leave the room. "Not yet," she added in a gentler voice. "Stay with me awhile."

It had happened exactly the way they all said: she'd found the girl—Lai—in a brothel in Tangier.

For no particular reason that was the city she'd picked out in which to die.

She'd gone there without telling anyone, rented a cheap room in a not very clean building operated by two Swedes. The first day she removed her sketchbooks from her suitcase and burned them one by one in the sink. It was a prelude—a gesture. First the work died—then the life. The concept amused her. It was such a perfect way to die—so premeditated, orderly.

On the second day she went into the city. In a filthy street market where merchants cried in shrill alien voices a lean man in a rumpled suit accosted her and told her about the brothel. She pulled away, feigning shock and disgust, but later near dusk after dinner in a dingy cafe she went that way, stepped through the open door, found a grotesque oily man sitting at a desk dwarfed by his bulk.

"May I be of assistance, madam?" he said in impecccable English.

"I was given this address—in the market. I'm an artist. I'm looking for subjects to paint."

"Ah, of course." He removed a ledger from a drawer and placed it in front of him.

"I would like…" She reached inside her purse and in a gesture of defiance removed all the cash she'd brought with her from Paris. She put the money down on the desk. "I want whatever it is I can have for this."

He nodded, licked his thumb, and counted the money with painstaking care. He wore a tailored gray suit, pink shirt, and a narrow dark tie. His features were vaguely Middle Eastern. She thought he was likely a Turk.

"A woman?" he said when he finished counting. "A girl perhaps. A young one."

"How young is young?" She was prepared to leave.

"No younger than you would wish, madam."

"Twenty then."

"White, black, Asian, Arab? Yellow hair, long hair, bald—?"

"It doesn't matter," said Meredith, feeling hopelessly degraded by the process.

"Of course not." The man's lips twitched sympathetically. She heard a bell ring in the distance. A door opened in the wall behind the desk and another man appeared. He could have been a twin of the first. The two whispered softly, not in English, and the second man said, "If you will accompany me, madam." His voice was a queer echo of the other's.

Past the door they climbed a steep flight of steps. At the top the man held open another door and bowed ponderously as she stepped by.

"Here?" said Meredith, pausing at the threshold.

"Oui, mademoiselle."

She continued on through. The door closed soundlessly behind her. On the other side was a cramped windowless cubicle lit by a single shaded bulb. There was a bed but no other furniture. Lying in the bed, a white sheet drawn up to her breasts, was the girl. At first Meredith did not look directly at her. "Are you here for me?"

"Yes."

"I—I'm sorry then." Meredith let out her breath. "Maybe I shouldn't have done this. Maybe I..."

She stopped then and full of self-loathing undressed quickly, letting her clothes fall in a disorderly heap. She was thinking: I'll be very fast about this and then go back to the hotel. It's only right that I should make an end of it this way.

She crossed to the bed, put one knee down, and started to crawl. All at once she stopped as the girl turned her head so that the light caught her face just right.

Gazing at her Meredith felt as if the hand of a giant had grabbed hold of her heart and given it a brutal squeeze.

"Who—who are you?" she managed.

The girl's head pivoted. "My name is Lai."

"My God," Meredith said in a husky voice she barely recognized as her own, *"what* are you?"

"I'm whatever you want me to be," she said.

Afterward she took the girl with her. The proprietor made no attempt to object. The money she'd given him was likely more than he saw in a year's time.

"I'm taking you home with me." she told the girl as she led her back to her room. "I'm Meredith Savard. I live in Paris. I'm rich. And I—I paint."

"I've never been to...Paris." She enunciated the word distinctly as if the city were not known to her.

The next day—together—they left Tangier by train.

"We're not going to that party tonight," Meredith finally said. "I've decided I'm not going to share you with anyone."

But she knew as soon as she spoke that never would be.

5

As Desmond Blue hastened through the nighttime streets of old Kabul accompanied by the disguised dwarf Louie Roth on the way to the offices of Dr. Ling Chi Ho, dentist and erstwhile criminal mastermind, he was reminded of an earlier occasion he had visited this fascinating city.

It was some years ago now—on his honeymoon. I was a different man then, thought Blue: tall, lean, lanky, dapper, handsome in his own peculiar way with a strong direct gaze, gentle mouth, firm sensitive jaw. *Doctor* Desmond Blue, psychoanalyst. (*Dezi to my friends.*) Not yet celebrated in any sense but a dedicated practitioner of an honest trade.

And madly in love too. With the lovely young woman he'd only recently wed.

Together they picked out a honeymoon itinerary. From New York (their home) to Kabul by way of Boston's Fenway Park, Dublin, London, Paris, Venice, and Istanbul. Stops later added would include Mumbai, Tokyo, Honolulu, and Dodger Stadium in Los Angeles.

But Kabul—really—why there? people invariably wanted to know. The other places along the way, well, fine; they all made perfectly splendid sense. Even the baseball parks, assuming one was a fan of that antique nineteenth century pastime. And especially considering neither of them had been abroad before. But Kabul? A notorious hell hole. No one visited Kabul unless they had to.

Blue recalled the answer with a grin as he gripped Louie's arm tightly to prevent his escape. A long-horned ox in care of a white-clad peasant lumbered past, dropping a load of manure in its wake. As Blue skirted around the pile he glanced quickly left and right at the dark shuttered houses they passed. Furtive men lurked in shadowy doorways ready to pounce upon the unwary. Louie as a known member of the criminal underworld was afforded safe passage down these mean streets. Alone, Blue would have been dead within minutes.

As for the Kabul honeymoon trip, it was actually her idea, not his. And how had she come by it? Simple. She'd done it with a fingertip dropped randomly on a map of the world and landing smack dab on Kabul. "That's where I want to go," she said and poor Dezi could only smile and say, "Yes, dear. Whatever you want is what I want too."

Scarlet was her name. (After that dreadful book yes—or more likely, even worse, the movie adaptation.) Scarlet Tewkesbury Cipriano Blue. Quick of tongue, sharp of mind, utterly devoid of deceit or dishonesty. And mad as a hatter too, according to official documents. (She was also blind and black but neither was thought to be as significant as her madness.)

They'd met—where else?—in the psychiatric ward of a public hospital in the South Bronx, New York City, not far from Yankee Stadium (on a clear day you could hear the roar of the crowd), where Dr. Desmond Blue, freshly graduated from a renowned psychoanalytic institute and already author of two brilliant (some said) treatises on the subject of the Will to Die, was serving an internship despite a flourishing private practice that already included among its patients the astronaut Carlotta McCoy.

Scarlet Tewkesbury Cipriano was—in the words of the doctor (not Blue) who had admitted her—a strange case. An attempted suicide. Her fifth at least. Barbiturate overdose this time. Saved only by a freakish quirk of fate when her husband Joey ("the Shark") Cipriano, a minor figure in the local mob, returned unexpectedly from work (he'd forgotten his lucky gun) and found his wife passed out in the bathtub in her wedding dress with her nose and mouth scant inches from going under.

Upon regaining consciousness at the hospital she took her husband's hand in hers, felt it carefully, and said, "Who are you supposed to be?" They'd been married less than a month. He was a funny looking white man with protruding teeth and a hooked nose, pushing fifty, who carried two guns (one of them lucky) wherever he went.

"I'm your goddamn husband, you stupid nigger bitch," he said, "and I just saved your dumb blind ass from drowning in the bathtub."

"Well, thank you very much for that," she said primly, "but what's a husband?"

Blue, who'd been hovering close to the bed (having already fallen hopelessly in love with his patient, a real no-no in the psychiatrist profession), overheard every word exchanged, intervened and told Joey ("the Shark") he would have to leave at once. (Joey pulled out his lucky gun and threatened to kill Blue on the spot but that's another story, not really relevant to the honeymoon trip to Kabul.)

The problem with Scarlet Tewkesbury Cipriano's mental state as it turned out was her unshakeable conviction that when she'd swallowed the twenty-nine green pills and put on her wedding dress and climbed into the bathtub filled with warm water was that she'd died and all this—the hospital, the doctors, the nurses, the other patients, Blue—all of this was purgatory. (She'd been raised a Catholic before her father in hock to the mob for gambling loses, gave her to Joey Cipriano in return for the forgiveness of his debts.)

"So you believe you're dead, do you?" Dr. Blue said at the start of their first fifty-minute session.

"That's right, Doc," Scarlet said. "I'm dead and this here is purgatory like where the sisters say you'll go if you've committed a bunch of sins."

"And what sins have you committed?"

"None that you need to know about unless you're God or Jesus."

"I'm not."

"Thank God for that then."

They both laughed heartily.

Six weeks later, after Scarlet Cipriano's release from the hospital as an incurable psychotic who offered no danger to herself or others ("How can I kill myself when I'm already dead?" she told the doctor who signed her release—guess who?) they were married in a civil ceremony and left on their honeymoon trip.

When the slugs suddenly appeared in the sky over Earth Blue was in Copenhagen attending a seminar on the effects of violent pornography on the male adolescent libido. When the seventy-seven golden ships flew over the city in formation Blue stood transfixed outside along with several colleagues. If only Dr. Jung could be here now, he thought, the man would be having an orgasm worthy of Reich.

It took a week after the Occupation for him to get a flight back to North America. By then many of those thought to have vanished in the ruined cities had begun to reappear with no memory of where they had been or why. Blue rented a beetle buggy in Boston and made the treacherous drive to New York. When he reached the great city he could not believe his eyes. There was nothing left of it—nothing at all. New York was a huge flat bowl of ash, soot, and debris.

The apartment building on the Upper East Side where he and Scarlet had made their home was a pile of rubble indistinguishable from the many other similar piles surrounding it.

Blue shed a quick tear and then went on with his search. He drove west—to Salt Lake City where, it was said, the dead had come back to life. Once there he scanned the faces of everyone he passed, dead and living alike, but there was no sign of his wife. After many futile days of searching, he found the niece—the young woman whose wedding Scarlet had come here to attend. "She—Scarlet—she's gone away," she said in a singsong voice, waving a hand vaguely at the horizon. "She left here on the seventh day." (The niece—like many of the resurrected dead—now officially to be called "spooks" when it was determined that calling them "zombies" was offensive—dated all of experience from the moment of her rebirth.)

"Gone—gone where?"

"She didn't say. She didn't know. She didn't care."

"But she's all right? She wasn't…damaged?"

From what Blue had observed here in Salt Lake at least ten percent of the resurrected spooks had suffered severe mental impairment.

"Certainly not. She's fine and dandy."

"But can she—can she see now?" It was the question he felt he had to ask.

"I wouldn't know. She never said. I guess you'll have to ask her that one yourself."

Blue drove to the nearest spook reservation outside Ely Nevada. The armed guard at the gate—there were armed guards posted at all the gates—insisted he didn't recognize the photograph Blue showed him. "There's only about fifty of them left here, mostly the ones with their brains scrambled. I'd recognize this one for sure. She's one pretty lady. Your wife, you say? You're a lucky man, mister. If I was you I'd count my blessings and go home."

"But I want to see her. I love her."

"She don't love you though."

Blue grabbed the guard by the front of his shirt and shook him, oblivious of the gun in his belt. "How can you know that if she's not here?"

The guard squirmed free of his grasp. "I know it, pal, because none of them do. None of them love anybody. They don't give gave a drizzly shit for any of us."

But Blue drove on. To the next nearest reservation and then the one after that. The reservations had sprung up mere days after the Occupation. They were governed by the spooks themselves although many occupied public land—former parks and the like. Only a few of the spooks had stayed in Salt Lake City. The rest left and wandered.

While driving through northern Arizona Blue picked up a hitch-hiker wearing clerical garb who turned out to be another spook from Salt Lake City. His name was Chesterfield, a former police detective. The two got to chatting and when Blue showed him Scarlet's photograph Chesterfield hesitated then nodded. "She does look familiar. I think I remember seeing her a few weeks back."

"Oh?" said Blue, concealing his excitement. Spooks tended to be protective of each other's privacy. "Where was that?"

"It must have been in Hollywood. There's a reservation there in what used to be a famous woman's clothing store. She was living there and helping out."

"Did you talk to her?"

"A few times. She was friendly enough. Why? She somebody important to you?"

"My wife," said Blue grimly.

"Oh. Sorry." Chesterfield lit another cigarette. Like most spooks he was a chain smoker. "I suppose I shouldn't have said anything. Getting your hopes up and all."

"I've been looking for her ever since the Occupation. I was in Copenhagen when it happened."

"Can I offer you some advice then?"

"What?"

"Stop."

"But why should—?"

"She won't be the same. She's not the same. None of us are. Death changes a person."

"I have to find that out for myself."

"She might not even recognize you."

"I'd rather die than live without her."

"Don't say that, friend-o. Don't ever say you'd rather die."

"Is it that horrible?" In his travels Blue had never heard a spook speak of the actuality of death and dying before.

"Horrible? Not really. In fact, it's more the opposite. And that's the problem. Dying is so amazing an experience, so overwhelming, that once you've been dead you can never really enjoy living again."

"I don't think I understand you."

"Well, wait then. You'll find out eventually." He laughed, tossed his cigarette out the window, immediately lit another. "But don't hurry it along either. That's all I'm trying to say. Wait till you don't have any other choice. Then die. But don't rush it. Don't go till you're damn well ready."

After he dropped Chesterfield in the outskirts of Sedona, Blue turned the beetle buggy around and headed west. To Hollywood. It took him the rest of the day and part of the night to get there.

At two a.m. he pulled up in front of the former clothing store at the corner of Hollywood and Vine and pounded on the locked door.

A uniformed guard appeared, a wizened old man with mean narrow eyes and a pistol on his belt.

Blue showed him the photo of his wife. "Her name is Scarlet Tewkesbury Cipriano Blue. A man I met on the road today—a spook named Chesterfield—told me she was living here."

"That she is," said the guard. He handed the photo back. "But that ain't the name she's using now. We call her Emerald Blaze."

"But she is here?" He tried peering past the guard into the dark interior. "I don't care what her name is. I have to see her."

"Who are you?"

"I'm her husband."

"Emerald ain't married."

It went on like this for a while. Finally, Blue offered the guard enough money—he'd taken to carrying a paper bag full of silver coins everywhere he went—that the guard agreed to go back and see.

He closed the door and went away.

"Emerald Blaze says she ain't never heard of anybody called you," he said when he finally came back.

"But I'm her legal husband. I have papers with me to prove it."

The guard spat past him onto the sidewalk. "Best to consider yourself divorced then," he said and placed his right hand on the butt of his pistol.

Blue stood his ground. "Please," he said. "You have to let me in."

The guard shook his head. "Not my call to make, buster. This is still a free country. It's my job to keep lifers like you from coming and harassing—"

"Desmond." Her voice was like a whisper from memory. She stood behind the guard looking past his shoulder.

He took a lunging step toward her, smelling her sweet perfume. "Scarlet," he tried to say.

She held up a hand. "Don't come any closer, Desmond. Jimmie will shoot you if you do."

"Why don't you want to see me, Scarlet?"

"I am *seeing* you, Desmond. Right now. For the first time. I am *seeing* you standing in front of me."

Which is when it really hit him for the first time.

She could see.

"Isn't there some place we could talk? In private?" He looked at the guard who was watching them intently, hand still on his pistol butt. "I won't harm you. You know that."

"All right. If you honestly think it will help." She turned and beckoned him to follow. "We can go to my room."

Blue went past the guard, through the door, and down a long hallway. They passed a long procession of other spooks pacing sleeplessly back and forth. Many wore costumes—clowns, cowboys, pirates, sailors, Roman centurions.

Scarlet wore blue jeans and a loose sweatshirt. Except for her eyes—and the heavy scent of perfume—she was exactly as he remembered her.

Her room was tiny—a bed and a dresser. There was a pile of books on the floor in a corner.

"You can read now," he said.

"Yes, of course." She sat down on the bed—it didn't look as if it had ever been slept in—and looked up at him. "You shouldn't have come here, Desmond. You should have let things alone. I thought of writing but with New York gone I didn't know how to reach you."

"I went there first after I got back from Copenhagen. I thought you might have gone there to wait for me. After that I went to Salt Lake City. When you weren't there either—your niece said you'd gone away—I searched everywhere else I could think of."

"But why?" she said. "You knew I was dead. Why didn't you let me be?"

"Because I love you. Why else?"

She sighed. "I'm sure you do. But I don't love you, Desmond. I can't. It's just not possible."

The coldness of her words pierced him like a knife. "Don't say that, Scarlet. Please."

"It's the truth."

"But why? Can't you at least tell me that much?"

"I would if I could. But I don't really know. I died and then I lived again. We all did. And afterward it wasn't the same. None of it was—not for any of us. Now go. Please." She stood up, opened the door, held it for him.

"Can I see you again?" he said.

"I'd rather you didn't."

"Are you sure?"

She had to think: "Yes, Yes, I'm sure."

* * * *

Afterward Blue's private detective business soon prospered. He developed a large clientele and a devoted following. He was famous around the world as a real life embodiment of the great Sherlock Holmes. He put on weight, hired retainers and secretaries, moved to a mansion in the Sahara Desert he chose regardless of geography to call Arabia Deserta and sponsored certain secret scientific experiments.

All the while he kept tabs on Scarlet. Every now and then—once every few months when there wasn't an active case to pursue—he visited her at whatever reservation she was currently living at. When they met Blue did most of the talking. He told her about his most recent cases, related tangled tales of mystery and intrigue, spoke openly of his occasional failures. Then he went away until a few months later when they met again.

This pattern remained intact until last spring when Blue went to the Youngstown Ohio Reservation where Scarlet now lived and the guard at the gate informed him that Emerald Blaze—as she called herself—was no longer there.

"Where is she? What happened? My sources told me she's still here."

"She was but—well, she died."

"Of course she did. That's why she's here. Are you trying to be funny or what?"

He wasn't trying to be funny. Scarlet was dead. Really dead this time. Finally so. Two nights earlier she had slashed her wrists, cut her throat, and bled to death in her room.

"They're doing it all time now," the guard explained. "Two or three every month. It's like a plague. A suicide plague."

"But, my God, why?" Blue said. "Did she leave a note, a message, any explanation?"

"Just a sheet of paper with two words scrawled on it."

"What two words?"

"*In time*. That's what she wrote. *In time.* And then she killed herself."

Blue went home then and from Arabia Deserta announced his intention to retire from the business of crime detection effective immediately. He shut himself up in his study for long periods, smoked opium by the pipe full, only rarely emerged.

But then Dr. Schwerner had appeared with his envelope of time photographs and Blue had recognized this as a case he dare not evade. He resumed the practice of detection once more.

Blue's last case.

Would this be the one that finally brought him face with that most elusive of entities: the naked truth.

Only time would tell.

You've got to be out of your gourd, Blue," grumbled Louie Roth as Blue dragged him through the maze of Kabul's tangle of back streets. "Don't you figure old Dr. Ling is going to sniff out something phony when you and me show up at his office in the middle of the night?"

"Why should he suspect anything? I'm not Blue the detective. I'm Bludoni the guru."

"That idiot disguise won't fool that sly devil five seconds."

"Which is why I intend to remain in the background, Louie, while you occupy center stage. Here, let's take another look."

Blue stopped under a street lamp, grabbed hold of Louie, jerked back his head, forced open his mouth, and examined his teeth.

"Excellent," he pronounced. "A literal rat's nest of ugly decay. There's enough rot in there to keep Dr. Ling drilling for hours."

"I'm telling you, Blue, nobody touches my teeth—nobody."

"I offer a bonus, Louie," said Blue wearily. "A lucrative bonus."

"The hell with your money. I can't stand pain. I have a low tolerance."

"Then it appears, my friend, you have a choice to make. Either the pain of Dr. Ling or the pain of Desmond Blue. When I set to work on your teeth with a pair of rusty pliers, there will be no anesthesia, I assure you of that." Taking hold of Louie's arm, Blue dragged him ahead. "Come along, Louie. The sooner we get this over with the sooner we can see about getting you a good set of dentures to replace the teeth you've lost."

The offices of Dr. Ling Chi Ho, D.D.S., occupied the top story of a squat brick building.

Blue pushed open the door and drew Louie in after him. As he had hoped no receptionist lurked in the darkened outer office at this late hour. He rang a bell and waited patiently, one hand firmly clasped to Louie's elbow.

A door in the far wall opened silently and the skull-like visage of an ancient Oriental peered through the gap. "May I be of service to you gentlemen?" said Dr. Ling Chi Ho in perfect British-accented English.

"It is my companion here who is in terrible agony," said Blue, thrusting Louie forward while remaining in the shadows himself. "He presently suffers from a terrible pain of the mouth." Blue had assumed a thick Eastern European accent and spoke in a guttural whisper. Over the years he'd learned that such seemingly superficial characteristics as tone of voice, stance, gait, and posture were frequently more crucial in determining a person's identity than facial features.

"Why, I believe it is little Louie Roth," said Dr. Ling with a smile of recognition.

"I've got some sort of awful toothache, Doc," said Louie, glancing back at Blue. "It hurts every once in a while anyhow."

"Then come ahead, my diminutive friend," said Dr. Ling, crooking a bony finger. "Let us see what we have here."

Louie gave Blue a final lingering look like a lamb being marched to slaughter and shuffled forward. Dr. Ling inserted a finger into his mouth and probed delicately. "Which one hurts, Louie? This one looks particularly ugly."

"Ouch!" Louie slammed his mouth shut as Dr. Ling withdrew his finger barely in the nick of time.

"I see at least three that will require prompt extraction," Dr. Ling said briskly. "So if you'll come with me, Louie, we can begin immediately."

"Hold on a second," said Louie, standing fast, "I want to know what kind of dope you're going to shoot me full of first. I'm a sensitive guy. I can't stand pain."

"Drugs, Louie?" said Dr. Ling with evident distaste. "I would hardly resort to such crude methods. No, I am a devout practitioner of the classic Vedantic technique of dentistry where the power of the mind over the body reigns paramount." He tapped his forehead. "When one refuses to acknowledge the existence of pain it simply withers away like a blossom without water."

"I ain't no blossom, Doc," said Louie, shrinking back.

"Ah, but I can show you how to transform yourself into one." Dr. Ling caught Louie's arm in a surprisingly firm grip and drew him toward the open door. "Allow me please to demonstrate. There won't be a moment of pain. You have my bonded word."

Once he was alone in the waiting room Blue stepped into the light and took a careful look around. A pair of matching filing cabinets stood beside a large desk. Blue tiptoed over to examine these when the outer door swung open and a stocky bluff-looking man swept inside. He was wearing a plaid sport coat, yellow slacks, and a blue-and-red polka dot tie that seemed to cover half his chest.

The man squinted owlishly at Blue. "Who the blazes are you?" he asked.

"Suffering patient," said Blue, hastily assuming his best Austro-Serbian accent. He grasped his jaw and emitted a low moan. "Dreadful ache of the tooth."

"And the doctor?" The man nodded at the door in the far wall. "Where the devil is he right now?"

"With another patient. Little buddy of mine. Also with a rotten tooth."

As if in confirmation a shrill child-like cry erupted from behind the closed door. The bluff man pursed his lips in apparent sympathy and looked eager to depart. "Would you, be so kind then as to inform Dr. Ling that Brother Xavier stopped by to say farewell? Thank him for his hospitality and assure him the next time I visit Kabul I will be certain to look him up."

Blue put on a blank expression, hardly daring to believe his good fortune. Brother Xavier already—and in the flesh. He murmured something affirmative and let out another realistic moan of his own. Just as he finished a second piercing cry echoed from beyond as well. Brother Xavier gave a shudder and hurriedly made his way out.

As soon as he was gone Blue raced over and leaned his ear against the door. He listened as heavy footsteps pounded down the stairs, then counted to ten and hastened in pursuit. Just as he reached the stairs Louie let out another terrible scream. Poor little fellow, thought Blue sorrowfully. Well, without suffering there can be no growth. He made a mental note to double whatever bonus the dwarf had coming.

Blue reached the street just in time to see the heavy bulk of Brother Xavier drop into the passenger compartment of a sidecar taxi. Blue drew back into the shadows until the little vehicle had drawn away from the curb, then raced into the street, waving his arms frantically. Luck was with him again for in no time another taxi came roaring up and squealed to a stop beside him.

It was a beat-up piston-driven Dodge sedan well aged. Blue leaped into the back and pointed at the other vehicle disappeared around the corner ahead. "Follow that cab!" he shouted. "Fifty dollars if you don't let it out of your sight!"

With a giggle of delight the driver shot away from the curb. Blue was thrown forcibly back by the acceleration. A broken spring poked him painfully in the spine.

"I used to run moonshine whiskey for a living back home in Alabama," the driver explained as he tore through the narrow streets of Kabul at a rapid clip, darting around camels, beeping bicyclists out of his path, scattering pedestrians left and right. "You won't find a faster buggy than this baby in all of Asia," he boasted.

Blue nodded tensely, his attention riveted on the sidecar ahead. Originally he had intended to confront Xavier openly and demand he share whatever secrets he possessed concerning the Sect but as he had earlier warned his associates this was a case in which nothing and no one could be taken at face value and the unexpected apparition of such an ambiguous figure as Dr. Ling Chi Ho had turned him cautious. It would be wisest to reconnoiter the landscape first, he had decided, before taking precipitous action.

"Don't get too close yet," Blue advised the driver. "I don't want the man in the sidecar realizing he's being followed."

"Gotcha, pal." The driver eased up on the accelerator.

* * * *

A short time later the sidecar turned onto the main highway leading out of the city proper. A cluster of bright lights appeared ahead. "That's the aeroport coming up," the driver explained. "Your pal must be planning to skip town."

Blue ordered the driver to continue to keep his distance until Brother Xavier had sufficient time to enter the main terminal building. Then Blue followed himself. Inside the nearly vacant cavern of the waiting room there was no sign of Brother Xavier however. Blue hurried over to the ticket booth and banged his fist on the counter. A sleepy-eyed man with long stringy hair and a droopy moustache popped out from underneath. The scent of hashish was on his breath. "What's up, pops?" said the ticket agent, clearly another Yankee expatriate.

"A man came in here a few moments ago," said Blue. "A heavy-set man in a loud jacket. I don't see him now. Can you inform me what's become of him?"

"Not my problem," said the agent with bureaucratic indifference. He started to drop behind the counter again. Angrily Blue reached out and caught him by the shirt collar.

"I don't care whether he's your problem or not. I want to know where that man has gone. Answer me or I'll report you to the authorities for drug use on duty."

"You're looking at the only authority around here," said the agent with a sneer. He straightened his collar. "The fellow you want sounds like the one that flew in here last night. I suppose he went out tarmac to fetch his aeroplane."

"The man has a plane of his own?"

"Leer jet. The classiest thing we've had around here in ages."

"And you think he may be already gone?"

"Gone or going. Why? What's the beef?"

"No beef but I'll want to hire an aeroplane of my own immediately. A jet also—and equipped with radar capable of tracking another aircraft."

"Why not ask for a magic carpet?" said the agent. "That I might be able to get for you. An aeroplane, no way."

Blue controlled his temper. He reached inside his smock and pulled out a handful of silver coins. "I require the aeroplane immediately."

The agent stared hungrily at the coins. "Now that you mention it maybe I can give you a hand. See that old bird over there?" He indicated a far corner of the big room where a man Blue had failed to notice before dressed in a bright orange aviator's jumpsuit lay curled up asleep on the floor. "He came in here earlier tonight and said he had his own aeroplane for hire. I told him the last time anybody hired an aeroplane in Kabul was three years before Noah's flood but he said he'd wait around just in case something came up. Ain't it a coincidence you showed up when you did?"

Blue like all detectives did not believe in coincidence. Yet he didn't appear to have any choice. He dropped the silver coins into the ticket agent's waiting hand and hurried over to where the man was sleeping. Leaning over, Blue poked him in the shoulder. "Sir?" he said. "Sir, may I have a private word with you concerning your aeroplane?"

The man raised his head slowly, revealing the weathered features of a sixty-year-old. "You pay good bread, my aeroplane flies. Where you bound, daddy-o?"

Blue explained in a hushed tone that he could not be sure, that he wished to follow another aeroplane.

"I know the one you mean," said aged pilot. "I saw it on the runway when I landed. Damn fast jet aeroplane too—like a good-looking whore on Saturday night—but not as fast as mine, I'm telling you."

"I'll give you five hundred in silver dollars now and another five hundred if we manage to follow him all the way to his destination."

The old man shook his head. "Not so quick, big boy. I've got to know what makes the fart stinky. You're talking to Georgi Gustanov, formerly highly decorated officer in Soviet Air Force, not to any local yokel. Are you a Red or something?"

"A Red?"

"A Communist. Marxist-Leninist son of a bitch."

Blue shook his head. "My sole political commitment is to the ideal of popular republican democracy."

"Then okay by me, I guess. I'll take you on that ride. Gustanov hates the fucking Reds. They boot me out of Soviet Air Force when I get too old. Load of horseshit, say I. Come along, plump partner. We must prepare for our mission most difficult."

Blue followed Georgi Gustanov out onto the concrete tarmac. The lighting here was poor and his confidence in the old man's flying abilities was minimal but again there seemed no other alternative at hand. On the way they passed a sleek jet as bright and shiny as a newly minted coin. Brother Xavier stood close to the fuselage chatting with a uniformed mechanic. Blue averted his face as they went past. "Hey, you crazy Russian," the mechanic shouted after them, laughing. "Shot down any slug spaceships lately."

"Fuck your sister's flabby bottom," Gustanov muttered underneath his breath. "These fools make fun of Gustanov," he explained. Jealous, you know. I earn the Star of Lenin for my service in the Soviet Air Force. Not one but two such. Let them dare say the same."

When they reached Gustanov's aircraft Blue felt a renewed stab of anxiety. The plane was a single-engine biplane so old and decrepit it looked as if it belonged in a museum. "Where did you get this thing?" he asked.

"Earned it with my service," Gustanov he said. "When I left the Soviet Air Force I took it with me. You want to fly like a bird or stand there flapping your jaw like a dummy?"

Blue was examining the plane—clearly stolen—with increasing concern. The wings looked as if they'd been glued on; there was rust and mold everywhere on the fuselage. "We may have to travel a considerable distance. Are you sure we can cross mountains in this?"

"Do birds sing in the springtime?" said Gustanov blithely. "Do pretty Georgian girls have large breasts and warm pussies? You show me the mountain, baby, and Gustanov will fly over top of it."

"The Himalayas," said Blue. "We may need oxygen for that."

"A snap for Gustanov. Just hold your breath, friend, till we get on the other side."

This didn't exactly reassure Blue as to the level of sanity involved here. Still, there seemed to be nothing else but to join the Russian in the cramped cockpit. There were two seats pressed snugly together. Gustanov strapped himself into one and began to study the myriad assortment of dials and gauges in front of him. He grumbled once or twice, pressed a button or two, jerked a lever, then seemed satisfied. Reaching under the seat he pulled out a badly scratched leather helmet with a dull red star affixed to the crown and placed it on his head. He pulled a pair of goggles down over his eyes. "When the other fool takes off, we follow. Hang onto your hat when we do."

* * * *

It was a quarter-hour later when Xavier's plane roared suddenly to life and began coasting down the runway.

Gustanov waited until it was airborne before starting his own engine. Blue was beginning to worry. "What if you lose him?"

"Can't," said Gustanov, gesturing at the instrument panel. "Got the radar locked. Best gizmo ever invented. See up above, down below, everywhere you want. Took it from a MiG-23—best aeroplane ever built."

"He could still outrun us, you know."

"Buffalo turds, friend. The last pilot to try and outrun Gustanov was named Mercury and I whipped his butt clean."

The old aeroplane vibrated wildly as Gustanov moved into his takeoff run. Blue shut his eyes and clenched his hands. The only way he knew for certain when the plane was airborne was when the vibrations lessened somewhat. He opened his eyes and gazed at the starry sky above. Below, the lights of Kabul winked and glowed. Blue tried to ignore the fact that there was solid ground down there too. He took a series of deep breaths, calming himself.

"Here is our little friend now," said Gustanov. In order to make himself heard over the roar of the engine he had to shout. He pointed a finger at the radar screen. There was a tiny blip in the far left moving at a rapid clip toward the edge of the screen.

"Look there," said Blue. "You've nearly lost him already. In another minute he'll be gone."

Gustanov grinned and jabbed a finger at the screen. "Keep your eyeball peeled and watch this, baby," he said. "Plenty can happen in sixty seconds flat. Hold onto your hat while we make like the wind."

Gustanov lunged forward, grabbed hold of the throttle, and gave a violent tug. The moment he did the plane seemed to spring forward through the air. The sudden increase in velocity pinned Blue against the seat. The plane vibrated crazily but somehow managed to hang together in one piece. Then there was a sudden eerie silence and the vibrations ceased. Blue moistened his lips tentatively and turned his head. "I believe I may owe you an apology, Captain."

"Apology accepted, baby." Gustanov edged back on the throttle and chuckled. "This bird of mine can sing sweet music when she wants, eh?" He nodded at the radar screen. "We right on top of the little dude now. There's two planes maybe faster in Europe—one in Asia. Africa a big horse laugh, America—who knows? Two or three times I fly over it but never land. They still have great tall buildings like in the movie *King Kong*?"

"A few," Blue said. He was beginning to relax after all. "The slugs flattened Manhattan of course."

"And Minsk," said Gustanov. "Lost many friends there, then they reappear elsewhere and pretend to be stupid."

"Savages you mean."

"No more so than many others." He reached up and removed the wig from on top of his head. He used it to wipe some of the sweat off his brow.

"How about a little nip now?" Gustanov said, reaching a hand under the seat and emerging with a bottle of one hundred twenty proof Vodka. He unscrewed the cap, tipped the bottle, and swallowed thirstily. Then he passed it to Blue who took a more tentative sip. His throat felt as if it had caught fire. He coughed and gagged.

"Good Christ, this is wretched stuff," said Blue.

"Private stock," said Gustanov, reclaiming the bottle. "When the new bunch in Kremlin booted me out of Soviet Air Force I took a reward with me. One thing is my plane, the other is basement full of vodka. Cheap stuff, sure, but hits the belly hard. Ready for more?"

"Not quite yet," Blue said, glancing at the radar screen. The reassuring blip of Brother Xavier's jet remained fixed in place.

"Let me know when you are. I was the one who shot it down, by the way. The day the slugs came. I went up in my aeroplane and blew it out of the sky before it knew I was there."

"You mean you were the one shot down the slug ship?"

"Oh, sure. That was me all right. *Blooey*. Right out of the sky. Am I scared? Ready to shit bricks? No way, Jose. Been in worse fixes in my time."

"I've often wondered about that," said Blue. "How is it you managed to shoot one of their ships down when no other aeroplane could get close?"

"Strategy, baby." Gustanov took another long swig from the bottle.

"I fly straight up to the golden ship till *blam* I hit the force field barrier. Then I stay right on top, *blam, blam, blam*. I am going half-crazy pounding myself to death but that makes me plenty pissed too. I think hey if they're burning up people and cities all over the world like my radio says then they got to have some kind of weapon and if they got a weapon then it's got to be coming out someplace. I fly all around that ship till I find the opening. Then I slip through."

Blue could see the sense in Gustanov's tactics though he doubted anyone else would have been insane enough to attempt something that desperate. "If you penetrated the barrier at the point where the weapon was being fired, why didn't they use it on you?"

"Good question, buddy. I slip through very quick, feel this awful heat like the inside of hell, figure I'm roasted to death, then nothing. I keep going. I fire my missiles. *Blam, blam*. Nothing happens. So—*bang*—I crash my plane right down on top of the spaceship and punch the cockpit ejection lever one second before. *Blooey*. I float to the ground with a parachute. Spaceship crashes. When I land Soviet soldiers have slug surrounded."

"Then you actually saw one of them?"

"Hard to say. I see a shadow, soldiers standing all around. Later they take them out and shoot them. Me, they don't touch. Why? Because I tell them I see nothing. Plus I'm one big Soviet hero now."

"Then you don't know what it actually looked like?"

"Like a big ugly slug, right? That's what they say."

"But you never actually saw it yourself?"

"Nope, I just shoot it down. And I also—hey!" Gustanov broke off, pointing out the cockpit window. "What goes on here? Somebody break a big pillow or something?"

Blue looked out the window and saw that it was indeed snowing. "Where do you think we are?" he asked.

"Over mountains."

"What mountains?"

"Himalayas maybe. They're plenty big and snowy."

"Aren't you sure?"

"Hell, no. I am a pilot not a thickheaded navigator. You tell me to follow that plane. I say okay, swell. You don't ask me where it's going."

Blue peered through the window, trying to see past the torrents of snow. He thought he could dimly make out the towering shapes of a chain of rugged mountains just ahead. "What's our present altitude?"

Gustanov shrugged. "Hard to say for sure."

"You do have an altimeter, don't you?"

"Sure. Right here." He tapped one of the dials on the instrument panel. "Broken though."

Suppressing his growing rage Blue leaned forward and again tried to peer through the haze of snow. Yes, those were definitely mountains up ahead.

Couldn't Gustanov see them too? All of a sudden one of the mountains loomed up very close. Blue yelled a warning. At the last moment Gustanov jerked back on the wheel. The plane soared upward at a steep angle. Through the window Blue saw the jagged slopes of a white mountain whizzing past. It looked close enough to reach out and touch.

When the plane finally leveled off he let out his breath. "Wasn't that rather close?"

Gustanov drank from his bottle. No sweat," he said. "I see it coming all the time."

"What about the other plane?"

Gustanov looked at the radar screen. "Up above us now."

"Maybe we ought to go that way too."

"Not a half bad idea."

After a few minutes steady climbing the plane broke through a layer of clouds and left the snowstorm behind. To the east a patch of light began to glow. Dawn was on its way.

"Down there is Tibet," said Gustanov after a while.

"I thought you weren't a thick-headed navigator."

Gustanov looked hurt. "Any good pilot must possess a keen knowledge of local geography."

"Does that include mountain ranges?"

"What's your hang-up, round belly? We didn't hit anything, did we? When we run into a mountain then you give Gustanov a ring and complain."

The clouds remained thick below them. It was difficult to believe that anything was alive down there. The white blip on the radar screen led them on.

Thirty minutes later Gustanov reported:

"Our friend is heading down, I think."

"Landing?"

"Looks good, yes. You want to set down also?"

"Perhaps it would be best to survey the situation from the air before actual landing."

Gustanov pursed his lips. "That kind of tough maybe."

"How so?"

"Not a whole lot of gas left to burn."

"Didn't you fill the tank before leaving Kabul?"

"Sure, but there's maybe a little leak. I plan to fix, then forget. Just a baby leak. No big sweat, brother."

"Exactly how much fuel do we have left?"

"Ten minutes, say—fifteen maybe."

"Then it appears we're going to be landing," Blue said wearily.

"Can land, can crash." Gustanov shrugged. "The choice is yours, baby."

The plane dipped through the clouds, emerging above a flat desolate plateau. Blue could see no signs of civilization anywhere.

"Five minutes gas left maybe," reported Gustanov.

"Are you certain your fuel gauge is even working?" Blue asked pointedly.

Gustanov chuckled. "Only a loony would go up in the sky with a broken fuel gauge."

The land rose gradually in front of them, wrinkling to form a chain of rocky hills. "Our friend has landed," said Gustanov.

"Where?"

"On the other side of the hills, I think."

"What's there?"

"When we get there take a look and see."

When they got there Blue took a long look.

Nestled in a narrow valley was a village that would have seemed more appropriate to nineteenth century Bavaria than Tibet. Amid a lush setting of trees and greenery a number of chalet-like cottages lay scattered across the landscape while in the center of these stood what had to be one of the largest, most imposing structures Blue had seen in his life: an enormous, apparently windowless concrete blockhouse. At the far end of the valley was a strip of black pavement where Xavier's plane sat parked.

"Land beside it?" asked Gustanov with a nod.

"We do not seem to have a great deal of choice in the matter."

"This sure is one weird-looking place."

"Yes."

"Vacation paradise maybe?"

"Something like that, I imagine."

Gustanov set the plane down solidly on the landing strip and braked cautiously. "Sure never heard of any goofy villages around here."

"I have a distinct feeling," said Blue, "that the residents have not gone out of their way to publicize its existence."

When the plane stopped at the end of the runway Blue looked out the cockpit window and saw three men watching them. One was expected—Brother Xavier. The other two were not—Dr. Ling Chi Ho and Louie Roth.

Louie raised a hand and waved at Blue. In the other hand he held a gun.

On the runaway Blue and Gustanov stood with their hands in the air. "I am beginning to realize," Blue said, "that I have been the victim of an elaborate con."

"Tell him, Xavier," said Louie.

"I apologize for any deception, Mr. Blue," said the little man. "But it did seem the simplest way of luring you here. In the name of the Preservation Society, let me welcome you to the city of Futura."

6

Roused by the steady knocking at the door to his room in the Grand Safari Hotel Dr. Gordon Schwerner rolled off the bed, came to his feet, staggered to the door and turned the lock.

Darby Spock dressed in a clean khaki suit and smelling strongly of fresh perfume brushed past him. He wore his .45 strapped to his hip. "What the bloody hell have you been up to, Schwerner? I've been out there pounding on the door like a maniac for five minutes. I was afraid that bloody bastard had murdered you."

Schwerner shook his head. "I guess I must have been sleeping. I suppose it was that shot he gave me."

"Well, if you ask me you're damned lucky that's all it was. These pygmies are a strange breed. Frankly they've always given me a rather severe case of the willies. Some say the whole bloody bunch dates back to the dawn of man. How's the leg, by the way?"

"It seems—" Schwerner broke off, stunned. The swelling in his leg had vanished and there was no lingering pain. He reached down and gingerly pinched the flesh just below his rolled-up pants. "That's odd. I seem to be perfectly all right. I wonder what he gave me."

Spock grunted. "Some native poison no doubt. Like I said you're damn lucky to be alive. But we'd better hurry. Mohammed bloody Bello is expecting us for dinner."

"Dinner? Already?" Schwerner glanced over his shoulder and saw through the window that it was dark. "I suppose I ought to change clothes."

Spock folded his arms and sat down on the bed. "I'll wait for you if you don't mind."

Feeling more than a little ill at ease Schwerner removed his torn and soiled garments and changed into a pair of gabardine slacks and a polo shirt. "Did they recover the van and jeep yet?"

"Only the van, I'm afraid. According to Bello the jeep was a total loss. I'm half inclined to believe him for a change though. That elephant gave it a hell of a whack."

"But we can still go on, can't we?"

"We've got to give it a try. We'll wait for tomorrow though. None of my boys has turned up yet. Bello says he's got people searching behind every bush but I'm beginning to have my doubts. Either way it's going to be bloody difficult without them."

"But we can manage?"

Spock nodded. "We're damn well going to have to."

They proceeded downstairs to the main dining room, a vast ornate chamber suitable for banquets. Each of the several dozen tables had been set with white linen although only one was presently occupied.

When they entered Mohammed Bello jumped up and waved to them cheerily.

They joined him at a table near the center of the room. "I've taken the liberty of ordering for the three of us," he said. "My chef is an absolute master at preparing buffalo steak."

Until now Schwerner had been unaware of how utterly famished he was. A lean man in a baggy tuxedo glided up to the table and poured a quantity of red wine into each of their glasses leaving the bottle behind on the table. When he moved away Schwerner caught the telltale scent of the dead and suddenly felt considerably less hungry than before.

Bello noticed his choked expression. "I apologize for any unpleasantness," he said, "but it's a strict policy of mine to forbid the wearing of perfume among my employees. I find it such an artificial affectation, don't you? All men should be proud of who and what they are. There is never a good reason to disguise reality."

Schwerner nodded politely, glancing across the table at Spock who was glowering in rage. "What about my boys?" he said gruffly. "Have you managed to round them up yet?"

Bello swung his head. "Alas, friend Darby, the news there is not good. Apparently our brief acquaintance, the rogue elephant, threw quite a scare into them. My pilot has spent many hours methodically searching from the air and found nary a sign of man nor beast. I hope this will not seriously impair your plans for the future."

"Oh, we'll make do," Spock said airily. "If necessary we can always stop off at the castle."

"Castle?" said Bello with a bemused frown.

"The Renaldo Castle." Spock's eyes narrowed. "Surely you've heard of it."

"That hoary old tale? Yes, of course. But surely no one lives there now."

"You don't know about the Vincentes?"

"The teachers of disturbed children?"

"They live at the castle."

"Oh, really?" Bello looked surprised. "No, I hadn't heard that. How very interesting. They must be my nearest neighbors. So that's your destination." He turned and looked at Schwerner. "The Renaldo Castle, is it?"

"Ah, no." Schwerner couldn't understand why Spock had felt it necessary to bring up the castle. "We've come here on a fishing expedition—I'm a devoted angler."

"Ah, the freshwater lakes. How stupid of me to have forgotten."

The spook in the tuxedo now returned bearing food. Schwerner held his breath till the man went away and then attacked his meal with a passion. Bello had spoken truthfully: the steak was indeed superb.

"All due credit must go to my chef," Bello said when Schwerner complimented him. "A meal such as this is a mere lark for him. Prior to coming to work for me he held sumptuous court in one of Dar-es-Salaam's most splendid restaurants."

"Dar-es-Salaam?" said Schwerner, paling. "You mean he's a spook too?"

"All of my employees are," Bello said smoothly. "It's a strict policy with me. Darby will tell you it's because I am such a horrible miser but the truth is it is only compassion that impels me."

Schwerner struggled not to let his revulsion show. He had traveled five days in the company of Darby Spock without any undue discomfort but somehow the thought of a spook actually touching the food he ate was deeply disturbing. He reached for his wine and swallowed a gulp.

"By the way," said Spock, jabbing his fork at Bello in an accusatory manner, "I still don't quite understand what it is you're up to out here." He had already put away several glasses of wine and was now pouring himself another. "And don't go giving me any nonsensical guff about how you've retired. You're up to something and I'd damn well like to know what it is."

Bello laughed. "Ah, friend Darby, you are such a suspicious fellow. Yet I have nothing to conceal. My work here is largely in the nature of a hobby. During your arrival did you perhaps notice the presence of a large, rather unsightly concrete warehouse?"

"I noticed it," said Spock. "What have you got hidden there? A heroin manufacturing plant?"

"Ah, Darby, always the jokester. But what say we make a bit of a game out of it? When I mention the word Africa what is the first thing that pops into each of your minds?"

"Death," said Spock.

"Wild animals," said Schwerner.

Bello beamed happily. "How amazing. In a real sense both you gentlemen have stumbled upon the correct solution. Death and wild animals—that is indeed at the root of my work here. As you are doubtlessly aware—especially you, Darby—the animal population of the African continent has been declining at a gradual but steady rate for the past century. It all began with the wholesale slaughter of many species by members of your own white Christian race during the late nineteenth and early twentieth centuries. Elephants in particular were prized for their ivory while zebra, leopards, and even hyenas were senselessly slaughtered so that they fancy women of New York and Paris could strut about wearing their pelts."

"That was all a bloody long time ago," said Spock, pouring yet another glass of wine. "What does it have to do with you—with now?"

"A very great deal, I am sorry to say, for this wanton slaughter had repercussions which reverberate to the present hour. Ecological cycles were violently disrupted, centuries-long feeding patterns permanently disturbed. As a consequence the great herds continued to dwindle in number until now they are threatened with final extinction."

"Hogwash," said Spook. "The big herds are all up north. The water is better there."

"Alas, Darby, I lived in the north for many years and there are no large herds there."

"Then you should have looked around better. How do you think I manage to make my living?"

"By sheer ability. By pure good fortune. And also as the last of the great white hunters the field is yours alone so to speak. If another attempted to compete with you there would surely be insufficient game to support two."

"You're talking through your bloody hat again, Bello."

He shook his head sorrowfully. "If only it were so."

"But even if you weren't what does this have to do with your warehouse?"

"I have chosen to devote the next several years of my life to doing whatever is possible to preserve and hopefully restore the natural wildlife of this marvelous continent. In the warehouse I have established an animal hospital and research laboratory. During my recent trip abroad I approached several of the world's leading animal biologists, offering them employment. In the meantime, my own people and I do what we can. So, gentlemen, if your sleep is disturbed tonight by the roar of a lion or the bellow of a hippopotamus, please think nothing of it. It will only be poor simple idealistic Mohammed Bello doing what he can to preserve Allah's most precious gift—the treasure of life itself."

Spock gulped his wine, glaring at Bello. An enormous spider appeared suddenly from nowhere and began a steady march across the tabletop. Spock doubled his fist and started to bring it down when Bello reached out with surprising speed and caught his wrist.

"Please, Darby. Need I reiterate how I feel about the sanctity of life?"

The spider plodded relentlessly on, tumbling off the far end of the table, regaining its legs, and then striding off across the floor in the direction of the kitchen.

Spock jerked his arm free of Bello's grasp. "This research you say you're conducting," he said in a low tone. "Does any of it just happen to involve elephant must?"

Bello shook his head. "As a matter of fact I have never—"

"And is that perhaps why the elephant that attacked us today was a rogue that wasn't really a rogue?"

Bello smiled uneasily. "Really, Darby, you grow far too suspicious. Whether that particular creature was infected or not I cannot say. The elephant is after all a singular beast, far more intelligent and less predictable than generally assumed. I can only assure you of one thing: I did not put him up to assaulting you. I love the animals of Africa, it is true, but I have not yet attained a point where I am able to, like the fabulous Dr. Doolittle of legend, communicate with them on a personal basis."

Spock belched. The whites of his eyes had turned a rabbity pink and the tip of his nose had taken on a crimson hue. "I wouldn't put it bloody past you to try though." He reached for the nearly empty bottle of wine and almost knocked it off the table. Catching it by the stem he pulled it toward him and emptied the remaining contents into his glass. "You've always reminded me of an animal yourself, Bello—a bloody spineless cobra."

His genial expression intact Mohammed Bello rose to his feet and bowed, first to Spock, then to Schwerner. "If you gentlemen will please excuse me I really must be about my duties. Should you experience any further needs feel free to regard my servants as if they were your own."

"I have a need right now," said Spock. He shook the empty bottle over his glass. "I'm bloody thirsty."

"I'll see that another of my finest is brought to your table."

"Better make it two. I feel especially thirsty tonight."

"Two bottles it shall be, friend Darby."

Bello turned on a heel and headed across the room, disappearing into the kitchen.

"Bloody spineless bastard," muttered Spock. "Foul shitless bung-hole."

"Now look here," said Schwerner, his voice tight. "Is it really necessary to insult the man over and over? He did save our lives after all—my life at least."

"Who asked your bloody opinion?"

"No one. But I think you ought to hear it. Desmond Blue hired you to serve as my guide and to otherwise assist me as necessary. I'm here on a case—an extremely delicate and important one—and I would much prefer if you kept your personal animosities to yourself. And why did you feel it necessary to mention the Renaldo Castle? The fact that we're going there was supposed to remain secret."

"I did it to see how that sly bastard would react. I wanted to see the guilt in his eyes."

"And...?"

Spock smiled grimly. "Bello's too canny to give his hand away that easily."

"Then listen here. From now on I really must insist upon a modicum of civil behavior. Whether you approve of Bello or not we're going to need his help to get back on the road tomorrow. If you find it impossible to comply with my wishes, then I strongly suggest you take your van and return to Zanzibar without me."

"And leave you here with that—that fiend?"

Schwerner folded his arms. "The decision is yours to make, Darby. My intention remains to press on and reach the Renaldo Castle. If you cannot assist me in that, perhaps Mohammed Bello can."

"He'll assist you right into your grave."

"The case I'm here to pursue does not involve Mohammed Bello."

"Are you sure of that?"

"I have no reason to think otherwise."

"Then I suggest you think on it again. If something rotten is going on—and I don't imagine you'd be here if it wasn't—then Bello's mixed up in it. You can damn near count on that. He's mixed up in it up to his bloody neck."

The waiter arrived then, gliding on soundless feet, and deposited two bottles of wine on the tabletop. Spock rose to his feet, grasped a bottle in each big hand, and moved unsteadily away. "I'm going to my room."

"As you wish. Get so drunk you can't move. It doesn't matter to me. But in the morning I'll expect you to be polite to Mohammed Bello. Do you understand that?"

"Go to the devil," said Spock. Then he grinned. "But I'll see you in the morning."

With a jaunty wave he sauntered off in the direction of the elevator.

Schwerner let him have a decent head start, then came to his feet and took the staircase up to his room.

* * * *

Alone in his room Schwerner lay down on the bed and made a serious stab at trying to concentrate on the case at hand. What about Mohammed Bello for instance? Was there any real basis to support Spock's vague allegations? Nothing that Schwerner could discern. In all the excitement of the last few hours he had perhaps tended to lose sight of his real reason for being here in the first place. Yet the central problem remained and until he actually reached the mysterious Renaldo Castle and discovered for himself the exact nature of its connection with the Sect conspiracy there wasn't much he could actually do.

A series of peculiar noises from outside drew his attention away from his thoughts to the window. He came to his feet, crossed over, and drew back the curtains. The room faced the front of the hotel and directly under the window a bright light illuminated a circular patch of lawn. In the distance beyond, Schwerner could make out the big concrete warehouse but there were other indistinct shapes in the darkness as well, shapes he could not immediately identify.

As he continued to watch, one of the shapes moved, lumbering forward into the light. To Schwerner's amazement the shape turned out to be an elephant, one only slightly smaller than the one that had attacked the jeep earlier. The elephant paused below the window, lifted its trunk in the air, and appeared to sniff the evening breeze. After a moment, lowering its trunk, it went on.

Schwerner shifted his gaze and concentrated on the other shapes beyond the ring of light. He was now able to identify several. One was clearly a male lion and another—somewhat farther away—a leopard. A third shape, larger than the others, he thought must be a rhinoceros or a hippo. The grounds of the hotel seemed to have become a veritable menagerie of wild beasts.

Schwerner let the curtains fall back and returned to the bed. He lay down on his back and put his hands behind his head. He felt oddly weary all at once, an aftereffect of the injection the pygmy doctor had given him no doubt. Whether he actually slept he was unsure.

It seemed only an instant later when someone was pounding frantically on the door.

It was Darby Spock, hair mussed, khaki jacket splattered with mud. "Let me in," he said breathlessly, pushing past Schwerner. "And shut the bloody door. I've discovered something important—something damnably important."

Schwerner closed the door. In spite of his disheveled appearance Spock no longer seemed the least bit drunk.

"What is it, Darby? What have you found?"

Spock's eyes darted about the room. "You don't happen to have something on hand to drink, do you?"

"Damn it, Spock, if you've managed to put away both bottles you took—"

"Come off it, Schwerner. I thought you were supposed to be a detective. It takes more than a few bottles of wine to get Darby Spock stinko. I was lulling that bastard Bello, that's what I was doing. I told you something rotten was going on here. Well, now I've bloody well found it out. That elephant attack today was no accident."

"What are you talking about?"

"It'll be easier to show than explain. Come along but be damned careful. Bello's sure to be lurking around somewhere close and if he catches us prowling about it'll be the end of us for sure."

Schwerner was reluctant to go along but Spock seemed sufficiently convinced that he had uncovered something important that he felt he had no choice. They went down to the lobby. "Can't you at least tell me where we're going?"

"Outside. To that bloody animal hospital of Bello's, that's where."

"We can't go out there. I saw an elephant from my window just a minute ago. And a lion too. They'll tear us apart."

"No, they won't. Not unless Bello tells them to. If they weren't safely tamed his own people couldn't freely move about either, could they? Now keep quiet and follow me."

They crossed the broad expanse of the lobby and slipped through the door. The electric light bathed them in an ethereal glow. From the lawn Schwerner could clearly make out the various animals lurking in the darkness beyond. There were many more here than he would have guessed—at least a half dozen lions that he could identify. Spock grabbed his sleeve and pulled him forward until they were outside the halo of illumination. They edged cautiously past a tawny lioness. The big cat sat licking a paw and paid them no more attention than she would a passing flea.

"If one of these things eats me alive," Schwerner muttered, "Desmond Blue will be most displeased."

"If one of them eats you alive," said Spock, "then I'm next on the bill of fare. So you can forget about Blue's ire."

The evening had turned chilly. Bent low to the ground the two men moved toward the concrete warehouse, then Spock swung sharply to the right so that they ended up approaching the building from the side rather than straight on. When they reached the windowless wall Spock knelt on the ground.

"Now what?" said Schwerner, crouching beside him.

"Put your head down here," said Spock. "There's a crack in the wall. Put your eye close and you can see everything inside."

Schwerner squatted down beside the wall. The crack was quite narrow but when he placed his eye against it he could indeed see inside the building. At first the light dazzled him but after a moment he began to make out certain shapes. The interior of the warehouse consisted of a single large room. In the middle of it lay an enormous gray shape near which stood two human figures dressed in white.

"I see two men—and something else, something big."

"That's the elephant," said Spock. "When I was here before I saw them bring it in."

"It's lying on its side."

"They knocked it out. With a tranquilizer gun. Can you see what they're doing to it?"

Schwerner stared hard. The two men in white were standing close to the elephant's head. There was a great raw open patch in the top of its skull and a circle of pink showing through, "They've cut a hole in the skull bone."

"Right. And they're planting something in the brain."

Schwerner pulled his head away from the wall. "Planting what?"

"Don't ask me. Some kind of electronic device, I'd wager. Something with which to drive the poor devils batty whenever Bello wants. Pavlov would be proud. These animals not only drool on command—they kill."

"You don't know that for sure, Darby."

"What else do I have to do, man? Draw you a picture? For God's sake, you've got eyes in your head the same as mine."

"They could be surgeons—veterinarians. Maybe the elephant is ill and they're operating. Bello did say it was an animal hospital."

"Hogwash," said Speck.

Schwerner again fastened his eye to the crack in the wall. One of the men had turned away from the elephant so that he was now facing Schwerner directly. Schwerner's breath caught in his throat and he emitted a gasp of surprise. "Good Lord." He drew his head back from the wall as if he had been burned.

"What is it?" said Spock. "What are they up to now?"

"I know one of those men."

"It's not bloody Bello, is it? He wasn't there before."

"No, not Bello. One of the men I was sent here to look for. One of those involved in my case."

The man whose face Schwerner had seen was none other than the blond-haired pinch-faced conspirator.

"See?" said Spock. "I told you this whole thing smelled to bloody heaven."

"I'd better keep an eye on him. Now that I've found him I don't want to lose him." Schwerner put his head back close to the wall and made certain the pinch-faced man was still there. He and the other man now appeared to be stitching up the wound in the elephant's skull. Schwerner leaned back on his heels and rubbed his chin.

"What are you going to do?" said Spock.

"Try and follow him, I suppose. Wait till he comes out and see where he goes. You'd better go back to the hotel, Darby. There's no reason for you to be involved in this now."

"Don't you want company?" Spock tapped the butt of his .45. "You can have this if you want."

Schwerner shook his head. "I'm not very good with firearms, I'm afraid."

"Well, do be careful, man. Remember, Bello is someplace around here too."

"I will," said Schwerner. "And thanks, Darby."

"Don't mention it, Gordon old chap."

Coming to his feet Schwerner edged cautiously around to the front of the warehouse facing the hotel. There were no trees or bushes close by, nothing to provide a satisfactory place of concealment. Schwerner lay down flat on his stomach, rested his chin on the ground, and fixed his attention on the faintly visible rectangle of the door. As soon as he had situated himself he was startled by a movement to his right but it was only Spock on his way back to the hotel.

As Schwerner waited in the darkness for the man he was waiting for to emerge the cold seeped into his body. The ground beneath him was wet and mud stuck to his clothes. He gritted his teeth and glanced at the luminous dial of his watch. It was already after midnight. Then it was one o'clock. Two. Around two-thirty a curious lion sidled up and sniffed the bottoms of his shoes. Schwerner froze in terror, praying that Spock was correct and the animal was harmless. After a few moments that seemed like hours the lion wandered off.

The explosion of light when it finally came caught Schwerner unprepared. He had been watching the rectangle of the door but it was the entire wall that rose up into the air with a noisy groan. He cursed his own stupidity. Of course it would be impossible to fit a full grown elephant through a man-sized door.

By the time his vision cleared the wall was already falling shut and the elephant had vanished in the dark. For a moment he was afraid he had lost the man too but then squinting he made out two dark figures outlined against the receding light. He waited until the wall clanged shut, then rose to his feet. His muscles had tightened from disuse and his legs ached dreadfully. He nearly fell before finding his balance. The two men were conversing in hushed tones. After a moment they separated. Schwerner didn't know what to do then—it was much too dark to tell which man was which—but then he caught a hint of an odor and knew that one of the men—the one heading away from the hotel—was a spook.

Schwerner followed the other man.

He moved off briskly toward the hotel, stopping only once on the way when he passed a pair of leopards. Crouching down the man patted the two beasts fondly, stroking their fur and speaking in a soothing voice. Then he went on.

As the man entered the circle of light in front of the hotel Schwerner hung back. He waited until the man had actually entered the hotel and then broke into a run. He barged through the door and into the lobby. If the man for some reason had chosen to linger Schwerner would have to think up a quick excuse for being out alone after dark but it would still be better than losing him entirely.

But the man was not there. The lobby was deserted.

Schwerner hurried to the staircase and listened intently. There was no sound of footsteps from above. Then he went to the elevator. The open cage stood vacant in front of him.

"Damn it," he muttered. "Damn it to hell and back."

A hand dropped on his shoulder. "Would you care for a little assistance?"

Schwerner turned. It was Spock, smiling broadly, a bottle of wine in one hand. "I thought you might be in need of an additional pair of eyes on the inside," he explained. "I've been waiting here all this time."

"Then you saw the man come in?"

"I saw him all right." He nodded toward the corridor to his left. "First door on the front side. If he'd tried to go farther you'd have caught him. He was barely gone when you came charging in."

"Did you get a good look at him?"

"Fairly good. I was crouched behind a fern."

"You didn't recognize him?"

"Never saw the man before in my life."

Schwerner looked down the corridor at the indicated door. "I'm going to try and talk to him."

"Are you sure that's wise? He'll know you were following him."

"Not if I'm careful. I'll tell him I was out looking for Mohammed Bello and heard a noise."

"You're sure he's the one you're after?"

"Positive. But I still want to find out all I can."

"I'll go with you." He laid a hand on his .45. "Never know when a chap like me might come in handy."

They went down the corridor. Schwerner raised a hand and rapped on the door. At first there was no response then a familiar voice called out, "Yes? Who is it please?"

"That's bloody Bello," whispered Spock.

"It's Dr. Schwerner. I wanted to—to ask you something. May I speak with you a moment?"

"Of course, Doctor. One brief instant please."

Schwerner turned to Spock. "Are you sure this is the room he went into?"

"Of course I'm bloody sure."

"Then what's Mohammed Bello doing in there?"

"That's something you'll have to take up with him. All I know is I saw your man go in there too."

It was several minutes before the door opened at last, revealing Bello's smiling face. Boldly, as if it were the most natural act in the world, Schwerner marched straight in, forcing Bello back into the room.

Schwerner looked quickly around. The room apparently served as an office of some sort. He saw a desk, a swivel chair, and a number of filing drawers. The one window was shut and covered by curtains. There were no doors—not even a closet door.

"You wanted to ask something, Doctor?" Bello was staring in some confusion at Schwerner's muddy clothes.

"Uh, yes. Yes, I did. I wanted to know if…" He broke off, wondering if Spock could have been mistaken. There was no place in the room large enough to conceal a man. The window was the only means of escape but surely he would have heard it open and close. "I wanted to know if you'd seen Spock," he finished rather lamely.

Bello's smile grew wider. "Why, there he is now. Standing right behind you."

Schwerner turned, feigning surprise. "Oh, there you are, Darby."

"Merely went out for a little early morning stroll," Spock explained. His words were slurred—as if he were drunk. "We spooks never sleep, you know. It makes life difficult at times. I think I miss dreaming more than anything else."

Then Schwerner figured it out. Desmond Blue, brilliant detective that he was, would have spotted the truth long before. The solution was really quite obvious. Bello was the only man in the room; there was no place to hide; escape was unlikely if not impossible.

Therefore...

Schwerner stared long and hard at the dark grinning face of Mohammed Bello. What he attempted to do was peer beneath the surface features and external flesh to the man beneath. He ignored the close-cropped hair, the thin beard, the flat nose, the black impenetrable eyes. Instead he concentrated on the size, shape, structure, and pattern of the bones.

And what he uncovered was a man he had twice glimpsed before: once in a photograph; once in the warehouse.

He didn't have to see the smear of make-up over the left eyebrow, the thin strip of white peeping through. That only confirmed what he already knew.

Mohammed Bello and the blond pinch-faced conspirator: they were one and the same person.

7

"Breakfast will be served within the quarter hour, sir."

Agonizingly Alfie Jarrett forced open his eyelids. The robot loomed over him in the dark, a single red light winking off and on in its forehead.

"Christ," he groaned. "What the time is it?"

"Almost five-thirty, sir. Mr. Hennesey said it would be acceptable to permit you to sleep a bit longer than usual this morning."

"Five-thirty? Are you out of your mind? Go back and tell Hennesey to go to hell. I'm going back to sleep."

"Oh, I couldn't allow you to do that, sir." One of the robot's pincer-like hands closed around Alfie's forearm, gripping the bones with impressive strength, "Mr. Hennesey would be terribly distressed if you failed to join him for breakfast."

"Who wants to eat in the middle of the night?"

"Early to bed, early to rise, sir. That's one of Hr. Hennesey's favorite maxims."

"Then tell Mr. Hennesey I didn't exactly get early to bed last night." He laughed suddenly in spite of himself. "I did have a little rise though."

"Sir?"

"Never mind." Alfie managed to kick the bedcovers aside and attain a sitting position. "Get out of here and let me get dressed."

"I'll wait for you in the hall, sir."

After the robot had lumbered out Alfie rose painfully to his feet and struggled into his clothes. Grabbing his toothbrush, he swept past the robot and slammed the bathroom door behind him. He splashed several handfuls of water on his face and the back of his neck and scrubbed his teeth and tongue clean. He still felt as if a couple drunken bats were flying around the inside of his head. In the window a dingy twilight seeped through. Alfie looked out past the antique museum of Market Street and into the melancholy wasteland beyond. The whole world seemed covered in a thick soupy fog.

"Okay," he told the robot when he returned to the hall. "I guess I'm ready for my poison now."

"It's only fried eggs and crispy bacon, sir," the robot said calmly.

"Same thing."

They went down the winding staircase. The more Alfie moved the more awake he felt but he wasn't sure if that was an improvement.

"You're Henry, aren't you?" he said to the robot.

"I'm honored that you remember me, sir."

"What about Reynal? Is he anywhere around?"

"Reynal does not involve himself with routine household chores, sir. He serves as Mr. Hennesey's chief engineer at the project site. I imagine you'd find Reynal out there presently."

"This Reynal is quite a bright fellow from what I hear."

"Among robots Reynal is exceptionally superior."

"What about Susannah?"

"Who, sir?"

"Mr. Hennesey's so-called daughter. Isn't she superior too?"

The robot emitted a peculiar squeaking noise which might have been intended as a chuckle, "Susannah is a human being, sir, not a robot."

"That's funny. Somebody told me different."

"Then they must have been pulling your leg, sir."

"Could be," said Alfie. But he didn't think so. He believed he could tell when somebody was lying or telling the truth and Tess

Hennesey hadn't been lying. What it meant was that the other robots didn't know any better. Whether that was important or not Alfie couldn't say but at least it was interesting.

In the kitchen John Hartford Hennesey was seated alone at the head of the table. Across the room near the stove stood a beautiful woman with coal black hair, blood red lips, and a tiny heart-shaped tattoo on her left cheekbone. She wore a maroon satin robe and silver slippers. For a second Alfie tensed. But it wasn't Tess, he realized. It was just Susannah.

"Morning, sir," he said to Hennesey, sounding so chipper he almost made himself sick. "Early to bed, early to rise, I always say."

"Well, pull up a chair, son, and prepare to dig in. You haven't had the opportunity of meeting my other daughter yet, I believe. Susannah, this is Mr. Jarrett. Alfie, this is Susannah."

"How do you do?" said Alfie. Susannah came over and deposited a plate laden with a half-dozen strips of crispy bacon, four pieces of toast, and three fried eggs sunny-side-up in front of him. "I hear you weren't feeling so hot last night when I arrived."

"Nothing to fret about, son," Hennesey answered for her. "Only a touch of the bug. Reynal got her fixed up in no time at all. Right, darling?"

"That's right, Father," said Susannah with a radiant womanly smile that would have fooled Alfie if he hadn't known better.

This whole scene was starting to turn weird enough so that Alfie decided to concentrate on his food. The meal turned out to be utterly delicious. "Where's Tess?" he asked after he finished wiping his plate clean.

"Still sleeping, I imagine," said Hennesey. "Tess is an inveterate late riser. We'll be fortunate to catch sight of that young lady much before noon."

"Must be nice," said Alfie who was starting to feel drowsy again. He gulped his coffee.

"Maybe so," said Hennesey. "But one thing's for certain: sleeping late is a luxury only the female of our species can afford to indulge. We men have too much to do in our lives to loll around in bed all day and all night. Edison once remarked that he could find no good reason at all for a man to sleep."

He removed a cigar from inside his coat and jammed it between his teeth. It wasn't there a split second before Susannah appeared with a burning match and ignited the tip. Leaning back in his chair Hennesey puffed sedately.

"I've got a nice little surprise in store for you this morning, son. Normally we'd head straight out to the project site and get to work but since today's sort of a special day—your first one here—I thought I'd take you hunting. Ever done much of that?"

"Can't say that I've had the opportunity, sir."

"But you're up for it, aren't you? You're not one of those damn fool bleeding-hearts who say hunting's a barbaric sport?"

"It's never bothered me, sir." Which was true enough, although now that he thought about it the idea of a man with a gun slaughtering some poor defenseless animal didn't strike him as especially civilized.

"I figured as much. If you weren't a born hunter you wouldn't be here right now. Hunting and space travel are damn near the same thing, you know. They're both based on the urge to conquer. You want to know how many different kinds of people there are in the world, son?"

Alfie decided to risk a wild guess: "Two?"

"Exactly. Two kinds of people and only two kinds. Want to know what I call them? I call them the sheep and the wolves."

It seemed to Alfie that he'd heard something like this before. "I suppose you and I, sir, we're the wolves," he said, venturing another wild guess.

"You bet we are. The lone wolf: smart, sly, cunning, gutsy, and scared of nothing that isn't ten times bigger and forty times meaner. An animal born to lead the pack, never to follow. Let the sheep do the following. That's how they end up in the slaughterhouse, you know—by following the Judas goat. The forest is the rightful domain of the wolf—the great timberland. No slaughterhouse for him. No, sir."

Above his head Alfie heard a floorboard creak. Tess? he wondered hopefully. Somehow Alfie was desperately eager to see her again. He was finding it difficult to concentrate on much of anything other than what had happened in his room last night.

Hennesey rambled on, waving his cigar: "I've studied history, son—I know the facts—and throughout the past you'll discover a symbiotic relationship has existed between the sheep and the wolves. The wolves lead—the sheep follow—and the human species prospers. But a number of years ago something went haywire. The wolves were driven out of the temple, the sheep took control in the cockpit, and the result was the anarchy and chaos that surrounds us today."

"Are you talking about the slug attack, sir?"

"Oh, phooey on the so-called slugs. I'm talking about something that happened well before them. If we wolves had been running the show the way we should have when the slugs showed up, they wouldn't have got much past Pluto before we blew them halfway back across the Milky Way. No, sir, what I'm talking about is socialism. Socialism and Red Communism. That's what the eggheads call it when the sheep take over."

"I thought a lot of Communists were killed when the slugs came too. In Russia and China, places like that."

"So? Who cares? If the sheep are running things it doesn't make the slightest difference because no one of them is any different from any other."

"Then it sounds to me like the world is in a lot of trouble, sir." He was remembering Tess's advice not to try and argue with her father.

"So it is, son. So it surely is. But history is a cyclic process. The wheel's constantly turning. My hope is that when you and I reach Centauri it will serve as an inspiration to others—to the other old wolves like me and the young ones like you crouched down in their dens—that good old-fashioned rugged individualism is the only way of accomplishing truly cosmic goals." Hennesey jabbed out his cigar in his plate and pushed himself upright. "But enough idle chatter. Susannah, fetch me my cane. Mr. Jarrett and I are heading out to put a few of our theories into practice."

"Yes, Father."

Outside a two-seater jeep sat parked on the other side of the white picket fence. There was a strange robot dressed in regular clothes seated behind the wheel, a creature almost human in the wealth of its facial detail. Alfie had a feeling this must be the fabled Reynal. The robot turned and looked at him and blinked both dark narrow eyes.

Alfie assisted Hennesey into the back seat, then climbed in beside him. Two big guns—rifles—lay on the floor between the seats. "Early in the morning like this is usually the best time to head out on a hunt," Hennesey confided. "Your wild game is apt to be too full of sleep to put up much of a battle. That way we can blow them down where they stand without getting our hair mussed."

"That sounds easy enough, sir."

Hennesey placed a hand on Alfie's knee. "It's meant to be, son. Hunting's not a sport, a game. Never think of it that way. Hunting's a life and death pursuit. There's no sport in that, is there?"

The robot swiveled its head and looked back over a shoulder. "Where to, Mr. Hennesey?" Inside its mouth Alfie spied what looked to be a full set of human teeth.

"What do you suggest, Reynal?"

"Well, last night on my regular inspection tour I spotted a group camped downtown near old Van Ness Avenue."

"How'd they look to you, Reynal? Fat and sassy?"

"No, sir. Lean and mean, I'd say. There were several small kidlets in the bunch too."

"Good. They always put up a tough fight. They're quick on their little feet. Let's head that way and see what there is to see."

Reynal pulled away from the curb. An early morning trolley jammed with robot passengers went bouncing past, bell clanging. Alfie wondered exactly what sort of animals he and Hennesey were supposed to be hunting. This was San Francisco after all and as far as Alfie could figure the only critters apt to be found here were rats, roaches, fleas, and a few mosquitoes.

The gate in the stone wall swung open at their approach. Reynal steered through the gap and headed into the ruins of the city. As they went on the fog thinned and gradually lifted.

"What about Miss Susannah, sir?" Reynal asked. His voice lacked the metallic clacking tone of most robots. "Didn't she want to come along as usual?"

"I decided not to bring her this time. Call this a boy's day out. It's too soon after her illness for something as tough as a hunt. You did a fine job doctoring her by the way. She seems almost as good as new, cooked Alfie and me a damn delicious breakfast this morning too."

"I don't believe I've had the pleasure of meeting the young man, sir."

"Of course. How impolite of me. Reynal, this is Mr. Jarrett. Alfie, meet Reynal. He's a robot like the rest of them but the next best thing to a real man in my opinion. Reynal's my good right hand out at the project site and damn near everywhere else around here too. The other robots are programmed to obey him same as any human so if you ever get any back talk from one of them take it to Reynal and he'll straighten them out."

Alfie leaned forward. "How do you do, Reynal?"

"Quite fine, Mr. Jarrett." Reynal removed one hand from the steering wheel, reached back, and squeezed Alfie's palm. The metal sheath that covered his hand was surprisingly soft and pliant and through it Alfie could swear he felt bones, not steel.

As the skeletal husks of buildings came into view Hennesey became more excited. His head waggled on his shoulders and he tensed forward in the seat, his weight balanced on the head of his cane. He nodded at the stark landscape surrounding them. "I was born in a little town in the Middle West same as you, Alfie, but to me it was always the great metropolitan cities that represented the true heartland of the old U.S.A. Farms, *phooey*, I always said; the true business of America was business. People always think of George Washington as a planter but he was also the richest man in the colonies and a keen student of business trends. Same with John Hancock. Wolves they were—both of them. Too bad a hardnosed fellow like the old general had to fall under the sway of a Red Communist agent like Hamilton late in life."

"Hamilton?" The name rang only a faint bell in the back of Alfie's mind. "I didn't know they even had Communists back then."

"The term, no; the breed, yes. The thing always precedes the deed. Keep that in mind, Alfie."

Reynal had slowed the jeep down to a crawl. As he went on talking, Hennesey swung his gaze back and forth, examining each side of the street with care. Most of the few remaining structures here were three and four-story brick apartment buildings. Alfie looked too but saw nothing.

"That's one of the funny features of communism," Hennesey went on in a low voice. "Although created and refined by men who were wolves through and through—Hamilton, Marx, Lenin, Roosevelt, Mao—once put into practice it quickly became the domain of the sheep. John Randolph of Roanoke—my personal hero—and Thomas Jefferson—who started out on the right tack before he went wrong—battled Hamilton every inch of the way. In my opinion if they had come out on top—Randolph especially—we'd live in a hell of a different world today."

"Did Hamilton become president then?"

"He never tried. Hamilton preferred to run things from behind the scenes. Like a puppet master. Then he died in a duel."

"Who killed him? This Randolph guy?"

"No. The duel was a big phony, you see. It was another Communist, a fellow named Burr, who supposedly pulled the trigger. Burr was even cannier than Hamilton. One theory is that Burr wanted to make a martyr out of Hamilton. My own idea—backed by research—is that Hamilton had finally figured out the consequences of his ideas and was ready to switch sides. It's all damned complicated of course. The more complicated things are, the harder they are to figure out. The Communists know this and take advantage of it."

The more he listened to Hennesey the more Alfie wondered who in American history wasn't a Communist.

Suddenly, the jeep squealed to a stop. Reynal pointed ahead. "Do you see that, Mr. Hennesey? That may be smoke over there."

Hennesey shielded his eyes against the glint of the morning sun. He grunted. "That's smoke, all right. Campfire, I'd wager. Let's go take us a look see, Alfie."

Using his cane for support Hennesey managed to climb over the side of the jeep and into the street. It was his left leg that seemed to be the bad one again today. He reached back, grabbed both rifles, and handed one to Alfie. "Reynal," he said, "you spotted it. You get to lead the way."

They headed down the street in single file, Alfie bringing up the rear. Both Reynal and Hennesey moved with stealth and caution. Alfie tried to do likewise. This whole thing was starting to worry him. He was beginning to have a pretty good hunch exactly what sort of game Hennesey was stalking and it made him uneasy.

They had drawn even with the gutted frame of a red-brick two-story apartment building when Alfie spotted a thin stream of gray smoke wafting through the cavity of a broken window. Clearly seeing the smoke as well, Hennesey stopped, grabbed hold of Alfie by the arm, and leaned over to whisper. "Take the front door. Kick it in if you have to. I'm going to try the window. With any luck we'll catch the buggers in a crossfire."

"But you can't just—"

"Not now. If they hear us that'll be the end of it. Now scoot."

Reluctantly Alfie headed for the door. Reynal, crossed the street and stood waiting on the opposite sidewalk, long arms folded on his chest.

Alfie looked over at him. He could have sworn the robot was grinning.

Alfie mounted the front steps on the balls of his feet. He held the rifle in one hand, the barrel aimed at the sky. With his other hand he gave the doorknob a twist. Over his shoulder he could see Hennesey creeping along stealthily, his cane tapping dully. When the old man reached the window he ducked low and raised a hand.

"Go," he mouthed. "Let's do it."

Alfie gave the door a hard push. It stuck at first and he had to kick hard before it flew open. Jamming the rifle under his arm he lunged through the opening and swung immediately to his right, crouching down.

There were four of them in the small room: two adults—a man and a woman—and two small children. A campfire smoldered in the center of the floor, the source of the smoke. The four turned and gaped at Alfie as he burst inside. The four were savages, dressed in grimy rags.

Before any of them could move, a voice bellowed through the window. "Freeze, you slimy bastards, and prepare to die!"

Hennesey's flushed excited face showed through the gap.

"Hey, wait!" Alfie yelled. "I don't think—!"

Hennesey's rifle barked—once, twice, three times. Alfie froze in his tracks, too stunned to move. Then something big and heavy smashed into his chest and he went sprawling. The rifle flew out of his hands and skidded across the floor. Another shot rang out from the window.

Then there was silence.

Slowly, cautiously, Alfie raised his head. He looked at the bare room, the fire, the smoke. Then he saw the bodies. Three of them— the two children and the woman. They looked dead.

"Did you see that shooting? Did you see that goddamn shooting?"

It was Hennesey. He had come around from the window and entered through the open door.

"Three shots, three bull's-eyes. You've got to hand it to—"

Suddenly his voice cracked. He grabbed at his chest with both hands. The rifle clattered to the floor. His face turned pale. Alfie rushed over and grabbed his elbow. "Maybe you'd better sit down, sir."

Hennesey nodded wordlessly and let Alfie help him to the floor. His breath came in harsh rasping gasps. "Damn heart," he managed to whisper.

"It always acts up when I need it most."

"Are you going to be all right, sir?"

He shook his head. "Get Reynal. He's got—"

"Here I am, Mr. Hennesey." Reynal knelt beside the old man. He popped something open in his fist and stuck it under Hennesey's nose. Hennesey inhaled, his chest rising and falling in quick frantic jerks. Gradually the color returned to his face. He pushed Reynal gently away.

"That'll do."

"You forgot to take your pill again this morning, sir?"

"Guess I must have. Thinking of the hunt. Always gets me excited and I forget things."

"You did well, sir." Reynal indicate the three dead bodies on the floor. "You got most of them, I see."

"That I did. Alfie here didn't get off a shot. The leader of the pack ran over him and right out the door. What happened, son? I thought you were a hunter."

Alfie was about to stammer a protest when suddenly one of the bodies on the floor moved. It was the woman. She sat up, wiped some of the blood off her face with a sleeve, and said, "That was some splendid shooting, Mr. Hennesey. I have to hand it to you. You sure snuck right up on us that time."

By now the two dead children were also sitting up and wiping at their faces.

"You didn't hear a thing did you, Mary-Margaret? Who was that old buzzard with you by the way? Was that Bad Jacob or Cobbler Tom? Whoever it was he sure knocked hell out of the boy here, didn't he?"

Hennesey laughed. "I'll see that the usual assortment of goodies is on its way out to you, Mary-Margaret. Reynal here will take care of it. You stay here and wait for him to come back. There'll be fresh meat and potatoes, green vegetables, maybe even some coffee. Milk for the children too of course."

"That will be just fine, sir. Children, tell Mr. Hennesey thank you. Tell him what a generous man he is."

"You're a generous man, Mr. Hennesey," they said together.

"Thanks, kids. That's kind of you to say."

"Can we have some cookies this time too, Mr. Hennesey?" said the smaller of the two, a boy.

"That you may, lad. Thanks for reminding me. Reynal, a bag of the cinnamon snaps for each of these tykes. Don't forget it."

Using his cane, Hennesey managed to boost himself back to his feet. "By the way, Mary-Margaret, you seen anything lately of that funny looking Chinaman that was hanging around here?"

The old woman seemed to think. She shook her head. "Can't say that I have, sir. He seems to have up and vanished all of a sudden like."

"Daffiest Chinaman you ever saw in your life," Hennesey told Alfie. "Had bright red hair like a Mick. Susannah and I brought him down one day. She got him in the belly, me in the head. Instead of thanking me, he said I was suffering from some kind of inferiority complex. Never heard anything like that before. Savage like all the rest out here but he talked like he was some kind of psychiatrist or something. I told him it might be best if he moved on and it sounds like he did."

The two of them joined Reynal back at the jeep. As they drove back toward Market Street, Hennesey leaned over and patted Alfie on the knee. "Don't let what happened back there break your spirit, son. Next time I'm sure you'll do better."

"I thought you'd actually shot those people, sir. I guess it startled me."

"Who me? Shoot people?" Hennesey grinned like a cat with its paw in the fish bowl. "Why, I'd never hurt a fly."

When they reached the pink gingerbread Victorian house Susannah stood waiting on the porch to greet them. Hennesey gave her a tender kiss on the cheek. "Guess what, darling?" he said. "We bagged three of them today. Old Mary-Margaret and two of her brood. Cobbler Tom got away."

"How did Alfie do?" she asked.

"Gave it his best shot. Can you believe though? He thought we were using live ammunition." Hennesey sniffed the air. "What's that I smell cooking? I'm hungry as a bear in a cave. Always get that way after a successful hunt."

"I've got a pot of beans cooking on the stove."

"What about Tess? She out of bed yet?"

"Tess came down just a few minutes after you left, Father. She took the Lincoln out to the project site."

"What did she want out there?"

"She didn't say."

"Funny girl, that one," he grunted. Wrapping an arm around Tess, he went on into the house.

Alfie hung back deliberately. To be truthful he'd about had his fill of John Hartford Hennesey for the time being. He sat on the porch steps, watched a couple trolleys go past, and then got up and went out to where Reynal was loading a bag of potatoes into the jeep.

"Need a hand with anything?" he asked.

"If you wish, sir." There wasn't a drop of sweat on him of course, although the day had turned warm. "This way."

Reynal led him to a building the sign on the front of which said was a feed and grain store. Inside it was full of crates and boxes of food. Reynal went all the way to the back and opened a heavy door. A blast of frigid air escaped through the gap. "We need to get a side of beef, sir, and some pork."

Once the jeep was packed Reynal got back behind the wheel again and started the motor. "Thanks for your help, Mr. Jarrett."

"You're taking all this to those savages out there then?"

"Oh, yes. Mr. Hennesey is a man of charity, sir. He tries to help the less fortunate when he can."

"As long as they pretend to let him shoot them."

"I doubt they mind, sir. It's all a game to them too."

"Maybe so. I hear you're the chief engineer on the project."

"That's what Mr. Hennesey is good enough to call me, yes."

"He wants me to be his co-pilot, you know."

"He told me that."

"What do you think? I've got to admit I'm nervous. It's a long trip to the stars and back."

"I don't think you have anything to worry about, sir."

"You don't, huh? You think the rocket will get off the ground then?"

"I think it'll do that and more. It'll reach Centauri, sir. And bring you safely back home as well."

"I'm happy to hear that." Alfie couldn't help wondering. Could a robot be programmed to tell lies. It was an interesting question.

"Well, I'd better get going. Savages don't like to stay in one place long. I need to get this food out to them before they move on." He reached for the ignition key and suddenly let out a yelp."

"What happened?" Alfie, looking down. "Did you hurt yourself."

"A loose wire, I think."

"Better be careful. Don't want to electrocute yourself."

"It was just a shock, sir."

Reynal tried the key again and this time it turned.

He drove off.

Alfie stood there for a long moment watching the jeep as it disappeared down the length of Market Street.

So, he asked himself, can a robot receive an electrical shock? Can it feel actual pain? It didn't seem to make sense. What would be the point?

He turned and crossed back to the house. He could hear voices coming from the kitchen. Hennesey and, he thought, Susannah. No Tess though. On silent feet he went up the stairs and down the hall to his own room.

Inside, he pulled his suitcase out from under the bed, popped open the lock, and pushed aside a pile of socks and underwear. Then he ran a hand along the inside of the suitcase until he heard a soft click. Reaching inside the open flap, he removed the set of photographs Blue had given him to memorize.

He went through the photographs one by one until he came to the one he wanted.

It was the third from the bottom. The one showing the hatchet-faced narrow-eyed conspirator.

Alfie stared at the photo, smoothing out the wrinkled features as he did, softening the fleshy forehead, turning the skin from olive to silver.

Then he looked again.

It was close—damn close.

"Howdy there, Reynal," he said softly.

8

By the time Peter Mark came fully awake and dashed downstairs Ginger Cunningham was nowhere to be seen. As he went past the living room he looked in and saw floating horizontally in the middle of the air the image of a huge naked black man. The man's eyes were shut, his head tilted back, his mouth open. Peter could only surmise that the man was either fast asleep or else in the throes of some kind of ecstatic state.

He moved quickly on.

In the kitchen Oscar Stovall stood by the stove, eyes dancing with excitement, hands twitching at his sides, feet in a state of constant motion. "This is it for sure," he said, rushing up to Peter. "I just talked to Fire Captain Brady and he said the whole department is going out on this one. Come on. Hurry up. We better get moving or we'll miss out on the fun."

Peter followed Stovall toward the door. From the living room a piercing scream suddenly rang out. Peter froze for an instant then hurried on. It was only Jayne's tridee. Outside an evening mist filled the air like a gentle shower. Stovall started the bug's electric motor. As soon as Peter joined him he sped off with a whining shriek.

Stovall drove tensely, hunched low over the wheel, his eyes barely clearing the dashboard. As he drove he kept humming to himself, the hypnotic tune rising and falling in a dissonant wail. When they reached the Fire House it was jumping with activity. Beetle buggies like vigilant sentries lined both sides of the street. Stovall slammed on the brakes, leaped out, and sprinted for the doors. Peter hurried after him.

Many of the men were already dressed and ready to go in slicker raincoats, high rubber boots, and hard metal hats. Fire Captain Brady sat perched behind the wheel of the big shiny red truck. "Regulars ride with me," he called out. "Volunteers take your own buggies. We all know where we're going. Let's get there in one piece."

Once he was dressed in his firefighter gear, Peter hopped on the back running board. Soon after, the truck rolled forward, siren wailing. As the truck surged down the street, swerving to avoid parked beetles, Peter held on as tight as he could. The wind slapped at his face. His eyes filled with tears. Behind, a procession of buggies followed. The fireman closest to him—it was Hiram Evers—was laughing with glee. The excitement was contagious. "Do you know where we're going?" Peter shouted at Evers.

"Damn straight I do. Don't you?"

"Oscar said it might be Roy Goldman."

"That's the target all right. Ain't it a horse laugh? That fat bastard hanging around the Fire House all day and now us paying him a private visit at night."

"Is it books do you think?"

"Damn straight it is." Evers leaned close and shouted in Peter's ear, "It's a whole damn library from what I heard. We'll be pouring flames on them from now till daylight. If you ask me that son of a bitch has it coming."

The siren let out another mournful wail as they rounded a sharp corner, seeming to gather speed. Evers began to hoot and holler, slapping his leg with his free hand. Peter tucked his chin against his chest and hung on for life and sanity.

The fire truck slid to a halt in front of a two-story blue stucco house in the shape of a railroad car. The address on the front said 451 Spruce Street. A dim light shone through the curtained front window. The houses on both sides were dark and empty looking. Oscar Stovall was the first man off the truck. Fire Captain Brady had to call him back.

"Not so fast, men. Let's get the hose ready first and bring some axes too. We may have to knock down the door if he tries to pull any funny business."

As the trailing buggies began to arrive the houses lining both sides of the street came to life. People in night clothes surged onto the sidewalks and stood gaping at the scene. As Peter helped unwind the fire hose from the back of the truck he noticed a strange car parked in front of the Goldman house. It hadn't been there a few moments earlier and seemed totally out of place in this clean neat neighborhood. It was one of the most garish cars Peter had ever seen, a hot pink Cadillac convertible with the top up and the window glass tinted so that it was impossible to see inside.

Hiram Evers noticed him looking. "Know who that is, don't you?"

Peter shook his head. "No, I was wondering."

"That's the man himself. Mayor Lucius B. Washington. A fire like this one and he always shows up. It makes you feel kind of proud to know he cares."

Fire Captain Brady led the way up the front walk, Oscar Stovall tagging at his heels. Brady banged his fist on the solid looking door and shouted, "Open up in there, Roy! We know you're there!" Peter didn't see how anyone could possibly sleep through the commotion.

When there was no immediate response from the house Brady turned to the men gathered behind him. "All right, boys, he's asking for it so let's give it to him. Chop that thing down."

Oscar Stovall sprang forward, axe in hand, and brought the blade down solidly with a loud *thunk.* Wood splintered, chunks spewing in the air. Two other men joined him, swinging their axes. A big spotlight on the hood of the fire truck had been trained on the scene, casting mammoth shadows. The crowd of nearby residents edged closer. Peter spotted Bob Jones clad in slippers and pajamas and at his side Laurel Brady in a flannel nightgown. Small children hugged stuffed animals and watched with wide eyes. A baby began to wail.

"Faster!" Brady shouted. "Damn it, men, this isn't a drill! Let's get in there and get to burning!"

The door burst open. Flinging down his ax, Stovall charged through the gap. Peter found himself propelled forward by the crush of men from behind. The firemen rushed down a short hallway and into the living room. A variety of lurid paintings hung from the walls. There were witches soaring on broomsticks, pale ethereal ghosts, a bat, three shadowy spirits rising from the sealed crypt of a country graveyard. The biggest painting of all, a full six feet by eight, hung over the fireplace. It showed nothing other than the huge grinning countenance of a black-furred yellow-eyed cat.

"The dirty sick son of a bitch," said Hiram Evers. His face livid, he stared at the paintings and shook his head from side to side.

The door leading from the living room to the rest of house was closed. Captain Brady tried the knob and when it refused to open gave the lock a violent kick. The door flew open. The firemen rushed into the dining room, through it, and into the kitchen. Brady opened another door and led the way down a narrow corridor. He seemed to know exactly where he was going.

Halfway to the end of the passageway a door stood to the left. Brady stopped here and signaled for silence. Through the door Peter could hear a rhythmic click-clicking sound. Brady grabbed the door-knob and gave a violent twist. The door swung open. On the other side sat Roy Goldman in front of a cluttered desk. His fingers raced across the keys of a typewriter. A set of earphones were perched on his head and faintly Peter could hear the roar of loud symphonic music. Was it Wagner or Mahler?

Fire Captain Brady crossed to the wall, bent down, and pulled the plug from its socket.

Goldman spun in his chair. When he saw the firemen his eyes grew huge. "What is the meaning of this?" he demanded in a surprisingly dignified voice.

"Maybe that's what we ought to be asking you, Roy," said Hiram Evers.

"Let me handle this," Brady said. "Roy, there's been a formal complaint lodged against you for a violation under article seventeen of the city charter. You know what that is, don't you?"

"I do, Captain, yes."

"The illegal possession of contraband flammable materials in a private domicile. What have you got to say for yourself?"

"It's a darn lie of course," said Goldman.

"And you're the darn liar," snapped Evers.

Roy Goldman rose to his feet. He pointed a finger. "You bunch of small-minded fools. You pack of halfwit witch hunters. I want you out of my house. I want you out of here this minute."

"Now hold on there, Roy," said Captain Brady. "There's no reason to get nasty. We're only doing our duty."

"I don't want to hear about your stupid duty. There's nothing here that's any of your business."

"Then what do you call that crap you were typing away at when we came in?" asked Evers.

Goldman's eyes narrowed. "That crap as you call it happens to constitute an act of creation. That's something an illiterate fool like you wouldn't know anything about, Hiram."

"Then you admit it's a book you're writing," said Evers.

"It's a manuscript—a manuscript of a novel I've been working in my own free time—and manuscripts do not fall under the provisions of your precious article seventeen. So now if you so-called gentlemen don't mind I'd like to ask you again to take your silly firemen costumes and stupid idiotic minds and get out of my house."

"I said to hold on, Roy," said Brady. "There's something I need to check first before anybody goes anywhere."

He crossed the room, circled around the desk, and stopped in front of the far wall. Another painting hung here, one depicting a human-like figure, its face half-eaten away, stalking a terrified woman down a dark city street. Averting his eyes Brady removed the painting from the wall. Goldman emitted a strangled cry and lunged toward him. Hiram Evers sprang forward and caught Goldman in a bear hug. "Try that, you bastard, and I'll knock you silly."

Behind the painting gaped a round hole in the plaster wall. "Well, well," Captain Brady said. "What have we here?"

"None of your darn business," said Roy Goldman. "You get away from there or else I'll—"

Brady thrust his hand inside the hole and pulled out a paper-bound book. He let the book fall to the floor, reached inside again, and pulled out another book. He dropped this one on top of the first and wiped his fingers on his coat. "All right, men," he said, "there's plenty more in there where these came from. Let's gather up the evidence and get to work."

A number of men led by Oscar Stovall hurried to the wall and began removing books. When they were finished there were at least three dozen stacked on the floor, including several in permanent cloth bindings.

Roy Goldman, all resistance gone, stood staring at his feet.

"That's the lot of them, Captain," reported Oscar Stovall, a feverish glint in his eyes. "Now do we take them out and burn them?"

"That's what the city charter says for us to do." Brady nodded at the floor. "Everybody grab a handful and let's get to burning."

"What about this bastard?" said Evers, meaning Roy Goldman.

"Bring him along too, I guess. He's got a perfect legal right to witness the disposal of his personal property."

Peter helped carry the books outside. He glanced at a few of the titles. Some he knew: *The Time Machine, Frankenstein, Alice in Wonderland.* Several others—*Dandelion Wine, The Man Who Sold the Moon, Foundation and Empire, More Than Human, Childhood's End*—were unknown to him. Most of the books sported cover paintings in the same lurid style as the paintings on the wall.

The firemen piled the books in a mound in the middle of the lawn close to the sidewalk. The crowd that had gathered earlier had in no way diminished. Peter heard a low murmur of excitement as Hiram Evers emerged from the house with Roy Goldman in his grasp.

Fire Captain Brady ordered his men to form a half circle around the books. Then he went over to the fire truck, grabbed the fire hose by the nozzle, and dragged it across the sidewalk. The pink convertible had not moved. As he stood with the other firemen Peter thought he saw the outline of a face pressed against the glass peering through a window.

Clutching the fire hose in one hand Fire Captain Brady faced the crowd. "Fellow citizens of Winesap," he said in a formal tone, "what we have here before us is a prima facie instance of a willful violation of article seventeen of our city charter. I hope this will serve as an object lesson to all of you—most especially the youngsters—as to what can occur when one man tries to take the law into his own hands." He turned on a heel with military precision and surveyed his men. "Peter Mark, you're new to our town. We'll let you do the honors tonight. Step forward, young fellow, and perform your duty."

Reluctantly Peter came forward. The watchful eyes of the crowd converged on him. Captain Brady handed him the hose. Peter looked down at the brass nozzle in some confusion.

"Just give that gizmo on the underside a good firm squeeze," Brady said in an undertone. "That's all there is to it. One good squirt should be plenty. We don't want to set the whole town on fire. Not with Mayor Washington himself here watching."

Peter nodded glumly and advanced on the books. The firemen backed away to give him room. He aimed the nozzle at the mound and wondered what was supposed to happen next. In the glare of the spotlight a few more titles leaped out at him: *The Left Hand of Darkness, Timescape, The Eclipse of Dawn.*

Peter gave the lever on the underside of the nozzle a gentle squeeze as instructed. Without warning a stream of fire gushed from the hose in an energetic burst. Peter cried out in alarm and nearly lost his grip. The pile of books exploded into flames. Peter staggered back and threw up his free hand to shield his eyes. The blast of heat was overwhelming in its intensity.

Fire Captain Brady ran forward and drew Peter back. "That was more than plenty enough, son," he said breathlessly. "You'll get more accustomed to the equipment later on."

Behind them the crowd burst into spontaneous applause. Peter wheeled, staring dully, and noticed little Ginger Cunningham standing among them. There was a knowing smirk on her face that cut right through him. He looked away. Oscar Stovall had crept up close to the crackling fire and was gazing down at the burning books with open rapture. Peter dropped the fire hose on the sidewalk, wandered into the street, and dropped down on the running board of the fire truck. In front of the house Roy Goldman had apparently fainted. Hiram Evers stood over him, glaring down in contempt. Peter lowered his gaze and held his head in his hands.

"A little too much excitement for some folk tonight, eh, son?" It was Captain Brady. He sat down beside Peter and rested his hands on his knees.

"I guess so, sir."

"Wait'll you get back to the Fire House and scrub some of that grime off your face. You'll feel as good as new again."

"I hope so." Portions of the crowd now came forward to obtain a closer view of the fire. Among them Peter again noticed Ginger Cunningham. When she saw him watching her, she raised a hand and saluted in recognition. Peter turned his head away, feeling suddenly ashamed. For some reason he very much wished that Ginger had not been present to see him light the blaze.

The flames died slowly, flaring up now and then as a new book caught fire from underneath.

A sudden movement inside the Goldman house diverted Peter's attention. He looked up just in time to see a face peering from the front window and then it was gone. It was difficult to be certain of anything at such a distance in the dark and yet Peter was sure of what he had just seen.

"Over there, sir," he said to Captain Brady. "In the window just now. I thought I saw somebody looking out."

Brady shook his head. "I don't see anyone."

"It was a woman, I think. She's gone now."

"Roy's wife, I imagine."

"His wife?"

"If Theda's in there I wish she'd come out and take him inside. He's going to catch pneumonia lying there in the cold and damp like that."

"Do you know her well?"

"Theda? Roy's wife? Can't say I do really. She keeps to herself and Roy's not exactly the most popular fellow in town himself. A lot of people wish he'd stayed away when he ran off to Chicago a few years back."

"Is that when he got married?"

"While he was away? I guess it must have been. He didn't have a wife when he left Winesap and when he came back she was with him. Strange looking woman too. Some kind of foreigner, I imagine. There's plenty of them in Chicago, I hear."

Peter came to his feet and went around to the other side of the fire truck where he couldn't be seen from the house. If he recognized the woman she would likely know him too. He had seen her once before. In Rome. With Pope Sergio.

The woman in the window—Mrs. Roy Goldman—was the swarthy, darkly beautiful female Sect conspirator.

A PROFILE: PETER MARK

The man known as Peter Mark was twenty-two years old when:

—he relinquished control of the jet-propelled aeroplane he was flying and let it dive spiraling toward the desert below...

—his face, throat, hands, and penis were totally destroyed in the subsequent fiery crash...

—Desmond Blue pulled him from the flaming wreckage miraculously alive...

—Dr. Gordon Schwerner grafted steel plates to correct the horrible wounds to his body...

—and for the first time he saw God.

As far as Peter was concerned his life had commenced at that critical instant—with God.

Of everything that had transpired before—his name, appearance, heritage, life—he never spoke.

Those who knew him well had developed theories of their own of course.

Alfie Jarrett for one theorized that Peter had been a young guy with a load of personal problems. Alfie also thought it probable that Peter had been born rich but like most kids with money his upbringing had been mean and miserable. Maybe his parents beat him or maybe they were both killed by the slugs and turned into spooks who gave him over to an aunt and uncle who raised and tortured him or maybe he was left alone with a pervert piano teacher who tried to grope him in the dark. There were all sorts of possible explanations, Alfie conceded, but explanations were pointless anyhow since all that mattered in life was who you were and what you were and never how come or what for.

Alfie also believed that Peter had once been a notorious rapist.

"Oh, come off it," said Crystal LaFleur. "Peter wouldn't hurt a rattlesnake that was ready to bite him."

Alfie went on to say he didn't think Peter had been any ordinary run of the mill stick it in and run off kind of rapist. Knowing Peter, he'd be more the type to go down selflessly on his victim's privates for like ten hours and only when she was ripe and ready, when she was moaning and cooing and panting and begging for it, would he slip it in and take his own pleasure.

"That shows you've never been raped," said Crystal with disgust.

"But," said Dr. Schwerner when Alfie tried his preposterous rape theory on him, "that still doesn't explain why the poor boy would try and take his own life."

"Who says he did? Maybe the plane wreck was an accident, something went haywire in the engine."

"No," said Schwerner flatly. "I was there when it happened and Peter never denied that it was a suicide attempt."

"Then who knows?" said Alfie. "Maybe there was something else that went wrong. I'll bet that was it. One night Peter picks up this dyke by mistake and she raises a fuss and it makes him feel rotten so he tries to kill himself. I'll bet you a million that's exactly what happened."

Schwerner was not only not a betting man, he was also firmly convinced that Alfie's ridiculous obsession with the less pleasant aspects of carnal lust such as rape and humiliation was more his problem than Peter's.

Besides, Schwerner had his own theory as to Peter's past history. Schwerner believed Peter must have been a great physician.

His youth would have presented no barriers. Genius as Schwerner well knew was often the province of the young. Peter had been a brilliant surgeon who transplanted pulsing hearts, sliced open tumorous brains, and shaved away carcinogenic growths. He lived alone in an austere room in a large metropolitan city and dedicated himself soul and body to the practice of his chosen craft. Then one afternoon he met a blind girl of no more than sixteen or seventeen selling flowers on the street and fell hopelessly and instantly in love. When she confessed to him that she'd been blind since birth and the doctors had long ago given up any hope of a cure, Peter refused to accept the judgment of science and soon devoted himself to nothing else than finding a cure for her blindness. After three years of research and study he believed he had found a way. The surgery took twelve incredibly tense hours to complete but in the end he was successful and when the lovely girl obtained her first sight of the beautiful world surrounding her she burst into tears of joy and fell limply into the arms of the man who had saved her from the curse of eternal darkness. Later they were married.

"My God, Gordon," said Nadia van Hauten softly. "I never imagined you were such a rank sentimentalist."

Schwerner frowned. "I only report the likely facts as I conceive them to be," he protested.

"You forgot to explain the suicide too," said Alfie.

"That came much later—by several months at least. The poor girl must have died—presumably in an accident, perhaps as a consequence of a rare incurable disease. In any event Peter knew that he could never live without her and so attempted to end his own life."

Crystal LaFleur said she didn't have the vaguest idea who or what Peter could live with or without or who he had been or who he had not been and furthermore she didn't think it was anybody else's damn business but as long as everybody was taking guesses then she, okay, she thought he must have been had been a musician. Everybody seemed to forget what a great guitarist he was. She further suspected, considering his age, that he had most likely played in a rock 'n' soul band. Not there was anything wrong in that—Crystal liked a lot of such music herself—but the truth was that travelling musicians weren't exactly noted for practicing monogamy while on the road. The way she saw it one time the band arrived on tour in St. Louis or Pittsburgh and some other empty city the slugs had flattened and while Peter was taking a nap the other guys went out and picked up three savage prostitutes off the street and brought them back to the hotel and started taking turns. Peter resisted joining in for a long time—he had a steady woman friend back in Hollywood whom he genuinely loved—but his maleness finally won out over his conscience and he had brief intercourse with one of women. Even though he felt terrible about it afterward he'd still done what he'd done and used the poor woman as if she were nothing more than a vessel for his own lust.

"That's the dumbest story I've ever heard in my life," said Alfie when Crystal first expounded this theory.

"That's because I'm not done yet," she said.

According to Crystal there existed in many cities a secret underground organization calling itself Women United for Life and Sanity. On occasion the members of the more militant faction of this group would deliberately inoculate themselves with virulent venereal diseases and then stalk the streets posing as prostitute savages in order to teach men who deserved it a lesson. As destiny would have it the three prostitutes picked up by the band in the ruins of Pittsburgh or St. Louis were members of this organization so that when Peter returned to Hollywood he unknowingly gave the terrible disease to his woman friend who subsequently died a slow horrible death. Realizing what must have occurred and what it signified concerning his own sexuality Peter logically decided that he could no longer bear to live in such a flawed male body and so attempted to kill himself.

"What about the disease?" Schwerner asked pointedly.

"What disease?"

"The one you claim Peter contracted from the supposed whore. If it killed his girlfriend, why didn't it kill him too."

"Because it works more gradually in men."

"Are you sure? His testicles are intact. We could examine the evidence to be sure."

"Mind your own business. Besides, maybe he was immune."

"Personally," said Nadia van Hauten, breaking in, "I'd like to hear more about these Women United for Life and Sanity. Did you make that up?"

Crystal winked. "It's not a half bad idea though, is it?"

Lacy Bach who had once been a Gypsy fortuneteller in a carnival and who honestly believed she'd sometimes succeeded in glimpsing the future also had a theory about Peter's early life though she seldom spoke of it. Lacy thought that Peter had probably been just an ordinary person little different from the billions of others around the globe. She didn't think it likely he had been a notorious rapist or a famous surgeon or a successful rock musician or anything like that. Lacy thought Peter had been a normal average decent young guy kind of person like what he was now except for the steel skin grafts on his face and hands. (Lacy was in love with Peter but felt that didn't necessarily distort her judgment.)

"And again it fails to explain the suicide attempt," said Schwerner.

"Are you sure?" mused Nadia. "After all, thousands if not millions of ordinary people kill themselves every year and nobody really knows why. What makes you think Peter is any different?"

Another problem with all these theories was that not one of them attempted to explain the jet aeroplane Peter was flying that day, how he'd come to be in it, who it belonged to, why its loss had never been reported.

The one person who might have been able to provide some illumination here was Desmond Blue.

But Blue, listening to these theories expounded, never volunteered a word. He just sat in his big easy chair, scratching the hound Baskerville behind it ears.

Then he belched.

9

Twenty-five kilometers north northeast of Brussels Pierre Chabrol lost control of his beetle buggy when the left front tire the struck a pothole in the highway. Pierre's new bug was a cherry red roadster—an Algerian-made Studebaker—so newly minted that it seemed to him to radiate youth and vigor so that only moments before as he drove along Pierre had been contemplating how truly fortunate he was to be the owner of such a magnificent machine. In the entire range of his acquaintanceship Pierre could recall only four others who possessed beetle buggies equally as splendid and all were wealthy Parisians while Pierre himself was merely a humble salesman of intimate female apparel. The purchase three weeks ago of the roadster had consumed all the funds he had meticulously set aside during ten years of such work, crisscrossing the European continent countless times, flattering department store owners, cajoling tight-fisted buyers, bestowing small gifts upon the wives and mistresses of floor managers. His own wife had recently informed him that he was an ingrate and a fool for squandering their savings in such a ridiculous manner while his only child, a daughter, insisted he had finally shown his true colors as a selfish and frivolous man. His boss, the head of the sales department in Paris, had made a loud joke about possible embezzlement but throughout it all Pierre retained his sincere conviction that what he had done had been well worth the cost. He was now at last a well-respected man. Where before he would sometimes wait thirsty and hungry as long as sixty minutes at his table in the small roadside cafes where he dined, this morning at breakfast his meal had scrupulously appeared in no less than seven minutes flat. A remarkable miraculous transformation, thought Pierre Chabrol, and all because of the new roadster.

Wrestling the wheel, braking with caution Pierre soon managed to bring the swerving bug back under control. Breathing hard, sweating profusely in his heavy linen suit he pulled off to the side of the road, climbed out, and inspected the wheel and axle. On his hands and knees in the gravel he promised himself if anything was damaged he would hold to blame the idiot Belgians for refusing to maintain their highways in a decent state of civilized repair. Because its suffering citizens could no longer afford to purchase magnificent buggies like his, the Belgian government saw no good reason to fix their ancient potholes. Pierre was not fond of Belgians. The only people worse in all Europe, he believed, were the Germans who at least made up for their chilly manners by serving as the most eager customers for his wares.

"Which way are you going?"

Pierre jumped in surprise, banging his head on the fender. Looking up he discovered standing over him a young man and woman dressed in summer garments. Both had blue eyes and yellow hair like Swedes.

"What do you want of me?" Pierre asked, rising awkwardly to his feet. "I'm only poor salesman."

"We'd like to ride in your vehicle," the young man said, pointing down the highway. "If you're going in the same direction we are."

"I—yes, I'm going to Berlin," Pierre said.

"Is Berlin on the way to Moscow?" the young woman asked. Her voice was similar in tone to that of the young man though colder and less personal.

"I suppose it could be, yes. I never go past the Polish border but I believe there's a regular daily train to Moscow."

"Then you can take us with you." The woman gave the man a push. By the time Pierre hastened around to open the door for them the two of them were already inside crunched together in the passenger seat.

"That's all you want from me then?" Pierre said, as he turned the ignition key. "Only a ride?"

"What else could we want?" the man asked.

"Well…money for one thing." Pierre tried a laugh. "There are a great many thieves along these roads. Especially here in Belgium." He drove back onto the highway and accelerated. "This bug is a new

Studebaker. It cost all of my life savings. You could have tried to steal it from me."

"We have no use for money," the man said.

"Or anything else of yours either," added the woman. "My name is Lai. His name is Jai. We are most happy to know you."

"Pierre Chabrol," he said with some relief. The two of them did appear sincere. "You are brother and sister perhaps?"

"Perhaps," said the woman—Lai—with an odd giggle. "Here comes another buggy too," she added, looking at the highway ahead. "Watch it go by. *Wheee*! It's very fast."

"A mere bucket of bolts," Pierre quickly corrected. "Compared to this Studebaker. Here, hold on tightly." He stepped down hard on the accelerator to give them an idea but let up before one of the many Belgian police sedans that patrolled the highway spotted him. "You must be Swedes. Or perhaps Norse. Your English is excellent by the way."

"We are both human beings," the young man—Jai—said, as if this were in dispute. He shifted his position in the seat so that he could look directly at Pierre. "A person we met in Paris—a man with coal black skin and ragged clothing—told us there was a creature in Moscow who was not human."

"The so-called slug—the Occupant? Yes, I suppose. No one's ever actually seen it as far as I know."

"We want to meet this creature. It's why we're traveling to Moscow."

"I'm not sure you'll be able to. The Russians are a secretive lot. They always have been. That's why I never go there."

"We intend the creature no harm. We have serious questions to ask it."

"That seems fair enough, but the Russians…" He shrugged. "They have their own ways." In truth Pierre did not much enjoy talking about the slugs. Or even thinking about them. His father, mother, and two dear sisters had all vanished on that terrible day in Bruges where they'd gone on vacation. If they had later returned as savages—as many had—he had remained happily ignorant of the fact.

"They won't stop us," Jai said.

"They can't," Lai agreed.

Pierre was beginning to feel uneasy again. He couldn't for the life of him think of any good reason for wanting to visit that murderous monster in Moscow. "Are you scientists of some kind? Is that why you're going there?"

Jai seemed confused.

"A scientist is what Dr. Schwerner is," Lai explained. "A maker."

"But we are not makers."

"No, but this creature might be. That's why we're going there to see it."

All of this was beginning to sound nonsensical to Pierre. He was regretting now his offer of a ride—made from fear alone.

He looked at his watch. "It's drawing close to two o'clock now," he said as pleasantly as he could manage. "This is the time I usually stop for lunch."

"We have no money for lunches," Jai said. "We have seldom eaten since we left the mansion."

"Then perhaps it would be best if I left you off here," Pierre said with rising hope. "That way you can catch another ride without having to wait while I have lunch."

"We don't mind. Time is of little interest to us. We'll go in and sit and sit and watch while you eat."

"I only have enough money for my own lunch, I'm afraid," he said. As he did, he wondered if that was wise. What if they saw it as another reason to rob him? If they took his new bug they could sell it along the way and then take a train directly to Moscow. Still, if they were going to rob him, wouldn't they have done it before now?

"I could buy you some coffee though," he said. "And perhaps a sweet roll you could share."

"We don't require food," Jai said.

"But we do like the taste," Lai added. "We will accept your offer of coffee and a sweet roll."

"There's a roadside café not far ahead now. We can stop there. And of course while we're eating you could look for other rides."

"No." Jai shook his head firmly. "We will stay in this buggy until we reach Berlin."

"That may not be your wisest course," Pierre said. "There are other faster vehicles on the highway than mine. In Germany especially. There are many fast bugs there—old ones—from before the time of the slugs."

"This is as fast as we care to go, thank you."

Pierre nodded, deciding to let the matter go and accept the inevitable. Perhaps the two of them were indeed a bit odd, slightly eccentric like the English and the Scots. But as long as they didn't harm him—or his property—what could it matter? They were company at least. Company was always welcome on a long drive.

A short time later Pierre turned off the main highway and followed a winding dirt road that led into a small village tucked between two hilly mounds. Outside a cafe where he had dined many times before, Pierre let his inherent kindness overcome his lingering anxiety and invited Lai and Jai to join him for lunch. He explained he'd found some extra money in one of his sample cases and he would be glad to buy them lunch in return for their pleasant company on the road.

It could all be charged against his expense account anyhow, he thought. All he had to do was claim they were prospective buyers.

And maybe they were. The woman was lovely. She would look fine in many of his top of the line items.

* * * *

After he'd eaten his fill—and once more the food arrived with a promptitude he found astounding—he felt considerably more relaxed. While waiting for the check to arrive he puffed on a cigarette and decided to satisfy his curiosity on one point. "Earlier I asked whether you two were sister and brother and you did not have a chance to reply. You look so nearly identical that I am frankly curious. Are you perhaps twins?"

The man smiled. "Everyone always says that when they see us together—but we aren't, not really."

"The resemblance is nevertheless uncanny."

"A brother and sister must have the same father and mother," he said as if reciting from a lesson, "and we don't—not really. Also a brother and sister cannot copulate together while Lai and I have a great many times."

Pierre felt a flush of embarrassment. Perhaps he was old-fashioned but it disturbed him to hear lovemaking spoken of quite so openly. "I would have been willing to wager you were at least cousins."

"Cousins?" Jai looked perplexed, "What are cousins?"

Pierre endeavored to explain. "Cousins are if your father and Lai's father were brothers or your mother and her—" He stopped, feeling perplexed himself. "You really don't know what cousins are?"

"We are friends and companions only," Lai put in from across the table.

"I see. That's fine." By now he was happy to drop the subject. "I was simply curious, that was all."

* * * *

When they returned to the buggy Pierre had to chase off several young boys who'd come to look and admire. Lai and Jai again slid into the passenger seat together while Pierre got behind the wheel, started the engine, and headed back onto the highway.

Because the roadster lacked headlights—an expensive accessory he'd chosen to forgo for reasons of economy—it would eventually be necessary to stop for night. His original intention had been to keep driving until he reached a certain hotel not far from the Rhine where he had stayed in the past but the lunch had consumed more time than anticipated and he now doubted he would be able to reach this preferred destination before dark. As diplomatically as possible he raised the subject with Lai and Jai, suggesting again that while he stopped for the night they should attempt to secure other transportation.

"We'll wait here in the bug until morning," Jai said. "Then we can resume our travels."

"But there's hardly room for both of you to sleep comfortably."

"We will not sleep then."

"But don't you have to? It's been a long day after all and—"

A sharp *bang* from the car's right front end suddenly boomed out. Pierre jerked the steering wheel fiercely to the left, let up on the accelerator, and punched the brake. A steady thump-thumping noise echoed as the car rolled to a stop at the side of the highway.

"What is it?" said Lai. "Why are you stopping so soon?"

"A blowout, I'm afraid. Idiot Belgians. They refuse to take proper care of their public roads."

He got out and went around to the front of the car to assess the damage. As expected the right front tire was flat to the rim. He opened the trunk, got out the jack, and headed back to the front.

That was when three men emerged from the woods at the side of the road. Two of them were carrying rifles and all three had woolen ski masks pulled down to hide their faces. Pierre froze in his tracks and raised his hands in the air. The jack slipped from his fingers and clattered as it landed in the gravel. "What do you want?" he cried out. "I've done nothing to harm you."

"Keep quiet and your hands in the air and you will not be harmed," said the man without a gun. He spoke in gutter French. "Move except when you're told and you'll be shot. Have your companions get out of the car with their hands in the air."

"You are highwaymen, aren't you?" He looked up and down the road seeking help but as usual there wasn't a vehicle in sight.

"Don't expect the police to come to your rescue. They know to steer clear of places they're not wanted."

By now Jai and Lai had stepped out of the bug. They held their hands in the air but looked puzzled and confused.

The highwayman smiled through the slit in his mask. "I see you were generous enough to bring your pretty young daughter with you," he said.

"She is not my daughter," Pierre said miserably.

The man laughed. "Then all the better for us," he said.

Jai and Lai still seemed totally confused by what was going open. As the two armed highwaymen went through car, removing Pierre's luggage and sample cases and pawing through the contents, Pierre tried to explain. "These are Belgian highwaymen," he said in English. "Robbers and thieves. They want to steal our valuables. If we cooperate they likely will not harm us."

"But we have no valuables." Lai said.

"I know but I do." He decided this was probably as good a time as any to take out his wallet. He did, dropping in on the ground. He slid the wristwatch off his arm and dropped it too. "There," he said. "That's all I have with me. All my money and everything else. Now will you go away and leave us alone to fix the tire you ruined?"

The other two thieves were still going through his sample cases, taking out various items of negligee, holding them up, and laughing.

"My lady will look smoking hot wearing this," said one, showing a lace corset.

"Your lady couldn't fit into that if she went on a six-month fast," said the other.

"What's up with you, Frenchie, anyway?" said the first man. "Are you a dirty pervert of some kind."

"No, I'm a salesman. These are samples I show to store buyers."

"A likely story," he said. He was looking at Lai. "I have an idea. Why doesn't the young lady here join us in the woods to try on a few of these samples while you change your flat tire. That way when we're done we can all drive off together."

Pierre did not like the sound of this. The man hadn't even looked at his wallet yet. Instead he was staring at Lai. He knew such thieves rarely harmed their victims which was the main reason the local police let them alone. But what if this was an exception? What if the plan was to take Lai into the woods, rape her, and then once Pierre fixed the car kill all three of them, bury the bodies, and sell the beetle buggy for whatever they could get.

But if so, what could he do about it? There were three of them, two with rifles. He noted that even going through the cases the two men never set down their weapons.

He was considering making a desperate run for the woods in hopes of at least saving himself when what happened next happened so swiftly he was never afterward sure of the exact sequence of events. It seemed that one moment the highwaymen were all looking at Lai and grinning and the next their rifles flew out of their hands, they grabbed hold of their heads, screamed incoherently, and fell to the ground.

It wasn't until Pierre crouched down beside the one nearest him and felt for a pulse that he realized the man was dead.

And so were the other two.

"My God," he said. "My God, you've killed him all."

Jai and Lai stood there looking down at the bodies on the ground.

"These men were going to kill us," Jai said.

"I realize that. But you—you don't even understand French, do you?" It seemed an absolutely stupid thing to say—but what else? None of this made sense.

"You fix the tire," Jai said. "We'll fix the rest."

And so they did. The two of them carried the bodies into the woods and came back while Pierre was still finishing with the tire. Then they helped put his samples back in their cases.

Within twenty minutes they were on the highway again.

Pierre's hands on the wheel wouldn't stop shaking.

Two hours later as darkness fell Pierre stopped in another village where there was a small inn. He invited the two of them to take rooms near him at his expense but Jai refused, saying neither would need sleep tonight.

In his room at the inn Pierre could barely sleep. Who were these two? What madness had he stumbled into? How could he ever manage to get himself out of this terrible awful horror?

In the morning stumbling exhausted outside into the chilly dawn he saw that his beetle buggy was gone.

His luggage, his sample cases, everything was piled neatly at the side of the road.

But the vehicle—his beautiful Algerian-made Studebaker roadster—was gone.

And so were the two of them—Jai and Lai—along with it.

BOOK FOUR

DENOUNCEMENTS

Punctuate the following sentence: that that is that that is not is
not is that not so

—Old Grammar School Joke

1

Once the footsteps of Mohammed Bello had receded, Darby
Spock turned on Dr. Gordon Schwerner with a fierce angry glare.
"Schwerner, you stupid son of a horse's behind," he said in disgust.
"Knowing what you do about that bloody fiend you seriously intend
to let him come bold as punch and announce that he plans on joining us tomorrow? Correct me if I'm mistaken but did you perhaps
neglect to insert your brain when you woke up from your nap this
afternoon?"

Schwerner shook his head, stifling an urge to yawn. He sat on the
edge of the bed in his suite while Spock prowled the carpet in front of
him. It was dawn, the day already seemed full, and he was exhausted.
"Darby, please. Use your head. What else could I have done? Inform
Bello that we're on to his game and demand an immediate explanation? I'm sorry but I don't happen to think that would be a wise tac-
tic. If he wants to join us in our trek, I say let him. He's the one I'm
here to investigate after all."

Spock snorted, picked up a bottle of wine off the floor, drank
thirstily. "And if the bloody bastard decides to assassinate us as we
sleep?"

"Then I guess we'd better not sleep." This time Schwerner did
yawn.

"That's simple enough for me," said Spock. "I'm a spook. I can go years without more than an occasional nap. But what about you, Schwerner? You poor lifer. You look half dead already."

Schwerner managed a weak grin. "I suppose I'll have to depend on you to watch over me, Darby. Besides if Bello had wanted to kill us he could have done as easily here as out on the veldt."

Spock gave another loud snort. "He's too much of a bloody coward either way."

"Why? There's no one here except us, him, and a few loyal spooks."

"Like all cowards Bello lacks the fortitude to look a man in the eye when he pulls the trigger."

"Then isn't it better to have him with us where we can keep an eye on him rather than letting him sneak up on us from behind?"

"Maybe." Spock nodded grudgingly and took another drink. "I just wish I knew what he wants with Maria—at the castle."

"I suppose that's what Desmond Blue sent me out here to find out. Of course you don't have to go along if you'd rather not. There's really nothing preventing you from taking your van and going back to Zanzibar. I imagine Bello will find some other means of transporting the two of us from here to the castle."

Spock looked appalled. "Schwerner, you bloody prig. What type of man do you take me for? If you think I'd even consider deserting you now and leaving you in the clutches of that villain then you're sadly mistaken. What do I have to be afraid of? The worst he can do is kill me and I'm already dead."

Schwerner managed a grateful smile between yawns. "I appreciate that, Darby. I truly do."

Spock took another swig from the bottle and belched. "To tell the truth I haven't had this much fun since the time I led three ravishingly nubile American schoolgirls on safari way back before our alien friends dropped in to wreak their havoc and a mischievous hippopotamus ate every stitch of clothing they possessed one afternoon while they were sunbathing. There are two universal constants, Schwerner. One is the velocity of light in a vacuum and the other is Darby Spock."

"You sound like a man of science now, Darby."

"I am as a matter of fact. Earned a degree in nuclear physics at dear old Cambridge years before you were likely born."

"How did you end up out here then?"

"Fate, I suppose you'd call it. I fell arse over heels in love with a visiting scholar from Canada. Lovely boy, brilliant as well. When I found I was only one of several dozen who'd shared the pleasures of his bed I lit out in a fit of pique for Africa to bury my sorrows in the lust of the hunt. My uncle Alan was already an established white hunter in Nairobi and taught me the skills of his trade. The next thing I knew years had passed, Uncle Alan had passed on, killed by a rogue leopard, and I'd inherited his safari company. Then the bloody slugs passed over a certain rather unique brothel in Dar-es-Salaam I was known to frequent between trips to the bush and I found myself suddenly stone dead."

"But you lived again?"

"So they tell me." He laid the empty bottle down on the floor. "Now's the time for me cut short the story of my life and let you get some sleep before it's time for us to set off again."

"Thank you, Darby. I do appreciate that."

"I'll be in the corridor if you need me," he said.

* * * *

The next thing Schwerner knew it was late morning and he and Spock were carrying their luggage downstairs and through the lobby to the waiting van. To neither's surprise Mohammed Bello was already up and awake ahead of them, perched in the middle seat, a broad smile on his face. Seated behind him were two enormous half-clad black men. When Schwerner slid into the front seat he immediately smelled the scent of the dead.

"What's going on here, Bello?" said Spock as he situated himself behind the wheel.

"Oh, nothing, friend Darby, nothing at all," said Bello. "It is a truly wonderful day and all is good and right and beautiful with the cosmos, I am sure."

"That means you're ready to leave, I presume."

"Ready indeed, Darby, ready indeed. With good fortune and the blessings of a beneficent Allah I calculate we should reach our intended destination sometime shortly after first light the day after to-morrow."

"The hell you say." Spock turned the ignition and listened to the engine cough and sputter. He pumped the accelerator a few times. "The bloody Renaldo Castle isn't more than two hundred klicks distant from here. We can cover the distance in a matter of hours."

"With the proper equipment no doubt but my mechanic regrets to inform me that your engine block has developed a small crack. Do not push it, he warns, or else it may explode in your face. Slow is sure, he tells me."

"You wouldn't mind if I stuck my head under the hood and looked for this alleged bloody crack of yours?"

"Not at all, Darby, though it is quite minute, I understand, and such a search may consume several precious daylight hours."

"Then never mind. If it wasn't there before I wouldn't put it past you to make sure it's there now." He looked past Bello to where a number of boxes and crates sat piled against the rear doors. "What about our gear?"

"Everything we may require has been safely packed and stored. There are bags for sleeping, a snug warm tent, a portable cooking stove, enough food for—"

"And my rifles?" The engine caught at last. Spock fed it more gas then let it idle.

"Your rifles?"

"Yes, Bello. Rifles. Guns. Weapons. Things that go bang-bang and sometimes make other things dead. I keep three rifles in the van and another in the boot of my jeep. I don't see a sign of them back there."

Bello turned his head and spoke rapidly in a native dialect to the spooks in the seat behind. They shook their heads in unified bafflement and looked appropriately blank.

"My men tell me they saw nothing of any rifles when they recovered your gear," said Bello. "Perhaps your errant boys returned to the site of their cowardice and committed an act of pillage."

"Balls," muttered Spock. He put his hand on his holster. "My .45 ought to serve well enough anyhow," he added in a louder voice. "And what about those two matching bucks of yours, Bello? You're not intending to bring them along, I hope."

"As servants only. To handle the more tedious matters of daily routine."

"Like cooking our meals, I suppose."

"Well, yes, that and—" Bello broke off and let his mouth remain open a moment in surprise. "Surely you do not object because they are among the deceased."

Spock laughed hollowly. "It's not a case of the kettle calling the pot black, no." He released the hand brake, shifted into first gear, and took his foot off the clutch. The van crept forward. "You're quite welcome to have them come along if you want."

Schwerner leaned over and whispered into Spock's ear. "Darby, are you sure that's a good idea? With them along we'll be outnumbered."

Spock winked. "Don't fret about them," he said in a soft voice. "As long as they remain dead I know them a damn sight better than bloody Bello does. I'll handle them. Trust me."

Spock drove with precision and care. Although there was no clear road to follow he appeared to know the lay of the land intimately and never hesitated. On occasion they drove past a few antelope or grazing gazelle and once a solitary lioness raced majestically alongside van. The sight of these creatures made Schwerner recall the scene the previous night in the warehouse and he couldn't help wondering if these animals had also been tampered with by Bello and then set loose to roam the veldt.

As Spock drove Bello kept up a steady stream of chatter. He seemed quite familiar with every square foot of land they passed and had at least one anecdote to go with every landmark. This scrub tree was where four Roman Catholic nuns had in colonial times been sexually ravaged by a now extinct breed of anthropoid ape and this hill was where a company of Roman soldiers in the third century B.C. had been hailed as gods and then ritually eaten alive by a tribe of heathen Negroes. Schwerner didn't believe a word of it. And it was hot too. Incredibly so. With the windows down for ventilation the blistering heat swept through the van like a tide.

After less than ninety minutes of actual travel Mohammed Bello broke off in the middle of one of his anecdotes—it concerned a captive white girl raised by hyenas—lunged forward and jerked the keys from the ignition slot. The engine stalled immediately.

Spock swung around in a fury. "What the devil do you think you're doing now?"

Bello leaned back, wagging a finger, and slipped the keys in his shirt pocket. "Remember what I cautioned before we departed, Darby. Slow is sure. We don't wish to push the engine more than necessary."

"There's nothing wrong with the bloody engine. Now give me those keys."

Bello shook his head defiantly. "I won't do that, Darby. I feel responsible for the welfare of us all. A two-hour wait is definitely in order."

"Two hours!"

Bello nodded. "I am sorry but it is for the best." He glanced back at the two spooks who seemed to be observing everything through watchful eyes. "Patience is a virtue, Darby. Surely a man of your wisdom and experience should be aware of that."

Spock looked at the two black men and gave a grunt. "All right. Have it your way. A two-hour wait it will be."

Now that the decision to stop had been made Schwerner opened his door and stepped to the ground. If Bello had deliberately intended to select the most desolate piece of land in all Africa, he could not have done a better job of it. From horizon to horizon there wasn't a tree or bush or even a good-sized boulder in sight. Schwerner slumped down in the meager coolness provided by the van's shadow and wiped his face with a sleeve. A short time later Bello dropped down beside him. Spock and the two spooks had apparently chosen to stay inside the sweltering van.

"Isn't this marvelous country?" said Bello as he gazed at the desolation surrounding them. "If I am not mistaken you scientists like to proclaim that the first humans trod the earth not far from this spot."

"Yes," said Schwerner without much enthusiasm. "The fossil evidence points convincingly in that direction."

"Isn't that fascinating? To think that here where you and I presently sit fifty million years ago other human creatures may also have sat discussing the wonders of existence and the beauty of the cosmos."

"I doubt very much that such primitive beings would have been capable of abstract conceptualization. Besides, *Homo erectus* dates back no more than two million years not fifty."

Bello did not appear be listening. His eyes swept the landscape like a hunter in search of prey. "I have developed a certain theory of my own I would much enjoy sharing with you. Perhaps for a man like yourself with such vast scientific learning it will seem either foolish or obvious but I would like to run it past you nevertheless. My theory proposes that unlike the currently nihilistic view there is indeed a definite purpose to human existence and that the riddle of this purpose will in time be revealed. Do you dispute this theory or regard it as hopelessly elementary?"

"Neither necessarily," said Schwerner, drawn into the conversation in spite of himself. "I'm an atheist personally but don't necessarily reject the possibility of purpose or meaning in the universe."

"But without a god to supply that meaning?"

"Correct. A meaningful universe is not dependent upon the existence of an omnipotent being."

"I see. A somewhat singular viewpoint then."

Schwerner shrugged. "If you insist."

"Then let me share another silly notion of mine, one that just came to me now as we sat here discussing philosophical possibilities. What if the solution to the great riddle of meaning in the universe was to be revealed to us right here and now? What if in a sudden burst of insight and inspiration the two of us saw the answer to everything we seek to know? What then? How would our lives be affected? Would we rush out to preach to others the enlightenment we had found, would we perhaps do nothing, kill ourselves, go on no different than before? What do you think, Doctor? You are a wise and learned man. You must have an opinion to express on this matter."

Schwerner stared at Bello. What was all this about? he wondered. Was Bello in this abstract discussion of ultimate purpose making some veiled allusion to the conspiracy of the Sect and its secret intentions? "When you speak of the riddle of meaning, Bello, what is it exactly that you have in mind? Is it a definite objective—a goal—a final end point?"

Bello nodded slowly. "What else could it be? We have already agreed, have we not, that human existence began here. Given a beginning there must also be an ending, yes?"

"And what might that ending be?" Schwerner asked.

Bello laughed suddenly. "You ask me this, Doctor? I, a mere humble businessman, a former gentleman farmer? I know nothing of such solemn matters. If there is such an end point, then others may know of when and how it will come. But not I, Mohammed Bello. I am at best a modest man. For instance, I have often heard it said that the universe is finite. If this is the case, then does it not indicate that time is also finite."

"It may be," said Schwerner.

"Then so too is knowledge yes?"

"I don't think it's necessarily that simple, no."

"Isn't it? I thought we'd both agreed that time and the universe itself are both finite."

"But because something is finite does not necessarily mean it's simple. Knowable, yes, at least in a theoretical sense, but—"

"Will you shut your eyes, Doctor?"

"What?" Schwerner stared.

"Your eyes—will you close them? It's an exercise I often perform myself when I'm here on the veldt. Close your eyes and try to see the land beyond. Try it."

"The land beyond what?"

"Just see it, Doctor. Please. For your own sake not mine."

In spite of his better judgment Schwerner shut his eyes. Imagination, he knew, was not one of his strong points so what happened next may well have occurred through the power of suggestion alone. All Schwerner knew was that as he sat there with his eyes shut, feeling the searing heat, smelling the stink of his own sweat, experiencing a tense knot of nausea at the base of his stomach, he did indeed begin to glimpse something. It wasn't entirely a matter of vision—of sight. His other senses were also involved—smell in particular. There was a brutal primitive quality to his perceptions. What did it signify? He couldn't be sure. The perceptions were there—completely real—but the words to describe or explain them were not.

"What the bloody hell is going on out here?"

Schwerner opened his eyes and found Darby Spock crouched down in front of him, one hand on his knee. Spock was glaring at Bello seated beside him. "Were you trying to put a bloody spell on the poor man? He looks positively dazed."

"No, Darby, I'm fine," Schwerner protested. But was he? Where had he been? What had he just now perceived?

Bello was smiling innocently. "The good doctor and I were merely pursuing a philosophical point."

"With your eyes shut?"

"We were seeking the end of the universe that we live in."

"Hogwash," said Spock, his breath smelling of whisky. "You were trying to put him in a trance. Hypnosis. I know the kind of tricks you have up your sleeve, Bello, and I'm telling you you're not about to get away with them here."

"As usual, friend Darby," said Bello with his grin intact, "you are the man with the last word." Coming to his feet he brushed the dust off his trousers and climbed back in the van.

"Now what was that all about?" Spock asked when they were alone.

"To tell the truth I'm not really sure," Schwerner admitted. "For a while I thought he was going to reveal something important but now I'm not really sure what happened."

"A bunch of crazy mumbo-jumbo it sounded like to me."

"I suppose that's what it was, yes," said Schwerner.

The two of them got back in the van. Although barely an hour had passed, Spock insisted it was time to be on their way again. Bello protested, citing the engine block, but Spock waved him off and turned the ignition. "I've refilled he radiator with fresh water. We'll be perfectly fine. Now be quiet, Bello, and let me drive."

* * * *

In the end the second part of the trip turned out to differ little from the first. The landscape remained as unvaried and desolate as before. After two hours and perhaps fifty additional kilometers, Bello once more pulled the key from the ignition. "Here's where we'll camp for the night," he announced as the van coasted to a halt.

"For the night!" cried Spock, slamming his fist against the steering wheel in frustration. "Damn it, Bello, it's barely four o'clock yet."

"But the engine, Darby. Think of the danger, the risk."

"Damn the risk," said Spock. With a string of muttered expletives he jerked open the door and sprang out. Schwerner, happy for the opportunity to stretch his legs, followed. The two spooks, exiting from the back, immediately got busy setting up camp. The spot Bello had picked out was not without its charms. Only a few yards away a shallow stream gurgled past. Schwerner went over, knelt down, and splashed water on his face and neck. Sitting down, he pulled off his heavy boots and dipped his feet in the water.

A shadow fell over him. Looking up he saw that Mohammed Bello had managed to creep close again with his usual stealth. "I see you have found the river, Doctor."

Schwerner doubted that this meager trickle deserved such an imposing title. "The cool water is quite refreshing after the long drive I have to admit."

Bello pointed to a nearby rise in the land. "Just over there, if memory serves, lies a small freshwater body of water. Lake Clarence, I believe it's called."

"I don't think I've ever heard the name."

"The natives have a different word. Lake Clarence is renowned for its golden bass."

Schwerner felt a tightening in his chest and throat. His heart thumped. "Did you say golden bass?"

"Oh, yes. Quite famous among serious anglers, I believe. Record breaking catches have been pulled from the waters of Lake Clarence. A pity we don't have time to wander over and try our luck."

"And it's nearby you say?" Schwerner looked longingly in the direction Bello had indicated.

"Less than a kilometer, I'd say. You're intrigued, I see. I'd forgotten you were an avid angler. Come, let us consult with friend Darby and see how he feels about a slight diversion."

Schwerner hurriedly pulled on his boots and trotted after Bello. A canvas tent had been set up beside the van and the two spooks were now busily stacking kindling preparatory to igniting a fire. Spock, pipe clenched in his teeth, sat on the ground with his spine propped against the van's front bumper.

He glanced up curiously as Bello and Schwerner came rushing toward him. "Now what's all the bloody excitement?" he asked.

Schwerner waved his arms excitedly "Bello says Lake Clarence lies just over that rise."

"So it does," said Spock. "although it's barely much more than a pond. I could have told you that. I am a reputable guide, you know."

"Bello also says the lake is full of golden bass."

"Could be. I wouldn't know. I never eat fish myself. The bones are incredibly dangerous. Millions choke to death eating fish every year."

"But I was wondering, Darby. Since we're so close to the lake, wouldn't it be possible to jaunt on over long enough for me to give it a go? I have rod and reel and tackle with me."

"You mean now?"

"It's not far. And there's several hours yet before nightfall."

Spock was looking suspiciously at Bello. "If you go, then I think the three of us should. Me to make sure you don't lose your way and Bello because I don't trust the bloody bastard here alone."

"No objection from me," said Bello, his obsequious smile back firmly in place. "The exercise will do me good."

"Then go get the equipment you need, Doctor and I'll grab my pistol. We may as well go now and that way be sure we're back before dark. Your men can continue setting up camp while we're gone, Bello."

"Excellent planning," said Bello. "I only wish I could join the good doctor in his sport but unfortunately my compunctions against the taking of life extend even to those simple creatures native to our oceans, lakes, rivers, and streams. Nevertheless, it would be my privilege to observe a dedicated angler as he plied his skill."

"And cut the bull too, Bello. Even I know the one necessity for successful fishing is to keep one's mouth shut. Fish can hear voices strangely enough. Which means once we reach Lake Clarence you're going to need to keep your bloody yap closed for a change."

Bello looked sober as drew a cross on his chest. "You have my bonded word on that, Darby."

"Now you're a Christian?"

"Only when giving my bonded word."

* * * *

Lake Clarence when reached it proved a severe disappointment for Schwerner. He couldn't have said with certainty exactly what he had anticipated but it most definitely was not this tepid muddy pond barely a stone's throw across. As he prepared his rod and reel for an initial cast he scanned the surface of the lake in hopes of detecting the telltale ringlets that would indicate the presence of fish. Spock touched his arm and pointed to an object dimly visible on the opposite shore, "Did you see that?" he asked in a whisper.

Schwerner strained his eyes. "No, what is it?"

"A skull. Antelope or zebra, I imagine. Poor bugger must have stopped for a drink. The water's no good here. Don't drink it for God's sake."

"But the golden bass. It doesn't affect them?"

"I wouldn't know anything about that. You'll have to talk to Bello. He's the self-proclaimed expert here."

Schwerner removed an intricately woven purple-and-gold fly from the kit he carried with him and attached it to the hook at the end of his line. Then cocking his elbow, he made his cast, the fly soaring neatly through the air. As soon as it struck the placid surface of the lake he gave several swift jerks on the rod and then began reeling the line gently back in, causing the fly to bob and weave through the muddy brown water. He was by no means certain this was the best technique to follow—the few expert anglers who had previously stalked the legendary golden bass were divided in their recommended approach—but it seemed a good basic method with which to begin. As he turned the reel with his right hand he maintained a steady grip on the rod with his left. He used a five-foot fiberglass pole, feathery light and sensitive to the touch though nothing to compare in quality with some of custom-built rods he had at home. The surrounding quiet was cathedral-like in its solemnity; even the omnipresent insects had fallen quiet. Spock and Bello sat side by side in the grass a few yards behind where Schwerner stood, Spock puffing contentedly on his pipe, the gray smoke curling around Bello's head like a wreath. Abruptly the tip of the fishing rod jerked and Schwerner felt an exploratory tug on the line. When he let go of the reel the line shot through the water with a zing.

Involuntarily Schwerner gave an excited shout. A strike—and so soon. He jerked the rod high in the air and slammed the heel of his hand, against the reel to jam the line. Then he let go of the reel and held his breath as whatever had hold of the line commenced a furious run. "I think I've got one," he said. "It's the bass—it's got to be."

"Here," said Spock who now stood at his side. "I want you to have this too."

Schwerner looked down at his feet and saw Spock's .45 on the ground. "You're going, Darby?"

"A bit of business I need to attend to back at camp. Almost forgot but it shouldn't take long."

"What about Bello?"

"You needn't worry about him." Spock nodded at where Mohammed Bello lay in the grass, his eyes shut and his mouth ajar. "He appears to be taking a snooze."

Schwerner returned his attention to the golden bass he'd hooked and for the next thirty minutes while the battle raged it was as if he was no longer a solitary man standing on the shore of a muddy lake in East Africa but had been transformed into a mechanical instrument, an extension of the hook, the fly, the lure, the line, the reel, the rod. It was always like this when the angling went right and it was because of this sensation of transcendence—this out of body experience—that he had come to feel as he did about the art and sport of angling.

At last with a final weary flick of the wrist Schwerner brought the golden bass ashore where it lay weakly flopping in the grass.

He waited until it was no longer moving and then stepped forward to claim his prize.

* * * *

As he was removing the steel hook from the gills of the dead fish a hand fell on his shoulder. "Caught the bugger, did you?" said Darby Spock.

Schwerner held up his trophy. "It's awesome, isn't it?"

Spock squinted. "The poor thing's hardly bigger than my forearm."

Schwerner looked hurt. "That poor thing as you call it fought me to a near standstill for going on thirty minutes."

"Why let it?" Spock said. "You could have blasted it with one well-placed bullet in the beginning and been done with it."

"That's not sport, Darby—that's slaughter."

"Well, sport or not I don't see how one little fish is supposed to feed three grown men."

"I can try and catch more," Schwerner suggested eagerly.

Spock looked up at the darkening sky. He shook head. "We'd better get back to camp. Besides chances are the fish here are as poisonous as the water they live in. Better just chop off its head and save the rest for stuffing and mounting later."

While Spock went over and shook the still sleeping Mohammed Bello awake, Schwerner took a last long look at his prize then tossed the dead fish into the lake.

He collected his gear and the three of them soon set off for the campsite.

* * * *

They arrived just as dusk was falling. Oddly, though everything seemed properly set up for the night, there was no sign of Bello's two spooks.

"I can't understand what could have become of them," he told Spock after looking around and calling them. "They know better than to wander off without permission."

"Maybe a passing lion grabbed them," Spock suggested. "Or another of your rogue elephants."

Bello shook his head. "In that case there would be bones. No, I just don't understand it, Darby. I can only hope they'll soon return." He moved off, cupping his hands to his mouth and shouting in an indecipherable tongue.

Spock pulled his pipe out of his pocket, knocked the ashes out of the bowl, and ground them underfoot. He saw Schwerner looking curiously at him and winked.

"This was your work, wasn't it?" said Schwerner in a soft voice. "It's what you said you wanted to take care of back here. What did you do? Drive them off?"

'Let's just say that I persuaded them to head for the hills."

"How?"

"A few words to the wise. Nothing that would mean anything to a lifer." He looked enigmatic. "I put the fear of bloody death into them, so to speak."

"Lucky Bello happened to fall asleep when he did."

"Luck had nothing to do with it. A sleeping potion I sometimes use on myself." He held up his pipe. "It appears to be equally effective when burned and smoked."

"What if you'd knocked me out too?"

"A few minutes sleep wouldn't have harmed you any."

"I would have missed my beautiful golden bass," Schwerner protested.

Spock patted him on the shoulder. "Let's not quarrel over what never happened, Gordon."

It was pitch dark before Bello finally returned to the campsite. "The ingrates," he said, dropping wearily down beside the fire. "I cannot comprehend such irresponsibility. I searched for a kilometer around and found no trace of them—nothing at all. I don't know what we're going to do without them."

"Oh, we'll muddle through somehow," Spock said blithely.

* * * *

The following morning shortly after daybreak they were again on their way. Recovered from his despair of the previous night Mohammed Bello was his usual animated self once more. This second day of travel proved little changed from the first. When they set off Spock announced that they would likely reach the Renaldo Castle sometime shortly before noon. By the time three o'clock arrived and Bello lunged forward to once again jerk the keys from the ignition they were still more than fifty kilometers short of their goal.

"Damn it, Bello," said Spock, "If we keep going like this we'll never get there before dark."

"But the engine, Darby," said Bello, springing out the door. "We must not endanger the engine," he called back to them.

As they labored to set up camp Schwerner was the first to notice the figures approaching from across the veldt, "What do you make of that?" he asked, going over to where Spock and Bello were at work putting up the tent.

Spock laid down the hammer he was using and looked. "Men," he said. "Three of them. On foot too."

"Are they from the castle?"

"I wouldn't imagine so." He nodded meaningfully at Bello. "It's still a considerable hike from here."

"What do you think they want?"

"Maybe we ought to ask them when they get here."

The three men turned out to be black Africans, each extraordinarily tall, close to seven feet, and dressed in colorful cotton robes and brilliantly feathered headdresses. The faces of all three were decorated with streaks of garish green and gold paint.

"Goniani," Spock murmured as the men drew near. "Odd to find them way out there."

"Didn't you tell me something about the Goniani before?"

"Yes. They're the same bunch that put an end to old Renaldo. These three are high priests too unless I miss my guess."

"They're not dangerous?" Schwerner had noticed the men were carrying spears.

"They've never molested me."

As the three Goniani priests continued their stately approach Bello broke away from Spock and Schwerner and dashed forward to meet them.

"Now what's got into him?" Schwerner asked.

"It's a mystery to me. But we'd best find out."

By the time Schwerner and Spock reached them Bello had been there long enough to have become embroiled in an angry dispute with one of Goniani. This man, the tallest of the three, who wore a monocle in the socket of his left eye, was waving his spear threateningly in the direction of Bello's stomach. Spock hastily inserted himself between the two and spoke rapidly in a clicking tongue unfamiliar to Schwerner.

The Goniani priest, still glowering at Bello, lowered his spear. "This brown pygmy," he told Spock in excellent English, "dared to question my presence in this land. The man is either a fool or insane."

"My companion is indeed a fool," Spock confirmed.

"I was merely attempting to ascertain their purpose in creeping up on us like that," said Bello, peering around Spock, behind whom he had found refuge.

"See?" cried the Goniani, raising his spear once more. "Again the fool speaks offensively."

Spock glanced back at Bello. "Keep your bloody mouth shut," he whispered, "if you value your life. This isn't your plantation out here. These three would as soon kill you as look at you."

Bello's jaw tightened but he said nothing more. Turning back to the Goniani, Spock held his hands in front of his waist. "I must apologize for the outburst of this fool. His tongue is like a racing gazelle. It is disconnected to his mind."

The Goniani dipped his head in a gesture of acknowledgement. "Such fools are a curse upon all men everywhere."

"My name is Spock—Darby Spock."

"You are known among the Goniani as a great hunter. I am Nylun Bobutu."

"You speak my own language with the fluency of one who has journeyed to distant lands."

"I know Oxford."

"And I Cambridge," Said Spock.

Bobutu might have smiled. "Then we are rivals."

"But brothers as well," Spock added cautiously. "My white companion is Schwerner, a renowned doctor. The brown fool is the slave-monger Mohammed Bello."

"Him I recognize only as feces," said Bobutu. "His name is spoken among the Goniani as a substance found in unclean latrines."

"This is so," Spock readily agreed. "And his mouth when open is a shimmering sea of brown shit."

"And his mind as tiny as a beetle's turd."

The two of them went on like this for some time, insulting Bello back and forth.

Spock chuckled fondly. "My companion and I would deem it a great honor to share our sustenance with three of the Goniani tribe."

Bobutu looked genuinely saddened. "Alas we dare not tarry. Our mission demands haste."

"Is this mission one that involves the nature and beauty of the cosmos?" asked Spock.

"It does," Bobutu said. "A wondrous child has been born whom we travel to worship and adore."

Despite the oddness of Bobutu's reply Spock's solemn expression never wavered. "May I inquire where this wondrous child may be found?"

"As yet the portents are uncertain. My comrades and I have walked nineteen days and slept eighteen nights. The stars have informed us only that four are now one and a fifth is awaited. At that moment we may venture forth to pay obeisance to the whole—to the child."

"A great honor."

"And also a stern duty."

Bello leaned close to Schwerner. "Have you ever heard such heathen mumbo-jumbo in your life?" he whispered.

"We wish you great success in your mission," Spock said.

"That which is certain must be certain." said Bobutu.

"I am nevertheless honored by your confidences."

"As we are honored by the wisdom of Darby Spock."

As if at a signal the three men bowed their heads in unison and without another word or a backward glance went around Spock and continued on their way across the veldt.

As soon as they were safely out of earshot Mohammed Bello said, "Did you ever in your life hear anything so repellent? A child has been born, he claims. That's blasphemy—the purest blasphemy. If you'd let me have my head, Darby, I would have told them so too."

"If I'd let you have your head," said Spock, "they would have trimmed it off at your shoulders. I've heard of this fellow Bobutu. He happens to be among the highest of the Goniani high priests. Trying to tell him about faith and blasphemy would be like trying to lecture Schwerner here about science or fish. What Bobutu has learned and forgotten is more than most of us will ever know."

By this time the three Goniani were dim specks in the distance. Spock turned back toward camp. Schwerner fell into step beside him. "What did you make of all that?" he asked.

"The part about the wondrous child, you mean?"

"Yes. It certainly sounded strange to me."

"Well, true, but who really knows anymore? The Goniani may be a queer bunch but their priests are highly respected throughout East Africa. And they ought to be—their priests were among the few the slugs didn't carry with them. Bobutu's no fool either. You can count on that."

"He certainly seemed to believe what he was saying."

"I've no doubt that he does."

"Do you?"

Spock laughed. "Now who's the one talking blasphemy?"

* * * *

As darkness descended Mohammed Bello busied himself preparing dinner. It was a faux chicken stew, he revealed, a specialty of the fabled kitchen of the Grand Safari Hotel. Cooked in a tangy broth the meal proved thoroughly excellent and Schwerner ate a good deal more than he should have. As the last remnants of daylight filtered from the sky Bello excused himself, crept away to the tent, and apparently went to sleep. Spock came to his feet, yawned, and announced that he was going to build a fire.

Schwerner lay on his back and looked at the vast field of stars blazing above, attempting to identify some of the more obscure constellations of the southern sky. He felt even more than usually tired himself and it was a struggle to keep his eyes from sliding shut.

"See anything interesting up there?" Spock asked.

Schwerner turned his head and found Spock sitting behind him. A short distance away a small fire was burning.

"Nothing I haven't seen before. I spent most of my early life in the Southern Hemisphere."

"No miraculous portents of any sort?"

"You mean like Bobutu?" Schwerner smiled. "I don't suppose I'd recognize one if I did."

"A pity actually. The stars make it more difficult in a way. Sitting here looking up at them it's hard to be so bloody certain that something like that couldn't happen. A wondrous child? Who can say? It was supposed to have happened once before, I hear. Around two thousand years ago, wasn't it?"

"That's one theory, yes." Because of the time photographs Schwerner was one of the few people alive who knew for certain that something had indeed happened two thousand years ago. The trouble was that the Jesus Christ he had seen in the photographs looked awfully human in his suffering. Which was, he had to admit, quite possibly the point.

"And it's a theory that's dead," Spock said. "As dead as I am."

"Well, that's only because of the visit from our mysterious Occupants in their golden ships. After that it was difficult for many to continue to believe in God as the creator and humankind as the center of His universe."

"For Christians perhaps. But to the Goniani for instance it made little difference. Yet suppose the star of Bethlehem appeared in the sky again tonight? How many of us supposedly civilized beings would regard it as a miracle? Few of course. A supernova, the scientists would explain. A natural cosmic phenomenon. Nothing miraculous there."

Schwerner was about to respond when a flare of motion in the northeastern quadrant attracted his attention back to the sky. He looked up just in time to catch a glimpse of the last faint spasm of an expiring meteor. A portent? he wondered with an inward smile. Bobutu would doubtlessly have thought so but to Schwerner as a man of science what he had observed was nothing more remarkable than a chunk of interplanetary debris captured by the gravity of Earth and then consumed by the friction of the atmosphere.

Like the Star of Bethlehem again. A natural cosmic event.

Suddenly he noticed that of all strange things Spock had apparently fallen asleep.

He reached over to rouse him when his own arm suddenly went numb.

A moment later he toppled over on his side, sound asleep himself.

2

A vicious pounding in his skull like a rapid succession of hammer blows drove Gordon Schwerner awake. He opened his eyes upon an extraordinarily brilliant white light that made him cry out in pain and shield his face with his hands.

A blinding white light?

There was only one conceivable source of such a light in the universe he knew.

A star.

Schwerner became aware that he was lying on his back with his face turned directly up to the sky.

The white light was the sun shining overhead.

And if the sun was overhead that meant it was the middle of the day—it was noon.

Schwerner leaped to his feet in a panic.

Swinging his head he looked everywhere around.

There was nothing to see. The tent, the van, the equipment and supplies—everything had vanished.

And with it—gone too—Mohammed Bello.

Darby Spock was asleep on the ground a short distance away. Schwerner knelt down and gave him a shake. "Spock, for God's sake, wake up, man. Mohammed Bello has disappeared. He's taken everything with him."

Spock's eyes popped open. When he saw the sun he flinched, moaned, and rolled away. "Bastard," he finally managed to murmur groggily. "Bloody fucking bastard."

"How did he do it?" said Schwerner. "How did he know we wouldn't wake up?"

"Because he put us to sleep—that's how." Spock had attained a sitting position. He massaged his face with the heels of his hands. "He doped us."

"Drugged?"

"My sleeping potion. The same bloody trick I played on him." Spock thrust the fingers of one hand inside his empty holster. "Bloody fucking bastard."

"But Bello doesn't smoke."

"He doesn't need to—he cooks. Remember that delicious faux chicken you and I so eagerly wolfed down last night? Spicy as a wog curry, wasn't it? Well, now we know why. When I catch up to him I'll wring his neck with my bare hands. I swear I will."

"Is that what you think we ought to do? Catch up to him?"

"I think we'd bloody well better give it a try," Spock said grimly. He stared at the desolate land around him. "But I won't lie to you, Schwerner. We're in a pickle here."

"We'll starve."

"No, we won't. We'll never live that long." Spock poked a hand inside his jacket and emitted a grunt. A moment later he drew out his flask and gave it a tentative shake. "Not bloody much of this left either."

"We can't very well subsist on liquor."

"We haven't a great deal of choice in the matter."

"The Renaldo Castle isn't—"

"Forget how far away it is." He waved both arms at the surrounding landscape. "We're talking about the East African veldt, man. It happens to be bloody hot out here if you haven't noticed. The castle could be a hop, skip, and jump away and we'd be dead of dehydration before we reached it."

"What about the Goniani priests? They said they'd been out here for nineteen days. They weren't carrying food or water that I could see."

"This is their world, their native habitat. They understand how to survive in it. Me, I know the veldt the way you might know a good whore after a two-hour trick but to the Goniani it's more like having a wife. And you can't top one of those for familiarity."

"Then what do we do?"

"We walk," said Spock, rising to his feet. "And I suppose we can hope."

"Now?"

"Unless you can offer a substantial reason for waiting until we become thirstier."

"Which way should we go? Toward the castle?"

"I suppose that's as good a route as any."

* * * *

Schwerner had hardly covered five hundred meters when his lips, mouth, and throat dried up and became like sandpaper. Spock on the other hand moved at a surprisingly energetic clip, seemingly unaffected by the brutal heat. Schwerner thought of the spook he had seen struck by the taxi in Zanzibar and began to feel resentful. What if he died out here while Spock lived? For some reason he felt that would be dreadfully unfair.

After another five hundred meters Schwerner grabbed hold of Spock's arm. "Can I have a drop of that whisky now?" he asked in a harsh rasping voice. "I can barely breathe."

Spock shook his head curtly and did not reduce his pace. "No, not yet."

"When?"

"We'll wait for dark."

"Dark? For God's sake, man," he cried.

"For dark. If you start gulping it down now, you'll merely dry out sooner. If you're truly desperate we can stop long enough for you to try and piss."

"I don't need to piss, damn it. I'm thirsty."

"That's what I mean. Piss in your boot, then drink it."

"I'd throw it up."

"Drink that too."

"You're not serious."

"It's been done, Schwerner. I can assure you of that."

"Well, not by me."

"We'll see."

* * * *

The land was flat. The land was featureless. The land was changeless and devoid of character. Schwerner searched in vain for anything that might remotely be regarded as a landmark. A lake for example. It wouldn't have to be a terribly large one. The water could be as dank and muddy as Lake Clarence. A pond would be acceptable. The trickle of a brook.

I'll cross over the water, he thought longingly, and lie down in the shade of the trees.

Then he saw the tree. It stood a short distance ahead, a twisted stunted thing like the skeleton of a dead child. Schwerner gazed at the tantalizing shade that curled beneath the trunk like the wanton hips of a willing woman. "Look," he said, pointing in awe. "We can rest there."

Spock shook his head. "I said not yet."

"For God's sake, man, are you a sadist?"

"A realist. If we stop now—in this bloody heat—we'll never get started again."

"So?"

"We'll die out here, man."

"You're not human, Spock. It doesn't bother you at all."

"I'm as human as you are, Schwerner, and believe me it bothers me."

"How do you know we're headed in the right direction?" They had gone past the tree now. Schwerner looked back as if to confirm its reality.

"I know."

"You haven't looked at your compass in hours."

"That's because bloody Bello ran off with it."

"Then we *are* lost."

Spock stopped and turned, placing his hands on his hips for emphasis. "Listen, Schwerner, and listen closely. I know exactly where we're going. I'm familiar with the terrain. I know the route. So don't concern yourself with it. In fact don't concern yourself with anything. Just keep your bloody mouth shut and try to conserve your strength."

"You can't silence me that easily, Spock."

"If it proves necessary—" Spock showed Schwerner a balled-up fist "—I'm prepared to use other means."

"If you knock me unconscious you'll have to carry me."

"The hell if I will. I'll leave you here to bloody well rot."

Schwerner fell silent. Not from fear—he was no coward—but rather out of calculation. If Spock wanted to play it that way—with violence—then he'd simply wait until dark and then kill him. Drop a rock on his big fat ugly spook head. To Schwerner it all seemed remarkably clear and this clarity of thought appeared to affect his physical well-being as well so that all at once he no longer felt tired or hungry or even especially thirsty. He felt in fact very much as though he were floating through the air, his feet like helium balloons, his arms at his sides flapping like the wings of a buoyant bird. The sensation was altogether pleasant. He started to giggle.

"Spock," he said after what seemed like an eternity of delirious floating.

"What now, Schwerner?"

"Tell me what it was like when you were dead."

Speck glanced back and frowned. "Are you all right, Gordon?"

"I'm fine—perfectly fine. I think it's a fair question. If I'm going to die I have a right to know."

"You're not going to die," Spock said flatly. "What's the matter with you, man?" Apparently they had stopped. Schwerner was no longer floating "Your face is as red as an apple and your skin—" he had hold of Schwerner's wrists "—you're as dry as an onion."

"I said I felt perfectly fine." Schwerner jerked his hands away. "Tell me what it was like. If you do I promise not to kill you later tonight. I won't drop a rock on your big fat spook head after all."

"Stay here. Sit. I'm going to go find us a place to rest."

"I don't want to rest," Schwerner said petulantly. "I want to die."

"Sit down and put your head between your legs."

His movements as stiff as a marionette Schwerner sat on the ground and let his head rest between his raised knees. "Cocksucker," he murmured. It was a word he'd never previously uttered in his life and the sound to his ears was as alien as the sound of church bells. "Cocksucker," he repeated in a firmer tone. "Motherfucker," he added. "Ass licker."

He tried to laugh but the pain in his throat was too terrible to endure. The tolling of church bells sounded incessantly in his ears like the cries of children at play.

* * * *

There was a wetness on his face and everything around him was cool and sweet, moist and dark. Then the sharp taste of whisky made him choke.

"Lie still," said Spock.

"I think I'm going to be sick."

"Then turn your head, damn it, so you won't choke on your own vomit."

"I can't. It hurts too much."

"Then lie still."

There wasn't any sun now. It was as though some god-like being with a giant hand had reached casually up and plucked it from the sky. It took a while for Schwerner to understand that what this signified was that night had fallen. A bead of moisture trickled down his chin. Reaching up, he rubbed his face, then tasted his fingertips with his swollen tongue. "Water," he said in wonder.

"An old well."

"You knew it was here?"

"I told you I'd gone this way before.""

"You could have told me there was a well."

"I'm sorry but there was the strong possibility we'd find it dry. I didn't want to get your hopes up unnecessarily. As it is I had to dig down a foot by hand before I struck water."

"Then we're not going to die after all."

"Not immediately at least. You've had a nasty touch of sunstroke but that will pass too."

"I could use another swallow of water."

"Lie here and rest a while longer. You'll have to walk to the well on your own. We've nothing to transport water with unfortunately. It's my bloody fault this happened. I thought you were stronger."

"I've never been a terribly active person," Schwerner admitted. "Even on the island the robots did all the real work."

"Robots? Island?"

He let his head rock from side to ride. "It's a long story, Darby."

"In the morning after a good night's sleep you'll feel stronger."

"But shouldn't we try to press on now? It seems to me it would be easier hiking after dark."

"Yes, but we both need rest. We pushed too hard today."

"I suppose you're right." Despite the darkness Schwerner could see Spock's face clearly. It seemed to radiate sympathy, compassion, and concern. Spock had even taken the shirt off his own back and placed it under Schwerner s head as a pillow. The pallid hairless flesh of Spock's bare chest made Schwerner think of death. He experienced a shudder of revulsion but that was promptly overwhelmed by a wave of gratitude. Spock had saved his life—that much was definite—and Schwerner found it difficult to cope with the complex emotions this engendered.

"Darby?" he said after a time.

"Yes, Gordon?"

"You're my friend, aren't you?"

"I suppose I am, yes."

"I've led a difficult life until now."

"You needn't tell me about it."

"That's not what I mean. It's...well, to tell you the truth I'm afraid of dying."

"I don't see why you should be. You're not apt to die for a goodly long while yet."

"But someday I will."

"Well…yes."

"Then couldn't you tell me? Just something to help me feel better prepared, something of what it was like for you."

Spock tugged at the bushy end of his moustache. "I was rather hoping that was merely your delirium talking earlier."

"It's been on my mind since we first met at the hotel in Zanzibar. I've never known a spook before and well…if you do tell me I won't tell anyone else. Not even Desmond Blue. I promise."

Spock was silent for a lengthy period. Then he said, "Let's get you some water first. I'll give you a hand over to the well."

"And then you'll tell me?"

He grunted. "I'll tell."

* * * *

When they returned from the short walk Schwerner sat down on the ground. He felt better now except for the hunger pangs in his stomach and a certain lightness in his head.

"Where do you want me to begin?" said Spock, sitting across from him.

"At the beginning. The moment you died. I want to know what happened next."

"Well, I woke up."

"Right away?"

"Who knows?" He was lighting his pipe "It certainly seemed that way, yes," he said through a veil of smoke.

"And you were still your own self? You occupied your own body?"

"I most assuredly did."

"Then there is an afterlife."

"For those of us taken during the Occupancy, there was, yes."

"Was it heaven do you think?"

"That I can't say. Some of us believe it was—they've even made a bit of a religion out of it in certain of the spook reservations—but I personally don't think so. Among the dead I'm somewhat of an agnostic. That's part of the reason the reservations have never held much appeal for me."

"You weren't anywhere on Earth though?"

"Most definitely not." His eyes took on a faraway look. "It was a considerable distance from here, I'll guarantee you that much."

"But it was a material place, a distinct world?"

"A material world but a far different one from this one. I woke up in my own body and all around others were waking too. We were within a deep river valley surrounded on both sides by snowcapped peaks. Others woke in other locales—some beside oceans or seas, some among green hills or mountain lakes. There seemed to be no clear-cut pattern. The chap waking closest to me for instance said he was a farmer from China. The others came from places all over the globe."

"What about those who were never reborn? The ones still missing? The millionaires and generals and presidents? Were they there too?"

"I never saw anyone like that. No one I've talked to ever did either."

"What happened to them, I wonder."

Spock balanced his pipe on a knee and shook his head. "Perhaps they were the ones that didn't get to go to heaven." He laughed. "They went somewhere else."

"And you were there in this river valley for the entire three days?"

"That I can't tell you. The whole time I was there it never grew dark and more often than not there seemed to be at least two suns in the sky, one larger and more luminous than the others. I never slept of course and I failed to keep track of the number of times I ate."

"Where did you obtain food?"

"Right off the ground. Or on trees. There was plenty of fruit and vegetables and even the grass one walked on turned out to be quite tasty. The river water itself was as sweet as a nectar."

"You know what it sounds like to me," said Schwerner. "It sounds like you were on an alien planet."

"That's the other popular theory of course. In fact, you'll find many spooks who'll believe it was the Occupant's home planet."

"Did you ever see them?"

"I saw something. Once or twice. High up in the sky. It could have been them. I don't know."

Schwerner sighed. "This isn't turning out to be especially helpful."

"I told you it wouldn't."

"But why have you spooks kept it all secret?"

"Because we figure it's nobody's business but ours. We're the ones who died—not you lifers."

"Still, don't you think the evidence ought to be systematically examined? By scientists if by no one else? What if there is a pattern? What if that place you went actually was the slugs' home world? Don't you think it would be important to know?"

"Why? So the rest of you could mount an expedition, go there and teach them a bloody lesson?"

"Of course not," said Schwerner. "Just so...so we'd know."

"*I* know," said Spock, touching his bare chest with the stem of his pip. "That's all that's important to me."

Schwerner thought this was a limited selfish viewpoint but could tell there would be little to gain by disputing the point with Spock. Besides, there were other matter he wanted to know about first. "What about the resurrection? What happened then?"

"That took place in more or less the same fashion as the other thing—when I died. All at once I felt extremely tired and couldn't keep my eyes open. I collapsed in the grass and went to sleep and seemed to wake a bare instant later. When I did I found myself back in Dar-es-Salaam again. I believe it was pretty much the same with everyone else. A few as you know came back minus a portion of their senses. But it wasn't dying that made them stupid. It was being forced to live again."

"Was that other place so...so wonderful?"

"Yes, it was."

Schwerner felt a bitter sensation that might have been envy. "Then why don't you kill yourself and get it over with? Have you ever considered that?"

"Now and then, yes." Spock smiled. "But if I did I'd have nothing left to look forward to, would I?" He rose to his feet. "Now unless you've something else to badger me about I'm going to fetch a drink of water."

"No. I guess you've told me everything you could."

"And you're not satisfied, are you?"

"I'm not. It seems to raise more questions than it answers."

"You ought to be accustomed to that. You're a scientist."

"Sometimes I wish I weren't."

"Oh?" said Spock, sounding sincerely surprised. "Then what do you wish you were?"

Schwerner considered for a moment. "I don't know. A priest maybe. They're the only ones who seem to have the answers for everything."

"Maybe that's why the Occupants got rid of them all."

By the time Spock returned from the well Schwerner had fallen asleep on the ground where he lay. As he slept he dreamed of a strange distant place where two suns like the eyes of a beast hovered in a cloudless sky. Around him rose the chiseled slopes of lofty mountains and there were also green trees and meadows of grass and various flowers in a multitude of sizes, shapes, and colors. He was alone in this place except for once when a gentle voice spoke from high overhead. Even though he strained his ears to hear what the voice was saying the words seemed to come in a language that was foreign to him.

* * * *

In the morning when Schwerner woke the sun was just inching past the flat line of the horizon. His lightheadedness had vanished with the night but the hunger pangs were even more agonizing than before. Spock, wide awake and no longer shirtless, sat beside him.

Schwerner started to rise.

Spock put out a hand and held him back. "Better not," he whispered, hardly moving his lips. "Take a look. We've visitors."

Schwerner raised his head far enough to see. Not more than twenty yards away stood motionless forms of three large male lions.

"My God," he said softly.

"They've been sitting out there since first light."

"Are they going to—to attack us?"

"I don't know."

"What if they do?"

"Then I suggest you run for your bloody life."

"Run? Run where?"

"That," said Spock, swiveling his head slowly, "I wish I knew."

Although the worst heat of the day still lay hours in the future Schwerner was almost instantly bathed in sweat. Supporting his weight on both elbows he held his head high enough off the ground so that he could observe the lions. How long he waited in that position was difficult to determine. It couldn't have been more than five or ten minutes but seemed far longer. In that time the lions never twitched more than a muscle but their eyes were constantly watchful and vigilant.

Then in a graceful motion one of the lions rose partially erect on its hind legs and lifted its nose, sniffing the air.

"Uh-oh," said Spock.

"Is it going to charge?"

"I'm afraid so."

"What can we—?"

"Get ready to run."

"But I won't—"

"Now!" cried Spock.

The lion charged. For Schwerner still on his back it seemed to take forever to roll over, place his legs beneath him, and stand upright. He broke into a mad frantic sprint but hadn't covered a dozen yards when something enormously powerful struck him solidly in the back. He pitched forward, his head in front of his body, and turned a half-somersault in the air before hitting the ground with both shoulders. He rolled over once, felt the air rush from his lungs, and lay motionless on his back. There was a terrible screaming sound in his ears that he assumed at first must be poor Spock. But the voice was his own. As he lay there too stunned to move he anticipated at any instant the weight of the lion crashing down on him, its foul breath in his face, its fangs and claws tearing and rending his flesh.

Something brushed his arm.

He screamed.

"Gordon," said a calm voice.

He looked up and saw Spock standing over him.

"You're not injured, are you?"

"I—no, I don't think so," Schwerner said. Reaching behind, he touched his shirt where the lion had struck him. The cloth was torn into shreds. He felt something moist. "I think I'm bleeding," he said.

"Let me have a look." Spock bent down. "Only a few minor scratches. Damn lucky you fell forward the way you did. If you'd gone under the bugger he'd have had you for sure."

"But the lion," said Schwerner. "What happened to it?"

"Look for yourself."

Schwerner followed Spock's gesturing hand and discovered all three lions stretched out on the ground not far away, their great shaggy heads tucked between their forepaws. They appeared to be asleep. "I don't understand," he said.

"Frankly neither do I. After the one went after you the other two broke in my direction. I figured I was a bloody goner for certain but then they just skidded to a stop as if somebody had whispered in their ears, lay down on the ground, and went straight off to sleep. I can't figure it."

"What should we do?"

"If you can walk we'd better try to get the hell away from here while we can."

"I can walk," said Schwerner with determination.

Spock helped him to his feet and together they set off at a rapid pace. They hadn't gone far when Schwerner heard a thunderous noise and turned his head to discover the enormous figure of an African elephant approaching from the left. "Here comes another one," he said, grabbing Spock's arm and preparing to run.

"No, wait." Spock held him back, "Look there."

Schwerner looked and saw a pair of riders mounted behind the elephant's head. Both were young and one appeared to be a girl. She waved her arms excitedly at them.

"Do you know her, Darby?" said Schwerner.

"I'm not sure." Spock glanced over his shoulder to confirm that the lions were still asleep. "Why don't we wait a moment and find out?"

When the elephant reached them it knelt on its forelegs and dipped its head so that the girl could slide off. Her clothing consisted of the bottom portion of a bikini swimsuit and nothing else. She wore her sandy blonde hair trimmed close to her shoulders and her square boyish face was covered with a light coating of freckles. The rest of her body was tanned and lean. She didn't look any older than eighteen or nineteen. "Hi," she said to Spock. "I'm Talia O'Brien. Remember me?" She spoke English with the flat accents of the American West.

"As a matter of fact I believe I do." He glanced at Schwerner. "Talia is one of the children from the castle," he said.

"And that's Phillip up there." She was pointing to the other rider—a boy—still perched on the elephant's neck. He stared down at them with dull vacant eyes.

"I don't believe I know Phillip," said Spock.

"He doesn't go out much." She tapped her forehead. "He's simple but very sweet."

"If you don't mind tremendously," said Spock, peering over his shoulder at the lions, "it might be wise for us to find another place to chat."

"Oh, those lions won't hurt you," Talia said.

"I'd still rather…"

"Okay if you want." She crossed briskly to the elephant and slapped it soundly on one side of its trunk. Obediently the elephant rose back to its full height and lumbered off. "Come along," she called to them, waving an arm. "Over this way."

Spock and Schwerner went after her, moving fast in order to keep pace with the elephant's giant strides. They hadn't gone far when a cloud of dust appeared in the distance. Talia walked back to them. "That must be Maria coming now."

"Damn that Bello," said Spock.

"Why? What's wrong?" said Schwerner.

"Bloody bastard took off with my perfume along with everything else."

"I certainly can't smell anything," said Schwerner.

"Well, I sure can," said Talia, making a face and squeezing her nostrils. "Both of you stink something awful. When's the last time you took a bath?"

In a short while a two-seat jeep pulled up beside them and a handsome dark-skinned woman with black opaque eyes smiled from underneath a pith helmet. "Darby Spock," she said. "So it truly is you."

"Hello, Maria," said Spock in a stiff formal tone that Schwerner had never heard him use before. "May I introduce a good friend of mine? Maria Vincente, Dr. Gordon Schwerner."

"A doctor?" she said with immediate interest.

"Not a physician, I'm afraid," Schwerner said somewhat apologetically. "A scientist."

"Oh, that's too bad. I am always so worried that the children do not receive adequate medical attention from Charles and myself but it is such a long drive to the coast that we can afford to take them only in the event of a true emergency." She turned her attention back to Spock. "Darby, we have not had a visit from you in months. I was afraid you were angry with us."

"Nothing of the sort, Maria," said Spock with what was for him a rare friendly smile. "As a matter of fact I was out this way in the middle of January."

"And you did not stop to say hello? How mean of you."

"Well, actually I intended to but…well, there was barbed wire all around your place. And warning notices. I wasn't sure I'd be welcome."

"Ah, yes, that." Her face clouded briefly but immediately brightened in another smile. "None of that was intended for you, Darby. You're always welcome in my home. Now do get in—both of you. We shall have you at the castle before you know it."

Spock and Schwerner climbed into the back of the jeep, Spock positioning himself so that it was Schwerner who ended up occupying the place directly behind Maria Vincente. It surprised Schwerner to realize that Spock was so concerned about his personal body odor. He was not a man Schwerner would have expected to care much what anyone else thought of him. Talia O'Brien had already remounted the elephant beside the blank-faced boy and the great beast was now only a gray spot in the distance.

"You wouldn't happen to have a swallow of water with you?" Spock asked as Maria released the brake and prodded the jeep forward, "The two of us have been stranded out here since early yesterday and we've hardly had a drop since then."

"I was afraid that might be the case," she said, reaching under the seat. Her hand emerged holding a canvas canteen which she passed over her shoulder to Schwerner. He drank gratefully, letting the cool water trickle down his chin, then handed the canteen to Spock who also drank in deep gurgling swallows. "Have you not eaten either?"

"Nary a bite," said Spock, wiping his mouth with the back of his hand. "It was getting rather hairy out in fact till your girl happened along. Quite a stroke of luck for us that was."

"It wasn't entirely luck," she said. As the jeep sped past the elephant Maria leaned out and waved at the two children aboard. Talia clasped both hands over her head and shook them exuberantly, her face creased in merry laughter.

"A most attractive girl," Schwerner said in a cautiously noncommittal tone.

"Yes, Talia is that," Maria agreed. "I do hope her costume—or lack of same—did not disturb you unduly."

"Ah, no—no, of course not," Schwerner said quickly. "I quite understand that it gets hot out here."

"It's not that actually. It's more because of Charles—my husband. He does not believe in the concealment of the body. He says that something or someone must have created our bodies in the first place and that to hide them from view is to insult not only ourselves but also our creator."

"I suppose that's a valid point of view, yes."

"Well, it's definitely his."

Spock broke in: "What did you mean, Maria, when you said it wasn't luck that led you to find us?"

"I meant that the three of us—Talia, Phillip, and I—have been out here searching for you since late yesterday."

"But you had no way of knowing we were here."

"No, but it seemed a likely supposition. Because of that Arab," she added by way of explanation.

"Mohammed bloody Bello?" said Spook, his face clouding darkly. "When did you see him?"

"Yesterday afternoon. He appeared at the castle quite without warning. Something must have gone wrong with the brakes of his vehicle for he crashed through the fence without stopping and ran straight into the castle wall. Charles and some of the children saw it happen and pulled him from the wreckage. A blow to the head had rendered him unconscious so they brought him inside and put him to bed. Charles said he did not think the man was injured too severely."

"Then Bello didn't tell you we were out here."

"No," she said with a shake of her head, "but I recognized your van and there were also various articles in the back with your name on them. I became concerned and decided it would be best to institute a search in case something had gone wrong. I do not fully understand what happened though. Did you and the Arab become accidentally separated? Is that what took place?"

"Something like that, yes," Spock said ambiguously.

"Well, he should have recovered by now and will likely be conscious by the time we reach the castle. You may chat with him then if you wish."

"Now that's a conversation I'm definitely anticipating," Spock said grimly.

* * * *

The Renaldo Castle when it came into view more than lived up to Spock's description. Schwerner was certain he had never seen anything remotely resembling it in his life. Unlike the somber dignified castles he had occasionally observed in out of the way corners of Britain and Germany the Renaldo Castle seemed to sprawl across the land as if placed where it was by sheer chance alone. The general impression was of a mountain of separate stone blocks tossed randomly in the air by giant hands and allowed to stand wherever they happened to fall. Maria aimed the jeep at a gap in the tall barbed wire fence. As they passed through the opening Schwerner observed a big rectangular sign printed in heavy block letters: *No Trespassing—Violators Shot on Sight*. He could quite understand why Spock reading that notice had been perplexed. "I will fix you something to eat right away," Maria said as the jeep approached the high castle wall. "I am sure you must both be utterly famished."

She parked the jeep in a courtyard close to what must have been intended as the front door, a thick wooden slab blocking a space big enough to admit four grown men side by side. In order to open the door Maria had to lean her full weight against it. "This place is very old and difficult to maintain," she explained, catching her breath. "But don't you think it is rather wonderful too?"

"It's certainly most impressive," Schwerner agreed. "This man Renaldo must have been a genius."

"Yes," she said, her voice suddenly glum. "Renaldo was brilliant in many ways."

* * * *

The coolness of the interior of the castle was like a welcome slap in the face after the searing heat outside. The three of them passed into a vast, sparsely furnished room, the stone ceiling of which loomed a good thirty feet overhead. "Why don't you rest here?" Maria said, pointing to an old couch and chair, "while I go to the kitchen to see if—"

The remainder of her sentence was cut off by a stampede of running feet. Schwerner turned his head and observed what appeared to be a pack of wild savages charging through the door. In truth they were only children—twenty or thirty in various shapes, sizes, sexes, and shades of skin. Maria emitted a cry of delight and held her arms open to receive them as the children swirled around her. Bending down she picked up one of the smaller ones—a girl—and held her close to her chest. The rest of the children surged onward toward Spock who with his pipe clenched between his teeth and a bemused smile on his face greeted them stoically. To his astonishment Schwerner noticed that hardly any of the children wore a stitch and the few that did—mostly the older ones—were no more modestly attired than Talia O'Brien. As the children swept around him in a wave Schwerner felt fingers clutching at his legs and tiny hands touching the skin of his hands and arms.

He looked helplessly across at Maria who gave him a warm smile. "Do not be afraid," she called out. "They mean no harm. They are only curious about strangers."

Schwerner had had little previous experience with children, whom he had always regarded as a strange and alien species. With the little girl still in her arms Maria vanished through the doorway to the left, leaving Spock and Schwerner to cope for themselves. Uncertain what was expected of him, Schwerner reached down tentatively and patted one of the heads nearest him. The head belonged to a skinny girl nine or ten years old who immediately responded by leaping straight up in the air and throwing both hands around Schwerner's neck.

Instinctively Schwerner hooked his arms around her waist to prevent both of them from falling over. Then the other children started giggling. Schwerner looked down to see what was supposed to be so funny only to discover to his horror that one of them had unfastened his fly and exposed his penis to view. "Look how tiny it is," said a boy, pointing with his finger. "It looks like an old carrot that's become wilted with age."

"Hey, stop that!" cried Schwerner, partly from embarrassment, partly from outrage. He tried to zip his fly back up but whenever he let go of the girl dangling from his neck she would slide down so as to get in the way and prevent him from reaching his crotch. "Darby!" he shouted in desperation. "Darby, please get them off me!"

"Hold onto your, uh, your hat, Schwerner. I'm on my way. Now children," he added in a soothing tone as he forced his way through them, "this really won't do. It's terribly bad form to humiliate a guest in this fashion." When he reached Schwerner, Spock loosened the girl's fingers from his neck and let her drop to the floor. As soon as he was free Schwerner grabbed his zipper and zipped it shut. "Come along, Gordon," Spock said, touching his arm. "Let's find a place to sit and wait for Maria. She must have gone to get something for us to eat."

"Are you sure it's safe to move?" Schwerner said. "They might try to tear me to pieces next."

"Oh, I think it's safe enough. They're only children after all."

Schwerner grunted and allowed Spock to lead him to the couch.

"I certainly hope you never intend to take up parenthood," Spock said as the two of them sat down.

"Well, I don't exactly see you racing out to have triplets either."

"If I could, perhaps I might. Spooks aren't fertile, you know."

"Oh." The pain implicit in Spock's words made Schwerner feel instantly guilty. "Actually I didn't know that. I'm sorry."

"It's one of the few aspects of existence you lifers have over us."

Their curiosity satisfied, the children were filing from the room, laughing and talking among themselves. With a fond expression Spock watched them go.

"But tell me honestly, Schwerner," he said, turning back, "don't you find this place rather remarkable?"

"I'm not sure that's precisely the term I'd use, no."

"Oh, don't be such a bloody stuffed shirt. Even you can see how open and responsive these children are. I sometimes think if I'd had a childhood like this instead of the proper English upbringing I suffered through I might have turned out a better man today. Perhaps you can understand now why I was anxious when it appeared something had gone wrong here."

"Would you mind if I asked you something personal?" said Schwerner.

"I probably would, yes," said Spock.

"You're in love with her, aren't you?"

"With Maria? Is it that bloody obvious?"

"It's pretty easy to spot, yes."

"Well, as a matter of fact, I do believe I am. The first time that's happened since I died. Not that it makes much of a bloody difference one way or the other."

"Maria doesn't love you then?"

"Of course not. Maria loves her work, the school, the children."

"And her husband?"

Spock shrugged. "She's loyal to him anyway."

"Well, I just hope whatever's wrong here it doesn't involve her."

"What makes you so certain something's wrong here? I told you nothing seems changed."

"Those signs are still there. And the barbed wire."

"I know. But maybe it doesn't mean anything. Perhaps all it is is another of Charles's many eccentricities."

"A peculiar kind of eccentricity, threatening to murder people on sight."

"Well, I told you he was rather peculiar."

"You don't sound as if you particularly approve of him, Darby."

At that moment Marie Vincente returned with a tray piled high with sandwiches and beer. "I sent the children outside to play," she told them as she placed the tray on the couch between them. "I felt we could all use a few moments tranquility."

Schwerner attacked the topmost of the sandwiches and gulped down the beer. "Thank you," he said through a mouthful of beef, white bread, and mayonnaise. "I guess the children caught me rather by surprise."

"They're not usually that unrestrained," she said. "But whenever I have to be away from the castle for any length of time they do become restless. Charles and I are the only parental figures many of them have ever known and they've come to depend upon us for perhaps too much."

"The responsibility must be enormous," said Schwerner.

"Oh, by the way." She looked over at Spock. "I spoke to Charles just now and he says that your friend Mr. Bello is much improved. He was able to describe to Charles the unfortunate circumstances that led to your separation."

"Now that's a story I'd love to hear," said Spock.

"He told Charles he had awakened before either of you and taken the van to go in search of firewood. Apparently he then suffered an unexpected flat tire and by the time he repaired the damage and returned to your camp the two of you had vanished. Desperate with fear he drove here in search of help but his brakes failed and he crashed into the wall and after that everything is an utter blank. He was quite overjoyed, said Charles, to discover both of you had reached the castle safely."

"I'll just bet he was," Spock said drily. "Speaking of my van though, how is it?"

She shook her head sorrowfully. "A total wreck, I'm sorry to say."

"Bloody stuff." He looked at Schwerner. "That's going to make it rather difficult when we're ready to leave."

"Perhaps I could drive you to the coast," Maria said tentatively. "I'd have to discuss it with Charles first of course."

"No, don't bother." Spock looked somber. "We'll find another way. I'll see if I can contact some of the local tribes."

"Don't you have a telephone or anything?" Schwerner asked.

Maria seemed uneasy. "To tell the truth, Doctor, Charles does not believe in telephones. It's another of his eccentricities. He flatly refuses to converse with anyone he cannot actually see. We did have a radio at one point—I insisted on it in the event of an emergency—but it broke down several months ago and we've not had the opportunity to have it repaired."

"Well, I'm sure something will turn up," Spock said, rising to his feet and brushing bread crumbs off his trousers. "The same room as usual, Maria?"

"I've had it prepared for you already, Darby," she said with a gracious smile. "Dr. Schwerner can have the room immediately adjoining yours."

"Fine. And Bello? Where have you got him tucked away?"

"His room is across the corridor from yours, Darby."

"Then as long as we're up there we'll have to drop by and say hello to the chap."

"You shouldn't stay long though," she cautioned. "With concussions there always remains the danger of a relapse. You don't want to tire him too soon."

"We'll be careful not to do that," said Spock.

"Then please do make yourselves at home. I must tend to the children now but I'll make certain you are informed of the hour for dinner."

Spock waited on his feet until Maria Vincente had departed then crooked a finger at Schwerner. "Come along, old top, and I'll show you where to lay down your head."

They ascended a stone staircase leading up to the second floor. Halfway to the top, passing a window, Schwerner looked out and saw in the courtyard below the figure of an African elephant. Standing in its shadow was someone he thought he recognized as the girl Talia.

At the top of the stairs they headed down a wide corridor. Three-quarters of the way to the end Spock swung left, opened a door, and went through. The room beyond was spacious and well-furnished. There was a wooden chest of drawers, a queen-sized bed, a writing desk, three chairs that looked like antiques, and a stone fireplace set in the wall. Their suitcases had been placed in the center of the carpeted floor. "Ah-ha," said Spock. "Let's see what we have here."

Bending down he pushed the suitcases aside and let out an exclamation of delight. "Well, look what I've found," he said, emerging with his .45 in his hand. He held the barrel close to his nose and sniffed. "Hasn't been fired either. There's some satisfaction in that at least."

Schwerner was inspecting his own suitcase. He opened it, looked inside, then closed it again. "I think this has been tampered with. I never leave my suitcase unlocked and there are several visible scratches around the lock too."

"Bello of course," said Spock. "I hope there's nothing in there you don't want him seeing."

"Nothing relevant to the case, no. Desmond Blue always insists we memorize everything, then burn the paper."

"Smart man. Nevertheless, I'd keep my eye peeled for snakes when I first go through there if I were you."

"You're not serious," said Schwerner.

Spock shrugged. "Perhaps not. Still, the bloody bastard has tried to kill us twice."

"Twice?"

"Those three lions this morning."

"You don't think Bello had anything to do with that?"

"I wouldn't put it past him. And don't forget the rogue elephant that turned out not to be a rogue. If Bello could pull that off then why not with lions too?"

Schwerner edged back from the suitcase, feeling ill at ease.

"How do you want to play this?" Spock asked, cocking his head at the door.

"With Bello you mean?"

"Do we confront him openly as the rat we know him to be or do we continue to play stupid?"

"Stupid," said Schwerner after a moment's reflection. "If we let him know we're aware of who and what he really is, he may run before I can learn his motive for being here."

"Well, you're the detective," said Spock, sounding less than convinced.

* * * *

The two of them crossed the hall to Bello's room. Spock first raised a fist as if to knock but thought better of it and gave the knob a turn instead. The door opened on a small cramped room with a double bed occupying most of it. In the faint light from window Schwerner dimly made out Mohammed Bello lying on his back, the top of his head swathed in bandages. His eyes were closed and his chest rose and fell with rhythmic regularity.

"He's asleep," said Schwerner, surprised.

"Want to give him a shake?"

"No, we'll try again later."

They'd turned to go when Schwerner happened to glance back and found Bello's eyes not only open but watching him intently. Startled, Bello flashed a wide toothy grin. "Why, Darby, Dr. Schwerner," he said in a voice weakened by pain, "do my eyes deceive me? Is this not an impossible dream? Do I hallucinate in a state of crazed delirium?"

"Cut the bull, Bello," Spock said. "They already told you we were here."

"Ah, yes, but dared I believe that my fondest prayers had been so promptly realized?"

Schwerner moved close to the bed and tried to put on a look compassion. "Maria told us about your accident. I hope you're feeling better."

"Oh, it's a mere nothing," said Bello, his expression strained. "A minor concussion, permanent brain damage unlikely. More importantly the two of you have miraculously escaped a terrible death. One minor point eludes me though. How exactly did dear Maria know of your presence on the veldt and send out a search party?"

"She recognized my van," Spock said. "Which you stole. They found us this morning as we were about to be devoured by lions."

"How extraordinarily miraculous," said Bello. He frowned "Yet the veldt is vast and the two of you so insignificant. It is indeed a wonder that you were found with such alacrity."

"I suppose that's true," said Spock, a puzzled frown crossing his face. "It certainly was a stroke of luck there."

"And did the dear Spanish lady also inform you of my own tragic tale of suffering and woe?"

"Maria gave us the story you've been telling her, yes. But there is one minor point I don't quite comprehend either. Why when you went to gather this alleged firewood in the middle of the night did you feel it necessary to take along our entire supply of food and water not to mention my personal sidearm?"

Schwerner gave Spock a cautionary look but Bello seemed undisturbed by the question. "That was done as a matter of general security of course. I remembered those three heathen witch doctors and feared they might attempt to creep up on you while you slept and make off with all our possessions even if they somehow chose to spare your lives."

"Then you did us a favor," Schwerner put in quickly, hoping he wasn't carrying the pose too far.

Bello beamed. "You praise me unduly, Doctor, for it is I after all who has foolishly destroyed our sole means of transport."

"An unavoidable accident," said Schwerner.

"Of course. And yet the consequences are nevertheless tragic. It now appears that none of us will soon be able to leave the gracious company of our host and hostess."

Bello's voice did not sound quite so sorrowful as he no doubt intended. Schwerner could not help speculating about the various levels of duplicity involved here. Bello was lying of course but at the same time he and Spock were lying too when they pretended to be unaware of Bello's deceit, but wasn't it also conceivable that Bello knew full well that they were lying and was himself lying in turn by pretending to be unaware that they were lying when they pretended to be unaware that he was lying?

"The only thing I care about," said Schwerner, "is that the three of us are alive and well. You must try to rest now, Mohammed. Recover your strength and then we can worry about how to get home."

"Your kind words, my two dear friends, constitute the best therapy any man could ask for."

Schwerner reached down and clasped Bello's hand in his. Behind him Spock made a choking noise as if suppressing a giggle. Schwerner stepped back, gave Bello a farewell wave, and followed Spock across the room to the door.

"Well," said Spock once they were safely outside in the hall, "I do have to hand it to you. I had no idea you were such an accomplished actor."

"You think we fooled him then?"

"With Bello who can say? Still, we did find out one thing for certain."

"What was that?"

"Those bloody lions. Did you notice how he neglected to bat an eyelash when I brought them up? The bastard was behind it. You can lay a hefty wager on that."

"He was already here at the castle when it happened though, wasn't he?"

"Which makes him doubly dangerous. We're going to have to keep on our toes every second."

Schwerner stroked his chin and cheeks, heard the rasp of his beard. "So what should we do next?"

"That's up to you," said Spock. "As for me I'm going to have a lie down for a few hours and let my head float away."

"I thought you didn't require sleep."

"Sleep, no. Rest, yes. My body's in splendid shape but my mind's beaten to bloody pulp."

"I think I'll have a walk around the castle then."

"Suit yourself but remember to be careful. If you bump into any lions while you're out wandering, don't stop to pass the time of day. Flee for your bloody life."

Schwerner promised he would, then grabbed his suitcase and went off into the next room. It was another smaller one like Mohammed Bello's but clean and comfortable nevertheless. He stripped off his torn and soiled garments and put on clean underwear, fresh socks, and a pair of green-and-red checked trousers. After shaving, he completed his wardrobe with a yellow knit shirt and a pair of black wing-tipped shoes. Then feeling more like himself than at any time since leaving Zanzibar he headed for the stairs.

He had just reached the top step when a sound coming from behind made him stop. Someone was strumming a guitar and singing an old folk ballad in a thin reedy male voice and although music was far from one of Schwerner's major passions the voice was sufficiently attractive that he paused to listen. The music seemed to be coming from the last door on the right-hand side of the corridor. When the song ended Schwerner lingered a moment to see if there would be more and when there was only silence started to go on his way. He had barely descended a step when a voice called out from above.

"Hey, you. Hold it right there."

Schwerner looked back and saw that a man had emerged from one of the rooms above. He was in his middle to late forties with gray-brown hair drawn into a ponytail, a lean weathered face, small bright eyes, and a shaggy fringe beard. He was also stark naked.

"What do you think you're up to out here?" the man asked.

"I was just—just listening to your song." He assumed this had to be the same man he'd heard playing and singing.

"And who might you be?"

"I'm Dr. Schwerner. Gordon Schwerner. You must be Charles Vincente."

"Never mind that. I asked you a specific question. Did Maria send you to spy on me or not?"

"Spy? Why, no—no, of course not. As I explained I was merely listening—"

"Don't lie to me."

Charles Vincente—if that was indeed who this was—advanced menacingly toward the head of the stairs. Past him Schwerner could see inside the open door of the room behind three children sitting on the floor. One he recognized—Phillip, the boy who'd been with Talia O'Brien on the veldt. The others were a plump boy of about twelve with a ruddy complexion and thick eyeglasses and a dark-skinned girl a few years older who did not appear to have any arms. All three children were like the man stark naked.

"Charles, stop that." A fifth person Schwerner hadn't noticed before stepped from the room and shut the door behind her. It was Talia O'Brien dressed in a lacey blouse, blue jeans, and moccasin slippers. "He's not spying on anyone. He's the man who came here with the white hunter Spock."

"The dead thing who's in love with my wife?"

"Right. Now leave this man alone and let him be. He's a guest in your house. You need to treat him as such."

"I do, do I?" Charles stood a moment regarding Schwerner below him and then suddenly extended his hand. "The hell with it," he said. "If you knew half the pain I've been through lately, you'd be paranoid too. Put her there, friend."

Schwerner reached out and took his hand. They shook. "I was just having a walk," he explained.

"You in a hurry or something?"

"Well, not really, no, but—"

"Good. Then I've got a question for you. You just heard this girl point out that this spook friend of yours is in love with my wife. All fine and dandy with me. I was in love with her once myself. But the question is, what is love? Everybody seems to have their own definition and none are the same. So what's yours?"

"You want to know my definition of love?"

"Yes, exactly. What is it?"

"Charles is a noted authority on the subject of love," Talia O'Brien put in, joining them. "He's written several well-known monographs on the subject of expansive love."

Love, admittedly, was not something Schwerner had spent much time thinking about. He'd never been in love as far as he knew. "Well, I suppose what love is…well, basically it's a strong affection, I guess."

"That's it?" Charles said in an incredulous tone. "You think love is nothing more than plain everyday garden-variety affection?"

"Well, a strong affection, I said."

"That's dumbest definition of love I've heard in my life," he cried, shaking his head.

"I'm afraid I'm not well-versed on the subject."

"You've never been in love?"

Schwerner nodded. "I don't think so, no."

Charles turned around and looked at Talia. "We've got to do something to help this poor fellow out."

She looked at Schwerner and smiled. "I couldn't agree with you more."

Flushing in spite of himself, Schwerner quickly stammered: "No, that's quite all right. I appreciate your concern but I don't really think—"

"Too young for you, huh?" He put his arm around Talia and pulled her close. She smiled up at him. "What about Maria then? She's more your type, huh? I don't know how she feels about you but I'd be glad to raise the subject if you want."

"What subject?"

"Why, you two having sex together, what else?"

Schwerner stared at him open mouthed. He couldn't tell for sure if they were toying with him or not. But either way he knew he didn't like it. "I'm afraid you'll have to excuse me now," he said stiffly. "I have somewhere I need to be."

And he headed down the stairs in a frantic rush.

He'd only just made it down to the main floor below when he heard footsteps following from behind.

He stopped and waited for her to catch up to him.

"I'm really sorry about that," Talia said when she reached him. "Charles has a habit of coming on strong like that when he meets new people. Not that we get all that many out here anyhow. He doesn't mean any harm by it."

"Well, he certainly seems to be an excitable personality."

"He's under a lot of pressure." She thought for a moment and then made a face. "At least he likes to think so. You're going for a walk you said? Mind if I tag along? I'll try and explain a few things about this place as we go along."

Schwerner had to admit that the thought of this pretty young girl's company wasn't displeasing. "I'd like that," he heard himself saying.

Outside it didn't seem any cooler than it had earlier in the day when he and Darby were wandering lost on the veldt. But somehow the heat seemed less oppressive now.

The two of them walked together side by side.

"So," said Schwerner after they'd gone a short distance around the castle, "was any of that back there meant seriously or were you two just having fun at my expense?"

"Oh, all of it was serious," she said. "One thing you'll learn about Charles, he's always very serious."

"But that ridiculous thing with Maria…I mean, really. What kind of way is that to talk about one's own wife?"

"She's his wife, sure, but that doesn't mean he owns her. She's not his property."

"I never implied she was. It's just—"

"Charles is a highly respected psychologist," she said. "His primary specialties are love and sex. He's a teacher too. A good one in my opinion. The best I've ever had."

"Is that why you're here then? You and the other children. You're students."

"Well, partly. We're all orphans too. Charles and Maria adopted us from back home in America."

"And brought you all to Africa?"

"Well, eventually, yes."

"There is one thing I'm confused about though. Whatever gave Charles the idea I might be spying on him? You said he was paranoid. Was that intended in the clinical sense?"

"I suppose." She shrugged. "He didn't use to be that way."

"What happened to change him?"

He saw her hesitate. "I really shouldn't be telling you any of this. It's supposed to be a secret."

"What is?"

"The experiment. The gestalt. The Linkage, we call it. Charles is the prime catalyst.

"I'm afraid I don't know what that means."

She turned and waved a hand at the castle. "How much of the history of this place do you know?"

"Well, some of it. Darby filled me in on the background of this Renaldo character—what eventually happened to him."

"Did he tell you what Renaldo was up to?"

"Slaughtering people, apparently. Some poor natives, I believe."

"No. That's the story they gave out at the time but it's not entirely accurate. What Renaldo was doing here did sometimes cause people to lose their minds. They'd go hopelessly mad and then—from fear, I imagine—he did kill a few of them. Mercifully though. They weren't going to get any better. They were hopelessly insane."

* * * *

"What does any of this have to do with Charles Vincente though?"

"Charles regards himself as Renaldo's chief disciple. Maria's one too. Or at least she was in the beginning. They first came to Africa searching for Renaldo's lost notebooks. When they found them where he'd hidden them here in the castle the notebooks confirmed Charles's theory as to the crucial flaw in Renaldo's experimental work. He'd chosen the wrong subjects to experiment on."

"Because they were African?"

"Because they were adults. Their minds were already set in stone. They lacked what Charles calls psychic flexibility. Charles figured with children it might work better. And it turned out he was right. It did."

"What did?"

"What I told you about. The Linkage."

"And what's the Linkage?"

"The Linkage is—" And then she stopped. "Look," she went on, "it's probably way easier to show you than try to explain. Meet me here in an hour. I'll go in and get the others and find us a good safe spot. It won't be perfect without Charles but since he's already blabbed it all himself, I guess the big secret isn't a secret anymore."

"Charles never mentioned any of this to me. Who did he tell? Darby Spock?"

"No, Charles would never tell Darby anything. He hates him. It was that other friend of yours. The one who wrecked the van."

"Mohammed Bello?"

"Yes, him."

"Good grief," he said. "Why did Charles tell him anything?"

"That I don't know. I wasn't there. I was out on veldt with Maria and Phillip saving you from being eaten by lions. You don't know how Charles is. He's been dying to blab to someone, you can be sure of that. The barbed wire fence, all those warning signs he posted— that was as much to save him from his own big mouth as to protect the rest of us. And there's Maria too. She's turned against the experiment. She says the Linkage is too much of a risk psychologically. Especially since it involves children. I'm going to be eighteen in five more days—"

"Happy Birthday," Schwerner heard himself say before he could stop himself. He felt foolish but Talia reached out, grabbed his hand, and squeezed.

"Thank you, Gordon," she said. "That was sweet of you. But like I was saying, the others kids are all younger than me. A couple are barely past puberty. Maria thinks they're too young to have their minds messed with. So will you wait here until I come back?"

"Yes, of course."

"I'll see you in an hour then." With a wave of her hand she turned and headed back into the castle.

He gave her a few minutes start and then followed.

* * * *

For the next fifty minutes Schwerner explored the castle from bottom to top. In that time he was able to get a peek into nearly every nook and cranny he passed. He climbed as high as the top floor and briefly peeped inside the basement. It was on the third floor above his own room that he came across the only signs of life he encountered when he heard Maria Vincente's strong patient voice coming through an open door as she instructed several of the children in the basics of algebraic equations. He saw nothing of Charles or Mohammed Bello. Presumably they were in their rooms—as was Darby. There was no sign of Talia either. He was careful not to stumble on her unawares, but still where could she be?

He found out when he returned at the time prescribed and heard voices from ahead.

He slowed down and crept cautiously forward.

Then he saw them. There were four of them. Three of the children—and Talia. At some point he'd apparently stopped thinking of Talia as a child. The four of them were seated in a circle in the tall grass. They were holding hands. All except one. The armless girl he'd seen in the room with Charles was there sitting cross-legged beside to Talia.

The other children were the chubby boy with glasses he'd also seen with Charles in the room and Phillip the boy who'd accompanied Talia and Maria on the elephant.

Their eyes were closed. They were naked. All four of them. Talia too.

Schwerner swallowed hard and stepped into the open.

The armless girl suddenly cried out: "I sense a disturbing presence."

Schwerner froze in his tracks.

A long moment passed.

"The presence stands near," the girl finally said.

This time all of them—including Talia—opened their eyes and stared at Schwerner.

"I meant no harm," he said, stepping forward. "I was taking a walk around the castle when I—"

"Rupture!" the girl cried. "The Linkage is ruptured!"

With that the four of them seemed to go limp all at once. Their bodies sagged. "What do you think you're doing here, intruder?" cried the armless girl.

Schwerner tried to explain. "I was only taking—"

"He's here, Carmen, because I invited him," Talia said. "I wanted him to observe the Linkage."

"But why?" said the chubby boy in a whiny tone. "You know Charles won't like it."

"I don't care what Charles likes. He's already told that other man—the one called Mohammed Bello."

"Only because he forced him."

"We don't know that for sure. Now shut up—all of you. That means you too, Waldo. I asked Dr. Schwerner to come and observe us in the Linkage because we may need his help. Gordon, won't you come sit next to me. Now that you've seen us I'll try and explain what's going on here."

Schwerner found the invitation too alluring to resist. He sat down in the tall grass next to the naked girl and tucked his long legs under him. Talia laid a hand on his knee and leaned close.

"Now let me try to explain," she said. "The four of us—plus Charles when he's here—we make up what's known as a synergic gestalt. That's Charles's term but it's a good one if you know what it means. Each of us is still a separate person—an individual entity—but linked together like this, fused, we're also another person, somebody different than any of us. Waldo is the brain of this other person—he's a genius—Carmen is the heart, Phillip the sensory organs, and me—I'm the arms and legs. Charles is the ego—the controlling force—the prime catalyst. He's the one who gives us direction."

"When he's here," Waldo muttered. "Which he isn't right now. And that's the dumbest explanation of a Gestalt Linkage I've ever heard."

"Shut your face." She looked at Schwerner again. "Do you understand what I'm trying to say, Gordon?"

"Well, partly," he admitted.

"That's what I mean. It's hard to explain. So—" she squeezed his leg again "—we'll have to show you. This isn't going to be easy. You'll have to take on Charles's role. You have to be our ego."

"But what do I—"

"You don't do anything," she said. "We do it together. The four of us combined, unified. You just sit there and relax and let it happen. You do have to be naked though. It works better without clothes on. They just get in the way of letting your mind be free. Charles says we were born naked and we need to learn to live naked. You don't mind, do you?"

Schwerner lied and said he didn't. With the least embarrassment he could manage, he stripped down to the buff. Oddly, once he was as naked as the rest, much of his self-consciousness went away.

Talia patted him reassuringly on the leg as he dropped back down beside her. It felt odd—the feel of the wind on parts of his body usually kept covered.

"Well, I still don't like it," Waldo said. "And don't tell me to shut up again either. If I decide to walk away and leave you alone the Linkage won't work, will it? I'm the brain, aren't I? The Linkage is nothing without me. What I want to know is how can we be sure this old guy isn't going to drive all of us crazy? Like what happened in Renaldo's day."

"Because he won't," Talia said. "Because I trust him. He'll be fine. And he's not that old. How old are you, Gordon?"

"Twenty-four," he said.

"And that's on the outside," she said. "On the inside he's even younger."

"But—" Waldo began.

But before he could say anything else there was a sudden gurgling noise. It was Phillip, his eyes wide, his tongue protruding from a corner of his mouth. For a moment Schwerner thought he was choking.

"See?" cried Talia triumphantly. "Phillip agrees. How about you, Carmen? What do you think?"

"I think…" She shut her eyes and seemed to concentrate. She was a stunningly beautiful girl, Schwerner realized, something her deformity had prevented him from noticing until now. Her skin was a deep copper hue like a sunset and her face bright, cheerful, and filled with peace.

Her eyes came open again. "I think Gordon is a troubled but sympathetic soul. He's uncertain but kind within. He's brilliant but far from wise."

"Good," Talia said curtly. "Now let's link." She closed her eyes and her breathing slowed. The others did the same. Schwerner tried to mimic them. For a long time absolutely nothing happened and he began to feel more than slightly absurd. Opening his eyes, he glanced around the circle. Beside him Talia's face and upper body were bathed in sweat as if she were straining to raise mountains. Hastily, Schwerner shut his eyes again and tried to relax—and concentrate.

Then Phillip spoke. At first Schwerner thought it must be Waldo—but the words were coming from Phillip's mouth instead.

"I perceive great conflict—terrible conflict followed by revelation. Annihilation will dawn and a dark man will appear. I see...a soul without form or shape."

"Deep Linkage," murmured Waldo. "Deep Linkage is near."

For Schwerner it was like being two places at once. Like being two people at once. One was himself and the other was something... larger. Greater. He was himself but he was each of them too. Each of them and all of them.

He was Waldo. (A boiling cauldron of fear and disgust; a mind like a clockwork universe.)

He was Carmen. (Serenity tinged with sorrow; pain and pity; a spirit of detachment.)

Phillip. (As dark as the inside of a tunnel with a light flickering at faintly at one end and within that spark of light shadows of himself, Spock, Bello, Maria, Charles, and someone else...someone almost recognizable.)

And Talia.

He was Talia, body and soul.

She sat in the stall feeling the taut muscles of her buttocks against the cold hard ground, the feel of wind on her face, hair brushing her shoulders like whispers.

"Rupture," said a distant voice. (Waldo again.) "The gestalt is ruptured."

And then it was all going.

Slipping.

Fading.

Gone.

"That," said Talia in a breathless voice, "was fantastic."

"Yes," he agreed.

"It's never been like that before. The wholeness, the oneness, the purity. You're the one who brought us together, Gordon."

"Yes, you did." It was Carmen smiling at him.

Talia was looking at Waldo. "Why did you stop it?" she asked him.

"I—" He raised a hand and wiped at his eyes. "I got scared. It was powerful."

"I think we were all afraid," Carmen said.

"Afraid we might not come back," Waldo said.

"Is that bad?" Talia asked.

"I don't know. But it sure is scary."

Phillip rose to his feet then and picked Carmen up in his arms. The two of them moved off through the grass and Waldo after wiping his eyes one more time followed.

That left Schwerner and Talia alone.

"I'd better get dressed," he said.

"Why? You look fine as you are."

And so do you, he thought. But he didn't say it aloud.

He was dressed and ready to go, wondering what he should say to her to explain how he felt, when she broke in to say: "Gordon, look up there."

She didn't point but her eyes moved.

He looked where she was looking.

A familiar face was peering down at them from a window in the castle high above. How long it might have been there was impossible to tell.

"Damn it," he said softly. "It's Mohammed Bello."

A PROFILE: TALIA O'BRIEN

(All her life ever since she was big enough to read on her own Talia O'Brien had wanted to be an authoress. It seemed to her the best possible life imaginable. If you didn't like the world you lived in or the people around you, then you could invent your own world and your own people and live there along with them for as long as you wanted. When she was living at the Renaldo Castle in East Africa her favorite writers among the many books in the library were the no-nonsense American stylists of the previous century with names like East, North, South, and West. As a budding authoress herself she wanted to compose tough hardboiled stories of her own that would echo with all sorts of resonances. The story she knew best was her own life so that was the story she first started to tell):

As far back as I can remember (*wrote Talia*) they called me Trina. Ma and Pop never did because they never really got to know me, having knocked themselves off when I was three years old. How come they did it nobody ever knew for sure. People did stuff like that back then and nobody ever found out why. The way it happened, Pop hanged himself in the garage with a strand of old piano wire while Ma shoved a spike loaded with Mexican brown into her arm, turned blue and never woke up again. The cops came around first and made jokes and then the welfare mothers grabbed up little Trina (me) and made her go live with Aunt Flo and Uncle Charlie in a different town, a different place. By then I was too old to cry more tears than I'd already shed.

My cousin Terri May was there too. We were like twins, doing everything together, growing up and learning the ropes of life, the ties that bind. At twelve I was lean and lanky, covered in freckles down to my skinny behind, far from beautiful. Terri May was all of that too and hard as the shell of a dragon's egg. She smoked weed like it was molasses and said her only goal in life was to run away and join a carnival and marry a one-legged sideshow clown named Crackers. Why Crackers? I asked her and she laughed and said 'cause I like crackers better than most anything else in the world. That was cousin Terri May for you all the way. Sometimes, she once told me, I think the whole world and everything in it is a paper bag full of puke and you and me, cuz, are the only real things floating in it. There was poetry in that little gal and her only thirteen when a truck run her over on her bike and killed her deader than a drowned rat.

This was in Texas, if I forgot to say so before in the first place. Half between Austin and San Antone, a crazy place full of madness, death, glitter, and gore. After the slugs came I lit out for California, figuring by then I needed to see things on my own. I was fourteen, full of piss and vinegar, and wrong on every count. I was on my own.

In Vegas I hooked up with a dealer calling himself Hyde. He asked how old I was and when I laughed he said that's what I tell 'em too. He called me his baby sister and had eyes that burned with unwanted knowledge. One night he came home late and said to me, baby sister, before the sun rises in the morning I'm gonna have killed a man. I asked him why and he said that was the one question I should never ask any man. He showed me his gun, stuck it in his mouth, pulled the trigger. The back of his head blew off in a burst of blood and brain and bone. It was fairly upchucking to look upon.

After that out in L.A. I joined a biker gang called the Dead Hombres. I sheared my hair crewcut short and wore jeans cut to the crotch, a studded leather vest, buckled engineer boots. I chewed Mexicali devil weed and spat profusely. Nobody in the gang knew I was still a virgin. Hell, some days I didn't know myself. The Dead Hombres were some mean lean brown boyz. My favorite was one known as Solomon Cruz and for a time we two figured on getting married in the church as soon as we were old enough. It never happened. An ice cold dude named Gringo in a rival gang known as the Caledonian Stompers called Solomon out and he had no choice but stand tall for himself, taking my cherry alongside the love that burned between us that would never die. Bullets flew that night like hard Texas hail and when it was done both Solomon and Gringo lay dead in the hot summertime L.A. streets. To drown my sorrows I went into an all-night diner called Frisco Jack's stinking of ancient grease and a million shed tears and shot up the place with Solomon's 9mm. In the ensuing confusion a fry cook in the back died. For some reason they wanted to hang it on me.

On my way out of town I caught a ride with a salesman who could have been Willy Loman's baby brother. (Or his doppelganger.).

We got to talking.

"When I was still with carnival," I told him as we drove through the hot ebony night, "I knew this clown who called himself Crackers."

"What was he like," he said to me, "this clown you knew who called himself Crackers?"

"About like what you'd expect a clown to be like," I said. "A jerk, a royal asswipe, hated everything and everybody, never a decent word to say except about the one thing he loved and could never get enough of?"

"What was that, darlin'?" he said.

Africa was still a long way off for me even then. Africa with its hills like big green elephants…

3

After parting from the girl Talia who said she needed to go in and help prepare dinner for the children, Schwerner headed off to his room. He briefly considered dropping in on Darby Spock to describe what he had experienced with the children in the tall grass beyond the castle walls but realized as he proceeded down the hall that he could barely keep his eyes open. The Gestalt Linkage had apparently taken a great deal out of him and it was also absurd to expect that he could have recovered this rapidly from his ordeal on the veldt. He went past Spock's room, entered his own, dropped down on the bed, and let his eyes slide shut of their own accord. He wanted to see if he could run over in his mind the details of the case as he knew them so far but before he could proceed consciousness deserted him like an anxious soldier the night before battle and he found himself entering a realm of blank and dreamless sleep.

It was Spock, smelling strongly of fresh perfume, who shook him awake. "You'd better get up, Gordon," he said when Schwerner opened his eyes. "We're late for dinner already."

"This soon?"

"It's past eight, I'm afraid."

Schwerner stumbled to his feet and disappeared into the bathroom to splash cold water on his face. When he returned he noticed that Spock was again wearing his .45 at his belt.

The two of them went downstairs and into the dining room. Charles and Maria were already in place at opposite ends of the table. Their expressions were dark and strained and Schwerner guessed that they had been quarreling before he and Spock arrived.

At Maria's invitation both men filled their plates with food on the table. The main course consisted of a thin fibrous meat—zebra, Maria explained when Schwerner asked—which proved unexpectedly palatable. Charles Vincente ignored the meal entirely. A gallon jug of red wine sat at his elbow. He filled his glass to the brim, drained it in a few swift gulps, then filled it again and took another big swallow.

The uncomfortable silence was broken by the arrival of Mohammed Bello, He came bustling into the room, paused to bow crisply in Maria's direction, then took his place on the far side of the table. A gauze bandage still covered the top of his skull but he seemed otherwise recovered from his injuries.

Spock glared as Bello heaped food on his plate and began eating as if on the brink of starvation. "I thought you were supposed to be dying," he said drily.

"Alas, friend Darby, how true." Bello spoke through a mouthful of meat and vegetables. He held up his left hand and showed a one-inch gap between thumb and forefinger. "My escape with my life was this close. Now a much blessed man I revel in the glory of my continued existence in this wonderful world."

"I regret that I can't join you in that," Spock said with a tight smile, "Being as I'm dead it would seem rather hypocritical of me."

"Dead only in the literal sense, friend Darby," insisted Bello. "Within—in the soul—you are a man of vigorous life."

Spock didn't seem to know quite how to respond to this flattery. Before he could say anything Bello shifted his attention to the still silent Charles Vincente and began questioning him about the nature and philosophy of the school. Charles responded smoothly and with increasing eagerness and as a result some of the tension in the room evaporated.

"This is truly marvelous work you are accomplishing here," said Bello, his fork jabbing the air in emphasis. "It's a favorite theory of mine that the mind of a child resembles the blank canvas of an artist and that it's the sacred duty of we adults to fill this empty space by sharing our own accrued wisdom. And you as well, Doctor," he added, stabbing his fork at Schwerner. "I believe you also take a strong interest in the welfare of the young."

Schwerner was puzzled. "Actually education is rather far outside my field of expertise."

Bello seemed confused. "How peculiar. I could have sworn I observed you earlier sitting outside in the company of several children and participating fully in their innocent childhood pastimes. Did my eyes play a trick on me?"

"Children?" Charles's head swung around. He looked suspiciously at Schwerner. "What were you up to this time, you lying bastard?"

Schwerner was startled by the fury of this outburst. "I was only talking with—"

"Talking with who?" Charles rose from his chair, fists doubled at his sides. "Tell me which children you were playing around with or I'll knock your fool head off."

"That pretty girl was one of them," Bello put in helpfully. "The one with the freckled face who rides the elephant. And the moron." He nodded to himself. "Yes, I especially recall the presence of the moron."

"And maybe a dark girl too," said Charles. "A girl without arms. And a fat ugly boy with pimples and wearing eyeglasses. Maybe they were all out there together, right?"

"Why, yes," said Bello, smiling. "Yes, I believe they were all there indeed."

Charles let out an angry snort, kicked back his chair, and moved around the table toward Schwerner. Spock sprang from his seat and stepped between the two men. "Now see here, Vincente. I'll thank you to keep your bloody hands to yourself."

Charles scowled. "Out of my way, spook. This bastard was spying on me. You heard him admit it yourself."

"One more step," Spock said, lowering a hand to his hip, "and I'll have to stop you."

Charles hesitated, eyes darting back and forth. He looked at Maria but she turned away. Bello observed the entire scene with avid interest.

"To hell with you too, Spock," Charles finally said. He spread his arms wide to indicate that he was addressing all of them. "To hell with the whole lot of you."

He grabbed the jug of wine off the table and tucked under his arm as he hurried from the room.

"A man of fervent passion," Bello murmured admiringly. He thrust another bite of meat into his mouth, jumped up, and sped from the room in pursuit of Vincente.

Spock dropped back down in his chair. "I'm dreadfully sorry, Maria, but I couldn't very well let him get away with that."

She nodded to indicate that she understood. "It's quite all right, Darby. Charles has no excuse to be acting that way."

"Not that bloody Bello helped much," said Spock. "He was egging him on the entire time." He looked at Schwerner. "You don't happen to know what that was all about, do you? Who are these children Charles is so concerned with?"

"I think I can answer that, Darby," Maria said. "The children Dr. Schwerner was with today are participants in an experiment Charles has been conducting, one he has become extremely sensitive about. I think it may have warped his judgment, made him confused and agitated."

"It must be a bloody important experiment for him to carry on like that," said Spock. "Can you tell me what it's about?"

"I don't think..." She paused, plainly uncertain whether to continue. Her chin rose and she looked determined. "I don't see why I should not tell you. The experiment is one that involves group consciousness. Gestalt Linkage is what Charles terms it. He received the idea from reading the private notebooks of Renaldo."

"Good lord," said Spock. "And how long has this been going on?"

"Ever since we first came to Africa, although in the beginning there was little progress and nothing important occurred. Charles first tried deep meditation with the children and when that proved futile he gave them psychotropic chemicals like LSD and mescaline until I found out about it and made him stop. It was three months ago when he brought together these particular four children that he began to obtain successful results."

"In what way?"

"The children appear to...their minds merge. Into a singular whole. A gestalt." She made a tight fist with her hand. "They become another person—an identity different from themselves."

"And was this also when Charles put up the barbed wire fence? And those warning signs?"

"It was, yes. Charles became anxious that someone would find out what he was doing and force him to stop. You must understand, Darby, that Charles has faced persecution so often in the past that he's come to anticipate it—even here."

"Maybe in a way he's right this time," Schwerner said.

Maria looked at him quizzically. "I do not understand, Doctor. What persecution do mean?"

"I'm talking about Mohammed Bello. I don't believe it's an accident that he's here."

"But he is your friend, is he not?"

"No," Schwerner said. "I'm a...a private agent. I was sent here by my employer to investigate Bello."

"He is a criminal?"

"In a sense he is, yes. Bello belongs to a—a secret conspiracy—a criminal enterprise. It's complicated, I'm afraid."

"But why should these criminals be interested in Charles or me or the children?"

"That I don't know yet," Schwerner admitted. "But I can assure you of this much. Mohammed Bello is a dangerous man—an evil man." The word, one he seldom used, escaped his lips with startling ease.

"Can't you make him go away and leave us alone?"

"I think it would be wiser to get to the bottom of this first," Spock put in.

"But he may try to harm the children?" she asked.

"If he tries anything like that," Spock said menacingly, "Schwerner and I will take care of him."

"Well, now you have made me feel as Charles does." She frowned. "I am as frightened as he. Ever since we came to this land I have experienced a sensation of foreboding that some horrible disaster would soon befall us. I spoke to Charles about my feelings and he insisted I was being silly and superstitious. But this feeling has not gone away. I do not like any of this. I do not like Charles's experiment and I do not like this Mohammed Bello."

"You can leave Bello to us," Spock said with more bluster than Schwerner could have managed. "He isn't apt to pull any tricks while the two of us are keeping a close eye on him."

Maria stood up, her expression strained. "You must excuse me now. I need to visit the children. They will have finished eating long ago and be wondering what has happened to me."

Schwerner and Spock came to their feet and remained standing while Maria made her departure. When they were alone again, Spock sat down with a grunt and looked at Schwerner. "How much of this had you already found out on your own?"

"Nearly all of it. I was with the children today when it happened—the Gestalt Linkage. They asked me to join them. And I—well, I did."

Spock looked solemn. "You mean this thing is actually real?"

"It is." Schwerner quickly described what had taken place in the tall grass with Talia, Waldo, Phillip, and Carmen.

"You're sure about all this?" said Spock. "You weren't simply hallucinating?"

"I don't hallucinate," Schwerner said stiffly.

"No, I don't suppose you do." Spock reached inside his jacket and pulled out his flask of whisky. "And this Linkage—how did you feel about it?"

"That's difficult to say."

"Please try. Frankly I'm interested."

"Well, it was...it was incredible, Darby. Amazing, fantastic and quite indescribable. I wasn't myself anymore. I was them—the four children—and I was also someone else too—a wholeness." He stopped, suddenly embarrassed. "I told you it was difficult to explain."

"No, you're doing a creditable job," Spock took a sip of whisky. "Now tell me something else too. Would it be possible for me to experience this gestalt, this Linkage?"

"Would you want to?"

"I would, yes." He nodded firmly.

"Well, according to what Talia told me it's dependent upon the character of the individual involved. For instance, she said it never worked well with Charles, though I gather that it did succeed when Bello was part of the Linkage."

"Bello? How in bloody hell—?"

"Charles invited him. Allowed him to participate in a partial Linkage. The children said he was...very controlling."

"Then this thing is already getting out of hand." With due deliberation Spock returned the whisky to his pocket. "So what do you suggest we do next, Schwerner?"

"I think what you told Maria is our wisest approach. We'll need to keep a close eye on Bello at all times. Perhaps we should stand alternate watches. Especially since you don't require sleep. We still need to discover precise motive behind him being here while at the same time preventing him from causing any unnecessary harm."

"It seems to me the first part is pretty damn obvious."

"It is?"

"Bello came here to control the Gestalt Linkage."

"He couldn't possibly have known about it beforehand."

Spock looked doubtful. "Your boss knew, didn't he? Why else would he send you here?"

"Yes, but that's different. Desmond has his own private sources of information."

"Well, apparently Bello has them too. Use your bloody imagination, man. Think of what this could mean in terms of human development. It's an enormous step forward, a major leap in evolutionary development."

"Aren't you exaggerating?"

Spock fixed him with a stare. "Am I? You know more about it than I do."

"Then perhaps you're not exaggerating," he conceded.

"As long as we're agreed on that I have one additional suggestion to offer. Since we know who Mohammed Bello is and why he's here, wouldn't it be simplest to dispose of him now before he does accomplish some genuine harm?"

"Assassinate him, you mean?"

"I suppose that's a way of putting it, yes."

Schwerner shook his head firmly. "I could never do anything like that, Darby."

"Fine. Then allow me. I could make it look like an accident. While drunk I stumbled into the wrong room, found a strange man in the bed, blew his bloody head off in a panic. The law out here is hardly noted for vigilance, plus I very much seriously doubt anyone will greatly miss Mr. Mohammed bloody Bello."

Schwerner continued to shake his head. "No. It wouldn't be right, Darby. I'm sure Desmond didn't send me out here to commit murder. He wanted me to uncover as much information as possible concerning an apparent conspiracy so that later he could reach down to its roots and destroy it completely. Bello must be receiving orders from somewhere. If I let you kill him, we'll never learn anything more."

"You don't think he'll talk, do you? That evil bastard is one tough cookie, I'm telling you that."

"I still have to try."

Spock sighed. "All right. You're the detective. I'm not." His tone indicated that he wasn't entirely convinced.

* * * *

The two of them headed upstairs to the second floor. Passing an open door halfway down the corridor, Schwerner looked in and saw Maria seated in a chair surrounded by a circle of tiny heads. There was a book open in her lap and she was reading aloud from the text. To his surprise Schwerner knew the book. *Alice's Adventures in Wonderland.* One of the many works of fantasy fiction in his parents' library. He'd read the book several times as a child, though he'd never much cared for it. The absurdist storyline made him uncomfortable.

"Now I wonder where in hell they're hiding," Spock muttered as he went past.

"Who's that, Darby?"

"Bloody Bello of course. And Charles. If we're going to put them under surveillance we'd better start now. Since sleep isn't a problem for me I'll stand first watch. You can take over tomorrow after breakfast."

"How exactly do we intend to handle this?"

"Find Bello first and then stick to him like tape."

"He won't like it."

"That, as you Americans say, is tough tiddy. If necessary, I'll hop into bed with him and spend the bloody night. Ah, listen up. Hear that? Our quarry is brought to bay."

He had stopped in front of Bello's room. Through it came the murmur of voices, one of which Schwerner recognized as Bello's.

"I'm going in," said Spock. "Before they can jump out the window. I'll see you later, Schwerner."

"In the morning after breakfast?"

"If not sooner."

Spock gave a farewell salute, thrust open the door without knocking, and entered the room. Through the gap Schwerner saw the startled faces of Bello and Charles. They sat side by side on the bed with their heads close together like two spinsters sharing fresh gossip.

"What do you want here, Spock?" Charles cried out in a slurred voice.

"Oh, nothing much, gentlemen. Just thought I'd drop by and shoot the breeze with a couple of old friends."

Spock shut the door behind him.

Schwerner lingered long enough to be sure Spock wasn't immediately ejected and then went on down to his own room. In spite of his earlier nap, he was once again feeling exhausted.

He entered the room, flicked on the overhead light, slipped out of his shoes, and unfastened his belt. He had lowered his trousers to his knees when a voice spoke nearby:

"Do you always greet female guests by dropping your drawers?"

His head jerked up and he saw Talia lying on top of the bed watching him with amused interest. This time to his relief she was fully dressed in sweater and jeans.

He jerked up his pants swiftly. "How did you get in here?"

She seemed to be enjoying his obvious embarrassment. "I walked in the door. What do you think?"

Recovering his composure, he fastened his belt. "You could have waited for me and knocked."

"It's more fun this way. Besides, I didn't feel like hanging around out in the hall. Charles and that slimy Arab were wandering around again. Charles is drunk by the way."

"Yes, I know." He had a sudden worried thought. "What about the others? Waldo and Phillip and Carmen? Do you know where they are?"

"Upstairs sleeping, I suppose. Phillip can never stay awake more than seven or eight hours at a time and I know Carmen was exhausted by the Linkage today. Waldo doesn't sleep much either but he likes to lay around in bed looking at dirty pictures and playing with his Uncle Pud."

Schwerner was feeling embarrassed again. "But they're all right?"

"Sure. Why wouldn't they be?"

That was a difficult question to answer without explaining everything else. "No real reason." He went over and sat down gingerly on the edge of the bed as far from her as he could. "Did you want something with me?"

"Oh, nothing in particular." Her voice was deliberately casual as if she too were being evasive. "I was just wondering what you thought about what happened today."

"Well, I thought…" Schwerner broke off, wanting to be sure of his words before he went on. "It was awesome—an extraordinary experience."

She looked at him carefully. "Then you liked it?"

"Yes. Certainly."

"The reason I ask, some people wouldn't. I know it can be scary—especially the first time. Loss of identity and all that. Why do you think Renaldo drove all those poor people mad and then had to kill them? He wasn't as careful as Charles and he didn't have Phillip to help make it work right but you see what I mean."

"What's so important about Phillip?"

"Haven't you noticed? He's got psychic powers. He's telekinetic for one thing and Waldo says he can read minds and plant thoughts. He's getting more powerful all the time too. The Linkage helps him grow."

"I don't accept the existence of psychic powers," Schwerner said stiffly.

She laughed. "Tell that to those lions out on the veldt that wanted to eat you alive. Ask them what it was that made them change their minds."

"Are you saying that was because of something Phillip did?"

"You can bank on it, brother."

Schwerner didn't argue. Events had been taking place so rapidly since the lions he hadn't really had time to think about what happened then.

Now another question occurred to him: "How many people know about the Linkage?"

"I never stopped to count," she admitted. "There's the four of us kids of course and most of the other children especially the older ones have some idea of what's going on. There's Charles and Maria. Throw in you and the Arab and I guess Spock and how many does that make?"

"I was actually more concerned with outsiders."

"Nobody like that, no. After Charles put up the fence we didn't get many…oh, wait. I almost forgot. The weird Chinese person."

"Who was that?"

"A huge fat guy with bright red hair that looked like an obvious wig. I stumbled on him one afternoon flaked out in the tall grass out by where we were today. He was a weird one, all right. I could barely understand a word he said. He kept getting his r's and l's mixed up." She chuckled, shaking her head. "He called me Missy Tara."

"Did he happen to mention his name?"

"Sure. It wasn't Chinese though. Bluto, he said. Maybe he meant Bruto. I had to laugh at that too. It made me think of an old Popeye the Sailor cartoon. Ever seen one of those? They're pretty good."

"What did this Bluto character want?"

"Well, he claimed he was a witch doctor. Which was pretty ridiculous to start with. Belonged to a lost tribe from Atlantis that now lived in the Congolese rain forest. The chief of the tribe was two thousand years old and rich as hell from uranium mining and all he ever wanted was to give away his fortune to good causes. This Bluto said the chief had sent him here to determine if we were worthy of a gift or not. I didn't believe a word he said."

"When was this?"

"A couple weeks ago. Maybe less."

Schwerner nodded. At least one mystery had been solved. How and where Desmond had obtained his information about the Vincentes and the school.

Talia was watching him closely. "You know something about this, don't you? You know who this phony Chinese character really was, don't you?"

Schwerner admitted he did. "His name is Desmond Blue. He's my employer."

"Desmond Blue, the great detective?"

"You know him?"

"I've heard of him. Who hasn't?"

"Desmond sent me here to investigate Mohammed Bello."

"Good. Because he frightens me. He frightens all of us. So what are you going to do? Arrest him?"

"I don't have that authority. Even if I did he hasn't necessarily committed a crime."

"And you won't kill either, I gather."

"Darby suggested that too. I'll tell you the same thing I told him. Not unless it proves to be the only viable alternative."

She seemed willing to accept that. "There is one other thing I ought to tell you though. Phillip thinks it's a real possibility. It's got him so excited he can hardly sit still. He thinks if we establish a Linkage again with you part of it we may lose control."

"I don't understand." He shook his head. "What does that mean? Lose control of what?"

"It means we could cease to exist as individuals and become the Linkage."

"I don't see how that's possible."

"Phillip thinks it is. He thinks it's where we've been heading all along. He says it may be inevitable."

"But Phillip is a—"

"A retard?" she said.

"That's not a word I'd use, no."

"Good. Because it's inaccurate. Phillip's a special person. He's a savant. That may be a cliché but it's also true. As for the Linkage, there's only one way of finding. We have to try it again—all of us— and find out what happens."

"I see."

"So are you ready?"

Before he could answer the door was flung open and Maria Vincente hurried in. "Dr. Schwerner, you must come quickly."

"Why? What is it? What's wrong?"

"It's Darby, Doctor." Her voice was shaking. "He has been injured. Hurt. You must come at once."

Schwerner was already on his feet. "Where is he?"

"I'll show you. It's in Mohammed Bello's room. I found Darby on the floor. He's unconscious."

"And Bello? Is he in there too?"

"I haven't seen him, no."

* * * *

They found Darby Spock in Bello's room sitting up on the bed wide awake. There was still blood on his forehead but his eyes were alert and awake. He started to shake his head to indicate that he was all right but the gesture broke off in a wince. "The bloody bugger cracked me on the head. I've been out cold on the floor ever since.'"

"Who did it?" Schwerner asked.

"Who do you bloody well think? Bello of course. Either him or else that—" He stopped, noting Maria's presence. "Either him or else somebody else here at the castle."

"You mean Charles," Maria said. "You can say it if you want, Darby. I know it's what everyone's thinking."

"I'm sorry, Maria."

"Don't be. Charles is the one who should be sorry."

"It may not have been his decision to make," Schwerner said. Then a sudden apprehension struck him. He looked at Maria and asked, "Do you know if any of the children are missing? Have you looked in on them lately? Do you know where they all are right now?"

The anxious look on her face confirmed that she didn't know. "That is why I came to this floor, Doctor. I always check on the children at least twice each night before going to bed. Talia was not in her room but I knew she would likely be with you. Then I came past here and I heard Darby groaning. I opened the door and found him on the floor covered in blood."

"A superficial head wound only," Spock said. "They always make you bleed like a stuck pig."

"We'd better look around and see if we can find the other children then," Schwerner said. "Three of them in particular. Phillip, Waldo, and Carmen. If they're with Bello—"

"I have a better idea," Talia broke in to say.

"What's that?" said Spock.

"I'm pretty sure I know where they are."

"Where?"

She stood up. "Where we all were earlier today."

"Good God," Schwerner said.

"We'll need a flashlight." Talia said.

Maria held up her hand. "I have one here. I thought I might need it."

"And your gun, Darby," said Schwerner.

"Right here." Spock slapped his holster. "Bello neglected to take it this time."

"Then we'd better get moving," Schwerner said. "They already have a head start."

* * * *

Schwerner and Talia led the way downstairs and out the door.

The weather had changed. Dramatically. A sheet of cold rain hit Schwerner square in the face as stepped outside and a fierce driving wind nearly knocked him over. He reached behind, took the flashlight from Maria, lowered his head, and plunged forward. In a matter of seconds his clothes were drenched. The pelting rain made it almost impossible to see and the force of the wind whipped the high grass lashing against his legs. "Carmen!" he called out when it seemed as if they'd come far enough. "Phillip, Waldo, Carmen, can you hear me?"

There was no response. But he hadn't really expected one. The wind swallowed his words as soon as he spoke. Staggering forward, head bent, chin pressed to his chest, Schwerner swung the flashlight in a wide arc. Then all at once there they were. Five faces rising out of the dark. He saw Carmen. Waldo. Phillip. Charles.

And in the middle of the circle sat Mohammed Bello.

"Charles, no!" Maria cried out, rushing forward. Schwerner held her back. "Don't," he said. "Not now."

The Linkage had clearly been formed.

"Bastard," said Spock. "Bloody bastard." He stood glaring at Bello. What role was he playing in the Linkage? Schwerner wondered. The one he'd played himself earlier? Or was that Charles? It was impossible to tell.

Sick with revulsion, afraid of what might come next, Schwerner grabbed Spock by his arm. "Shoot him, Darby," he said, indicating Bello. "Kill him."

Spock didn't argue. His hand dropped to his hip and the .45 rose in his hand. He aimed the weapon steadily.

But nothing happened.

"Shoot him, I said!" cried Schwerner.

Spock's face was a ghostly pale mask drenched by the rain. His jaw was clamped tightly shut. His eyes bulged in his head. "Damn it, Schwerner, I am trying. But I can't do it. Something's stopping me. My bloody finger won't budge on the trigger."

Schwerner realized what had to be happening. "Phillip!" he called out. "Stop it! Let Spock go! He's only trying to help!"

But the boy's moon face was blank and expressionless. His eyes burned like embers. Those aren't Phillip's eyes, Schwerner thought. They're Bello's. He's the one controlling this.

Spock let out a frustrated cry as his hand clutching the gun shook. The gun popped free of his hand, flew through the air, and landed in the wet grass close to where Bello was sitting cross-legged. He looked down at the gun, smiled thinly, and his eyes rolled back in his head.

Schwerner continued to hold the flashlight in his hand, the harsh glow illuminating the scene in lurid shadows. Behind him stood Maria murmuring softly to herself and Talia just gaped and stared as if unable to believe anything she was seeing.

Then the Linkage disappeared. The three children, Bello, and Charles. One moment they were there in the long grass.

The next they were gone.

Then they were back again.

"My God," Spock said with a gasp. "Did you see that?"

But now something had changed. Schwerner saw it clearly. The smile on Bello's face was gone. In its place was something else. A look of utter terror.

Seeing this, Schwerner lunged forward. He couldn't have said for sure what he intended. He wanted to reach the children—Carmen especially—she was the nearest—and pull them free of the Linkage before—

"Schwerner!" It was Spock's voice. "Schwerner, don't move. Look behind you. Slowly, man. Damn it, I said slowly. See what's in back of you."

Schwerner turned his head. Slowly, yes, very slowly—and saw behind him three pair of gleaming yellow eyes shining in the dark.

The lions. The lions from the veldt.

What in the name of madness were they doing here?

He looked back at Bello and saw that the terror on his face hadn't gone away. If anything it was even stronger than before.

Then the lions leaped.

It was over in a few seconds.

Mohammed Bello was dead—torn to shreds.

The children—and Charles—looked like sleepers coming suddenly awake.

"Don't anyone move," Spock cautioned. "Not while they're still here."

He meant the lions. But even as he spoke they were moving off. Shortly afterward they vanished into the surrounding darkness as swiftly as they'd first appeared.

* * * *

The next day the sun was shining again as bright as ever and they had visitors. Nylun Bobutu and the Goniani high priests.

They asked to see Mohammed Bello's dead body.

"We burned it,'" Spock told them. "Charles insisted upon it. He called him the devil—the evil one."

"But h is dead?" Bobutu said. "That much is certain?"

"It is indeed," Spock said. "I can assure you of that."

* * * *

Later in the day a whirring noise invaded the afternoon stillness. Schwerner looked up at the sky and at first thought he was seeing a giant bird. As the object descended it assumed the shape of a helio-plane.

The helio-plane landed a short distance away. A door in the side slid back and a woman dressed in an aviator's silk jumpsuit leaped out.

Schwerner recognized Crystal LaFleur.

"Hey, Doc!" she yelled, waving to him. "Doc, get your ass over here. Desmond wants you right away!"

By then Schwerner was beyond surprise.

He hurried across to where the helio-plane sat and thrust his head inside. Desmond Blue sat strapped into the rear passenger seat. "Ah, Doctor Schwerner, there you are at last. Do climb in. We're returning at once to Arabia Deserta. I have an aeroplane waiting in Nairobi."

"But I've found out so much already," Schwerner said. "One of the Sect conspirators was here all along. He died last night—killed by lions—and the children—"

"Yes, yes, I know all that," Blue said with a dismissive wave. "Now do get in. We need to move quickly."

"But, Desmond, I can't just—can't I at least say goodbye?" He looked back to see if Talia was among those who'd hurried out to look at the helio-plane.

But she wasn't there.

"Damn it," said Blue, "get in or I'll have Crystal here drag by your short hairs."

Crystal was standing just in back of Schwerner. She hissed in his ear: "Better do as he says, Doc. Desmond's been acting worse than a cranky old grizzly the last few days."

With a last forlorn look at the Renaldo Castle, Schwerner climbed into the passenger seat.

"Fasten your safety belt, Doc," Crystal said, jumping in next to him. "The air's been bit rocky around here lately."

A moment later the helio-plane climbed into the broad blue African sky.

Hands clenched in his lap, Schwerner never looked back.

For the first time in his life that he could remember there were tears flooding his eyes.

4

Naked except for a black satin bra and matching silk panties, Eric Jorgenson, a wraith-like blond with extraordinarily soft smooth skin, stood in front of the mirror in his two-room Berlin apartment and peered critically at the reflection looking back at him from the polished glass. Tonight, he thought with grim determination, I shall become as never before Petra in spirit and soul as well as flesh.

He went into the bathroom, shaved for the third time today, then returned to the living room where his wardrobe for the evening lay spread out on the couch. Eric dressed with meticulous care. Fishnet stockings. Satin garter belt. A blouse of crinkly leather. Short zippered skirt of a similar fabric. Blue suede laced boots. A silver medallion necklace that glinted in the light. Thin copper bracelets, one on each wrist.

Eric returned to the bathroom to apply his make-up. As he knew from past experience moderation here was absolutely essential, for too little in the way of cosmetic coating would permit Eric to peep unnaturally through while too heavy an application would cause Petra to resemble the painted whore she most definitely was not. Facial cream therefore. A light brushing with powder. Some rouge. Red lipstick. Touch of purple eyeliner. False lashes.

Only at the end did Eric reach down and remove from its hiding place the shoulder-length tresses of genuine human golden-red hair that at last transformed Petra from bizarre grotesque into a creature of stunning and womanly beauty.

As he maneuvered toward the door that led to the street a final transfiguration overwhelmed the respectable young man who labored during the day as a junior accountant in the firm of Belham & Belham mortgagors. His step turned light and airy. His chin tilted at a fey angle. His shoulders arched, hips swayed gently. Pausing with one hand on the knob Eric shut his eyes and whispered words of encouragement to Petra. He let the caressing touch of the feminine garments seep inward through his skin to inundate—he hoped—the spirit and soul of Petra's womanliness.

Then with confidence she stepped outside.

The time was nearly eight, a warm evening. The district where Eric resided contained decaying homes for the former working classes. On occasion in the past neighbors had glimpsed Petra entering or leaving the apartment. At this very moment in fact Petra could observe the moon white face of the retired schoolteacher watching from across the street. What did the little old man think? she wondered. Who was this strange and beautiful woman who had just emerged through the studious young man's door? Sister? Friend? Co-worker? Lover? Whore?

Aha, thought Petra, if only you knew, old man, you would—she smiled at the thought—vomit.

A taxi drew up beside her. Raising her skirt modestly, Petra slid into the rear seat of the beetle buggy. The driver was a stiff-necked man with coal black hair, Hitlerian cowlick, and a toothbrush moustache. He smiled at her through the rearview mirror. "Where do you wish to be taken, beautiful lady?"

She gave him the address and when he looked confused added, "The Cafe of Monsters." She looked him at the mirror. "You know it, do you not?"

"A pretty-pretty girl such as you," he sputtered. "To that den of freaks?"

Petra smiled. "This pretty girl is also a pretty-pretty boy underneath."

The taxi leaped away from the curb. The driver drove without caution. "So you are a damn queer," he said without anger when stopped by a red signal as a freight train trundled past. "You could have fooled this fellow for sure."

"What do you mean by this word 'queer?'" she asked politely.

"I mean a man who enjoys dressing in the clothes of a woman."

"A pervert," she said primly.

"And you are not?"

"Oh, no. I am a special person. A phenomenon. I am Eric and also Petra. Which do you prefer by the way?"

He ground the gears noisily, accelerating. "A freak is what I call you."

"Perhaps. But someday your grandchildren will be freaks also."

The driver might well have become enraged—Petra had been beaten many times, once violently gang-raped by five Polish shoulders while visiting friends in Warsaw—but the man only shrugged. "I have no children of my own. Let the others do as they want. They will anyway." He laughed. "The same as you, sweetie."

Petra was never ashamed of being who and what she was. Cautious, yes. Secretive—often! But ashamed? No—never! Once a certain powerful man who was her occasional lover suggested taking steps to annihilate Eric completely. "I know an excellent physician who will perform such surgery quietly."

He had doubtlessly intended to please her. Instead, Petra was revolted. "I will gladly do it," she said, lying naked in his arms, "but you must join me."

He laughed, thinking she joked. "But I have a good use for this thing of mine," he said.

"Do you not think Eric has a use for his?"

To destroy Eric would be to destroy Petra's own uniqueness—her duality—and Petra would no more do that than remove her clothes here in this taxi so that the stupid driver could see for himself that she was indeed phenomenal.

"Here we are, pretty lady," the driver announced as the taxi glided to a halt.

The Cafe of Monsters was located in a dingy factory-laden section of the old eastern zone. Petra paid the driver what she owed and on a whim added a substantial tip. He started to thank her profusely, then thought better of it and sped quickly away. She waved after him, laughing. "You could have fooled this fellow for sure!" she shouted into the stillness of the night.

The entrance to the Cafe of Monsters was an unmarked gate in a brick wall. Petra passed through it, moved down a well-lighted passageway, and came to a door. She knocked twice, paused, then knocked four times in rapid succession. The door swung inward and two identical heads peered around the corner. Familiar music reached her ears. Bix Beiderbecke: "Singin' the Blues." A great favorite among many at the Cafe of Monsters.

"Ah, Petra, my darling, it is you at long last." The proprietor of the cafe: Herman/Victor Lindstrom. It was Herman, the twin on the left, who spoke. Victor as usual lately appeared to be asleep. Petra worried that Victor suffered from a serious malady—a tumor in his already weakened brain. A horrible fate for both halves of a pair of conjoined twins. "We have not seen you here at the Cafe of Monsters for many days."

"Eric has been working extra hours," she explained. "The government is trying to collect taxes from the widows of the wealthy once again."

Herman laughed at this rich funny joke. He and Victor were wrinkled old men who had once traveled widely throughout Europe as star attractions in a seamy sideshow carnival. They had appeared before the Kaiser himself, Herman sometimes boasted when drunk, and had avoided death in the concentration camps because their many admirers extended to Herr Hitler himself. The brothers were joined at the hip by a narrow two-inch band of flesh. The surgery to separate them would have been a relatively simple operation even a half-century ago but Petra doubted that either had ever considered it. Now at their advanced age it was unlikely either would survive the violent parting.

"The Baron has been asking for you, Petra," said the old man with a sly wink.

"He is here then—tonight?" She felt a tremor of anticipatory pleasure.

"I believe I saw him only a short time ago." The brothers stepped aside to allow her to pass. The familiar fused odor of perfume and sweat made her instantly lightheaded as she plunged ahead into the room. At the bar—tended by one of the Lindstrom grandchildren, a handsome boy who attended university—she ordered tonic water. While the boy poured her drink, Petra cocked her head and surveyed the room. For a Sunday the cafe was remarkably full. At the nearest table she recognized Bo, Po, and Zo, three Hungarian pinheads of indeterminate age and gender who were among the Baron's many favorites. But he was not with them tonight. Petra's eyes moved on. Halfway across the room she spotted the towering head and broad shoulders of Hedda, the Norwegian giantess, another with whom the Baron was taken, but Hedda was with three Russian soldiers and again there was no sign of the Baron.

As she turned to sign for her tonic water, a hand came down on her bare forearm. Thinking it must be the Baron, Petra swiveled with an eager smile but it was only Rosie the dog-faced lady. Even in this roomful of freaks, Rosie stood out. She was hardly five feet in height and almost as wide as she was tall. Her face was a thatch of matted gray fur in the lower half of which sprouted a hairy muzzle with a round black nose at the tip. Her eyes were small and feral and her voice when she spoke was a growl. "Looking for the Baron, Petra dear?"

"No, not particularly." Petra did not especially care for Rosie. She stank always of urine and sometimes of feces as well. The joke around the Café of Monsters was that the fleas that infested Rosie's fur were the least of her many charms.

"There he is. Right over there. With the new couple."

"We have a new couple?"

"There. Don't you see them?"

Looking around the room once more, this time Petra saw them. The table was the last in the room next to the jukebox nearly hidden from view by the swaying dancers—dwarfs mostly—who cavorted in vague rhythm to a Count Basie tune. The Baron sat with his tuxedoed back turned toward her, the slack features of his second sightless face concealed in the shadowy half-light.

The two seated across the table—the new couple—were blond and striking. The man wore a cotton open-necked shirt as tight across his chest as a second layer of skin while the woman—his sister, his twin?—was wearing something sequined, tiny, and strapless that showed her pale white skin to startling advantage. Petra experienced an immediate stab of jealousy. "What do they think they're doing here?" she demanded. "Herman should never have let them in."

"The Baron insisted," said Rosie.

"He should know better too." She resisted the urge for another, stronger drink. "The Café of Monsters is not a circus freak show for the amusement of rich fools."

"The Baron says they're phenomenal."

"I don't see how—or where."

"They're identical twins."

"So? They're unattached. Even Victor could see that much."

"If he ever wakes up again." Rosie laughed. "But the Baron says it doesn't matter. They're phenomenal, he says, simply by being what they are. He's biologically male and she female. True identical twins from a single egg must by necessity be of the same sex. The Baron says he's looked closely himself and it's all quite true. Some think—" she somehow giggled deep in her throat "—he's done more than simply look."

"This I must see this for myself."

Drink in hand, her studied aloofness set aside, Petra forced her way across the room. Moving through the maze of dancers, she pushed several aside. One old dwarf dressed in a cheap plaid suit three sizes too big swore at her in a shrill piping voice. "Watch where you're going, stupid whore. Big fat freak." She hardly heard a word. What Rosie had said about the new couple was no doubt true. Apart from the clothes they wore, it would not have been possible to tell one from the other. As she drew closer the Baron's second face seemed to sense her approach. She could feel those blank vacant eyes that always made her queasy staring at her. Just as she reached the table the Baron turned his head and saw her. An annoyed look passed over his features but quickly faded. "Ah, Petra love," he said with his usual glibness. "I have been searching for you everywhere all through the night."

The Baron was an impeccably dressed man in his middle forties with chiseled Prussian features, a shaven head—"so that my poor other face might see if it only could"—and eyes that rarely blinked.

He lived in a splendid house in the oldest section of Berlin and had been a regular patron of the Café of Monsters since it first opened when Eric was still a confused boy playing dress-up in his sister's bedroom closet.

"Aren't you going to introduce me to your new friends, Baron?" Petra asked with a disarming smoothness as she grabbed a chair from the next table and slid neatly into it, her skirt rising to show the bare flesh above her stockinged thigh.

The Baron reached over and pulled the skirt down past her knee. "Petra," he said, "this is Lai and that is Jai." The first was the man—the second the woman. "They have only recently arrived in our city."

"You're both quite lovely," Petra said with all due honesty. From behind a barking laugh sounded out. Rosie, thought Petra, turning to see that the dog-faced woman had indeed followed her across the room. "Get yourself a chair, dear," she said. "There's always room for another friend at the table."

While Rosie sauntered off in search of chair, Petra stared openly at Lai and Jai. The woman stared blankly back as if bored while the man met her gaze with equal interest.

"I don't quite understand you, Petra," he said. "I thought everyone here was a freak of some kind. But you're only a man pretending to be a woman. That's not freakish, is it?"

Rosie was back now with her chair. She sat at the Baron's left and waving a furry arm said, "Yes, Petra dear, why don't you enlighten the lovely young man? Surely there should be no secrets among friends. Show him what you have hidden under that tiny little skirt of yours? Many of us here are quite curious to see."

Petra looked at the Baron who gave no sign that he was even listening. He fixed a cigarette in his holder, lit it, and then reached across the table laying a hand on each of the two seated across from him.

"What I have and what I am is my concern," she said. "I'm human. We all are. Even you, dear Rosie, though sometimes it's difficult to keep that in mind."

The Baron laughed explosively, smoke pouring out his nose.

The woman—Jai—seemed to snap from her trance. "Why, that's what we are too, Petra," she said. "We're human. Right, Lai? We're human beings, aren't we?"

"Yes," he said, "that's what we are."

"And all true humans are freaks," the Baron finished up. "Now that we've exhausted that subject, perhaps it's time to move on." He raised a hand and waved it in the air. "More drinks all around! We're dying of thirst over here."

While waiters scurried around taking orders and fetching drinks, the Baron took out a thin brown cigarette, inserted it in his holder, lit it, and sucked in a lungful of smoke. He passed the holder across the table to Petra.

"Here," he said. "This always puts you in a better mood, my dear."

His other hand came down on her leg. He reached up under her skirt and dug his nails painfully into the flesh of her thigh.

She took the harsh smoke into her lungs, held it as long as she could, and then passed the cigarette on to Jai.

"When we leave I want Petra to come with us," Jai blurted out to the Baron. The cigarette holder dangled from his mouth. Through the thin fabric of her dress Petra could see her nipples.

"I wouldn't have it any other way," the Baron said. "Not only must Petra come but Eric as well."

"Eric?" said Jai, looking around curiously. "Who is that?"

"Petra's dear…brother."

"But I don't see anyone. Where is he?"

"Oh, right here." The Baron pointed his thumb at Petra's lap. "There is Eric down there swaddled beneath a layer of nylon and lace. We seldom get to see Eric here at the Cafe of Monsters but when he does appear he's always memorable."

Petra lowered her eyes, more in embarrassment than shame. Only once at the Baron's insistence had she appeared at the Café as Eric. Afterward at his house he had seemed particularly aroused—and brutal. She refused to ever do it again.

"I still don't understand," Jai said. She handed the cigarette back to Petra who took another long deep drag, letting the hot smoke curl down her throat and into her lungs. The drug did not seem to be either opium or hashish but something else, something altogether different, that went straight to her loins.

"What about me?" said a faraway voice. Petra turned her head and saw Rosie beside her. "You said it was all right for me to sit with you tonight, Baron. Can I come home with you too?"

"Why not, dear?" he said, leaning forward as if to plant a kiss on her furry cheek but stopping just short. He raised his head and looked around the table. "Unless someone else here wishes to raise an objection."

"No," Petra said sharply. "I don't want Rosie to come along."

The Baron smiled archly. "I don't recall soliciting your opinion, darling."

"You don't want to go with us, Rosie," Petra said. She had no clear idea what the Baron was up to but knew whatever it was poor Rosie in the end would suffer.

"But the Baron said I could."

"And I say no. You're not ready. Trust me. I know."

"Ready for what?"

"To be fucked to death like a mad bitch cur," the Baron cried out. His words were slurred. His hands waggled in the air. Petra had never seen him like this. The drug in the cigarette—whatever it was—was affecting him as nothing else before.

Rosie giggled. "Oh, I'm more than ready for that," she said.

"There may be other activities as well," the Baron added in a mysterious tone.

"Like what?" Rosie said, leaning avidly forward.

"You mean you can't guess?"

She barked out another odd laugh. "Oh, I can do that, Baron."

"I knew you had a splendid imagination, Rosie."

By now Petra had lost interest in the conversation. She'd done what she could to save Rosie. What happened now was up to her. The cigarette came around the table again and this time she took an even deeper lungful, letting the potent smoke flow through her body like a medicine. She let her eyes shift back and forth from Jai to Lai and back again. Which was which—and did it even matter? She moved her eyes more rapidly, trying not to blink, and watched as the twin images blurred into one, fusing like two separate streams converging to form a river. The effect reminded her of a movie she'd once seen about a madman who wore a painted mask to conceal a disfiguring injury. At the end burned to death in a horrible conflagration, Petra vividly recalled how the mask had melted as the orange red flames consumed it, the nose flowing, the ears shriveling, the cheeks and lips and eyes dripping blood. But all of that was repulsive. And Lai and Jai were beautiful. Watching them now she felt as if she were gazing upon something classical and remote like the chiseled remnants of a Grecian urn.

She passed the cigarette to Jai who drew smoke and handed it on to Lai. Jai then hunched forward, speaking softly so that only Petra could hear. "You're a beautiful human person. We've heard so much about you but we never realized you were like this—the way you are."

"You heard it from the Baron?"

"And others too. We've met them all by now. Bo and Po and Zo. So delightfully charming. And Hedda the giantess. And there was a woman last night so huge when she took off her dress she seemed to burst outward like a giant bomb. The Baron wanted to fuck her while we watched but Lai said no, that would be wrong. We were already thinking of you then, I'm sure. You're the only one that's really like us, you know."

"I'm only a poor misunderstood drag queen." It was what she always said when pressed. But this time it didn't seem right—even to her own ears. What was going on? Who were these two?

"I want us to all have sex together," she said in a voice that sounded like she was trying to yell.

"You do, do you?" It was the Baron. He laughed uproariously as he staggered to his feet. "Then come along. Let's go. All of you—all of us. We'll have a party to end all parties."

As they went out, Herman bowed to each of them at the door. He looked worried if not frightened. "Come back tomorrow," he said. "All of you do come back. The Cafe of Monsters will be here tomorrow. And the day after—and the one after that too. You'll always have a home here—remember that—a home for any and all who are unique."

"I never heard him say that before," Rosie said as they went out.

A hand struck Petra in the back, pushed her forward. "The poor fool is dying on his feet," the Baron said, "and everyone knows it but him. Don't let him ruin the night for the rest of us."

His long car was waiting at the curb. The five of them piled inside. The driver, a bear of a man in a black leather coat like the Gestapo wore, held the doors open. Petra found herself in the front seat with the driver and Rosie. No one spoke as the car glided through vacant streets. Petra gazed out the window as factories and grim warehouses marched past in weary succession. Then came a district of flashing neon and painted windows—restaurants and nightclubs, beer halls and coffeehouses—and finally pockets of trees and grass and here and there scattered houses, great huge mansions like oases appearing suddenly out of the desert. The Baron's home was the last of these. The long black car entered through an iron gate that swung open automatically as it approached. The house had originally belonged to the Baron's maternal great-grandfather, a high ranking official during the Nazi period later hanged as a war criminal. The Baron enjoyed the irony, since the Nazis had begun their campaign of mass extermination among the very people—the freaks—who were now his own kind. "When you kill a Jew or a Gypsy you kill his many unborn descendants as well. But when you kill a bearded lady or a dwarf or hermaphrodite or a man with a second face in the back of his head, then you kill only the individual because another like him may be born to anyone anytime and the breed of freaks will continue unto the next generation and all that follow."

They crossed the lawn in a group and entered the house. Wasting no time in formalities, the Baron led the way up the winding staircase to the room at the top of house that Petra knew well. A burst of light flared as they entered and Rosie for one threw back her head and gasped in awe like an unbeliever stricken by a glimpse of the face of the one true God. The ceiling was a vast window revealing the stars while the walls were enormous mirrors reflecting each of them back and forth in ever diminishing images. The floor was as a giant mattress. Rhythmic music began to reverberate.

She felt hands around her neck. It was the Baron of course. She had been anticipating this, knowing he would surely seek to humiliate her as always did when others were present—and often when they weren't. She steeled herself not to resist, knowing by now what would happen if she did. She dropped to her knees. He shoved her down on her stomach. She felt his fingers removing her clothes with dexterity. Her tiny skirt was gone in a whisk and then the stockings and garters. When he jerked the silk panties down past her ankles she lay naked from the waist down. She knew what he intended next. It was his way of denying her uniqueness and asserting his personal control. She tried always to pity him.

Closing her eyes, she strained to relax and await his entrance.

"No, don't," said a soft voice. It was one of them. Until now she hadn't noticed that their voices were identical. With her eyes shut she couldn't possibly tell one from the other.

"You told us Petra was unique," said whichever of them had spoken before. (Or maybe the other; there was no way of knowing.)

"But she is," said the Baron.

"We want to see. You said you'd show us."

"All right, if you insist," he said irritably. "Petra, roll over and show them what you have there."

"No," she said, her face pressed to the floor.

"I said do it." He struck her. She cried out. He struck her again. Harder. "Show them, I said."

"Please, Petra," said Jai, crouching beside her. Lai was on the other knelt on the other side. Gentle hands brushed her face, stroked her hair. Tenderly. She (he?) removed the blonde wig. "We only want to know for sure."

She did as he (she) asked, turning on her back and sealing her eyes against the anticipated shame. The Baron reached down and brutally pushed her legs further apart. Whenever this happened Petra always thought back to the time when as a child the older boys forced Eric into the woods and made him undress and display himself in front of them while they laughed and called out ugly horrid names, and then they—

It was no different then what the Baron did now and the shame she felt, that was the shame now too.

Lai continued to stroke Eric's short hair. Opening his eyes, he saw the delight in her face. "It's true," Jai (Lai) told Lai (Jai). "Petra and Eric are like us."

"As I told you," said the Baron. "A true freak! Like me! Like all of us! Like everyone! Now allow me—"

"No! Get away!" cried Jai (Lai). "Leave him (her) be. We need to be alone with this person who is like us. Take this one who is like a poor sad dog. She will have you gladly."

'Rosie?" he cried. "Are you mad? I don't want Rosie."

"No, Baron," said Jai. "We dislike you," said Lai from the same mouth. "Last night you watched and saw us as we are but now if you do not wish to be hurt you will do as we say."

The Baron's face showed a bewildering flicker of emotions—including fear. Across the room Eric saw Rosie off by herself in a corner and watching the scene in front of her with a mixture of curiosity and wonder, her own physical image multiplied over and over in the mirrored walls behind her.

"You cannot speak to me that way," the Baron said. "No one can."

Jai, ignoring him, reached down and drew Eric to his feet. She helped him dress and then, as Petra, watched as she strode forward and slapped the Baron hard on his face. She slapped him again, drawing blood, as Rosie cried out in delighted surprise.

Then he turned and held out her hands and the three of them stood together as one.

The Baron tried to speak through the blood in his mouth but his body stiffened and jerked. He staggered on his feet, then crossed the room and Rosie hurried forward to meet him. As Petra and Eric, Jai and Lai, Lai and Jai, Eric and Petra watched Rosie took the Baron in her short stubby arms, threw him down on the floor, and took him as if he were the dog in heat and she the man, giggling merrily all the time.

By then the three of them were on their way out. Down the winding staircase and into the waiting long car.

The driver turned as they climbed in. "Where to, children?" he asked.

"To Moscow!" they cried as one. "Take us to Moscow!"

5

Alfie Jarrett was bored out of his mind.

It didn't seem fair.

All of last year trapped within the stifling walls of the Arabia Deserta mansion all he could think about was *case case case*, how much he wanted a case, needed a case, any case, something to break the monotony, and now that it had finally happened, now that a lightning bolt of good fortune had actualized his fondest wishes, the best he could do was wander around all day like a holy fool in a trance struggling to keep his eyes open and not yawn in people's faces. It was a genuine letdown was what it was. A crime and a pity. This case was just too odd, Alfie felt. A conspiracy that wasn't a secret, a sect that had no name. Given a good dishonest murderer, thief, kidnapper, rapist, spy, pederast, and he'd have been as dizzily happy as a goat in a garbage dump. So what did he get instead? He got a crazy old coot of a millionaire with two beautiful daughters—one of whom wasn't human—several dozen clanking beeping robots, a spaceship which contrary to all accepted laws of physics was supposed to hurl people—including himself—to the stars and back faster than the speed of light.

The fate of the human race lay in the balance (so said Desmond Blue) and what was Alife doing all day?

He was playing checkers with a goddamn robot. (And worse: losing every game too.)

Alfie had been here in the ruins of old San Francisco going on ten days now. Ever since his second day, a routine had been established. Each morning come the crack of dawn the robot Henry entered his room, red light blinking, and drove him up and out of a restless dream-spattered sleep. Stumbling to his feet, Alfie threw on some clothes, weaved a bleary path downstairs to the kitchen where an annoyingly chipper old man with an ornate handlebar moustache and an artificial leg that never seemed to be the same one two days in a row was waiting for him, John Hartford Hennesey in the flesh along with his absolutely gorgeous daughter Susannah, who was in fact a robot, for another invariably scrumptious breakfast. Hennesey's other equally beautiful daughter, the very much human flesh and blood Tess, never appeared this early in the day. How or why she was excused from the ritual of dawn-arising Alfie never did find out and the one time he'd grumpily inquired of Hennesey the old man had launched into a lengthy harangue on the subject of Susan B. Anthony and nineteenth-century proto-communism and Alfie had said to heck with it and gone back to his fried eggs and crispy fried bacon.

After that it was outside to robot-infested Market Street and into the Lincoln Continental for the drive past the stone wall that circled the compound and out through the ruins of the great city to the wooden shack underneath which the secret starship project lay concealed. Most mornings a fog as thick as molasses covered the landscape which only served to deepen Alfie's gloom. As he drove Hennesey babbled, gabbled, yammered, and raved. Alfie seldom bothered to listen anymore and took special care to keep his own contributions to the conversation at a minimum. One trouble with Hennesey—and there were a great many—was that a person couldn't say cheese to him without him promptly launching into a diatribe on the subject of pre-Occupancy Wisconsin and the socialist/communist/welfare state established there by some politician named Fightin' Bob or Tailgunner Joe. (Hennessey himself seemed to get the two confused, assuming there really were two of them.) Another time when the subject of hobbies somehow came up, how it was essential for any hardworking man to have one to fall back on—Hennesey's being the conquest of the known universe—Alfie committed the major blunder of volunteering that his own hobby was the growing of tulips, fuchsias and other such flowers.

Hennesey's big head swiveled around on his shoulders and he gave Alfie a careful onceover. "I know tulips are Dutch," he said, "but what's a fuchsia?"

Alfie had already surmised that he'd just done a very dumb thing. "It's a plant, sir. With red, pink, or purple flowers."

Hennesey chuckled. "So you like raising flowers, do you?"

Alfie bristled. "What of it?"

"Nothing, son, nothing at all. Only I once came within a hairsbreadth of putting you out of business."

"I'm not in a business," Alfie grumbled. But to no avail.

Hennesey went on heedlessly.

"There was this fellow I knew back in the old days, a genuine honest-to-goodness genius, who invented an artificial flower. I was going to handle the marketing for him but the damn fool went and poisoned himself while developing a nerve gas that would kill a person in less time than it takes to snap your fingers. The dumbbell never wrote a thing down either."

"I wouldn't have been interested in artificial flowers anyway," Alfie said. "The part I enjoy is watching them grow."

"Ours grew."

"Then how were they different from real flowers?"

"They were different because they were better. Our flowers came equipped with a special scent based on the chemical components of the finest, most expensive perfumes and a design so perfect that every pedal was the exact replica of every other pedal. More than that, son, our flowers didn't require water, soil, sunlight or bird droppings in order to thrive. They were things of rare and precious beauty, I'm telling you."

"What makes a flower beautiful," said Alfie, "is that it's one of a kind. You can't mass produce something like that."

Hennesey gave a hearty laugh. "Son, that's the dumbest thing I've heard in twenty years. Your trouble, like so many kids today, is that you don't understand the nature of the free enterprise system."

It wouldn't have shocked Alfie one whole hell of a lot to find out that was true.

* * * *

Once they reached the wooden shack at the edge of the surf and rode the hidden elevator down to the secret cavern below, Hennesey turned all business. Reynal, the robot chief engineer, who was in actuality a disguised human being and apparently also a member of the mysterious Sect conspiracy, was normally there ahead of them and he and Hennesey would immediately wander off with their heads together in intimate consultation. A couple times as a matter of duty Alfie hung close and eavesdropped but the conversation was ninety percent gibberish to him—photons and quarks and time-space distortions—and the remaining ten percent didn't seem especially significant.

Come nine or ten o'clock and it was time for Hennesey to take the long ride up the scaffolding to check on the Hennesey Drive. Alfie begged off accompanying Hennesey on these excursions since heights made his nose bleed and besides—though he never dared confess this part to Hennesey—just the sight of that lean silver needle rising a hundred feet in the air gave him a severe case of the nervous willies. About this time too Reynal disappeared for the remainder of the day. Hennesey gave him various errands to perform. He might drive into the rubble of the city to see to the welfare of certain savages or else take the longer trip across the bridge to Berkeley or up to Nuevo Sacramento to place orders for various parts and supplies needed for the project. Alfie was eager to tag along with Reynal on these jaunts—anything to get away for a while—but when he broached the possibility Hennesey snapped back that Alfie was too valuable to the project to be allowed to go gallivanting around the countryside all day.

So with Reynal gone and Hennesey a hundred feet in the air Alfie was left largely on his own. This was usually when he'd drag out the black-and-white checkerboard he'd drawn with a felt tip pen on a slab of old cardboard and toss twelve pennies on one side and twelve nickels on the other and try to corral one of the passing robots into a game. Eight times out of eight the tin bastards trounced him with ease, a fact that did little to improve Alfie's mood for the remainder of the day. One afternoon Hennesey descended earlier than usual from the scaffolding and happened to limp past just as a game was winding down. The old man paused and looked on, puffing his cigar and leaning on his cane. When the game was finished and Alfie vanquished he said, "This looks like a barrel of fun. What do you call it, son?"

Alfie looked up. "Why, it's checkers, sir. Haven't you ever played?"

"Can't say that I have. Poker's more my game."

"Well," said Alfie, visions of victory dancing in his head, "how'd you like to give it a shot?"

Hennesey studied his gold pocket watch. "The rules aren't too complicated?"

"Not in the least. I can teach you how to play in five minutes flat."

"All right." Hennesey squatted down next to Alfie. "Deal me in, son."

Ten minutes later as Hennessey claimed the last of Alfie's checkers, Alfie reached out and angrily knocked over the board.

"You don't want another game, son? Make it double or nothing this time?"

Alfie gave the old man a careful look. "Are you sure you've never played checkers before?"

"Whatever gave you that silly idea?"

"You did. You asked me to explain the rules."

"Guess I did at that." He chuckled. "So how about double or zero, lad? You up for it or not?"

Every other day or so Tess Hennesey would put in an appearance at the project site, seldom arriving much before late afternoon. She wore a completely different outfit each time. Alfie's personal favorite so far consisted of a pair of skin tight blood red satin shorts slashed to the groin and a matching halter top that was barely more than a thin strip of transparent fabric. Neither garment made much of an effort to conceal the fact that the female body underneath was absolutely and totally naked.

As soon as Tess stepped from the elevator a swirl of activity coursed in her wake. She buttonholed robots, examined computer printouts, studied blueprints, and rode the platform up and down the length of the rocket. If Alfie wasn't too wrapped up in his current game of checkers he'd listen in while Tess and her father talked but their conversation also seemed limited to technical matters—gravitational curvature, hydrogen ion displacement, and so on. Hennesey always listened to Tess with an air of perfunctory detachment as if he were only humoring her by pretending an interest but Alfie noticed that as soon as Tess left Hennesey invariably called the robots together and gave them a whole new set of tasks to perform.

And of course it was Tess who on Alfie's first full day in San Francisco had discovered the malfunction in the Hennesey Drive that would have sent the ship—the *Lazarus*—drifting through the cosmos toward oblivion while anyone with the bad luck to be on board gradually went bonkers. Naturally Alfie had immediately suspected Reynal of committing an act of sabotage and that night after dinner before everyone went up to bed he cornered Tess in the living room and asked if she was positive the malfunction had been as serious as she claimed. She looked at him with a sort of crooked smile, said that if it wasn't she'd wasted a lot of years in a lot of places studying physics, mathematics, and applied engineering, and slipped away before he could ask anything more.

Those few brief moments in the living room turned out to constitute one of the rare private encounters Alfie had with Tess over the next several days, a circumstance he had certainly not anticipated after his initial night in the household. As a matter of fact, that second night as soon as he reached his room—sharply at nine, Hennesey's official lights-out hour—he stripped off his clothes, pulled back the curtains surrounding his bed, and flopped down on the mattress to await the arrival of Tess so that the two of them could carry on from where they had left off the night before. It wasn't as if he was in love with the woman or anything like that but some of the acts she had willingly performed last night—and a few she had mentioned in passing as she gathered up her night clothes to steal away—were well beyond the knowledge of even the most accomplished whores in Tangier during their lewdest, most imaginative moments. What Alfie felt toward Tess Hennesey was a kind of gargantuan hard-on commencing at the top of his skull and extending down to the soles of his feet. The only thing that disturbed him about that night was the way events had transpired. He was personally more accustomed to assuming the aggressor role and had already determined that tonight would be different in that regard. Tess wouldn't catch him off guard a second time and when he finished with her sometime in the wee hours of the early morning he was sure she'd have discovered for the first time in her life the true meaning of the word satisfaction.

By midnight when Tess had still not appeared Alfie began to feel annoyed. If he'd had any idea which room was hers he'd have gone there right then and taken her as she lay unawares if necessary. Unfortunately, he hadn't had the foresight to ask and the possibility of stumbling in on Susannah or, much worse, old Hennesey himself by mistake was enough to keep him pinned in his own room. Not that he doubted she'd be showing up soon; she was just being cautious, he was sure. A woman like Tess in the kind of heat she was in was no more apt to pass up what he had to offer than a hungry tomcat was going to ignore the biggest fattest mouse in creation when it went sashaying by, twitching its tail.

By three o'clock a wide awake Alfie had to concede that he might possibly have miscalculated. By then he was so wrought up from anticipation that he couldn't have slept anyhow. Dropping a hand to his groin he proceeded to jerk himself off in a blind frenzy that bordered on self-mutilation. Even after that he still lay rigidly awake. Twice during the next hour just as he seemed to be drifting off he thought he heard furtive creeping noises from beyond the door and knew it had to be Tess coming after all. The second time he hopped out of bed and stuck his head into the hallway but there was nothing there. Damn her anyway, he thought, crawling back into bed. Damn her eyes to hell and back.

Shortly after four when he finished masturbating to completion a third time he fell into a deep dreamless sleep.

* * * *

What seemed microseconds later here came Henry the robot, bolts rattling, pincers clanking, red light winking, announcing in an obscenely cheery tone that morning had arrived, sir, and it was now past time to rise and shine and greet the brand new day with a warm and hearty handshake.

"Oh stuff a duck," muttered Alfie, jamming his face into his pillow.

Downstairs in the dining room there was no sign of Tess. Susannah stood at the stove flipping flapjacks on a hot griddle and even the sight of her manufactured loveliness was enough to get Alfie charged up again. At breakfast he shoved food grimly down his throat, chewing furiously, and tried his best to ignore Hennesey as he blithely rattled on about wolves and sheep, cats and chickens, pigs and ducks, cows and grasshoppers.

Later that day Tess did put in a brief appearance at the project site. (Wearing those blood red satin shorts again, legs as smooth and long as one of Hennesey's embittered rants.)

Alfie went boldly up to her and demanded to know in his strongest, most masculine tone if she'd had a good night's sleep or not.

"Wonderful," she said, flashing him a bored smile. She turned her attention immediately back to her father and informed him that she'd be going up to Nuevo Sacramento with Reynal later today and was there anything he needed for the project.

Chuckling fondly, Hennesey gave her a quick peck on the cheek. "Nothing you need to fret your pretty little head over, darling," he said. "Reynal will take care of all those pesky details. You just relax and have yourself a fine time in the big city. Do some shopping. New clothes. Put yourself in a good frame of mind."

That night sometime around one as Alfie lay wide awake continuing to hope that the previous night had been a fluke and Tess would show up at any moment to make things right when the door to his room swung open and a young woman with emerald green eyes, coal black hair, and blood red lips glided through the gap, her ripe body encased in a nightgown so scanty that it seemed a mere afterthought,

Alfie sprang upright in bed and held out his arms. "Tess, goddamn it, I knew you'd come."

Only it wasn't Tess.

Alfie recognized Susannah from her tentative, somewhat uncertain stride.

"What did you just call me?" she said as she slipped into bed next him.

"Oh, nothing," he said sullenly.

"I thought for a second there you called me Tess."

"You do look a little like her, you know. It was a natural mistake."

"But Tess would never come to your room like this." She laughed airily as if this were the most absurd thought in the world. "Tess is so serious. She doesn't have time for frivolities."

"Why not? Tess is a woman too, isn't she? She has those same natural bodily urges like all the rest of you."

She laid her head on his bare chest and looked up at him with eyes like a fawn. "Sometimes I wonder about that."

That night Alfie finally succeeded in obtaining a good night's sleep—but only after he managed to successfully steer Susannah out the door. No matter how horny he might be, sex with a robot just wasn't his thing.

The next day when Tess appeared at the project site shortly after three in a sea-green wraparound skirt and little else, Alfie had to pinch himself in the groin to keep from violating her on the spot.

She didn't visit his room that night either.

Or the next one after.

Eventually the point came when Alfie figured he had to make a definite decision. Springing out of bed—it was sometime past two in the morning—he pulled on his pants and stepped into the hall. He was convinced by now that Tess was simply playing hard to get—an old female trick dating back to Eve and Adam—and that if he went to her instead of waiting for her to come to him everything would work out swell in the end.

Alfie had by now found out that the room immediately next to his was empty and the one across from it was a small bathroom so he headed down the hall past the stairwell to the first door in the opposite wing. Leaning his ear against the wood he was rewarded by the sound of violent snoring coming from within. Convinced that this could not possibly be Tess, he started to move on when an anxious voice cried out from the other side of the door: "Carlotta? Carlotta, is that you, dear?"

Alfie froze in his tracks. The voice was Hennesey's.

He heard heavy footsteps thumping across the floor, the sound of something dragging, and then the rattle of a doorknob. Before Alfie could duck for cover the door popped open and Hennesey's head poked through the gap. As Alfie might have expected the old man wore a floor-length flannel nightshirt and a stocking cap with a tassel at the peak. When he saw Alfie standing in front of him his expression seemed disappointed. "Oh, it's only you, lad."

"I—uh—yes, sir. I couldn't sleep."

"Well, you certainly shouldn't be wandering around out here in the cold. Not at this time of night. The robots have their orders, you know."

"They do? What orders are those?"

"To shoot intruders on sight of course. Blazes, son, if one of them had spotted you, it might have blown you to pulp before you could Jack Roosevelt Robinson. Now you mosey on back to your own room right real quick and take care from now on. I need you alive when we take off for Centauri."

"Uh, yes, sir. Thank you, sir."

Relieved that Hennesey hadn't been more suspicious Alfie hurried back to his own room and once in bed beneath the rather fey countenance of John Randolph od Roanoke resumed his regular evening activity of restlessly tossing and turning. As he did so he thought about the fact that both Tess and Susannah had somehow managed to reach his room without being shot by killer robots roaming the halls. Was it possible Hennesey might have been making the whole thing up? Maybe he had his own reasons for wanting to make sure Alfie stayed in his room all night?

* * * *

The next morning when Henry came to rouse him, Alfie asked about the robot patrols.

"That's correct, sir," said the robot. "And since Reynal only assigns the least intelligent models to such routine duty there is a distinct possibility one might fail to recognize you before it was too late."

"What about the immediate family though? Couldn't the same thing happen to them?"

"I suppose it could, sir. These are very stupid robots we are discussing. Of course…"

Alfie glanced up from where he was tying his shoelaces. "Of course, what?"

"Well, I'm not supposed to tell anyone but since you are Mr. Hennesey's co-pilot I suppose it's all right. The robot sentries pass through the house only every hour on the hour. The schedule is quite strict. Their primary function is to protect the grounds from intrusion by savages or other unfortunates. The chances of anyone actually reaching the inside of the house are remote."

"Who else knows about this schedule? Does Hennesey?"

"I wouldn't know, sir. Mr. Hennesey tends to leave such details to the discretion of Reynal. All we robots are programmed to obey Reynal absolutely though oddly enough Miss Susannah happened to question me about this same subject not long ago."

"And Tess?"

"Miss Tess has surely known all along, sir." Henry let out one of his wry gurgling pseudo-chuckles at this point. There's little that goes on here in Old San Francisco of which Miss Tess in not aware."

Since he had been able to find out so much with such relative ease, Alfie decided to press Henry further. "Is everybody's bedroom located on this same floor?"

"All of the family, yes. Only Reynal and I have rooms elsewhere in the house."

"That's Mr. Hennesey's room on the other side of the stairwell then, right?"

"Yes, sir. A neat and cozy room it is too."

"And Tess?" he ventured. "Which room is, uh, hers?"

"The one at the very end of the wing. Personally, I feel that Miss Tess has the most splendid room in the entire house. I helped her redecorate it myself the last time she visited. You ought to examine it yourself, sir, if the opportunity arises. Miss Tess's taste in interior décor is most sublime."

Alfie couldn't help grinning. Whether Henry knew it or not he had every intention of examining Tess Hennesey's bedroom at the earliest available opportunity.

* * * *

In his own bed that night a fully dressed Alfie could barely restrain his eagerness to be off. It seemed to take hours for nine o'clock to become ten and twice that long before it was eleven. After another eternal hour, midnight arrived and as he had each hour on the hour Alfie listened with ears cocked to hear any heavy clanking noises that might indicate that the robot patrol was going by.

Ten minutes later, having heard nothing, he threw back the bedcovers, crept to the door, and peeked out.

The hallway was dark and empty. Alfie slipped out. As he went past Hennesey's door he rose on the tips of his toes and stole silently by. When he reached the door at the end supposedly belonging to Tess he first put his ear against the wood. Hearing nothing from inside but refusing to let that deter him, he grabbed the knob and gave it a turn.

Nothing happened.

The door was locked.

Damn! thought Alfie. Now what?

He stood there a moment uncertain how to proceed. Then, his frustration providing added strength, he raised his fist and banged lightly on the door with his knuckles.

"Tess," he hissed, leaning close. "It's me—Alfie. Let me in, Tess."

Not a sound from inside. Nothing. No eager patter of bare feet. No door hurled open. No warm passionate welcoming embrace.

He knocked again. Louder this time. He knocked three more times, waited for a count of twenty, then knocked again four times.

Still nothing. Not a sound.

What now? he asked himself. The rational thing would be to hurry back to his own room, retrieve his shiv from under the mattress where he'd secreted it, return here, kneel down in front of the door, slit his wrists, his throat and belly, and bleed out on the spot.

But the pulse of life beat too powerfully in the chest of Alfie Jarrett for suicide to offer a viable alternative. He considered breaking the door down instead but it looked awfully solid to him—they really knew how to build things in the old days—and in the end, head bowed, he turned to retrace his steps to his own lonely bed before the robot patrol wandered by and blew him away like a discarded cigarette butt in a cloud of gunsmoke.

He'd taken only a few steps when a stream of light flooded the hall. The slender curvaceous body of a nearly nude young woman blocked his path.

Tess? thought Alfie with crazed hope.

But it was only Susannah. It seemed her room was the next one down the hall.

"What are you doing out here in the dark, Alfie?" she asked.

"I was just—"

He stopped himself. To heck with the idiot lies, he thought. Especially idiot lies aimed at a robot.

"I was looking for Tess," he said. "Henry told me her room's the one over there."

"Oh, it is," she said. "But I think she took the car out earlier tonight. She often does that and sometimes doesn't come back until morning. What did you want with her? Maybe I could help."

He swallowed hard. Looking at her in that filmy thing that might have been a kind of nightgown, it was difficult keeping in mind that beneath that smooth sheeny skin lay a maze of tangled wires, transistors, and circuitry.

"I wanted to ask her something about the project," he said. "A problem I just now thought of."

"But it's after midnight."

"I know but I couldn't sleep."

Susannah moistened her lips with her tongue. "I bet I could help you with that," she said, turning and looking invitingly at the open door to her own room.

"I'm sorry," he said grimly. "I really can't. I—I have to get back to my room."

And with that he scurried away, heading down the hall and feeling once again very much like a holy fool in a daze.

Damn you, Desmond Blue, he thought as he stepped through the door to his own room and slammed it shut behind him.

* * * *

In the morning just as Alfie entered the kitchen Susannah Hennesey suffered a breakdown while whipping up a batch of scrambled eggs at the stove. When it happened the sound of the spring snapping somewhere in her innards was as sharp and clear as a clap of thunder. Thick blue smoke poured from her mouth and nostrils and there was a stench of ozone in the air. Hennesey sprang up from the table and rushed over as swiftly as his artificial leg would permit, grabbed his robot daughter by the ears, and gave her head a vicious jerk that would have snapped the neck of anyone human. Susannah froze instantly in place, one hand still clutching the wood spatula. Muttering under his breath Hennesey limped past Alfie, returning a short time later accompanied by Reynal who picked up Susannah under one arm and carted her from the room.

"Well, son," said Hennesey, acknowledging Alfie's presence for the first time, "I guess you and I are going to have to take potluck this morning."

He peered inside a cupboard. "Here's something that ought to stick to the ribs." He tossed a can of pork and beans across the room to Alfie, retaining one for himself. "You'll have to find something open it with, son," he said, "and get yourself a fork too while you're at it."

Apparently the repairs necessary to put Susannah Hennesey right proved relatively simple for she was back in place by dinner that night. Later, shortly before lights-out, as Alfie lay in bed with his clothes on wondering whether he ought to make another stab at finding Tess, there was a gentle knock at the door. When he got up to open it he found Susannah waiting in the hall. She had on a cotton bathrobe buttoned to the neck and her hair was done up in a severe maidenly bun. "May I talk to you, Alfie?"

"Uh, sure, why not?" he said, stepping back out of the way. "Come in."

She remained on her feet a fair distant away as he sat down on the edge of the bed. "I wanted to apologize to you," she said. "For the selfish way I've been acting."

"What way is that?'

"Only thinking about myself. The things I want instead of what's best for everyone. So I've decided to postpone copulating with you for the next seven days. After that whatever you want will decide. Does that sound fair to you?"

He acted like he was thinking the matter over. "Sure. Completely fair. But why seven days? What happens then?"

"Don't you know?" She seemed genuinely taken aback.

He tried to think. But nothing sprang immediately to mind. "I guess I don't," he admitted.

"That's the day before you and Father leave on your trip."

"We're going on a trip? Where to?"

"There." She raised a finger, pointing at the ceiling. "Up there."

"We're going up on the roof. What for?"

"Beyond that, Alfie. You're going to the stars."

"Holy shit! You're kidding me, right? Seven days? We're leaving in seven days?"

"Well, eight. Reynal mentioned it to me this morning when I was making breakfast. That's why I had that stupid breakdown of mine. My circuitry overloaded with grief and pity. Reynal says it's because I'm still confused about my sexual identity."

"My God," he said softly.

"You don't sound very excited. Reynal said you would be. He said you'd go bonkers when you heard the news."

"Oh, I'm bonkers all right. I'm so bonkers I'm about ready to have a breakdown of my own."

She looked frightened. "Should I go and get Reynal to come and fix you?"

She turned toward the door.

"No, don't," he said, holding up a hand. "It's all right. I was just shocked, that's all. I wonder why you're your father hasn't said any-thing."

"Reynal says he's saving it for a surprise. Farther loves surprises. You should see how he hides my gifts on Christmas morning."

"I can't wait."

She laughed. "You won't have to."

"I won't?"

"No, because both of you will be on your way to Centauri by then. There won't be a Christmas this year. Father says if I'm good he'll hide my gifts in advance but I'm not to look for them until the day itself."

"That's good of him."

She clapped her hands together. "I'm so glad you think so. Guess what gift I asked for this year?

"I don't know. A new car? World peace?" He was barely listening to his own voice by now.

"Way better than that. I asked for you, Alfie. It's you I want for Christmas."

"I won't be here, remember? I'll be on my way to the stars with your father.".

I know that but—" she sighed "—a girl can always dream, can't she?"

* * * *

The next morning, unwilling to mess around further, Alfie asked Hennesey straight out on the drive to the project site exactly when the *Lazarus* was scheduled to leave Earth for Alpha Centauri and beyond. Interrupted in the middle of a sentence—part of a harangue concerning certain suppressed articles of the U.S. Constitution— Hennesey glowered. "What's it to you, boy?"

"Well, I am going with you, aren't I?"

"Of course you're going with me."

"Then shouldn't I know the date we're leaving?"

"I'm afraid I don't follow you on that one. Why do you want to know the date?"

"Well, because, I've got plans to make, business that's got to be cleared up. You said yourself we might be gone for years."

"And I also counseled you at the time you accepted your position here that all such personal matters should be resolved before you reached San Francisco. Are you confessing that you deliberately disregarded my specific orders? Some might construe that as mutiny, son."

"It's not mutiny. It's just—" He stopped himself, not really wanting to get too far on the old man's bad side. There was still the case to consider. "I've got a life insurance policy. A big one. I want to make sure the premiums are kept up while I'm gone."

"Tell Reynal. He'll take care of it for you. He takes care of everything like that for me."

Alfie could see that he was going to have to be more direct if he wanted to get anything out of Hennesey. "There's a rumor going around that we're leaving in eight days. Is it true or isn't it?"

Hennesey gave him another suspicious look. "Who blabber-mouth told you that?'

"I don't remember. Does it matter? Are we going then or aren't we?"

"Of course we're going."

"But *when*?" By now Alfie was yelling. Not at the top of his voice—but close enough. So much for patience as a virtue, he thought.

Hennesey stopped the car. There was no need for him to pull off to the side of the road. Since there wasn't any other traffic.

"Look, son," he said, "I'm not normally a tight-lipped man but on a project of this magnitude security must stand paramount. If those superstitious SOB's over there on the other side ever caught wind of what we're up to over here they'd raise so much cane the devil himself would want a bite. It's the sheep we've got to keep our eyes on, Alfie. We wolves have to be careful to secure our balls where nobody else knows they're there. Even my own dear children don't know the exact day we're lifting off."

"Susannah knows. Reynal told her. I bet Tess knows too."

"Tess is different. Her I trust."

"But not Susannah?"

"Susannah's a robot. I'd assumed a bright boy like you would have figured that out by now."

"I did. She told me so herself. She also told me I was going to be her early Christmas gift from you to her eight days from now."

"Seven," Hennesey said.

"What?"

"Seven days. Susannah gets to have you for one night and the next morning come dawn's first light, *blooey!* off to the stars we fly."

"My God," said Alfie. "Then it really is true."

"You said you wanted to know, didn't you?"

Hennesey turned the key and re-started the engine.

Off to the project they drove.

A PROFILE: TESS HENNESEY

One autumn evening at dusk Tess Hennesey, thirteen years old with her mother five months gone, stood on the eastern shore of Puget Sound a few miles south of what was left of the ruins of Olympia looking down at the gray green waves lapping at her feet and realized with an intensity she had not previously experienced that the only willful act a person in her place at her time of life could commit while still retaining any integrity as a human being was to run away.

As an insight it wasn't terribly welcome; by nature Tess was not a venturesome person.

The log house a short distance away where her father would now be sitting, talking on the phone or dictating letters to one of his battalion of secretaries or possibly just thinking up new and unique ways of making money was a warm, cozy, and comfortable environment while the outside world seemed different: a grim cold place.

When Tess looked up again she immediately noticed the odd looking boat—like a loaf of bread with a single smokestack jutting from its middle—floating serenely a short distance away. She heard the steady thumping of an engine and saw puffs of white smoke streaming into the sky. There were people on board the boat too. She saw a number of figures standing on the deck and when she squinted and looked harder she saw that several of them were waving to her, as if beckoning.

That was all she needed. Tess tossed off her clothes, left them where they lay, and waded out until the bitterly cold water lapped at her waist. Then she began to swim. She was fortunate to reach the boat without cramping from the chill. Strong arms hoisted her up out of the water. When she began to shiver uncontrollably, teeth chattering, a blanket was thrown around her shoulders. "Here, drink this," said a voice. The cup was hot to the touch. She swallowed the coffee in lusty gulps.

There were eight people on board the boat. Three were grown men, three women, and the others a boy and girl a few years older than she was. Two of the men and one of the women wore white pancake make-up on their faces. Another had a round cherry fake nose pasted on top of her own.

"Who are you people anyway?" she asked. "Are you clowns or something?

"Yes," said the woman with the bright red nose. "That's what we are, all right. We're something."

"We're players," said the boy nearest her own age. "Actors. Want to join us?"

She said, "Yes, I think I'd like that."

"Great," he said. "Then finish your coffee and we'll go below. We'll show you who you're going to be."

"I'm Tess Hennesey," she said.

"Well, that's a start anyhow," put in one of the men with the white make-up on his face.

They all laughed at that.

"Bu do put on some warm clothes first," said the woman with the red nose who seemed older by a few years than the others, "before you freeze your little tail end off."

After Tess finished her coffee they took her below deck and gave her a baggy blue suit, a top hat, and a pair of red sneakers way too big for her feet. Then they made up her face.

"Perfect," said the boy, standing back. "You fit the role to a T."

"What role is that?" she asked.

"One we haven't figured out for sure yet."

"My mother and father were in Olympia when the slugs came," she said to forestall any questions. "I'm an orphan now."

"How curious," said another of the men, this one wearing only a bathing suit derby hat, and bow tie. "That's what we are too. We're the Orphans of the Storm."

"What storm is that?"

"Whatever one you want."

Later they took her to meet Bimbo. Bimbo was a big shaggy brown bear. "Bimbo dances," said the red-nosed woman. "Not very well, I'm afraid, though for a bear not badly either. We're on our way to Seattle to put on our show and at the end Bimbo comes out and dances a waltz."

"I'd like to see that," said Tess.

"Oh, you will," they said together.

And all of them laughed at that too.

They steamed north and docked for the night at a marina in the town of Gig Harbor. Tess found out a little more about each of them. The one with the bow tie was called Koko. Koko had been an architect in a firm in San Francisco before the slugs came. "But I thought they destroyed San Francisco," she said, "and took everybody in it away with them."

"That's what I thought too," he said, "yet here I am." Koko had built the steamboat all by himself starting from scratch. Later Stefen—which was the boy's name—told her that Koko had survived the destruction of San Francisco because he happened to be away on business in Boston when it happened. His wife and four children had stayed behind and he never saw any of them again although he'd searched in all the ruined cities to see if they'd come back as savages.

"But they hadn't?" she said.

"Koko never said."

Among the others, Zarilla and Devon, the two men in the pancake make-up, were magicians. Zarilla could pull doves out of a hat, make almost anything solid disappear, and escape from all sorts of locks and chains including a strait jacket. Devon's specialty was sawing the girl Rory, who was Stefan's older sister, in half. "So far," he boasted, "I've been one hundred percent successful but you never know, do you?"

The older woman with the red nose was Jane, a former astronaut who'd orbited the Earth over a thousand times. She told Tess in confidence that she knew Tess's father, John Hartford Hennesey. "You've got to give him time," she said. "The poor man's got a heart as big as Jupiter but he's grieving right now. I'll send him a cablegram and let him know you're safe."

"I don't want to go back there," Tess said. "I like it here."

"I'm sure you do. But when you are ready to go let me know and I'll make sure you get home in one piece."

The next night in Seattle Tess at the end of the show danced a slow waltz with Bimbo the bear. Rory showed her the steps she needed to make. She wore her regular costume of a blue suit, top hat, and floppy red sneakers. Everyone gathered at the waterfront park to see the show leaped up when she started to dance and clapped their hands. Some called out "Bravo!" in excited voices. Tess felt dizzy with the thrill of it all. Her hands were wet from sweating. Jane told her all that was normal and it would eventually pass.

At the end of the show they all got back aboard the boat and headed north for their next show.

In time they went as far as Alaska.

Then they turned around and steamed back down the coast again, stopping frequently along the way to put on another show.

It was a year before they reached Olympia again. Tess was four-teen by then. She told Jane she was now ready to go home again. "I had a lot of fun and learned so very much," she said, "and I'll miss you all like crazy but I have to see my Father again. I worry about him."

They let her off at the same place they'd first seen her on the beach. Koko brought the boat in close so that she could wade ashore and not have to swim.

The clothes she had been wearing that day were still there on the beach. They were neatly folded as if waiting for her to return but time had done its work and they were wet and soiled and covered in pine needles and pitch. Her father was waiting in the cabin. He broke into tears when he first saw her.

6

When Alfie Jarrett came down to breakfast and found John Hart-ford Hennesey and his "daughter" Susannah (who was really a robot) waiting in the dining room he came to a sudden and irrevocable decision.

He'd had his fill.

If he was forced to spend one more day cooped up in a hollowed-out underground cavern playing checkers with a bunch of brainless tinheads who always beat him anyway while a few yards away final preparations were being completed on the starship designed to carry him light-years into outer space he knew he'd damn well crack up once and for all. He needed a break—he was getting desperate.

Before he could say anything though, Hennesey gave him a cheery welcoming smile. "Flapjacks this morning, son," he said, rubbing his belly in anticipation. "Better pitch right in before me and the little gal eat them all up."

"I—uh—I don't think I'll be able to join you this morning, sir." Alfie tried looking unwell. "I'm feeling kind of under the weather."

"Nothing serious, I hope," said Hennesey, plainly concerned.

"Just a touch of nausea, sir. I think I ought to go back to bed though."

"Well, do as you want," Hennesey said airily, "but I'm afraid I'm going to have to dock you for the time."

Since Alfie hadn't received a penny of salary yet he raised no objections. Using both hands he hugged his stomach and let out a few realistic moans.

While he was still in the middle of a moan Tess Hennesey swept into the room. She was wearing what could best be described as a blue velvet sash that hugged her hips like a glove and above that a white tee-shirt like a second layer of skin. Her bare legs from the bottom of her rear end to the tops of her open-toed sandals resembled a pair of sleek ivory columns. "Is someone in here dying?" she asked, sliding into a chair at the breakfast table.

"It's poor Alfie," said Susannah from the stove where she was flipping another stack of pancakes. "He says he has the nausea."

"Oh, poor boy," said Tess, turning her cool green eyes in his direction. "I came down early this morning specifically to ask if he wanted to join me for a picnic on the beach."

Alfie had trouble believing his ears. For nearly two weeks now Tess Hennesey had paid him about as much attention as if he were a wisp of the wind—and now this. Removing his hands from his midriff he tried to look the picture of absolute health and good cheer.

"Uh-uh," said Hennesey flatly, pausing with his fork in mid-air. "That boy's sick. And besides, darling, you know I don't believe in leisure time activities when there's important work to be done."

Alfie felt a surge of raw fury. Important work, the old goat called it. What important work? Playing checkers with robots?

"You can't make him work when he's ill," Susannah put in helpfully.

"And he can't go traipsing off on any picnics either," said Hennesey.

"I'm sure I'll feel better in a little while," Alfie ventured.

"Can't afford to take the chance," Hennesey said. "Not with the fellow that's going star-hopping with me. Now you get up to your room, lad, and if I hear of you leaving that bed I'll take a switch to you myself."

Alfie glanced hopefully at Tess for assistance but her face was an inscrutable blank. In a rage he stalked upstairs to his room, flopped on the bed, shut his eyes, and tried to control the pounding in his skull. He might not be as nauseated as he claimed but he did feel a hell of a migraine coming on.

A few minutes later the door opened and Henry the house robot came bustling in, a tray gripped in one steel pincer. At first Alfie assumed it must be his uneaten breakfast sent up by a worried Susannah but when he took a closer look he saw several vials, a tablespoon, and a glass of water. "What's all this, Henry?" he said.

"It's your medicine, sir."

"I never asked for medicine."

"Miss Tess instructed me to bring it, sir. She informed me that you had been taken violently ill."

"Well, she was wrong. You can tell her I feel as healthy as a bull moose."

"Miss Tess was thinking you might say that, sir, but was quite insistent nevertheless that you imbibe the medicine. She was positive it would do you a world of good."

"Then you can tell her from me I don't need a world of good." He tried to rise from the bed but Henry stuck out a metal hand and pushed him gently but firmly down.

"Damn it, Henry, let me go," Alfie said.

"I'm afraid I can't do that, sir."

Alfie squirmed. "I swear I'll kill you, you tinhead son of a bitch."

"Miss Tess was adamant, sir. She wishes you to swallow at least one tablespoon of each preparation. Now please cooperate. It will prove easier for the both of us."

Alfie could see little alternative. Closing his eyes, doubling his fists, screwing up his face tight as a drum, he let the robot insert the spoon between his lips. It turned out—he couldn't help counting—there were seven different concoctions to swallow. The only significant distinction he could detect among them was that some tasted more dreadful than others.

"Now there, sir," said Henry, handing him the glass of water. "You must admit that you feel better already."

"I feel like—" Alfie began. He got no further. Springing up out of bed he sprinted past the robot and managed to make it to the bathroom just in time.

He was rinsing his mouth at the sink when he heard footsteps "Henry tells me you're feeling healthy as a bull moose."

He glared at Tess. "Through no help of yours. You tried to poison me."

"Oh, phooey. Just because you had a little throw up. Look at it this way. Now that you've cleansed your body of the bad stuff, whatever's left is good, right?"

"You're starting to sound as screwy as your old man."

"Does that mean you don't want to go picnicking with me?" she teased.

"I never said that."

"Good. Because Father's gone out to the project site and I just ordered Henry to pack us a lunch basket. I've got to stop by my room to change into something more appropriate for the beach but you go down and keep Suzie company and then we'll head out."

Alfie staggered downstairs to the kitchen where he found Susannah scrubbing the breakfast dishes. When he told her he was feeling a hundred times better she smiled happily but wagged a finger of warning. "Just be sure you don't try to rush out and help Father with the project. You've been working too hard as it is. If you don't go on that picnic with Tess I swear I'll never ask you to copulate with me ever again."

Alfie didn't require a whole lot more persuading. Especially when Tess reappeared dressed in something more appropriate for the beach: blue terrycloth shorts and a miniscule halter top.

They took the jeep. It was typical San Francisco day—cold and damp. Tess's long hair waved in the breeze. They drove through a district of flattened houses and crushed buildings and then after the road gave out up and down a seemingly endless series of sand dunes.

"Isn't there anything you want to say to me?" Alfie asked, breaking the long silence. "We really haven't seen much of each other lately."

"I know. I've been busy every day."

"I wasn't necessarily talking about the daytime."

She gave a high-pitched laugh. "Why, Alfie. I never knew you cared."

"It's not that. I was just surprised. I thought we had a pretty good time that first night."

"I wouldn't say otherwise, dear." She removed one hand from the wheel and squeezed his knee. "If I hurt your feelings, I'm sorry. I told you I've been busy—that's all."

"You seem to have plenty of time to run up to Nuevo Sacramento with Reynal every few days."

"That's business too," she said.

"What sort of business?"

She looked at him out of the corner of an eye. "The project—what else?"

"That's what I've been wondering."

"Isn't today a beautiful day?" she asked, deliberately changing the subject. "Doesn't a day like this make you glad you're alive?"

As a matter of fact, Alfie thought, today was anything but a beautiful day. As far as being glad to be alive, what exactly was the alternative? Being dead? And wasn't that what was worrying him right now?

"Now what's your problem?" she said. "You look like your pet dog Spot got squashed by a battle tank. I hate men who sulk."

"I'm not sulking. I wish I was. Anything would beat being lost in space forever with a broken down spaceship and John Hartford Hennesey."

"Oh, Father's not so bad once you get used to him and the *Lazarus* isn't going to break down. Its systems have been tested time and again in every conceivable fashion."

"I'm more worried about the thing that's supposed to make it go than the ship itself."

"The drive you mean?"

"The famous Hennesey Drive, yes."

"Well, don't worry about that either."

"I thought it was supposed to be impossible to travel faster than the speed of light."

"What gave you that idea?"

"Einstein did."

"Einstein was wrong."

"That's what your father keeps telling me too but he never gets around to explaining why he's so sure he's right and Einstein's wrong."

"That's because he doesn't the vaguest idea. Father is a business-man, not a theoretical physicist."

"Then who is? All I see around here besides him are robots. They're smart enough, I suppose, but they can't really think for themselves, right?"

"Aren't you forgetting somebody who can?"

"Am I? Like who?"

"Like me," she said.

"You?" He started to snort, then recalled that it was Tess who had discovered the supposed malfunction in the drive.

"I'm the one who designed the Hennesey Drive," she said. "De-signed it and built it. It's my baby. If it doesn't work, blame me."

"But you're not a scientist."

"When we get back to the house, have me show you my degrees. I attended some of the best universities in the world—several of them in fact."

"Your father told me you were an actress."

"I was that too for a while. I danced with a bear and wrote poetry. I had a novel published in England two years ago. People there still read books. Anything else you want to know about me?"

He scrutinized her carefully. "Is all of that really true?"

"True enough," she said.

"How old are you?"

"Older than Einstein was when he came up with his theory."

They had reached the ocean now. Tess pulled up a few yards short of the water's edge, hopped out of the jeep carrying the wicker basket Henry had packed and a blanket. Alfie tagged after her. The wind was fierce here. Alfie walked with his head down to keep the sand from blowing in his eyes. "This is nuts," he grumbled. "We'll freeze to death." He was wearing only swimming trunks and a tee shirt himself.

"I find it invigorating," she said. She walked with her head held high. When they reached the line where dry sand became hard and wet she spread the blanket on the ground. Alfie gazed at her bare legs. Not a sign of a goose bump.

"So what's to eat?" he said. "Something hot, I hope."

Tess pried the lid off the basket and looked inside. "There's supposed to be four different kinds of sandwiches and some potato salad." She pulled out a bottle. "And there's wine—pinot noir."

"I'll have a glass of that. And a sandwich. Any kind as long as it's not liverwurst."

Tess removed the cork from the bottle and handed a glass of wine to Alfie. He drank it down, trying not to gag. It was probably great stuff but he rarely drank alcohol of any kind. He liked to keep his mind clear. Especially when, like now, he was on his case.

The sandwich was tuna salad. He wolfed it down, making up for the breakfast he had missed. Maybe it was because they were sitting now instead of standing but the wind didn't as fierce. He gazed out across the water, watching the waves come rolling in.

"The project site is over that way," Tess said, misinterpreting his gaze. She pointed down the beach. "About a dozen kilometers from here, I'd say."

"Thanks for reminding me." He made a face.

"Still scared, huh?"

"So sue me."

"Why? You'll go down in history. The first man ever to reach the stars."

"The first dead man you mean."

"Don't be morbid." She jumped to her feet. "I'm going for a swim," she announced.

"Now I know you're nuts. It's freezing out there."

"You don't want to join me?"

"Uh-uh. You couldn't drag me in."

"Have it your own way."

She stepped out of her shorts, unfastened the halter top, and trotted down to where the waves were lapping in. When she reached the water's edge she turned, shouted something he couldn't hear over the roar of the surf, and dived in.

Alfie came to his feet and watched her bobbing head and sleek tanned body as she sliced through the incoming waves like a scythe. It almost looked like fun, Alfie thought, but he was shivering just standing here. He couldn't imagine how it felt out there in the water. After a few minutes he lost sight of her. He sat down to wait, pouring himself another glass of wine. This one went down easier than the first. A fellow could get used to this, he thought. He poured another.

By the time he finished the third glass he thought he could see her heading back in. He walked down close to the water, bringing her clothes with him as he did. There was something hard and metallic wrapped inside her shorts. He pulled out whatever it was. It turned out to be a gun. A .22 caliber revolver. He checked. It was loaded all right.

He was still holding the gun in his hand a few minutes later when she stood up in the surf a few yards from shore and walked the rest of the way in. She took her clothes from his hand and stepped into her shorts. "What are you doing with that thing?" she asked, indicating the gun. She was dripping wet but still not shivering.

"I was going to ask you that," he said, holding the gun out to her.

She took the gun from him and held it balanced in her hand. "I was planning on using it to shoot you with it if I couldn't lure you out into the ocean with my body."

"And if you could?"

"Then I was going to make sure you drowned out there."

"But I didn't."

"Nope."

"And you didn't either. Shoot me, I mean."

"I haven't yet, no."

"Why not?"

"I guess I must have changed my mind," she said.

She walked past him back to where the blanket lay on the sand and sat down. She poured a glass of wine and drank it down.

Alfie sat down next to her.

"Look," she said, hugging her legs with her arms so that her bare breasts didn't show, "I know who you are."

"Me too," he said with a shark-like grin. "I'm Alfie Jarrett, the astronaut."

"You're Alfie Jarrett, the private detective. You work for a man named Desmond Blue. He sent you here undercover to stop the project. I hired a detective of my own in Nuevo Sacramento. He knew who you were the second I showed him a photo."

"Billy Badger his name?"

"That's right."

"Good detective. No Desmond Blue—but there's worse. He's wrong about one thing though. I'm not here about your project. I didn't even know about it till your father told me. Desmond probably knows, but Desmond knows everything."

"So why are you here then?"

"Your robot Reynal. If he really is a robot. Which I doubt."

"What about him?"

"Have you ever heard of something called the Conspiracy of the Sect?"

She thought for a long moment, brushing errant strands of wet hair out of her eyes as she did. "Did you just make that one up?"

He shook his head and then as briefly as possible tried to fill her in on everything he knew about the Sect.

"And you think Reynal's one of them?"

"I know he is. Like I told you, I've seen his picture. In the past. He was there when horrible things happened."

"But he's here now too."

"That's right."

"And you don't know why?"

"I have a pretty fair idea actually."

"The project."

"Exactly. The single most important event in the history of the human race. You said so yourself."

"And you think he's going to try and stop it?"

"Maybe. I don't know for sure."

"Why don't you ask him?"

"I'm not that dumb."

"No," she said, "I don't think you are either." She looked down at the gun in her hand and then tossed it aside. She squirmed out of her shorts and stretched out beside him. "Okay, I believe you," she said. "Now get rid of that ridiculous bathing suit and let's get warm, for God's sake."

* * * *

On the way back to the compound Tess stopped on the crest of a high hill overlooking the ruins of the city. The twisted superstructure of a burned-out high rise loomed off to their left.

"What's up?" he asked as she hopped out of the jeep.

"A couple of savages I know who live up here." She reached back in and grabbed the picnic basket. "They have children. I want to leave them the rest of the food."

Alfie looked at the dark building. "Maybe I better go in with you."

She laughed and touched the bulge in the elastic band of her shorts. "Don't worry. I'm packing."

While she was gone Alfie climbed out of the jeep and walked around, trying to keep warm. From up here it was possible to view the remnants of both great bridges that had once linked the city to the rest of the world. The steel remains glinted in the fading dying afternoon light.

When Tess emerged from the building behind, the empty picnic basket swung in her hand. She got behind the wheel and started the engine.

"That's funny," Alfie said from beside her.

"What is?" She released the handbrake.

"See over there?" He pointed. "On the bridge? It looks like a whole bunch of people walking across."

Tess followed his pointing finger to the Bay Bridge. After a while she made a fist out of her hand and slammed it down hard on top of the dashboard. "Goddamn it," she said.

"What's wrong?"

"Those people. There must be hundreds of them. You know who they are, don't you?"

"Savages, I suppose."

"No, they're not savages."

"Then who are—?" he began but the rest of his words were drowned beneath a roar of acceleration and a screech of tires.

A PROFILE: CARLOTTA MCCOY HENNESEY

When she and her friend from the old days had completed for the time being the activity primarily responsible for bringing them together tonight Carlotta McCoy Hennesey slid out of bed, put on a robe without bothering to button it, stepped cautiously through the darkened room, and flicked on the overhead light.

"Ouch," said the man in the bed, shielding his eyes.

"You don't mind?" said Carlotta. She sat in a chair in front of a fake wood desk, pushed a stack of hotel stationery aside, found an open pack of cigarettes, put one in her mouth, and set it to burning with a butane lighter. "I don't like to smoke in the dark. If you can't see the smoke there's no taste."

"Since when do you smoke?"

"Since about a month ago. It's odd but I find that I rather enjoy it."

"Aren't you worried about cancer?"

"It's not something I think about, no." Carlotta tipped an ash with her fingernail. It missed the edge of the ashtray by an infinitesimal amount.

"I'm glad this happened," said the man. His hair was trimmed in a sort of pageboy bob that splayed out on the pillow like a silvery halo. It had been shorter and darker when Carlotta had known him before but like her he was no heavier now than then. In his work—like her—he could not afford to be.

"It was pleasant seeing you again too," she agreed.

"I was shocked when you called. I just never thought…it's been what now?"

"Nearly thirteen years," she said.

"Since a week before your marriage, I believe. The night of your last press conference."

"Which no one paid any attention to."

"I did."

"It was the second to the last story on your newscast."

"That wasn't my fault."

"I know. It was mine. I made the error of believing people could see past the tips of their own noses. I stupidly thought they could see as far as the Moon. I was mistaken."

"That's all you ever really cared about, isn't it?"

"This planet is a dying world."

"I suppose if I agreed with that I'd feel the same as you."

"You don't?"

"We'll muddle through. We always have."

She flicked another ash and this time hit her target. "I had to come to San Francisco anyway. My analyst is here and I needed to talk to her."

"Then you've been here before?"

"Oh, yes. As a matter of fact, I kept an apartment on Telegraph Hill for several years when I was seeing her regularly."

"You never called me then."

"Not then, no."

"Is she any good? Your psychiatrist, I mean."

"One of the best, they say."

"Has she helped?"

"She can't send rockets to the Moon, no."

"Unlike John Hartford Hennesey?"

"The Moon, no. That's too costly even for him."

"Where then? Earth orbit perhaps?"

"You're pumping me." Her cigarette had burned down close to the filter where it always tasted bitter. She laid it in the ashtray and let it burn itself out. "Who are you asking for? Yourself or your network?"

"Whichever you prefer. There have been rumors."

"Then it had better be for you only. If it ever came out publicly and got talked about, somebody would find a way to stop us."

"Us? You're not doing this alone? Somebody's going with you?"

"My husband is."

"Hennesey? My God."

"It'll make a helluva news story, won't it?"

"Is that why you married him? Everyone naturally assumed it was because he was as rich as Midas but I could never quite fathom that, not knowing you. Was it because he was probably the only man in the world deranged enough to finance his own private space program?"

"I married John because I thought he was the most fascinating man I'd ever met in my life. And also because no one else ever asked me."

"I must have."

"No, never. I'd remember, trust me."

"I interviewed Hennesey once. All he wanted to talk about was politics. To me he sounded like every other right wing lunatic out there."

"His enthusiasms do run deep. He's almost feminine in that. I respect him for it even if I don't agree."

"And the little girl? Tess is it?"

"That's her. And she's not a little girl anymore. She's twelve going on thirty."

"Pretty?"

"At the moment, no. She's at that gawky age when few girls are and the boys are even worse. She will be though. And she's smart. Smarter than either one of us."

"What does Hennesey think of her?"

"He adores her."

"And you?"

"He adores me too." She laughed. "Though I frighten him sometimes too, I think."

"Then I'm honestly shocked you'd want to come here and risk spoiling all that. What if he found out?"

"He won't." She lit another cigarette and even though her mouth was dry and the smoke tasted hot she inhaled deeply. "I'm doing this for me."

"Why? Is something wrong with you? Are you ill? You're not dying, are you?"

"Aren't we all?"

"That doesn't answer my question. You're not planning to get yourself killed up there, I hope."

"I'm not planning on anything, no."

"If it's not safe, I'll stop you. I'm not going to let that lunatic murder both you and him in some crazy scheme."

"It's perfectly safe. I wouldn't do it otherwise. Our technicians are all former NASA people—the best there is in the world."

"Should I believe you?"

She said, "Yes," and stubbed out the cigarette. She then went over to the bed and said, "Do you mind if we keep the light on this time?"

"I don't if you don't. You used to be…rather shy about it."

"Sometimes I just like to know what's going on." She tossed her shoulders, removing the robe. "Scoot over, baby doll," she said, with a laugh.

In the morning at dawn seventy-seven golden ships flew through the sky.

7

When Tess Hennesey pulled up in front of her father's pink gingerbread Victorian house, Alfie Jarrett in the seat beside her could tell right away that something was amiss. Parked on the sidewalk alongside John Hartford Hennesey's Lincoln Continental were two post-Occupancy beetle buggies, custom electric jobs. "Looks like we've got company," he said.

"I see," said Tess. "Damn it."

As he hurried up the walk after her Alfie could hear the braying of Hennesey's voice sounding from within. They found him in the living room surrounded by antique furnishings, his back to the wall. His face was beet red with fury and there was a shotgun cradled in his arms.

He swung the barrel back and forth between the two men who stood shifting nervously in front of him. Both were clean-looking and well-dressed, with narrow cunning eyes. Alfie's first impression was instinctive: cops, he thought.

When he saw Tess, Hennesey relaxed. The barrel of the shotgun dipped an inch and he ceased to swing it back and forth. "Gentlemen," he said in a voice considerably calmer than he looked, "allow me to introduce my daughter Tess and my associate Mr. Jarrett."

The two men did not appear to know quite what to make of Alfie or Tess. Especially Tess. Her scanty beach attire in particular seemed to put them ill at ease.

"These men," Hennesey went on, speaking to Tess, "claim to be agents of the so-called government of the United States and, believe it or not, the jackasses insist they have a right to come on my private property and tell me how to live my life."

"What exactly do you men want here?" Tess said.

The meaner looking of the two agents—there was a jagged scar running down the right half of his face below the eye—gave Tess the kind of appraising look that made Alfie want to reach for his shiv. "I'm Agent Herbert Coolidge," he said. "My colleague and I are here in an attempt to reason with your father before something unpleasant occurs."

"They've got a supposed court order," said Hennesey, "signed by a Communist judge. Can you believe that one, darling? A court order directed at me?"

"What sort of court order is it you have?" Tess asked.

"One forbidding your father from proceeding further with this insane scheme of his," Coolidge said.

"Scheme, he calls it," said an outraged Hennesey. The barrel of his shotgun jerked menacingly. "The single greatest event in human history and lamebrain here calls it a scheme."

"Why did you have to tell them anything about it at all?" Tess asked, turning to her father.

"I didn't, darling," Hennesey said meekly. "Not a word. The sneaks already knew everything."

"Perhaps you could reason with your father, Miss Hennesey," the other agent said. He was younger, in his twenties, with a pockmarked face and the air of someone who thought he was handsome. He tried to force a smile at Tess but the muscles in his face ended up leering instead. "A lot of innocent people could be harmed unless the law is obeyed."

Tess shook her head coolly. "This city—what's left of it—the land and everything on it belongs to my father. You have no legal right being here. What he does on his own property is his business alone."

"That's telling them, buttercup," Hennesey cheered. "Kick them where it hurts."

"I'm afraid there's more involved here than just you folk," said Coolidge, taking charge again. "This, uh, spaceship he's apparently built and hidden someplace, what if it were to explode and blanket the entire area with deadly radiation?"

"That can't happen," Tess said patiently. "The ship isn't nuclear powered."

"Well, there could be other horrible accidents," the younger agent put in, still leering. Alfie wished Tess would put on a robe or something.

"No, there couldn't be," she snapped. "My father sought the advice and of every major scientific and engineering mind in the world while developing this project and I can assure you that it's absolutely safe."

"We're really glad to hear that," said the man in an effort at obsequiousness that started Alfie's stomach churning.

Coolidge was looking solemn. "That's not the only factor either. People are also concerned about the possible future consequences of this—ah—endeavor of yours."

"People?" Tess said. "What people?"

"Everybody in the government, Miss. Probably most of the rest of the world besides."

"The world has no idea what we're doing here."

"I'm sorry to say they do." Coolidge produced a newspaper from somewhere inside his jacket and handed it to Tess. Alfie leaned over and peered past her shoulder. The newspaper was a Nuevo Sacramento sheet, a sleazy tabloid on ragged newsprint. The headline was a bright red screamer: *Millionaire Eccentric Plans Revenge Starship Launch!!* Beneath the headline was a blurry photograph of Hennesey that looked a good two decades old.

"We never wanted this any of this," Tess said. "The project was supposed to remain secret."

"It's a little late for that now, I'm afraid," said the younger agent, taking back the newspaper. "The whole world knows what you're up to out here."

"I don't get it," Alfie put in to remind them he was here. "What's this 'revenge starship' stuff all about?"

"It's the slugs," the agent said. "The rumor going around is that Mr. Hennesey here intends to go out into space, find them, and pay them back for what they did to us."

"That's absurd," said Tess.

"Is it?" Coolidge eyed Hennessey. "What do you have to say about it sir?"

"I say phooey," Hennesey said. "This lad here and I are sailing off to the stars for one reason only: we're going to give the human race a real shot at a real future. The slugs can go straight to hell and stay there as much as I give a hoot."

Tess looked at the agent holding the newspaper. "I want to know where all this came from," she said.

"Does it matter?" Coolidge said.

"If we have a spy in our midst," she said, glancing back at Alfie, "I want to know who it is."

"As a matter of fact," Coolidge said, "our source was anonymous. I assume the same is true for the newspaper. You aren't denying any of it though, are you?"

"The revenge part certainly."

"And the rest of it?"

"Sheep," interjected Hennesey. His eyes were vague, his face pale. His hands trembled and his forehead and upper lip were beaded with sweat. "That's what your sources are, flatfoot—they're sheep. Them and you and the whole blessed human race. A big fat herd of mindless, gutless, balls-free sheep and the only one in the world who can save you from yourselves is John Hartford Hennesey."

Coolidge continued to speak to Tess: "I think you really need to listen to what I'm saying here, Miss Hennesey. My partner and I aren't simply here to put a stop to your work. We also want to offer you our protection. Ever since the first rumors of this scheme of yours got out, there's been a great deal of hysterical overreaction. I'm particularly concerned about some of your nearby neighbors. There's a strong possibility of overt vigilante activity. If I could go back to the settlements in Berkeley and Nuevo Sacramento and assure people that the situation here is under control I think it would be best for all concerned."

"It is under control," said Tess. "I told you that already. There's no danger whatsoever."

"I'm afraid we're going to have to come up with something more substantial than that. I want you to show me where this spaceship is hidden and I want to be allowed to place it under armed guard."

"That's not possible," said Tess.

"Vigilantes," muttered Hennesey. "Mobs, I call them." His voice rose into a shout. "Herds of goddamn sheep." He staggered forward, the shotgun waving in the air. "Out of here, coppers. Out of my house and off my property."

Tess looked anxious "I think my father's right," she said quickly, her expression turning anxious. "I really think you ought to go now."

The younger agent looked ready to leave but Coolidge was made of sterner stuff. His right hand was edging toward his belt. Alfie poised himself to spring, wishing above all else for the hard cool steel of his shiv. He'd taken on more than a few cops hand to hand over the years in the service of Desmond Blue and remembered that some had been a lot tougher than they looked. And Coolidge looked tough to start with.

Just then Henry the robot lumbered into the room from the kitchen. Jammed between the steel pincers of his right hand was a big black beautiful revolver. His aim was steady. "I can escort these gentlemen to the door if you wish, Mr. Hennesey."

No one spoke for a moment then Coolidge seemed to make up his mind. "All right." He gave a grunt. "We've done everything we can here. If none of you people wants to listen to reason we can't very well force you."

He stepped toward the door, his younger partner slipping out ahead of him after a last leering look at Tess.

Alfie and Henry followed them out and stood on the porch watching until their beetle buggies drove off.

"They'll be back," said Tess, who'd followed them out. "When they do they won't come alone either."

"Do you wish me to alert the robots of possible intrusions, Miss Tess?" asked Henry.

"You'd better do that, yes. First though head out to the gate and make sure those two actually left. Then go find Reynal at the project site and ask him to come and take charge at the gate. No one is to be allowed inside. Tell him to instruct the robots accordingly. Absolutely no one whatsoever."

"I fully understand, Miss Tess." Still carrying the revolver Henry headed for the Lincoln.

"What about those people we saw on the bridge on our way here?" Alfie asked her when they were alone. "You think they might have something to do with this."

"They're Coolidge's vigilantes, I imagine."

"Then you think he was telling the truth?"

"I'm afraid so. And once he gets over there and tells them what happened here I'll bet anything they'll be coming the rest of the way across."

"To do what?"

"God only knows," she said wearily.

They turned and went into the house. As they entered the living room Alfie heard a thud. A short distance ahead John Hartford Hennesey lay sprawled on the floor. Perspiration soaked through his shirt and his eyes were rolled up in their sockets so that only the whites showed. "Water," cried Tess, racing across the room. "Bring me some water."

Before Alfie could move Susannah emerged from the kitchen clutching a glass of water. She knelt beside Hennesey while Tess cupped his head in her lap as if it were something precious and fragile. Susannah placed the glass against the old man's bloodless chin and tilted it at a steep angle. Some of the water ran down his face, drenching his shirt, but his eyes cleared and he emitted a moan. "Sheep," he mumbled. "Nothing but sheep."

"We'd better get him upstairs to bed," Tess said.

"No," moaned Hennesey. "No rest. No sleep. Work. Job to be done. Sheep at the gates. Blind stupid sheep. No guts, no balls. The lone wolf must show its fangs."

"Father, hush. You're not feeling well," Tess and Susannah between them managed to get the old man to his feet. Once he was upright.

Susannah bent down, leaned her shoulder against his stomach, and lifted him effortlessly off the floor. She carted him away in the direction of the stairs. "Damn it," said Tess, watching them go. "Damn it to hell. This is the worst possible thing that could've happened."

"Don't you think he'll be all right?"

"I don't mean Father. I mean those two men—and that damn mob of theirs."

"Can't the robots hold them off?"

"That depends on a variety of factors. Father's kept them supplied with buckshot, tear gas, and other anti-riot gear. I always thought he was being paranoid but now I know better. Still, if there's enough of them wanting in here and they're angry or frightened enough, anything could happen."

"Maybe I ought to head out that way and take a look around too." He was also thinking of Reynal being the one in charge of their safety.

"No, not you," said Tess. "I'll go. You stay here and watch over Father. He'll be anxious when he comes to. You need to tell him… tell him no matter what, we're going ahead with the launch exactly as scheduled."

"How soon is it?" said Alfie.

She looked at him closely. "Don't you know?"

"I was told one week from today. At dawn."

"That's as good a time as any."

"Good Lord."

"I know." She stood up, pecked him on the cheek. "I said I'd trust you and I will. Now go in and wait with Father. When I get back we can talk more."

He watched her drive off in the jeep. *One week*, he told himself. *One week from today. When the sun comes up.* Christ Jesus, what was he sup-posed to do? Go through with this thing? Wouldn't Desmond Blue get the shock of his life when he found out that his loyal retainer, good old Alfie Jarrett, had decamped to the stars in a faster-than-light spaceship piloted by an addle-brained madman?

* * * *

Alfie went upstairs to Hennesey's bedroom, rapped on the door, and let himself inside.

The interior of the room was pretty much what he would have imagined: a cozy dimly-lit cavern heavy with the smell of antiquity. Oil paintings hung from every square foot of available wall space. Most resembled the John Randolph painting in his own room—portraits of famous historical figures dressed in odd clothes and powdered wigs—but the painting that most strongly attracted his attention was different. It hung directly above the bed and showed a handsome woman in her middle thirties with close-cropped brunette hair and sharp boned features. The resemblance to Tess (and Susannah too of course) was strong.

Hennesey lay on his back in the middle of the bed, his head propped on pillows. Susannah sat in a chair beside him.

"Alfie?" Hennesey managed in a breathy whisper. His eyes opened in a narrow squint. "Son, is that you?"

"Yes, sir, it's me—Alfie."

Susannah rose to her feet and stepped away from the bed. Alfie took her place reluctantly. The close atmosphere in the room made him uncomfortable. The scent of approaching death filled the air. He knew it well from his years as a faith healer.

Hennesey's hand snaked out from under the covers and gripped Alfie by the wrist. "Co-pilot," he said, "the stars beckon. Can you feel them, son? They're calling to us."

"Sure I can, sir." He made his chin bob up and down. "That's why I'm here. Tess asked me to give you a message. She said to tell you, no matter what, the launch will take place exactly as scheduled."

"Course it will. And I'll be there to see it off. A little touch of the colic is all this is." He coughed. "This foul damnable climate. Like Mark Twain said, the coldest winter he ever endured was a summer in San Francisco." His eyes closed again now, his voice came as dreamy as a song. "The stars, son. Doesn't it make you want to weep? In a short while you and me—a couple of human beings with all the sins and frailties of the breed—we're going to be out there among those stars. Isn't it enough to steal your breath away? Isn't it enough to dazzle your brain?"

"It certainly is, sir," said Alfie, not untruthfully.

"You know what this reminds me of?" A smile crossed his face. "It reminds me of a woman. Not any ordinary woman but that one special woman we each have in our lives, the one we see at first only in our dreams from the time we're first weaned until—and I truly believe this—each of us is permitted to glimpse her in the flesh if only for a brief instant in time."

"I guess I haven't seen mine yet, sir."

Hennesey did not appear to have heard him.

"Carlotta was her name. Carlotta McCoy. I made her my wife, son. All those years I dreamed of her and then one day there she was on the TV. I found her, hunted her down, and I married her. Smartest move I ever made in my life. The day she died I bawled worse than a baby."

"How did it happen, sir? Was she ill?"

"No, she was right here."

"Here?"

"In San Francisco, boy. The day the slugs came. She was here then."

"Oh," Alfie said.

"And that same night back home after I got done bawling my eyes out and drinking a bottle of good bourbon whiskey straight down was when I had my other dream."

|

"What dream was that, sir?"

"The one where I saw the Equation. The one that rules everything, son. The Cosmic Equation, I call it. One and one is one. They showed it to me. The slugs did. During their Occupation when they moved the deck chairs around on us. They told me who they were and why they were here. It was because of the equation—because of cosmic fusion. Two atoms of hydrogen fusing to form one of helium. Everything comes from that, son. The Big Bang. The Ultimate Squash. All of it."

"I guess that's right, sir." He had no idea what Hennesey was talking about.

"Billions and billions of hot white stars expending their energy. I make no assertions of scientific knowledge, Alfie. I'm an ignorant businessman, nothing more. Tell me something, Alfie. Have you ever lain with a woman?'

With Susannah present he hesitated to be overly frank. "Well, a few times," he admitted. "When I was younger."

"Me too. In fact before my marriage to Carlotta I carried quite the reputation as a lady's man. A regular Don Pierre. So you know I know what I'm talking about when I tell you that too is part of the cosmic equation. Think about it. One and one is one. That's how it works, isn't it? Same as how the stars make other stars which eventually form planets and on those planets there's life. That's us, Alfie. And what do we do? We reproduce. Cosmic fusion again. One plus one is one."

His voice had grown weak again. He let out a sigh. Susannah, hurrying over, hovered worriedly.

"Whether you believe me or not isn't the important thing, son," he said. "Not right now anyhow. But when get out there into space and you see it all around you—the stars and the galaxies—and the light—always the light—a universe of light we live in—that's when you'll understand."

"I hope so, sir."

Hennessey's eyes closed. His breathing was shallow. Alfie got up from the chair, gestured at Susannah to take his place, and tiptoed into the hall.

* * * *

Back in his own room, Alfie reached under the mattress, and emerged holding his shiv. He strapped it to his ankle above the sock using a thin elastic band he found in his suitcase. Then, feeling more like himself again, he went back downstairs and out onto the porch.

The sky was turning dark already. It looked like a cool night on its way, though a clear one too. A few stars were already out. Alfie sat down on the bottom step and stretched his legs in front of him. Market Street was quiet. The trolleys didn't seem to be running and the costumed robots had vanished like props in a play that had closed out of town. He assumed they'd all been sent out to stand guard at the wall.

He stayed on the porch until Tess drove up at the wheel of the jeep. She'd changed clothes and was now wearing what looked like a pilot's jumpsuit. Henry pulled up behind her in the Lincoln.

"How is he?" she asked as she came hurrying up the walk.

"Not real good," Alfie said. "I don't know if that was a heart attack or what but he's in pretty bad shape. He's asleep now but Susannah tells me his pulse is getting weaker all the time. I think we'd better get him to a doctor right away."

"There isn't time for that," she said.

"Then you'd better make time or else you're going to have a dead father on your hands."

Tess shook her head and waited for Henry to march past into the house. Then she added: "If he's going to die then this is the way he'd want it. Besides, I don't think we could get a doctor to come here now. Not with what's going on."

"It's that bad, is it?"

"There's a mob of at least a thousand people gathered by the wall, demanding to be let in. Nothing really bad has happened yet but it's only a matter of time till they get worked up enough to break through the gate."

"Can't the robots stop them?"

"Not without using physical force and they can't do that. Don't let Henry and his rifle fool you. That's all a bluff. All our robots are programmed never to do harm to a human being. Father's idea. He got it from an old book."

"Not a very smart book if it ends up getting us killed."

"It won't," she said. "Because we won't be here when they break in."

"Where are we going? Nuevo Sacramento?"

"Farther than that." She raised her head and looked at the sky.

"Christ," said Alfie. He could feel his knees turning weak. "You don't mean what I think you mean, do you?"

She nodded. "I changed the schedule. The *Lazarus* is taking off at midnight tonight. The weather's good and everything essential is as ready now as it ever will be."

"Your father's not," he said. "He's in no condition for something like that."

"If we wait—even forgetting about the mob out there or those thugs form the government that are spurring them along—do you honestly think he'll get any better?"

"I'm no doctor, Tess."

"You're not blind either."

"No, but it'll kill him. The take-off, the trip. We both know that."

"It may. But what else can we do?"

"How about we take the Lincoln, bust through the gate, and get the hell out of here."

"No," she said flatly. "Father's never run from anything in his life and neither have I."

"But you're not the one that's going to the stars."

"Of course I am," she snapped. "Haven't you figured that much out by now? I thought you were supposed to be the brilliant detective." She was suddenly moving past him—into the house. "Wait for me in the jeep," she called. "When I get back we're going out to the project site."

Alfie started to say something but before he could come up with the right words Tess was gone. He went out and waited in the jeep. He knew he ought to be feeling stunned or shocked or bewildered but oddly he didn't feel that way at all. Maybe he *had* known it all along.

Tess was back inside ten minutes with a big suitcase in her arms. The contrast between the mundane act of packing a bag and the launching of a spaceship to the stars made it hard not to laugh.

Tess started the jeep and took off down empty Market Street. "Henry will follow in the Lincoln," she said. "Susannah will bring Father."

"He's awake?"

"Yes, and he seems better," she said without much enthusiasm.

"Did you tell him you were going instead of me?"

"He knew that already too."

Alfie was astonished. "But I—are you sure about that?"

"Absolutely. My mother was an astronaut, you know. Before she and Father married. They tell me I take after her. And then there's the Hennesey Drive. I invented it. I have to go along."

"But I thought—"

She laughed. "He told you that old story, didn't he? About the dream he supposedly had the night the slugs came. The cosmic fusion equation. One and one is one."

"He did mention it, yes. I thought he was delirious."

"Maybe he was." She shook her head. "By now I'm wondering if he's starting to believe it himself. Here we are now."

* * * *

In the glow of the headlights the wooden shack swam into view. As Tess applied the brakes, Alfie sniffed the salty ocean air. They climbed out of the jeep and went inside. Tess used one of the electronic remotes to call up the elevator from below. They descended in silence. The elevator doors slid open. Alfie stepped out, tilted his head, and stared at the shimmering shape of the silver starship a hundred feet above.

"You got here sooner than I anticipated," said a voice.

Alfie swung his head. A robot emerged from the shadows underneath the ship's tailfins. It was Reynal.

"What are you doing here?" Tess said. "I thought I told you to remain at the wall."

"I'm afraid it's too late to do anything about the wall."

"The mob broke through?"

"I let them in."

"Why did—?"

She stopped as Reynal moved into the light. There was a gun in his hand. "I regret having to resort to such crude methods but I'd rather hoped that mob of idiots would be enough to stop your coming here. It appears I underestimated your tenacity, Tess. Your decision to move up the launch schedule also caught me unprepared."

Tess turned on Alfie. "Do you know anything about all this?"

"About Reynal here?" Alfie raised his hands in the air. "He's the reason I came here. I tried telling you that before. He's your informant too, I'm sure."

Tess looked at Reynal. "There's nothing you can do to stop us now," she said. "Everything's set and synchronized. The *Lazarus* is going to lift-off at midnight no matter what."

"Let it. As long as there's no one aboard I'm content. My only interest lies in making certain that when it does leave no one goes with it. This—" he gave the gun a shake "—should take care of that."

"But why?" said Tess in a gentler tone.

Reynal looked momentarily perplexed. "To be frank with you I haven't the slightest idea. I do only as told."

"Like a robot?" she said.

Reynal smiled. "Yes. Like a robot."

"And who's your programmer?" put in Alfie.

He kept hoping for a lapse in Reynal's attentiveness, one long enough for him to reach the shiv strapped to his ankle. But so far it hadn't happened.

"You don't really expect me to answer that, do you?" Reynal said.

"Why not? You're going to kill us anyway, aren't you? You or the mob or somebody is."

"As a matter of fact I sincerely hope not. My mission here is to root out and whenever possible eliminate the deviant aspects of human history. In the considered opinion of those I represent this attempt by Mr. Hennesey to reach the stars qualifies as such behavior. I assure you I mean you no direct harm. If injury should occur through the natural working out of events I cannot be held personally responsible."

"Wow," said Alfie. "Now that's a prime load of bull if I ever heard it. I mean, you crucified Jesus, right? You had a hand in it anyhow. You were there. Are you calling the son of God a deviant?"

Reynal stared at Alfie as if he'd lost his mind. "Are you trying to be funny?"

"There's nothing funny about it. I saw the photographs. You and your comrades throughout time."

The elevator began to hum. They all turned and watched as it descended. When the doors opened three figures emerged. In the lead—astonishingly—came John Hartford Hennesey. He wore his usual frock coat, red satin vest, string tie, and baggy striped trousers. Susannah and Henry followed after him. Although Hennesey appeared to lean on his cane somewhat more heavily than usual, his face was hearty, his eyes clear. He went up to Tess without paying any notice to Alfie or Reynal and said, "Guess what, darling? Those damn sheep attacked our home." He shook his head in amazement. "A whole mob of the nincompoops. Can you believe it? They had the utter gall to stand in the middle of the Market Street—*my* Market Street—and demand that I come out and answer to them."

"What did you do, Mr. Hennesey?" asked Reynal politely.

"What do you think I did?" He swung his head in Reynal's direction but did not seem to be aware of the gun in his hand. "I hopped straight out of bed, slipped into my finest clothes, and went running out to confront the damn fools." He chuckled at the memory. "Walked right through the middle of them as if they weren't even there. Got in my car and drove here. The damn fools didn't have the gumption to try and stop me either. One or two made a move but I stared them down like dirt."

"They didn't follow you, did they?" Tess asked, looking worried.

He snickered. The way I drive, nobody's apt to follow me anywhere. Eighty-five miles an hour the whole trip. Ask Susannah here. I took three years off the poor child's life." His gaze wandered to the starship and he paused to stare up at it in wonder. "Well, son," he said in a changed tone "maybe we ought to hop aboard, eh?" He was speaking to Alfie now. "No sense hanging around here with our mouths open when the stars are beckoning."

"I'm afraid Reynal has a different idea, sir."

"Reynal? What does Reynal have to do with anything? Reynal's a robot. He does what he's told." Hennesey put a hand in his vest and removed his gold pocket watch. "We haven't much time for silliness if we're blasting off at twelve."

"I don't intend to be silly, Mr. Hennesey," Reynal said, wagging his gun. This time he made sure Hennesey saw it in his hand. I'm afraid you'll have to postpone your voyage."

"Never," said Hennesey, tight-lipped. "Come midnight the *Lazarus* rises like its namesake or my name's not Hennesey."

"I'm afraid I really must insist, sir." Reynal's eyes betrayed his uncertainty. Clearly he wasn't entirely sure what to make of the old man's present state of mind. Hennesey might not be any crazier than usual but even that degree of crazy was enough to cause problems. "You must stay where you are, Mr. Hennesey. If you don't I'll be forced to shoot."

"Oh, phooey," said Hennesey. Cane swinging, right leg dragging he headed for the ship.

"Father, don't," Tess said. "Reynal's serious. He could shoot you."

Hennesey didn't seem to hear. He waved a hand at Alfie. "Hurry along now, son. Time's as precious as a diamond in the sky when you're about to make history."

Alfie figured there would be no better moment than right now to make his move. As Reynal raised his gun and pointed it at Hennesey, Alfie dropped to a knee, grabbed his shiv, and threw it in the same quick motion.

But Susannah moved faster than he had. By the time the knife left his hand, she was already on top of Reynal. He fired twice as she charged but the bullets seemed to have no effect.

As she crushed him underneath her he got off another shot at point blank range. The bullet tore a hole in her throat. A stream of pink fluid squirted from wound. A sharp acrid stench filled the air.

"Darling!" Hennesey cried. "Daughter!"

But it was too late for Reynal. He wasn't moving. He lay motionless on the floor with Susannah on top of him.

"Darling," moaned Hennesey, crouching beside her. "Daughter, you saved my life."

Alfie pushed himself back to his feet. He walked over and picked up his shiv from off the floor. He looked at the bodies lying nearby on the floor. Tess joined him. "My God," she said, "what an unbelievable mess."

"What happened? Reynal looks…he looks dead."

"He is. Susannah crushed him. If I remember right she weighs something like a ton."

"But—"

"She's a robot, Alfie. Remember?"

Hennesey cradled what was left of Susannah's head in his hands. He gazed up at Alfie and Tess.

"I believe she's dead too," he said in a stricken voice. "That deranged madman Reynal murdered her."

But Susannah was clearly not dead—despite considerable evidence to the contrary. Her eyes were open and she was smiling. "Don't forget the *Lazarus,* Father." Her voice was a whisper as fluid continued to leak from her wounds. "It must be time for you to go."

"Oh no, darling," Hennesey said stiffly. "I won't do that. I won't leave you now."

Alfie looked at Tess. "You want him or not?"

"Of course I want him."

"Then I'll get him for you." Alfie swung back his arm, turned his hand into a horizontal flat plane, and caught Hennesey cleanly in the back of his neck.

He fell forward in a heap.

"Henry," Alfie said, "please take Colonel Hennesey aboard his ship. It's time for him to leave."

Lights blinking, Henry moved to comply. Tess and Alfie stood watching as he carried Hennesey toward the waiting ship.

"So," Alfie heard himself saying, "are you sure you couldn't do with some company?"

"For God's sake." Her head snapped back and she gaped at him. "What did you just say?"

"Company," said Alfie, finding it difficult to look her in the eye. "You know, me come along too. The way we originally planned or thought we planned or whatever the hell it was." His skin felt warm as if he were flushing from embarrassment but that was impossible because he was never embarrassed. "What I mean is, I couldn't go before because I had my job to do for Desmond Blue but now that Reynal's dead that's pretty much the end of that and I guess I could leave a note for Blue and tell him everything that's happened and then—"

"No.' She put a hand on his chest and gave a push. "Enough. If you go crazy on me too, I don't know what I'll do."

"I'm not crazy," he said. "Not in that sense anyhow. Desmond says I'm a cultural sociopath with psychopathic tendencies but right now I think I'm…well, maybe I'm just bored. Or in love. One or the other or both. I told you I'm a man of action. Well, this is Blue's last case. After this I'll need something else to fill my time."

"Take up knitting," she said.

"Look, I'm serious, Tess—I really am."

She shook her head. "There's only room for two people on board the *Lazarus*."

"Well, your father won't…"

"I know." She lowered her hands. "He won't live long. But if he at least reaches space—if he knows the trip's started and there's no turning back—he'll be happy."

"And you'll be alone."

"That's fine. There'll be plenty to keep me occupied, books I've wanted to read for years, tapes and films and music. There are certain classical problems in mathematics I could play around with for decades and never arrive at a concrete solution. And who can tell what miracles a good dose of solitude may bring about? Maybe by the time I get back I'll have a unified field theory to announce."

"There's more to life than books and numbers, Tess."

"You mean like—whoa." She stopped and took a long breath, regarding him with her hands on her hips. "No, don't tell me. It's me you're in love with me, right?"

He started to shake his head but couldn't complete the gesture. "You think that's possible?"

"I think it's definitely starting to look that way."

"So what are we going to do about it?"

"Me, nothing. There's nothing I can do, Alfie. I told you why already. The cold equations. There's only room for two."

"You're sure about that?"

"I am. Yes. Let's be honest here. Think about it for a minute. You and me cooped up on the *Lazarus* for years. You know how long it would take before we loathed the sight of one another? Neither one of us is apt to win any awards for congeniality."

"Well, if you're sure…" He looked past her to the *Lazarus*. The platform was on its way back down the side of the ship. Henry rode alone. "I just didn't want you thinking I was scared, that was all."

"I knew better than that." She took a couple steps back away from him. "And do me one more favor, please. Take care of Susannah. Take her back with you to wherever you came from and see that she's get repaired. She may have saved our lives just now."

"I can do that, yes. There's a doctor I work with—Dr. Schwerner—he can fix about anything."

"And treat her especially sweet when she recovers. I think you owe her that."

"What do you mean by especially sweet?"

She winked. "You might start by copulating with her. I don't pay a lot of compliments but you're not half bad at it. For a cultural sociopath with psychopathic tendencies that is."

"Susannah's a robot."

"So? She's a human robot, isn't she? He's got all the features you might need. Father made sure of that."

"She's still only a machine."

"So are we, Alfie dear. So are all of us. Haven't you figured that much out yet? Even after our makers paid us a visit and did a reboot?"

She turned away then and without another word or even a fleeting farewell glance back she headed toward the waiting *Lazarus*. For some reason Alfie just didn't feel like standing here watching her go. Instead he knelt down beside Susannah and asked her how she was feeling. Her eyes were still open and alert but she didn't respond except perhaps for a faint smile. There was an awful lot of pale pink fluid on the floor around her, a sticky pool of it.

A shadow fell over him. It was Henry. "Miss Tess says we need to vacate the cavern, sir." Distantly Alfie heard the steady whine as the platform rose up the side of the ship with Tess presumably aboard. "When the *Lazarus* leaves there may be certain disruptions in the local space-time continuum that will be most unpleasant to experience."

"Yes, I see." Alfie came back to his feet. "Bring Susannah with you, Henry, and we'll get out of here."

"And Reynal, sir?"

"Reynal's dead, Henry. When Susannah fell on him she must have crushed him."

"He wasn't actually a robot, sir. I don't know whether you knew that."

"I figured it out."

"That's good, sir."

After Henry left carrying the heavy Susannah in his arms, Alfie paused for one last look at the *Lazarus*. As he did a mental vision of a ravishingly beautiful young woman with coal black hair, blood red lips, and a tiny heart-shaped tattoo flooded his mind.

Then with a sigh he hurried off the join Henry and Susannah in the elevator.

* * * *

They took the jeep, Henry driving, Susannah in the back. In the passenger seat Alfie could see a black cloud of smoke rising from the vicinity of Market Street. He told Henry to drive along the beach until they reached the wall and then they'd have to get out and wade on foot the rest of the way. He was afraid if they tried to drive through the gate they might run into parts of the mob or Coolidge and his partner or something even worse.

They'd just emerged from the water, Henry carrying Susannah easily in his arms across the wet sand, when what felt like a mild earthquake lasting perhaps thirty seconds shook the ground underneath. The *Lazarus*, he thought. On its way to the stars. What else could it be?'

They continued on into the ruins of San Francisco. Alfie had no clear destination in mind. Henry suggested they try looking up some of the friendlier savages in hopes of obtaining temporary refuge for the rest of the night. Alfie said he supposed that was as good an idea as any. They plodded on through the streets, climbing hills, pushing aside piles of rubble and debris, until they came to a red brick two-story apartment building that looked vaguely familiar. Henry shifted Susannah into the crook of his arm and banged on the front door with one steel pincer.

"If you're looking for love or riches," said a voice from within, "you've come to the wrong place."

"It's Henry, Miss Mary-Margaret. Henry from the Hennesey Compound."

"You alone?"

"Mr. Jarrett is with me, ma'am."

Alfie heard a chuckle. The door swung back on its hinges. He stepped into a dim room lit only by candlelight. When Mary-Margaret saw Susannah she let out a cry of concern and led Henry to a bundle of rags that might have been somebody's bed. "Lay her down here, Henry. She looks badly hurt. What happened to the poor child?"

"She was shot, Miss Mary-Margaret."

"Isn't there anything we can do for her?"

"Only treat her with sympathy, ma'am. I'll need to obtain spare parts in order to begin the necessary repairs."

Mary-Margaret accepted this without apparent surprise. In the faint light Alfie detected two men sitting cross-legged in a corner of the room. They were playing cards.

"Cobbler Tom," Henry whispered to him, indicating a short dark man dressed in a burlap smock. "I don't believe I recognize the stout fellow with him. He must be new savage in town."

"But not that new overall," said Desmond Blue, turning away from the card game and tossing Alfie a quick salute.

"Desmond, for God's sake," cried Alfie. "What the hell are you doing here?"

"Hush, Alfie," said Blue, tugging on an ear. He studied the cards in his hand. "Can't you see I'm trying to concentrate. I'll be with you in a moment."

"How did you find me?"

"I didn't find you—you found me. Now please be good enough to seal your mouth and let me play."

"And I raise you twenty more," said Cobbler Tom, tossing what looked like several sea shells into the pot. "Show me what you've got, big man."

Later after Blue had run out of shells his eyes lit on the robot. "Why, Henry. How have you been lately?"

"Quite well personally, sir. I must apologize for my failure to recognize you at first. The last time you were here if I'm not mistaken you were of Oriental extraction."

"A brief aberration only."

"Mr. Hennesey has gone to the stars. Miss Tess as well."

"Yes, I know. We felt it when their ship left. Crystal should be along shortly. She's out checking on the helio-plane. When she gets back we can go."

"You mean we're done here?" Alfie said.

"So it would seem."

"But the Sect? What about them? They were here, you know. They tried to stop Hennesey from going to stars."

"That's one interpretation of the data, yes." Blue stood up as the door opened and Crystal stepped through. She grinned at Alfie. "So the prodigal returns."

"I'm happy to see you too, sweetheart."

"Don't you wish."

"Bring the injured young lady along, would you, Henry?" Blue said. "I believe we can all fit into the helio-plane if we squeeze. We need to get her to where she can receive adequate care.

"She's only a robot, sir," Henry said apologetically as he picked up Susannah in his arms. "She's only modelled to resemble a young lady."

"There's a difference?" said Blue.

8

As the train drove deeper into her native land, Anna Provosky turned from the window and contemplated the gnarled aged fingers clasped in her lap.

Three hours since the train had crossed Polish border bearing her home for the first time in four decades and she was only now recovering from the disillusionment of that event. It was the anticipation which had spoiled it for her, the expectation mingled of dread and joy, so that when the moment finally came after all the many years she had felt hardly a thing, only an idle curiosity as she pressed her face to the window and wondered why rich passionate Russia seemed no different at all from the drab dull uninspiring Poland left behind.

She had waited too long. Had she come home twenty years earlier—even perhaps ten—the emotions which had then still churned within her would have been sufficient to transform the instant of homecoming into something precious and memorable. Now she was just another old woman who had come home to Russia not to live but rather to die and that in itself was more than enough to counter any pleasure she might feel at her homecoming. The crossing of the border turned out to be an act no more significant than the digging of a grave as a prelude to the burial of a corpse. And she the corpse— Anna Provosky. *Prima ballerina assoluta.*

Forty years ago when she fled Russia there had been no more famous woman in the world. Anna had never quite adjusted to the obscurity of her later life. Here in this packed railway coach none of her fellow passengers, many of whom had been with her since Paris, had offered her a second glance. If they only knew, she thought. And yet even if they had known, what would it have meant to them? They were young; she was not. They were the living; she the dying. In her mind she remained the sloe-eyed raven-haired long-limbed beauty who had dazzled the cultured elite of four continents. In those years of her youth—and she had been a great star at seventeen—when she entered a room all eyes turned to follow. But now the doctors said death was inevitable. The cancer had spread throughout her body. Now she was going home to die.

Perhaps she should have come back before. To have seen what it was like. The current Soviet government no longer presented an obstacle to those who had once fled its iron embrace. Politics had never greatly concerned her anyhow. She could scarcely recall the name of the grim-faced father figure who had distantly presided over the nation during its last decadent days. She remembered Greta more clearly. The last of her many lovers. The black American girl. Half her age. A prodigious dancer, all bones and skin, without flesh or extraneous muscle. Greta had gone to Florence to examine the great religious art and vanished there when the golden ships of the slugs passed overhead during their Occupancy. Why her? No one could answer that of course. She was just gone. Taken away presumably. In the years since for Anna, her grief eating away at her every moment waking or sleeping, she had not watched one minute of ballet. Even on that horrible device called the television.

The train appeared to be slowing. A country stationhouse with a bony horse and rickety cart standing out front. The old Russia. The one she had known briefly as a child before the years of training, the years at the institute. Brakes screeched. Doors flew open, banged shut. Anna glanced up as two new passengers entered the coach, peered uncertainly about, and then took seats across the aisle from her. A boy and girl. Husband and wife? she wondered. Lovers more likely; they were young. Not brother and sister despite the surface resemblance. That you could always tell. The boy sat nearest her across the aisle.

The train pulled out of the station, gathering speed.

Before she knew what she was doing, Anna leaned across and said, "Excuse me, please."

The boy's head turned with a look that momentarily froze her blood. Anna knew that look. Had seen it before. With Greta and the many before Greta. The look of a lover waking in the morning. "I—I—" she stammered.

And then, recovering, she plunged on with dignity, sill speaking Russian: "Would you mind much telling me how far is the distance to Moscow?"

The boy wore a heavy jacket, woolen cap, cotton pants, laced boots. A white frothy layer of snow clung to him. He shook his head, smiled, and looked at his companion. Leaning past him, the girl said in a voice that was warm and friendly, "I believe it will be three hours yet before we arrive."

"Thank you very much," Anna said, ready to withdraw back into her solitude.

"We are going there also," the girl persevered. "Jai and I have someone we must see."

"Yes, I understand."

"My name is Lai," the girl added.

Such odd names, thought Anna. Not Russian, though the girl at least spoke the language well enough. "Once long ago I lived in Moscow," Anna said in an unexpected burst of candor.

"We have never been there before. Is Moscow a beautiful city? Like Paris?"

"No. Moscow is…drab." She had to search her mind for the right word in Russian. So long since she had spoken the language of her own childhood. "When I lived there as a young woman I had a *dacha*—a large house in the country. I spent most of my time there when I was not performing."

"You were a…a dancer?"

"Yes. How did you know?" She couldn't possibly remember. She was barely Greta's age. Greta's age when they first met. There were films of course. Films and tapes. But who watched those? None this girl's age.

"And now you are traveling there again to live?"

"To Moscow, yes, though not to my old *dacha*. I shall have to find a small apartment."

"You are ill?"

Anna nodded. "Somewhat, yes."

"With the disease of cancer?"

"Why, yes. How did you—?"

"And you will die soon?"

"I—I will, yes." She looked down at her hands in her lap but when she glanced up again the girl continued to watch her. "I am Anna Provosky," she said. "Once I was *prima ballerina assoluta*. There are seldom more than five or six such in the world at any one time."

A different voice broke in: "You are truly her? You are Anna Provosky?"

She saw a man close to her own age standing in the aisle. His appearance was vaguely distinguished in a rather disheveled manner with a pair of tortoise shell eyeglasses perched on the nub of a nose. She thought he was probably a physician or perhaps a retired university professor.

"I am Anna, yes."

"Anna Provosky was once a fine dancer," Lai explained to the man. "She was *prima ballerina assoluta*."

"I know. I knew her well. I saw you perform many times, Anna Provosky. When I was a young medical student. You were magnificent. A goddess of the dance." The man removed his eyeglasses and rubbed his eyes. "I suspected it was you when I entered the car but did not wish to intrude on your privacy. I remember when you fled Russia—a day of mourning for all patriots who love the arts."

"You are most kind to say that," Anna said.

"And now at last you have returned to dance for us again?"

Anna did not know whether to laugh or scream. "I have returned, yes, but I no longer dance. I'm an old woman now. Too old for that."

"No, never," he protested.

The man was only being kind. But she wished he'd stop. Some things were best left unspoken.

"I think Anna Provosky is the most beautiful woman I've ever known in my life," Lai said.

Anna gaped at her in astonishment.

The man then produced paper and pen and asked for her auto-graph. Anna signed her name without thinking.

Gripping the paper tightly in his hand, the man waved it over his head. "Look," he called out in a loud voice. "Here is Anna Provosky. Anna Provosky has come back to Russia."

With that the others came forward. A thin woman in red. A boy of perhaps fourteen. Old men. Young men. Women and girls together. Anna signed her name many times over and over again. She answered their questions. Yes, she was going home to Moscow. No, she would not be dancing. Too old for that now. Retired twenty years. *You were beautiful when you danced. Like an angel on wings. We loved you, Anna Provosky. Prima ballerina assoluta.*

By the time the last of them returned to their seats her fingers ached from writing her name.

A hand reached across the aisle and gripped hers. "I must speak with you," said Lai. "Please."

Anna moved over to window to give her room to sit beside her. "What is it you wish of me…Lai?"

"To help you—Jai and I." She spoke in a whisper—in French now. "We think we can help you."

"Help me? But how? I have no need for money or—"

"Not money. No. It is important only that you dance again. These people—did you not hear them?—they all want it so badly."

"But that's a matter of age, not will. I will be sixty-one on my next birthday." A day she would likely never live long enough to see. "I am too old."

"But that is why can help. We are young and strong. We have many great powers."

Anna waved a dismissive hand. "I am not a superstitious person. Forget your spells and your potions, your salves and your magical ointments. I have tried them all, believe me, child. There is nothing more to be done."

The girl looked hurt. "Please, Anna. You don't understand. We are strong because we are different."

"Different? In what way are you different?"

"In many ways—many that we do not yet fully understand." She seemed perplexed. "The one we seek in Moscow may be able to explain."

"Then I do not understand why it is that you think you can be of help to me."

"You once loved to dance, did you not?"

"I did indeed. It was my life."

"Then you stopped?"

"Yes."

"Why?"

"Because someone—a person I loved very much—was taken away from me. In the beginning I danced for my own joy and if others appreciated my art, that was an added pleasure but not an essential one. Later when I became famous the applause of the audience became more important to me. By the end I danced for only the one person and when she was taken from me I stopped."

"But you could start again?"

"I told you no. It is not possible. It's an absurd idea—preposterous. Do you want to make me the laughing stock of the ballet world?" Her voice had grown shrill. Some of those in the nearest seats turned and looked. But like Lai she was speaking French now. "Please," she whispered, grasping the girl's hand. "You must let me be."

"Tell me about this person you loved."

"Why?" Anna felt a spasm of fear. She had never spoken to anyone of Greta before.

"Because Jai and I do not understand love very well. Wherever we go people seem moved by it and yet because we are different we need to learn more."

"What are you? Who are you?"

Lai shook her head. "Please. If only you'll tell me about love, what it means, how it feels, we can then help you."

Anna told her: "Greta was her name. She was a black girl from America I met in Paris when I was already no longer young. Greta was a dancer too—a fine dancer though not a great one. She possessed excellent form, subtle grace, but she lacked inner feeling—the spirit of fire—"

"How did you know you loved her?"

Anna concentrated upon her own memories trying to slow them down so that she could feel them again and perhaps describe them, "Because when I looked at Greta I saw my own self reflected through her eyes but it was myself in a changed light—transformed as though the person I knew myself to be had become someone else, someone greater and more beautiful." She looked at her hands. "You make me talk like a fool—a mystic."

"Then you loved her because she resembled you?" Lai asked with sudden hope.

"To some extent, yes, but not totally, no. If Greta had been too much like me, then there would have been no love."

"I don't understand."

"I know. I'm sorry. It's very difficult to speak of these things—these feelings."

"But Jai is like me and I am like him."

"And you're in love?"

"No. Yes. We don't know."

Anna glanced across and discovered Jai's intent gaze fixed upon her. A chill swept through her. Desperately she turned her attention back to Lai. "You truly can help me, then?"

"Yes. But only if you want us to."

"I—yes. I want it."

"I'm glad." Lai rose to her feet and offered her hand to Anna Provosky. "You will come with me now?"

Anna hesitated. "To where?"

"To where we won't be disturbed."

Anna stood. They went down the aisle together, hands locked. The train swayed under their feet like a drunkard. Anna gripped the backs of the seats they passed to steady her balance.

Two cars down Lai stopped in front of a door and produced a key. She turned the lock and stepped inside.

It was a stateroom. Unoccupied. Empty. There was a bed down out of in the wall.

"Where did you get that key?" she asked fearfully.

Lai smiled. "From the conductor?"

"You stole it?"

"Yes." Lai came forward and embraced Anna. She kissed her on the lips. Slowly and deeply but without much passion.

Then she stepped back.

"Who are you?" Anna said, sounding breathless.

"My name is Lai."

"Yes, I know that much but...where are you from?"

"The desert. In Africa. Jai and I were born there but ran away."

Anna spread her arms. "I'm afraid I still don't understand."

Lai leaned down and touched Anna's long white hair and stroked it. "You are very beautiful," she said and pushed her back on the bed. She lay down beside Anna and began removing her clothes. When she was naked Lai held her again and rubbed her breasts gently. "Tell me more about Greta," she said. "I want to know more."

"Why?" said Anna, desire now coupled with a growing fear. But she couldn't stop herself.

"Because you said Greta went away and I can't understand how that could happen. Not when you're so…so lovely." She pressed her face into Anna's hair.

"Greta was in the city of San Francisco when the ships passed overhead," Anna said heavily. "When they left they took her with them."

"Who did?"

"The ones called slugs. Or Occupants, others say. They flew over cities towns. People died and lived again. Others just disappeared. Greta was one of those."

"Why?"

"That no one knows."

"But there was a reason?"

"No one knows that either."

Hazy sunlight penetrated the window glass turning the air in the room a pale amber shade. Someone tried the doorknob, knocked twice, and went away. The conductor? Jai? Who else could it be?

Lai held her close now. The feel of her—her touch—was overwhelming.

"You never looked for her? For your Greta?"

"There was nowhere to look. They were gone. The people the Occupants took with them."

"Did you cry?"

"Cry?"

"Weep. When you found Greta was gone did you weep for her?"

"Yes—no. I don't honestly remember."

But Anna began to cry now. She turned her face away.

"Please. No more questions. I came here to forget not to remember. I don't want to remember."

She turned her head back and let out a shriek of dismay. Lai was gone. Instead a naked man lay beside her.

It was Jai.

"What are you doing here? What happened to Lai?"

"I am Lai," he said in a soft voice that made her shiver. He kissed her. "I am going to help you."

His skin was pale and smooth, hairless as a woman. Anna shut her eyes as tight as she could—until all she saw were gold and violet starbursts of kaleidoscopic light on the backs of her eyelids. Why are they doing this to me? she wondered. What if she yelled or screamed or cried out for help? They would surely be jailed—both of them—or worse. She a renowned personage with many admirers aboard this train. She heard footsteps in the corridor. Voices. The bed sagged under his heavy weight as he rolled closer to her. Anna made up her mind to remain still. She would not resist. She would remain supine and motionless beneath this boy—this man—as he touched her shoulders, pressing down—as he lay on top of her with hands kneading her flesh, moist lips and tongue licking and kissing her cheeks, mouth, throat, breasts. At his touch her thighs came apart.

He pushed a finger inside her.

"Don't hurt me," she said. "Perform whatever filthy act you desire but do not cause me pain. Please. I'm not a young woman. I'm not strong."

He said nothing. His touch though firm was gentle. "We love you, Anna Provosky," he said. She noticed how similar his voice was to that of the woman—the girl. It could have been either speaking. Anna forced her eyes open. His face was close, a hazy blur like snow blown on the wind. Then all at once he thrust inside her. Anna heard a distant voice murmur: Oh yes yes please that is fine. It does not hurt. Fuck me deeper. Good. Like that. Your prick huge inside me."

The voice was hers, using words she hadn't spoken in years, Russian words, long forgotten.

She kicked her heels, rocked her hips, fingernails digging into his smooth hairless back, shoulders like a woman, like Lai, like Greta, like—"I love you," she whispered in his ear. "I love you, Lai." Her thighs like sticky marmalade. All right. Yes. That's fine now. It's a good hard fuck you're giving me. Keep it up. Fine. Slap my ass with your balls. Lovely. Faster. Harder. Make me come. Are you making me come? Shove it in hard and quick. Fuck that quim. Fuck it good so I come. Fuck my quim with your big hard prick. Now. Fuck hard. Fuck me. God. Holy fuck. That's making me come. Holy sweet Jesus Christ come. It's your prick that's making me come."

It brought to her mind a memory. As a child—long before she began to dance professionally—Anna believed she must have been about eleven years old—she had ventured one evening to the dark basement room of her mother's younger brother who was then staying with the family in their summer home on the Black Sea. It was a big lovely house with pet poodles and hounds for the hunt and a dock for motorboats and places to swim in the warm salty sea water. In his room her uncle showed her a silver bracelet encrusted with yellow jewels that sparkled like the eyes of a cat. When she told him what a wonderful gift it was he asked if she would take off her clothes for him. He said he had seen her swimming in the morning in her yellow bathing suit and he wanted to feast his eyes upon her beautiful skin. She told him she couldn't do that, it would be wrong, but when he pleaded and tears ran down his face, she relented to the extent of removing all her clothes except for her white cotton panties. He asked her to put on the bracelet and after she did he told her shyly that he would like to rub her and put his finger inside her. He then leaned back on the bed, opened his trousers, and pulled out his erect penis. If she recalled accurately after the passage of so many years he stroked it no more than four or five times before it spurted semen onto the carpet. It was a blue shag carpet as thick as a lawn and the white stains made her think of the tracks of a slug. "Look," she said, pointing. "You peed all in white." He fastened his trousers, took her in his lap and stroked her hair as he often had before. He said, "Please, Anna, my beautiful darling, you must never speak of this to anyone. If they found out they would despise me."

Anna gave him her solemn promise. Her mother's younger brother drew her white cotton panties down her legs and rubbed her naked form with the heel of his hand and pressed his lips against it.

Anna left his room, her new bracelet jangling on her wrist.

The next day after swimming she went to his room again but he had gone. "Younger brother has gone to join the army," her mother told her and they never spoke of him again.

The woman who lay on top rolled away. "No more, Anna. It is done."

Lai stood up and began to dress.

Anna peered up at her from the bed. "But I don't want you to leave."

She put a finger to her mouth. "I must. We must."

She stepped into the corridor and was gone.

Later, Anna began to dress. As she was finishing she felt the train lurch to a stop. Curious, she lowered the window and looked out. The train stood in a huge, poorly illuminated cavern like the tomb of an ancient pharaoh. A man in a shabby gray suit stood on the nearby platform staring at his watch. She called out to him and asked where they were.

"Moscow," he said, speaking Russian.

"But that is not possible. We cannot—"

"I have lived in Moscow fifty years, madam," he said stiffly. "I ought to know where I am."

She slammed the window shut, hurried out the door, and went back to her seat.

The uniformed conductor appeared and helped her gather up her luggage. "The young boy and the girl who were seated across from me," she said when they stood on the platform. "The two who looked like twins. Did you perhaps notice if they left the train?"

"Not that I recall. Perhaps they moved to a different coach."

"They were going only as far as Moscow."

"Then they must have disembarked, Anna Provosky."

"You know me?" she asked in surprise. The conductor had not been among those in the car when her identity was revealed.

He removed his cap and held it over his heart. "How could I not know the young and beautiful *prima ballerina assoluta* Anna Provosky?"

In the glass of the window Anna now saw her own face looking back at her. The smooth soft flesh of her cheeks. The firm taut skin of her chin. The coal black hair. Gone was the old woman who had once peered back at her from the mirror glass.

As she crossed the station carrying her own suitcase she rose on the tips of her toes. It was a mad instinctive gesture but she didn't seem to have control over herself as she turned a pirouette—right there on the platform—her arms whirling at her sides like the wings of a dove as she spun around and around in intricate delirious circles and she didn't stop, couldn't stop, until she overheard the applause welling up all around and the voices crying out aloud, "Bravo, Anna Provosky, bravo!"

9

A week after the fire at Roy Goldman's house the mob came and carried Peter Mark outside, tied him to a pole, and burned him at the stake.

He was naked. Lashed securely with his hands tied behind his back. Flames licked at his feet and ankles while the smoke rising from the fire filled his mouth, nostrils, and lungs, making it difficult to breathe, painful to swallow, nearly impossible to think coherently. Peter was convinced that a silly mistake had been made, for surely there was no earthly reason why he should have to die in this inhuman fashion. He was a godly man who tried very hard to be decent. No one could deny that—could they?

Around him the mob stood watching. Through the hazy blur of the smoke Peter saw them link hands and began to move in a somber circle. The people were dressed identically in slicker yellow raincoats, black rubber boots, and hard metal hats. Among them he identified the warm friendly face of Fire Captain Sam Brady. Hiram Evers was another familiar figure and Oscar Stovall was present too, his eyes shiny with excitement. Peter discovered Jayne Stovall at her husband's side and next to her an enormous fat man whom Peter only belatedly recognized as his employer Desmond Blue. As he peered through the smoke Peter was able also to make out both Alfie Jarrett—who at least appeared downcast—and Dr. Gordon Schwerner. Peter made an effort to call out to those he knew best—Alfie in particular—beseeching them to please intercede with the others to release him from this terrible fate.

But no one seemed to hear. Instead their voices rose in a chant: "Burn, witch, burn!" they shouted. "Burn, witch, burn!" Peter swallowed hard. "I'm not a witch!" he cried back, though even as he spoke he wondered if he was telling the truth. Could any man truly know the darker recesses of his own soul? Nothing was impossible after all. Witch? Demon? An incarnation of Satan himself? Peter wished he could be as certain of his own innocence as his words claimed.

The flames leaped higher. Looking down Peter observed the skin of his legs turning crisp and black and he smelled the sickly stench of burning flesh, his own. He wondered if perhaps a full confession might yet save him. (Surely the wounds he had suffered so far were not beyond the capacity of Dr. Schwerner to repair)

But when he tried to speak he found that his tongue and lips were so badly blistered and swollen that the words emerged as gibberish. The circle continued to move about him. He now spotted Nadia, Crystal, and Lacy among them, the three of them looking as lovely as ever in spite of the baggy raincoats they wore, and close beside them the slim long-legged figure of young Ginger Cunningham. Theda Goldman was also present—the darkly beautiful female conspirator. "Burn, witch, burn!" she shouted with the others. Peter felt the flames licking up his inner thighs and lapping at his genitals. To his shock he felt himself coming erect. In a burst of—

* * * *

"Hey, Peter, wake up, buddy. Hiram Evers is here to see you. He's down in the kitchen."

The disembodied voice invaded Peter's dream like an intruder from separate world. His eyes snapped open and when they did the smell of burning flesh left the air. He lay on his back in his bed in his room in the Stovall house, the covers in a knot at his feet. Hastily he looked down to be sure he was still wearing his shorts.

Ginger Cunningham giggled. "You don't have to worry. I've seen a few of those things before."

"You have?" said Peter, surprised. "Where?"

"Where do you think? On the stupid tridee. I used to sneak in and watch some of Jayne's shows with her. It got boring pretty quick. Seen one, seen them all."

"Yes, I suppose." Still embarrassed, Peter managed to sit up. "I never really thought of it that way."

Ginger lit a cigarette and blew smoke. She looked at him carefully. She was wearing her yellow shorts and white tee shirt. "What's wrong with you anyhow? You look like somebody smacked you over the head with a brick."

"I was having a nightmare when you woke me up."

"No kidding?" She looked impressed. "I never have nightmares anymore."

"But you dream?"

"Not that for a long time either. I think the tridee does it. Watch too much and it steals away your dreams. I quit watching but the dreams never came back. I guess that part of my brain got burned out for good."

"I'm not sure that's possible," Peter said. "I think you ought to give it more time. Then you'll dream again."

"I hope so." She gave a sigh. "I don't mind losing the nightmares but dreaming's kind of fun, don't you agree?"

"Oh, yes. Very much so. Even if that nightmare I was having just now wasn't much fun. What does Hiram want with me I wonder. I'm not scheduled for duty till this evening. He didn't say anything, did he?"

"Who? Him?" She snorted. "He's not the kind to go around spilling his beans in front of a kid. Have you ever noticed how the dumber the adult the snootier he acts around children?"

"You think Hiram Evers is dumb?"

"No, not dumb," she said after a moment's thought. "He's more the stupid kind."

"There's a difference?"

"Sure. Dumb means not having any smarts. Oscar and Jayne— they're both dumber than a post. They can't help it. Stupid means having the smarts but not knowing what to do with them. Those are the ones you've got to watch out for."

"Thanks. I'll try and remember that."

She grinned. "The advice will cost you two bucks. Psychiatrist rates."

Peter shooed her out of the room so that he could dress. As he went past the living room on his way to find Hiram, he glanced in and saw Jayne crouched naked in the middle of the floor while gigantic fleshy entities swam past through the air. With a shudder, he hurried on into the kitchen. Hiram Evers sat at the table, a can of beer in his hand. When he saw Peter he held out the beer. "Care for a swig?"

"No, thank you. I just woke up."

"Me too." Evers belched. "Makes a good solid breakfast if you view it in the right light."

"I think I'd rather have coffee."

"Help yourself. Fresh pot on the stove. I kicked Jayne's fat ass long enough to get her to make us some."

Peter crossed to the stove, poured himself a cup of coffee, and sipped cautiously. "Ginger said you wanted to see me."

"That's right. I've got a message to pass along. He lowered his voice. "It's about the Goldman fire."

"Yes, what about it?" Peter didn't particularly like being reminded of that night. Especially his own role in the proceedings. Twice in the past week he had secretly visited the Goldman home on Spruce Street hoping to apologize to Roy for what he'd done but on both occasions no one had responded to his stealthy knocking even though he felt certain someone had been at home. Of course it might have been Theda instead of Roy and he had to admit he wasn't terribly eager to confront her—not yet anyhow. "What message is that, Hiram?"

"It's concerning your work that night. It was damned impressive. I'm authorized to tell you that."

"I don't understand. Who authorized you to tell me that?"

Evers crushed the empty beer can in his fist. His voice dropped into a whisper. "Who do you think? The mayor. Lucius B. Washington himself. He said for me to give you the good word."

"You know him?"

Evers winked furtively. "Let's just say him and me have a personal acquaintance that dates back a few years. And he'd like to have a little chat with you too."

"The mayor would?"

"That's right. I don't know if you know but he was there that night."

"I did notice his car."

Evers chuckled. "Hard to miss that baby, ain't it? Garish as the lipstick on a three-dollar whore." He tossed the flattened beer can over his shoulder. It missed the trash container by a good distance and rattled across the linoleum floor. "There's been a fair amount of talk regarding you this past week, by the way. Some of the boys felt you hadn't entirely proved yourself yet—one fire's only one fire, they said—but I stuck up for you and the mayor finally came down on my side. I told him that a smart boy's a smart boy and not apt to turn dumb all at once."

"I'm afraid I don't entirely understand what you're talking about," Peter said.

Evers winked and stood up. "Maybe you shouldn't. The mayor likes to do his own talking. You ready to go then?"

Peter gulped the remainder of his coffee. "You mean right now?"

"The mayor's not a man to be kept waiting."

The two of them went out the back door into the yard. Peter spotted Ginger Cunningham perched in the crook of a tree. She gave him a big friendly wave as he passed underneath. He and Evers circled the house and crossed the street. Oscar Stovall, emerging from his beetle buggy, shuffled past them headed for the front door. Peter nodded and said hello but Stovall did not seem either to hear or see him.

"Kind of simpleminded, ain't he?" said Evers as they got in his bug.

"Oscar is a little odd, I guess," Peter agreed.

"Odd ain't the word for it. Nutty is better." Evers started the electric motor and drew away from the curb. "Anybody told you about the time he flipped his wig?"

"I don't believe so, no."

"It occurred three, maybe four years ago. Oscar was always a little odd—crazy as hell about being a fireman for instance—but nobody ever thought much of it. Then one time he didn't show up for work three days in a row and we started getting worried. Fire Captain Brady and me drove over to see what was up. Found Oscar flat on his back in the living room watching some loony show on the tridee. There was a stubble on his face and he acted dead to the world except for the way his eyes were wide open and staring like a catfish on a hook. Looked to me like he hadn't slept or ate in days and his lips were swollen and cracked like he wasn't drinking water either. There was crap and piss in his britches too—you could smell it on him. The captain went over and switched off the tridee but it didn't seem to help none. Oscar just lay there like a zombie. The mayor finally had to send him up to Chicago for treatment. Shrinks, I guess. They sent him back after a few weeks and said he was better. At least he could walk and talk and get to Fire House in time to work his shift.

Now they say Oscar hardly ever watches tridee. They say he doesn't have to. He can see the pictures in his head any time he wants just by thinking about them."

"Where was Jayne when this happened?"

"She was right there with him. Not that it seemed to bother her much. She ate her dinners and took her naps and got up and went to the potty whenever nature gave a holler. When we shut off the tridee though, then she went bananas. Went straight for my eyes and tried to claw me blind. Once we got Oscar out of there we switched it back on for her. She was okay then."

"Does it ever affect you that way? Watching tridee all the time I mean?"

Evers swiveled his head and grinned. "Hell, bud, I know better than to watch that shit."

"But I thought—"

"I'm a music lover. The German Romantics in particular. My old woman likes to eyeball a show now and then but she never was exactly noted as an intellectual giant either. Folks tell me you hardly give it a glance yourself."

Peter couldn't help wondering who these folks were who were talking telling things about him. Oscar undoubtedly was one and perhaps Jayne as well. "I'm usually too tired after work."

"And maybe too smart too." He chuckled. "I told you the mayor has his eye on you. He's a pretty keen judge of character, that man."

"What about him? The mayor I mean. Does he watch much tridee?"

Evers slapped the steering wheel in his glee. "Now I know you got to be shitting me," he said.

* * * *

It was another warm lovely bucolic day in Winesap with the sun suspended like a big golden eye in the dead center of an azure sky. Peter turned and watched the afternoon pedestrians strolling by. He saw entire families out enjoying the day with mothers and fathers and white-haired grandparents and sometimes as many as a half-dozen children. He observed the sweethearts also. It was a delight watching them strolling along hand in hand, utterly oblivious to the existence of anything or anyone else in the world except themselves.

"On a day like this," he told Evers, "I don't see why anybody would want to stay cooped up indoors with tridee."

"Sure enough. But wait'll tonight. We try and keep the intensity low on days like this. It's the only way to get people outside now and then for their own health."

"You mean you can regulate the effects of the tridee?"

"The mayor's got the switch right in the middle of his desk. But I shouldn't be shooting off my mouth. The mayor likes to spring his own explanations."

"Jayne was watching tridee today," Peter pointed out.

Evers smirked. "Like I said that girl's got the constitution of a Missouri mule. The brains too if you ask me."

* * * *

Evers parked beneath the flashing neon sign of Pearson's Family Drugstore.

He slid out from under the bug's wheel and beckoned Peter to follow. Inside the drugstore an owl-eyed man with a fringe of gray hair stood behind the counter to the right of the soda fountain. "Howdy, Hiram," he said without much enthusiasm.

"Mayor in the back, Mr. Pearson?"

"I believe I may have heard him slip in a short time ago."

Evers's eyes narrowed with suspicion. "What do you mean by that?"

"Why, nothing. I just—"

"You didn't happen to maybe tiptoe back and try to sneak yourself a peek?"

"Of course not, Hiram. I know I'm never supposed to—"

"And don't you forget it either. The mayor's a generous man with his friends but when people cross him they have a tendency to regret it later on."

"I know that, Hiram."

"Good for you." Evers reached across the counter and patted Mr. Pearson on the shoulder. "This way," he said to Peter.

They went around the counter, climbed a short flight of steps, and paused in front of a door. In order to open it Evers had to use two separate keys. When the second lock clicked Evers swiveled his head and caught Mr. Pearson watching from below. The druggist looked hurriedly away. "The mayor don't care much for snoops," Evers told Peter in a voice meant to carry. They went through the door.

"I don't understand," Peter said as Evers relocked the door. "What's the mayor doing back here?"

"This is where his office is."

"What about City Hall?"

"Oh, he's got a suite of rooms over there too but he likes it best back here. Mayor Washington is a man of the people—even if hardly anybody has ever seen his face—and a place like this is where you find people."

They walked down a long corridor with numerous small rooms opening off it. Through the doors Peter saw narrow cots, wooden stools and benches, porcelain sinks. Each room seemed identically furnished. From behind a closed door he heard the raucous laughter of a woman punctuated by the fierce grunting of a man.

"What are these rooms for?" he asked Evers.

"They're rentals—transient rentals."

"Why would anybody want to rent a room back here?"

"For recreational purposes."

"Recreation?"

"Also known as screwing. This is the town whorehouse, friend. Prices range from a low of ten dollars up to a two-lady special for a hundred and sixty-five. If you want I can introduce you to a little doll who'll give you the ride of your life for fifty bucks and tip."

"I'm a little short of cash right now," said Peter.

"Sure. Anytime you're interested though just come see me."

"I'll remember that." At the end of the corridor stood another door. Evers raised his fist and knocked three times. He paused momentarily then knocked twice more.

"Evers?" said a deep melodious voice from beyond the door.

"Yes, sir. I brought that new fireman you wanted to see."

"Good. Bring him in."

Evers unlatched another pair of locks and ushered Peter inside. The room was small, cramped, and windowless, dominated by a huge mahogany desk. To one side of the desk sat a man Peter recognized: it was Bob Jones engaged to Fire Captain Brady's daughter Laurel. The only other person in the room was a man of forty or fifty seated directly behind the desk. He was dressed in a shiny chartreuse suit with a matching wide-brimmed hat and a black tie held fast to the front of his pink silk shirt by a diamond stick-pin. There were jeweled rings on most his fingers and a thin moustache under his nose. The size, shape, and color of his eyes were concealed behind sunglasses.

Peter stared in disbelief.

A smile spread slowly across the man's face. "Surprised aren't you?" he asked in the same voice Peter had heard through the door.

"I just never thought…"

"You never thought the Mayor of Winesap would turn out to be as black as the ace of spades."

Peter nodded reluctantly. "There don't seem to be any other people of color in town," he explained.

"Not unless you count white as a color. Which technically it isn't. I'm Lucius B. Washington." The mayor pointed at the chair presently occupied by Bob Jones. "Come over here and sit down, Peter, and let's see if we can find out a few things about each other's individual philosophies of life before we get down to discussing business."

Bob Jones obediently vacated the chair and crossed to stand beside Hiram Evers. Peter sat down in his place and tried to make himself comfortable. "What is it you'd like to know, sir?"

"The same things as you, I suspect: in other words—everything, the works."

"I really don't know where to—"

"Try the beginning. The cold hard facts if you please. We'll start there and then drift on to more abstract terrain. You're from Chicago, Evers informs me."

"Yes, sir. I was a fireman there too."

"And did you like it? Chicago, I mean. The urban life experience as a whole?"

"Well, I guess so. It certainly wasn't as peaceful as Winesap but—"

"I'm also a city man. From Boston originally. I attended school there. Would you doubt my word if I told you that I hold a master's degree in abstract philosophy from Harvard University?"

At the moment Peter didn't feel in an especially skeptical frame of mind. "I'd believe you, sir."

"In that case—" the mayor leaned back and folded his hands in a gesture of satisfaction "—how would you like to venture a guess as to the manner in which I made my living subsequent to graduation?"

"I don't know. I suppose you were a teacher of some kind."

"Incorrect." The mayor grew solemn. "A true philosopher can never masquerade as a mere teacher—he must remain a student. What do you know of the science and art of cat fighting?"

Peter was taken aback. "I'm sorry, sir. Did you say cats?"

"I did."

"I don't think I've ever heard of anything like that."

"It was enormously popular once." The mayor's voice assumed a tone of nostalgic reverie. "Especially in the central core neighborhoods of our once great cities. I functioned as a promoter primarily—an arranger of bouts—though I did own and manage a few elite scrappers of my own. A beautiful sport—a way of life—and the perfect milieu for the abstract philosopher. Your Taiwanese Alley Tom is the finest of fighting breeds—all claws and teeth and guts and cunning. I'd send agents to Louisiana, Tijuana, all the significant ports, to capture them in the wild. Place two of them in a ring six feet square, strike a bell, and let them go at it. I promoted some championship bouts that lasted upwards of four and five hours.

The combatants would gnaw each other's limbs off and then slither around the ring on their bellies like snakes to continue the battle. At times one had to pry the fangs of the victor loose from the throat of the vanquished. At other times it couldn't be done and the poor creature would have to be destroyed before it starved to death."

"Weren't things like that against the law?" asked Peter, his stomach queasy.

The mayor looked amused. "Undeniably. But there is surely a higher law that exists in a realm far beyond the human sphere. That's what drew me to the sport in the first place. I alluded to the fact that I am by profession a philosopher and the cat in its inner character is the most truly existential of animals. No other dares live so fully in the single instant of the present. How old are you, Peter?"

"About twenty-five, I think."

"Then you're old enough to recall the days before the slugs came and changed everything for better or worse. I had a bout scheduled that day in West Oakland. A tough old Tom named Vargas—champion of northern Mexico—versus a Taiwanese gray known as Chang II. It was a special promotion of mine—tickets priced at a flat one hundred dollars up—and the only spectators were pimps. Pimps were always notable connoisseurs of the sport of cat fighting and invariably among my most dedicated customers. Partway through the bout a flash of blinding white light burst in the air. When my vision cleared I discovered that everyone present excluding myself and the cats had vanished. I don't imagine you knew that, did you? Not only did the Occupants go after all the warmongers, capitalists, and political hacks among us they also eliminated every pimp in the world."

Peter shook his head. "I'd never heard that before."

"It's a fact. Though they did spare the hookers—the women—for which reason I have always regarded their visit as an act of justice."

Peter could have argued the point but refrained.

"Confronted with this reality," the mayor went on, "I therefore responded as any philosopher would by embracing the new reality imposed on us from without. I got in my car—a little beetle buggy, by the way, not the Cadillac you'd naturally assume—and drove straight here to this fair city. Since then Winesap has been my home."

"What made you decide to come to Winesap?"

"In the glove compartment of my car I kept a road map of the United States. Before setting out I removed the stickpin from my tie and jabbed it in the map at random. The point stuck here in Winesap. Due to the chaotic state of the world at the time my journey consumed more than a few days. When I arrived here I purchased a copy of the local newspaper from a rack and discovered that a special mayoral election was in progress, the incumbent having been taken by the slugs. I hired a printer to print some posters and began to publicize myself as a write-in candidate. After I had expended more than nine-tenths of my stake in voter outreach—some might call it bribes—the ballots were counted and I was officially pronounced the winner. Subsequently, I have been re-elected every fourth year by popular acclamation."

"And your race—your color—it didn't make any difference?"

"I was careful in my campaign literature not to include a distracting photograph. Are you by any chance familiar with the writings of Mr. Sherwood Anderson or the plays of Thornton Wilder?"

Peter shook his head quickly. The mayor's question sounded like a trap to him. "I never touch books, sir. I'm a fireman."

"A pity. They're excellent works—quite insightful. Anderson and Wilder taught me something important: that beneath the veneer of hayseed serenity that pervades your typical Midwestern town there lurks as much rot as anywhere else. Did friend Evers happen to enlighten you as to the nature of the private rooms we maintain here?"

"He said they were used by…by prostitutes."

"And did he go into any details about these lovely ladies? Like, for example, where and whence they come?"

"Only that one of them was—he said she was very competent at her trade."

"I kept my trap shut otherwise, Mr. Mayor," Evers put in from his place by the door. "I gave the lad here a personal recommendation but went no further."

"They're our local ladies," the mayor told Peter. "Each and every one of them. Most are simple housewives, though we've got a few schoolteachers and nurses too, spinsters for the most part, the kind that can't attract or hold a man under ordinary circumstances. Bob Jones over there handles recruitment and says he often has a young schoolgirl come up to him and beg for the chance to work in Pearson's back rooms like her teacher told her she should. But I have a strict policy there. A girl has to graduate high school first. Take Bob Jones's little fiancée as an example. That girl could well—"

"Laurel?" Peter interrupted, stunned. "Do you mean Laurel Brady?"

"Yes, I believe that is her name. Now Laurel is a bright girl and could undoubtedly find work anywhere she wanted. But nevertheless every Friday evening here she is down in room fourteen servicing as many as—"

"But Laurel is Fire Captain Brady's daughter."

"So I believe, yes, but since the good captain's reservation here is for Tuesdays and Thursdays when his good wife has her bridge club over—there's no chance of him bumping into the girl when she's, ah, professionally engaged. I bring all this up only to provide you an insight into my electoral success here in Winesap. I try to give the people what they want and what they want is what I give them. There are exceptions of course."

"He means Roy Goldman," Hiram Evers said.

"Mr. Evers told me about the little chat you were having with Roy the other day."

"But it was nothing," Peter tried explaining: "Roy just dropped some coins and I tried to—"

"Oh, I know the cover story." The mayor waved a hand. "And for the moment I do not choose to question it. Roy Goldman is a fascinating character. Talented too. Have you read any of his work?"

Peter gave his head a hasty shake.

"There's one story in particular that sticks in my mind. A tale about an aging alcoholic living in a nameless hotel in an anonymous city. The man has a wooden leg, the result of a war wound, and as the story begins he is passed out in a drunken stupor on the floor of his room in a puddle of curdled vomit. A curious cockroach waddles up and slips inside the hollow core of the leg by means of a small crack in the wood. When the man awakes he notices the crack and seals it up with tape. The cockroach, unable to escape, proceeds to burrow up inside the man's stump, eating flesh as he goes. The story continues in this vein for several thousand words, the viewpoint alternating between the roach and the man being eaten alive. At the end of the story all that is left is an empty pile of skin on the floor. When I complimented Roy on the sagacity of the allegory he admitted that the alcoholic was intended to represent the people of Winesap and the cockroach was yours truly."

"You know Roy then?" said Peter, surprised.

"I do indeed. Roy and I met much as you and I have today when he first returned to Winesap. I made him the same offer then as the one I'm about to make you."

"What offer is that, sir?"

"An offer of freedom—the freedom to be miserable."

"That doesn't sound very appealing."

"Are you sure? Give it some thought. Take me as an example. I am not now and never have been a happy man. Nor do I expect or desire to be. Those individuals I most admire—from Marcus Aurelius through Thomas Aquinas to John Donne, Kant, Kierkegaard, Dostoevsky, and Kafka. Rotten terrible miserable unhappy little men all of them. Unhappy—why? Unhappy, I say, because they—we—because we think. Roy refused my offer by the way. He said he couldn't dispute my analysis that the more people thought, the more miserable they were, but he just couldn't go along with my policy of burning books for the greater happiness of all. He said it was censorship and censorship was wrong."

"No gratitude," said Evers from his corner. "Mayor here offered Roy the chance to read all the damn books he wanted in return for a little support come election time and the damn fool turned him down."

"He ran against me."

"And got his butt whipped."

"But not after he first tried—what was the phrase he used?—he tried to expose me. Ran all over town telling people that Mayor Lucius B. Washington was a coal black coon from out west in Oakland who wore diamond rings on his fingers and dressed in loud colorful attire. 'That's not the Mayor Washington we know," the voters to a man replied. I was re-elected in a landslide. So what do you think, Peter? My offer good enough for you? Or do you want to be another Roy Goldman and stand fast?"

Peter looked around the room. Hiram Evers and Bob Jones were both watching intently.

"So what you're offering me," Peter said, "is the freedom to be miserable by—"

"By any means you care to avail yourself of," he said.

"Including reading books?"

"If that's your bent, yes."

"And in return you want—what?"

"You'll be expected to go to work for me—starting immediately—in the same capacity as Mr. Evers and Mr. Jones here—as a sort of unpaid confidential agent. Now neither of them is particularly interested in books but both are willing to forgo immediate gratification in return for the deeper pleasures—the unhappiness—of exercising power over their fellow townspeople. Your needs, I sense, are nearer my own. And you come most highly recommended. I can assure you of that."

"Who by?" Peter asked, puzzled. He couldn't think of anyone. Hiram Evers didn't really know him that well and Bob Jones barely at all. Who else could it be?"

"By a trusted friend of both of us," the mayor said. "You'll continue your normal day-to-day duties at the Fire House but you'll also be expected to keep your eyes and ears open and inform me at once of anything relevant you come across."

"You want me to be a kind of spy then. You want me to inform on people who are hiding books. Is that it?"

"If you come across any—which would frankly surprise me—apart from dear Roy, that is—then certainly you should let us know. But I'm more concerned with what people are thinking and who it is that's doing this thinking. As I've emphasized before, thought and unhappiness are the same and if unhappiness exists in Winesap I want to be apprised of it immediately since it's my sworn duty as mayor to quash it at its source."

Peter let his head bob slowly up and down. Whether he liked it or not going to work for the mayor made sense. It would provide him a perfect excuse for snooping around town in pursuit of the case.

"It sounds pretty good to me, sir. It's a fair offer."

He put out his hand to shake.

There was a grating noise as the rings on the mayor's fingers scraped the steel of Peter's hand.

"Glad to have you aboard, Peter. Now if you'll excuse me—" he came to his feet "—I have another appointment to keep. Mr. Jones, would you please check the alley and make certain the coast is clear?"

"You betcha, Mayor." Bob Jones crossed, the room, unbolted a door in the opposite wall, and opened it. A splash of yellow sunlight poured into the room.

"There's a little girl out there on her bike."

"Chase her away, please."

Jones looked back. "No, forget it. She's gone already."

The mayor came around his desk, nodded a quick farewell, grabbed a pork pie hat off the rack, and slipped out the door. Bob Jones kept watch out the window until a door slammed and a gas engine coughed loudly to life.

Hiram Evers sauntered over and slapped Peter on the back. "That was a damn smart decision you made there, boy," he said, "Working for the mayor is the only way to keep your noodle straight in this town. Otherwise you'll end up in the loony bin with Oscar and Roy."

"Then I guess I should thank you," Peter said. "For recommending me to the mayor."

Evers seemed amused. "Hell, that wasn't me."

"Then who was it, I wonder."

"The mayor's lady friend, I'll bet. She's the only other person he sees much of. Bet that's where he's headed right now in fact. Likes a little noontime action every now and then."

"He has a lady friend? Not any of the ones in the rooms out there?"

"He won't touch those with a ten-foot stick. Nope, his lady is a real lady."

"Who is she?"

"Theda Goldman, that's who."

Evers and Bob Jones were both grinning ear to ear.

A PROFILE: GINGER CUNNINGHAM

Cute perky little Ginger Cunningham with her carrot orange hair, pert turned-up nose and wobbly-knobby knees felt next to nothing (like a big round zero) when at age seven years, nine months, twelve days Momsie and Pops snuck out of the two-room apartment on Locust Street and flew the coop once and forever. But poop, she thought—so what?—because even way later when she grew up tall and lean and gorgeous and all of twelve she remembered them only as smells (tobacco, beer, sweat) and sounds (the whine of a can opener) and certainly not as faces or voices, all of which had slipped totally from her memory like last night's bad dream.

After they left Ginger lived alone and never put a foot outdoors. There was nothing much in the apartment they hadn't taken with them anyhow—a little food, no money, nothing else—just one old dog-eared magazine she read again and again. The magazine was *True Mystery Cases* and only three of its ten articles were intact.

The first of these told the story of Warren the pig-faced boy from Alabama who (with his Bowie knife) slit open the bellies of pregnant women (after first forcing them to commit acts of degradation) and ate the flesh of their unborn infants alive.

The second article told of the notorious Santa Isadora Hipster Cult Murders of thirty years earlier and raised the speculation based on newly discovered evidence that a strange woman described only as swarthy and darkly beautiful (and possibly of Eastern European extraction) had been the real brains behind the whole ten days of slaughter.

The third article was Ginger's favorite: The Case of the Mystic Mussulman. The detective involved wasn't the usual dumb beefy cop with liver spots on his hands but a private detective named Desmond Blue who (according to the article) lived in a mansion called Arabia Deserta in the middle of the Sahara.

In any event, thanks to complaints from neighbors noticing the newspapers piling up on the doorstep, a pair of policemen finally came by, kicked down the door, and discovered the abandoned Ginger sitting in the middle of an otherwise empty living room reading her detective magazine.

They took her to the Home for Wayward Children to await the return of her parents (which never happened) or her adoption by a good local Christian family (which didn't seem to be happening either). She took her detective magazine with her and read those three articles over and over again at night in bed when she was supposed to be sleeping and instead she'd be looking out the window and watching the clouds roll by and making silly shapes out of them like dogs and fish, chickens and elephants.

Then Aunt Martha (who was fat) and Uncle Jim (who wasn't) wrote a letter and said they'd be glad to take her to live with them until her parents came back (which of course never happened).

The house Aunt Martha and Uncle Jim lived in was on the outskirts of town near the abandoned railroad tracks. There were already six children living with them. None were theirs but like Ginger were wards of the court for whose support a stipend was paid on the first of every month based on the age and medical disability (if any) of the child involved. Four of the children were mean and ugly and older and ignored Ginger entirely but the other two—a brother and sister—were closer to her own age.

But they didn't like her either as it turned out (and vice versa) so Ginger spent most of her time reading her magazine and making plans on how to run away before Aunt Martha or Uncle Jim spanked her again which they seemed to do on a regular basis the second of every month after the checks arrived and they'd drunk up all the whiskey they'd bought the day before.

Then the county came by and told Aunt Martha and Uncle Jim they needed to send Ginger to school or else their payments would be cut off. Her second grade teacher's name was Miss Blixon, with a hawk nose and beady eyes, who announced in a sonorous tone to whole class that Ginger was a genius who could already read at the twelfth grade level and she was sending a note home with her so that her parents would know.

When Aunt Martha and Uncle Jim read the note they got frightened. The last thing they needed was for one of their foster children to stand out from the rest because that could mean only one thing and that thing was trouble.

That was when they started locking her in the closet at nights. At first she didn't like that much because being in the dark closet made it impossible to read any of the three articles in her magazine (or anything else either for that matter) or look out the window (there was no window in the closet) and watch the clouds rolling by and pretending they were animals such as monkeys, crocodiles, and hippopotami.

Because of the closet, she started not going home right after school like the other kids. Instead, she started spending time at the town library. It was a good place to hang out for a little girl who was a genius already reading at a twelfth grade level. While there she read and re-read the three articles in her detective magazine till she finally grew tired of them and went on to teach herself to read in four different languages—Spanish, French, German and, Latin—a few books in each of which the library had set aside in a special section no one except Ginger ever went into.

That was where she was one fine afternoon when Roy Goldman came by the library to see if they had any of the books he'd written (they didn't of course) and spotted her back there. He said, "Hi there, little girl, what are you doing hiding way back here where nobody else ever goes?"

She told him: "Just reading." And held up a copy of *Don Quixote* in the original Spanish and showed him she was already on page 983.

Since *Don Quixote* was one of Roy's favorite books and because the poor little girl looked both sad and abused he decided the best thing would be for somebody more reliable than Aunt Martha and Uncle Jim to adopt her.

So on his way home from the library he stopped off to see Mayor Lucius B. Washington in his office, the mayor having once told him concerning another matter, "Anytime you want something just drop by, Roy, my door's always open to a creative artist like you."

That was when Ginger went to live with the Stovall family, Oscar and Jayne. Jayne had dull eyes and a puffy face and Oscar was a real choice nut but harmless, so it was a distinct and definite improvement over anywhere she had lived before. She still had the true detective magazine with her and read the three articles once a week or so and sometimes Jayne would come into her bedroom late at night and crawl under the covers with her and they'd hug and talk and cuddle like sisters and a couple times Jayne started crying and said she really wished she was dead and buried. Sometimes when Oscar was off at the Fire House the round-faced Roy would come around and he and Jayne would go off together into the bedroom but after they were done in there doing who knows what (Ginger knew but would never tell) and Jayne was back in the living room with her tridee Roy would come and ask Ginger about the books she'd read recently—her new favorite was *The Wonderful Wizard of Oz* and its many sequels—and he would warn her to be careful because now with the library officially shut down people weren't allowed to have any books at all in their homes and if they did—even one book—the books would be burned.

Then a man with a steel face and steel hands came to live with them too and Ginger discovered he was an associate of Desmond Blue, the detective she'd read about and admired in one of the three articles in her detective magazine. She put a shadow on him too then and saw him go in with Hiram Evers to meet with the mayor.

10

Peter Mark was a half-block from the two-story pale blue stucco house on Spruce Street where Mr. and Mrs. Roy Goldman lived when he spotted Mayor Lucius B. Washington's hot pink Cadillac parked in their driveway bold as life. Its discovery—and the fact that its presence here supported everything Hiram Evers and Bob Jones had told him about the mayor and Theda Goldman—caused Peter to slow his step and look warily around. There was nothing in particular to see but that lack—coupled with the silence in the air—made him anxious and he recalled how during his walk from downtown he had not once passed another human being.

The same sidewalks which only a short time before had teemed with pedestrians—whole families out for their afternoon strolls—had abruptly turned as empty and desolate as a desert. Of course there was a logical explanation: the weather had turned chilly. A hard wind whipped through the treetops and rattled the leaves. As Peter paused and stood listening he heard the mechanical rasp of voices emanating from the nearer houses and noticed in the windows of several the flickering of tridee images.

The citizens of Winesap had all gone home to get warm and be entertained; there was surely nothing sinister in that. Nevertheless, the silent emptiness continued to disturb him. There was something unnatural about it—something abnormal and almost perverse.

The house next to the Goldman home was vacant. Peter crossed the lawn and dropped down beside the concrete porch from where he could observe the blue stucco house. Except for the mayor's car in the driveway there wasn't a sign of life. The curtains were tightly drawn and there was a black burnt patch in the lawn showing where the book-burning had occurred. Peter edged away from the shelter of the porch and trotted in a straight line toward the Goldman house. When he reached the wall he threw himself flat against it, paused to collect his breath, and then began to maneuver toward the back, ducking his head whenever he passed a window. If Mayor Washington was actually inside with Theda Goldman, Peter wanted to confirm the fact with his own eyes. He wasn't entirely certain what such a discovery might entail in terms of the case but knew it would likely be important.

The back yard was a wild thatch of greenery. Peter saw an uncovered wooden porch jutting out from the rear of the house. The door leading inside appeared to be slightly ajar. Peter headed that way, stepping cautiously through the untrimmed grass. Grasshoppers leaped from his path. Bees buzzed noisily around his head.

He had nearly reached the porch when he first noticed the voices. They were soft and hushed, the words unclear. One of the voices—

he paused to listen—was that of a woman while the other—though he couldn't be certain—sounded like Mayor Washington. Peter put a foot on the bottom step and pressed down tentatively with his full weight. When there was no incriminating creak he began to ascend.

There were four steps in all. Two long strides brought him to the brink of the door. He peered through the gap and discovered looming at the end of a short passageway the squat hulk of an electric stove and the lean silhouette of a refrigerator. The voices he had heard were only slightly more distinct now but seemed to be coming from fairly close ahead. Peter took a deep breath and steeled himself for action. Having come this far he couldn't turn back. He would have to press onward until the thing was done.

Grasping the edge of the door he drew it toward him. The hinges squeaked. Peter slipped through and crept furtively forward, moving delicately on the balls of his feet like a dancer.

He found them in a corner of the kitchen bathed in shadows. The mayor lay flat on his back with his head facing Peter. The woman—

Theda Goldman—sat on his hips. Peter heard the squishy sound as their bodies ground together and looked away. But he had already seen too much. He observed the woman—the fleshy woman—the knotted muscles of her thighs, the plateau of her belly and abdomen, the fullness of her swaying breasts. His skin began to tingle. He was sweating.

Peter knew he ought to run. There was no reason to linger now. He had found everything there was to know and ought now to hurry back to the refuge of his room to ponder in solitude and arrive at a clear and rational conclusion as to what specific actions should follow.

But his feet refused to budge. His eyes remained fixed.

Theda Goldman saw him. Her lips parted. She was smiling. Her head bobbed up and down. She extended a hand, crooked a finger, beckoned to him.

Peter stepped forward before he could make himself stop. Theda showed her teeth, ran her tongue across her lips, mouthed a name—his name.

Peter took another step. What did it matter? Alfie would never have hesitated—not even Schwerner would have. Peter was a man like them, wasn't he? He was made of blood and bones, flesh and muscle, balls and—

The mayor moaned. The sound served to snap the spell which held Peter. He threw his weight back on his heels, stumbled down the passageway, crashed through the door, staggered across the porch, and fell off the edge.

He picked himself up in an instant and ran. He circled the house. Cut across the lawn. Dashed into the street. Peter let the wind guide and direct him. His chest was on fire and threatened to burst. There didn't seem to be enough air in the world to fill his lungs. Still he ran, refusing to pause, knees churning like pistons, his feet seeming to soar above the ground without touching. He ran and ran and when he finally stopped, dropping to his hands and knees, there was a sound in his ears like a series of small explosions.

Peter lay on his back in a field of grass. He turned his head from side to side and eventually recognized the corner lot where children gathered on hot afternoons to play baseball, A short distance away the wind whipped through the infield dirt but here in the outfield all was tranquil and serene.

Of course he was finished—through. What had happened just now—his fall from grace—could neither be explained nor forgiven. As soon as his strength returned he would leave Winesap. He'd send Desmond Blue a cablegram—a simple message of resignation—and someone else would come in his place—Alfie or Schwerner or perhaps even Desmond himself—and then Theda Goldman and all the evil that she—

"Ah, there you are."

Peter lifted his head and saw a little girl in yellow shorts and white tee shirt approaching.

She was smoking a cigarette, pushing a bicycle.

"Ginger?" he said, sitting up, "What are you doing here?"

"Looking for you." She propped the bike on its kickstand and dropped down beside him. "How did you ever get all the way over here?"

"Well, I was... I was running."

"I know. I saw you take off like a rocket."

"You saw me?"

"You see...well, I've kind of been shadowing you lately."

He felt a flush of shame and turned his face away.

"What made you act like that anyway?" she asked. "I was scared you'd flipped out for good."

He shook his head. "You wouldn't understand."

"Try me. I'm smart for my age."

"They were having sexual congress, fornicating—the mayor and Theda Goldman. I saw them."

"So?"

He sighed. "It just…it just disturbed me, that's all."

"How come?"

"I found it disgusting."

"Why?"

"Look, it's a long story."

"The story of your life?"

He looked at her questioningly. "How did you know that?"

"I'm a good guesser." She stretched out in the lawn beside him and stuck a blade of grass in her mouth. So go ahead and tell me." The wind brushed her hair, spilling it across her face. "I'm in no big hurry."

So Peter told her. The story of his life. It was the first time he'd ever told anyone and perhaps it was because Ginger was so young that it seemed more as if he were talking to himself than to another person. He started at the beginning. With his birth.

"My mother was a famous person—if I told you her name you'd know her—and my father was even more famous. But they weren't married and my father wasn't in a position to acknowledge his parentage so I lived with my mother and saw my father only two or three times a year at most."

"That sounds familiar," she said.

"What does?"

"Having a lousy father."

Peter went on: "Then the slugs came. I was still a boy when that happened. We three were together, vacationing in a secluded resort in the Italian Alps where no one would know us. One morning I woke up and I was frightened. Things didn't seem right. There were There were portents in sky. I went to their room—which I'd been warned never to do—and opened the door. They weren't there. They were gone. Disappeared. Taken. I knew it the moment I looked in and saw the empty bed.

"You had a traumatic episode?"

"I…yes. I suppose I did."

"Then what?"

"Well, I went into shock. A catatonic fugue state, the doctors called it. I neither moved nor spoke. They sent me to a sanitarium in Switzerland where they used shock therapy to try and bring me around. Eventually it worked to the extent that I emerged from my fugue state but even then I still never talked. The sanitarium had a huge library. It had once belonged to Dr. Jung, a great psychiatrist. I spent all day in the library and often slept there at night. I read every book I could find on religion and philosophy and the so-called occult sciences. I felt I'd found the answer to many of the dilemmas I'd faced in the work of Gnostic scholars like Valentinus, Menander, and of course Simon Magus. All human suffering is physical in origin, I learned, a product of the flesh, while beauty, the divine spark, is a function of the buried soul. That was when I realized what I had to do. I opened my mouth and spoke for the first time in months and I told the doctors I was now ready to be released. They were flabbergasted hearing me speak and I was concerned some of them might go into traumatic shock themselves."

She laughed at that. "I wish I'd been there to see it."

"Well, of course they had to release me because by then I was officially an adult and of course I was very wealthy thanks to my parents. That was the first thing I took care of after my release. I gave all my money away. It's amazing how quickly it can be done when you really put your mind to it. I also gave away all my material possessions—houses, boats, aeroplanes, the works—everything I'd inherited. When I had nothing left, then I was ready to proceed on to the next step."

"You were going to bump yourself off," she said.

"How did you know that?"

She tapped the side of her head. "It only figures. I warned you I was a bright kid."

"Well, that was it all right: suicide. I now owned only one thing. An aeroplane—an experimental jet that had belonged to my father. Flying was my one great passion. So up in the air I went—over the

Mediterranean—and at twenty thousand feet I cut the engine, went into a dive and waited to die."

"Which you did," she said in a heavy mournful tone.

"Of course not." He frowned in irritation. "But I was badly hurt. I crashed somewhere in the Sahara Desert. In Morocco, I think, or perhaps Mali. But I was alive. Two men found my body in the twisted wreckage of the plane. One was a doctor, a scientist, who set to work saving me. When I recovered consciousness, I discovered that parts of my body had been replaced with polished steel. In other words, I had achieved my goal of physical transcendence without actually dying. I was prepared then to live out the remainder of my life on a purely spiritual plane. And I did too—until today."

"When you got excited?"

He gave a sad nod. "Well, yes. Yes, I did."

"The way Mrs. G. was keening and moaning I almost got turned myself—and I'm pre-pubescent."

"You mean you saw them too—what they were doing?"

"It was kind of hard to miss. When you're peeking in the window the way I was."

"Well, I'm sorry then."

"Why? What for?"

"What you saw is nothing a child your age should be exposed to."

"Hey, look, just because you had a little traumatic shock doesn't mean the rest of us can't have some fun seeing things we shouldn't."

"I don't know. Maybe you're right. A man I know—one of the two who saved my life in the desert—says I take too many things too seriously for my own good."

"That sounds like something Desmond Blue might say."

He stared at her. "You know Desmond?"

"He's my hero. I've been reading about him since I was a little kid. Studying all his famous cases. Why do you think I've been shadowing you everywhere you go? I found out you worked for him. I heard you and Roy talking the other day."

"I see." He looked glum. What kind of detective was he when a twelve-year-old girl knew more about what was going on than he did?

"Oh, by the way," she said, "if you're still fretting about burning Roy's library, you don't have to be. The books he had in his house were only there for show. The real thing—his real library—is a hundred times bigger and he's got them all hidden away at the old Berryman place up in the hills above town. I know you have to have heard of it."

"The name does sound familiar," he said.

"It ought to. One of Desmond Blue's greatest cases. Way before my time but there's people in town who remember it like it was yesterday. That's how come Roy knew it was the perfect place to hide his books. Everybody's scared to go up there. Even Fire Captain Brady, I bet."

"Then could you do me a favor, Ginger?" he said.

"What's that? Help you blow your brains out? No way. You want to do that, you're on your own." Ginger had a triumphant smile on her face.

"I guess that could wait," Peter said meekly.

"Till the case is over?"

"Well, at least until then."

"That's what I thought. She stood up. There were grass stains on her bare knees. "So tell me what it is you want me to do? If it's part of a real case—a Desmond Blue case—you name it, I'll do it."

"I'd like for you to keep an eye on Theda Goldman. For tonight at least. Do it without letting her see you. Do you think you can?"

"I tailed you all over town without you spotting me, didn't I? And you're supposed to be a detective. Theda should be a snap."

"Don't underestimate her. Theda's extremely dangerous and she…she's evil, I think. I saw it in her eyes just now."

"That wasn't the only part of her you saw just now."

Peter felt his skin tingle and was glad he was physically incapable of blushing. "Couldn't we forget about that."

"Sorry. I was baiting you. It's a rotten characteristic a lot of bright children have. I read that in a casebook once."

Peter came to his feet. The sun was already dipping below the horizon while the wind if anything seemed to have increased in velocity. He could feel dust pinging off his mask-like face and became acutely aware of the passage of time. "Look, Ginger, I have to get over to the Fire House. I was supposed to start my shift an hour ago. You ride your bike home, have something to eat, and then—"

"I'm not hungry," she said, showing a smile. "Too excited, I guess."

"Well, if you're sure. But be positive you keep a close watch on Theda. See who goes in and out of the house—especially Mayor Washington—and if she leaves for any reason try your best to follow her. After what happened this afternoon I think there's a strong possibility something important may occur as soon as tonight. She knows I'm aware of her presence here in Winesap and she may do something desperate as a result. I wouldn't go to work at all except that if I'm wrong I don't want to draw undue attention to myself. In the morning meet me in my room and I'll take over from there."

"Got you." Ginger stood up and held out her hand. "Partners?" she said.

Peter grasped her hand, squeezing cautiously. "Partners," he confirmed.

* * * *

When a short time later Peter walked into Fire House there was only one person at the card table. Hiram Evers glanced up from the solitaire hand spread in front of him and scowled, "Where the blazes you been hiding all day?"

"I'm sorry," Peter said. "I must have lost track of the time."

"The mayor was looking for you earlier and he was mad as a plucked hen when I couldn't turn you up."

Peter felt his mouth go dry. Had Theda Goldman moved against him already? He began to worry that it had been a mistake to come here as though nothing had happened. "I went for a walk around town. I ended up over at the ball field."

"In this weather?"

"I guess it has been kind of windy."

"Windy ain't the word. It's cold enough out there to freeze the pimples off a zombie's butt end."

"What did the mayor want with me?" Peter tried to sound casual. He sat down across the table from Evers.

"He didn't say. Something to do with this new policy of his, I imagine."

"What new policy is that?"

"This curfew thing—whatever you want to call it."

"I don't think I've heard about that."

"Then you're about the only one who hasn't. From now until further notice nobody's to go outside without a good excuse. All schools and businesses are shut down for the duration of the emergency. The mayor wants me and Bob Jones and probably you and some of the other Fire House boys to ride around town looking for violators, toss them in the clink if we catch any. The last time I can remember anybody getting put in jail was Harry Moss when he wouldn't stop flashing his dick in front of old ladies."

"But what would be the point of that? The curfew I mean. Won't people eventually starve when they run out of food?"

"The mayor's gonna set up a Meals on Wheels program. Use us firemen to do the delivering. I don't like it but what can you do?"

"I still don't understand," Peter said, shaking his head. "What's the point of it?"

"Making sure nobody can get away, I suppose."

"Get away from what?"

"The tridee, that's what." Evers dropped his voice as if suddenly concerned that someone might be listening in. "The mayor's turned the intensity level way the hell up. Watch ten minutes of that crap now and you're hooked for life."

"Did he tell you why?"

"Not a word. But I can guess. Whole thing happened right after he got back from banging dear Mrs. Goldman one more time. I figure she must have put the bee in his ear. The trouble is the two of them are gonna end up frying every brain in town and we'll all end up like the village idiot Stovalls."

"Where is everybody anyhow?" Peter said, lifting his head and looking around. Except for the two of them the Fire House seemed empty. "Shouldn't there be two volunteers here along with us?"

Evers spat on the floor. "That's supposed to be the rule but since starting tomorrow we're gonna be driving around town arresting numbskulls and delivering food I guess the rules don't apply no more." He spat again. "It's almost enough to make a fellow quit this day job except if I did I'd have to go home with the rest of them and watch tridee all day."

"I see."

"But I'm sure as hell keeping my beetle buggy good and charged up. If this town blows its stack the way I figure it might, I plan to be three counties away when the shit hits the fan. You want to come along with me, you're welcome."

"Why, thank you, Hiram," Peter said. "I appreciate the offer."

"Don't mention it. Us sane folk gotta stick together. It's like what happened during the French Revolution. You start chopping off heads it's hard to know when to stop." He picked up the deck of cards and shuffled. "Call your game, Pete," he said. "Long as we're cooped up here we might as well stay gainfully occupied."

"Gin rummy?" said Peter, who was finding it difficult to concentrate.

"Nickel a point."

Evers dealt out the cards.

* * * *

As the long night wore on Peter considered the advisability of sneaking away to see what was taking place elsewhere in town but had to bear in mind the possibility—however remote—that this whole thing might be a set-up and that Evers was here to see what his response might be and report back to the mayor. The entire shift therefore went by with the two of them seated at the card table and when it was over Hiram Evers was seventeen dollars and forty-five cents richer.

"That ought to rent me a decent whore my first night in Chicago if worse comes to worse," Evers said, rising to his feet and stretching. Outside the sun was up and shining. "I hear they got women for sale up there shave themselves bald all over."

"It must be another new fad," said Peter, who had never heard anything remotely of the kind.

"Well, it's certainly something to think about, ain't it?"

That was when the telephone rang. Evers went over and answered. He spoke briefly before hanging up the receiver with a bang. "That was Bob Jones. He says the mayor just phoned and said he was cancelling all further Fire House shifts starting immediately. For the duration of the emergency, he said. Looks like you and me might be the last two sailors off the boat, Pete."

As the two men stepped into the still chilly dawn Peter asked, "What are you going to do now, Hiram?"

"Me, I'm going home and grabbing some shuteye first if the old lady'll keep the volume on the tridee low enough to let me get my forty winks. Then I'll mosey on over to Pearson's and see if the mayor's come to his senses yet. See you there maybe?"

"I'll try," Peter said, without making a definite commitment. He wanted to keep his options open till he had a clearer idea of what exactly was going on.

"There's just one other thing I'd like to be sure of first," said Evers, holding lightly onto Peter's arm.

"What's that?"

"It's you, Pete. What your interest in all this happens to be. It was Theda Goldman recommended you to the mayor in the first place, I believe. She an old friend of yours from Chicago or something like that?"

"Oh, no," Peter said quickly. "I never met her before the night of the fire at her house."

"And she just kind of all of a sudden took a liking to you, huh?"

"I—I guess she must have," Peter said.

"Must be those hot pants of hers heating up again. If I was you, Peter," he winked lewdly, "I'd keep Mr. Pickle in my pants for the time being. That lady don't mean nobody no good. That includes you, pal."

"Thanks for the advice, Hiram. I'll keep that in mind."

"Stick with your little orphan friend. It's safer that way."

So Evers must know about Ginger and him too, Peter thought. "I—I'll do that."

"Smart idea."

Evers walked away, whistling.

* * * *

As he drew close to the Stovall house Peter noticed a lone figure sitting hunched on the front porch.

It was Roy Goldman.

He seemed to be asleep.

Peter gave him a shake. "Hey, Roy. Wake up."

Goldman's eyes popped open behind the thick lenses of his glasses. He seemed confused at first and then suddenly joyful. Springing to his feet he grabbed the bewildered Peter in a warm embrace. "Boy, am I ever glad to see you, buddy."

"Why? What is it? What are you doing here?"

"Waiting for you. You've got to help me."

"Help you how?"

"It's Jayne." Goldman jerked his head at the door behind. "She's in there alone. I think it's got her trapped."

"What does?"

"The tridee. I stood right next to her and screamed in her ear at the top of my lungs. It didn't faze her. Something awful is going on. It's like she's in a catatonic fugue state."

Peter quickly filled Goldman in on the mayor's new policy requiring everyone to stay indoors. "And Hiram says the mayor's also turned up the intensity of the tridee."

"That explains it then." His eyes burned with hate. "Well, he's gone too far this time, I'm telling you. I've been patient until now—bided my time—but after this—after what he's done to Jayne—turned her into a zombie—I swear I'll destroy him. I love her, Peter. I always have. Without her my life is meaningless."

To Peters astonishment Goldman began to cry. Peter sat down next to him and put a soothing arm around his shoulders. "What about your own wife, Roy? Don't you love her too?"

His head jerked up then. "Are you kidding? Theda's not my wife."

"But isn't she—?"

"She's a friend, sure. A sympathizer. Theda and I are working together to overthrow the mayor and every ugly thing he stands for. But, look, we don't have time to stand here talking. We've got to get in there and help Jayne. Say you'll go in with me, Peter. Please. I don't think I can do it alone."

"I'll be glad to help, Roy."

"God bless you," Goldman gave Peter another big hug and then stood up. He reached for the door and grabbed the knob. "Are you with me or not?" he said, his voice heavy with drama.

"I guess I am—sure."

"Then let's do it." Goldman hurled open the door. The moment he did a blast of sound poured through like a wave. Goldman lowered his head, clenched his fists at his sides, and plunged into the house. Peter went after him.

They reeled down the hall and turned into the living room.

As soon as he stepped inside, Peter staggered and nearly fell. It was far worse in here than he'd expected. The noise alone was awesome—unbearable—a blaring cacophony of discordantly clashing sounds—music, voices, bangs, clangs, clatters—all fused together into an anarchic symphony of lunatic noise—while the images that floated in the air seemed to make no sense at all. Color-drenched visions churned chaotically. A few shapes were clearly human—faces, figures, parts of the body—while others were puffy indistinct shapes that might have been meant to represent almost anything imaginable. A huge gray-and-black blot—a boulder perhaps—came speeding through the air. In spite of his awareness that it couldn't be real Peter automatically threw himself flat on the floor as it rocketed past overhead.

He felt a tug on his arm and looked up. Roy Goldman bent down trying to shout, but the noise level in the room made it impossible to understand a word. Peter shook his head. Goldman pointed with a finger. Peter followed his gesture and discovered in a corner a pair of shapes that seemed somewhat more substantial than the others flowing around them. It was Stovalls—Jayne and Oscar both. They were naked.

"Over there!" Goldman shouted, waving at Peter. "Let's get Jayne out of here first!"

The two men crept across the floor. A soldier in battle fatigues crawled past overhead. There was a horrible explosion and the man's belly burst open, spraying blood and gore. Peter covered his head with his hands but when he dared look again the soldier had vanished.

Goldman reached Jayne first. Kneeling down he put his lips close to her ear. The veins in his throat stood out like wires as he screamed at her. She appeared not to hear. He grabbed her arm and jerked on it. There was still no response.

Peter hurried around to the other side, put his arms under Jayne's shoulders and hauled her to her feet. She neither resisted nor helped him. When he tried to get her to stand on her own, her knees buckled under her. He'd have to drag her outside. But when he started doing just that, she suddenly began to fight back, squirming and kicking. A rocket came soaring out of nowhere aimed straight at his face. Automatically, Peter threw up his hands to shield himself. Jayne dropped to the floor. By the time the rocket had passed she'd crawled back to the sanctuary of the corner again.

Peter got Roy Goldman's attention. He pointed at Jayne. "You get her ankles!" he yelled. "I'll get her arms! We'll have to carry her out together! And don't pay any attention to all that stuff in the air! None of it's real!"

Goldman nodded. A disembodied breast a full meter wide floated past like a flesh-colored blimp. A chorus of hounds began to howl in unison.

Between the two of them, Goldman and Peter managed to lift Jayne off the floor. She was as limp as a rag doll. But when they started to carry her toward the door, she began to squirm and kick again. Caught by surprise, Goldman lost his hold on one ankle. When he reached down to grab it again Jayne kicked him hard in the face. He let out a yell and fell flat on the floor. Peter reluctantly let go of Jayne and bent down to help. "Are you hurt, Roy?" Peter shouted.

There was no answer. Goldman's expression was slack, his eyes vacant and staring into empty space. Clearly the tridee had him now. Peter knew there was only one thing to do.

He slapped him across the face as hard as he could.

Goldman seemed to snap back awake again. "Get me out of here," he mouthed. "Hurry. Please."

Peter took hold of Goldman around the waist and hauled him through the room, ignoring as well as he could the tangled imagery flowing around him. He made it to the door, pushed it open, and carried Goldman outside into the clean fresh air of the day. He set him down on the lawn and then hurried back to kick the door shut again.

"It isn't any use," Goldman said when Peter dropped down beside him. "We'll never get her out of there. If it hadn't been for you, I'd be in there myself."

"I know. I felt it too."

"Then there's only one thing left." Goldman managed to come to his feet.

Peter looked up at him. "You're not going back in there, I hope."

"No. That would be pointless. We both know that wouldn't work. We have to go to the source. The mayor. He's the one in control. We have to stop him."

He turned and hurried across the lawn.

Peter chased after him. "Roy, wait," he called. "What is it you have in mind?"

Goldman stood at the curb next to his beetle buggy. "Are you still with me or not?"

"I'm not sure," Peter admitted, wondering if this was really what he ought to be doing. And what about Theda? What was her place in all this? Roy said she was his friend, his ally. They were working together. But how could that be?

While Peter stood there pondering, Goldman went around and climbed inside the buggy. He started the engine, looked back at Peter. "I said are you coming or aren't you?"

When Peter didn't answer he drove off, tires squealing as he rocketed around the nearest corner.

"What got into Roy?" said a voice.

Peter turned around and saw Ginger Cunningham standing with her bike.

"It's the tridee," he said. "The mayor's turned up the intensity and everybody's gone crazy."

"I know. I heard. It's why I'm staying out here till it blows over."

"I think Roy's gone to try and kill the mayor."

She laughed. "Fat chance of that. Roy couldn't kill a bug if it rolled over on its back and said please squash me."

"No, he's serious. It's Jayne." He nodded back at the house. "She's trapped in the living room. Oscar's in there too."

"Good. Best place for them both."

He suddenly remembered something. "What are you doing here anyhow? I thought you were supposed to be keeping an eye on Theda Goldman."

"I did. That's why I came to get you. Something's up."

"What is?"

"Theda. She's up at the old Berryman place. You know, where Roy hides his books. She's been in there since the sun came up this morning. Roy dropped her off there. It must have been before he came here and found out his lady love's gone batty again. I tried to look in the window and see what she's up to but you can't. Some-body's painted over the glass with black paint. Guess who?"

"That's odd," he said.

"What did I tell you?" She slapped the handlebars. "So why don't you climb on and we'll go have a look around?"

"At the Berryman place?"

"The old haunted house, right. Unless you've got a better idea."

He didn't. "I'm still worried about Roy though."

"Don't be. Like I said he'll be fine. The mayor pulls this every few months. Turns up the intensity level, makes sure everybody's hooked in nice and tight, then dials things back down again."

"Really?"

"Would I lie to you? Now hop on. We better get to moving."

Peter hopped on. They wobbled off down the street, picking up speed as they went.

A PROFILE: THE BERRYMAN FAMILY

There is fact and there is conjecture and there also is truth, the latter most often consisting of a careful fusing of the two preceding. In profiling the Berryman family of Winesap, Illinois, it is therefore prudent to commence with a statement of fact, proceed to a recitation of conjecture, and conclude with a tentative version of the truth.

The facts are these:

The first Berryman to appear in Winesap was old Josiah Berry-man who arrived in town mounted on a mule in the year of Senator Douglas's controversial Kansas-Nebraska Act. Old Josiah was a man of considerable stature, black-bearded, with bleak sunken eyes and lips as thin and straight as iron rails. With the gold coins he carried in his leather saddlebags, he purchased title to two plots of land within the town limits: the first at the corner of Main and Poplar downtown and the second perched at the summit of a high hill then nameless but later popularly known as Berryman Hill. With his own two hands old Josiah Berryman raised a modest wood cabin on the hilltop and then with a roof over his head proceeded to devote his days to construct-ing on the Main and Poplar lot a large single-roomed building, above the doorway of which when finished he nailed a neat hand-lettered sign reading, "Berryman's General Store." In the store old Josiah

Berryman came to stock a variety of materials including seeds and grains, hand tools and farm implements, linens and yard goods. Berryman's General Store was an immediate success with the citizens of Winesap since prior to its existence the nearest such store had been a twenty-seven-mile overland trip away and this success coming in spite of the fact that old Josiah Berryman was an unfriendly, reticent man who never spoke one word when a lesser number would serve as well.

It was during the first summer of the War of the Slaveowner's Rebellion when Josiah Berryman closed his store early one afternoon, bolting the doors securely and shuttering the windows, and rode forth from town on his mule. He was absent sixteen days and when he reappeared on a buckboard drawn by two mules there rode at his side a scrawny woman with the eyes like a hawk and a bonnet pulled down to cover her ears. In July of the following year this woman was delivered in the hilltop cabin of a boy named Josiah Berryman Jr. and within an hour of the birth of her son she was pronounced dead—the certificates of both birth and death endorsed simultaneously by a single hand, one Dr. Sheridan Cuthcart.

No citizen of Winesap—with the obvious if brief exception of Dr. Cuthcart—was to set eyes upon young Josiah Berryman Jr. until nine years after his birth when he appeared one day without warning behind the counter of his father's general store and set immediately to work as if he had been there every day of his life. By this time the store was three times its original size and sold among other products the famous McCormick reapers from Chicago. When a delegation of ladies shortly thereafter confronted Josiah Berryman Sr. to enquire as to why his son was not enrolled in the town school, he looked at them with a chilling stare and uttered three distinct words in his own defense: "Ain't no necessity." Since the boy could clearly read and write adequately and perform basic arithmetical calculations—no one could recollect even a minor error in one of his bills—the ladies chose to let the matter drop.

In the year of the Great Pullman Strike five events occurred one after another in Winesap like birds in a line of flight. Firstly, old Josiah Berryman expired suddenly of apparent brain fever one humid summer afternoon while working the counter of his store. Secondly, young Josiah Berryman Jr. erected on the hilltop lot with the assistance of town labor a three-story house painted white and blue with twin turrets and more than twenty-five glass windows. Thirdly, the old wood cabin was battered to the ground by men armed with axes and the lumber carted away to be sold as firewood. Fourthly, a second Berryman General Store was opened in a nearby town amid much ceremony and hoopla including a brass band that played a selection of patriotic songs. And fifthly and lastly, Josiah Berryman Jr. appeared on Main Street one afternoon riding in an open carriage drawn by two white horses and perched at his side was a plump rosy-cheeked woman with the yellow eyes of a cat, whom he later introduced around town as his bride. The year following on a stormy night Dr. Jason Fullerton was summoned to the house on the hilltop and when he returned home some hours later was ghostly pale of face, filthy drunk, and wealthier than he had ever been before. Still drunk, Dr. Fullerton committed suicide two months later and another ten months after that a new doctor, one Vincent Byers, visited the Berryman house to deliver a healthy strapping eight-pound boy given the name William James Berryman whose mother like her husband's own mother failed to survive the birth of her child by more than an hour.

By the year of Teddy Roosevelt's Bull Moose campaign there existed a total of forty-seven Berryman General Stores scattered throughout the townships and hamlets of rural Illinois, Indiana, Ohio, and Missouri, and there could no longer be the slightest question that Josiah Berryman Jr. was far and away the richest man not only in Winesap but the surrounding counties as well. He was more sociable than his late father had been and even though he was never known to accept an invitation to any gathering, public or private, he was quite willing to utter as many as seven and eight words at a clip in response to such pointed queries as "How are you today, sir?" or "What do you think of this screwy weather we've been having lately, Mr. Berryman?"

His son—William James—was even more outgoing. Bright, cheerful, gay, inordinately popular with his peers, he attended public schools in Winesap until the year of the sinking of the *Lusitania,* at which time to the dismay of many local mothers with adolescent daughters he departed town by train one glorious autumn day in order to attend a university in the East, an institution known as Princeton. There were afterward rumors—neither denied nor confirmed by his father—that the boy had seen service as a lieutenant in the American Expeditionary Force and suffered a grievous wound while saving the lives of nine of his company while under horrendous Hun fire in the Belleau Wood. It wasn't in fact until a full nine years later—in the month of Lindbergh's transatlantic odyssey—that William James Berryman returned to the town of his birth on the occasion of his father's tragic demise while at the wheel of his brand new Cadillac sedan after running through the town's one and only red light and colliding with a telephone pole. After consulting with the Springfield lawyers who had hastened by train to oversee the estate of the deceased, young William James Berryman entered the town's most notorious speakeasy, took up a table, purchased a bottle of the worst Detroit bootleg gin available, and proceeded to get rip roaring drunk. At some point after midnight with quick and dexterous hands he managed to remove every last shred of clothing from the supple frame of a former high school classmate, one Molly Gray, revealing to the eyes of those fortunate enough to be present her vanilla breasts, curlicue nipples, and pubic bush like the pelt of a Golden Seal.

For over a week William James Berryman remained in seclusion within the speakeasy's four walls—never forced to imbibe alone, it should be noted—and would most certainly have been placed under arrest as a common drunk had it not been for the fact that even men as hard of heart as the town's four police officers could not help sympathizing with the grief of a young man only lately deprived of the succor of his extremely wealthy father.

On the tenth day his friends arrived. It was a wholly unprecedented event for the town as the two dozen noisy young men clad in striped jackets and straw boaters poured forth from the train, engaging a fleet of taxis at the station to ferry them up to the Berryman hilltop house. That was when the party commenced, and from that day forward jangly jazz music oozed from the house at all hours night and day with the relentlessness of ocean waves crashing on the beach while young daughters were warned by vigilant parents to stay well clear of that iniquitous hilltop den, a caution violated only twice—once by the aforementioned Molly Gray, who stayed a month and a half, and once by Beatrice Nye, who stayed only one night but who later gave birth in a distant town to twin boys.

The party went on for weeks and weeks and while some of the young men in their jackets and boaters did indeed soon depart others quickly arrived to take their place. It was on a cool day early in November when the female stranger sashayed from the train with a platinum hairdo, scent of city perfume, wad of chewing gum in her cheek, skirt as tight as a sailor's knot, breasts like almonds, legs like candelabra sheathed in silk stockings, and drawled at the station agent, "Hey, honey, gimme a sheet of paper, a pencil." She then composed a short note, folded the paper neatly in two, and instructed the agent—Theodore Bilbo—to give it to the taxi driver—Benjamin Latimore—to deliver into the hands of William James Berryman personally. The note (as testified to by both Messiers Brady and Latimore) read as follows:

> BILLY BOY—Well here I is. What a gay shithole you live in baby
> If you've found the right preacher then I'm still your gal Sal.

The very next day the Reverend Maxfield Blake of Bishop, Missouri, arrived in Winesap by train, taxied up to the hilltop house, remained inside less than an hour, and emerged white as a bedsheet, never uttering one word and rewarding his driver—Ben Latimore again—with the most generous tip of his entire taxi driving career.

The great party ended that day. The young men in their striped jackets and straw boaters descended in mass from the big house on the top of Berryman Hill like a swarm of locust in search of new fields to devour and by nightfall were gone from the town forever. William James Berryman, sallow of cheek, scarlet of eye, stubble of chin, followed the next day, catching the noon express to Chicago, where he proceeded to fill the next half-century of his life managing the vicissitudes of the family mercantile fortune. Less than a week after his departure a mischievous boy named Spike O'Donnell, assuming the hilltop house to be vacant, snuck up close to have a quick looksee when a young woman with platinum hair wearing a pink satin nightgown threw open the front door and shouted, "Hey, little shithead, get the fuck off my property!" Over the years that followed deliveries of food arrived weekly at the house, the yard was kept neat and tidy by hired workmen, bills were paid diligently always on time, lights were seen burning from dusk to dawn, and on occasion a passing motorist would report having glimpsed the pale face of a woman peering forlornly from a high window like a sea captain's wife awaiting a long overdue ship.

In the year of the hippie riot at the Democratic National Convention in Chicago a telephone voice claiming to be William James Berryman requested Tom Dobbs of the mortuary firm Dobbs & Dobbs to see that a hearse was dispatched to the Berryman home and when the vehicle arrived a short time later the driver discovered on the front porch bundled in a bedsheet the copse of a middle-aged Caucasian female dead as a mackerel. The woman was subsequently—and quietly—interred in the town cemetery beneath a marble headstone engraved Sally Marx Berryman (1906-1968) RIP, and shortly thereafter when a gang of out-of-town thieves attempted to break into the Berryman house they found the doors securely bolted from the inside and the windows covered with wire mesh that glowed red hot if tampered with. The regular weekly deliveries of food continued; workmen tidied and kept up the yard; bills were paid diligently on time; lights burned from dusk to dawn; but no further faces were glimpsed in any of the windows.

Then came the fatal year when the entities popularly known as the slugs or Occupants visited Earth, stopped time in its tracks, and proceeded to make certain alterations and revisions to the status quo of the universe including the destruction of several cities and the apparent death or disappearance of a considerable number of leading personages. Although the direct effects of the Occupancy upon the hamlet Winesap were minimal (loses limited to a mayor, several preachers, one priest and a rabbi) it was a mere two days afterward when a frail old man in a chauffeured limousine passed through downtown Winesap and was promptly identified by those few senior enough to recall as none other than William James Berryman. The limousine climbed to the house on the hilltop where the old man produced a set of keys from a pocket, unlatched the front door, stepped inside, and did not reemerge for some thirty-seven minutes. When he did he got only as far as the bottom porch step before keeling over and when rushed to the city hospital was solemnly pronounced dead on arrival.

Such are the facts as generally known regarding the Berrymans of Winesap Illinois.

What follows is sheer conjecture:

—that Josiah Berryman Sr. had signed a pact in blood with the devil guaranteeing himself earthly riches in return for the souls of himself and all his male descendants;

—that William James Berryman had attempted to void this pact by fleeing first to Princeton, then to war, and finally to Chicago but had been drawn inexorably back to the house of his ancestors to die in his footsteps;

—that the nameless wives of both Josiah Berryman Sr. and Josiah Berryman Jr. were consorts of Satan sent to mate with the Berrymans and bring forth the cursed children who bore that blighted name;

—that the young woman with the platinum hair—Sally Marx Berryman—was the devil's own whore spurned by the pure and decent soul of William James Berryman; or that Sally Marx Berryman was actually an angel of divine mercy sent from heaven to stand guard over the pure and decent soul of William James Berryman; opinions here differed;

—that all Berrymans were nothing but a bunch of blood-sucking vampires out of the swamps of Transylvania who hung upside down from the rafters and could turn themselves into wolves and rats and chickens and only silver bullets drenched in the menstrual blood of a virgin could kill them;

—that something—some *thing*—lived in the attic (or basement) of the Berryman house;

—that there was a logical scientific explanation; that Josiah Berryman Sr. was an embezzler; that Sally Marx was the granddaughter of one those he embezzled and who sought to extort money from William James Berryman who shot and killed her and then hired another woman, an obscure actress, to impersonate her for forty years;

—that the wife of Josiah Berryman Sr. was his own third cousin and that the sin of incest cursed the Berryman name unto the last generation;

—that William James Berryman was a homosexual invert who married the beautiful Sally Marx in an attempt to rid himself of his own foul tendencies only to fail to assert his manhood on his wedding night and fled his home in shame;

—that things living in the Berryman house crept out on moonless nights to devour bad children as they slept;

—that Sally Marx was in actuality the illegitimate daughter of Josiah Berryman Jr. and that Marx was her adoptive name and that she never married;

—that Josiah Berryman Jr. left his entire fortune to his daughter Sally Marx and this was how William James Berryman survived the Occupancy (by two days anyhow) when every other person of his wealth and fortune vanished;

—that William James Berryman was flat broke by the time of the Occupancy, having lost his inherited fortune over the years in blackmail payments and deals with the devil;

—that the Occupants came to Earth in search of William James Berryman and somehow managed to miss him;

—that God was behind everything that happened;

—that there was no God and never had been;

—that there had been a God once upon a time but the Occupants took Him away with them when they left;

—that everything was a conspiracy;

—that nothing in the whole cosmos made an iota of sense if you ever sat back and really put your mind to thinking about it.

But all of the above was pure conjecture until fused with the facts in case in order to produce—magically—the truth:

There was absolutely nothing unusual or extraordinary about Josiah Berryman Sr. He was a man much like the majority of men of his time, born in a New England farming community of dirt poor Puritan stock, naturally glum and reticent even as a boy who spent the best years of his youth laboring like an animal in the rocky fields of other men until he at last managed to put together a big enough stake to allow him to set out west in search of a life of his own. He chose Winesap in which to settle down because his rear end was blistered from mule-riding and he opened his general store at the corner of Poplar and Main because his stake was too small for a hotel or a saloon and because he'd be damned in the eyes of the Lord before he'd grub one more minute in the black soil he'd come to loathe. The scrawny eagle-eyed woman he married was one Lucy Farley Faraday, fifth, last, and homeliest daughter of a Massachusetts mill hand, who twelve years before during a drunken poker game had granted Josiah Berryman Sr. the sole right to her hand should he ever succeed in accumulating a fortune worth sneezing at. Josiah Berryman Sr. did not forget this promise and when the time came returned to claim as his bride the woman who had waited patiently all those years for the only man who had ever wanted her because the truth was that for whatever reason Josiah Berryman Sr. loved Lucy Farley Faraday in that deep and mysterious sense that silent men often love when they love at all and when she died giving birth to the son they both desperately sought he came naturally to despise the sight of the boy, driving him day and night like a senseless beast behind the counter of his general store until the boy—to the shock of both—came to resemble his father in almost every aspect that mattered.

There was thus nothing unusual or extraordinary about Josiah Berryman Jr. either except perhaps for the burning will to make himself rich which derived largely from simple exhaustion after all those backbreaking years behind the counter of his father's general store and his observation that rich men certainly seemed to work less hard than poor men. The woman he came to marry—plump and cat-eyed—was Harriet Shaw Stevenson, younger sister of a drummer who traveled in caps and bonnets and who once described her to the storekeeper as a young lady of beauty and wonder and since Josiah Berryman Jr. strongly felt the need for a wife to tend the big hilltop house he married her even when she proved to be neither beautiful nor wondrous.

Soon enough like his own father before him Josiah Berryman Jr. came to love the woman he'd married in a deep and mysterious sense that kept his heart pounding when she entered a room and their lips met and hands touched and it was like nothing he had ever guessed existed under God's heaven. After a year of marriage came the stormy night when Dr. Jason Fullerton was summoned from the town below to deliver the child born and named Josiah Berryman III and when Dr. Fullerton emerged from the birthing room he first made Josiah Berryman Jr. share a bottle of whiskey with him and then reported that although the boy was healthy enough he wasn't entirely right either since he was gnarled and twisted like a tree kept out of the sun and had no ears and a thing like a snout instead of a nose and hair that covered his body like a rug even though he had just been born and hands that hung down to his kneecaps, In revulsion and horror after viewing his son Josiah Berryman Jr. gave Dr. Fullerton a substantial sum to keep his mouth shut and the boy was placed in a windowless basement room behind a thick oak door where no one but his parents would ever see him or know for sure that he existed. A year later a second healthy son came along and was given the name William James Berryman and within an hour of his birth his mother was dead with the consequence that Josiah Berryman Jr. who had loved only once in his life came to love a second time after stumbling downstairs to the basement room and hurling open the thick oak door and clutching the twisted body of his eldest son in arms. They hugged and comforted one another and for years afterward Josiah Berryman Jr. spent many pleasurable hours in the company of Josiah Berryman III and sometimes his other son William James Berryman would creep downstairs and put his ear against the basement door and hear voices murmuring from within—the father whom he recognized and another soft voice that meant nothing to him. It wasn't until William James Berryman was grown and ready to depart by train for Princeton that his father revealed the secret and led him to the basement room and opened the door with a set of keys and said here is your brother and what William James Berryman saw was a naked monster covered in fur with burning yellow eyes and breath that came from a snout and pushing his father aside he fled wordlessly from the basement room and went east to Princeton and then to war and finally to years of self-imposed exile in Paris and New York City until word arrived of the death of Josiah Berryman Jr. He returned home at once to claim the fortune which he now believed would alone give meaning to his life but when he entered the old house on the hilltop a quartet of solemn lawyers from Springfield advised that the entire estate had been left in the name of his older brother Josiah Berryman III who—it was their understanding—was a permanent invalid unable to receive visitors. William James Berryman reacted hysterically when he heard this and went into town and got rip roaring drunk and sent telegrams to everyone he knew and said come on out and meet me at the old homestead here and we'll have ourselves one hell of a blast. A hell of a blast it was too with hot jazz music playing on the gramophone all day and night and every few hours William James Berryman slipped away to deposit a tray of food outside the thick oak door in the basement and when he came back it would always be gone. One afternoon as he slept in the same bed he had occupied as a child he woke to a gentle touch and looked up to discover a monster looming over him. Well, what is it you want now, brother? he asked in a voice heavy with bitterness. Do you intend to turn me out? It is your home and your fortune and I have no right to be here except at your tolerance but Josiah Berryman III speaking in a calm cultivated voice explained that all he wanted was to reach a fair and equitable bargain, that he had little personal need for wealth and would gladly relinquish control of the family fortune in return for something he could actually use. He then went on to describe how in the years he had lived alone in this house with only his father for company he had devoted the bulk of his energies to a careful and fastidious exploration of his intellectual self, that he had read diligently and thought extensively in all matters of science and art and philosophy and had by now attained a stature in life where he believed it was time to explore a different aspect of his character, namely his physical self—his body and emotions and passions—but that in order to do this properly he would require another human being with whom to share his quest. William James Berryman asked his brother if he would mind telling him what the hell he was talking about and Josiah Berryman III replied that he was talking about a woman—someone who would be his wife. William James Berryman said he thought that was the most ridiculous thing he'd heard in his life but the next day remembered a girl he'd known in New York named Sally Marx who was always out for the main chance and sent her a carefully worded cablegram explaining how she could live like a queen till the day she died. When Sally Marx appeared in Winesap a few days later William James Berryman had her brought to the house on the hilltop and finally at her insistence led the way downstairs to the basement room and said here is your husband and she looked and laughed and said you must be out of your mind if you think anything is going to get me to marry that monster but Josiah Berryman III interceded and asked that he and Sally Marx be left alone for one hour and when William James Berryman came back he found Sally Marx quiet and subdued and subtly changed with her clothes slightly disarrayed and her make-up smeared and she told him that they had decided to go ahead and see this thing through. The wedding took place the following day in the basement room and afterward William James Berryman closed up the house and shook hands with his brother and stared long and hard at his sister-in-law and told them that if either ever needed any-

thing he'd be in Chicago drunk on his ass. After decades of silence
there came a phone call one afternoon in which Josiah Berryman III
said that Sally Marx was dead and William James Berryman promised to have the matter taken care of with another woman on her way
inside the week, a young and lovely girl, but Josiah Berryman III said
that would not be necessary because he intended to devote the remaining years of his life to completing the careful and diligent exploration of his spiritual self that he began some years earlier with absolutely amazing results thus far and William James Berryman
suggested that if that was indeed the case then perhaps it would be in
the interest of both if a final legal transfer of the family estate could
now be transacted but Josiah Berryman III just laughed and told his
brother that wouldn't be a very wise, that it would in fact be the last
thing in the world either would want to have happen now. More years
went by and one day the slugs came to Earth and took millions of
people away with them and William James Berryman was brought to
the realization that the sole reason he was still alive was because his
brother must now be dead. He journeyed to Winesap to see for himself and when he entered the big hilltop house it was dark and silent
and filled with dangling cobwebs and shifting shadows and when he
went downstairs and opened the heavy oak door there was no one in
the room, only a sheet of fresh white paper neatly folded on the floor.
William James Berryman picked up the paper and read the message
written there and shook his head and stared at the high ceiling and the
invisible sky that lay beyond it and whatever mysterious realm might
lie beyond that. *I've been called and gone away*, said the note, and
understanding the probable meaning and possible implications of
that simple declarative sentence William James Berryman burned the
note and scattered the ashes and mounted the stairs and headed outside but his heart hadn't been worth a plug nickel in ages and the
front porch was as far as he'd got.

(In the years that followed the Berryman fortune became the subject of much complex litigation with the end result that the old house
on the hill in Winesap was allowed to fall into ruin and one day a
round-faced man with a crew cut and thick eyeglasses broke into
the house and went to the basement and set to work with carpenter's
tools he had brought with him. The noise of his work prompted a
handful of stories about ghosts haunting the old house but when a

short time later various townspeople began to vanish amid tales of madness and despair only a very few persons thought to draw any connection between the one and the other. Nevertheless, a private detective named Desmond Blue was hired to look into the mystery and he wandered around town several days asking seemingly aimless question until one moonless night dressed all in black he crept up to the old house on the hilltop and slipped silently through the back door and descended on soft feet toward a light burning in the basement.)

11

The old blue-and-white relic of the Berryman place stood at the top of the hill on the outskirts of Winesap, the Heartland City of America. As Ginger Cunningham pedaled her bike up the winding road that led past the house, her breath came in short sharp gasps. Perched on the handlebars, Peter Mark kept offering to switch places but Ginger was stubborn as only a girl of twelve can be and told him there wasn't any need. "I'm a whole lot tougher than I look," she assured him, in between gasps. "I just smoke too much."

The first thing Peter noticed when they drew up in front of the house was Roy Goldman's beetle buggy parked in the jungle of weeds and burnt yellow grass that served as a front lawn with the driver's side door hanging wide open. The fierce wind which had blown all night had eased with the coming of day but it was still powerful enough to send Ginger's hair flapping across her face. Brushing it aside, she nodded at the bug. "Looks like Roy beat us here. So now what?"

"I guess we go inside and find out what's going on."

She seemed hesitant. "You're sure about that?"

"Why? You're not afraid, are you?"

"This old place gives me the chilly willies. I followed Roy up here and looked in the window that one time but I've never gone inside. It's supposed to be haunted, you know."

"Don't be silly. There's no such thing as ghosts," Peter assured her. "Even if there were, Desmond got rid of them the time he was here."

What if he missed one?"

"Well, then I guess we—"

He stopped at the sound of a loud engine. Both he and Ginger managed to duck down out of sight just as a large truck drove into view around the corner of the house, bumped across the yard spraying dirt and weeds in its wake, and headed off down the road toward town. Peter popped his head up long enough to catch a glimpse of a dazed looking Roy Goldman behind the wheel.

"You want to go after him?" Ginger asked, nodding at her bike.

"Not yet. Let's check out the house first and see what's inside. Theda's still in there, remember."

"I just hope she's alone. No ghosts, I mean."

"You can stay out here if you want."

"Thanks but no, thanks. I may be a chicken but I'm not a dumb chicken. Besides, if you run trouble somebody's got to be there to bail you out."

Peter used his shoulder to force open the front door. The lock was old and rusty and gave way with ease. Immediately inside was a big empty room with a low ceiling. Cobwebs hung like dusty icicles in the corners while dust balls drifted lazily across the floor propelled by unseen drafts. Peter wandered through two more similar rooms until he reached another door near the back of the house. He tried the knob. The door opened on a flight of stairs leading down into the basement below.

"Isn't this the part where the detective pulls out his gat?" Ginger said.

"I don't have a gun."

"Now he tells me."

"Come on," he said. "Let's have a look."

They went down the steps, moving cautiously. The basement turned out to be a far cry from the dust-choked rooms above. It was clean and neat. The walls looked recently painted. Florescent lights in the ceiling gave off an eerie glow.

"Hello!" Peter called out. "Anybody home?"

There was no answer.

Much of the space had been partitioned off into a several small separate rooms, barely more than cubicles. Peter started to look inside the nearest but Ginger pulled him back.

"Don't," she said.

Peter looked at her in surprise. "Why not?"

"I don't know. Just don't—okay?"

He shrugged. "Well, if you want. But what about the books? Can you tell me where it was you saw them?"

She considered a moment and then pointed down the central passageway. "Down that way, I think. It was around the back of the house where I found the window and looked through."

Peter went first, glancing inside the various small rooms as they went past. They all looked empty. Eventually they ran into a concrete wall, turned right, and followed another passageway past still more cubicles. At its end the passageway opened into a much larger room.

Ginger pointed to a window high up on the opposite wall. "That's where I looked through," she said. "The books were here—piled up in boxes."

"Well, there's nothing here now."

"Roy must be moving them. In that truck he was driving, I bet."

"Seems likely."

"What do you think? Is he trying to skip town?"

"He didn't act that way this morning, no.

"I don't think he'd leave without Jayne anyway. He must have something else in mind. So what do we do?"

"Try to catch up with him, I guess."

"On the bike?"

"I guess so."

Peter started to turn to retrace his steps but something caught his eye. In a far corner under the window there was a single book lying on the floor.

He went over and picked it up. It was an old book, bound in black leather and smelling of antiquity. He opened it to the title page:

Mysterion
Marcel de Sarnot
Paris
MDCCXCV

"1795, Peter said. "Just as the Reign of Terror ended."

He flipped through the pages with Ginger hanging over his shoulder. "What language is that? It's not French, is it?"

"No, it's Latin."

"Can you read it?"

"A little," he said.

"What's it about?"

"Nothing," he said, slamming the book shut. His face was flushed.

"Is it that scary?"

"No. It's…it's pornographic."

"You mean it's a dirty book?"

"Yes, very."

"That doesn't sound like Roy. But you never know, right? Maybe underneath all the blubber he's a raging sex fiend at heart."

Then a new voice suddenly sounded: "I don't believe that belongs to you."

Peter turned at the sound. Theda Goldman stood looking at him, her hand extended. There was a gun in it.

"Give it here, please," she said.

"Why should I?" Peter held the book away. "So you can burn it?"

"Burn it? Burn a book? Me? So far as I'm aware, you're the only one here who's made a habit of burning books."

Peter prickled with guilt. "You know why I did that. It was because of you and your…your conspiracy. The Sect."

"That's absurd," she said.

"Is it? You can't deny that you're behind everything that's happened in this town."

"Why can't I? I only arrived in Winesap a short time ago."

"You're forgetting something, aren't you? I saw you yesterday with Mayor Washington. You'll never get me to believe that what's going on here—the curfew, the tridee, everything else—that it's not all because of you."

"I may have offered a suggestion or two but it was purely for Roy's benefit, not mine."

"Roy? He's one of you too?"

"My God." She tittered with amusement. "Not hardly."

"Then why try to blame him for your own—your own sins?"

She balanced a hand on her hip and peered at him long and hard. "Precisely how much do you know, Mr. Mark?"

"A lot more than you think," said Peter, trying to brazen it out.

"So you keep saying but I get the strong impression—"

There was a sudden sharp noise like the snapping of a taut spring.

Theda peered quizzically up at the ceiling.

Clang!

A metal slab dropped down from the above, sliding firmly into place and cutting the room neatly in half with Theda on one side and Peter and Ginger on the other.

From the other side of the slab, Peter heard Theda scream.

He couldn't believe their luck. "Come on," he yelled at Ginger. "Let's get out of here."

The two of them turned and ran back in the direction they'd come from. Behind, he heard what he thought was a gunshot. It made only a hollow pinging noise coming from the other side of the steel slab. He looked back and saw to his surprise that the slab was moving.

He stopped and pointed. "Good God," he said, "she'll be crushed."

In the silence they could hear Theda scream. She fired off another shot. It pinged.

"Wow," said Ginger, "just like Edgar Allan Poe."

"What do you mean?"

"In Poe's story 'The Pit and the Pendulum,' one of the devices the Inquisition uses to torture people is a room where the walls slowly move inward and crush whoever's inside."

"That's ghastly," he said.

"Well, it's only a story."

There were more screams coming from Theda. Louder and more frantic. Peter looked around the room. "There must be some way of stopping it. Do you see any controls?"

"Not here—no."

He went over and banged on steel wall. It continued to slide forward inches at a time. "Theda, the controls!" he called out. "Where are they? How do I turn this thing it off?"

The muffled voice from the other side was hard to understand.

"I think she said upstairs," Ginger said.

"Did you say upstairs?" he shouted. "Theda, are the controls up there?"

This time her voice was loud enough to be audible. "Yes! In the master bedroom! Hurry! My God, please hurry!"

Peter raced for the staircase. He had just reached the bottom step when from behind a long strangled cry of anguish and horror resounded.

Then another sound: *clang!*

As the metal slab rose back into place in the ceiling.

He sat down on the bottom step and put his head in his hands.

"Want to go back and take a look?" Ginger said.

"No! And you're not going back there either!" He grabbed her arm. "Let's get out of here!"

"I told you the place was haunted," she said, as he pulled her up the stairs.

* * * *

Once outside they stopped and tried catching their breath. Ginger reached under the waistband of her shorts, extracted a crumbled package of Camel cigarettes, stuck one in the corner of her mouth, and lit it with a match. She exhaled a cloud of dirty gray smoke. "I'm sorry," she said. "I suppose I should've told you."

"Told me what?" said Peter.

"When I looked through the window that time it wasn't just the books I saw. I also saw Roy playing around with those rooms down there. They've got all sorts of weird stuff rigged up in them. Pits and pendulums—the whole works. Torture chambers."

"And Roy did that?"

"I doubt it. I think they've been there a long time. Since the Berrymans maybe."

"I see," he said.

"Well, at least you got away with that book she wanted."

He looked down it. The book—*Mysterion*—was still in his hand. "But it's just…filth."

Peter stood up and took a last look back at the house. "We'd better get going," he said, pointing.

In the town below smoke could now be seen rising in the wind.

* * * *

They took Roy's beetle buggy. The keys were still in the ignition.

As they headed back down the winding road leading into Winesap, Peter spotted a dozen separate places where smoke could be seen rising into the sky. "Fires," he said grimly. "Lots of fires everywhere."

"What do you think it means?" Ginger said from beside him. She'd lit another of her Camel cigarettes.

"I don't know," he said, "but with this wind it could really get nasty."

The hill swooped to an end and they entered the tree-lined streets of residential Winesap. Peter spotted one of the columns of smoke not too far ahead and aimed the bug in that direction. The sidewalks were as empty as before. Through the windows of the houses they passed the telltale flicker of tridee could be seen.

When they reached the fire, Peter left the bug in the middle of the street and hopped out. Dense clouds of smoke drifted from the broken windows of a white frame house while flames driven by the wind danced across the roof. A family of four dressed in pajamas and robes—father, mother, two small boys—stood on the lawn, gazing back at their burning home. Peter hurried over and asked the man, "Is this your house, sir?"

"Sure is," he said in an oddly detached voice. "Looks like she's going to burn right on down to the ground, don't it?"

"Shouldn't you call somebody?" Peter said.

"Who you got in mind, friend?"

"Well, the fire department, I suppose."

The man laughed. "Hells bells, they already been here and gone. Who do you think started the fire?"

"You mean you had books hidden in there?"

"What would I be doing with a stupid book? No, a man brought them by first. A big pile of them. Brought them into the living room where we were watching a show and left them there. Then the fire-man showed up and lit them on fire like it was a Fourth of July bon-fire. He helped us get out before we got burned up too."

"I really don't want to miss my program," the woman was say-ing, tugging on her husband's sleeve. "You sure it wouldn't be all right to go back in and catch the end?"

"The fireman said it wasn't safe, remember?"

Peter went back to the car and started the engine.

"Where now?" Ginger asked. "More fires?"

"No." Peter drove off, pumping the throttle. "Pearson's Drug-store. I want to see what the mayor has to say. He's the only person in town who can stop this madness before it's too late."

"I'd say maybe it already is," Ginger said, looking at the clouds of smoke filling the sky. "Too late, I mean."

They hadn't gone more than a few blocks when a wailing noise from behind caused Peter to pull off to the side of the road. A bright red fire engine went roaring past, siren howling.

"Did you see him?" Ginger asked.

There had been one man only in the truck—the driver. It was Oscar Stovall.

"I saw him," Peter said, shifting gears. The bug took off. "It was Oscar."

"Well, now what do we do?"

"Let's see if we can find out where he's going."

The siren made it easy to tail the fire truck as it tore through the town's central business district, swerved onto Main Street, and squealed to a stop in front of the flashing neon sign of Pearson's Family Drugstore. Oscar Stovall dressed in a black slicker raincoat and red metal hat sprang out of the driver's seat, grabbed the hose from the back of the truck, and dragged it across the road.

Peter drew up behind the truck, sprang out, and tried to intercept Stovall before he could reach the store.

But he was too late.

As Peter drew close there was a sudden whooshing noise and a geyser of flame spurted from the hose.

Peter threw up a hand to shield his eyes from the glow.

Ginger grabbed hold of him. "There was a big pile of books in there—in the store. I saw them in the window."

Oblivious to them or anything else, Oscar Stovall continued to spray the front of the building with flame.

Peter hurried over to the fire engine, grabbed the lever, and turned off the pump.

But it was already too late. The whole building was a mass of flame and smoke. A sheet of crimson fire raced across the front of the store, consuming everything in its path. The big front window collapsed inward in an explosion of broken glass.

Peter intercepted Stovall on his way back to the truck. His face was aglow with excitement. He didn't seem to recognize Peter. "Out of my way," he growled. "This is official fire department business."

"Oscar, wait," Peter said, grabbing his arm as he tried to push past. "Don't you understand? This is all a trick. You're being fooled. Roy Goldman planted those books. They're his."

"Don't matter," Stovall said, jerking his arm away. "Books are books. They all need to be burned. Every filthy one of them. Burn them till they're nothing but ash. It's my job—my duty. Nobody else cares anymore. Even Mayor Washington. It's all up to me."

Peter saw only one option left. He waited until Stovall got half-way past him and then threw a quick left hook. His hard steel fist neatly clipped Stovall on the jaw. His eyes rolled back in his head and his knees sagged. Peter caught him under the arms and eased him down into the street.

Then he went back inside the truck, took the keys out of the ignition, and tucked them safely away in a pocket.

Back at Roy's bug a familiar figure was standing beside Ginger watching the fire burn. It was Mayor Lucius B. Washington dressed in a natty purple suit and porkpie hat.

"Nice bit of fisticuffs there, son," he said, with an appreciative nod.

Pete pointed at the raging conflagration consuming the drugstore. "Don't you think we ought to try and figure a way of putting these fires out before they spread and burn down the entire town."

"You needn't worry about that," the mayor said. "People are safe. I had the entire area evacuated some time ago—right when Roy was first delivering his books all around town."

"And you didn't try to stop him?" said Peter, aghast.

The mayor shrugged. "It seemed a tad late in the game for that, don't you think? Besides, son, I'm afraid our town fire department long ago lost whatever skills it may have possessed when it comes to putting fires out."

* * * *

"You don't sound overly upset by it."

"How can I be? I was fooled fair and honest same as everybody else in town. Roy Goldman was a far more effective antagonist than I ever imagined."

"You mean Theda, don't you?"

"Theda, Roy, what's the difference? The idea was always the same. Increase the intensity of the tridee, create a town of zombies, and then strip them of everything they have. It worked beautifully—up to a point. Unfortunately—" he looked at the burning building and shook his head "—after that point was reached it turned into a disaster."

"Theda's dead," Ginger said, coming up to them. "She was crushed to death when one of the torture rooms at the Berryman place malfunctioned."

"Ah, really?" The mayor looked momentarily saddened. "I warned them about that. I warned them no good would come from—" he paused and smiled weakly "I told them no good would come from playing with fire. But they wouldn't listen to me."

He turned away then and crossed the street, still smiling vaguely. The hot pink Cadillac was parked at the curb.

In a burst of anger Peter went after him.

"Damn it," he said. "What's wrong with you? You act like you don't care. Your whole town is burning to the ground and you strut around like it's one big joke."

"Mr. Mark," the mayor said, placing a hand on his shoulder, "you are seriously in error when you say that. This town is not my town and it never has been."

"You're the mayor, aren't you?"

"I bear the official title, yes, but the fact remains I despise these people—loathe everything about them—everything they are, everything they stand for. Do I make myself clear? These people are not just white, Mr. Mark. They're bleached to the bone. I wish them nothing but the purest hell forever and a day."

Then he got in his car and drove off.

Watching him go, Peter made no effort to stop him.

When he went back to Ginger, Hiram Evers and Bob Jones were standing beside her solemnly watching the flames licking at what little remained of the town drugstore.

"What a horrible, wicked man," Peter said.

"And the only honest one I ever met in my life," Evers said.

"That's no excuse. Not for all this." Peter made a gesture.

"What makes you think he wanted one? An excuse I mean?"

Peter went back and got in the beetle buggy. Ginger slid in beside him. "I know I've said this before," she said, "but one more time. What's next?"

"Let's go home."

"To Stovalls' you mean?"

"I do, yes."

"Roy's probably there too."

"That's what I was thinking."

* * * *

They proceeded through town. The smell of smoke and fire was like a foul pollutant saturating the air. Twice they had to detour widely to avoid fires, some of which appeared to be consuming entire blocks. The wind had by no means lessened and Peter doubted that much of the town would remain standing come nightfall.

There were more people out in the streets now, especially those areas nearest the major blazes, all looking utterly lost and forlorn. Where would these people go? Peter wondered. How would they live? Did any of them still possess the strength of character necessary to begin the process of rebuilding? To be honest Peter doubted it. Winesap, Illinois—the Heartland City of America—would soon be as dead and gone as ancient Carthage or fabled Troy.

The truck Roy Goldman had been driving was parked in the middle of the lawn in front of the Stovall house. Peter and Ginger climbed out of the buggy and walked toward the porch. Roy Goldman and Jayne Stovall were sitting on the steps waiting for them. Jayne's eyes were unexpectedly bright and alert. Roy had a book open in his lap.

It looked like another copy of de Sarnot's *Mysterion*.

He raised his head and smiled as Peter and Ginger drew near.

"Well, what did I tell you?" he said. "I said I had a plan to solve everything and I darn well did, didn't I?"

"You call this solving everything?" Peter said.

"Sure do." He turned and looked at the open door behind him. "Thirty minutes ago the tridee feed went dead once and for all. If that's not a solution I don't know what is."

"Mayor Washington's left town," Ginger said.

"See?" Goldman looked triumphant. "I told you so, didn't I? Now all we have to do is put everything back together again the way it used to be and everyone can be happy." He put his arm around Jayne and pulled her close. "Isn't that right, sweetheart?" He kissed her on the cheek.

"And how are you going to do that?"

"I don't know yet. We'll find a way. People are always at their best when faced with the worst. The darkest hour is just before the dawn. Don't you agree?"

A whirring noise attracted Peter's attention to the sky. He looked up and discovered, hovering directly overhead, the familiar shape of a helio-plane.

It appeared to be descending.

"I wonder who that could be," Ginger said.

Peter didn't have to wonder. He knew who it was. "It's Desmond Blue."

"He likes making dramatic entrances, huh?"

"That he does."

* * * *

A short time later the helio-plane set down in the middle of the street. A door in the cockpit slid back and a familiar face looked out. Crystal LaFleur waved an arm, beckoning Peter over.

"Who's that?" Ginger said. "It's not Desmond Blue."

"No, of course not. It's Crystal. But Desmond's in there somewhere, I'm sure. Come along, you can meet him."

The two of them went out into the street and waited for the helio-plane blades to stop rotating.

Blue leaned out of the copter as Peter approached. "Get in the back," he said, jerking a thumb. "The young lady too. Miss Ginger Cunningham, I believe."

"That's right, Mr. Blue."

"How'd you like to go to work for me, dear?"

"I'd love it."

"Good. Sit up front there with Crystal and make a note of every move she makes. You're going to learn to be our auxiliary helio-plane pilot for starters. Make sure you're careful to note every last detail. The lives of the rest of us may well depend upon it. Peter, in the back with me," Blue added, pointing to the empty seat beside him. "We two have much to discuss."

Once they were all inside, Crystal pulled back on the throttle and the helio-plane lifted off into the dark smoky sky. From the air Winesap below looked as if it were in the middle of a war zone. Fires burned out of control everywhere.

"I failed, Desmond," Peter reported, watching the fires burn. "The woman posing as Thelma Goldman is dead. Killed in a freak accident at the old Berryman house. Mayor Washington left town and Roy Goldman, the last time I saw him, thought he had won."

"Good," Blue said. "That'll serve them all right."

"Did you hear me?" He could barely hear himself over the whirr of the helio-plane blade. "I said I failed."

"I know. I heard you. I'm afraid I rather expected as such."

"Then why did you send me here?"

"My usual reasons for sending people places. To further their education. But enough idle chatter. Did you bring me the book or not?"

Once again, Peter had almost forgotten he had it in his hand. "You mean this?" Peter held out the copy of *Mysterion* by Marcel de Sarnot he had found in the Berryman basement.

"I do indeed," Blue said, grabbing the book from Peter's hand. He laid it open in his lap and began turning pages rapidly. When he got to the beginning of the text, he leaned his head down and began to read.

"But, Desmond, I wanted to tell you—"

"Hush. Can't you see that I'm trying to read."

"But I thought—"

Blue reached up and jerked the flaps of his deerstalker cap down over his ears.

With a sigh Peter turned to the window. The heartland below was like a green and gold garden as the helio-plane plowed through the sky in pursuit of a private destiny.

12

"Well, well, well," murmured Vasily Andreev, thrusting his eagle's beak of a nose close to the ceiling-high pane of shatter-proof glass that divided the spacious room into equal halves.

On the opposite side of the barrier the prisoner gazed calmly back at him.

"So here we are together one more night, my old companion," Andreev went on. "And how did your day proceed, my friend? Did the doctors come to stab and pick at you? Were there silly scientists with their graphs and charts and theories?"

Without waiting for a reply he knew would never come, Andreev leaned back and let out a sputtering laugh. In truth it had been a good many years since the doctors and scientists had last visited the prisoner with any degree of regularity. Still, he enjoyed teasing his old friend now and then. After what it and its presumed fellows—the so-called "slugs"—had done to the poor stupid human species a tiny bit of turnabout was only fair play.

With a fart, Andreev turned and shuffled across his half of the room, bald head wobbling on a spindly neck. He crossed to the one window and peered through the steel mesh at the distant ribbon of the street some thirty-three stories below. The building was located in an obscure district of the old Moscow—the prisoner its sole remaining permanent occupant. In prior years when the Union of Soviet Socialist Republics had flourished as a sovereign national entity, things had been different. This same building had then served as an exclusive retreat for personages high in the government and party. Andreev, who for a time had numbered among such men, smiled remotely at the recollection. The young girls who had lived here then—Bulgarians, a great many of them—had been chosen for their passive natures. A private sanctuary for the insertion of powerful pricks into not unwilling quims. Or so the fools had blindly believed. Andreev had himself monitored the many long hours of film and videotape, the more explosive portions of which he still retained in a secret vault in a secure location. Not that any of it mattered anymore. Only the sheer entertainment value remained—and a certain lingering nostalgia for a better time now passed. The dead could not be blackmailed, as they existed in the one realm safely beyond the long reach of shame or fear.

"I believe it's snowing again," he announced, backing away from the window. Vasily Andreev was perhaps the only adult Russian who still cherished the sensation of falling snow. He took his chair, sat, stretched his legs, and punched his belly, eliciting a burp. The prisoner's half of the room was without furniture of any kind. There was a separate bathroom—a porcelain cubicle, originally a brilliant white, now gray, equipped with a modern flush toilet—an early but needless addition to the scheme of things since it had soon been clear that the prisoner had no practical use for such a device, as it apparently managed to eliminate its bodily wastes internally without recourse to the traditional turd. Andreev did not understand the process involved—he was no scientist, after all—though he had once overheard a distinguished biologist pontificating at length on the matter and had no reason to question the man's professional reliability. Or his sanity. Still, he sometimes wondered: what other foul human habits did this creature lack? Did it sweat? Fart? Burp? After many years without a bath, what was the current state of its body odor? An intriguing question doubtlessly but not one that Andreev would ever likely solve: he and the prisoner were each restricted to their separate but equal domains. No physical intercourse was permitted. The reason: fear of contamination. Not mine, thought Andreev with amusement—but its. The doctors and scientists fretted that should the prisoner perish while in human hands its fellows might return to Earth, swooping down to wreak a terrible vengeance. Andreev was skeptical. Having come once and done what needed to be done, why come again? The universe eschewed redundancy—no two snowflakes were identical, no two tulips or stars. The prisoner clearly expected nothing. In all its time here not once had its eyes strayed to the ceiling in a hopeful gaze.

Andreev winked conspiratorially. "Soon, my good friend," he promised, wagging a finger, "soon I will begin."

He referred to his nightly discourse. In the beginning while standing duty here, Andreev had filled the long hours from dusk to dawn by reading aloud to the prisoner. The subjects he pursued—not of his own choosing—were varied: human history, universal cosmology, the myriad occult sciences. Soon he grew bored. He laid his books aside and instead talked extemporaneously to the prisoner. Did it listen? Did it hear? It gave no sign. Nevertheless, Andreev went on talking. For hours and hours on end. Talking as he'd never dared talk before. Talked until his throat grew raw, his lips cracked and bled, his tongue swelled to the size of a sausage. Andreev had never been a voluble man. As the head of the nameless Soviet intelligence service assigned the task of monitoring the loyalty of all the other many Soviet intelligence agencies, he had rarely been called upon to speak more than a half dozen words at a time. The room was bugged of course. On the second night after he began talking, two burly men in trench coats—both former colleagues—burst in and attempted to remove Andreev in handcuffs. Observing this through the plate-glass barrier that divided the room neatly in half, the prisoner went at once into the bathroom—its first and only such visit!—and thrust what was presumed to be its head into the toilet bowl. Terror soon reigned supreme. Andreev was promptly released. As soon as the handcuffs came off, the prisoner removed its head from the porcelain bowl and again (presumably) breathed the air of life. Andreev shook off the men in trench coats. He went back to talking again. In the years since, he had seldom ceased.

"A damn fine joke," he told his alien friend. "What you and the others did. Coming to Earth and scaring the pants off an entire species so that now not only are they afraid of you but of me as well."

Andreev wiped his nose. He was thinking now of the other time the prisoner had saved his life—the first time. Shortly before the arrival of the slugs in their seventy-seven golden ships, Andreev had been placed under arrest. He had long anticipated such an occurrence, knowing better than most the razor-thin line that separates fear from loathing. For six long days he underwent the familiar rituals of interrogation. Needles plunged through the flesh of the tongue. Electric prods rubbing against the testicles. Hot irons inserted into the anal cavity. His torturers had demanded to know the location of the secret vault housing his private files—documents, films, tapes. Vasily Andreev could have told them of course and spared himself the pain. Devoutly Christian, however—a condition he had for years flaunted, once wearing a jeweled crucifix while visiting the Kremlin itself—his interest in the agonies of martyrdom was considerable. Did God indeed visit those suffering and ease their pain? After six days he still had no answer. His torturers gave up too. His execution was ordered. Early one spring morning. A dusty prison courtyard. A keen high dry light. Hard brick wall. Andreev refused the proffered blindfold. A squad of sloe-eyed young soldiers raised their weapons. *Ready! Aim! Fire!*

At *fire!* the soldiers vanished. *Poof!* In an instant they—and their officers—were gone.

"God has saved me!" Andreev shouted at the top of his lungs.

Later he found out he was mistaken. God had not intervened.

Instead, it was the ones in the golden ships: the Occupants, they were called. The mysterious creatures who had come to Earth, suspended time itself and then—

Well, that was the problem. Then what? They had taken tens of thousands away with them. They had destroyed certain cities, towns, villages.

But their intent—their purpose—their motive?

No one knew.

Except—presumably—the prisoner.

And it wasn't telling.

"Now let me tell you about my time among the sewer rats," said Andreev, standing now and approaching the glass barrier that separated him from the prisoner. "I know you've heard this story often before but I suspect it must be a favorite of yours as it is of mine. It was during a time when I had fallen out of favor with my superiors. Whispers reached my ears of pending arrest, perhaps execution. I was still a relatively young man at the time and life seemed if not precious at least worth preserving. While sitting on a park bench one afternoon contemplating my fate, I happened to notice a particularly fat gray rat scurrying past. Curious, I stood and followed and saw the rat slip through an open grate and into the sewers below. On an impulse, I chose to follow. For a full year after my initial descent, I made my home in the sewers, feasting on what garbage drifted past, dressed in weeds and leaves washed down by the rain and melting snows. I soon felt more rat than human, a confusion that was to haunt me for some time to come. The rat is a haughty beast, however. It has no use for the human being, I should add. The rat regards our species with haughty contempt. My own early efforts to communicate with the rats were spurned. It took that full first year for me to learn their language well enough to converse with them, their language consisting more of gesture, movement, faint wriggling of the eyes, nose, whiskers, and snout than sound. Although I am personally fluent in some two dozen human languages none to my knowledge—not even the higher dialect of the warrior caste of the Samira tribesmen of Inner Mongolia known to only seven living men besides myself—can approach in complexity and sophistication the language of the sewer rat. When a man learns to speak as a rat he must also come to think and believe as a rat and that was my soon privileged condition. The most important of these beliefs is the philosophic concept that all turds will come to those who wait. If it's gold bullion you seek, seek it not among the rats of the sewers, for gold bullion sinks without a trace. If you seek diamonds the same is true—on the bottom. But excrement floats and if you wait patiently, then a pile must surely soon float past. Among the rats are certain holy individuals known as *vishees*—waiters-for-excrement—who do nothing in life but lurk in obscure places examining all that floats past in search of the unattainable: the perfect turd. These holy *vishees* are protected, fed, and sexed by the other rats. For a period of several months at the end of my sojourn I too served as a *vishee* and in that period while examining literally thousands of turds of all imaginable varieties, I saw only one that I could honestly describe as approaching perfection and on that occasion—I admit this freely—I broke down and wept as a blind man blessed with the chance to glimpse the stars one night of his life might weep. I did not recover my senses for many days afterward.

"The religion of the rats is also a complex and sophisticated one. In the beginning, they believe, God created this universe out of the leavings of another failed universe and on the second day He built a great city to cover the globe of the world. On the third day God constructed beneath this city an intricate system of sewers and on the fourth day from a single hair plucked from his own tail he created the rats and other vermin to inhabit it. After that God went away to another place to create another universe and it wasn't until much later that a rat named Moleete, driven by hunger, created the first human beings and sent them forth to roam the surface world in order to produce the leavings upon which to this day all rats feed. While I cannot accept this narrative in its entirety—I remain as always a devout Christian of the Orthodox faith—neither can I deny it out of hand. The purpose of human life is to keep rats fed—so say the little creatures themselves—and my own experience among them has demonstrated to me the distinct possibility of this being true. It is also an unarguable fact that you Occupants did not during your sway over our little world harm one single solitary rat. Personally, I take this as a sign.

"I was not the first human being to live among the rats. At least one other had preceded me. I suspect you have heard me speak of him before: Jesus of Nazareth. According to what I learned from several wise old *vishees,* Jesus did not perish as long assumed upon the cross but instead merely fell into a deep coma. On a later night several merciful rats crept forth from their underworld lair and removed the unconscious savior from his tomb, subsequently using their knowledge of arcane medicine to return him to life. Jesus remained among the sewer rats of Jerusalem until his natural demise many years afterward, a melancholy old man embittered by his treatment at the hands of his fellow humans with black haunted eyes and hands and feet that bled periodically from his old wounds. Jesus left a number of children behind and I met at least two rats who claimed descent from his seed and in both I detected a certain thrust to the jaw and hook to the nose that led me to believe that the blood of the Hebrews might well flow in their veins.

"The rats' formulation of substantive evil is personified in the corporeal form of the domestic feline—the house cat. The cats of the sewers are a special breed growing at times to as much as three meters in length and weighing upwards of several hundred kilograms. These cats are so huge and fierce that all rats would long ago have been exterminated had they not proved more skillful and wily at unified communal action. I can fondly recall the tremendous thrill of witnessing as many as one hundred rats—myself most proudly among them—tackling one of these giant cats and bringing it down under the sheer weight of our righteous numbers. No rat will ever eat the flesh of a cat, I might add, for to do so would be to take into one's own body the evil of the beast. To this day I carry on my flesh scars from violent encounters with cats."

Andreev unbuttoned his shirt and exposed his chest to view. There among the black and gray hairs were a number of pale streaks that might well have been made by the claws of some huge animal.

"The rats revere only one creature above themselves," Andreev continued, fastening his shirt, "and that is the duck. I was not aware of this—no rat will speak casually of the duck—until once while splashing at the edge of a slime pool with two female acquaintances

I heard a loud quacking noise approaching from an adjacent tunnel. My two companions instantly prostrated themselves on their sleek underbellies and covered their eyes with their delicate forepaws. A short time later the duck floated into view. There are not many such creatures living in the sewers but those few are much the essence of their species with their silver down like silk and their glistening beaks like bars of gold. As the duck swept past I dared to raise my head and peer directly at it. Our eyes met, locking briefly, and in that instant I felt the searing warmth of its benevolent all-embracing love like a blast of hot Gobi wind. Later I beseeched my companions to explain what had transpired and was told that the duck is revered among the rats as the one true *blex*, a term I can translate only as *God/It/Being*. The basis for this reverence comes from the undeniable ability of the duck to flourish equally in the three primary states of cosmic matter: water, air, and earth. Even the great cats will not harm a duck, worshipping them also. On my way home each morning after my work here I pause to feed the ducks in the park from bits of bread kept in my pockets for just such a purpose."

Andreev reached into his trousers and brought forth several chunks of moldy black bread.

He went on: "My life among the rats of the sewers was happier and more content than any I had ever dreamed possible and I soon ceased to think of that other human world that must presumably still exist above. After seven years had passed I was swimming in one of the uppermost tunnels accompanied by my current wife and three of my older children when a flash of blinding light like the curse of some ancient god suddenly burst upon us. I was struck momentarily senseless and before I knew what was happening had been grasped and lifted up and placed down on something hard and slick and hot. Barely conscious, I was soon transported against my will to the street above. The month was July. The men who had raised me were sewer workers assigned to repair a clogged drain and I, they believed, had just been rescued from an unspeakable fate. Before I could loosen my tongue to protest—the language of Russia was but a dim memory buried in the back of my brain—I had been taken to hospital. What followed I will not bother to delineate: the charges of lunacy lodged against me, the cruel months spent in the asylum, my eventual release due to the intervention of a former comrade who recalled my prior service to the state and wished to make use of me again. As soon as I was able I returned to the sewers but the rats upon sensing my presence darted swiftly away. I called and called, using their own language, and at last spied two gleaming yellow eyes and recognized the venerable form of Biiwi, oldest and wisest of *vishees*. He inquired as to what I might want and I replied that my sole desire was to return to the only life I had ever loved. He told me that, alas, that would not be possible, for a great myth had sprung up around my experiences, the tale of a mighty white rat—that is me, Andreev—who had been visited by the spirit of the duck and raised to a higher level where he sprouted wings and beak and became as a *blex* in the heavens. For me to return to the sewers now would be to render absurd the substance of this myth and while those wise in the ways of the cosmos did not interpret the story in a literal way, the young—the children—those to whom the future must be entrusted—they could not be so bluntly disillusioned.

"And so, grievous of heart, I went away, throwing myself into my new work as head of a secret intelligence service monitoring the activities of all the other many secret intelligence agencies. The rest is, as they say, history."

His throat raw from so much uninterrupted talking Andreev paused to collect his breath. The prisoner watched with rapt attention.

Andreev continued: "But that story, as intriguing as it no doubt is, is as nothing compared to what occurred a year later when—"

There was a knock at the door.

Andreev swung his head in astonishment.

No one had knocked at the door in a great many years. Even the sentries who stood guard below were under strict orders never to venture above the ground floor.

Again came the knock.

"Who is it?" Andreev called, approaching the door.

"A friend," said soft and gentle voice like the music of the great Tchaikovsky.

Andreev hurled open the door before recalling that he had no friends other than the prisoner.

On the other side stood a beautiful young woman with a faint birthmark in the shape of a five-pointed star showing just below the nipple of her left breast.

The woman was naked.

She wet her lips with the tip of her tongue. "Vasily Andreev?" she asked.

"What do you want?" he stammered, stepping back into the room.

"I want you, Vasily Andreev," she replied, and closed the door behind her.

13

Dressed in a dingy gray smock and torn leggings Desmond Blue, the world's greatest detective, sat sprawled at his ease in a soft chair in a windowless room somewhere in the colony of Futura in the province of Tibet. Blue, eyes narrowed, brow furrowed, swung his gaze slowly back and forth between the two men who presently stood confronting him. The first of these was a lean, blond-bearded, stunningly handsome man garbed in brown burlap while the other was squint-eyed, pudgy, and wore a green-and-pink silk shirt decorated with painted images of pineapples, volcanoes, and hula dancers. Blue faced the first man as he spoke:

"If I've caused you any embarrassment, Signor Donatello, then you have my sincere apologies. My motives were of the purest sort, I assure you."

"You told lies about me," the man said grimly.

"Ah, but did I?" said Blue with a wink. "Let's be watchful of our terms. To me—and to the law—a lie must consist of a conscious act of deception rendered with malicious intent while what I uttered was a mere accusation that I had no basis believing either correct or incorrect."

"He splits hairs with a razor," Mario Donatello told the other man with disgust. "He knows he tell lies about me but will not come out and admit it."

"I think Donatello's may be right, Blue," the other man said. "If he's not a member of this Sect of yours, you ought to have the decency to say so."

Blue leaned forward and spread his arms in a gesture of helplessness. "Brother Xavier, if I could then I most assuredly would, but how can I possibly know? Apparently, I've failed to make myself clear. I am not myself a member of the organization known as the Sect. I am thus unfamiliar with its membership list."

"Isaac says that you are a member," Donatello said.

"No. Isaac said that the probability of my being a member was greater than 99%? Since I'm not a member, then the less than one percent probability was the correct one."

"Then how is it, if you are not one of them, you knew of my presence here in Futura?" Donatello asked.

"Oh, I have my means," Blue said airily. "After all, Signor Donatello, I am a detective."

"But you could also be a member of the Sect."

"I could, yes, but as I've already stated I am not. Brother Xavier, has any attempt been made to contact my client, Pope Sergio in Rome?"

Yes," Xavier said, his face growing long, "I attempted to place such a call myself and learned to my sorrow that His Holiness recently suffered a major attack of the blood and now lies critically ill in a public hospital near the site of the empty Vatican ruins."

"A pity," said Blue. "I am deeply grieved."

"Even though it happens to be extremely convenient for you as well?" said Donatello.

"Enough," Blue said. He emitted a mighty sigh. "Since skepticism continues to plague my every word I must as a consequence fall back upon my rights as a human being. I therefore demand to be confronted by my accuser. I wish to meet this Isaac at once and have him charge me to my face."

"Impossible," said Xavier curtly.

"But why?" said Blue.

"Because—because you're a conspirator. A suspected conspirator. We can hardly trust you alone with Isaac."

"Then bind my wrists." Blue held both hands limply out. "Use chains if you must. But again as a human being I stand on my rights."

Xavier shifted uncomfortably. "He does have a point. I suppose it is only fair."

"I see nothing to be gained by any such meeting," said Donatello.

"But if we're not sure…"

"Damn it, of course we are. Isaac is infallible—that much we know—and if he states that Blue is a conspirator then the man is a conspirator."

"Gentlemen, please," broke in Blue. "I am not unwilling to strike a compromise. If after meeting with Isaac I have failed to convince both him and you of my ultimate innocence, then I promise to go any place of your choosing and there voluntarily incarcerate myself for the remainder of my natural years. In other words, I am willing to relieve you of the awesome responsibility of taking the law into your own hands. If guilty I will serve my sentence. If innocent I demand freedom."

"If he's that sure of himself," said Xavier, "I don't see how we can refuse."

"It is your decision, Brother Xavier." Donatello thrust a hand inside his burlap robes and withdrew a shiny handgun. "But if he attempts any monkey business on the way I shall personally blow his brains out."

"Fair enough, gentlemen," said Blue. He came to his feet.

* * * *

Brother Xavier crossed the room, unbolted the door, and ushered Blue and Donatello out into the corridor. Two guards armed with rifles stood flanking the door. As the three men emerged, the guards fell into step behind them.

All Blue knew was that he was being held captive somewhere inside the enormous concrete blockhouse he had observed from the air. As Brother Xavier led the way through a maze of windowless corridors, Blue soon gave up any hope of keeping a mental map of their route. At times they passed others going in the opposite direction. Most were dressed like Donatello in mendicant burlap robes. Many stared curiously at Blue as they went past but said nothing.

"Quite a busy place you have here," Blue remarked to Brother Xavier after another group went by.

Xavier beamed with pride. "Those here at Futura are devoted to our cause."

"Which is what?" asked Blue.

Donatello frowned. "Surely as a conspirator you must know."

"As a matter of fact," Blue said archly, "I do not."

Xavier shrugged. "Our cause is the systematic ordering of all that is known of yesterday in order that we can project the exact nature of tomorrow."

"Ah, I see. You're prophets then. The Pope said something to me about preserving the past in the event of some future calamity."

"That was the mission of the early Preservationists, yes. The society dates back to the fourteenth century, another period when many feared the imminent collapse of human civilization. In recent times, however, we have come to understand that preservation is only one part of our overall task. Projection is also necessary in order to become aware of what will occur and thus take steps to meet it."

"Then you are you claiming to be able to predict the future, correct?"

"Yes."

"And how is this done? Not by examining the entrails of dead sheep or dealing cards from a shuffled deck, I assume."

"Through logic and deduction. Once the past is fully known, then the future is as readily readable as the pages of a book."

Blue shook his head. "I'm afraid I can't fully go along with you on that one, Brother Xavier. And I speak here as a practicing detective for whom the techniques of deduction are the blood of my life. Uncertainty is a universal phenomenon."

"Given sufficient data, any conclusion can be reached. Here in Futura we are in possession of that data."

"Where? How?"

"I will leave that for Isaac to explain."

"And how long have you been making these predictions of yours?"

"Since Isaac joined us."

"This Isaac must be quite the fellow then."

Both Xavier and Donatello laughed. "That he is indeed, Mr. Blue."

"And so you successfully predicted the Occupancy, I gather?"

"There I'm afraid—" Xavier began hesitantly.

"There we lacked sufficient data," Donatello said. "Since the question of whether another intelligent species existed in the cosmos was purely speculative, no basis existed for a firm projection."

"And still doesn't I assume."

"What do you mean?"

"You don't know whether they're coming back or not."

"No. No, we don't."

"Then what sort of events can you predict?"

"Human events with human causes," Xavier said. "The future revival of the world economy for instance. I can give you a date for that. The establishment of a powerful centralized monarchy in northern Brazil—that is set for the year after next either in July or early August. Even something as seemingly random as an aeroliner crash over Sweden within the next nine days is predictable?"

"How so?"

"By the methods I described. By examining every shred of known data regarding air travel safety from the time of the Montgolfier Brothers until today. After that, statistical techniques take over and an exact prediction can be easily arrived at."

"And you're never mistaken?"

"Not when sufficient data exists, no."

"And what are you doing about it then?"

"Doing?"

"This air crash. What steps have you taken to avert it?"

Donatello gave an irritated grunt. "We could hardly do anything like that, Blue."

"Why not?"

"Because the continued survival of the Preservation Society—of Futura—depends upon absolute secrecy."

"Then why not offer up an anonymous tip?"

"No one in authority would believe it."

"Not the first time perhaps. But after you were correct once, they'd surely take you far more seriously the next time. Or the time after that."

"I think you're deliberately confusing our purpose, Mr. Blue. The idea is not for us to alter the future but rather to know it and thus to understand it."

"Come now, Brother Xavier. The future is not a thing embedded in solid granite. We both know better than that."

Xavier turned his head and stared at Blue. "Do you sincerely believe that, Mr. Blue?"

"If I didn't I would never have come here."

"Isaac says you came here to destroy us," Donatello put in.

"And I say Isaac is wrong."

They'd come to the end of a long corridor. Blue's best estimate was that they were now somewhere very near the geographical center of the blockhouse. They passed into a circular, brightly illuminated room with bare walls and a high ceiling. A woman in a loose-fitting yellow smock sat behind a desk piled high with books and papers. When the woman saw Blue her face broke into a tentative smile.

"Nora?" said Blue, halting where he stood. "Nora Malloy?"

Her smile became more certain. "Then you do remember me, Desmond?"

"My God, how could I possibly forget?" He hastened forward and caught her hands in his, pressing down tenderly. Nora Malloy was a slender dark-haired woman with strong cheekbones, a fleshy mouth, and wide sparkling eyes. "It was," said Blue, "only yesterday that we parted."

She laughed, shaking her head. "Oh, a good deal longer ago than that, Desmond."

"For me it was only yesterday."

She threw back her head, laughing even harder. "You always were a romantic, Desmond."

"You know this man, Nora?" Donatello asked in a tight voice.

"Desmond Blue and I were great friends a very long time ago," she said.

"You never mentioned it before."

"I didn't feel it was anyone's business." Her gaze continued to rest on Blue. "You've put on a few pounds, I see."

Blue patted his stomach with a fond hand. "I have striven to enjoy life as I've found it. But you, Nora—you're quite as lovely as ever."

"And you're still a private detective?"

"When a case worth pursing presents itself, yes. One such brought me here, although your esteemed colleagues suspect other motives."

"Desmond Blue is the best and wisest man I've ever known in my life," Nora said to the two men.

"That will be up to Isaac to decide," Donatello said stiffly.

"Then I suggest you go in and get it over with. Desmond and I have much to talk over between us."

"Isaac is free then?"

"For this I'm sure he is. You're all three welcome to enter. The others—" she looked at the armed guards "—will have to stay out."

Donatello looked as if he was ready to object. "Are you sure that's a wise idea, Nora?"

"Of course I am. Desmond can hardly mean to harm Isaac."

"Well, if he does it will on your head not ours."

"So be it," she said. She came around the desk and took Blue by the arm. This way, Desmond. I'm sure Isaac is very much looking forward to meeting you. I know he's a great fan of your many past cases."

* * * *

The room beyond the door was white, cool, square, and apparently vacant. Blue swung his gaze from side to side, seeing nothing more interesting than a slight indentation in the wall near the ceiling that looked like the opening for a speaker.

He was about to ask Nora to explain what was going on when a reedy, boyishly adolescent voice filled the air. "Nora," it said. "Nora, is that you again?"

"It's me, Isaac."

"Is he with you? Desmond Blue? Is that really him?"

"He's standing here next to me," she said.

"Then hold on a sec while I get the cameras rolling. This I definitely want a record of." There was a brief pause and then a shrill whistle sounded. "Gosh, he sure is fat."

Blue glanced at Nora. "Isaac?" he asked.

She waved at the wall, smiling. "All ten cubic kilometers of him. Embedded in solid concrete."

"A computer," he said.

"The largest, most complex, and most sophisticated ever built."

"And it talks?"

"More than that, Desmond, Isaac is alive. As fully conscious as you, me, or any human. The big difference is, while each of us knows a little of this or a little of that, Isaac knows everything."

Blue looked skeptical. "I don't believe that's possible."

"Then you're wrong, Mr. Blue," said Isaac's voice through the wall. "You're wrong, I'm right, and I predicted it would happen exactly this way. Didn't I Xavier? Didn't I tell you he'd be wrong about me?"

"Yes, you did," Brother Xavier confirmed.

"Blue turned his head and looked back at Nora. "If I'm wrong, it's not the first time. I've been wrong before, I'm afraid."

"Of course you have," said Isaac. "I could cite many instances if you wish."

"No, that's quite all right," Blue said. "I concede that I'm only human."

"But do tell me something if you please. In the case of the Krakow Ruby. Do you remember that one?"

"Quite well," said Blue. "It was among my more notable triumphs."

"Well, you arrested the wrong person. It wasn't Matthew Burnside who stole that jewel."

"I recovered it on his person. Concealed in a fold of artificial skin on the underside of his scrotum."

"True enough. But he wasn't the one who put it there."

"You have another suspect?"

"I do. Richard Powell. The renegade chemist. He drugged poor Burnside with an Amazonian potion that left no chemical residue and while the poor man was in a stupor planted not only the jewel but the various clues you errantly pursued to arrest the wrong man. It was all a set-up, Mr. Blue, a neat frame. Powell was after the hand of Burnside's fiancé, the comely young Miss Habersham, heir to a fortune worth more than fifty point forty-seven times the value of the purloined ruby. In the end Powell got the girl—thanks to another of his hypnotic potions—and poor Burnside got twenty years at hard labor thanks to your testimony."

"You're sure of this?" said Blue.

"Of course. The data are quite conclusive. I'm as sure of Powell's guilt as I am of the fact that you are a member of the secret society known as the Sect."

"But," said Blue, "I'm not."

"Of course you are."

"Then that settles that," Donatello said. He raised his gun and pointed the muzzle at Blue. "Shall we go? Remember the terms of the agreement we made. Once your guilt was established, you would offer no further resistance."

"Hey, wait—hold on," Isaac called out. "I'm not done talking with Mr. Blue about his cases yet. There are a few others where the conclusions reached were—"

"Never mind that," Donatello said. "This Blue is a most dangerous man. He's been sent here to destroy us and everything we stand for. We must—"

"Gentlemen!" It was Nora Malloy, her voice rising above the rest of them. "All of you need to be quiet and let Desmond speak for himself."

"Thank you, Nora," Blue said in the ensuing silence. "First off, Isaac, as to my arrest of the supposedly innocent Andrew Burnside, you are quite correct. He was indeed not guilty of that one particular crime, the theft of the Krakow Ruby. But as I knew at the time he was in fact the notorious master thief Jimmie Fingers who had stolen the crown jewels of the impoverished Balkan Kingdom of East Uberia leading to a widespread famine in which tens of thousands of innocent tribesmen perished. Unable to bring him to justice for that dastardly crime, I instead allowed the false evidence tying him to the theft of the Krakow Ruby to stand. As for Richard Powell, the chemist, he and I were working in tandem throughout. He was much in love with the comely Miss Habersham regardless of the size of her fortune and has since, I'm happy to say, made her a most kind and loving husband."

"None of which contradicts my analysis of the facts," Isaac pointed out.

"No, it does not. But in crime—as in life—and perhaps in history as well—the facts are not always supreme. Now if you don't mind, Isaac, I'd like to ask you a few quick questions of my own."

"Go ahead, Mr. Blue," said the voice from the speaker. "I'll answer truthfully, that much you can count on."

"I'm sure I can, Isaac. So tell me this then. Am I correct in my understanding that you charge me with being a member of a secret conspiratorial organization known as the Sect?"

"I do, Mr. Blue. I'm sorry but the facts are clear."

"What facts may I inquire?"

"In the course of arriving at a judgment I've examined the sum total of all data at my disposal concerning the Sect conspiracy dating back to eleventh century prior to the Christian Era. Additionally, I've referred to the vast quantities of data at my disposal pertaining to your own life and activities as well as a great amount of peripheral data."

"Could you be more explicit about the latter?"

"To do so would mean producing a printout in excess of fourteen billion words."

"He's right about that, Desmond," said Nora. "The sheer quantity of data available to Isaac is staggering."

"I see," said Blue, looking less than happy. "Then let me be clear on one point. Isaac, am I correct in stating that your judgment concerning my belonging to the Sect is based solely upon the data stored in your memory banks?"

"Why, yes, Mr. Blue. It's all I ever have to go on. But that's fine because it's pretty much all there is."

"Then I have only one further question. This data—is there any possibility that some parts of it may be inaccurate?"

"You mean something that seems to contradict everything else?"

"I do."

"In that case—"

"All right, Blue," Donatello broke in. "You said one further question. You asked it."

"Donatello, please," Nora snapped. "Desmond, I think you may be on to something here."

"I think so too, Nora. So then, Isaac, this contradictory datum that involves me, can you specify its exact content?"

"It's just the one lone fact, Mr. Blue."

"What fact is that?"

"The fact that you're a member of the Sect."

"And this unsupported fact—in just those words—this is contained in your memory banks?"

"It is."

"And you accepted it?"

"I received definite instructions that I should accept it as valid while dismissing anything that contradicted it."

"How did you receive these instructions?"

"They were introduced into my circuits by voice some four days ago."

"In other words," said Blue, "first you were told it was a fact that I was a member of the Sect and then you were instructed to disregard anything indicating otherwise."

"That's exactly what happened, Mr. Blue."

"And who did this?"

"I couldn't say. The cameras in this room were disconnected prior to the data input."

"Desmond," Nora said softly. "There would have to be a verbal passkey. Before Isaac can accept verbal input, a specific passkey must be used. It's a random eleven-digit number and changes hourly."

"How many people have access to this code?"

She thought for a moment. "Just six. No—counting me, it would be seven."

"And no one else could discover this key by accident or design?"

"I don't see how."

"Then," said Blue, "it would appear that whoever wanted to foster the incorrect belief of my conspiratorial status was one of this group of seven."

Nora didn't seem pleased by the prospect. "It appears that way, yes."

Brother Xavier was shaking his big head slowly back and forth. "I just can't believe it. Those seven—why, that would include the three of us here plus...plus all the best people in Futura. Why would anyone want to slander Blue in such a despicable way?"

"There can be only one conceivable reason," Blue said bluntly. "To prevent me from pursing my investigation of the case."

"But that would mean—"

"It would mean," Blue said, "that whoever did this is one of them. Nora, gentlemen, I am most sorry to have to report that you have in your midst a member of the Sect."

"Wow," broke in Isaac in a voice filled with delight. "This is turning out to be just like a real detective story."

* * * *

The next afternoon found Blue seated on the front steps of his assigned chalet on the outskirts of the Futura colony gazing out at the sparkling vista of the high crystalline peaks of the holy Himalayas. The air was cool, the wind mild, and the sun beamed benignly down.

The man seated on the steps beside Blue was thinner, older, and wearing an orange jumpsuit and opaque aviator's goggles.

His name was Georgi Gustanov. He had once served as a fighter pilot in the Soviet Air Force.

"This joint is fairly groovy turf," Gustanov was saying. "But also sort of dull boring to boot. Since they let me out of that stupid cell where I was locked up like a yellow bitch dog, everybody I bump into wants to be oh-so-serious like a bunch of fish at school. I approach a pretty girl—even an ugly one with hairy blackhead and wop moustache—and suggest how about later a hanky-panky roll in the hay and you know what they tell Gustanov?"

"I wouldn't have the foggiest notion, Georgi," Blue said, his gaze riveted on the inscrutable mountains.

"They say, 'Georgi, old sport, we dig you muchly as pal and boon companion but in this neck of the woods we try damn hard to keep the private parts private. We got this precious important work to do in saving human civilization and no time for silly shit like humping like camels.' You tell me something, please, Boss, since everybody here say you some kind of brilliant breed of cat, since when is a roll in the hay some kind of silly shit?"

"I'm afraid that must be regarded as one of the few subjects that lie outside the scope of my general expertise," said Blue.

"You don't roll in the hay, daddy-o?"

"I've been celibate ever since the loss of my dear wife."

"But if she's gone away someplace else, then why not fuck your brains out? You're famous, man, like Gustanov once was. Why not take the advantage?"

"Because it wouldn't seem right to me, Georgi."

"Right? Wrong? What's that got to do with screwing? Cats, dogs, horses, camels. They all fuck. You think they give diddly squat about the right and wrong of it?"

"I'm not one of them."

"If you say so." He shook his head wearily. "You not only a brilliant breed of cat, dad, but also some kind of weird-o saint. How you stand that and not start eating weeds?"

Blue emitted a sigh. "I fear that like many you grossly overstate the necessity of sexual release, Georgi. Many great men have retained their celibacy for lengthy periods without suffering undue harm. Sir Isaac Newton died a virgin at age eighty-five years while the philosopher Kant followed an identical path. The example of Jesus Christ is too well known to bear repetition."

"So who wants to be one of those cuckoos?" Gustanov stuck a thumb in his ear and wriggled the fingers. "Man, you playing some kind of loony tune upstairs if you ask me."

"Georgi, the limits of your perceptions sorrow me. How can you concern yourself with a purely physical act when this glorious natural view lies in front of your eyes?"

Removing his goggles Gustanov squinted. "What glorious view you talking about?"

"These mountains in front of us at the moment are like the outstretched fingers of an omnipotent god."

"These?" Gustanov chuckled. "You know what they remind me of? Not fingers. Not God. What they remind me of is those cute little white goosebumps you sometimes find on a pretty lady's bare bottom."

"Your mind," said Blue, "is stuck in a rut."

"Pretty good rut to be stuck in though." Gustanov put on his goggles again. "Hey, here comes company."

Blue had also noticed the figure approaching from the direction of the central blockhouse. "Yes, I see."

"Who you think it is?"

"I wouldn't know."

"Your chickadee, I bet."

Blue frowned. "I have no chickadee, Georgi."

"You know who I mean. That sweet dish with the soulful eyes. She's kind of old for a boy-child like me but very foxy middle aged baby nonetheless."

"If the person to whom you're referring is Nora Malloy," said Blue, "she is merely an old friend."

"She digs you though."

"Don't be crude."

"What's crude about digging somebody?"

* * * *

As the figure drew close it did indeed prove to be Nora Malloy. In truth Blue had been anticipating her arrival the past several hours. When Nora reached the steps of the chalet Blue rose to his feet and bowed in formal greeting. Gustanov remained seated and waved a hand. "How things happening, lady of beauty and eternal delight?"

Nora laughed. "Hello, Captain Gustanov. Desmond."

"I was just admiring the glorious view," said Blue.

"And me," said Gustanov, "I was just admiring the much more glorious view since a certain beautiful lady appeared in my goggles."

Nora to Blue's utter astonishment—and dismay—blushed visibly. "You're a horrid flatterer, Georgi."

"You bet a dime I am, sweetie. It's one of my more famous tendencies." He came to his feet. "One other famous tendency is knowing when to split the scene when not wanted. Unless you got a girlie friend or two coming by for a little orgy action, I now go to pine away inside a cold cruel room with nothing to keep me company but my poor tired hand."

Gustanov disappeared into the innards of the chalet where he could be heard from time to time stomping noisily about.

Nora was smiling. "You certainly seem to have a penchant for attracting colorful friends, Desmond."

"There are times when color can become a shade tiresome," said Blue. "Won't you please sit down, Nora?"

She dropped onto the step vacated by Gustanov and for a time the two of them simply observed the mountain peaks in mutual silence.

Then Nora said: "Any luck today?"

Blue shook his head. "I completed my painstaking perusal of the Isaac's Vatican files pertaining to the Sect and confirmed my original suspicion. The file has definitely been tampered with, crucial documents removed."

"Do you think it was the same person who planted the false information with Isaac concerning you?"

"That would be the logical supposition, yes."

"Then your trip here has been a total waste of time."

"I wouldn't necessarily say that."

She looked up eagerly. "Then you have found something valuable?"

"I found you," he said.

This time Nora didn't blush. "You're starting to sound like Captain Gustanov."

"Lord save me," said Blue.

Again, there was silence. The mountains looming before them in their impassive magnitude seemed to function against casual conversation.

It was Blue who spoke first: "I believe you have come with a proposal to offer me."

She looked surprised. "Who told you that?"

"No one. I deduced it. Having a practicing detective so close at hand experienced at ferreting out secrets, it would seem only logical to engage his services to rid yourselves of an unwanted infiltrator. I assume therefore that you wish to hire me."

"Not me, Desmond. This is Isaac's idea. I think he wants another chance to watch you at work. He got a kick out of seeing you in action last night."

"You opposed him?"

"I wasn't convinced it was the best idea. The only thing that seems to interest you is this case of yours—the Sect. We in the Preservation Society have to concern ourselves with a broader sphere than that."

"This conspiracy is as much your enemy as mine, Nora. Perhaps more so."

She nodded without necessarily agreeing. "When would you want to begin?"

Blue looked up at the sky, then at his watch, then up at the sky again. "I have found over the years that my mind tends to operate at its most efficient in the hours immediately after dawn. For that reason, I would prefer to delay until morning tomorrow before commencing the hunt. At that time—let us say six o'clock—I would like to meet with all seven suspects in Isaac's inner den."

"Seven? Then you include me?"

Blue spread his hands. "In my capacity as a detective I must. In addition, prior to tomorrow's meeting, I want to have a private chat alone with Isaac. I don't want any of the suspects to be aware of this."

"Except me, I gather."

He laid his hand on hers. "Obviously."

"Then I'll see that it's arranged. An hour from now in my office. Will that work for you?"

"Perfectly."

Wait one hour after I leave here and then come to my office. Do you think you can locate it?"

"I'll try my best."

"Then we'll see each other then."

A PROFILE: NORA MALLOY

As far back as her memory went—into the thirty-third month of her life—Nora Malloy had been seeing things before they happened. As a girl growing up on a horse ranch in rural Idaho, these visions had from the beginning seemed a natural part of her life, no different from what her other senses—eyes, ears, nose—told her. It wasn't until she was nine-years-old and saw Mr. and Mrs. Davies and their two babies from a neighboring ranch burning alive that she mentioned one of these visions to her mother and asked what it meant.

"You just had a bad dream, Nora," her mother said, looking at her oddly.

"But I wasn't asleep."

"You were daydreaming then."

"But my eyes weren't closed."

"They don't have to be."

"Do you have daydreams too?"

"No," she said softly, giving her head a tired shake. "I don't have daydreams anymore."

It was a month later when the Davies family returning from a trip to Boise skidded off an icy highway into a ravine and died in a fiery wreck.

After the funeral Nora hid in the barn and thought harder than she'd ever had to think before in her life. Her mother looked at her oddly when she finally emerged but said nothing.

At sixteen Nora had a vision of a lean handsome man with red hair and friendly eyes. She often glimpsed unknown faces in her visions. New teachers who did not arrive until the following term, friends who later moved in from Montana or Kansas, her own brother Nathaniel six weeks before he was born, and once, when she was fourteen, two brawny men with brown sweaty faces whom she met only five days later while walking home in the rain from school as their car rattled to a stop beside her and one of them leaned out the window and flashed her a toothless grin and said she should hop right in because they'd give her a lift the rest of the way home and that way she wouldn't get wet. But Nora said no. Nora said they weren't really going to do that. They were going to drive off the road, rape, and murder her. She had seen it in a vision and knew it to be true.

After that she jumped a fence and ran all the way home.

* * * *

The man with the red hair was different though. Months passed and then years and she kept having the same visions of him at regular intervals. But the man never appeared. Eventually, when she at college in eastern Washington, she figured out who he had to be, why the visions involving him were so strong and so frequent. It was because—she realized this with a start: *Why, he's the one I'm going to fall in love with,* she thought.

Up until that time Nora had never fallen in love with anyone. She'd gone through her crushes as most bright teenage girls did but they were soon over and except for a few days of sighs and sniffling disguised as anguish meant nothing.

But this man was different.

Who was he? Where was he? How could she find him? The visions rarely extended further than the man's beaming smiling face. After high school she took a bus trip with her two best friends to Seattle and Portland—to see big cities for the first time—and while there she kept her eyes peeled, looking everywhere for him. But she didn't find him.

And then one day she had another vision and suddenly cried out, "He's in New York!"

Her roommate, a studious girl, a biology major, looked up over her glasses. "Who's in New York? King Kong?"

"No—yes. They're both there."

And that was because in her vision—in the background—she had seen the spire of the Empire State Building.

Nora did not go immediately racing back right away. New York was a big city—eight million people—and far away. Plus, she didn't know for sure that he even lived there—only that someday in the future he'd be there—maybe as a visitor, a tourist. And there was no way of knowing when that would be; because her visions never told her that.

When she finally reached New York, it was because she'd taken a job in Seattle at a small private press and had come there to meet with a new young writer who'd submitted the manuscript of a novel that showed considerable promise.

But no, he wasn't the man with red hair—as she'd rather absurdly hoped—but was instead a middle aged dentist with a wife and two adopted children from Africa who like many middle aged dentists liked to write on the side. (His novel when it appeared disappeared into the great void of the unmentioned and unreviewed like most novels written by middle aged dentists.)

As she wandered aimlessly through the nighttime streets of Manhattan peering into the faces of every man she passed who might remotely resemble the man with the red hair, she finally ended up, spent and exhausted, in front of a small reparatory cinema showing a double features of classic films from the distant past.

She bought a ticket, went inside, and as was her habit when going to the movies alone—which she often did—took a seat three rows from the front.

There was only one other person in the same row. He sat at one end next to the aisle and she sat at the other end.

She waited until the intermission between the showing of the two films before going over and sitting next to him.

"Did you enjoy the movie?" she asked.

"Not really, no."

"Why didn't you?"

"Because I'm a mystery buff and that flashback—well, it destroyed the suspense for me. The movie was only halfway finished and yet we knew all the answers."

"I don't think that was what the real story was about though."

He looked at her with interest for the first time since she'd sat down. "Then what was it about?"

"What he did to her. James Stewart. The way he made her change herself to suit him. First the hair and the clothes and then finally her personality, her self. He turned her into somebody she wasn't in order to please himself. It's an allegory—about the act of artistic creation—and so much more besides."

"Wow," he said.

She laughed. "You don't agree?"

"I didn't say that, did I?"

They left halfway through the second feature and went home together. To his apartment. His name was Desmond (which she didn't like) Blue (which she did) and it was still another five or six days before they became lovers.

What astonished Nora more than anything else was that the man with the red hair had turned out to be—of all things—a psychiatrist.

She asked him once if that was all he had ever wanted to be.

"Well, there was a period when I was younger when I wanted to play third base for the Chicago Cubs."

"I don't mean when you were a boy."

"Who said anything about being a boy? That was last month."

"I meant seriously."

"All right. Seriously then, I've always to be a detective."

"A policeman you mean?"

"Of course not. A private eye. A sleuth. I think I ended up becoming a psychiatrist because it was the closet I could come to being a private detective while remaining respectable."

"Is being respectable important to you?"

"Not in the least."

"Then why did—?"

He laid his hand over her mouth. "Shhh," he said. "That's the kind of question I spend all day asking my patients."

It was a while after they'd fallen in love before Nora got around to telling Desmond about her visions of future events. His being a psychiatrist made her leery at first, afraid if she told him he'd think she was mad and start playing games with her head, but when she found out he wasn't that kind of psychiatrist, she felt reassured.

Still, it was a while before she said anything.

They were having dinner at home one sweltering August night—spaghetti and scrambled eggs, his favorite—before she let it slip out.

He peered at her over the rim of his wine glass. "You can predict the future?"

"Not predict it, no. I just see flashes of it."

"Can you see who's going to win the Yankee game tonight?"

"Not something like that, no. I don't get to pick and choose any-way. I just have visions—see pictures."

"And they always come true?"

"Only if I don't do something to make them change first." She told him about the two men on her way home from school who would have raped and murdered her if she hadn't run away first."

"You saved your own life in other words."

"I guess I did at that."

"Have you ever had one of these visions involving me?"

"Before I met you, I did, yes. Before I came to New York."

"But that's something that's now already happened. We've met. We're lovers. Isn't there anything you've seen in one of your visions about me that hasn't happened yet but very soon might?"

She thought about that for a moment, then shook her head. "I can't tell you."

"Why not?"

"Because of the way it works. The future isn't set in stone—it shifts, changes constantly back and forth. If I said I saw you wearing a pink shirt and a black tie—"

"You haven't, I hope."

"No, that was just as example. But suppose I did."

"Couldn't we make it a white shirt and a blue tie?"

"Whichever. But even if I did see you dressed that way you'd still have the ability to decide to wear something entirely different. You'd still have free will."

"So what if you write it down and stick it in a sealed envelope and afterward, after it happens, we can open the envelope and see how close to correct you were? Could we do that?"

"No," she said. "You don't believe me, do you?"

"To be honest, I don't know. That's all I can tell you."

"But you find it hard to accept."

He nodded, spreading his hands. "I've never have been much of a mystic, Nora."

"You will be."

"Is that a prediction?" He smiled slowly.

"Just an opinion." She laughed.

She didn't raise the subject again and neither did he and they went on with their lives as before. It was a definite relief to discover that what had once seemed to dominate her life—her visions—could in time become a peripheral matter like hating the smell of certain cheeses or wanting to throw up whenever she rode the subway for more than a mile or two.

Then came the night when she woke up screaming. And she hadn't fallen asleep yet in the first place.

"Nora?" he said, shaking her. "Nora, are you all right?"

She looked right through him as if he wasn't there.

"Nora?" He touched her shoulder tentatively. "Nora, please. Tell me what's wrong."

"Desmond?"

"Of course."

"Desmond, I saw something."

"Here?" He looked around the darkened bedroom. "Where?"

"Not there." She touched her forehead with a fingertip. "I saw it here."

"Oh," he said. "You were having a dream."

"It wasn't a dream."

"Then what was it?"

"Do you remember what I told once, how sometimes I have visions of the future."

He nodded. "Yes, I remember your telling me that."

"Well, I—"

"You saw something?" he said eagerly. "What was it? Tell me."

"I—no, never mind."

"You don't want to tell me?"

"I...I'm not sure. Maybe later on. Can you just let me think?"

What Nora had seen was the burning of the Earth.

* * * *

She left New York the next day. Packed her things while he was at the office and caught a plane leaving within the hour. The first place she went she saw it again—the vision of burning—but the next place it wasn't there. She stayed awhile and then moved on. Some places— San Francisco, Jerusalem, Venice—she saw it and others—Boston, Boise, Seattle, Paris—she did not. And while there were many times when she wished she could reach up and tear the inner eye out of its socket there were other times when she felt peculiarly and wholly at peace with herself and the cosmos as if this horrible future she saw was the right and proper one.

She tried not to think about Desmond Blue.

She never told him about her vision. For good reason, she felt. To save his life. Because in her vision of the burning of the world she had seen him alive and unharmed walking through the rubble of a dead city and she feared that if she told him what she'd seen he might do something to try and stop it and as a result alter the fact of his own survival.

It was better that he remain ignorant—and alive.

Wasn't it?

14

It was seven-thirty the morning of the fifteenth when Desmond Blue walked into Nora Malloy's white-walled office and found her alone at her desk. When she saw Blue, Nora looked up and wagged a finger as if chastising an errant puppy and pointed over her shoulder at the clock on the wall. "The others have been waiting in there since six. Where have you been, Desmond?"

Blue bowed with gravity. "I chose deliberately to delay my arrival in order better to lay the groundwork for subsequent events."

"In other words you want to make them squirm."

"I also wished to ensure that I myself did no squirming."

Nora looked past Blue to where a second man stood slightly behind him. "I didn't know he was going to be part of this."

She meant Georgi Gustanov garbed in his usual aviator's jumpsuit and goggles but uncharacteristically silent.

"Every successful detective needs his Dr. Watson," said Blue. "And Isaac?"

"He had me inform the others he was meditating on a matter of significance and could not possibly be disturbed for any reason."

"Excellent," said Blue.

"That was your idea too?"

"His actually. Isaac is aware as few flesh-and-blood people that the best means by which to avoid telling a lie is to say nothing at all."

"I wish I knew what you two were up to."

"The truth, Nora. Only the truth." Blue nodded at the door. "Shall we proceed?"

They entered Isaac's inner chamber. As soon as Blue appeared he was met by an angry explosion of six voices all trying to shout at once.

He held his hands in the air.

"Ladies and gentlemen, please. We must maintain proper decorum if we are to succeed in our task."

"You're late, Blue," said Mario Donatello, pushing in front of the rest. "This is an absolute outrage—an act of deliberate humiliation to all concerned. Our time is valuable."

"In that case," Blue said, "I'll try not to take long." He let his eyes rove among the seven suspects. "And surely justice is worth any expenditure of time in its behalf."

An elderly black man with a fringe of white hair spoke up: "I think we'd all like to know for starters what exactly is going on here, Mr. Blue."

"Fair enough," Blue clasped his hands behind his back and rocked on his heels. "Ladies and gentlemen, for reasons I presume have been adequately discussed among you, it is apparent that one of you is not entirely who or what he or she appears on the surface to be. The inner circle of the Preservation Society—your circle, my friends—has been infiltrated by an agent serving the sinister interests of the so-called Sect, a conspiracy whose roots and designs are evil, pure evil. Isaac has sought to employ my services to ferret out the identity of this infiltrator and for that purpose I have requested your presence here this morning so that together we may dispose of the matter with a minimum of fuss to all concerned. Now, Nora—" Blue turned slightly "—will you do us the honor of introducing me to those here I've not previously had the pleasure?"

"Certainly, Desmond." Nora said.

The first person she introduced to Blue was a wiry youthful-looking man named Kevin O'Gar, the society's chief librarian. Blue recalled him as an Irish lyric poet of more than modest gifts who'd last published a rather thin volume of verse more than a decade earlier.

The second person introduced was an attractive copper-skinned woman named Orinda Mercado. Blue recognized her as the author of an extraordinarily popular "psychohistory" of contemporary events, the primary thesis of which was that the Occupation was the consequence of a mass human death wish.

The third individual was the academic sociologist Irwin Levitsky, a Marxist-Stalinist scholar who made no apologies for it. (Gustanov at the door gave a derisive snort.)

The fourth and final stranger in the room, the elderly black man, Nora introduced, as Ezra Dent. "Ezra," she explained, "is the senior member of the society and our resident software genius here in Futura. He more than anyone is responsible for the existence of Isaac."

The black man smiled. "I'm his daddy more or less," he said in a warm drawling voice. "Little Isaac is my only legitimate son."

With Donatello, Brother Xavier, and Nora that made seven.

Blue stepped back and once more surveyed the group as a whole. "Now that we have all had the opportunity to—" he began.

Donatello broke in: "One moment, Blue. That Russian lunatic with the absurd goggles. I demand to know on whose authority he's here."

"On mine of course. I've asked Captain Gustanov to join us as my assistant."

"Why do you need an assistant?"

"Georgi, why don't you explain?"

With a broad grin Gustanov thrust a hand into the side pocket of his jumpsuit and extracted a heavy black instrument, which he slapped meaningfully against his palm. "Comrade Blue has invited me to act as his sergeant-at-arms and designated thumper. As soon as we figure out which of you is the bad cat, then I get to thump the son-of-a-bitch a hard one up against the side of his head with my thumper."

"Surely you don't anticipate exposing the infiltrator so easily, Mr. Blue," Brother Xavier said.

"As a matter of fact," said Blue, "I have little doubt whatsoever that our task will be accomplished within the next hour." He glanced at his watch. "It is presently eight-oh-three. You have my guarantee that come nine-oh-three all of you—minus one of course—will have exited this room in complete innocence."

"And how do you intend to pull this off?" said Kevin O'Gar with an angry glower. "Is it going to be physical torture or the more traditional third-degree?"

"Neither," Blue said smoothly, "I believe the second-degree will suffice. Ladies and gentlemen." He clapped his hands to get their full attention. "May I ask you to please form a semi-circle facing the wall behind us?"

"What the hell for?" asked Irwin Jacob Levitsky with a suspicious frown.

"Now that," said Blue with a wry wink, "is for me to know and for you to find out."

With a minimum of additional grumbling the seven formed the semi-circle Blue had asked for. He remained alone at the front of the room until the formation was complete. Then at his signal the lights in the room dimmed and on the wall a series of concentric circles appeared, alternating red and yellow in color. Music began to play and the circles pulsated in rhythm to the beat.

"This is Isaac's work," Donatello said. "Nora told us he was busy meditating."

"Apparently he's finished," Blue said.

"This is absurd."

"No," said O'Gar, who was watching the pulsating circles on the wall, "I think it's meant to be hypnotism."

Blue let the lights and music go on for several minutes before again raising a hand.

At his signal silence filled the room.

Blue jabbed with a finger. "Miss Mercado, shall we begin with you?"

Orinda Mercado tore her gaze away from the wall with obvious difficulty. "I—yes, Mr. Blue."

"Your mother," he said. "Could you tell me something about her?"

"My mother? But what does—?"

"The question, Miss Mercado. Please endeavor to respond."

"My mother is dead," she said.

"I'm sorry to hear that." Blue's jabbing finger moved on to the next in line—Ezra Dent. "And you, Mr. Dent. What can you tell me about your mother?"

The black man smiled fondly. "Dead also, Mr. Blue, though you needn't feel sorry about it. She led a fine, full life. Warm, gentle, loving, and as strong as the earth."

"And yours?" said Blue, pointing at Donatello.

"My mother was a whore," he said stiffly.

"And your father?"

"His identity was unknown to me. Likely to her as well."

"Did you have any uncles?"

"Often a new one every few days." This time he smiled.

"These were blood uncles?"

"Of course they weren't." Donatello let his annoyance show. "I assume you know these questions are utterly nonsensical. An attempt to embarrass me in front of the others, I gather."

"Please," Blue said wearily. "Again, I must ask for your patience and your indulgence. My methods are sometimes less than direct, I admit, but they rarely fail. The sooner we get on with the interrogations, the sooner we will achieve a solution to our mystery. Now, Signor Donatello, I persist. What can you tell me about your blood uncles?"

"The only real uncle I ever knew was my mother's oldest brother. A big hairy man, a cobbler. I disliked the man intensely. My mother loathed him as well. I would surmise that at some point when they were young he had taken her sexually by force."

"Raped her you mean?"

"I believe that's the legal term for it, yes."

"Where was this?"

"Where? In Italy. Where do you think?"

"North or South?"

"In Naples. I lived nowhere else."

Again Blue's finger moved on. "Mr. O'Gar, have you ever had cause to visit Naples in the spring?"

"I don't believe I ever—no, wait. Now that you bring it up I did indeed pass through there once long ago. The weather was clear, the bay was beautiful, the season was spring, there was a lovely dark-eyed girl."

"You're certain of all this?"

"After so many years, alas, no. Memories grow hazy you know."

"Please try to remember. It may prove crucial."

O'Gar shut his eyes. After a long moment he smiled. "It was summer—August, I'm afraid—otherwise everything was as I stated."

"Ah," said Blue. Again, his finger moved on. "Mr. Levitsky, what have you to say for yourself?"

"Concerning what? My mother?"

"No, we're past that now. Italy. Have you ever visited Italy in the month of August?"

"Not if I could possibly avoid it."

"Then your response is negative?"

"Honestly, I'm not positive. Italy is not a country I'm overly fond of. Especially the South below Rome. A filthy place filled with filthy people. Excuse me, Signor Donatello, for speaking candidly. It's only my own opinion."

"And mine, Mr. Levitsky," Donatello said. "Remember, I was born and grew up there."

So you told us," Blue said. "Now Mr. Dent—" he pointed at the door "—you may go, please."

"I, sir?"

"I see no further reason for you to remain."

With a brief backward glance at the others, Ezra Dent made his departure. Gustanov held the door open for him and closed it once he'd passed through.

"So it's one down and six to go, is it, Blue?" Donatello said. "Or are you playing a different game?"

"This is no game."

"You could certainly have fooled me."

"At this point," Blue said, "I wish to modify my tactics somewhat. From now on I will ask a single question which each of you will respond to in turn. I'll begin with you, Signor Donatello. Which of the others here do suspect of being the infiltrator?"

Donatello looked narrowly at Blue. "How would I possibly know that?"

"I didn't ask what You knew. I asked what you suspected."

"Then I suspect—" his teeth gritted in a tight smile "—the black man, Dent."

Blue swung his arm, pointing. "Miss Mercado, your opinion please?"

"I'd rather not say—really."

"I must insist. Fair is fair and every one will have his or her chance."

"Well, in that case, if I really have to—and it's only a wild guess, nothing more—then I'd have to pick Irwin here. But that's only because—"

"You filthy liar," said Levitsky. "You know very well it can't be me. If it's anyone it's you with your bizarre psychohistories."

"Nora," said Blue. "Your turn next."

"I haven't the slightest idea, Desmond. And that's the truth."

"Yes, I know." Blue pointed. "Brother Xavier?"

The monk shook his big head. "I won't say either."

"But you have an opinion?"

"I do, yes, but I prefer not to accuse someone without evidence. And I have no evidence."

Blue nodded. "An interesting point of view. Donatello then. Who do you think it is?"

"Goddamn, I told you already: it's the old fool Dent."

"Are you willing to say that again?"

"I am. Dent, Dent, Dent. Is that enough for you?"

"No. Because I don't believe you."

"Then—" he swung his head "—then let's make it Brother Xavier here. Since he suspects me I will return the favor."

"But I don't suspect you, Mario," Xavier said. "I never intended—"

"Signor Donatello," Blue said, eyes narrowing. "what makes you think Brother Xavier suspects you?"

"It's rather obvious, isn't it? The monk has never trusted me. I came here a man of wealth and fame—an unreconstructed sinner. In addition, I—"

"But you are in error," Blue said. "Brother Xavier suspects only himself."

"Why do you say that?" Xavier asked with an air of shock.

"Why?" Smiling, Blue stepped close to him. "Am I mistaken?"

"Well...no, I suppose in a sense you aren't. I know perhaps as much about the Sect as anyone. I am fully cognizant of the extent of their powers. Drugs, hypnotism, all the modern devices of mind control—none of this is beyond them. It is entirely conceivable that any of one of us—or more—could be carrying out their will without being consciously aware of it. That includes myself."

"Please go, Brother Xavier," said Blue.

"Go?"

"Yes. I thank you for sharing your theory but it is not the correct one."

"But how can you—?"

"Oh, I know," said Blue, tapping his skull with a knuckle. "Believe me—I do."

Brother Xavier left the room.

Blue waited a moment and then nodded to himself. "Mr. O'Gar, you also."

"Me, Mr. Blue?"

"Yes, go."

"Certainly. With pleasure."

Kevin O'Gar exited the room without a backward glance.

Blue shifted his gaze, "Mr. Levitsky, I don't believe we've heard from you in response to our open question. Not officially at least. Whom do you suspect?"

"Well, frankly, it seems clear enough to me." Levitsky jerked a thumb in the direction of Orinda Mercado. "This woman here—her deliberate distortions of recorded history—these in themselves constitute sufficient evidence to link her—"

"Good God," said Blue softly. "You are certain of this?"

"I am indeed. Most absolutely."

Blue pursed his lips, frowning in concentration. "Miss Mercado, you had better leave us now."

With a faintly bemused expression Orinda Mercado exited the room. As she went past Georgi Gustanov he emitted a long low admiring whistle.

Levitsky began an angry protest but Blue silenced him with a curt head shake.

"Now, gentlemen, Nora," he said, "I would strongly recommend that we all work together to bring this matter to a swift and satisfactory conclusion. I'm most gratified to find that our gathering has turned out to be an intimate affair after all."

The three remaining suspects—Donatello, Levitsky, Nora Malloy—each looked at the others with a mixture of curiosity and doubt. Soft music had begun playing again; the colorful concentric circles danced across the wall.

Blue said, "Our next exercise will be one likely familiar to all—a word association game. I'll start the boulder rolling down the hill with a word and then point to one of you to respond with the first word that comes immediately to mind and then on to the next person I point to who will respond to the previous response and so on. Is all this clear?"

It was indeed clear.

"Excellent," said Blue, rubbing his hands eager in anticipation. "Then for our first word I choose one appropriate for the occasion: *evil*. Mr. Levitsky, over to you."

"This is not only asinine but worse. It's Freudian."

"Mr. Levitsky, please." Blue looked at his watch. "We're nearly done here. *Evil* is the word."

"Then *good*," said Levitsky.

"Excellent! Perfect! I see you know the game. Nora, your turn. The word to you is now *good*."

"Ah...*evil?*" She seemed uncertain.

"Already taken. We need to move on. Try another."

"God then."

"Wonderful! Brilliant! This game going so well. Signor Donatello, your turn. The word is *God*."

"*Satan,*" he said after a pause.

"The exercise will not work properly," Blue said, "unless you respond immediately—without hesitation. Act without thinking, as our existentialist friends say. Mr. Levitsky, over to you. The word is now *Satan*."

"*Money,*" he said with a smile.

Blue pointed. "Signor Donatello?"

Donatello said: "*Pleasure.*"

Nora: "*Love.*"

Levitsky: "*Lust.*"

Nora: "*Soap.*"

Blue started. "Did you say *soap?*"

She looked embarrassed. "Well, you did tell us to say whatever popped into our minds first. I guess lust makes me feel like taking a bath."

"Signor Donatello, the word to you is s*oap*."

"*Water,*" he said.

"*Purity*," said Nora.

Levitsky: "*Death.*"

Donatello: "*Blood.*"

Levitsky: "*Murder.*"

Donatello: "*Evil.*"

Nora: No, wait. He said it again. He said *evil* again.""

Blue rocked with merriment. "So he did. Did you all catch that? We began with my *evil* and we ended with evil. The circle is thus complete. The serpent swallows its own tail. It happens that way nearly every time," he added in a confidential tone.

Levitsky seemed considerably less amused. "It proves nothing," he muttered.

"True," said Blue. "And yet even the discovery of nothing may at times serve as an essential clue—I need only refer to the classic instance of the dog that failed to bark in the night." He took another look at his watch. "Time runs short, I fear, so rather than proceeding to another word I think we'll leap straight ahead into the next phase of the investigation."

Swiveling, he faced the wall and bowed. "Isaac," he said, "you may please join us now."

"Oh, I've been here all along, Mr. Blue," said the boyish voice from the wall speaker. "I've been having lots of fun listening in."

Blue now faced the others. "Over the years during which I've devoted myself first as a physician and then as a detective to the study of the human species I have gradually become aware of the critical significance in overall character development of the image of the father. In view of that for our next exercise I'd like us all to band together in an effort at concocting a model father figure satisfactory to all. Nora, you may begin. Your own father—was he a tall or a short man?"

"Tall," she said. "He was a rancher, remember. Though for a child every adult seems tall. Especially men."

"Isaac," said Blue over his shoulder, "can you provide us with a tall man, please?"

"Lickety-split, Mr. Blue." On the wall where the concentric circles had played there now appeared the gargantuan shadow-like outline of a human figure. A tall man.

"Now hold on here," said Levitsky. "I thought the purpose of this exercise was to uncover the identity of a spy among, not to waste time with a lot of psychological claptrap and humbug."

Blue looked offended. "My methods may at times appear arcane," he admitted, "but need I remind all of you of one indisputable fact? One of the three of you is the infiltrator we seek. Bearing that in mind, I would strongly urge you to watch your words accordingly."

"Are you threatening me, Blue."

"Only if you're prepared to confess your guilt."

"*My* guilt? Why, I'm hardly—"

"As you wish. Then let us proceed." Blue turned back to Nora. "How does Isaac's image of a father strike you? Credible or not?"

"Well, it does seem a bit on the exaggerated side. My father may have been a tall man but he wasn't a giant."

"We aren't seeking verisimilitude here, Nora—only essence."

"In that case, fine." She shrugged.

"Mr. Levitsky," said Blue, "what can you tell us about your own father?"

Glowering, Levitsky responded with obvious reluctance: "He wasn't tall. He was a shrunken little dwarf."

"Is he alive today?"

"I wouldn't have the slightest idea."

"Then the two of you were not close?"

"I hated the pig."

"Then what about his eyes? Can you describe them? Were they sly, avaricious, or what?"

"All of the above and more. The eyes of a rodent. He also had a long crooked nose and a swarthy complexion if that's what you're getting at."

"At the moment," Blue said, "I'm content to get at the truth only. Isaac, can you give us two dark eyes please?"

The outline on the wall vanished for an instant and when it reappeared a pair of narrow black eyes showed in the otherwise blank countenance of the face.

Blue looked at Donatello. "Would you care to take charge of the facial hair?"

Donatello was gazing at the figure on the wall with an uneasy expression. "That doesn't resemble my father at all."

"It's not intended to represent any particular individual—it's a composite creation of the subconscious."

"Jungian rot," muttered Levitsky.

"What do you want me to do?" said Donatello.

"The hair. Color, style, texture, so on.

"I'm afraid my father was as bald as an eggplant. He enjoyed being so. His great hero was the thug Mussolini."

"Isaac," said Blue, "one bald head please."

"Coming right up, Mr. Blue."

The top portion of the figure winked out of existence and when it reappeared the head was covered with what appeared to be a black hood. Only the eyes showed through a pair of narrow slits and they burned like fiery orbs.

"I said *bald*. My father was bald. What is this thing with the hood?"

"Again," said Blue, "let me reiterate. What we seek to create here is an idealized representation of a father, not a particular man."

"But it's still wrong. My father wore a big white moustache and a—a long shaggy beard. Put all of that in too. And get rid of that ridiculous hood. It's utter nonsense."

Blue spoke over his shoulder: "Did you catch that, Isaac?"

"I've the ears of an elephant, Mr. Blue."

The figure disappeared again but when it came back The only apparent alteration was the addition of what seemed to be ankle-length black robes.

Donatello looked stunned. "*Bastard*," he whispered. "Damn your filthy lies."

Ignoring him, Blue turned to Levitsky. "What do you think of our creation so far, sir?"

"If you're trying to draw the devil, then I think you've hit the mark. Otherwise, don't ask me what's going on. I told you this was a silly waste of time."

"Nora?"

"I don't know what it's supposed to signify, Desmond, but Irwin is right—it's rather terrifying."

"Signor Donatello? What about you? Does our little representation terrify you also?"

"Of course not. As I said it means nothing to me. It's not my father or anyone else's. I've never seen anyone looking like that in my life. It's ugly, disgusting. Get it off the wall. This is all a filthy trick aimed at me. It's stupid, meaningless."

"I wonder about that," said Blue. "What it means to me," he added, advancing toward Donatello, "is that a short time ago you assured us that your father was unknown to you. So which is it, my friend? Which is the lie and which is the truth? Is that your father up there on the wall or is it perhaps someone else you know? Is it the devil himself we see there?'

At this point Donatello broke and ran, moving with surprising speed and dexterity. Blue reached out to grab him but his fingers fell short. Gustanov at the door pulled out his sap and swung it in a downward arc but Donatello ducked deftly beneath the blow and came up with his right fist cocked. The punch caught Gustanov in the jaw and sent him sprawling.

Donatello was out the door and gone.

Blue took Nora by the arm. "Come, dear. Let's get you out of here."

They crossed the room to where Gustanov was rising to his feet. "Goddamn, daddy-o," he said, rubbing his chin, "that yo-yo's got him one mean son of a bitch punch."

"I'm sorry, Georgi," Blue said. "I didn't anticipate him doing that. Can you do me one more favor and escort Nora back to our chalet? Take Mr. Levitsky out with you too. I have a few minor matters to go over with Isaac first and then I'll join you."

"Sounds good to me, Boss." Gustanov cocked a finger at Levitsky. "Come along, pard. The big man wants to be alone with the thing in the wall."

* * * *

After the others had gone, Blue pulled up a chair, sat down, and looked up at the speaker. "So, Isaac," he said, "what do you have to say now?"

"If you mean about Donatello turning out to be the Sect infiltrator? I'm as surprised as you are, Mr. Blue."

"And I'm not surprised at all. Since I assume you put him up to it."

"Me?"

"Of course. Who else? This might be as good a time as any for you to drop the façade of adolescent boyishness. It certainly never fooled me."

"I know. I never thought it would." His tone of his voice had changed. He no longer sounded like a brash boy of thirteen. He now sounded exactly like Desmond Blue. "This better?"

"It'll do."

"Fine. Now you said you had a few minor matters you wanted to go over with me. Can I ask what those are?"

"Only one thing really. Now that we both know the identity of the Sect agent here in Futura—"

"We do?"

"Of course. It's you."

"Me?" said Isaac, still using Blue's voice.

"You. Then the next obvious question needing an answer is: are you also the one in charge?"

"In charge of what?"

"The Sect. The conspiracy at the dark heart of human history since the dawn of time.

"Me? Oh, goodness no. Like God, I'm more in the nature of a cosmic observer. I prefer to keep my distance from you people when I can."

"Then who is? I assume you know."

"I do, yes."

"And you won't tell me?"

"I won't. But—I will show you. Here, look."

As Blue sat there, a three-dimensional hologramic image formed in the air in front of him. It was the same gargantuan dark-robed, blazing-eyed figure that had appeared on the wall earlier.

"I've seen this before, Isaac."

"Step closer, please."

Blue stood up and approached the hologram.

"Now touch it."

Extended a hand, Blue let the tips of his fingers brush the dark shape. The touch was cold. He shuddered.

"Now lift the hood and take a look."

Blue slipped his fingers underneath the hood.

"You don't have to look if you don't want to," Isaac said.

Blue lifted the hood.

He looked at the face underneath.

15

"So what's become of Gustanov?" Blue said as he stepped inside the chalet and found Nora Malloy sitting alone on the sofa. "You haven't misplaced him, I hope."

"I suspect he's misplaced himself," Nora said. "A woman called shortly after we got here and invited him to her room for afternoon tea. He went racing out of here like the devil was in his pants."

"A most apt simile," said Blue, dropping down heavily in the chair across from her.

"You don't look well, Desmond."

"I don't feel well either."

"Maybe you ought to try and get some rest."

"I can't—not now. As soon as Georgi returns we're on our way back home."

"Then you found what you wanted here?"

"With Donatello's exposure you mean?"

"Oh, I forget to tell you. He's apparently disappeared. No one can find him anywhere in Futura."

"I thought that might be the case. Gone back to that cult of his assume."

"The Sect?" she said.

"That's what they call themselves, yes."

She smiled, shaking her head. "Desmond, please. I know better than that. I'm sure you do too. Donatello is only doing what Isaac told him to do."

"And what should I do about it then?"

"What can you do?"

"Nothing."

"Exactly. So that's what you should do."

"You don't think he's a danger? Isaac, I mean."

"No more than a great many other things."

"Like the Occupants?"

"Our masters."

"You mean our makers."

"Or both?"

She smiled. "Sounds like the beginning a mystery story to me."

* * * *

"Come and sit beside me, Desmond," Nora said. She patted the cushion. "I think we could both use a little closeness now."

He got up and went over and sat down with another heavy sigh. "I don't suppose drugs are permitted here in your sterile Futura? I've given up my dear opium for the duration but a bit of weed would go well right now."

"Would a glass of cognac suffice?"

"You have some?"

"There's two bottles in the kitchen. Gustanov must have got hold of them somehow. I can pour you a glass."

"And one for yourself as well."

Desmond Blue remained on the sofa, eyes focused on the mahogany floor until Nora returned. They touched glasses, sipped.

"Nora?" said Blue.

"Yes, Desmond?"

"Would you be willing—I know this is badly timed and crudely put—but would you be willing—for old time's sake if nothing else—would you be willing to make love with me?"

"I was beginning to think you were never going to ask."

"I've been celibate for ages, you know. And I've become grossly fat."

"That's an exaggeration."

"I have to bend over and squint to see my own kneecaps."

"Why would you want to see your kneecaps? They're only bones. I foresaw all this, you know."

"I was rather hoping you had."

"It turns out well in the end."

"That's good to know."

"Yes, isn't it?"

He leaned over and kissed her then.

BOOK FIVE

COSMIC FUSION

"He adjusted himself to beams falling, and then no more of them fell, and he adjusted himself to them not falling."

—Dashiell Hammett, *The Maltese Falcon*

A PROFILE: MARCEL DE SARNOT

The following excerpts are taken from *Mysterion* by Marcel de Sarnot, privately printed, Paris, 1795. Translated from the original Latin by Arnold Hope Grimthorpe & Desmond Blue:

"…authoress and I first rendezvoused behind the lace curtains of that white room which was to become for us a holy shrine devoted to the shameless fervor of our unleashed passions. Although I had long since been captivated by her fair charms from afar, the revelation of her naked beauty nevertheless swept over me that first day as if it were a sheet of fierce hot lightning: her firm breasts like miniature hills sculpted from ivory; the sleek, burnished skin of her slender, yet womanly thighs; the fleshy sheen of her smooth, flat abdomen; the curled, raven-black hair which graced the moist lips that stood expectant sentry before the tunnel of her desire. Unable to withstand the heaving tide of my fevered emotion, I took her radiant loveliness into my arms and ravished her full red lips with warm, lustful kisses.

'Become naked, my darling Marcel,' she whispered breathlessly into my ear. 'I beseech you not to keep me waiting another dread moment before granting my eyes the privilege of feasting upon the glorious essence of your tumescent manhood.' Instantly, I rushed to obey her command with fingers which fumbled like those of a young stable boy, mesmerized as I was by the nearness of her undraped beauty. When at last my blood-swelled organ burst forth into the pale afternoon light, I heard her tumultuous sighs. 'Oh, it is a grand fat one, my love!' she cried out. 'Already I adore it as though it lay pulsating deep within my womb!' Immediately, like a senseless slave, I hastened to fulfill the promise of…"(Page 5.)

* * * *

"…darling authoress commenced her oral ministrations upon the palpitating flesh of my staff, as she had so often divinely done in days past, and yet it was as though our passion was newly reborn each new day. A spasm of almost religious frenzy seemed to overwhelm her pink, wet, nibbling tongue as it bathed and caressed the entirety of my throbbing membrane, and it was as if that lust which surely enflamed her loins now lay concentrated like a pinprick of molten heat in the private sensations of her round and ravenous mouth. As I observed her flailing head impaled upon my organ, her silken hair spread upon my loins like the outstretched wings of a bird, I heard the sound of my own voice calling out in incoherent phrases, and, in a mad delirium, I reached down, clasped my hands upon her fair cheeks, and pressed savagely inward in order more fully to experience the maddening embrace of her warm, wet, suckling mouth…" (Pages 54-55.)

* * * *

"…tremendous heaving sensation deep within my loins and became dimly aware that no physical force known to mankind could now restrain the liquid flow from soon bursting forth like a great gushing river into the open chasm of her waiting mouth. I cupped her chin within my hands and fought to penetrate yet deeper the blessed cavity of her lips hearing the cat-like purring of her voice as the initial jets of hot liquid sprayed the back of her throat, bloating and stretching that hungry mouth as she strained gluttonously to swallow the spurting needles of my…" (Page 99.)

* * * *

"…struggled like a Roman stoic to avoid rushing heedlessly ahead, while I gazed in open rapture at the mute figure of my beloved authoress crouched in front of me in an attitude that was both mockery and acceptance of the holy rite of prayer, and I understood instinctively that for her our lust had now assumed the aspect of a true religion combining both flesh and spirit as one. The smooth orbs of her nether region undulated in tiny circles, thrusting beseechingly back at me as though crying out wordlessly for that swift impalement which would bring a unity, while I imperviously sought to extend the anticipation of that sacred instant when I would lunge between those pale ivory moons, which I worshiped like heathen idols, and work my will upon her darkest, most private realm. For a brief moment, I allowed the engorged tip of my organ to slip within the pink crevasse, simultaneously pressing the fleshy globes of her derriere snugly together with my trembling hands, so that my staff was trapped as if in the grip of a velvet glove, and then, first drawing back and lunging forward, I ran my tongue along the full length of her spine until I attained that clenched, puckered opening where her..." (Page 189.)

* * * *

"...continued to scream as my spent lust fired bolt after bolt of lightning-hot juice into the black depths of her nether zone. When at last
I withdrew, temporarily satiated, I found my own voice shouting words which I did not at first comprehend:
"'Who are you? What manner of being is this whom I ravish? You seem woman, and yet you are also child. You seem a lady, and yet you are wench. You seem human, and yet you are beast. You seem angel, and yet you are devil.'
"'My dearest Marcel,' she replied, after a silence, 'I beseech you not to ask such questions. I am the all of the all, that which has been, that which now is, and that which soon shall be. Love me for what I offer, but seek no deeper knowledge, please.'
"And then it was too late for mere words, as my passion rebounded with a surge, and I hastened to invade..." (Page 194)

1

"Good Lord in heaven," snarled Desmond Blue as he hurled the ancient leatherbound book across the length of the room where it banged hard against the wall and slid to the floor. "What sheer unmitigated trash!"
Clustered around Blue in the study, his three devoted retainers each raised their head and started in unison: a sullen Alfie Jarrett, unlit cigarette dangling from his lip; a haunted Dr. Gordon Schwerner, tanned and forlorn after his East African sojourn; a distant Peter Mark, curled on the carpet at Blue's feet with one steel hand rhythmically stroking the nappy fur of the hound Baskerville.

In addition, seated knee to knee on the loveseat perched Blue's battery of comely and efficient confidential secretaries—Nadia van Hauten, Crystal LaFleur, Lacy Bach—each with a pen poised expectantly above an open notepad.

Georgi Gustanov decked out in a crisp new orange jumpsuit leaned against the door, his arms folded on his chest.

"And with that," said Blue, indicating the book he had just hurled, "I complete my review of the investigative evidence collected in the matter of the Case of the Sect Conspiracy."

"Are you saying, Desmond," said Dr. Schwerner, "that all the work we put in on this case was for naught?"

"Not in the least, Doctor," said Blue, leaning back in his chair. "In your own investigation, for instance, you were privileged to witness what I can only regard as the most significant leap in human evolution since the day an anonymous man-ape in Africa decided to use a bone as a weapon with which to slay an enemy. Instead of the isolated lives each of has suffered alone for the past many millennia, you witnessed the birth of a new form of human consciousness, a fused synergic gestalt able to leave our frail physical bodies behind and enter realms of inner space previously denied to us."

"I suppose that's true," said a still downcast Dr. Schwerner.

"But you regret the loss of a certain young woman, do you not?" said Blue.

"I'm afraid I do. I think I may have fallen in love with Talia. I'm not sure. I've never been in love before. But it feels that way."

"Then cherish her memory, Doctor."

"That's it, Desmond?"

Blue smiled. "It's more than many have, Gordon. It's why we call it love."

Blue wheeled around and jabbed a finger. "As for you, Alfie," he said, "you too were privileged to witness a significant event in human history, our leap into outer space. To the stars, Alfie—to the stars and beyond. The dream of many of us since we were young children obsessed with fantastic tales of space and time. With all of the universe open to human expansion I foresee a day when the domain of our species extends from one end of the galaxy to the other. What marvels await our descendants, what wonders they will experience. The mind must reel and bogle at the prospect."

"Sure," said Alfie, not sounding entirely convinced. "But I still don't see why Tess had to go. She could have sent a robot along with her old man."

"You loved her too, I gather."

He shrugged. "I suppose so, sure."

"Then like I told Gordon, cherish her memory."

"But, Desmond," broke in Peter Mark from the floor below, "what about me? I didn't witness anything like Gordon and Alfie did. All I saw in Winesap were a bunch of mean miserable ugly people burning books and frying their brains on tridee. What kind of great evolutionary leap do you call that?"

"I don't," said Blue. "But when there's utopia there must always be dystopia to set it off. We're not perfect beings, Peter. Far from it. The yin and yang as my Chinese friends term it. The light and the dark. As for little Ginger Cunningham, cherish her memory too. And, please remember, Peter—" he smiled "she'll grow older as you grow wiser."

"Hey, hold on a minute, Mr. Private Eye." It was Georgi Gustanov pushing off from the wall. "All these horse feathers you spout are all swell and good in their place. I, Gustanov, love a pretty lady as much as anybody." He tossed a wink at the three secretaries. "But that's not what the good Holy Father hired you to investigate, is it? What about this bunch of nogoodniks known as the Sect? What are you doing about them? They kill Jesus and make a hero out of Hitler and you let them run free. What about this big boss of theirs the smarty machine that lives in the wall in Futura showed you his face? What are you doing about bumping him off for good?"

"Alas, Georgi," said Blue, looking suddenly weary. He spread his arms. "There isn't much I can do.'

"Why not when you saw who he was under the black hood?"

"I failed to recognize him. A complete review of the known data failed to render any identification. The man is completely unknown to history."

"And your diligent workers here? They all pretty sharp dudes. They can't spot him either?"

"I don't know if they can or not."

"You haven't shown them the picture?"

"What picture?"

"The one I saw you sneak."

"Oh." Blue's eyes narrowed into slits. "How do you know about that?"

"I know because I got eyes in my head. I see the little camera hidden in your fat hand. I got ears too. I hear the camera go *click*. So show us what you got."

"It's not the clearest photograph in the world. The conditions under which it was taken were dreadful."

"Still it's the best you got, right?"

"I suppose." Reluctantly, Blue reached into the folds of his robe and drew out a small three-by-five black-and-white photograph. The image was hazy and indistinct at best.

He first handed it to Peter still seated at his feet. "Anybody you recognize?" he said.

Peter gazed at the photograph, squinting through the steel mask of his face. "I'm sorry, Desmond. No, I don't recognize him."

Peter stood up, crossed over, and handed the photograph to Alfie. He gave it a careful look.

"Nope. Nobody I ever saw anywhere. Ugly looking creep though."

Then it was Dr. Schwerner's turn. He stared at the photograph long and hard—with the cool detachment of a scientist.

"No," he said. "I fail to recognize this person."

Schwerner took the photograph over to where the three secretaries sat.

Nadia looked first. "Nope, sorry," she said.

Crystal pushed errant strands of hair out of her eyes, leaned in close. "Afraid not, no."

"I don't think…" Lacy began. She finally shook her head. "Not me either, Desmond. Sorry."

"As I feared," said Blue, rising heavily to his feet. He moved to reclaim the photograph.

"Hey, hold on," cried Gustanov, darting forward. "You got one more good set of eyes in this room needing a look."

He plucked the photograph out of Lacy's hand, held it up to the light.

"Son of a goddamn bitch!"

Blue halted in his tracks. "You know him, Giorgi? You recognize this man?"

"I sure as bat shit do! This is him! The bastard of all known bastards! The scheming monster who tortures babies and laughs at their screams! The one who—!"

"A name, Georgi, does he have a name?"

"He sure as heavy owl shit does. A name like a bad tumor in the gut. Andreev is the name. Vasily Andreev. The son of a bitch who runs state security for all the goddamn Red Communist Empire."

"Where can this Andreev be found?"

"In Moscow, man! Where else? Andreev is the one who guards the slug. You will find him there with his captive friend!"

2

That which follows constitutes the sworn final testament of one Vasily Andreev, a human being first, a citizen of the Russian homeland second, and is intended as an accurate, complete, and faithful account of certain events occurring near the end of a rarely satisfying, seldom glorious existence.

To wit my own miserable life:

After the one naked and lovely young woman has caressed and fondled my body and after what I assume is her companion—as yet unseen by me—has slunk around behind my back and struck me on the head with a blunt instrument I am for some time rendered unconscious.

When I wake I open my eyes a crack but do not budge a muscle or utter a sound, for like all men possessed of native cunning I prefer to take stock of my current environment before inserting my physical self within it.

At first all I am able to discern most directly in front of me consists of nothing other than an indistinct blur of motion but then a familiar sound reaches my ears which I soon identify as the lustful moaning of considerable passion. Very much puzzled I give my eyes some hurried blinks and this time am able to detect certain phenomena with clarity.

Not far distant from where my wounded head rests upon the floor—let us estimate two meters—I discover three individuals locked in a state of carnal embrace that somewhat resembles a sandwich composed of flesh-and-blood elements. In the middle—assuming the role of the meat—kneels my dear old friend the captive while in front I further recognize the comely features of that naked young woman who not long ago professed a strong desire for Vasily Andreev himself.

At the rear of this grouping squats yet another naked person, a young blond man with a large and erect male sex organ—a prick!—jutting forth from his loins.

Whoever this fellow may be—he could from his looks be a twin of the woman—it is apparent that he is at present making use of this prick in order to violate the nether regions of my captive.

So what goes on here? I inquire of myself. Is it old Andreev who has gone batshit insane or is it the world itself which has again turned upside down?

Unable to reconcile the evidence of my eyes with the knowledge of my brain I turn my gaze to the naked young woman and here I discover the presence of the five-pointed birthmark I previously observed slightly below the bud of her left nipple. I further note the fullness of her hips, the leanness of her belly, the taut stretched skin of her thighs and flanks. It is an exceedingly pleasant vision even for one such as I, Andreev, who has only an intellectual interest in matters of this sort but as my gaze shifts toward the nexus where her legs meet her torso I come across yet another anomaly for between her thighs the shaft of yet a second prick lies swollen. Now hold on, I think, nearly speaking aloud with surprise. This cannot be.

Who is going crazy this time?

Eventually after much due deliberation I reach an inescapable conclusion: what is happening here, that which I am presently observing, is simply an act of sexual congress in which the three are but replaceable components of a singular indivisible whole.

As for my captive, she/he as always resembles the clear-eyed moon-faced twelve-year-old boy/girl I first pulled from the wreckage of her/his ship on the day of our reckoning.

In other words, she/he has at last found his/her own kind.

Sensing my gaze upon him/ her, she/he shouts out a message in Russian, the first words he/she has ever uttered to my knowledge.

It is at this point sadly that I fall into a swoon and by the time my senses recover the three of them are gone. Alone now, I rise to my knees and begin to crawl across the floor, twisting my head as I go and discovering a large, perfectly round hole in the surface of the plate glass barrier that for so long kept me apart from my captive.

I then raise the alarm and with salty tears of remorse clouding my vision I await my inevitable fate at the hands of those fools who know no better.

Amen.

3

In a dim cold windowless room tucked away in a bottom cellar of a nameless prison not far from the empty shell of the Kremlin, Desmond Blue sits across a low wooden table from a sad-eyed sallow-cheeked man with a long hooked eagle's beak of a nose. This man, one Vasily Andreev, has just concluded relating the full story of how he has come to be condemned to die as a traitor to his species.

Blue gazes at Andreev intently. "And the rest of it, sir?"

"There is no more, Mr. Blue."

"The words the Occupant spoke to you—you neglected to relate them."

Andreev shook his head. "That must remain my secret, I am afraid."

"You are going to die, I believe."

"At dawn I will be shot."

"And yet you do not wish to divulge these words short of the grave?"

"I cannot."

"It is an awesome responsibility you take upon yourself, Vasily Andreev."

Andreev seemed to hesitate. "It is not easy," he admitted.

"Then tell me. You say you know of my reputation. Then you must also know that I am a man who can be trusted."

"It is not because of you that I am silent."

"Who then?"

"Them." He jerked his head at the ceiling in a gesture of contempt. "For twenty years my captive chose to retain his/her silence with them and when the moment came to share her/his innermost thoughts it was to me—Vasily Andreev—that he/she spoke. I cannot betray that trust."

"Have you been tortured?"

"Of course." Andreev pulled his hands from under the table and held them up in front of his face. The thumb and all four fingers of his right hand were bloody stumps while the left hand though intact was a twisted mass of broken bone and exposed gristle. "They also removed my testicles with pliers and pulled my teeth with razors. Or was it the other way around?" He shakes his head. "None of that matters now."

"But you told them nothing?"

"Only as much as I have told you. They did not believe even that."

"I do," Blue said.

Andreev shrugged. "That is your privilege."

"Is there no way I can convince you to confide in me?"

Andreev thought for a moment. "Why is it that you want to know?"

"Curiosity," said Blue. "Simple—and human—curiosity."

"An honest response." Andreev nodded his head. "And the only one that I could possibly accept."

"Then you'll tell me?" said Blue.

"This room..." Andreev shifted his eyes.

"It is secure," said Blue. "A condition obtained only through a considerable outlay of funds, I might add."

"They will not keep their word."

"Which is why I also wear this." Blue opened his shirt and showed Andreev a metallic device strapped to his chest. "This scrambling mechanism devised for me by my associate Dr. Schwerner is completely infallible."

"Then there remains only a single obstacle before I can speak freely."

"Which is?" said Blue.

"How may I be sure you are who you claim?"

"My photograph has often appeared—"

"That means nothing."

"My fingerprints are—"

"Easily faked."

"Then how," said Blue, "may I convince you?"

Andreev looked sly. "Answer four questions."

"What sort of questions?"

"You are, I believe, a man renowned for your knowledge and erudition. As such these questions should pose no problem for you."

"Please proceed," said Blue.

"Give me the name of the first of the anti-popes."

"Hippolytus," said Blue. "St. Hippolytus, that is."

"What can you tell me of his martyrdom?"

"He perished while laboring in the Sardinian quarries to which he had been banished because of his Christian faith."

"Who banished him?"

"Emperor Maximinus Thrax."

"On which Biblical book did Hippolytus compose a learned commentary?"

"The Book of Daniel, though I personally dispute several of his assertions."

"Thank you," said Andreev. "I think that will suffice." He smiled thinly. "Those men holding positions of authority today are a devious lot but they lack the imagination necessary to engage a theologian to impersonate you. I am convinced you are who you say you are, Mr. Blue."

"Then you will tell me now?" Blue edged closer to the table. "The words your captive confided in me before his escape."

As you wish." Andreev leaned forward and spoke distinctly and deliberately, selecting each individual word with painstaking care before uttering it aloud: "What my friend told me was that he and his fellows came to Earth in order to—"

"Yes?"

"To reboot our program, he said."

4

A PROFILE: THE CONSPIRACY OF THE SECT

Reprinted from the Neah Bay WA Review of Books, Volume XIX, number 9, pg 11):

The Conspiracy of the Sect, a novel, by Arnold Hope Grimthorpe, Hornblower & Smoak Publishers, New York, Beirut, and Bombay, 25 cents, paperbound.

Yet another banal attempt by a writer of no discernable gifts to raise the ante of the genre known among its largely male adolescent cognoscenti as "science fiction" (or shortened more crassly "sci-fi) to the status of the serious novel of merit.

As with other such attempts (barring the occasional modest success of a slumming Huxley or a befuddled Orwell), the stench of pretentious failure exudes from its 192 closely packed pages like that of a fish left too long out the Frigidaire.

Arnold Hope Grimthorpe, according to a brief publisher's note appended to the garishly illustrated wraparound cover (remove at once, would be my advice), is the author of some 47 previous works within this primitive sub-genre, the titles of which my poor suffering fingers refuse to type. Suffice to say, I've read none of these and given the wretched assemblage of ponderous adverbs and stuttering adjectives in the current volume I would as soon volunteer to undergo torture in the dankest dungeon of a Latin American banana republic.

The "story" presented here, if such it can claim to be, is predicated upon the ludicrous assumption of a conspiratorial band known familiarly as "the Sect" which throughout history has wielded an undue influence over human affairs, bearing responsibility for such vexed events as the crucifixion of the Christ, the assassination of Lincoln, World Wars One, Two, and if necessary Three, and the failure of the Chicago National League baseball team to win a World Series in the lifetime of anyone living. (The latter my own jest, I admit.)

A time traveling "camera," a concept purloined without due credit from the young Mr. Wells and his titular "machine," is sent back in time to photograph past cataclysmic events, the results of which upon examination divulge the apparent presence of certain individuals of a dastardly bent at many dark moments over history.

A band of three (pace M. Dumas pere's musketeers, if not Hollywood's stooges) led by a portly detective stolen from many previous sources (I count nine. ranging from Poe to Stout) is enlisted to combat this menace. From here the plot unspools to its fated climax of such overarching banality that I was reminded again with a shudder of my salad days as an undergraduate under the edifying hand of the great scholar Professor Dr. Leavis.

In any event at this point I must rise and cry to the heavens: *Hogwash!*

To summarize then: highly recommended to those pimply youths of an onanistic bent age fourteen and below.

To all others (using my signature scale ranging from one to 99 stars): I rate this: ½* (at best.)

5

When Desmond Blue leaves the secret prison after completing his interview with the condemned eschatological traitor Vasily Andreev via its burnished steel gate and enters the cool shifting light of false dawn, Georgi Gustanov and Crystal LaFleur stand waiting bundled up against the cold in fur coats and heavy mittens.

"Any luck with the son of a bitch inside?" Gustanov asks.

"Yes and no," says Blue with a thoughtful shrug.

As the three of them proceed along the empty pre-dawn boulevard still damp from the traces of a brief earlier snowfall, Blue reaches out and tosses a heavy arm around the shoulders of each of his companions so that the three of them observed from afar might be mistaken for a single unified entity rather than the separate and distinct individuals they are.

"Well, boss," says Crystal, "what now? Where to next?"

"For you, my dear, that's your own choice. This is a fascinating city. Perhaps friend Gustanov could show you around."

"My pleasure," says the aviator.

"Why not?" she agrees. "As long as he keeps his Russian paws to himself before I bust him another in the chops."

Gustanov thrusts hands under his armpits and winces robustly. "Lesson already learned, my dear."

Even Crystal has to laugh at that.

"As for myself," says Blue, "I intend to visit a local hotel where a certain lady of my acquaintance awaits a rendezvous."

"The beauteous Nora Malloy, perhaps?" suggests Gustanov.

"Could well be," confirms Blue.

"And the case," says Crystal. "What about your case?"

"The case," said Blue "is solved."

"You know who did it?"

"I do. Who, what, where, when, how. I know it and yet knowing it I also know nothing."

"Sounds like a paradox to me."

"It rather does, doesn't it?"

The three of them traverse an additional block. On the opposite side stands a majestic gray stone building like an enormous animal poised to spring. The building is absolutely dark except for high up near the top a single glimmering rectangle of white light. A neatly lettered sign in Cyrillic announces that the Dziga Vertov Institute can be found within.

Blue smiles at the irony. Here it was that the captive Occupant had once been held.

At that exact moment a deep eschatological silence grips the air as if a giant fist has suddenly reached down and caught the world in its grasp.

The three of them raise their heads as one to the pink-hued dawning sky above only to see—

6

I am a former medical doctor officially retired and living in the green country some distance beyond the city of Moscow with a woman, my wife, whom I love. I am not a person well-versed in such disciplines as literature, mathematics, or the various speculative philosophies but during the time of my youth was supremely quick with my eyes and most reliably steady with my hands so that for a period during the Soviet Socialist epoch I served as the personal physician to several individuals of high rank and power. The majority of these were kind and gracious men, more benevolent and generous than was ever known by the public at large.

In due time a number of these men in appreciation of my labors bestowed upon me a fine country *dacha* to which I retired at the age of fifty-seven years. It was then also that I elected at last to marry, choosing as my wife a woman somewhat younger than myself, barely thirty, though not pretty, being heavy in the hips and chest with a bulky figure and rather too much given to hair on her arms and upper legs. She was an intellectual however, a space scientist and author of published works on lunar disconformities and extraterrestrial crater formation, and also always reading from thin books containing poetry that had for me no more meaning than a ripple of words like water rushing past in a stream. This is the same woman to whom today I remain married and it would be an untruth to say that a single unpleasant thought has ever crossed my mind relating to her during the time of our shared life together.

When the beings from somewhere else came in their golden ships and laid waste to the material world the pensions from the government which had sustained us in relative luxury ceased arriving. I attempted to pack our belongings for the journey back to Moscow but my wife intervened by saying, "No, we will never go there again. We will have to give up this great house but it has always been too large for comfort for the two us alone and we will find another dwelling, even a cottage, but we will not go back to that place where nothing green lives."

The cottage she found for us shortly thereafter was modest to a fault but in the time since we have lived there in comparative tranquility while I treat the illnesses of my neighbors, often accepting payment in kind of food and clothing to keep us warm and well fed in the long winters while my wife sits in her rocking chair evenings in her shapeless cotton dresses reading from the pile of poetry books that remain constantly at her side and sometimes we converse softly until it seems as though some unknown force must be holding back the first flush of dawn.

On this cool night at the end of autumn it is raining when the three strange ones come to our door. The roof of our cottage is sorely in need of repair but I am now too old now for climbing ladders and my wife is perhaps too heavy to try. The water runs down into buckets strategically arranged, often making pleasant musical noises as it does. When the knocking comes, my wife looks up from her book and says, "Now who can that be, husband?"

"A patient?" I say.

"In this dreadful rain?"

"Perhaps it is an emergency."

At the door stand three pretty young men bundled in heavy coats with blond locks spilling out from beneath their leather caps. They stand silent and motionless before me.

I have seen none of them before but hurriedly invite them inside to escape the cold and wet.

My wife in her rocking chair gazes at them uncertainly. I wonder if she knows who they are.

"You are the doctor?" one asks me.

"I am one, yes."

"Then you must help us. There are things growing inside our bodies and we do not know what they are."

"Tumors?" I ask.

"No, not that," another of them responds after a pause.

I look at my wife whose judgment is always keen and see in her eyes an unspoken warning but I am still a doctor even though officially retired and these three are like strange children and it is late and cold and there is a fierce rain pouring down outside. "Please come into the back room with me and I will conduct a physical examination."

As I pass my wife's chair she averts her eyes and I feel a momentary flush of shame at having ignored her unstated wishes. In the examination room I request the young men to remove their clothes and they shed their coats and caps and stand naked before me. Although my eyesight is not as sharp as it once was, I am able to discern at once that something odd has happened here, for the genitals of all three are peculiarly deformed. There are gaps where the skin should be smooth and much that should not be present is easily observable. There exist, I know, certain phenomena of nature of which I have read in medical texts but never previously seen with my own eyes. The three also bear identical birthmarks in the shape of a five-pointed star below the nipple of the left breast.

My sensitive hearing detects the sound of my wife pacing back and forth in the next room. She is not normally fond of walking and her restlessness only intensifies my anxiety. "These things you believe are growing inside your bodies," I say. "Where do you think they are located?"

The three all point at their abdomens a few centimeters below the navel.

I conduct a thorough examination and when I am finished say, "You are all pregnant." I do not look at them as I speak these words.

"What does that mean?" says one. "What does pregnant mean?"

"You are going to give birth to children—babies."

"And they are growing inside us now?"

"In your bellies, yes. Your—your wombs."

"When will these children be born?"

"I cannot be certain. Soon perhaps. The heartbeats are strong and I detected some movement. But you are not normal and I cannot be sure."

I remain in the room until they are dressed and then open the door for them.

My wife is sitting in her chair again. She observes in silence as I lead them to the door.

"Wait," she says. "It is still raining outside. They should stay with us until this storm has passed."

"No," I say sharply. "We do not have the room."

"They can sleep here in the living room."

"No, that is not possible." I hold the door until the three have stepped forth into the rain and then close it quickly and drop the wooden bolt.

"That was most unlike you," my wife says, "forcing them into such weather when they are already ill."

"They are not ill," I say.

She rocks in her chair, book open in her lap, but I know that she is not reading.

I sit between her feet and rest my head on her knee, listening to the rain descending drop by drop into the wooden buckets.

After some time she asks, "Who were they?"

I shake my head helplessly.

"At first I was afraid of them and then…"

"I know. I too was afraid."

"Do you want to kiss me now?"

"I do."

"I want it too."

Without laying aside the book she leans back in the rocking chair, shifting her hips slightly and placing her feet one on each side as I kneel below. Extending my arms, I take hold of her cotton dress and fold the hem past her waist, tucking it carefully beneath her.

"All right, my Alyosha?" she asks.

I lower my head and open my mouth, allowing my tongue initially to caress and then to penetrate the warm wet odiferous channel. My eyes are shut. I see nothing.

Outside the rain has stopped falling.

The chair rocks gently to and froe.

"I am coming," she says.

7

A silence grips the air as if held in the palm of a giant hand and the three of them with their heads thrown back gazing at the sky above where, hovering, looms the shimmering disc of a single lone golden ship.

"Well, well, says Blue in a steady voice. His hands continue to rest on the shoulders of the others. "So they've come back, have they?"

THE END

www.ingramcontent.com/pod-product-compliance
Lightning Source LLC
Chambersburg PA
CBHW020625020726
47494CB00001B/52